P9-BBN-688

BY LARRY MCMURTRY

Streets of Laredo
The Evening Star
Buffalo Girls
Some Can Whistle
Anything for Billy
Film Flam: Essays on Hollywood
Texasville
Lonesome Dove
The Desert Rose
Cadillac Jack
Somebody's Darling
Terms of Endearment
All My Friends Are Going to Be Strangers
Moving On
The Last Picture Show
In a Narrow Grave: Essays on Texas
Leaving Cheyenne
Horseman, Pass By

Streets of

SIMON & SCHUSTER

NEW YORK   LONDON   TORONTO   SYDNEY   TOKYO   SINGAPORE

Laredo

a novel by

Larry McMurtry

SIMON & SCHUSTER
Simon & Schuster Building
Rockefeller Center
1230 Avenue of the Americas
New York, New York 10020

This book is a work of fiction. Names, characters, places and incidents are either products of the author's imagination or are used fictitiously. Any resemblance to actual events or locales or persons, living or dead, is entirely coincidental.

Copyright © 1993 by Larry McMurtry

All rights reserved
including the right of reproduction
in whole or in part in any form.

SIMON & SCHUSTER and colophon
are registered trademarks of Simon & Schuster Inc.

Designed by Levavi & Levavi
Manufactured in the United States of America

10   9   8   7   6   5   4   3

Library of Congress Cataloging-in-Publication Data
McMurtry, Larry.
    Streets of Laredo : a novel / by Larry McMurtry.
       p.   cm.
    Sequel to: Lonesome dove.
    I. Title.
PS3563.A319S7   1993
813′.54—dc20   93-19279
                                                        CIP
ISBN: 0-671-79281-4

For Diana and Sara Ossana

So for the mother's sake the child was dear,
And dearer was the mother for the child. . . .

Coleridge, "Sonnet to a Friend"

America still inhabits solitude; for a long time
yet her wilderness will be her manners. . . .

Chateaubriand, 1827

We beat the drum lowly and shook the spurs slowly,
And bitterly wept as we bore him along;
For we all loved our comrade, so brave and so handsome,
We all loved our comrade, although he'd done wrong. . . .

"Streets of Laredo," c. 1860

Intreate mee not to leave thee,
or to returne from following after thee. . . .

Ruth 1:16

Part
I

A Salaried Man

1.

"Most train robbers ain't smart, which is a lucky thing for the railroads," Call said. "Five smart train robbers could bust every railroad in this country."

"This young Mexican is smart," Brookshire said, but before he could elaborate, the wind lifted his hat right off his head. He was forced to chase it—not the first time he had been forced to chase his hat since arriving in Amarillo. He had taken to ramming his hat down on his head nearly to his eyebrows, but the Texas winds were of a different order than the winds he had been accustomed to in Brooklyn, where he lived. Somehow, time after time, the Texas winds lifted his hat. Before he could even get a hand up to grab it, there it went. It was just a common fedora; but on the other hand, it was his only hat, and it was not his custom to go through life bareheaded, at least not while he was conducting business for the railroad. Colonel Terry would not have approved. Brookshire was only a salaried man, and he could not afford to ignore Colonel Terry's preferences in such matters.

This time the hat rode the wind like a fat bird—it had a twenty-yard lead on its owner before it hit the ground, and when it did hit, it rolled rapidly along the gritty street. Fortunately for Brookshire, a wagon was parked to the south of the station, and the hat eventually lodged against one of the wagon wheels. He strolled over and picked it up, trying to appear nonchalant, though in fact, he was more than a little out of sorts.

At the behest of his superiors—Colonel Terry in particular; Colonel Terry, the president of the railroad, was the only superior who counted—Brookshire had journeyed all the way from New York to hire a bandit killer. Brookshire was an accountant. Hiring bandit killers wasn't his line of work, but the man who normally handled the task, Big Johnny Roberts, had accidentally swallowed a wine cork and choked to death, just as he was about to depart for Texas. From Colonel Terry's point of view, it was a nuisance; he took a look around the office and before Brookshire knew it, he was on a train going west, in Johnny Roberts's stead. In his years with the railroad, he had performed a number of services, but never in a place where his hat blew off every time he turned a corner. Having to chase his hat was an aggravation, but the real reason he was out of sorts was because he wasn't at all impressed with the killer he had been instructed to hire.

About the best thing Brookshire could find to say for the small, weary-looking man standing in front of the little shack of a depot, a saddle and a duffle roll stacked beside him, was that he had been punctual. He had ridden in at dawn, hitching his sorrel mare outside the hotel precisely at seven a.m., the time agreed upon. Still, Brookshire had barely been able to conceal his shock when he saw how old the man was. Of course, Brookshire was aware of his reputation: no one in the West had a reputation to equal Woodrow Call's. In Brookshire's view, reputation did not catch bandits—at least it didn't catch bandits who covered country as rapidly as young Joey Garza. The young Mexican was said to be only nineteen years old, whereas Captain Call, from the look of him, was edging seventy.

Nonetheless, Brookshire had been ordered to hire Woodrow Call and no one else. More than that, he had been entrusted with a fancy, engraved Colt revolver which Colonel Terry had sent along as a special gift.

To Brookshire's dismay, Captain Call scarcely glanced at the gun. He didn't even bother to lift it out of its rosewood box. He didn't twirl the chamber or admire the fine engraving.

"Thanks, but I'll pass," he said. He seemed more grateful for the coffee. Of course, it was wintry, and the old Ranger was only wearing a light coat.

"Good Lord, what will I tell Colonel Terry?" Brookshire asked. "This gun probably cost him five hundred dollars. This engraving is handwork. It don't come cheap."

"Why, the Colonel can keep it himself, then," Call said. "I appreciate the thought, but I've no place to keep a fancy weapon. I'd have to deposit it in a bank, and I prefer to avoid banks.

"I generally depend on the rifle, not the pistol," he added. "If you're close enough to a killer to be in reach of a pistol bullet, then generally you're too close."

"Good Lord," Brookshire said, again. He knew Colonel Terry well enough to know that he wasn't going to be pleased when told that his gift had not been wanted. Colonel Terry hadn't been a colonel for nothing, either. Having such an expensive present rejected by a fellow who just looked like an old cowpoke would undoubtedly put him in a temper, in which case Brookshire and anyone else who happened to be in the office would have to scramble to keep their jobs.

Call saw that the man was upset—he supposed, really, that he ought to accept the gun. That would be the polite thing. But in the past few years, governors and presidents of railroads and senators and rich men were always offering him fancy weapons, or expensive saddles, or the use of their railroad cars, or even fine horses—and always, something in him resisted.

For one thing, he despised fancy gear. He rode a plain saddle, and all that he required in a weapon was that it be reliable and accurate.

For another thing, he had never met a governor or a president of a railroad or a senator or a rich man that he liked or felt comfortable with. Why place himself in some arrogant fool's debt for the sake of a gun he'd never shoot nor probably even load?

Only a few days before, Call and Charles Goodnight had discussed the matter of gifts from the rich and powerful. It had
been the day, in fact, that Goodnight had ridden out to the little
line cabin he let Call use when he was between jobs, and handed
Call the telegram asking him to meet a Mr. Ned Brookshire in
Amarillo at seven a.m., in the lobby of the best hotel.

Goodnight himself was famous; probably as famous as a cattleman could get. He had also been offered twenty-five or thirty
engraved Winchesters in recent years, but, like Call, he was
skeptical of the rich and powerful and seldom felt comfortable
in their company.

Throughout most of their lives, which had only occasionally
intersected, Woodrow Call and Charles Goodnight had not exactly gotten along. Somehow in the old days, the Indian-fighting
days, they had rubbed one another the wrong way almost
every time they met. Even now, they did not exactly consider
themselves friends. Once a week or so, when Goodnight was
around his home ranch, he had formed the habit of riding out
to the little line cabin to check on his guest, the famous Texas
Ranger.

The shack sat not far from the north rim of the Palo Duro
Canyon. Often the two men would sit, largely in silence, looking
down into the canyon until dusk and then darkness filled it. In
the dusk and shadows they saw their history; in the fading
afterlight they saw the fallen: the Rangers, the Indians, the cowboys.

"Let a man give you a fancy gun and he'll tell everybody in
five counties that he's your friend, when in fact, you may despise him," Goodnight said, spitting. "I don't number too many
rich fools among my friends—how about you?"

"I have not had a friend for several years," Call said. Only
after he said it did it occur to him that the remark might sound
a little odd—as if he were asking for sympathy.

"Of course, there's Pea and there's Bol," he added, hastily.
"Bol's out of his head, but I count him a friend."

"Oh, your cook, I think he fed me once," Goodnight said. "If
he's out of his head, how do you keep up with him?"

"I left him with a family in San Antonio," Call said. "When I get a job down near the border I sometimes put him on his mule and take him with me. There's another family in Nuevo Laredo I can board him with when it comes time to do the work.

"He enjoys a little travel," Call added. "He's still got his memories—he just can't put any two of them together."

"Hell, I can barely sort out two memories myself," Goodnight said. "It's what I get for living too long. My head fills up and sloshes over, like a damn bucket. Whatever sloshes out is lost. I doubt I still know half of what I knew when I was fifty years old."

"You take too many train trips," Call observed, in a mild tone.

"I thought we were talking about my bad memory," Goodnight said, squinting at him. "What's train travel got to do with it?"

"All this traveling by train weakens the memory—it's bound to," Call said. "A man that travels horseback needs to remember where the water holes are, but a man that rides in a train can forget about water holes, because trains don't drink."

Goodnight let that observation soak in for a few minutes.

"I was never lost, night or day," he said finally. "How about you?"

"I got turned around once, in Mexico," Call said. "It was a cloudy night. My horse fell and got up pointed in the wrong direction. I was yawny that night and didn't notice till morning."

"Was you mad at the horse when you did notice?" Goodnight asked.

"I was mad at myself," Call said.

"Well, this is a pointless conversation," Goodnight said, turning abruptly toward his horse. Without another word, he mounted and rode away. He had always been abrupt, Call reflected. When Charles Goodnight concluded that a conversation had overrun its point, he was apt to make a swift departure.

While Mr. Brookshire was walking back across the street, trying to whack the dust out of his fedora by hitting it against his leg, the train he and Call had been waiting for came in sight. It was the train that would, in time, deliver them to San Antonio.

Call was trying to think of a polite way to inform Mr. Brookshire that the fedora wouldn't do in a windy place like Texas. A hat that kept blowing off could lead to no end of trouble when dealing with a bandit as advanced as Joey Garza.

Even more, Call wished Brookshire could be persuaded just to go on back to New York, leaving him to deal with the young Mexican bandit alone. Traveling across the West with errand boys such as Mr. Brookshire took considerably more energy than tracking the bandits themselves. Call had little to say to such men, but they invariably had much to say to him. Six hundred miles of Mr. Brookshire's conversation was not something he looked forward to.

"This wind puts me in mind of Chicago," Brookshire said, when he returned to where Call was standing. He didn't bother putting his hat back on his head. Instead, he clutched it tightly in both hands.

"I've not visited Chicago," Call said, to be polite.

"The wind's not like this back home," Brookshire said. "Back home I can go for months without my hat blowing off my head a single time. I got off the train here yesterday, and I've been chasing my hat ever since."

The train wheezed and screeched to a halt. When it had come to a full stop, Captain Call picked up his saddle and duffle roll. Brookshire, to his surprise, suddenly found that he was feeling a little desperate—he felt that he didn't dare move. The wind had become even more severe, and he had the sickening sense that he, not his hat, was about to blow away. There wasn't a tree in sight that he could see: just endless plain. Unless he could roll up against a wagon wheel, as his hat had, there would be nothing to stop him for days, if he blew away. He knew it was an absurd feeling: grown men, especially heavy men such as himself, didn't just blow away. Yet the feeling persisted, and every time he happened to glance across the street and see nothing—nothing at all except grass and sky—the feeling got worse.

Call noticed that Brookshire had an odd look on his face. The

[18]

man stood with his fedora clutched to his stomach, looking as if he were afraid to move, yet he was standing on perfectly level ground on a sunny winter day.

"Are you ill, Mr. Brookshire?" Call asked. After all, the man had been polite; he had agreed to Call's terms and had cheerfully paid for the coffee as well.

"I'd like to get on the train," Brookshire said. "I believe I'll soon perk up if I could just get on the train."

"Why, here it is, right behind you," Call told him. "I assume you've got the tickets. We can step right on."

"I'm afraid I've left my valise—you see, that's my problem," Brookshire admitted.

"Oh, at the hotel?" Call asked.

"Yes, it's right in the lobby," Brookshire said, looking at the ground. He did not feel it would be wise to look across the street again. It was when he looked across the street that the blowing-away sensation seized him the most fiercely.

"Well, the train just pulled in—it'll be here awhile, I expect," Call said. "You've got plenty of time to go get your valise."

Then he looked again and realized that his traveling companion was having some sort of attack. Brookshire was frozen, his eyes fixed on his feet. He didn't appear to be capable of moving —walking the hundred yards to the hotel was, for the moment, clearly beyond him.

"I can't do it," Brookshire muttered. "I can't do it. I'd just like to get on the train."

He paused, his eyes still on his feet.

"What I'd like very much is to get on the train," he said, again.

Call immediately set down his saddle and duffle roll and took Mr. Brookshire's arm. The man was close to panic, and when a man was close to panic, discussion rarely helped.

"Here, I'll just escort you to your car," he said, holding Brookshire's arm. Brookshire took one small step, and then another. Soon Call had him situated in a railroad seat. Brookshire's chest began to heave and the sweat poured off him, but at least, Call reckoned, the panic was broken.

"Just stay here and settle in," Call said. "I'll stroll over to the hotel and pick up that valise."

"Grateful," was all Brookshire could say. What he really wanted to do was crawl under the seat, but of course, that would be impossible—anyway, the railroad car had walls. He wasn't going to blow away.

A few minutes later, Captain Call came walking in with the valise and with his own saddle and duffle roll. He sat down across from Brookshire as if nothing untoward had happened. But Brookshire knew that something had happened—something *very* untoward. He was embarrassed and also deeply grateful to the Captain. Not only had he guided him onto the train and then walked two hundred yards out of his way to fetch the valise, but he had done both things politely. He hadn't asked Brookshire *why* he couldn't walk a hundred yards and tote his own baggage; he just accepted that it was an impossibility and put him on the train without a fuss.

Brookshire worked for people who never let him forget that he was an underling. Captain Call hadn't been especially friendly when they met that morning, but he hadn't treated Brookshire as an underling. When he noticed that a crisis was occurring, he had dealt with it efficiently and with no evident feelings of contempt for Brookshire's weakness.

It was exceptional behavior, in Brookshire's view. He had met with a good deal of exceptional behavior in his years with Colonel Terry, but most of it had been exceptionally bad. He was not used to decent treatment, but he had received it from Captain Call. When his heart finally stopped pounding, he took another look at the man who sat across the aisle from him.

Call was smoking. If he even remembered that something out of the ordinary had happened on the railroad platform, he gave no sign.

The train started and they were soon cutting a narrow furrow through the endless miles of prairie. The stiff wind was still blowing, ruffling the surface of the sea of grass.

"Does your hat ever blow off, Captain?" Brookshire asked.

"Rarely," Call said.

[20]

"You see, I've got mine trained," he added, looking over at the man from Brooklyn. "You're new to these parts—it takes you a while to get yours trained just right."

"I doubt mine will ever be trained—I'll probably have to chase it all over Texas," Brookshire said.

Then, relaxing, he fell asleep. When he awoke and looked out the window, there was nothing to see but grass. Captain Call seemed not to have moved. He was still smoking. The stock of a rifle protruded from his duffle roll. Brookshire felt glad Call was there. It was a long way to San Antonio—if he had no one to share the ride with, he might get the blowing-away feeling again. Probably, after all, his superiors had been right in their choice of bandit killers. Most likely Captain Call could do the job.

"How long have you been a lawman, Captain?" he inquired, to be polite.

Call didn't turn his head.

"I ain't a lawman," he said. "I work for myself."

After that, a silence grew. Brookshire felt rather as he felt when he went to a dance. Somehow he had stepped off on the wrong foot.

"Well, you picked an exciting line of work, I'd have to say," he said.

Captain Call didn't answer. Brookshire felt at a loss. He began to regret having made the remark—he began to regret having spoken at all. He sighed. The Captain still said nothing. Brookshire realized he didn't know much about Texans. Perhaps they just weren't inclined to conversation. Certainly Captain Call didn't appear to be much inclined to it. He didn't appear to be excited about his line of work, either.

Brookshire began to miss Katie, his wife. Katie wasn't lavish with her conversation, either. A month might pass with the two of them scarcely exchanging more than three or four words. But the plains outside the window were vast and empty. The wind was still blowing, rippling and sometimes flattening the top of the grass.

Brookshire began to wish, very much, that he could go home

to Brooklyn. If only he were in Brooklyn and not in Texas, he might not feel so low. If he were in Brooklyn, he felt sure he would be sitting with Katie, in their cozy kitchen. Katie might not say much, but in their cozy kitchen, the wind never blew.

2.

Lorena woke to the sound of the baby coughing. Pea Eye was up walking her, trying to get her quiet. For a minute or two, Lorena let him: she felt too sad to move—sad, or mad, or a mixture; even without a sick child she was apt to feel that way on nights before Pea Eye had to leave.

"I guess she's croupy," Pea Eye said.

"Give her to me," Lorena said. Wearily, she propped up a little, took the baby, and gave her the breast.

"It's not the croup, it's that dry cough—you ought to recognize the difference by now," Lorena said. "The boys all had the same cough—Clarie didn't have it."

As she said it she heard Clarie go past their bedroom, on her way to milk. Clarie was the oldest; at fifteen she already had more energy than most grown men, and she didn't have to be told to do the chores. Even Pea Eye admitted that there were days when his Clarie could outwork him, and Pea Eye was neither lazy nor weak.

"I guess I'm just the worrying kind," Pea Eye said, relieved that the baby had stopped coughing, if only in order to nurse.

"There's other diseases children can have besides croup," Lorena reminded him.

"Seems like every time I have to leave, someone around here

is sick," Pea Eye said. "I'll be dreary company for the Captain, worrying about you and the children."

He *would* worry about them, Lorena felt sure, but right at the moment what he wanted was sympathy, and right at the moment, sympathy was the last thing she was in the mood to give him.

"You're the one going off to get shot at," she reminded him —there was anger in her voice; she couldn't suppress it.

"Clarie and I can take care of things here," she said. "If we have trouble the neighbors will help us—I'm their only school-teacher. They'll fetch me a doctor if Laurie gets worse."

When the little girl finished nursing, Lorena held her out to Pea Eye. He took her with him to the kitchen—he needed to get the coffee started. It was a four-hour trot to the railroad where he was supposed to meet the Captain. He needed to be on his way soon. But when he tried to saucer his coffee—he had long ago formed the habit of drinking his coffee from a saucer—Laurie wiggled, causing him to pour too hard. Most of the coffee splashed out. When Lorena came into the kitchen Pea Eye was looking for a rag. He needed to wipe up his spill.

"I wish you'd learn to drink coffee out of a cup, like the rest of us," Lorena said.

"It's just a habit I got into when I was rangering," Pea Eye said. "I didn't have no babies to hold in those days. I could concentrate better. I was just a bachelor most of my life—same as the Captain is."

"You were never the same as the Captain is," Lorena informed him. She took the baby and scooted a chair well back from the table, so coffee wouldn't drip on her gown.

"I hadn't learned to be married yet, in those days," Pea Eye said, mildly. Lorie seemed slightly out of temper—he thought it best to take a mild line at such times.

"No, you hadn't learned to be married—I had to teach you, and I'm still at it," Lorena said. "We're both lucky. Clara got me started on my education and I got you started being a husband."

"Both lucky, but I'm luckier," Pea Eye said. "I'd rather be

[24]

married than do them fractions, or whatever they are that you teach the brats.

"At least I would if it's you that I'm married to," he said, reflecting.

"I don't like it that he keeps taking you away from us," Lorena said. She felt it was better to say it than to choke on it, and she had choked on it a good many times.

"Why can't he take someone younger, if he needs help with a bandit?" she asked. "Besides that, he don't even ask! He just sends those telegrams and orders you to come, as if he owned you."

Though Pea Eye had not yet admitted it out loud to Lorie, he himself had begun to dread the arrival of the telegrams. The Captain dispatched them to the little office in Quitaque; they were delivered, within a week or two, by a cowboy or a mule skinner, any traveler who happened to be coming their way. They were short telegrams; even so, Lorena had to read them to him. She had learned to read years ago, and he hadn't. It was a little embarrassing, being the husband of a schoolteacher, while being unable to read. Clarie, of course, could read like a whiz —she had won the local spelling bee every year since she turned six. Pea Eye had always meant to learn, and he still meant to learn, but meanwhile, he had the farm to farm, and farming it generally kept him busy from sunup until sundown. In the harvesting season, it kept him busy from well before sunup until well after dark.

Usually the Captain's telegrams would consist of a single sentence informing him of a date, a time, and a place where the Captain wanted him to appear. Short as they were, though, Lorena never failed to flush with anger while reading them to him. A deep flush would spread up her cheeks, nearly to her eyes; the vein on her forehead would stand out, and the little scar on her upper lip would seem whiter in contrast to her darkening face. She rarely said anything in words. Her blood said it for her.

Now, down on one knee in the kitchen, trying to wipe up the spilled coffee with a dishrag, Pea Eye felt such a heavy sadness descend on him that for a moment he would have liked just to lie down beneath it and let it crush him. Little Laurie was only three months old. Lorena had school to teach and the baby and the three boys to look after, and yet here he was, about to go away and leave them again, just because some railroad man wanted the Captain to run down a bandit.

Of course, Clarie was nearly grown and would be a big help to her mother, but knowing that wouldn't keep him from feeling low the whole trip—every night and morning he'd miss Lorie and the children; he would also worry constantly about the farm chores that weren't getting done. Even if little Laurie hadn't taken the croup—he considered her sickness the croup, though Lorie didn't—he wouldn't have wanted to go. It was beginning to bother Pea Eye a good deal that the Captain just couldn't seem to recognize that he was married. Not only was he married, but he was the father of five children. He had other things to do besides chase bandits. When he left he would be doing one duty, but at the same time he'd be neglecting others, and the ones he'd be neglecting were important. It meant feeling miserable and guilty for several weeks, and he didn't look forward to feeling that way. The truth was, half the time he felt miserable and guilty even when he wasn't neglecting his wife, or his children, or his chores.

"I've heard it's a young bandit, this time," Pea Eye said. "Maybe it won't take too long."

"Why wouldn't it, if the man's young?" Lorena asked.

"The Captain's got too much experience," Pea Eye said. "The young ones seldom give him much trouble."

"If it's going to be so easy, why does he need you?" she asked.

Pea Eye didn't answer because he didn't know. Twice he had gone to Wyoming with the Captain. Once they had gone to Yuma, Arizona, an exceptionally hot place in Pea Eye's view. Several times they'd gone to Oklahoma, and once or twice, into Old Mexico. But normally, they were able to corner their quarry somewhere in Texas. A few hard cases fought to the end, but the majority of the outlaws—bank robbers, mostly—realized once they were up against the famous Captain Call, it was time to surrender. As soon as they gave up, Pea Eye's duties really began. He was in charge of seeing they were handcuffed properly, or tied to their horses, or whatever the situation required. Compared to Indian fighting, it was not particularly dangerous work. He rarely had to fire his gun or even draw it.

It hardly seemed important enough to leave home for; yet here he was, preparing to leave home and feeling blue all the way down to his bones as a result.

"I expect I'll worry the whole way," Pea Eye said. "But at least I'll be paid cash money."

Lorena was silent. She hated the mornings when Pea Eye had to leave; hated the night before he left; just plain hated the whole period after one of the telegrams came. She knew Pea Eye no longer wanted to leave. Living with her, working the farm, helping her with the children, was what he wanted to do. She didn't doubt his love, or his devotion, or his loyalty, or his strength. All these were at her service, except when Captain Call needed some part of them to be at *his* service.

Lorena had resolved, though, not to help Pea Eye leave. The fact that he had a loyalty to the Captain was part of the bargain she had made when she married him. Clara Allen—the woman Clarie was named for—had told her how it would be in that respect, and Clara had been right. Were Pea Eye not loyal to the Captain, who had employed him most of his life, he wouldn't be likely to bring much loyalty to her, either. Clara pointed that out.

But she would not help Pea Eye leave. She wasn't going to pass a benediction on it.

As she was sitting in silence avoiding Pea Eye's miserable gaze, Clarie came in from the milking shed with a brimming pail of milk. It was a cold morning; the bucket steamed a little, and Clarie had color in her cheeks. Lorena couldn't help smiling. Even in unhappy moments, the sight of her beautiful young daughter was apt to make her smile. Clarie got a cheesecloth, spread it carefully over the old milk strainer, and slowly poured the hot, foamy milk through it.

"I'll help you, Ma, while Pa's gone," Clarie said.

"Why, yes, you'll help me, when you can spare the time from Roy Benson," Lorena said. Clarie was a young woman, and the cowboys were already coming around. The gawky Benson boy was particularly attentive.

"Oh, Ma, don't talk about him," Clarie protested, embarrassed.

"Like I say, it's cash money," Pea Eye said, feeling that his problem had somehow been forgotten. It was often that way with women, it seemed. One minute Lorie would be drilling holes in him with her eyes, and the next minute she and Clarie would be combing one another's hair and singing tunes.

"We heard you," Lorena said. It was true that her wages for the schoolteaching were apt to be a side of beef or hand-me-down clothes for the children, or a horse that was getting along in years and might do to pull her buggy. Her wages were likely to be whatever folks could spare. It was a fair arrangement; indeed, the only possible arrangement in a place where there were still only a scattering of homesteads and not many settlements.

Pea Eye had only brought up the cash money in order to remind Lorena that the Captain didn't expect him to work for nothing. Having cash money never hurt.

Another bad aspect of the bandit-catching trips was that the very fact Lorena had secured enough education to become a schoolteacher, caused some tension between Pea Eye and the Captain. Lorena's educational accomplishments filled Pea Eye with pride, and he liked to talk about them. It was Clara Allen, the woman who sheltered Lorena in Nebraska, who had seen to it that Lorena learned to read and write and figure. Perhaps that was why the Captain got so stiff every time Pea Eye bragged about his smart wife. Clara and the Captain rubbed one another the wrong way. That was no reason, though, in Pea Eye's view, why he should be any less proud of Lorena's scholarly skills.

Clara had gone all the way to St. Louis to find acceptable teachers for Lorena, and of course, the teachers were expected to instruct Clara's two daughters as well. Clara boarded the teachers in her own home, often for months at a stretch. Betsey, her oldest daughter, had even married one of them.

Everyone agreed that Lorena was the sharpest pupil in that part of Nebraska. For a time, Clara ordered books for her, but soon Lorena was ordering them for herself. It was a proud day for all concerned when Lorena received her diploma from the correspondence college in Trenton, New Jersey.

Once they bought the farm in Texas the neighbors soon found out about Lorena's diploma, and they promptly persuaded her to teach their children. Her first classes were held in a barn. Charles Goodnight rode by one day, saw her teaching in the cold, drafty barn, and wrote a check on the spot sufficient to allow the community to construct a one-room schoolhouse on a bluff overlooking the Red River. The school was a five-mile buggy ride each way from their farm, but Lorena drove it without complaint. When their babies came she took them with her, lining an old cartridge case with quilts to make a crib.

To Pea Eye, and to many citizens of the plains, it was impressive that Lorena would care enough about her teaching to bounce her children ten miles over the prairie every day. She didn't want to disappoint her pupils, most of whom could only expect three or four years of schooling at best. Once the boys got to be nine or ten, they would be needed for work. The Benson boy who liked Clarie so much was still in school at fourteen, but that was exceptional. Even the girls would be needed in the fields by the time they were eleven or twelve.

Lorena thought Captain Call resented the fact that his old partner, Gus McCrae, had left her his half of the proceeds from the herd the Hat Creek outfit had trailed from Texas to Montana. Lorena's half didn't amount to that much money—not enough to resent, in Pea Eye's view. The whole Montana scheme had collapsed in less than two years. Gus was killed before they even established the ranch. Dish Boggett, their top hand, quit the first winter. The Captain left that spring. Newt— the Captain's son, most people thought, although the Captain himself had never owned to it—had been killed late in the summer when the Hell Bitch, the mare the Captain gave him,

[29]

reared and fell back on him. The saddle horn crushed his rib cage, and crushed his heart as well. It was the view of everyone who knew horses that, while an able ranch manager, Newt was much too inexperienced to trust with a horse as mean and as smart as the Hell Bitch. Still, the Captain had given Newt the horse, and Newt felt obliged to ride her. He rode her, and one day she killed him, just as Lippy and Jasper and one or two others had predicted she would.

After Newt's death the ranch soon fell into disorder; the Captain had to come back and sell it. Cattle prices were down, so he didn't get much, but Lorena's half enabled her and Pea Eye to buy the farm in Texas.

Lorena's view, expressed to Clara, not to Pea, was that the Captain wasn't prepared to forgive her hard past.

"He don't think whores should become schoolteachers," she said.

To Pea Eye, Lorena advanced a different theory.

"He didn't like it that Gus liked me," she said. "Now that you married me I've taken two men from him. I took Gus and then I took you. He'll never forgive it, but I don't care."

Pea Eye preferred to put such difficult questions out of his mind. With so much farm work to do and no one to do it but himself—none of the boys was old enough to plow—he had little time to spare for speculation. If he had more time, he wouldn't have used it trying to figure out why the Captain did things the way he did, or why he liked people or didn't like people. The Captain was as he was, and to Pea Eye, that was just life. Lorena and Clara could discuss it until they were blue in the face: no talk would change the Captain.

It bothered Pea Eye considerably that the Captain had never ridden over to see their farm or meet their children. His shack on the Goodnight place was not that far away. Pea Eye was proud of the farm and doubly proud of his children. He would have liked to introduce the Captain to his family and show him around the farm.

Instead, in only half an hour, he would have to leave his wife and children to go help a man who didn't like his wife and had

never met his children. The thought made Pea Eye sick at heart.
Catching bandits was tricky work. There was no telling how long
it might take. Little Laurie was tiny. She had come nearly a
month early and was going to have to struggle through a bitter
Panhandle winter. Pea Eye loved little Laurie with all his heart.
He thought she looked just like her mother, and could not get
enough of looking at her. He had bought a rabbit fur robe from
an old deaf Kiowa man who lived on the Quitaque. The robe
made a nice warm lining for the cartridge-box crib. Lorena kept
assuring him that it was a snug enough crib now that it was lined
with rabbit fur, but still Pea Eye worried. The cold was bitter.
Winter never failed to carry off several little ones from neigh-
boring farms and ranches. Pea Eye had many dreams in which
little Laurie died. It tormented him to think she might not be
there to look at when he returned.

For days he had been choking his fear down—no need to
burden Lorie with his worries—but suddenly, kneeling on the
kitchen floor and trying unsuccessfully to wipe up the spilled
coffee, fear and sadness came rushing up from inside him, too
swiftly and too powerfully for him to control.

"I don't want to go, this time!" he said. "What if Laurie dies
while I'm gone?"

He thought Lorena would be mighty surprised to hear him
say that he didn't want to go with the Captain. Never before had
he even suggested that he might not accompany Captain Call if
the Captain needed him.

Lorena didn't seem surprised, though. Perhaps she was too
busy with Laurie. Because Laurie was so tiny, she was a fitful
nurser, giving up sometimes before she had taken enough milk
to satisfy her. Lorie had just given her the breast again, hoping
she would take enough nourishment to keep her asleep for a
while.

"What if we all died, while you was gone?" Lorena asked,
calmly. She didn't want any agitated talk while the baby was at
the breast. But her husband had to be very upset to say such a
thing, and she didn't want to ignore his distress, either.

"Well, I'd never get over it, if any of you died," Pea Eye said.

"You would—people get over anything—I've got over worse than dying myself, and you know it," Lorena said. "But that's in the past. You don't need to worry so much. I'm not going to die, and I won't let this baby die, either. I won't let any of our children die."

Pea Eye stood up, but despite Lorie's calm words, he felt trembly. He felt he could trust Lorie—if she said she'd keep their family alive, he knew she would do her best. But people did their best and died anyway. Sometimes their children outlived them. That was the natural order; but sometimes, they didn't. He knew Lorie meant well when she told him not to worry, but he also knew that he would worry anyway.

The Captain would be unlikely to sympathize, because he didn't understand it. Captain Call had always been a single man. He had no one to miss, much less anyone to worry about.

"I never finished cleaning those guns," Pea Eye said distractedly, looking down at his wife. August, the youngest boy, not yet two, came wandering into the kitchen just then. He was rubbing his eyes with his fists.

"Hongry," he said, only half awake. He began to crawl into his mother's lap.

"You cleaned them enough to smell like gun grease all night," Lorena said. August had a runny nose, and she held out her hand for Pea Eye's rag.

"This is a dishrag," he said, still distracted.

"It was—now it's a snot rag," Lorena said. August arched his back and tried to duck away—he hated having his nose wiped. But his mother was too skilled for him. She pinned him to her with an elbow and wiped it anyway.

"You should take care of your weapons, if you're going after a killer," she said. "I don't want you neglecting important things, even if I complain about you being smelly."

"I don't want to go," Pea Eye said. "I just don't want to go, this time."

There was a silence, broken only by August's whimpering, and the soft sucking sound the baby made as she drew on the nipple. Pea Eye had just said the words Lorena had long hoped to hear, but the fact was, she hadn't gotten her sleep out—she was drowsy and would have liked to go back to bed. It was a hopeless wish: August was up, and Ben and Georgie would be crawling out of bed any time. Whether she liked it or not, the day had begun. She had long resented Pea Eye's blind loyalty to the Captain but knew there was nothing she could do about it. Mainly, she just tried to shut her mind to it.

Clara had told her that was how it would be, but Clara had advised her to marry Pea Eye anyway.

"He's simple—sometimes that's good," Clara said. "He's gentle, too, but he's not weak. His horses respect him. I tend to trust a horse's respect.

"He doesn't talk much, though," she added.

"I don't care whether he talks or not," Lorena said. "I wouldn't marry a man just for conversation. I'd rather read, now that I know how, than listen to any man talk."

"You're going to have to propose to Pea Eye, you know," Clara said. "He has no inkling that you want him. I doubt it's ever crossed his mind, that he could aspire to a beauty like you."

Pea Eye had been working for Clara about a year, at that time. July Johnson, the former sheriff from Arkansas who had loved Clara deeply but failed to win her, drowned trying to ford the Republican River with a herd of seventy young horses. July had no judgment about horses, or water, or women, as it turned out. His son, Martin, was going to know more, but that was because Martin had her to teach him, Clara reflected.

After Newt's death and the breakup of the Hat Creek outfit, Pea Eye had drifted south, meaning to descend the ladder of rivers until he got home to Texas. But, as luck would have it— the best piece of luck in his whole life, in his view—he showed up in Ogallala at a time when Clara was shorthanded, and she hired him on the spot.

Out her window, as she was advising Lorena to marry him, Clara could see Pea Eye in the lots, trying to halter-break a young sorrel colt. Of course, Pea Eye was older; too old, in a way, for Lorena. But people couldn't have everything. Clara herself would have liked a husband. She considered herself to be reasonably good-looking, she attempted to be considerate, and thought she was tolerably easy to get along with. But she had no husband, and no prospects. Decent men were scarce, and she knew that Pea Eye was a decent man. Lorena had little to gain by waiting for someone better to come along, and Clara told her so.

Looking at her husband, so shaky from the thought of leaving her that he could barely stand up, Lorena knew that Clara Allen had been right. He was loyal to her, and loyalty from men was a rarity in her life. Even Gus McCrae, her greatest love, had really been in love with Clara and would have left her to marry Clara, if he could have persuaded Clara to have him. Someday, Lorena imagined, some bandit would finally outshoot Captain Call, and she would finally have Pea Eye all to herself—if he could just stay alive, in the meantime.

Coffee was still dripping off the table—Pea Eye had made a poor job of wiping up his spill. He patted August on the head and left the room. In a few minutes he came back, wearing his hat and carrying his slicker. He didn't have his guns.

"Are your guns so dirty you're planning to leave them?" she asked, surprised. Never before had he left without his guns.

"I won't need them," Pea Eye said. "I'm just going to the railroad, to tell the Captain I can't go on no more chases with him."

Though it was exactly what she wanted to hear, Lorena felt a little frightened. Pea Eye had followed the Captain wherever the Captain went for many, many years, so many that she didn't know how many, and Pea Eye probably didn't know, either. Rangering with the Captain had been Pea Eye's life until she took him from it. For Pea Eye to end it now, just because the baby woke up coughing, represented a big change—indeed, a bigger change than she had anticipated having to face, on that particular day.

"Pea," she said, "you don't have to do this just because of me. You don't have to do it because of the children, either. We aren't in any danger, and we'll all be here when you get back."

Only lately had she been able to remember to say "aren't" rather than "ain't." She was proud of herself for remembering it so early in the morning, when she was sleepy.

"All I ever asked is that you be careful," she said. "Help this man if you want to. Just don't get killed for him."

"I ain't going to get killed for him, because I ain't going," Pea Eye said. "I've got too many obligations here. This chasing bandits has got to end sometime."

He walked out to the little smokehouse and got a slab of bacon. When he returned to the kitchen the three boys, Ben, Georgie, and August, were all propped up in their chairs, looking sleepy and eating bread soaked in the warm milk Clarie had brought in. It was their usual breakfast, although sometimes, if Lorena was up early, she made porridge. Clarie sat on a stool, churning—they had run out of butter the night before.

"You boys help your ma, while I'm gone," Pea Eye said, forgetting that he wasn't really going, this time.

Lorena turned to look at him, wondering if he had changed his mind. That would have been unlike him. It might take Pea Eye a while to make *up* his mind, but once he made it up, he rarely doubled back on himself.

"Oh," Pea Eye said, realizing from Lorie's look that he had made a slip of the tongue.

"Help your mother this morning," he said. "I'll be back this afternoon."

"Daddy, buy me a gun," Ben said. Ben was nine, and fascinated with firearms.

"No, he's not buying you a gun," Lorena said. "You'd just shoot Georgie, and I can't spare Georgie."

Georgie, seven, was straw-headed and buck-toothed, but he was Lorena's favorite, anyway. She couldn't help it. Every time she looked at Georgie, she felt her heart swell. He had a bit of a stammer, but he would grow out of it, probably.

"I'll sh-sh-sh-shoot h-h-him," Georgie countered.

Pea Eye picked up his slicker, and put on his hat. He looked at Lorena, who met his eye. She didn't say anything, but there was something disquieting in her look. Of course, that was nothing new. There was something disquieting in most of Lorena's looks.

Pea Eye tried to think of something more to say, but failed. He had never been a man of many words, and being married to a schoolteacher hadn't changed him much. Hundreds of Lorie's looks, like this one, left him baffled.

"See you for supper," he said, finally.

"If you don't show up, I'll know you changed your mind," Lorena said. "He might talk you into going yet."

"No, he won't talk me into going," Pea Eye said.

All the same, loping across the plains, he dreaded the meeting he was riding to. It was a fine, crisp day, but Pea Eye didn't feel fine. He had never said no to the Captain, and now he would have to. The Captain wasn't going to like the news, either—the Captain definitely wasn't going to like the news.

3.

When Captain Call saw Pea Eye standing by the railroad track, with no duffle and no firearms, he knew that the moment of change had come. It was an unpleasant shock, but it was not a surprise. Lorena had been tightening her hold on Pea Eye year by year. In the last two years, particularly, Pea Eye's reluctance to accompany him had been evident, and had even begun to affect his work. Half the time on their trips, he was too homesick, or woman-sick, to function as skillfully as he once had, and his skill had its limits, even when he was a young man.

"Well, I guess I've stopped this train for nothing, if you ain't getting on," Call said. He was annoyed, and he knew Pea Eye knew it, but since Pea Eye had arrived without his equipment, he saw no profit in forcing the issue.

"I'd better just go," Call said. "Good luck with your farm."

He shook Pea Eye's hand and got back on the train, which, in a moment, left. Soon even the caboose had vanished from Pea Eye's view, swallowed up by the sea of grass as surely as a boat would have been by the curving sea. Pea Eye walked slowly over and caught his horse; it had grazed some distance away. He felt stunned: the Captain was gone. The Captain hadn't even argued with him, though he had looked a good deal put out. Of course, he noticed immediately that Pea hadn't brought his guns.

"Forget your arsenal?" the Captain asked, when he first stepped off the train.

"No, I didn't forget it, I just left it at home," Pea Eye said. A man in a fedora had been looking out the window of the train, at them. Pea Eye was uncomfortable anyway, and being stared at by a man in a fedora hat didn't help.

"Oh, that's Brookshire, he's with the railroad," the Captain said, glancing around at the man. "He'll have to replace that hat, if he expects to travel very far with me. A man who can't keep his hat on his head won't be much help, in Mexico."

"I guess I won't be being no help in Mexico neither, Captain," Pea Eye said. "I've got a wife and five children, and one's a baby. The time's come for me to stay home."

Though Call had been expecting such a decision from Pea Eye for some time, hearing it was still a shock. He had paid Pea especially well on the last few trips, hoping to overcome his reluctance—it took money to farm, and what little Lorena had inherited from Gus must have been long gone by now.

But Call knew Pea Eye too well to suppose that money, or anything else, would prevail much longer. Pea Eye was through with rangering, and Call had to admit that what they were doing was only the shadow of rangering, anyway.

Call always felt angry when he anticipated Pea Eye's desertion —and, in his eyes, it was desertion—but, there by the train tracks, on the windy plain just north of Quanah, he swallowed the anger down, shook Pea Eye's hand, and got back on the train. The woman had won. In the end, it seemed they always did.

Brookshire was startled when he saw the Captain come back alone. The man looked testy. Then the train pulled away, leaving the tall man and the grazing horses behind, on the prairie.

"What's wrong with your man?" Brookshire asked. "Was he sick?"

"No, he's not sick, he's married," Call said. "Running down bandits don't tempt him no more."

"But I thought it was arranged," Brookshire said, more than a little alarmed. His instructions from Colonel Terry had been to let Call bring his man. Pea Eye himself was a legend, in a small way—Brookshire had been looking forward to meeting him. It was said that he had escaped from the Cheyenne Indians and had walked over one hundred miles, naked, to bring help to the other famous ranger, Augustus McCrae. Not many men could have walked one hundred miles naked, in Cheyenne country, and survived. Brookshire doubted that he could walk one hundred miles naked across New Jersey, and yet New Jersey was settled country, and his home state to boot.

He had hoped to meet the man and hear about his adventures. So far, he was certainly not hearing about many of Captain Call's. It would have been entertaining to hear about the hundred-mile walk, but evidently, it was not to be.

"I apologize—he's always been a reliable man," Call said. "He served with me more than thirty years—he's the last man I would have thought likely to marry. He never sought women, when he rode with me."

"Oh well, I married myself," Brookshire said, thinking of Katie's fat legs. Those legs had once had great appeal to him, but their appeal had diminished over the years. There were times when he missed Katie, and times when he didn't. When he wasn't missing her, he sometimes considered that he had been a fool, to tie himself down. Indeed, he was hoping that one bonus from his long train trip might be a Mexican girl. The popular view in Brooklyn was that Mexican girls were pretty, lively, and cheap.

"Who'll we get to replace him?" he asked, remembering that Colonel Terry expected results—and not next year, either. Joey Garza had struck seven times, stopping trains in remote areas of the Southwest, where trains were rarely bothered. He had killed eleven men so far, seemingly selecting his victims at random. Seven of the dead had been passengers; the rest, crew. Four of the seven trains had been carrying military payrolls, and one of the seven had Leland Stanford aboard. At that time, Leland Stanford was thought to be the richest man in California. The boy had taken his rings, his watch, and the fine silk sheets off the bed in his private car. He also took his diamond cuff links.

[39]

Leland Stanford was not a man who took kindly to having his sheets removed by a young Mexican not yet out of his teens. It was Stanford who stoked the fire under Colonel Terry, prompting him to hire expensive help such as Captain Woodrow Call.

It disturbed Brookshire that their plan had already gone awry, though they were still hundreds of miles from the border, and no doubt, many more hundreds of miles from where Joey Garza was to be found, *if* he was found.

One thing could be said with certainty about Colonel Terry: he did not like for plans to go awry. If some did go awry anyway, someone invariably got blamed, and most of the time that someone was Brookshire.

"I'll be lucky not to get fired," Brookshire said—he was mainly just thinking out loud.

"Why? Pea Eye was never your responsibility," Call said. "You never even met the man, and can't be blamed for the fact that he married and settled down."

"I can be blamed for anything," Brookshire assured him. "I'm one of those people everybody blames, when there's a misfortune."

For several minutes he sat with his head down, feeling sorry for himself. It seemed to him that life was nothing but one misfortune after another, and he got blamed for them all. He had been the seventh boy in a family of eight children. His mother had blamed him for not being the little girl she had hoped for; his father blamed him for not being able to go out in the world and get rich. His brothers blamed him for being a runt; and in the army, he was blamed for being a coward.

That one was fair, he had to admit. He *was* a coward, more or less. Fisticuffs appalled him, and gunfire alarmed him violently. He didn't like storms or lightning, and preferred to live on the first floor of apartment buildings, so escape would be easier in case of fire. He had been afraid that Katie wouldn't marry him, and once she did, he began to fear she would leave him, or else die.

But of all the things he had managed to be frightened of in his life, Colonel Terry's anger was unquestionably the most powerful. Brookshire feared the Terry temper so much that he would rather bite his tongue off than give the Colonel even the smallest particle of bad news.

Call didn't doubt what Brookshire said. A man who couldn't even control his hat was likely to attract a lot of blame. In that respect, Call reflected, Brookshire was not unlike Pea Eye himself. Pea had a strange tendency to assume that any bad turn of fortune was probably his fault. On the long cattle drive to Montana, various things happened that could not easily have been prevented. One morning the little Texas bull that all the cowboys feared got into a fight with a grizzly. The grizzly definitely didn't fear the bull; the fight was more or less a draw, though the bull got much of his hide ripped off, in the process of holding his own.

For reasons that no one could fathom, Pea Eye decided the encounter was his fault. He felt he should either have roped the bull, or shot the bear, though neither, in Call's view, would have been sensible procedure. If he had roped the bull, it might well have jerked Pea's horse down, in which case the bear would have got them both. If Pea had tried to kill the grizzly with a sidearm, the bear might have turned on the cowboys, instead of on the bull.

Five years and more later, Pea Eye was still worrying about his role in the encounter. What it showed was that people weren't sensible, when it came to assigning or assuming blame.

People were rarely sensible about anything, in Call's opinion. He had taken, he thought, a sensible approach to Pea Eye's desertion while he was actually in the man's presence—but now that he wasn't actually faced with his old corporal, Call found that his anger was rising. He had taken Pea Eye into his troop of Rangers when the latter was no more than a boy, too young to be an official member of any military organization. But, because the boy looked honest, Call had bent the rules, which were more bendable then than they would become.

Now, it seemed, Pea Eye had deserted him in favor of matrimony, and the desertion left a bitter taste in his mouth. Call had supposed that if he could count on any of his old troop, he could count on Pea. Yet it turned out to be Lorena, once a whore, now a schoolteacher, who could count on Pea.

Call had no doubt that Clara Allen had been behind the match, and though fifteen years had passed, he still resented her interference. It was one thing to educate Lorena; whores had as much right to improve themselves as anybody else. But it was another thing to arrange matters so that the girl could take his most trusted helper.

Dish Boggett, the best of the Hat Creek cowboys and far better on horseback than Pea had ever been, had mooned over Lorena for years. Why couldn't Clara have nudged the girl into accepting Dish? Up to that time Pea had shown no great inclination to domesticity, though he briefly courted, or was courted by, a rather bossy widow in the village of Lonesome Dove. The trail drive had ended that, if there'd been anything to end.

Because of Clara's meddling, or Lorena's boldness, or a combination of the two, Call was riding south with only a Yankee office worker, to go after the most enterprising young bandit to show up on the border in a decade or more.

It galled Call—when he next encountered Pea Eye, he intended to make that clear.

"I regret now that I didn't force him," Call said to Brookshire. "It leaves us shorthanded. It's just that I never expected to have to force Pea Eye. He's always followed me, before."

Brookshire noticed that the Captain looked a little tight around the mouth.

"How long has your friend been married?" he asked.

"Fifteen years, I suppose. He had a number of children, though I have not met them," Call said.

"You have not married yourself, I take it?" Brookshire asked, cautiously. He did not want to annoy the man, as he clearly had earlier in the day by asking him how long he had been a lawman.

"Oh no," Call said. "It's one thing I never tried. But you're married, and you're here. Your wife hasn't stopped you from doing your duty."

"Why, Katie wouldn't care if I went to China," Brookshire

said. "She's got her sewing, and then there's the cat. She's very fond of the cat."

Call said nothing. He knew women were sometimes fond of cats, though the reason for the attraction escaped him.

"So what will we do for a second man, now that your deputy has declined?" Brookshire asked. "Know any good gun hands in San Antonio?"

"Nobody reliable," Call said. "I don't know what a gun hand is, but if I ever happened to meet one I doubt I'd want to hire him."

"No offense," Brookshire said. "That's just what we call them in New York."

"I would rather do the job alone than to take someone unreliable, particularly if we have to go into Mexico," Call said.

"We might, I guess," Brookshire said. "He did rob that train with the governor of Coahuila on it. That was his worst act, after robbing Mr. Stanford."

"I doubt he knew the governor was on the train," Call said. "That was just luck. I doubt he ever heard of Mr. Stanford, either. I hadn't myself, until you mentioned him."

"Maybe I ought to wire the Colonel," Brookshire suggested. "The Colonel could raise an army, if he wanted to. I'm sure he can find us one man."

"No," Call said. "I'll do my own looking. Your Colonel might find the wrong fellow."

"I leave it to you, Captain," Brookshire said.

Call didn't answer. The question of Pea Eye's replacement was not one he was ready to consider. He was still brooding about Pea Eye, the man who hadn't come. His temper kept rising, too. It rose so high that it took all his self-restraint to keep from stopping the train and going after Pea Eye. Part of his anger was directed at himself for having been so mild and meek in the face of plain desertion. Of course, in strict terms, it *wasn't* desertion; no war was on, he himself wasn't even a Ranger anymore, and neither was Pea. The man wasn't really in his employ, and they were just going to eliminate a bandit, no very glorious cause or glorious work, either.

But then, none of their work had been glorious. It had all been bloody, hard, and tiring, from their first foray against the Kiowa until now. There were no bugles, no parades, and very few certainties, in the life they led as Rangers. Call had killed several men, Indian, white, and Mexican, whose courage he admired; in some cases he had even admired their ideals. Many times, going into battle, a portion of his sympathies had been with the enemy. The Mexicans along the border had been robbed, by treaty, of country and cattle that had been their grandparents'; the Comanche and the Kiowa had to watch the settlement of hunting grounds that had been theirs for many generations.

Call didn't blame the Mexicans for fighting. He didn't blame the Comanche or the Kiowa, either. Had he been them, he would have fought just as hard. He was pledged to arrest them or remove them, not to judge them.

But he *did* blame Pea Eye for not coming with him on the trip. Of course, the reasons Pea gave were not empty excuses: he did have a wife to care for, children to raise, and a farm to work.

In Call's view, there was an obligation stronger than those, and that obligation was loyalty. It seemed to him the highest principle, loyalty. He preferred it to honor. He had never been exactly sure what men meant when they spoke of their honor, though it had been a popular word during the time of the War. He *was* sure, though, what he meant when he spoke of loyalty. A man didn't desert his comrades, his troop, his leader. If he did he was, in Call's book, worthless.

Jake Spoon, a friend he had ended up having to hang—there was an example of a man without loyalty. Jake had rangered with Gus and Call. He was as pleasant and engaging a man as Call had ever known. But he had no loyalty, as he had proven in Kansas, when he ran off with a gang of thieving killers. When they caught him, Jake could scarcely believe that his old compañeros would hang him—but they hung him.

Pea Eye's case was far less extreme, of course. He hadn't thrown in with killers and thieves; he had merely married. Pea was not a man who could be said to be without loyalty. But he had *changed* loyalties, and what did that say? The whole point of loyalty was not to change: stick with those who stuck with you. Pea Eye had proven his loyalty countless times, on the old trails. But then he had chosen a new trail.

Thinking about the matter caused Call to alternate between anger and sorrow. One minute he wanted to ride over to the Quitaque and order Pea Eye to get his rifle and saddle and come; but the next moment, he felt he ought to respect Pea Eye's choice and leave him in peace with his wife, his children, and his farm. He himself would have enjoyed the trip south a great deal more if Pea had been along, but then, he was not in the business for enjoyment, he guessed. He was in the business to make a living. Once, there had been more to it than that, or at least, he had convinced himself that there was more to it. The politicians said that the killing he had done was necessary. Call was no longer so sure it *had* been necessary. But even if it had always been, in the main, a way to make a living, loyalty to one's own was still the first duty, and he felt a painful pressure in his breast when he thought of Pea Eye's defection.

Brookshire looked at the long plain outside the train window and sighed. The train seemed to creep. There was nothing but the horizon to measure its progress by, and the horizon was just an endless line. He remembered that he had some books in his valise—dime novels he had provided himself with in Kansas City, in case he came down with the doldrums during his travels.

There was also a pack of cards in his valise. On the whole, he preferred card playing to reading. Card playing didn't wear the mind down so.

"Captain, are you a card-playing man?" he asked, hopefully. A good game of cards would go a long way toward relieving the tedium of train travel.

"No," Call said.

"Well, I didn't really think you were," Brookshire said. He sighed, and rummaged in his valise until he found the dime novels. He pulled them out, glanced at them, and put them

[45]

back where he found them. After a little more rummaging, he located the pack of cards.

"I reckon it'll be solitaire, then," he said, with another hopeful glance at the Captain.

Captain Woodrow Call didn't say a word.

4.

On his way home, Pea Eye made a detour in order to ride by the schoolhouse. The little building was perched on a low bluff overlooking the Red River. He could see it, in spots, from fifteen miles away.

Pea rarely went to the school. On the few occasions when he did show up there, Lorena made it plain that he should state his business and then go on about it. The school was her place. On an active day, she had as many as thirty children to manage, and she needed to pay attention. Clarie was so good with spelling, and also with arithmetic, that Lorena sometimes let her daughter help her with the little kids. But she was the schoolmistress, and most of what had to be done, she did.

Still, Pea Eye felt an urgent need to see his wife, even though he knew she would not be at her most welcoming. At first, when Captain Call politely shook his hand and got back on the train, Pea felt relieved. The Captain didn't seem quite himself, but at least he hadn't been angry, and he had not attempted to insist that Pea Eye go with him.

But Pea Eye's relief scarcely lasted until he was out of sight of the train. He felt good for a few minutes, but then he began to feel strange. It was as if he were leaking—emptying out, like a bucket that had bullet holes in it. He began to feel sad—the same sadness he had felt in bed the night before. He had lain beside Lorena then, warmed by her body, wishing he didn't have to go anywhere. Now, it was clear that he wouldn't have to go. He could be with his wife and children, and get on with his many chores. The spring winds had blown a corner off the roof of the barn. All summer and fall he had meant to get it mended, but he hadn't. Now, he could attend to it, and to other much needed repairs as well. He could do whatever he wanted to, around the place.

Yet he felt so sad he could hardly keep from crying. His memories were getting mixed up with his feelings. Thinking of the barn with the leaky roof reminded him of the barn that had belonged to the Hat Creek outfit, way south in Lonesome Dove. That barn had no roof at all, for years. Of course, it seldom rained in Lonesome Dove, so the stock didn't suffer much, as it would have if that barn had been in the Panhandle. But the stock wasn't really what was on Pea Eye's mind, or in his memory. What was on his mind was the old Hat Creek outfit itself— his old compañeros, the men he had ridden with for years. Captain Call, of course, and Gus McCrae and Deets and Newt and Dish Boggett, old Bol the cook, and Jake Spoon; Soupy and Jasper Fant and all the rest. Now they were scattered, not merely all over the cattle country, but between life and death as well. Gus had died in Miles City, Montana, of gangrene in his leg. Deets was killed by an Indian boy in Wyoming; Jake, they had to hang in Kansas. Then the boy Newt, a good boy whom Pea had always liked and respected, had the life crushed out of him by the Hell Bitch, way up on the Milk River.

Pea loved his wife and children, and he couldn't imagine life without them. He hadn't wanted to go with the Captain, and he still didn't. But, despite that, he missed his old partners of the trail. The boys would never ride out together again; they would never be an outfit again. It was sad, but it was life.

He knew, too, that the Captain must have had a hard time holding his temper, when he discovered that he would have to go after Joey Garza alone. The matter of the bandit didn't worry Pea Eye, though. He couldn't imagine a bandit that the Captain couldn't subdue. That was just the order of things. It was Lorena, though, who kept pointing out that the order of things could change.

"Nothing's permanent," she insisted. "We'll get old, and the children will grow up."

"I'll get old first—I guess I'm old now," Pea Eye answered. "You won't get old for a long time."

"I don't know about that," Lorena said. "I've borne five children. It don't make you younger."

Now, riding beside the pale river with its wide sandy bed, occasionally catching a glimpse of the schoolhouse where his wife spent her days, Pea Eye had to admit that the order of things *had* changed. This was one of the days when it changed.

Lorena saw Pea Eye coming, through the glass window of the school room. The glass had to be ordered from Fort Worth, and the whole of the Quitaque community was proud of it. Few were the settlers who could afford glass windows for themselves.

"Here comes your pa," she said to Clarie. "I wonder if Captain Call lit into him?"

"He better not have. He don't own my pa," Clarie said. She deeply resented the Captain, a man she had never met. He had never even come to meet her and the other children, yet he loomed in her life because of the power he had to take her father away. She knew her father felt obligated to the Captain, but she didn't know why. It wasn't the Captain who had given her mother the money to buy the farm. Her mother resented the old man, too. Clarie knew that, from eavesdropping on her parents. Half the arguments she had overheard as she was growing up had to do with Captain Call. They were not arguments, really. Her father didn't know how to argue, or didn't want to, but her mother certainly knew how to argue. Her mother said many ugly things when she was mad. Mostly, her father just quietly obeyed her mother. He tried his best to do what she wanted him to do. The only times he didn't was when the Captain needed him. Then, he just saddled up and left.

"I thought he went with the Captain," Clarie said, surprised to see her father coming.

"No, he didn't go," Lorena said. "He finally stood up to the man."

"Goodness!" Clarie said. It was a big shock, a big change. "Are you glad, Ma?"

"I will be when I know I can trust it," Lorena said.

She had been about to test some of the older children in multiplication, but she closed her arithmetic book and went to the back door of the school. Pea Eye rode up, looking a little hangdog. He knew she didn't really like for him to show up at the school. She didn't like to see him looking hangdog, either, though—it made her feel that she must have been mean to him. She didn't want to feel that she had been mean to Pea. In the years of their marriage he had never raised his voice, much less his hand, to her in anger. He knew she wasn't an angel, and yet, year in and year out, Pea treated her like one. A man that steady was rare, and she knew it.

Still, the fact was, she was busy. She had an arithmetic class to teach, and few of her pupils were adept at arithmetic.

"Well, the Captain left without me," Pea Eye said quietly. He felt out of place; he always did, when he visited Lorie at the schoolhouse. He wasn't really even sure why he had come. He felt sad inside, and just wanted to be with his wife for a few minutes.

"Did he fuss at you?" Lorena asked. She was touched, that Pea had come. She lived with many doubts, but she never had to doubt that Pea Eye needed her. If he needed anything, he needed her. At the moment he looked gloomy and pale; lately he had been waking up with bad headaches.

"Are you sick, honey?" She asked, softening suddenly. Why was she so stiff with him, so often? He just seemed to bring it out in her, for no better reason than that he loved her to distraction. She liked it that he loved her, but she wished, sometimes, that he wouldn't be so obvious about it.

"No, he just shook my hand and left," Pea Eye said.

"Have you got one of those headaches?" she asked.

"It's pounding," Pea admitted. "This horse has got a stiff trot."

It isn't the stiff trot, it's the stiff wife, Lorena thought to herself—no point in saying it to Pea. He usually didn't know he was being punished, even when he was being punished severely.

"Wait a minute," she said, turning back into the schoolhouse. Clarie was comforting a little boy who had wet his pants. The child's mother had gone berserk that winter and had to be sent away. Two days out of three, the little boy wet his pants in the schoolroom. He missed his mother badly.

"Clarie, you better go home with your pa," Lorena said. "He's feeling poorly."

"But Ma, Roy and I were going to study together," Clarie protested, looking across the room at Roy Benson. Roy was the tallest boy in the school, by several inches, and he was also the nicest. He was nearly as tall as her pa—maybe that was why she liked him so.

"You can study with Roy tomorrow—your pa needs you today," Lorena said.

"But who'll help you with Laurie and the boys, on the way home?" Clarie asked, trying hard to come up with a good reason why she should stay. Roy's folks were thinking of taking him out of school, since he couldn't be spared from the ranch work much longer. She hated to miss even one day with Roy. The Benson ranch was fifteen miles from their farm. Clarie felt she would never get to see him, once he left school.

"Since when have I not been able to get home with my own children?" Lorena asked, a little impatiently. She was anxious to get Clarie and Pea Eye gone. The children were beginning to act up, as they always did when her attention wavered for more than a minute or two. Roy Benson was usually the instigator, too. He was a bright boy, but full of the devil.

"Well, you can take care of them, but Laurie is my sister and I like to help with her," Clarie said.

"You do help, but now I need you to help your father," Lorena said. "I wouldn't ask it, if I didn't need it."

Clarie gave up. The look in her mother's eye was a look you didn't argue with, if you were smart.

"Can I just go tell Roy I can't study with him today?" she asked.

"I'll tell him," Lorena said. "He ain't made of air, Clarie. He'll be here tomorrow."

"Ma, you said 'ain't,' " Clarie told her, startled. Her mother's grammar only slipped when she was angry, or in a hurry.

"Yes, because you're vexing me," Lorena said. "You know I slip up, when you vex me."

"Roy might not be here tomorrow," Clarie said, returning to the original point at issue. "His folks might make him work, and then I'll never get to see him."

She felt bitter. Roy was the only nice boy she knew, and now his folks might make him leave her, in order to help with the cow work.

But, bitter or not, she knew it was unwise to provoke her mother past a certain point, and that point was not far away. With another futile glance at Roy—he was teasing a little kid and did not see her—she went outside and obediently climbed up behind her father. Windmill, her father's big gray horse, grunted, but at least didn't break wind. For some reason, hearing horses break wind embarrassed her keenly; at least it did when there was a man around, even if the man was her father.

"Pa, do you like Roy Benson?" she asked, as they were trotting homeward.

"Roy? He's gangly, but then so am I," Pea Eye said.

5.

Billy Williams had to walk the last five miles into Ojinaga because he lost his horse. It was a ridiculous accident. It was sure to hurt his reputation as the last of the great scouts, and his reputation had been slipping badly, anyway.

The horse became misplaced as a result of the fact that Billy had to answer a call of nature. He had been riding at a sharp clip, all the way from Piedras Negras—the news he had was so urgent that it prompted him to neglect the call until disgrace was at hand. Then, he failed to tether his mount properly and the horse wandered off. Perhaps because of the sharp clip he had maintaincd, or the tequila he had drunk while maintaining it, Billy relaxed so much in the course of his call of nature that he dozed off for a few minutes, still squatting. That in itself was nothing new, since he often nodded off for a few minutes while squatting in response to nature's call. Squatting was a position he found completely comfortable; in fact, it was one of the few that he did find comfortable. When he stood up straight, he coughed too much. His diagnosis was that a couple of his ribs were poking into a lung, the result of an encounter a few years back with a buffalo cow that looked dead but wasn't.

Lying flat on his back was not a good position, either. A headache usually accompanied that position, probably because Billy never lay flat on his back unless he was dead drunk.

The fact was, his horse wasn't very far away; Billy just couldn't see him. His vision had once been so sharp that he could see a small green worm on a small green leaf, at a distance of thirty yards. Now, he couldn't even see his own horse if the horse was thirty yards away. It was a sad state for a great scout to have come to.

"Willie, you best retire," his friend Roy Bean told him the last time the two of them visited. "A man as blind as you are ought not to be riding this river. You could fall in a hole and be swallowed up and that would be that."

Roy Bean didn't deliver that opinion with much concern in his voice. Like most of Roy Bean's pronouncements, this one got said mainly because the man was vain and arrogant. He had never been able to get enough of the sound of his own voice, though it held no particular charm for anyone but himself.

"You're blind drunk nine days out of ten—what keeps *you* from falling in a hole and being swallowed up?" Billy asked.

"The fact is, I sit here in this chair in this saloon, not nine days out of ten but ten days out of ten," Roy Bean said. "If I could sit here in this chair eleven days out of ten, I would. I don't go wandering off where there might be a hole that could swallow me up."

That point was hard to dispute. Roy Bean seldom left his chair; even seldomer did he leave his saloon; and never, so far as anyone living knew, had he been outside the town of Langtry, Texas, a town that consisted mainly of Roy Bean's saloon.

"But then I ain't the last of the great scouts," Roy Bean said. "I don't have to go traipsing through the gullies. I got no reputation to maintain."

"I won't fall in no hole," Billy assured him. "I won't get swallowed up, neither.

"I would have to be a lot blinder than this, before I quit tracking," Billy added, though that claim was bravado. Traveling was becoming more and more worrisome, and as for tracking, he probably could track an elephant if he could stay in hearing distance of it. But tracking anything smaller, including his own horse, was a hopeless matter.

[54]

"Well, if you do avoid holes, there's the problem of killers," Roy Bean reminded him. "You can't see in front of you, or behind you, or to the side. The dumbest killer in the West could sneak up on you and cut your throat."

Billy refrained from comment. The two of them were sitting in Roy's dirty, flyblown saloon while they were having the discussion. The saloon was hot as well as filthy, and the liquor cost too much, but it was the only saloon around and contained the only liquor to be had along that stretch of the border.

Roy Bean, out of a combination of boredom, greed, and vanity, had recently appointed himself judge of a vast jurisdiction —the trans-Pecos West—and nowadays hung people freely, often over differences amounting to no more than fifty cents. It was an ominous practice, in Billy's view; he had often found himself having differences with Roy Bean amounting to considerably more than fifty cents. Roy had been told by many of his constituents that he shouldn't hang people over such paltry sums, and of course, he had a ready reply.

"A man that will steal fifty cents would just as soon steal a million dollars, and he would, if the opportunity presented itself," Roy said.

"Roy, the opportunity ain't going to present itself, not around here," Billy pointed out. "Nobody around here *has* a million dollars to steal. Not many of them has fifty cents, not in cash money."

"Well, I have fifty cents," Roy said. "I mean to keep it, too."

"If I was to steal it, would you hang me?" Billy asked. He didn't suppose Roy to be a man of much tolerance, but he thought he'd ask the question anyway.

"I'd hang you as soon as I could find my rope," Roy said amiably.

"We've known one another a long time," Billy reminded him. "I've nursed you through several fevers and I once killed a Mexican who had it in for you. I expect he would have cut your throat, later in life, if I hadn't laid him out."

"What'd you shoot this Mexican fellow with?" Roy asked. He was a master of the diversionary question.

Billy had to stop and think. Several years had passed since the encounter, and his memory had grown almost as cloudy as his eyesight.

"It wasn't no Colt," he said, finally. "I don't remember what it was. A gun of some kind. What difference does it make? He's dead, which is one reason you're alive. Now you're telling me you'd hang me for fifty cents. I consider that harsh."

"Well, I don't know that I could put my hands on my hanging rope, in a hurry," Roy said. "You might escape, if you were agile."

"Who said you could be a judge, anyway?" Billy inquired. "I'd want to see some papers on it, before I let you hang me."

"Since when can you read law papers?" Roy asked. "I've known you for too long and I've never seen you read anything, unless you count a pack of cards."

"I could read if it was that or be hung," Billy said. "You can't just say you're a judge and have it be true. There has to be some papers on it, somewhere."

"Out here west of the Pecos you can be a judge if you want to bad enough," Roy said. "I want to bad enough."

"Suppose I only stole a dime?" Billy asked. "What would happen then?"

"Same sentence, if you stole it from me," Roy said. "I need my dimes. If you stole ten cents from a Mexican I might let you off.

"The loss of any sum is more than I can tolerate, officially," he added.

"I can't tell that you've ever amounted to much, Roy," Billy informed him. "It's irritating that you set up to be a judge of your fellowman, so late in life. It's all because of this saloon. It's the only saloon around here, and that's why you think you can be a judge."

"I admit it was a timely purchase," Roy said.

"You didn't purchase it, you shot the owner," Billy reminded him. "Tom Sykes, I knew him. He was nothing but a cutthroat himself."

"That's right—so I purchased his saloon with a bullet," Roy said. "Three bullets in all. Tom wasn't eager to die."

"That's still cheap," Billy said.

"Not as cheap as one bullet," Roy said. "The sad truth is, my marksmanship has declined. In my prime, I would not have had to expend that much ammunition on Tommy Sykes."

Because of the saloon, it was necessary to put up with Roy, but the more urgent necessity was to get to Ojinaga and give Maria the news he had picked up in Piedras Negras. It was a great annoyance to Billy that because of a long shit and a short nap he had lost his horse. But that was the truth of it, and there was nothing he could do but limp along.

By the time he finally stumbled up to Maria's house, Billy was exhausted. His head was swimming from the strain of the long walk, and he was sweating a rainstorm. He had to grope his way through Maria's goats. Her goats seemed to think he had come hurrying all the way from Piedras Negras just to feed them.

Maria heard the goats bleating and went out to have a look. Someone had seen a cougar, near the village; she didn't want a cougar getting one of her goats. But they were only bleating at Billy Williams, who looked as if he might fall on his face at any moment.

"Where's your horse?" she asked, walking out to have a better look at him. She had known Billy Williams for many years. Sometimes she let him stay at her house, because he loved her children and would help her with them, far more than any of her husbands ever had. He also loved her, but that was not a matter she allowed him to discuss.

"Where's Joey? I got bad news," Billy said, stopping amid the goats. Maria frightened him a little. She always had. He presumed nothing when he came to her house.

"Joey left—I don't know where he went," Maria said.

"Damn the luck," Billy said. "I've traveled a long way to bring him some news and now I'm tired. I'm tired and I'm blind and I'm old and I'm thirsty."

"You can sleep in the saddle shed," Maria said. "Come in—

I'll feed you and give you coffee. I can't do nothing about your other problems."

"I'd rather have a bottle of beer, if you can spare one," Billy said, limping into the house. "I seldom walk in the heat, and I wouldn't have today, but my horse escaped."

"I don't keep beer in my house," Maria said. "You know that. You stay here. If you want beer you'll have to go to the cantina."

"Well, what's the harm in beer?" Billy asked, wishing Maria didn't sound so stern. He didn't know why he had asked for beer, since he knew she didn't keep it. Maria had been wonderfully beautiful once; probably she was still beautiful. Because of his poor eyesight, all he could see when he looked at her face was a dim outline. He had to fill in the outline with his memories. When he was younger he had coveted her greatly. He would have married her, or given her anything, for a taste of her favors, but he had never tasted them. He still did covet Maria, although he couldn't really see her now, except in his memories.

"The harm is not in the beer," Maria told him. "The harm is in men. Drunk men. Some of them beat women. Some of them have beaten me. If you want beer, go to the cantina, but tell me your news first."

"This is important news," Billy said. He saw a water bucket sitting by the stove, with a dipper in it. He limped over and helped himself to a dipperful. The water was cool and sweet. Before he knew it he had helped himself to three dipperfuls.

"Don't you even know which direction Joey went?" Billy asked.

Maria didn't answer. She didn't like to answer questions—not about her son Joey, not about anything. What she knew was hers; no one had a right to it, unless it was her children, and even their rights had limits. Much of what she knew was for no one to know. It was hers, and by knowing it she had survived. People were curious; women were even worse than men, in that respect; but that was not her problem.

"Where does the wind go?" she said. "Joey's young. A thousand miles isn't long to Joey."

[58]

"No, and a thousand miles might not be far enough, either—this time," Billy said.

Maria just looked at him. He was in disgusting condition, filthy and drunk. His weak eyes dripped rheum down his cheeks, which were red from years of drinking. But he had been loyal to her and her children for many years. Billy was the only man who had been good to Joey, when Joey was small. He had bought Joey his first saddle. He just walked up with it one day and gave it to Joey, when Joey was six. It was Joey's happiest day, the day Billy brought him the saddle.

Maria was with Juan Castro then, her second husband, and her worst. Juan Castro was so jealous that Maria never dared tell him that Joey was her son, so she pretended he was her dead sister's child. Even so, in that same year, Juan Castro sold Joey to the Apaches. Maria was away in Agua Prieta, helping her mother die. When she returned to Ojinaga and found her son gone, she was wild. She told Juan Castro she would kill him the first time he went to sleep. He beat her—he had beaten her many times—and left. Maria never saw him again, but she didn't have to kill him. His own brother did it, in a fight over a horse.

At that point, she went to Billy Williams and begged him to go trade with the Apaches to get her son back. Maria had never sold herself. She had never been with any man she didn't want. But she was desperate; she offered to be with Billy Williams, if he would go save her son. She had never said such words to a man before. She considered herself a modest woman. She had picked badly, when it came to men, but she had picked for love. Joey was her firstborn, and she knew the Apaches would kill him if he angered them, or else they would trade him themselves, farther and farther north, so that she could never find him.

Maria didn't want to live if Joey was lost, and yet, she had her children to raise, the two she had by Juan Castro. Rafael, the boy, had no mind and would die without her care; Teresa, the girl, was bright and pretty and quick, but born blind. Rafael lived with the goats and the chickens. Teresa, his sister, was never far from him, for she was the only one who could understand Rafael's jumbled words.

Maria knew she wouldn't have the strength to raise her damaged children unless she got Joey back. If she lost her firstborn, she would give up. She would whore, or do worse than whore. Billy was said to be a good scout, since he could talk the Indian tongues. For the sake of her children, she didn't want to give up.

So she went to Billy Williams and offered herself. To her surprise, Billy Williams, who had often pursued her and even tried to marry her, looked embarrassed.

"Oh no, that wouldn't be right—I couldn't have that," Billy said. He tilted his chair back, as if to remove himself from the slightest temptation.

For a moment, Maria felt hopeless. She had nothing else to offer, and now the man was refusing what he had often sought.

"It wouldn't be right," Billy repeated. "Don't disturb yourself about it, Mary. I'll find Joey."

He found Joey, far to the north, in the Sierra Madre, but the Apaches wouldn't trade him. All he could tell Maria was that Joey looked healthy and could speak Apache better than he could.

A year later, when Maria was so unhappy Billy feared she would die, he went again to the Sierra Madre; but again, he had to return and report failure. He had taken enough money that time to buy Joey, but Joey was nowhere to be found. He had escaped, and even the Apaches couldn't catch him. Since then, no one had caught him. He showed up in Ojinaga a week after Billy's return, just as Maria was slipping into hopelessness.

Later, Joey claimed that it was his years with the Apaches that enabled him to rob gringo trains so easily. The Apaches held a hard school, but they knew much. Joey learned what they knew, and he had not forgotten it.

"Tell me your news," Maria said. "I'm here and Joey's not."

"The railroad's hired Woodrow Call, that's it," Billy said—he was glad to have it out. "You know who that is, don't you?"

"I should—he hung my father and my brother," Maria said. "And my brother-in-law. My sister's a widow, because of Call."

"Well, that's who they've hired," Billy said. "It's a compliment, I guess. A railroad wouldn't spend that kind of money on just any bandit."

"Do you know Call?" Maria asked. The name sent a chill through her. She had loved her father and her brother. They had done no more than take back horses that the Texans had taken from them. No living man had caused her as much grief as Woodrow Call: not the four husbands, three of whom beat her; not the gringos, who insulted her, assuming that because she was a brown woman, she was a whore.

Now Call wanted Joey. He wanted her firstborn.

"I know the man, but the acquaintance ain't real fresh," Billy said. "I rangered for him about a month once, but he turned me out for drinking on patrol. I'm older than he is, and I've drunk when I had a thirst, all my life. It don't affect my vigilance much, but the Captain didn't believe me. Or didn't like me or something. He turned me out."

"Would you recognize him?" Maria asked.

"Why, yes. I expect I would," Billy said.

"If he comes here, show him to me," Maria said.

"Why, so you can kill him?" Billy said.

Maria didn't answer. Billy knew better than to repeat the question. Repeating questions only made Maria close up more tightly.

"What was your last husband's name?" he asked, changing the subject. "It's slipped my mind."

"Roberto Sanchez," Maria said.

"I don't see him—did he leave?" he asked.

"He left," Maria said.

"That makes four husbands, by my count," Billy said. "The two mean ones and Benito and this one. I don't know if this one was mean."

"Why are you counting my husbands?" Maria asked. Despite herself, she felt some amusement. Poor, skinny, and blind as he was, Billy still had some life in him. He was still interested in her, enough to want to know if her husband was around. Life still amused him. Once, it had amused them both, a lot. They had danced together, laughed together. There were times when it still amused Maria, but those times were rare. It interested her, though, that an old man with no money and almost no eyesight could still derive amusement from the things humans did. And he could still want her.

"I just like to keep track of your husbands. It's my pastime," Billy said. "Why did Señor Sanchez leave, if I ain't prying?"

"You're prying," Maria said.

"My feet hurt, tell me anyway," Billy said.

Maria smiled. Billy couldn't see the smile, but he could tell that her tone was a little less severe. He wished he could see her face. All he could see was a sort of outline.

"He left me because he didn't like me," Maria said.

"Why, he married you—why didn't he like you?" Billy asked.

"He liked the way I look," Maria said. "He mistook that for me."

"I sympathize with him, I've often made the same mistake," Billy said. "I'm sure I'd make it again, if I could see better."

"I think Joey went to Crow Town," Maria said. She didn't want to talk about her husbands, or her dealings with men.

"Crow Town, good Lord," Billy said.

"Joey is young," Maria said. "He likes such places."

"I'm old, I don't," Billy said. "I'd almost rather crawl off and die than go to Crow Town."

"Who said you had to go?" Maria asked.

"Woodrow Call has hung enough Mexicans," BIlly said. "I better go and warn Joey. Swift as he is, he might get away. If my going to Crow Town will help, then I'll go to Crow Town."

"You don't listen," Maria said. "You don't let me talk, and when I do you don't listen. I'll go to Crow Town myself."

"*You'll* go?" Billy said. "How long do you think you'll last, in that stink hole?"

"Long enough to warn my son," Maria said.

"No, I'll go. Joey relies on me to keep him informed about lawmen and such," Billy said.

[62]

"You lost your horse," Maria reminded him.

"Well, it ain't the only horse," Billy said. "I can get another horse.

"I doubt even Woodrow Call would go to Crow Town," he added. "Everybody that lives there hates him. He'd have to kill the whole town."

"You've forgotten how he is," Maria said. "If he's hired to go there, he'll go. If they sent him to kill Joey he'll go wherever Joey is."

"Well, I mean to get there first, even if I have to walk," Billy said. "The man turned me out. I can't forget it."

Thinking about Crow Town gave him such a terrible thirst that he limped off to the cantina and bought two bottles of tequila. There was an outhouse behind the cantina that afforded him a little shade, and he sat down in the shade and drank one bottle rapidly. Midway through the second bottle, as he was about to pass out, a vaquero came riding up, leading Billy's lost horse.

"I found your horse, old man," Pedro, the vaquero, said.

Billy found that the mere thought of his horse, not to mention the sight of him, to the extent he could see him, made him furious. The willful beast had caused him not only discomfort but embarrassment. For a man of his prestige to have to walk into a one-saloon town such as Ojinaga was little short of disgraceful.

Without hesitation, but not without difficulty, he managed to extract his pistol from its holster. His hand didn't seem to want to go where his brain told it to. His hand often rebelled in such fashion when he was drunk. But he eventually got the pistol more or less firmly in his grasp, and without worrying too much about aiming, he emptied it in the direction of Pedro and the horse. Of course, he had no wish to injure Pedro, who was a decent vaquero. He only meant to shoot the horse, in the head, if possible. But the only casualty of the fusillade was a little white goat who happened to be standing idly by, just in the wrong spot.

"*Gracias*," Pedro said, tipping his hat to the old man who

leaned against the outhouse wall. "That's one less goat to get in my way."

Pedro was a little disgusted. The old man had once been a renowned scout. He had been good enough to track Indians, it was said. He had once been a notable shot, too. Now he couldn't hit his own horse, at a distance of twenty yards. In Pedro's view, it would be better for such men to die and not go around shooting other people's goats.

Later, Billy found a bush that offered better shade than the light outhouse. He finished the second bottle of tequila and took a little nap. When he awoke, with an empty bottle and an empty gun beside him, Maria was kneeling by his legs. She seemed to be looping a rope around his legs. Her spotted mare was standing with her. He could just make out the spots. Then he was being dragged, slowly. If the dragging had been rapid, it would have upset his stomach. When the dragging stopped, he was behind Maria's house, near the pump. Before Billy could give the matter more thought, he found himself under a waterfall. Cold water was splashing in his face. He felt he could drown, if he wasn't lucky, from the flood of water. But when it stopped splashing, he was not drowned. He tried to raise up and bumped his head hard on Maria's pump. She had been pumping water in his face.

"I have to go find Joey," Maria said. "Look after my children. Don't let anything happen to them."

"Well, I won't," Billy said. "Are you armed?"

"No, I don't like guns," Maria said.

"You ought to take my pistol. You'd be safer," he told her.

"I don't want your gun, Billy," Maria said. "If I have a gun some man might take it away from me and beat me with it. I want you to stay here and see that Rafael and Teresa come to no harm."

But Billy persisted; finally, Maria took the gun. As she rode away on her spotted mare, Billy realized that she had called him by his name. That was a change. It had been several years since Maria had called him by his name.

6.

When Bolivar saw the Captain, he began to cry.

"*Capitán, capitán,*" he said, sobbing. Call had grown used to it, since Bol cried every time he showed up. But Brookshire, meeting the old man for the first time, was embarrassed. The place where the old man boarded was only a hovel made of mud, or of a mudlike substance, at least.

Soon Josefeta, the mother of the family that cared for Bolivar, was crying too.

"God sent you just in time, Captain," she said, in a shaking voice. "We can't have Bolivar with us, no more. Roberto has no patience with him. He hits him."

"Well, he oughtn't to hit him," Call said. "What's Bol done, to bring it on?"

"Last week he set himself on fire," Josefeta said. "Sometimes he cuts himself. In the night he cries out and wakes the children."

Call sighed. Bol's hair was snow white. He was still crying and shaking.

"He needs a haircut," Call said. The old man's hair was nearly to his shoulders, making him look shakier than he was.

"Last time we cut it he grabbed the scissors and tried to stab Ramon," Josefeta said. "Then he cut himself. I think he wants to end his life. It's a mortal sin."

Call had a good deal of respect for Josefeta. She had nine or ten children and a husband who was apparently none too nice. The money he paid her for keeping Bol was probably about all that kept the family going. He knew that dealing with the old man must be a trial, but he had not supposed it to be such a severe trial that they were considering putting the old man out.

Brookshire was appalled. The old man was sure to be an impediment to their travels, although the Captain had made it clear that they were only taking him as far as Laredo. Still, in Brookshire's reckoning, every minute counted. That was Colonel Terry's philosophy, too; of that there could be no doubt. The Colonel expected them to catch Joey Garza before he robbed any more trains, particularly any more trains that might happen to be carrying a military payroll. The military did not take kindly to having its money snatched. Hints had been received; the military let it be known that they might have to find other modes of conveyance if the young Mexican struck one more time.

One of Josefeta's little boys came around the house, leading Bolivar's mule. The boy had saddled it for him. It was with some difficulty that they managed to hoist Bolivar onto the mule's skinny back. The experience darkened Brookshire's mood even more. The old fellow could not even mount his own mule unassisted. But Captain Call seemed undisturbed. He was patient with Bolivar, and he gave the woman a nice sum of money for the trouble she'd had.

"I'm sorry for the trouble, Josefeta," Call said. "He's just old, and wandering in his mind. Maybe a little travel will improve his spirits."

As they got ready to depart, children began to gather around the old man and his mule. They seemed to be about half and half, boys and girls, and all were weeping.

"We don't want him to go, we love him," Josefeta said. "Only Roberto has no more patience. I'm afraid something bad will happen."

Brookshire had been worried all morning, but, as they made

their way at a slow pace toward the outskirts of town, he found that the heat was so great it overwhelmed even his capacity for worry. It was winter on the plains, but summer still in San Antonio. At night Brookshire lay in his little hotel room, as hot as if he slept in a box with a stove under it. His underclothes were soaked, his bedclothes soaked. He sweated so much that he awoke in a puddle. The hotel room had windows, but no breeze blew through them. All that came through them was mosquitoes, wasps, and other flying bugs. Each morning he woke up feeling more fatigued than he felt when he went to bed.

If the Captain was bothered by the heat, it didn't show. If he was bothered by anything, it didn't show. He had taken Brookshire with him to visit the sheriff of San Antonio. Call wanted to see if the man might have a reliable deputy he could spare.

"Mr. Brookshire represents the railroad," Call said. He thought that was enough information to give out.

Being introduced as if he were Colonel Terry, or somebody important, perked Brookshire up briefly. It made him feel like a banker—he had often regretted that he hadn't become a banker. It was a breeze to his vanity, going around with the famous Ranger. But long before evening came, Brookshire had sweated out his vanity. The one cheering thing he could think of was that his wife, Katie, wasn't along. Katie disapproved of sweat. She considered it uncivilized. In her view, nice people didn't get drunk, spit in public, break wind, or sweat. On occasion, in the summertime, when the Brooklyn heat was at its most intense, Katie even denied him her favors in order to maintain her standards in regard to sweat.

Walking around San Antonio in the heat, or lying in his little box of a room at night, Brookshire had at least one thing to be grateful for: he and Katie weren't leading their conjugal life in south Texas. Feeling as she did about sweat, life would be bleak if they lived in San Antonio, where even the briefest embrace would be bound to give rise to a good deal of sweat.

A sheriff in the town, a young man much in awe of the Captain, had no deputies to spare, so the Captain spent the rest of the day looking at horses and pack mules, or choosing the equipment they would need on a journey up the river.

It was at this point that Brookshire gave the Captain a bad start. When Colonel Terry instructed his people to send the Captain a telegram, he meant, of course, to make it clear that Brookshire was to accompany him from beginning to end; that is, until Joey Garza was dead, or caught. The Colonel didn't spend money recklessly. Brookshire was a trained accountant. For more than twenty years, he had kept up with the Colonel's bills. The only bills he wasn't allowed to see were those that pertained to the Colonel's mistress, a mystery woman named Miss Cora. No one in the office had ever seen Miss Cora, though it was known that the Colonel kept her in an apartment on Fifth Avenue. Once in a while a bill for flowers or jewelry would get misdirected and arrive in the office, a circumstance that invariably threw the Colonel into a temper.

"Why, that idiot, that's for Cora," he would say, snatching the bill and stuffing it into his pocket. The Colonel's wife, another mystery figure, was known in the office as Miss Eleanora. She was thought to be prim, and her primness, in the minds of the office workers, explained Miss Cora and the apartment on Fifth Avenue, and the jewelry, and the flowers.

Now and then, seeing one of the misdirected bills—they were always from establishments of high repute—Brookshire would dream a little. He would imagine that he was as rich as the Colonel and able to keep a nice girlie, one whose standards in the matter of sweat were not as high as Katie's. He thought of this girlie as his Miss Belle, for he liked the name Belle. Of course, it was just a little dream. Brookshire knew that he would never be as rich as the Colonel, and even if he did acquire a little more money he might never find a girl named Belle who would care to live in an apartment on Fifth Avenue and receive flowers and jewelry, from him. It was just his little dream.

The point, though, that startled Captain Call was that Colonel Terry expected Brookshire and his ledger books to accompany Call on his chase. The Captain had been promised his expenses, as well as a substantial bonus, in the event of rapid success. An expedition, even a small one, was bound to incur expenses, so naturally, Brookshire was expected to keep a full accounting. Mostly, when trouble had arisen in the past, it had involved dirty work on the part of Colonel Terry's rivals in Chicago or Cleveland or Buffalo—someplace civilized. In those cases, Brookshire's job was to rein in the Pinkertons. As a rule, Pinkertons were inclined to be casual about money, and the Colonel wasn't.

Employing Captain Call to catch Joey Garza was not as simple as hiring the Pinkertons to beat up a switch buster. There was only one point of similarity, which was that in both cases, the Colonel's money was being spent. And when the Colonel's money was being spent, he expected a full accounting.

"Why? Doesn't the man trust me?" Call asked, when Brookshire revealed that he was expected to accompany him.

"The Colonel don't trust God," Brookshire said. The comment just slipped out. Colonel Terry's unwillingness to trust was not lost on any of his employees. He was constantly popping into the office to inspect their work. When Brookshire turned in his ledgers at the end of each week, the Colonel sat right down, took out his big magnifying glass, and went over the pages line by line.

Call was inspecting a stout gray gelding that he thought might do, when Brookshire revealed that he was expected to come along. Call had just lifted the horse's foreleg, in order to inspect the hoof. He was going into rocky country and the animals would need good feet. The notion that Brookshire, a man who couldn't keep his hat on his head, was planning to go with him into Mexico had never occurred to Call. Bol, shaky as he was, would be less of an impediment. At least Bol was used to hard living, and he was Mexican. Brookshire seemed to be a decent man, but decency was one thing, experience entirely another. Call had no idea whether the man could even ride.

"But Mr. Brookshire," he said. "You're not equipped, and this isn't your line of work. I know you're a family man, and there is some danger involved. To be blunt, I'd rather not take you."

"I'd rather not go, neither, but what choice do I have?" Brookshire asked. "I'm a salaried man. I work for Colonel Terry. He expects me to keep the daily accounts—besides that, he expects reports."

"Reports?" Call asked.

"Yes, I'm expected to report," Brookshire said. It was clear from the Captain's stern look that he was not pleased with what he was hearing.

"If you capture the young Mexican, or kill him, the Colonel's going to want to know right away," Brookshire added. "He's a stickler for promptness."

"I expect he's a stickler for results, too," Call said. "What if I don't catch the young bandit promptly enough? What if he manages to rob the army a few more times?"

Brookshire felt uncomfortable with the question. He had not been the only one in the office to voice doubts about the Captain's age. Of course, everyone admired Call's reputation. He had undoubtedly been the best there was, once; in his prime, Joey Garza probably wouldn't have lasted a week, with the Captain in pursuit.

But now the man was old, and looked it. If Colonel Terry could see him, he would probably have taken back his offer, or at least reduced the stipend.

"I hope I'm not getting deaf," Call said. "I didn't hear you answer. What happens if I ain't quick enough?"

"He'll fire you in a minute," Brookshire said.

"I'm glad you admit it," Call said. "I'll get Joey Garza for you, but I can't say when I'll get him, and God couldn't either. Mexico is a big place—so is West Texas. We might not be handy to a telegraph office the day the Colonel decides to fire me."

"Captain, just catch the bandit," Brookshire said. "Don't worry about Colonel Terry, too much. Worrying about the Colonel is my job."

"Couldn't you get another job?" Call asked. "I don't think you enjoy this one too much. This Colonel of yours sounds like he's rough on the help."

Brookshire didn't deny it, but refrained from confirming it.

He had learned to be cautious in remarking about the Colonel. Remarks uttered hundreds of miles from the office nonetheless had a way of reaching the man's ear.

"I like a loyal man," Call said, seeing that Brookshire had nothing to say. "I think you are a loyal man. But being loyal don't mean you're suited for this work. It's unreasonable of your boss to expect you to do work you're not trained for."

"He is unreasonable, though," Brookshire said, before he could check his tongue. "He expects me to go, and I better go. I admit I ain't qualified. I'm about as unqualified a man as you could find anywhere. But here I am. I'm expected to go."

"Send the Colonel a telegram," Call suggested. "Tell him you've caught the Texas itch. Tell him the doctor says you're not to ride for six weeks."

"What's the Texas itch?" Brookshire asked, wondering if he would catch it. "How do you get it?"

"You just get it," Call said, amused. The man was so green it was almost painful to see. Call couldn't help thinking what a time his old friend Gus McCrae would have had with Mr. Brookshire. Gus would have joshed him within an inch of his life. No doubt he could have thought up diseases far more frightening than the Texas itch.

"Well, I don't want it," Brookshire said.

"I don't want to take you off and get you killed, either," Call said. "Can you shoot?"

"I can point a rifle, fairly well," Brookshire said. "I learned that much in the War, but then they made me a medical orderly. I haven't pointed a rifle since."

"How long since you've ridden a horse?" Call asked.

"My experience with horses is mostly limited to horse cabs," Brookshire admitted. "I may not have personally ridden a horse myself in a fair number of years.

"I did sit on a camel once," he remembered. "It was at the Hippodrome. It was the Colonel's birthday."

"What's the Hippodrome?" Call asked.

"It's a show place," Brookshire said. "Buffalo Bill has performed there—I've seen him three times. I even saw old Sitting

[71]

Bull. The Colonel has met Buffalo Bill, and Sitting Bull too, I expect."

Call said nothing.

"Have you met Mr. Cody?" Brookshire inquired, feeling a little uneasy. Stern as the Captain could be when he spoke, he was even more stern when he kept silent.

"I've not had the pleasure," Call said, dryly. He considered Cody a show-off and braggart. No doubt he had killed a number of buffalo, but any man with a gun and a reasonably good aim could have killed a number of buffalo back when there were millions of them. Once, while in El Paso, Call had seen a picture of some of the Indians who worked in Cody's show. The Indians were Sioux, and they were playing baseball. Call supposed, when he reflected on it, there was no reason why Sioux Indians shouldn't play baseball. What else did they have to do? There was no reason why they shouldn't be paid money to race around a ring and pretend to rob stagecoaches, either. Cody was clearly a man of some enterprise; he figured out that people who had never seen a free Indian, much less fought one, would pay money to watch such things. There might be no harm in it, but it didn't cause him to be eager to make the acquaintance of Bill Cody, or of Sitting Bull, either.

"Anyway, the Colonel insisted that I sit on the camel and get my picture took," Brookshire said. It had been innocent enough —just a birthday party at the Hippodrome—but Brookshire felt merely mentioning it had taken him down a notch in the Captain's estimation. He didn't suppose he had ever occupied a very high place in the Captain's estimation, but he couldn't afford to drop many more notches.

"You can't ride and you don't know whether you can shoot," the Captain said, in a tone that was not unkind. "Your hat blows off every few minutes, and the heat don't suit you. We may have to cross a desert or two, to catch Joey Garza. We may never catch up with him, and if we do he might shoot us both."

"Shoot you?" Brookshire said, surprised. "Why, I don't expect he could shoot you."

"He might," Call said. "He's said to be a notable shot."

"But you've got a reputation," Brookshire said. "The Colonel wouldn't have hired you, otherwise."

"There's one sure thing about my reputation, Mr. Brookshire," Call said. "It won't stop a bullet. That's why I'd rather not take you with me. I don't want to take you off and get you killed."

"Killed?" Brookshire said. "Why would I get killed?"

It occurred to Brookshire that the heat might have affected his hearing. He had worked for the railroad for many years, but never before had the question of dying arisen. Accountants didn't get killed, not even traveling accountants such as himself. During the worst troubles in the Chicago yards, he had still rested comfortably in a hotel room at night and had even allowed himself a nip of brandy now and then.

"Killed or not, the Colonel expects me to go," Brookshire repeated, in a voice that wavered a little.

"Try him with the Texas itch, while I inspect these horses," Call said. "You'll have ample time to send your telegram."

Brookshire did send a telegram. He didn't mention any disease or disability, for that might only cause the Colonel to put him out to pasture. After much thought and a few trial runs, he whittled his telegram down to a sentence and a query:

Captain Call unwilling to take me on the expedition. Stop. Advise. Brookshire.

The reply was immediate, and also brief:

Insist that you accompany Call. Stop. No compromises entertained. Terry.

Brookshire showed the telegram to Call, just before they set off to collect Bolivar. Call looked at it and handed it back to him.

"I'll compromise, if he won't," Call said. "I'll try you as far as Laredo. You can help me watch Bol. Sometimes he wanders off, in the night. You can ride one of the spare horses."

"Could I have a gun?" Brookshire asked.

"What kind of gun?" Call asked.

"A rifle, I guess," Brookshire said. "Or a shotgun, and a few pistols. I believe I'd feel more comfortable if I was armed."

"Help yourself," Call said. "There's a hardware store right across the street. I've got to see a blacksmith and buy some extra horseshoes. I'll see if I can locate you a saddle, while I'm at it. I'll be ready in thirty minutes."

Call arrived back thirty minutes later, riding one horse and leading two more plus a pair of mules, to find that Brookshire had equipped himself with two large Colt revolvers, a Winchester, and an eight-gauge shotgun.

"Good Lord," Call said. "What do you expect to do with an eight-gauge shotgun?"

"Well, the fellow in the hardware store recommended it," Brookshire said, defensively. He had been proud of his big shotgun, but now the Captain was looking askance at it, and his confidence began to sag.

The Captain picked up the gun and hefted it to his shoulder a time or two.

"It'll take a whole mule, just to carry the shells," he remarked, handing the shotgun back to Brookshire.

"The man said it would be useful for self-defense," Brookshire said.

"I can't dispute that," Call said. "It'll kick you into next week, but if you survive the kick, you probably won't have to worry much about the enemy."

"The revolvers are the newest model," Brookshire said, unhappily. The sense that he was totally unfit for what he was about to do struck him with renewed force. But the die seemed cast. Captain Call had turned away, and he was methodically strapping baggage onto one of the pack mules.

From there they went to retrieve the old Mexican who was out of his mind. By the time the full heat of the day arrived, they had left the last mud hovel behind and were headed across a dusty, thorny plain toward the Mexican border. The horse that had been chosen for Brookshire was a thin sorrel named Dob.

"I don't understand the name," Brookshire said, wishing the

beast's spine weren't so thin. He had expected his saddle to afford him more comfort than it did.

"It's just a name," Call said. "Maybe he was named after a dirt dobber, but that's just a guess."

Brookshire was wondering if Colonel Terry would honor the bill for Dob. The horse had cost eighty-five dollars, a vast sum in Brookshire's mind. What if Colonel Terry had only meant to allow him a sixty-dollar horse? Where would the difference come from?

Call had insisted that Brookshire dispense with the fedora and buy a proper felt hat. He had also insisted on equipping him with rough clothes, boots, even *chapaderos*, the leggings that were necessary in the brush country near the border.

The result, Call had to admit, made the man look ridiculous, not only in his eyes, but in the eyes of almost everyone who saw him. Somehow, his Yankeeness was more potent with the clothes—he looked like nothing so much as a New York accountant who had been forced to assume a costume that was completely out of keeping with his nature.

Brookshire himself had felt quite self-conscious in his new clothes, but once they rode out of San Antonio, he found that how he looked was the least of his worries. His new hat seemed to weigh several times as much as his beloved fedora. He had not considered the fedora beloved until he tried the new hat, which, besides being heavy, fitted him so tightly that it gave him a headache. The heat didn't help his headache, nor did the boots help his feet.

"They squeeze, don't they," Brookshire said, but Captain Call looked as if he had no idea what Brookshire could be talking about. The Captain's boots apparently didn't squeeze.

To Brookshire's surprise and dismay, sitting on Dob was somewhat like sitting on a saw. The horse was very lean, and the saddle narrow and hard. Though his head hurt and his feet hurt, and he felt that within a few miles he would probably be sawed in two, none of these discomforts was as troubling to Brookshire as the nature of the country they were traveling through. He had not supposed there could be country so bleak and inhospitable anywhere in the American nation. The ground was covered with flat cactuses; the Captain called them prickly pear. There were also thick, gray thornbushes called chaparral, interlaced amid the equally thorny mesquite. Several times they encountered rattlesnakes, which buzzed alarmingly. Though it was only midafternoon, Brookshire was feeling tired. But looking at the ground beneath him, he had a hard time imagining where he was going to sleep.

The one thing he didn't expect he would have to fear was a chill. The sky was not like the skies of home. It was vast, and instead of being blue, it was white, not with cloud but with heat.

Captain Call was not satisfied with the behavior of one of the mules. The beast was skittish. He jumped around so much that the Captain was finally forced to get down and lash the baggage more securely.

"Do snakes crawl around at night?" Brookshire asked.

"That's when they hunt," Call said. "I'm sorry I chose this mule."

The mule, as if annoyed by the comment, tried to bite Call, who whacked him on the nose with a glove.

"I expect I'd better replace him in Laredo," Call said. "I'm glad Bol's calmed down. He usually does, once we get moving."

Indeed, the old Mexican seemed much calmer. Once in a while, he muttered something in Spanish, but his eyes were dreamy, and he seemed happy to be on a mule.

Brookshire found that, despite the many discomforts and the prospect of a thorny sleep, he was not entirely discontented. The clothes took some getting used to, particularly the boots. He was sweating so much that Katie would probably divorce him on sight, in her shock at discovering that he contained such reservoirs of sweat.

Still, it was an adventure, the first of his life, unless you counted the War; but he had been so young and so scared during the War that he couldn't enjoy himself.

Now, though, he was riding out of San Antonio, bound for Mexico, with the famous Captain Call. They were going in search of a dangerous Mexican bandit, Joey Garza. It might be uncomfortable, but it was exciting, too. He owned four guns, and they were loaded. He was on his own in the West—on his own, except for Captain Call. Colonel Terry couldn't find him to yell at him. He couldn't even yell at him by telegram, not for a while. The Captain had said it would take about three days to reach Laredo. Brookshire felt that he would be an accomplished horseman by the time they got there. Perhaps he would be an accomplished shot, too.

That night, to his surprise, he slept heavily, so heavily that if any snakes crawled over him, he didn't notice. Breakfast was only coffee. The Captain suggested that Brookshire familiarize himself with his guns by loading them and unloading them a few times, to learn the mechanisms. While the Captain was making coffee, Brookshire did just that. The eight-gauge was the easiest. All he had to do was open the breech and stuff two of the big shells into the barrels.

"Hold it tight, if you ever shoot it," the Captain said. "I doubt either one of those mules could kick as hard as that gun."

"I don't believe I'll shoot it," Brookshire said.

Indeed, he had no intention of ever shooting the big gun, not unless he was heavily besieged. He was about to unload it and put the shells back in their case when, to his dismay, old Bolivar suddenly jumped up, grabbed the shotgun, and fired both barrels at the nearest mule. The shotgun kicked the old man so hard that he fell backward over a saddle, dropping the gun. With scarcely a kick the mule died, its stomach blown away.

"He shot the wrong mule, dern it," the Captain said. "This was the good mule." He was disgusted with himself for not keeping a closer eye on the old man. Bol's fancies were apt to get away from him, particularly in the mornings.

"*Los indios,*" Bol said, jumping up. Call grabbed the shotgun.

"No Indians, Bol, just mules," Call said, in pity. He wondered what happened to an old man's brain to disturb it so that it could confuse a mule with an Indian. He himself would be old soon, if he lived. He could not help wondering if a morning or an evening would come when he was as confused as Bol, confused enough that he could mistake a brown mule for a brown man.

"We'll have to split this baggage until we get to the border and replace this mule," he said. He soon had it divided among his mount, the sorry mule, and Brookshire's lean sorrel.

Seeing the dead mule, its side blown away, destroyed Brookshire's taste for coffee. In the War, he had seen a great many dead horses and mules, but that had been a long time ago.

"How much did the mule cost, Captain?" he asked, as they were mounting. He had his ledger in his saddlebags, and he wanted to record the lost property before he forgot.

"Forty-five dollars," Call said.

"I'll make an entry—I'm the accountant," Brookshire said. "I should have entered all this yesterday, but I was getting used to my new clothes and I forgot."

"One decent mule and two shotgun shells. If your boss is such a stickler, I'd be sure I listed the shells," Call said.

7.

Joey Garza had first gone to Crow Town when he was seventeen. A cowboy, so drunk he had forgotten which side of the border he was on, insulted Maria in the streets in Ojinaga. When Maria tried to walk away, the cowboy opened his pants and showed himself to her. Joey was standing in front of their house, a few yards away. He agreed with the gringo. His mother was a whore. Why else would she have had four husbands? But he had been wanting to kill a Texan, and the cowboy was right there handy. Joey put a pistol in his belt, walked past Maria who was hurrying home, her eyes down, and went over to the gringo, who was attempting to button up. Without saying a word, Joey stuck his pistol in the man's face and blew his brains out. The cowboy was too drunk even to realize that he was about to die. But Maria knew. She felt death in Joey when he walked past her. Joey was smiling, but not at her. She knew her son didn't like her. He was smiling because of the death he was about to deal. Joey's smile soon became part of the legend the gringos made about him: Joey Garza always smiled before he killed.

Maria gave Joey her horse and made him leave. She knew the gringos would be back to kill him. He had to leave. She didn't suppose he had killed the cowboy because of the insult to her, either. Joey didn't do things for other people. He did things for himself. It didn't matter to him that a drunk gringo had showed himself to his mother. He just wanted to kill, and chose that moment, and that man.

When the men came from the ranch where the dead cowboy had worked, they beat her with a lariat and then pretended they were going to hang her with the same rope. After they pretended to hang her, they beat her again. Maria wanted to be silent, but the men were determined; she cried out. It was merely for pleasure that the men beat her; they didn't expect her to tell them where to find Joey.

It was easier to beat her than to go look for Joey. She knew it wouldn't end with the beating, either, and it didn't. Later that night, after they had been to the cantina, the men came to her house. Maria had given Joey her horse; she had no way to flee, and anyway, she could not leave her children.

What happened in her house was worse than the beating. Maria had never been used by men who hated her. She was a modest woman and had not supposed she would have to bear such shame, such humiliation. She fought, but as a woman without spirit would fight: her spirit had become a crow. It flew to Crow Town to be with her son, the son she had to love, despite the bitter knowledge that he was no good.

The white men from the ranch across the border were men without purpose. Even degrading Maria was not purpose enough to interest them for long. They degraded her until they lost interest in degrading her, and then they left.

As deep as the shame of being handled by men in their lust, was the pain of knowing that she would not have Joey much longer. When the men left, Maria cried until she was empty. For days, she would fill up with tears, and then cry until she was empty. Whether Joey lived or not, Maria knew she had lost her son—the good son she had until Juan Castro sold him. That son was gone, farther away even than Crow Town. He was only seventeen, but already he belonged to death.

When Joey returned, Maria told him that. Joey only laughed.

"We all belong to death, Mother," he said.

"You're too young to say that to me," Maria said angrily. "I don't belong to death. I brought you out of me. I want you to stay alive. You have only killed one American. You should go to the mountains. The whites won't hunt you for long."

"I don't like the mountains," Joey said. Then he left, just in time. The next day, four lawmen came. The bad one named Doniphan, the hard sheriff, only watched while the others did the work. The lawmen were rougher than the cowboys. They tied Maria's feet together and loped around the village, dragging her. After that, they dragged her into a prickly pear. Then, they strapped her over a mule and took her across the river. The river was up; their horses had to swim, and so did the mule. In the middle of the river the men let the mule go. Maria and the mule were swept far downstream. Maria thought she would drown.

But the mule finally struggled up the rocky bank, hitting Maria's head against a rock as it struggled. Maria heard the men laughing; not the sheriff, but the others. They kept her in jail for a month, during which time she was feverish from the festering cactus wounds. Because they kept her handcuffed, she could only draw out a few thorns. She could only sleep slumped against a wall. If she lay down, she merely mashed the cactus thorns deeper into her flesh.

Though the lawmen never said it, Maria knew they were keeping her in jail in hopes that Joey would try to free her. The lawmen didn't know that her son disliked her. Only she knew it. Joey wouldn't try to free her. He had no loyalty to her.

But she had loyalty. She ignored the lawmen's questions. She wouldn't tell them which way Joey went. They didn't degrade her, but they starved her. Some days she would get nothing, and when they did feed her it would only be a tortilla and a little water. She grew tired and very weak.

When they finally let her out, Maria was so weak she couldn't walk across the street. She didn't have the strength to walk to the river, much less to cross it. She fell and had to crawl to the shade of a small mesquite tree to rest. While she was resting, she began to think about dying. Her body would heal, but she didn't know about her spirit. Her spirit smelled old. It no longer

[81]

smelled like the spirit of a woman who wanted to be a woman, a woman who wanted to live. Her spirit smelled too bad to her. She thought she ought to die and let it go to some new life, someone who smelled like birth and not like death.

But there was Rafael, and Teresa. She couldn't die. While she was resting and trying to summon the will to go on living, Billy Williams found her. He rode into town, rather drunk, and saw a brown woman sitting under a tree. That was not uncommon in Presidio. He had almost ridden past before he saw that the brown woman was Maria.

"Good God, Mary," he said, and immediately brought her water, and then more water. He went to the house of a Mexican woman and begged a little menudo, but Maria was too weak to eat.

Seeing Maria's condition, Billy began to boil. Her hands were almost black from poor circulation caused by the handcuffs. Most of her cactus wounds had festered.

"I despise lawmen," he said. "I despise their stinkin' hearts."

He went back to his horse, his face red with anger, and yanked his rifle out of its scabbard.

"What are you doing?" Maria asked, alarmed.

"I am going to kill those sorry dogs," Billy said.

"No, take me home, I'm sick," Maria said.

"All right, then—I will kill them later," Billy said.

Tom Johnson, the oldest of Doniphan's deputies, came and watched as Billy carefully loaded Maria onto his horse.

"I didn't know you fancied Mexican whores, Billy," Tom Johnson said.

"I fancy cutting your stinkin' heart out, Tom," Billy said. "I expect I'll come back and do it, once I take Mary home."

The lawman laughed. "You old-timers have got rough tongues," he said. "Do you fancy all whores, or just this one?"

He turned to see if his deputy, Joe Means, was coming to watch the fun. He only glanced off for a second, it seemed, but when he turned back toward Billy Williams, there was a crack and his right ear went numb. He thought a wasp might have got him, but when he put his hand up to his head he found that his ear was just dangling by a little strip of skin. Blood was pouring down his cheek.

"What'd you do, Billy?" Tom asked, astonished. The old man was walking toward him, a big knife in his hand. Tom became frightened; these old scouts were unpredictable. He thought he should draw his gun, but he felt paralyzed. Before he could reach for his weapon, the old man was there. He severed the little strip of skin that held the ear. Then he shook the severed ear in front of the shocked lawman's eyes.

"It could just as easy be your stinkin' heart," he said. Then he stuffed the ear in the man's shirt pocket and backed away. He didn't think Tom Johnson would recover from his shock in time to shoot him, but there was no point in taking chances.

Tom Johnson walked back to the jail, still in shock. Joe Means had his boot off and was shaving a callus off his right big toe when Tom Johnson walked in. Blood covered one side of Tom's face, so much blood that Joe almost slit his toe instead of the callus. His first thought was Apaches. Tom had only left the jail a minute before. Could the man have somehow gotten scalped?

"Good God, Tom, where's your other ear?" Joe Means asked, horrified.

"It's in my shirt pocket," Tom said, numbly. It didn't occur to him that the remark might sound odd. After all, Joe had asked where the ear was, and the ear did happen to be in his shirt pocket.

The line would be repeated along the border for the rest of Tom Johnson's life. He considered himself an able lawman. If nothing else, he outlasted his friend Joe Means by more than three decades. Joe was killed the very next year by a rattlesnake. He had ridden home one night, rather in his cups, and had the misfortune to step off his horse right onto a coiled rattlesnake. Normally, the snake would have rattled loudly enough to have warned Joe, but it was Joe's bad luck that the snake had broken off all but one of its rattles. If it rattled its one rattle, Joe didn't hear it. Most men didn't die of snakebite, but Joe Means gave up the ghost within twenty-four hours. He was mourned by few in the town of Presidio. Joe had a tendency to be surly, since being a deputy had gone to his head. He frequently arrested people for minor offenses that a more seasoned lawman would have overlooked.

Tom Johnson felt he was a seasoned lawman, but that was lost on the populace, such as it was. All anyone on the border could remember was that he had once kept his ear in his shirt pocket. Tom took to drink. When drunk, he often cursed Billy Williams. He didn't forget the Mexican woman, either. She had been the start of it all. It was because of her that he had become a figure of fun along the border. If he ever had occasion to arrest her again, he meant to do worse than he had done. In the meantime, there were other brown women in Presidio or across the river that he could wreak vengeance on, and he did. Any brown woman who got taken to Tom Johnson's jail knew she was in for trouble. Two suffered so much that they died. Several times Tom Johnson had gone to Ojinaga meaning to arrest Maria herself, to show her she could not get away with making a mockery of a white lawman. In his memory, Maria had mocked him.

But for some reason, when the moment came, he didn't arrest her. Sometimes he took a substitute. He would take another unlucky brown woman, strap her on a mule, and pull her across the river. Once, in a drunken moment, he told a cowboy in a bar that the reason he wasn't arresting Maria was because he wanted her to worry. He wanted her to wake up thinking about what he would do to her the next time.

Billy Williams laughed when the cowboy told him that story.

"That ain't why he leaves Mary alone," he said.

"Well, he said it was," the cowboy said.

"He leaves her alone because he knows if he harms her I'll do worse than shoot his ear off," Billy said. "Next time, I'll tie him to a stump and cut his stinkin' heart out."

"Whoa," the cowboy said. His name was Ben Bridesall. "You'd cut a deputy sheriff's heart out?"

"I would," Billy assured him.

"Whoa, that's strong talk," Ben said again. "Killing a lawman's as bad as stealing horses, in the law's eyes. You better keep a

[84]

fast horse handy, if you do that. They'll chase you clean to Canada."

"I wouldn't go to Canada," Billy said. "I'd go to Crow Town."

"That might do it," Ben said. "They'd have to want you pretty bad to come and get you there."

8.

Maria was a midwife, the only one in Ojinaga. She did not want to be gone to Crow Town too long; several women in the village would need her soon. Crow Town lay two hundred miles north of the border, in the sandhills. Maria had never been there, but she knew its reputation—everyone knew its reputation, an evil one. In earlier times, slaves had been traded in the sandhills; stolen children, white or brown; stolen women. To have gone to Crow Town and survived was a mark of pride to the young pistoleros along the border.

Years before, when the buffalo were being killed, a large remnant of the great southern herd had wandered south, off the plain and into the sandhills. There they were pursued by the Kiowa and Comanche, and by the most unremitting of the buffalo hunters. More than fifteen thousand were slaughtered by the buffalo hunters, in a last great frenzy of killing. The skins were piled in great heaps, awaiting wagons to transport them east. But the hide market collapsed, and the wagons never came. The towering heaps of hides slowly rotted. The ropes that bound them into piles were chewed by rodents. In the fierce winds of winter and spring the hide stacks began to blow apart. Wolves, coyotes, and badgers played with them. Soon the hides swarmed with lice and fleas. The thousands of hides were scattered throughout the sandhills. One spring, two years after the last buffalo had died, cowboys began to see crows in the sand-hills, crows and crows and then more crows. Something in the hides, some nit or flea, attracted the crows. At night, hundreds roosted on the few piles of hides that remained. In the daytime, a crowd of wheeling crows could be seen from far away. At certain times of the year, thousands of crows could be seen, and heard. Their cawing was audible thirty miles away.

An Indian named Blue Skin built the first structure in Crow Town, a one-room adobe hut. Blue Skin was shot by a vaquero, on the run from trouble in Mexico. The vaquero took Blue Skin's hut. He lived in it for a while, and then went back to Mexico. The hides continued to rot; more and more crows came, to caw and to wheel.

Then a Basque sheepherder built himself a little shack, not far from Blue Skin's hut. The Basque had been horse-whipped in Kansas for bringing sheep into cattle lands. The sandhills of the Pecos were not yet cattle land, and only Charles Goodnight and his partner, Loving, passed through them with cattle. The Basque felt that he wouldn't be bothered, since the land was too poor for cattle; sheep could barely survive it. Then the famous killer John Wesley Hardin passed through and killed the Basque, on a whim. John Wesley found the crows amusing.

"If there was another building or two here we could call it Crow Town," he said, speaking to his horse. John Wesley Hardin traveled alone. What conversation he made, he made with his horse. He repeated the remark in El Paso, and the name stuck.

Later, with the law after him, John Wesley fled to Crow Town. Two rough brothers from Chicago were sharing Blue Skin's hut. It was kill neither or kill both; fatigued, John Wesley chose to kill neither. He contented himself with a tent the old Basque had left. The soil around Crow Town boiled with fleas, from the thousands of rotting hides, but John Wesley wasn't bothered by fleas. His only problem with Crow Town, the community he had named, was the unavailability of victims. He didn't have to kill every day, or even every month or every year,

[87]

but he did like to have people handy, in case the killing mood came on.

He left, but returned to Crow Town whenever he needed a respite after some killing spree. Every year he found more people there—adobes that were smaller and more crude than the one Blue Skin had built, low frame houses and ragged tents. Finally, there were twelve houses and a little saloon. An Irishman named Patrick O'Brien owned the saloon. Whiskey deliveries were few and far between. When wagons did arrive Patrick O'Brien stacked the whiskey around his house, to the height of his roof. He had unpredictable customers, and was nervous about running out of liquor.

It was risky, stacking whiskey outside in such country. Patrick slept with four guns in his bed, and often had to run outside and empty two or three of them into the darkness, to protect his whiskey.

In Crow Town, where the sound of cawing could be heard night and day, the tamer types of citizens rarely appeared. Most of those who rode in were bad ones; not a few of them were worse than bad. Many a traveler had been casually shot down in the street, his death watched only by the crows. The crows rested in the skinny mesquite. Sometimes they walked among the buildings, as if they were people. The air, even on nice spring days, had a kind of rotten smell, the legacy of thousands of rotting hides.

Behind the town was a low, sandy hill with one skinny mesquite tree on it. Bodies of the dead were casually buried there; most of them would be dug up again, within a day or two, by enterprising varmints.

The most enterprising of the varmints was a giant feral hog, which showed up one Sunday and consumed substantial portions of three bodies. The locals, annoyed by the impudence of the swine, assembled a hasty firing squad and fired a fusillade at it; but, to their amazement, the hog defied them. It didn't die, or even retreat. It kept on eating. In the night it disappeared and was not seen for a month. Then one day, it reappeared and ate an unfortunate mule skinner who had been gored by his own ox. The ox, normally a placid creature, suddenly went insane and killed the mule skinner, though he had coaxed it across the prairies for eight years.

In time, the great pig grew bolder. Sometimes it would walk through town, attended by a contingent of crows, who would flank it or walk ahead of it, cawing. When the pig stretched out to sleep in the hot sun, several crows would attend it, cleaning nits and ticks out of its hide. The poor people who worked in the sandhills feared the pig. They called it the devil pig.

The pig disappeared for long stretches, only to reappear just when people had begun to hope that it had gone forever. The most superstitious of the poor people believed the pig walked down to hell to receive instructions from the devil, entering through a long tunnel that was said to open in the riverbank, just south of Boquillas. Sightings of the pig came from all points of the compass: from as far east as Abilene, as far north as Tascosa, and as far south as Piedras Negras. An old woman who lived near Boquillas claimed to have seen it go into the tunnel that led to hell.

Only the handful of people who stayed in Crow Town ever got used to the crows. Gamblers or outlaws who passed through found their cawing so distracting, they almost went mad. One famous gambler, known throughout the West as Tennessee Bob, became so maddened by the cawing that he pulled his revolver in the midst of a card game and blew his own brains out—and he'd been holding a winning hand, too. Tennessee Bob had played cards successfully from Dodge to Deadwood to Yuma, and he was playing cards successfully in Crow Town. What he couldn't deal with was the cacophony of the crows.

Tennessee Bob's real name was Sam Howard. Like most of the temporary residents of Crow Town, he had gone there because he had more or less used up the West. His career had taken him from Memphis to Abilene, from Abilene to Dodge City, from Dodge City to Silver City, from Silver City to Denver, from Denver to Deadwood, from Deadwood to Cheyenne, from Cheyenne to Tombstone, and from Tombstone to Crow Town. Other renegades, whether Mexicans, Swedes, Indians,

Irish, or American, took the same route in different order. What they shared was a sense that there weren't too many places left where life was so cheap that the law wouldn't bother trying to preserve it. Why send Rangers, or the army, to clean out a dirty little village in the sandhills, whose residents were so quarrelsome that they could be counted on to eliminate one another themselves, at the rate of one or two a month?

Renegades of all descriptions could reside in Crow Town and feel themselves safe from the law—they just weren't safe from one another. The few women who came there enjoyed no illusions about their safety. They weren't safe from anyone, and they knew it.

Very few lawmen ventured into the sandhills.

"I doubt even Woodrow Call would go to Crow Town," Billy Williams said, some two months before Maria left. He was discussing the matter in Maria's kitchen with an experienced smuggler named Olin Roy, whose specialty was moving gold across the border, at the behest of corrupt Mexican generals who were afraid they would be robbed by generals yet more corrupt.

Olin Roy was a large man, weighing just over three hundred pounds. He had trouble finding mounts that could carry him swiftly over the distances he sometimes had to cover.

"I expect Call would go to Crow Town if he felt like it," Olin said. "Probably he don't feel like it, though."

Maria overheard the conversation. She could not have avoided it, since Billy and Olin were in her kitchen. Olin Roy had once tried to marry her. She had refused him, but he still had hopes. He and Billy were opposites in one respect: Billy was always drunk, Olin always sober. Though large, Olin was delicate in his appetites. He could stomach only the mildest of peppers, preferring to diet on raw eggs stirred into a little sugary milk. In his travels, eggs were often unavailable to him. As a concession to the great fondness Maria knew he bore her, she tried to have eggs on hand when he came to visit. She could tell that Olin appreciated such small attentions.

When Billy and Olin were in Ojinaga at the same time, Maria was careful. She was no man's woman, but men were men and she had a lot of trouble with men who became confused about her affections.

Her first husband, Carlos Garza, was so jealous that he would fight any man who turned his eyes in Maria's direction. She was beautiful then; men often turned their eyes; there were many fights. She tried to soothe Carlos, to see that he rose content from their bed, but her love, though she gave it all, was not enough. Even if he had just left her bed, jealousy burned in Carlos's dark eyes. He loved, but he could not trust, and when she became pregnant with Joey he beat her and accused her of taking a lover. He would not accept that the child was his.

For Maria, his distrust brought pain and shock. She was young, and she had given herself body and soul to Carlos. She could not understand how he could think she would accept another man. She wanted no other man, could not even imagine wanting one. Only Carlos Garza could move her. He was very handsome, and he could move her with a touch or a look. Many times she begged him not to be foolish, not to fight over things that wouldn't happen, over feelings she didn't have. But Carlos was like a deaf man. From him, Maria learned that few men trusted women. Carlos heard only his own fears. Maria's words meant nothing, for to Carlos, women were liars.

When Joey was one year old, Carlos noticed a soldier turn his eyes to Maria. She was making tortillas, outside in the sun. The soldier, a fat *Federale*, was sitting in a wagon, across the street. It was a hot day. Probably the soldier was hungry, and only wanted a few of the tortillas Maria was making. But Carlos didn't think the soldier only wanted tortillas. Maria had seen the man look, but her mind was on her task. Carlos was supposed to be carrying water. She thought he was at the river, until she heard the sound of his voice, raised in anger. The soldier had a crowbar, since the *Federales* had been repairing the telegraph. She saw the soldier strike Carlos once, but he struck so hard that Maria was a widow before she could even run across the street. Carlos had been right about the soldier, too. Three weeks later, he was back in Ojinaga. Maria spat on him in full view of several *Federales*. She expected to be killed, but in fact, the man was a coward and did nothing. For a year, Maria felt guilty. She felt she had not done enough to make Carlos happy. If she had done even a little more, perhaps Carlos would not have been so tormented by jealousy. If he had lived, surely in time he would have come to accept that she wanted no other man.

But Carlos died, leaving Joey fatherless and herself a widow. Since then, she had been cautious around males. She treated them carefully, as vaqueros treated bulls. Everyone knew that bulls were at their most dangerous when they fought, and at such times, the loser was more dangerous than the winner.

Maria didn't want Billy and Olin to fight. She valued their experience and their affection and didn't want to lose one of them in a silly fight.

"I don't think either of you know this Woodrow Call," Maria said.

"I know him, but I'll be perfectly happy to leave him alone," Olin said.

The two men fell silent. Mention of Call seemed to remind them of the uncertainty of life, along the border.

"I'll do better than that," Olin added. "I'd ride about a hundred miles out of my way, to avoid the man."

"Didn't you sell Call the horse that killed his boy?" Billy asked.

"No, no," Olin said, wishing the legend of the Hell Bitch would just die.

"Why, I thought you sold her to Call," Billy said. "That's what everybody thinks."

"I did once own that mare," Olin admitted. "At the time, I had no idea Call had a son for her to kill."

It was growing dark; great shadows stretched into Chihuahua. The two men talked too much history, too much about things that were past. Bad things had happened to her, too, but she did not like to dwell on them. A certain restlessness took her, when she heard too much about the past. She still liked to laugh, to dance a little in the cantina. Roberto Sanchez, her last husband, had not been a very good man, but despite that, she missed him. She would have liked to have a husband. She enjoyed being with a man at night, and not just a pistolero or a man of

the cantina. She wanted a man who was not so prone to com-
ings and goings, one who would spend months or even years
with her; someone whose hands she liked, whose ways she liked.
Perhaps this man, if she could find him, would also like her
ways, and would welcome the laughter in her. Not all men liked
happiness in a woman; they seemed to fear her laughter. Was it
only men who were supposed to laugh?

Of her four husbands, only Benito, the third, had laughed
with her. Carlos and Juan, her first two husbands, had been too
jealous. Juan was also too violent. Roberto Sanchez had been
too restless; he didn't like to stay put. He could not even stay in
bed all night, much less stay with her for months. He didn't live
in the past, though. Men who lived in the past brought out *her*
restlessness. Life was there, in the house, in the yard, in the
town; in the bedroom, in her hands, in her womb. It was not in
the past. The bad things that had happened to her had not killed
her. They had not even killed the laughter in her.

She became a little annoyed at Billy and Olin, because they
so easily turned their eyes backward. Men were odd. One day
they were hard, far too hard; the next day they were soft, far too
soft. They were like porcupines: prickly on the outside, but with
soft bellies.

Benito, her third husband, had not even been prickly on the
outside. He never scolded her, and would never have thought
of striking her. His only fault was laziness. Benito would lie in
bed all day, looking at her with his big eyes. If she happened to
stop in her chores, to pause near the bed, Benito would put out
a hand.

"Is that all you can think about?" she asked one day, flattered
if a little flustered. "I'm old—why do you want me?"

Benito shrugged, and smiled his little-boy smile. He was
younger than Joey, Benito—not in years, but in feeling. Joey
had never been young. Benito would never have been old, even
if he had lived. But Benito got a toothache, a bad one. After a
month, the toothache was so bad, Benito could scarcely think.
He ceased putting out his hand to Maria, when she stopped
near the bed. Maria wanted him to let her pull the tooth, or let

the priest pull it, or the blacksmith, or anyone. But Benito kept shaking off this advice. He had beautiful white teeth and was vain about them. He wanted to keep them all.

"Why, so you will look beautiful in heaven?" Maria asked, vexed by his attitude.

"Yes, I want to look handsome in heaven," Benito agreed, smiling shyly. He thought it was a worthy goal, though he could tell it didn't please Maria. Her nostrils flared a little, when she looked at him, flared as a mare's might flare.

"Who says you will even go to heaven?" Maria asked. "You are too lazy. You never get out of bed. When I'm gone you might become a sinner, you might have to go to the bad place."

"When you're gone? I don't want you to be gone," Benito said. The thought of being without his Maria frightened him terribly. What would he do? Who would take care of him? Everyone agreed that Maria was the most competent person in Ojinaga. His clothes were only simple clothes, but they were always cleaner than other men's clothes. His meals were tastier than the meals other men's wives cooked for them. Sometimes Maria walked far down the river, looking for chilies or herbs that would make her posole more tasty.

But it was not only her competence that he needed. There was her smile, her cool hands, her soft breasts. The thought that he might lose all that caused him a moment of panic. He wondered if he pleased Maria, really pleased her, in their embraces. She seemed to be pleased, but she was a woman. It was hard to tell; perhaps she was merely pretending. Perhaps she had already found a lover—he suspected the butcher, Gordo Dominguez. Gordo had always wanted Maria, and perhaps he wanted her now. Perhaps they were doing things that were more pleasing than anything else Benito was able to do. Maybe Maria liked what Gordo did so much that she was preparing to run away with him.

Maria saw the worry in her husband's eyes, for there was no missing it.

"An angel might come and get me," she said, smiling. The

[94]

remark was intended to show Benito that she was teasing. No angel ever came to Chihuahua. She was not going to heaven.

"I need you, the angel can't have you," Benito said. He felt a quick desire for his wife, which overpowered his toothache. He was so insistent that Maria closed the door and went to the bed. Few people in Ojinaga closed their doors, in the hot mornings. She wondered what people would think might be happening.

But neither Maria's competence nor Benito's insistence dulled the toothache for long. In a few more days, it hurt so badly that he couldn't eat the tasty meals, or appreciate the clean clothes, or be affected by the soft breasts.

"Go to Chihuahua City," Maria said. "There's a dentist there."

"But it's a long way," Benito complained.

"It's a long time that you've been sick, too," Maria told him. "You might die."

Finally, one day the toothache got so bad that Benito decided to go to Chihuahua City, after all. Maria fixed him a poultice of hot cornmeal to hold against his tooth. She gave him the gentlest of goodbye kisses. His jaw was very swollen.

"I wish you would come," he mumbled. "I hate to ride so far alone."

"I have the children," Maria said, looking at them. Teresa was holding her new chick, just born the day before. Rafael sat with his goat, singing a little song whose words only he understood. Brother and sister were happy together. They were never apart more than a few minutes. Sometimes Rafael led Teresa; always, Teresa thought for Rafael. Though they were happy together, it made Maria sad to look at them and to know that they would never be as other children were. They were damaged; Joey was damaged, too. His limbs were normal, his eyes were clear, but his soul was sick. The children were only a little unhappy; yet, because of them, at times Maria felt a failure. None of her children were as other children were, and they would never be. She felt she didn't know how to be a mother. Though she was a midwife, and a good one, in her own birthings

[95]

something went wrong. She didn't know what errors she had committed, to cause her children to be so damaged.

She could not feel that she was a good wife, either. Benito was lazy, and she had not tried to cure him of it. She let him be as he was. Two of her husbands had been killed, and now a third one was sick. She felt oppressed. She did her best, and yet, the knowledge she had was often the wrong knowledge.

"The dentist better not hurt," Benito said. "I don't want to ride all the way to Chihuahua City to be hurt."

"You'll be glad you went," Maria said. "You'll feel so much better, that I won't be able to fight you off, even when the children are in bed."

Later, she was to cry and cry over that remark. When she made it, she did not realize that it would be the last thing she would ever say to Benito, who didn't make it to Chihuahua City, or to the dentist. Less than ten miles from Ojinaga his horse was shot out from under him. Benito tried to run, but the killer roped him and hoisted him up the side of a large boulder. Then the killer cut off his hands and feet, with a machete. The killer loosened the rope and rode away, leaving Benito to bleed to death. Benito crawled almost three hundred yards, back toward Ojinaga, before he died.

The killer was never found. The *Federales* came, but they didn't look very hard. Benito's mother and sisters were more upset by his mutilation than by the death. They felt it might mean that Benito's soul would be rejected by God. They felt he might never be allowed to rest.

Maria didn't worry about Benito being allowed to rest. He was good at resting. It made her smile, to think of him resting; now he could rest forever. He was not a traveling man; it may have been what she liked best about him. He was always there where she could find him, in the bed.

Benito had been a kind man. Maria knew she would miss his touch. He had been more kind to her than her father, her brothers, her uncles, her other husbands. It was wrong that he should die so cruelly; but at least he had crossed the border, into a land where there was no pain. Maria didn't believe in hell. If there was a hell it came to you in life. The Texans brought it. They had evil in them and they had exercised their evil on her, when they caught her in her house. That was hell, and it had happened to her in her own house. Hell was not happening to Benito. He had always liked to rest, and now he was resting.

But he would not be able to put out his hand to her, when she came near the bed; she would not be able to take his hand and guide it to her. Maria felt that the killer might have known what she and Benito did, when she shut the doors, in the morning. Perhaps that was why the hands were taken, she didn't know. Some old ones still made necklaces of fingers; perhaps someone had taken Benito's hands and feet, to be made into necklaces. Maria didn't know, would never know.

Beneath Maria's sorrow was anger. She felt a loyalty to Benito, and though her sorrow was deep, her anger was deeper. Her first two husbands were selfish men. They would have taken younger women, given time. But Benito wanted no one but her —he would never have taken a younger woman. That knowledge fueled her anger. Someday the killer might reveal himself to her. When that happened, she would take her own vengeance, even if it resulted in her death.

She would have liked to sit on the bed and touch Benito's hands, one more time. But it couldn't be.

"Do you think the killer is in Mexico or Texas?" she asked Joey, a day or two after the funeral. He had gone to the place and looked at the ground, but if he reached any conclusions he kept them to himself.

"Texas or Mexico, what's the difference?" Joey asked. He liked to take questions and make them into other questions.

There were times when her son was so insolent that she wanted to slap him. He toyed with her, in a way that made her angry. He was a smart boy, but too good-looking. He thought his looks gave him the right to be disrespectful to his mother. Joey was blond, a *güero*. He would look at Maria insolently, waiting for her next question. It did not occur to him to be helpful. It would not have occurred to his father, either. He would rather twist her questions, make them into other questions.

"One is Texas and the gringos own it," Maria said. "This is Mexico. We own it. That's a difference."

"It's two names for the same place," Joey said. "We should own it all. It was ours once, and we didn't have to smile at gringos when we crossed the river."

"I don't smile at gringos, but Texas was never mine," Maria said. "I'm a woman—nothing is mine. Not even my children. Not even you."

"I am nobody's," Joey said, smugly.

Maria suddenly slapped him. He was too much like all men. He was insolent, and he didn't care that she was sad about Benito, the only kind husband she had ever had.

Joey didn't move, when she slapped him; the cold came into his eyes. He had a hat on when she hit him, a little white sombrero. Her slap knocked it off. Joey picked it up quickly and examined it carefully, to see if it was smudged. He turned it around and around in his hands. He was particular about his clothes. The tiniest speck would spoil the hat, for Joey.

"That is the last time you hit me, Mother," Joey said, carefully setting the hat back on his head.

Maria slapped him again, harder, and again the spotless white hat got knocked to the floor.

"You're my son," she said. "I'll slap you when you need it."

Joey picked up his hat and took it outside, to dust it off. He left, and was gone for a week. When he returned he didn't speak to Maria. He took his dirty clothes out of his saddlebags, and handed them to her, to clean. He was riding a black horse. Maria had never seen the horse before, or the saddle. He was also wearing silver spurs.

Maria didn't ask Joey about the horse. She went outside, to Rafael and Teresa. They were sitting with their chickens and goats, under a little tree. Rafael was chanting one of his melancholy songs. Rafael was a big boy, and much nicer than Joey, only Rafael was lost in his mind. Maria grew sad, thinking about it. She gathered her washing and started to walk to the river. Rafael followed, with two of his goats. Teresa stopped to talk to an old woman who was grinding corn. Teresa was popular in the village. She was so quick and got around so well that some people almost forgot she was blind.

Her children dirtied a lot of clothes. It took Maria three trips to get all the clothes to the place where the women washed. That morning, because it was late, only one woman was there, old Estela. Old Estela had borne thirteen children, and outlived them all. One drowned in a flood and the rest were killed by diseases. Old Estela had only a few clothes to wash because she had no family. Once she told Maria that she came to the river because she heard the voices of her dead children call, from the water. She had convinced herself that her children were not really dead. They lived in the river, with the frogs and the fish and the little snakes. God had given them gills, like the fish had, so they could breathe. Old Estela knew they were there; every morning, she heard them.

Rafael helped Maria with the clothes. There were one or two simple tasks he could do, and he always did them. He liked to beat the clothes against the rocks, and to spread them so that the cold water ran over them. Once in a while a shirt would slip away, before he could place a rock on it. Then Rafael would have to wade in the water to retrieve it. The sheep, disturbed by seeing him in the water, would set up a bleating. Sometimes Teresa would follow them. She knew the path to the river, and all the other paths around the village. Teresa and Rafael did not like to be apart too long. They needed one another. Teresa could not sleep, except with Rafael. He had become her eyes; she became his mind. It touched Maria, that her boy and her girl were so careful to help one another.

"Do you hear your children today, Estela?" Maria asked.

"I hear the girls," Estela said, in her tiny crack of a voice. "They are over by that bush, where the coyote drinks."

Near the bush, the water made a rilling sound.

"The boys, I don't hear them," Estela said. "Maybe they have gone to Piedras Negras."

"I think that's where my boy went," Maria said, thinking of the black horse and the silver spurs.

9.

Joey Garza journeyed to the City of Mexico in search of a better gun. When he was seventeen, an old prospector named Lichtenberg had come through Ojinaga, carrying a little case made of fine leather, with a crest stamped on it in gold. Joey was interested in fine things. He admired the little case, and wanted to know what was in it. Old Tomas, who had once worked for the German on one of his prospecting ventures, said it was where Señor Lichtenberg carried his rifle.

Joey thought that a gun carried inside a case would be useless when trouble arrived. If trouble arrived, it usually arrived quickly. The Apaches who bought him from Juan Castro could kill you several times, in several ways, while you were trying to get a rifle out of a leather case. Joey had seen them kill people who had their guns in their hands, but were too terrified to fire. Because they were terrified of dying, they died.

The old German was very tired, when he reached Ojinaga. He was weaving on his feet. He politely asked Maria for board, and he gave her a gold coin, which she accepted. Then he removed his high-topped boots and was soon asleep. He took no precautions at all with his possessions.

Maria had a husband then, Roberto Sanchez. He came home from the cantina to find that Maria had rented their bed. He took the gold coin from her, but raged anyway, about the loss of the bed. Due to a fear of scorpions, Roberto hated to sleep on the ground. He was a fool, Joey thought. Scorpions could come in a house and bite people, they often did. Roberto raged for a long time, but Maria finally persuaded him that renting the bed was a smart move. One night on the ground wouldn't hurt them. She herself would clean the ground, to make sure no scorpions were there to bother them. Roberto Sanchez was still drinking tequila, but he finally stumbled after Maria.

Rafael, the idiot boy, was playing with a chicken behind the house while he sang a little idiot song. A sad tone came into his voice when he saw his mother go into the darkness. Teresa sat near Rafael. When she heard the sad note enter the song she scooted closer to Rafael and put her fingers to his lips, to feel from his breath what sadness he felt. She herself didn't care that her mother had gone out of the house. She heard her go, but for Teresa it only meant that she could whisper through the night, to Rafael, and not be scolded. Teresa loved whispering to her brother at night. In the darkness she felt that she and Rafael were the same. Neither could see, and it didn't matter that Rafael sang songs that had meaning only to him.

As soon as Maria and Roberto left, Joey took the little case into another room, where he lit a lamp and examined it carefully. It had a small lock, but he opened it with a piece of wire.

Inside the case, resting in velvet grooves, was a rifle, the most beautiful Joey Garza had ever seen. The barrel was heavy; it weighed as much as most rifles. In Joey's mind that gave the gun dignity. This rifle was not merely a gun; it was so beautifully crafted that holding it made him feel powerful. The stock was of polished wood, and the trigger guards curved beautifully. The German rifle was the most desirable weapon Joey had ever seen. He determined at once that he must have it, or one that was as good or better. If he had to kill the old German, he would do it, but he didn't intend to kill him right away.

Almost as fascinating as the rifle was a little spyglass that nestled in its own velvet groove. It had a fitting that attached it to the gun barrel. Joey attached it, and looked through the spyglass. Even in the dark room, lit only by the flickering lamp, he could see what the spyglass did. It brought the target near, even when the target was far. He slipped outside and practiced sighting through the spyglass, with only the moon and stars for light. He wished it were day. At first light, he meant to take the gun and sight through the spyglass. Having the spyglass was like having a better eye. The rifle was so well balanced that Joey knew he could kill from great distances with it. He could lie on a roof in Ojinaga and kill gringos across the river in Presidio. If the wind was blowing strongly the gringos would never even hear the report of the rifle. Three gringos could be walking in the street, and in a second, two of them would be dead. The third would have no idea who was shooting.

Joey considered stealing the rifle, then and there. He could leave and go where no one would ever find him. He knew the mountains to the south, in the great bend of the river, and knew the Madre. He could live in the mountains for years, eating the roasts of fat mule deer. But the old prospector's rifle was the first fine gun he had ever seen. In the City of Mexico there were bound to be many, and perhaps some that were even finer.

He sat outside his mother's house until almost dawn, simply holding the gun in his hands. Then he detached the little spyglass, took the rifle apart, and put it carefully back in its case. He felt divided; impatient, yet patient. He wanted to take the rifle and go, but he also wanted to learn patience. Among the Apaches, the best hunters and the best man killers were the most patient men in the tribe. Though it was hard to wait, they waited. The best hunters did not take the first deer they saw; they waited for the fattest deer. They shot when they were sure, and Joey resolved to do the same. He would shoot when he was sure.

When the old German woke up the next morning, Joey politely asked about the little case. The old man seemed surprised, but after he had several cups of Maria's strong coffee, he opened the little case and showed Joey the rifle. He explained the function of the little spyglass, and showed Joey how to attach it. Joey pretended to be amazed, when he looked through the little glass.

Later in the morning, the old German walked up and asked Joey if he would like to shoot with him. He suggested a little contest.

"If we shoot I will beat you," Joey said. He had nothing against the old man until he saw him looking at his mother, when she was bending over, getting a tick off her old dog's ear. His mother loved the old brown dog for some reason, though the dog was mangy and had a broken tail, and a sore that had never really healed, from where a javelina had gored him.

Joey considered his mother a whore, and if Roberto Sanchez died he had no doubt she would take another man. Only a whore would seek four husbands, Joey thought, but that didn't lessen his hatred of the men who helped his mother whore. The minute he saw old Lichtenberg looking at his mother's bosom he decided to kill him someday. For now, he would be content with a shooting lesson.

Joey took some melons far down the river and lined them up on rocks.

"But they are too far," Lichtenberg complained, when Joey came walking back. There was something about the light-skinned Mexican boy that was a little disturbing. He had a coldness in his face like some of the Indians had, particularly the Indians in the mountains. His mother was a desirable woman, though. Lichtenberg had meant to leave that morning, but he thought he might stay a few days. Perhaps for a coin or two the woman would go with him. In his travels in Mexico he had paid for many brown women. He could afford to pay for one more.

First, though, he would show the cold blond boy, the *güero*, how to shoot.

"You first," Lichtenberg said. "When you miss, I will shoot."

Joey had lined up eight melons on the rocks. He took the beautiful rifle with the heavy barrel and caused the eight melons to explode, one by one.

Lichtenberg was startled. The boy could never have shot such a gun before, yet he hadn't missed. One of his own beliefs was that Indians had better eyesight than white men. In the Madre the Indians would sometimes see things he could not see at all.

Often they would mention landmarks that to them were obvious but that he could not see until he had walked several hours. This boy must have some Indian in him, Lichtenberg thought.

Joey set up eight more melons. Lichtenberg, on his mettle, burst them all.

"A draw," Lichtenberg said, relieved. His hand was shaky that day. It would have been embarrassing to be beaten with his own gun, by a boy who had never shot a German rifle before.

"Can we shoot again?" Joey asked, politely. "I will find something smaller."

Lichtenberg was not eager. He would have been happy with a draw. But the boy had a challenge in his tone that he, as a German, could not simply ignore.

This time, Joey chose prickly pear apples, handling them carefully, so as not to get the tiny, fuzzy stickers in his fingers.

"Would you like to shoot first?" he asked the old man politely.

"No—you first," Lichtenberg said. He was sorry he had been polite to the boy. Better to have stayed in the hut and waited for the woman's husband to leave. Then he could have tried his money. He had a bad feeling about the shooting. It was as if the boy was the teacher, the one with confidence. He had young eyes, eyes that were accustomed to the distances of Chihuahua, to the space that the great eagles looked across. Lichtenberg didn't know if he could hit a prickly pear apple at such a distance, even with his scope.

Joey hit ten apples. He balanced the gun beautifully and aimed only for an instant, before firing. When he finished he politely gave the gun to Lichtenberg, who took it and missed five times. Twice he hit the rock beneath the little red apples, the bullets whining off down the valley. The rest of the time he shot high. After the fifth miss, he quit. He did not feel it would be a good day. The Mexican woman wouldn't accept his coin; his horse might go lame; a snake might bite him; he might be robbed; he would not find any gold, or even a stream in which to pan for it. A sense of the melancholy of life began to crush him. Why had he come to this stinking village, in a stinking country, where neither the water nor the food agreed with him?

Why had he left Prussia? He had known Bismarck once—if he had stayed in Prussia he might have been a minister, or a rich man; not a tired, wandering prospector, going from village to village, trying to scrape up a few flecks of gold. Any day he might be killed, by a bandit, an Indian, anyone he happened to meet. Now he had been defeated by a boy who could shoot his own rifle better than he could. He walked slowly back to Maria's hut and put the rifle back in its case. For a moment, looking across the hot plain, he considered shooting himself with it. One bullet and he would not have to go on with such an uncomfortable existence, traveling on a horse that was narrow-backed and surly.

But he put the gun back in its case. In a few minutes he began to feel a little better. The sun shone beautifully, and the coffee that Maria brewed had a fine aroma. Lichtenberg loved coffee. He had thought of going south, far south, where they grew coffee in the mountains. He decided not to kill himself, because of the coffee smells and the comely woman. Her husband was a brute, that was clear. The brute had made it known that he did not like Lichtenberg sleeping in his house. The husband smelled of drink. But the woman was very comely. The husband might go away, and even if he didn't go away, Lichtenberg could always look.

For her part, Maria wished the old German would go. She saw him looking at her. There were many men who showed their lust in their eyes; she could not keep them all from looking at her.

Roberto, her husband, had a harelip. He had once worked across the river, for a big ranch, shoeing horses—the cowboys teased him about his harelip, so much that he hated all whites, and the old German was very white. In the wrong mood, if he intercepted one of the old man's lustful looks, Roberto might take a knife to him, or an axe, or a gun.

A more likely problem, though, was that Joey would rob him of something valuable. Joey was a quick and gifted thief. Although the old man's clothes were ragged, from neglect and hard wear, many of the things he owned were nice. There was the fine rifle, and, in another leather case, a set of mining instruments. His belt had a silver buckle, and he wore a ring with a green stone in it. Maria had not touched his bags, but he had produced the gold coin from one of them and might have other gold coins in his valise.

Joey might steal any of it, Maria knew that. He might steal it out of curiosity. Joey liked to look at interesting things, particularly weapons. There was no telling what the old German might have that Joey would like to steal, but if he did steal something, trouble would come from across the river. The hard sheriff, Doniphan, liked nothing better than to beat Mexicans who stole things. The river meant nothing to Doniphan. The notion that Mexico was a nation with rights, like other nations, and with a border that needed to be respected, made Joey laugh. Mexico was a nation of whores, lazy men, Indians, and bandits, in Doniphan's view. He crossed the border when it suited him, taking any prisoners he wanted to take. In Ojinaga there was no one to stand up to him.

If Joey stole from the old German, he would steal and go. When Doniphan arrived, with his rough deputies and their quirts, it would not be Joey who would suffer their vengeance. It would be Roberto Sanchez, or some man on the street that they just happened to notice—the shoemaker, perhaps. They were not coming to do justice; they were coming to hurt Mexicans.

There would be less danger if the old German would just go, before Roberto lost his temper or Joey stole from him. But if Maria hoped for something, it seemed that that fact alone, the fact of her hope, made the something not occur. The old German didn't go. He drank tequila all day, smoked cigars, made water frequently, and wiped the sweat off his face with a fine silk handkerchief.

When he was not drinking or wiping sweat off his forehead, he looked at Maria, or talked to Joey.

"Are there many rifles like this in your country?" Joey asked him.

"Oh yes, many," Lichtenberg replied.

"Would I find some in the City of Mexico, if I went there?" Joey asked.

"You would find beautiful guns, but what would you buy them with? You are just a poor boy!" Lichtenberg said, startled that this youth, living in a filthy village, would aspire to travel to the City of Mexico, in search of a rifle.

"I would buy them with money," Joey said.

There was something a little frightening about the boy, Lichtenberg thought. A chill in his look, or in his tone. He reminded Lichtenberg of someone he had once known, long ago, an Austrian named Blier, a young count and assassin whose task it was to murder Hungarian rebels. There were many Hungarian rebels, and the Emperor wanted to avoid the expense of many trials. Young Blier killed forty rebels before they caught him and impaled him on a pole. Count Blier died hard, but he had done his job, saving the Emperor the expense of forty trials.

Lichtenberg had not known Count Blier well, but he had been with him a few times and remembered the look in his eyes. This boy, Joey, had the same eyes. Such eyes could look on a hundred deaths, or a thousand, without pity. Lichtenberg had seen men executed, both in Mexico and in Europe. He had seen them shaking in front of firing squads, or crying and begging as the noose was put around their necks. Some lost their water, as they awaited death; some emptied their bowels as well. He could not, without pity, look upon men staining themselves as their deaths came near.

But Count Blier could see it without pity; and so, probably, could this boy Joey, a boy who could outshoot him with his own gun. Joey was very good-looking. He was a *güero*, as they said in Mexico; *güero*, almost white. In certain moods, Lichtenberg might have offered him a coin. Boys were usually easier than women, but not this boy, this *güero* with eyes like the famous Count Blier's.

Maria saw Joey looking at the old German's things. His eyes turned again and again to the rifle case. She also saw that the old German looked at Joey as he looked at her. She wished the man would go; too much trouble would come, of his visit. But when you wished men to go they never did, and the old German was no exception. He stayed for four nights. Four times she had to persuade Roberto to sleep on the ground. He didn't like it. He cursed her and he cursed the German, but he only hit her once, and he didn't bother the German.

On the fifth morning, as Lichtenberg was leaving, Joey stole six coins from his valise. Lichtenberg was drunk when he left, and didn't notice. Joey went down the river and bought a horse, a black gelding, three years old. When he rode home with it, Maria knew he had robbed the German. Her best hope was that the old German wouldn't notice. Otherwise, Doniphan and his deputies would come.

"I didn't know you owned a horse," Maria said to Joey. "Yesterday you didn't own a horse."

"I only stole six coins, Mother," Joey said. "If the old man comes back, I'll just kill him."

"What if Doniphan comes?" Maria asked.

"Tell him to find me in the City of Mexico," Joey said.

That night, he left. After four or five days, Maria relaxed a little. Lichtenberg was many miles away. Even if he missed the coins, he wouldn't come back. A year later, she learned that the old man had drowned in Sonora. He had attempted to cross a wash, when the wash was running, and the water had swept him away. The vaquero who found his body took some silver ore from his saddlebags, but Lichtenberg was dead and could not tell where he had found the silver.

The news of his death made Maria feel light. That night, she danced in the cantina, and several vaqueros fell in love with her. When she danced, she often became happy, became welcoming, and men fell in love with her. It was the death of the German that allowed her to feel light. If he was dead, she was safe from his vengeance. Only when men were dead could she feel really safe from their vengeance. If he were alive, old Lichtenberg might ride in someday, with Doniphan to back him up, and beat her half to death, because Joey had stolen those coins.

In the City of Mexico, Joey Garza felt at home for the first time. He felt that he had come to the place where he belonged. All night there were people in the streets. The air was soft, the ringing of the church bells beautiful. Young priests went barefoot in the street, particularly around the great cathedral. Joey was not a worshiper, but he loved the great cathedral. Several times he came back to stand inside, happy just to look at the high ceiling and the great space it contained. In Ojinaga all the ceilings were low. As he walked in the night, whores followed him, because of his horse. They thought he was rich, for in the City of Mexico not many boys his age had fine black geldings.

Joey ignored the whores, and didn't frequent the cantinas. He had come for a gun—if possible, one with a little spyglass on it. It took him three days to find the gun he wanted. An old trader had it, a Frenchman, a man with a vast belly and empty eyes. Joey had the urge to stick a knife in the man's belly, to see if he could cause the emptiness to leave his eyes. Perhaps as he died, the man would look alive for a few moments. When Joey showed him the five coins—he had spent one on the gelding— the man didn't say a word. He just put the rifle away and nodded for Joey to get out of his shop.

That night, Joey walked the cantinas, looking for card players who were winning. In a cantina not far from the great cathedral, he saw a small man with quick hands who had many gold coins. When the man had enough of the card game, he put the coins in a little sack and had a whore carry it. When a second whore wanted to go with him, he shoved her away. Joey followed the man for a while, as he lurched along. He kept sticking his hand under the dress of the young whore. It reminded Joey of the way Benito had behaved with his mother; of how all men behaved with his mother. All her husbands put their hands on her, in the house. They didn't care who saw them.

Joey followed the man and the whore until they were well away from the cantina. As he was walking along a cobbled street, he saw a cobblestone that had come loose. Joey believed in omens. The loose cobblestone meant that it was time for him to act. He picked up the cobblestone, came quickly up behind the small man, and smashed his head with it. He grabbed the whore and took the sack of money from her. The whore became frightened, and fled.

Joey did not check to see whether the small man was dead. He took the sack of coins, got his horse, and rode to the edge of the City of Mexico, where he slept. The next day, he walked into the fat Frenchman's shop, jingling the coins. The fat man didn't change expressions, but he sold Joey the rifle. Later, Joey bought some bullets, two pistols, and a fine saddle. He went to stand in the great cathedral once more, and then rode north, out of Mexico.

Ten days later, on the Texas border west of Laredo, Joey robbed his first train. The robbery was an accident, in a sense. The train was stopped at a water tank. It was a train carrying sheep. Two sheepherders and the four men who ran the train were standing around the water tank, smoking. Joey was three hundred yards away. The heat was so great that it cast a haze. No one from the train crew had seen him. Joey decided it was an excellent chance to practice with his new rifle, so he tied his horse and crept a little closer to the men. He shot the two sheepherders first; it was easy to tell they were sheepherders because they wore huge sombreros and looked shaggy, like the animals they cared for. Joey then shot two of the railroad men, the two fat ones. He didn't like fat people, there were too many of them in the world. Juan Castro and Roberto Sanchez, two of the husbands his mother whored with, had been fat. As a child, he had often wakened to see a fat body on his mother's. Her husbands grunted like pigs, when they were on her. Shooting the fat railroad men was only a small revenge, for the pain his whoring mother had caused him.

The two other railroad men began to run, not into the train, but down the river, toward Laredo. Joey watched them run. He was trying to judge what would be a fair distance to shoot, a distance that would allow his rifle to perform at its best.

When the man in the lead was about four hundred yards away, Joey looked through the spyglass and shot. He aimed for the neck, but the man was running downhill and his aim was

[110]

a little high. The bullet blew the man's face off. Joey rode over later to inspect the body, and most of the man's face was gone.

The sixth man ran for his life. He sped along the river so fast that it annoyed Joey. Jocy loped away, on the black gelding, letting the man see him, letting him think that he had abandoned the hunt. The man slowed to a trot, and then to a walk. Joey loped down the river, until he was well in front of the man. He was satisfied with his rifle; now he wanted to try his new pistols, and at close range.

The man from the train finally stumbled out of a gully, not thirty yards from where Joey sat on the black horse. The man was terrified. He began to plead, and name the saints.

Hearing the saints named only angered Joey. A priest in the village had the habit of twisting his ear cruelly, while talking to him about the saints. Joey began to shoot at the weeping, pleading man, but, to his annoyance, shooting a pistol proved far more difficult than shooting his fine rifle. He emptied the two pistols, twelve shots, and did no more than nick the man's arm. Joey threw the pistols away, disgusted. They were poor weapons. He was not ready to admit that his aim was bad.

Joey rode to a little rise, overlooking the river. When the man was about seventy yards away, Joey took out the great rifle and shot the man twice, aiming for his knees. He did not mean to cut the man's arms and legs off, as he had Benito's, but he did mean to cripple him. The man's knees were shattered, and he writhed on the ground, screaming. When he passed out, Joey rode close to look at him. His legs were leaking a pool of blood. Probably the man would bleed to death, as Benito had. Benito had made his mother whore like a beast, on all fours. Joey had seen them in the bed, many times, in the early morning. Benito would be behind his mother, prodding her as bulls prodded, or dogs. That was why Joey followed him, roped him, and cut off his hands and feet with the machete, so that he would not prod his mother on all fours again.

The railroad man was not so guilty, but he looked a little like Benito, which was his misfortune. His mother didn't even know that Joey had seen her, in her shame, or that he had followed Benito and killed him.

Later, in a cooler mood, Joey went back and got his pistols. He shot the bleeding railroad man at close range, ten yards away. Then he rode back to the train. He had never been on a train, and was curious about it. The men he had killed must have some possessions. There might be things he would want, among their baggage.

What he found far exceeded his expectations. Three of the men had Winchesters, fairly new. Winchesters he could sell.

Besides the rifles he found two watches, a nice knife, a razor with ivory sides, a little shaving brush, and some soap that smelled like the soap a woman might use. The soap surprised Joey. The men were just men, not clean, not neat. He wondered which one had used the fancy soap.

He also found three hundred Yankee dollars, in gold. Finding the money stunned him. Three hundred dollars was more than all the people in the village of Ojinaga had, put together. It was more money than he had ever expected to see. And yet this was just a poor train, carrying a few hundred sheep.

If such a train yielded several guns, the knife, the razor, the watches, the nice-smelling soap, and the three hundred dollars, what would he find if he robbed a train with many people on it? What if he robbed a train with rich gringos on it? What would they have?

Joey had only killed the men to try out his new rifle. He had not been particularly interested in robbing the train. But now that he had robbed it, he began to think it might be interesting to rob a better train, a train with wealthy people on it, people who would own interesting things.

Once Joey had combed through the men's effects again—he had missed two coins and a nice pocketknife—he prepared to ride away, into Texas. When they discovered the bodies they would expect him to go into Mexico, but they did not think very well, the Texans. He thought he might go to San Antonio and buy things with his new money.

As he prepared to ride away, he paused for a moment to

consider the sheep. There were several hundred of them stuffed into the hot boxcars. The day was very hot, and the sheep had no water, no food. If he didn't let them out, or if someone didn't find the train, all the sheep would be dead.

Joey thought about letting the sheep out; he could use them for target practice. He could let them graze a few hundred yards away and pick them off with his great gun, pretending they were gringos. But his ammunition was limited. He did not have cartridges to waste on sheep. His brother, Rafael, lived with sheep and goats. He would have brought them into the house, if his mother had permitted it. Rafael, with his curly, dirty hair, looked like a sheep. He sang like a sheep, too. His little songs were like bleats. Teresa defended Rafael fiercely. Once, when Joey was teasing him, she had managed to grab a knife and stick him in the shoulder, through his shirt. Because Teresa was blind, he had underestimated her. When he laughed at Rafael, Teresa grabbed the knife and struck at the sound. Joey knocked her down and kicked her, but the damage was done. She had made a hole in his shirt. It was a new shirt, too, one that he had bargained for in Presidio. It was a shock, to discover that a blind girl could be so quick.

Remembering Rafael and Teresa and his ruined shirt hardened Joey's mind toward the sheep. He did not let them out. He merely whistled at them a few times, as he loped beside the cars that held them prisoner.

Seven hundred and twelve sheep died in the boxcars. The cars were covered with buzzards when the railroad men found the train. The sky was so black with buzzards that they could be seen for fifty miles. The men from the railroad had to wrap wet blankets around their heads in order to be able to run in and disconnect the cars that held the hundreds of dead and melting sheep. The buzzards were so thick around the sides of the cars that the men had to beat them away with clubs. The couplings of the cars were fouled so badly that some men fainted and some ran away. They could not breathe long enough to work the couplings loose. Finally, they had to be content with taking the engine, and even that was covered with buzzards.

"You know how flies will swarm on meat," Goodnight told Call. Goodnight had been in south Texas at the time and took an interest in the incident.

"Yes, they swarm," Call said.

"I'm told the buzzards swarmed on that train like big flies," Goodnight said. "The Garza boy wasn't known at the time, but it sounds like him, to me. Not too many people would ride off and leave seven hundred sheep to die."

"Seven hundred and twelve," Call said.

"Well, I wasn't there to count, so I don't know why they think they know that," Goodnight said. He was often annoyed by Woodrow Call's pedantry, when it came to matters of that sort.

"I expect the railroad knew beforehand—that's probably how they got the figure," Call said.

"Then I doubt it was accurate," Goodnight said. "I never met a railroad man who could count animals on the hoof, particularly sheep."

"Sheep all look alike," Call said.

"That ain't my point," Goodnight said. "An animal's an animal. The problem is, most people can't count accurately. I never met a railroad man who could count the legs of a three-legged cat."

The more Goodnight thought about human incapacity, of which he had witnessed a great deal, the more he warmed to his subject.

"I can't say that it's just railroad men," he said. "People can't count animals. I am one of the few that can."

"What's the most you ever counted in one count?" Call asked. The man's irascibility had always put him off slightly, though he knew that he himself had a reputation for being a fair rival to Goodnight, in that area.

"Eleven thousand eight hundred and fourteen cattle," Goodnight said, without hesitation. "That was four herds. I counted them into a holding pasture in Pueblo, Colorado, the last time I made the trip. It should have been eleven thousand eight hundred and forty-eight. We lost thirty-four head, or rather, Bill Starr did. I entrusted him with the second herd, which was a mistake. I like Bill, but he was deficient in a sense, and he still is."

"Those sheep would have been hell to count, once they burst," Call said.

Goodnight had driven a wagon into Clarendon, to bring back some groceries and a few posthole diggers, and Call, riding a horse that in Goodnight's opinion, was beneath his standards, fell in with him on the return trip. Joey Garza had just robbed his third train, killing five people, all of them white. But Goodnight was not thinking of the young killer on the border. He was still thinking about human incapacity.

"Do you think a man can acquire sense, or would he have to be born with it?" he asked Call.

"Sense?" Call asked. "Cow sense, or weather sense, or what kind?"

"I thought I was asking the questions," Goodnight said. "You're known to be direct—just be direct. Are you born with sense or do you acquire it, a little at a time?"

"I didn't know much when I was twenty," Call replied. "I believe I make better decisions now."

"I thought your best decision was to take that herd to Montana," Goodnight said. "It was bold, because the Indians weren't whipped. They got your partner and they might have got you. But it was a good decision, anyway. Montana was there waiting. It needed someone to come and put a herd in it."

Call said nothing. The man was tactless, to bring up Montana. Goodnight and virtually every adult in the West, if they were interested in the cattle trade, knew what a failure his Montana venture had been.

"It might have been smart if I had known how to run a ranch," Call said, finally. "I didn't. Gus was able. He could run pretty much anything. But he died before we got started. The whole venture was a total failure."

"I don't see it that way," Goodnight said.

"Well, it wasn't your ranch," Call pointed out.

"No, it wasn't my ranch, but I hate to see you thinking like a banker," Goodnight said. "From a banker's point of view, all my ventures have been failures, including this one I'm venturing now, this Palo Duro ranch. The lawyers will take it away from me, before I'm dead. Lawyers and bankers are like shit beetles. They'll finally carry off everything I've built up, like they carried off your ranch up above the Yellowstone.

"I would have liked to see the Yellowstone—I've heard it's mighty fine country, up there," he added. "If I could get around like I used to, I'd ride up to the Yellowstone, just to be able to say I'd seen it."

"You ought to go—it *is* fine country," Call said.

Goodnight rode in silence for several miles. He had to pop his little team of mules hard with the reins to get them to pull the wagon up the bank once they forded Cow Creek.

"I'm no student of the ledger sheets," he said, a little angrily, once they left Cow Creek behind.

Call found Goodnight's way of talking hard to follow. They hadn't been talking of banks or ledger sheets. What did the man mean?

"Bankers live by ledger sheets," Goodnight informed him. "They decide you're a failure if your balance hits zero, or if you can't pay your note. You're a damn fool for thinking like a banker."

"I don't think like a banker," Call assured him. "I don't even have a bank account."

"It was a bold thing, driving that herd to the Yellowstone," Goodnight said. "You went right through the Sioux and the Cheyenne. It was a bold thing. You ought not to let the bankers tell you you're a failure because you went broke. I've been broke nine times in my life, and I may be broke again, before I'm through. But I've never been lost, day or night, rain or shine, and I ain't a failure."

"I wonder if Roy Bean knows anything about the Garza boy?" Call asked.

"He might," Goodnight said. "He's got a good eye for thieves, that's because he's tight. Roy Bean would hang a man over a fart, if he didn't like the smell."

Call found the conversation tiring. He had only fallen in with

[116]

Goodnight to be sociable; after all, he was the man's guest. He trotted ahead for a bit, thinking about the seven hundred and twelve dead sheep. He had seen the bones of the Comanche horse herd, the one Colonel MacKenzie had destroyed. But those were just bones, cleaned by the winds and the sun. Seven hundred dead sheep crammed into boxcars was a different story.

"If I was the railroad I expect I'd just burn those boxcars," he said, when he dropped back even with Goodnight.

"Would you accompany me, if I decide to make that trip to the Yellowstone?" Goodnight asked, as they rode up to his barn.

"No, you'll have to find other company, if you go," Call said. "I'd rather be shut of Montana. You can't miss the river, though."

"I told you I've never been lost, day or night," Goodnight said. "I can generally locate a river."

"I expect so, I don't know why I said it," Call replied. The man was a famous plainsman. Of course he could find the Yellowstone River.

"I am not good at conversation, goodbye," he said, but Goodnight was already unloading the posthole diggers, and didn't answer.

10.

Brookshire knew the minute he walked into the telegraph office in Laredo that there was trouble—big trouble. No fewer than seven telegrams awaited him, all from Colonel Terry. Two telegrams from Colonel Terry was so unusual that it usually meant war had been declared. Brookshire had never expected to be unlucky enough to receive seven at one time. And yet it had occurred, in the hot town of Laredo.

"Ain't you gonna open them?" the old telegraph clerk said. His name was Johnny Whitman and he had been a telegraph operator on the border for twenty-nine years. Never before had he received seven telegrams for one person, only to have that person refuse to open them and share the excitement. Perhaps there was a war. Perhaps troops were on their way from San Antonio with orders to kill all the Mexicans. If that was so, and Johnny Whitman hoped it was, there would be rapid business for a few months.

Brookshire knew the man wanted him to open the telegrams and share the news with him, but he didn't care. Seven telegrams from Colonel Terry could only mean one thing. The Garza boy had struck again, before Captain Call could do his job.

If that was the case, then at least one of the telegrams might be informing him that he was fired. In that event, he wouldn't have to worry about Colonel Terry's fiery temper anymore, but he would certainly have to worry about Katie's. She did not like change, Katie. He had a job and she expected him to keep it. News that he was fired would undoubtedly cause her temper to flare up.

It had been nippy in Amarillo. Winter was supposed to be nippy, and Brookshire hadn't minded. Then in San Antonio, which was still in the same state, it had been hot, mighty hot. He didn't suppose it could get any hotter than it had been in San Antonio, but after a few hours in Laredo, he was forced to admit an error. Laredo, which was in the same state, was hotter still.

Their arrival in Laredo had been unpleasant on other grounds, too. Bolivar had begun to cry and wail. When they crossed the river into Nuevo Laredo, Bolivar knew that the Captain was about to leave him.

"No, *capitán*, no!" he pleaded. "I want to go. I can ride and shoot."

"Yes, and you have shot," Call reminded him. "You shot our best mule, and for no reason."

Bolivar had a vague memory of shooting a mule. He had shot it in the stomach with a big gun. Now, though, he couldn't remember why. Perhaps the mule had tried to bite him; mules were known to bite.

"I thought I was shooting the devil," Bolivar said, in hopes of convincing the Captain that shooting the mule had been an act prompted by forces stronger than himself.

"No, you thought it was an Indian," Call said. "You have to stay here, Bol—you might get hurt if I take you. I'll be back for you when I head home."

Soon he was handing money to a small, tired-looking Mexican woman who was not unlike the woman he had given money to in San Antonio. Brookshire decided the old man must have been a superlative cook, for the Captain to keep supporting him all these years.

Bolivar didn't appreciate the fact that the Captain had another decent family to place him with, though. He wanted to ride the river with the Captain, to ride and shoot, kill or be killed. At the thought that he would have to stay with the woman and the children again, he began to weep, and he was still weeping when the Captain and Brookshire rode off.

"Be quiet, you're old, you need to rest," Juanita said. She was not happy to see the old man. He caused many problems. But she needed the money. He was not a bad old man; just noisy, and sometimes a little violent to himself.

Brookshire stumbled out of the telegraph office, pale with shock, and took the seven telegrams to Captain Call, who was talking with the local sheriff, a young man named Jekyll, who sported a walrus mustache. Call was trying to find out the local gossip about the Garza boy.

To the surprise of both Call and the sheriff, Brookshire simply thrust the seven telegrams into Call's hands.

"Would you read them, please? I'm too worried," he said.

Call led Brookshire a little distance down the road, to a shade tree, before opening the first of the telegrams. He knew Sheriff Jekyll was dead curious about the information they contained, but he preferred to take the cautious, rather than the polite, approach. The less information got spread around, the better.

"Well, it's bad," Call said, when he had read all seven telegrams. "He's done it again, and somebody else has started doing it too."

He gave Brookshire the telegrams, and Brookshire read them quickly. Three more trains had been struck.

"Three! Three, my God!" Brookshire exclaimed. Even one more train robbery would have been a calamity, but three amounted almost to a world catastrophe. News that an earthquake had leveled New York City could not have been more unwelcome.

"I don't see anything about a second robber—where's that?" Brookshire asked.

"The telegrams don't say it—it's the distances that say it,"

Call said. "According to this, a train was robbed in Van Horn one afternoon and another in Deming, New Mexico, the next morning. Nobody's swift enough to cover that distance in twelve hours."

Call methodically arranged the telegrams in order and read Brookshire the totals: two crew and three passengers killed near Van Horn, little money taken; two crew and two passengers killed near Falfurrias, little money taken; and three crew and four passengers killed near Deming, another military payroll lost.

"O Lord, spare us," Brookshire said. "That's another payroll lost—the army will be mad, for sure."

"It's the passengers the Lord should have spared," Call said. "That's sixteen lives lost, in a little over a week, Mr. Brookshire. I fought Indians for fifteen years on the frontier and I lost six men. This is not a robber we're after, it's a killer—or two killers, it looks like now."

"If there's two robbers, or two killers, who's the other one?" Brookshire asked.

"I don't know," Call said.

"Well, one of them's a robber, too," Brookshire said. "He's taken three payrolls and lots of trinkets."

"Yes, he takes the money," Call said. "Or they take the money, because it's there. But the killings worry me more. How many were killed before I took this job?"

Brookshire tried to think. Three robberies had occurred before he left New York; another occurred while he was in Chicago. The one with the sheep wasn't on Colonel Terry's railroad, so Brookshire didn't count it, though he supposed he ought to count the dead men. It seemed to him that there had been three or four deaths each time, but he wasn't sure. Six had died on the sheep train, and now there were another sixteen dead. The count was in the thirties somewhere, so there was no denying it was a startling death toll. His regiment had only lost forty men, during the entire Civil War. Of course, his regiment had not been in the thickest of the action; still, the War had been carnage from start to finish and it was a

[121]

shock to realize that one Mexican boy, in the course of a few months, had taken more lives than his regiment had lost in the War.

"I doubt Wesley Hardin has killed that many people yet," Call said. "And Wesley Hardin is a bad one."

Near the livery stable, where Call had encountered Sheriff Jekyll, a large log had been rolled into the shade, to make a sitting place. Two old men with only a few teeth between them were sitting on it, whittling with small pocketknives. Call went over and sat on the log too. He was annoyed with himself for not having taken the casualty figures more seriously, sooner. The numbers had been available, but numbers were usually exaggerated. He had fought several fierce battles, with both Indians and Mexicans, in which no one was killed on either side. Usually there were wounds, but fighting men were not easily killed. In the War, of course, the great engagements had left hundreds or even thousands dead, but frontier fighting was of a different order. In the worst Indian fight he had engaged in, he had only been able to say positively that two Indians were killed —he buried the two himself.

Call rarely saw a newspaper and had not followed the Garza boy's murdering that closely. He had assumed that the figures were exaggerated. Let one or two people get killed in a feud or a ruckus, and as the story went up and down the trail, the figure would swell until it became twenty or thirty. Before the Garza boy showed up, the most notorious outlaw in the West was Billy the Kid, who was said to have killed a man for every year of his life, when he was nineteen. But Dish Boggett, the gifted Hat Creek cowboy who was now selling hardware in Lincoln County, New Mexico, where the troubles occurred, assured Call that the boy had only killed four or five men. Goodnight, who had been in Lincoln County while the range war was going on, agreed with that figure.

If the information in the telegrams was true, Joey Garza had quickly eclipsed Billy the Kid as a killer.

In his conversation with Sheriff Jekyll, Call had asked if anyone knew how the Garza boy got the trains to stop. One man, working without a gang, would have to be inventive to stop a train.

"He piles rocks on the tracks," Sheriff Jekyll said. "He ain't lazy. He works in the night, piling up rocks, till he gets a kind of wall."

"But a locomotive going full speed could bust through a pile of rocks, surely," Call said.

"Maybe, but the train might derail, and then you'd be in a pickle," the sheriff replied.

"If Joey Garza's after you, you're in a pickle anyway," a lanky deputy named Ted Plunkert observed.

"If it was me, and I was driving the dern train and I seen a pile of rocks and thought Joey Garza had piled it up, I'd pour on the steam," the deputy added.

Sheriff Jekyll looked startled and embarrassed by his deputy's remark. It had never occurred to him that Ted Plunkert would venture an opinion of any kind, in the presence of the great Captain Call. Ted Plunkert had not made a comment of such length and complexity since Jekyll had hired him. What could have prompted him to wag his tongue for five minutes when he, the sheriff, was discussing serious matters with Captain Woodrow Call?

"Ted, you were not consulted," Sheriff Jekyll said bluntly.

"I'll consult him—he's making better sense than you are," Call said, no less bluntly. He didn't like Jekyll's manner, which was fawning yet superior. Many young lawmen took a similar tone with him, nowadays.

Sheriff Jekyll blushed scarlet. Call thought the man might have a seizure, he was so embarrassed.

"Well, the engineer can plow on, if he wants to risk it," the sheriff said.

"It's run or fight, if you're dealing with Joey," Deputy Plunkert said. "I doubt I'd be ashamed to run, if he had the drop on me."

"Are you employed steady, or would you consider accompanying me?" Call asked. He liked the deputy's dry manner and matter-of-fact outlook.

"It's steady, but it's warm," the deputy said. "I wouldn't mind going to higher country, where there might be a breeze once a month or so."

"Now, Plunkert, who asked you into this conversation?" Sheriff Jekyll said. He considered it damn unneighborly of the Captain to try and hire his deputy. He didn't much care for Ted Plunkert, but if he left, there would be no one but himself to sweep out the jail.

Call sat on the log, by the toothless old men, and considered the situation. Survivors of the robberies claimed there was no gang. A single blond Mexican boy, well mounted, showed up and took their finer possessions. Though some of the passengers were armed, something in the boy's manner kept them from using their arms in their own defense. The lost payrolls had come to almost a million dollars in cash. Dozens of watches and rings and jewels had been taken, and the people killed had not been offering any resistance. The boy stopped trains carrying a score or more passengers, robbed them, killed a few, and left, only to strike again, far away, when it suited him.

In Call's experience, it was unusual for criminals to have such confidence. One reason they ran in packs was because confidence was one quality they seemed to lack. It was also unusual for criminals to have much ability. When they succeeded, it was usually because they had circumstance on their side. It might be that the Garza boy was an exception—a criminal with real ability.

Brookshire was so upset that he could not keep still. He saw Captain Call sitting on the log with the two old men. Obviously, the Captain was thinking matters over. Brookshire tried to allow him his privacy, but it was hard. Another telegram could arrive from Colonel Terry at any moment, informing them that they were both fired. The Colonel had never been loath to change help.

Brookshire found himself edging a little closer to the log where the Captain sat. If only they could get started, he might feel a little better.

"Ain't we gonna start soon?" he asked. "Joey Garza could be getting farther and farther away."

"That's just a guess, though," Call said. "He might be headed back down the river toward us, for all we know."

"What are we going to do?" Brookshire asked. "The Colonel won't sit still for much more of this."

"Nobody's asking him to sit still," Call said. "He can catch the next train and come out here and catch the boy himself, if he's impatient."

"Oh, but he won't want to," Brookshire assured him. "The Colonel don't like to leave New York—he's too attached to Miss Cora, for one thing."

"Do you still want to go with me?" Call asked. He had taken a liking to Brookshire. The man was incompetent, and he usually despised incompetence, but for some reason, Brookshire's incompetence made him likable. There was something brave in it. For a man who could neither ride nor shoot, to be willing to travel over some of the roughest stretches of the West in pursuit of a young killer who had already accounted for nearly forty lives, took guts.

"I *have* to go with you," Brookshire said. "I've been ordered."

"Suppose you didn't have to go, though," Call said. "Suppose you could choose."

"But Captain, I *can't* choose," Brookshire reminded him. "I work for Colonel Terry. I can't choose. I don't think I've ever chosen. I wouldn't know how."

Captain Call just looked at him. Brookshire was so taken aback, by the question and the look, that he didn't know what to say. Why ask him what he would do if he could choose? He had never chosen. He had taken the only job he had been offered, married the only woman who would agree to marriage. He was just a husband and a salaried man. Choice didn't play any part in his life. His choices were made for him, by people who were smarter than he was: Colonel Terry and Katie, to name two. Captain Call was also smarter than he was, Brookshire felt sure. Why had he asked such a question?

[125]

Call was wondering if the man would survive. There was no answer to the question, of course, but it was a matter he always pondered, when he led men into danger. It was also a question he could as well ask of himself. If the years had taught him anything, it was that survival was a matter that could not be predicted with any accuracy. Time and again, on the frontier, men who were well experienced and well equipped rode off one day and got killed. Gus McCrae, his old partner, was as competent as any man he had ever known, and yet, Gus had ridden off on a kind of frolic, in Montana, and ended up dead. None of the Hat Creek cowboys had been as competent as Gus, or Deets—the black man who had served him so well for so long—yet, Gus and Deets were dead, and some of the least competent—Soupy, for example, or Jasper Fant—were still alive and flourishing. There was no degree of competence that would assure anyone of survival, and no scale that would tell a commander which man would live and which man would die. If you added it all up reasonably, then Brookshire would be the first to fall, if there was a fight; and most people would expect that he himself would be the last. But it might not happen that way. Joey Garza was said to have a fine rifle, with a telescope sight. Several cowboys had turned up dead, on the Pecos ranches, shot while riding alone, far from their headquarters. It might be that Joey Garza was killing people who never saw him, never suspected that he was anywhere near. Instinct, however well honed, could not necessarily warn one that a young killer, hidden behind a rock four hundred yards away, with the sun at his back, was looking through a telescope sight, about to squeeze the trigger. If Joey Garza happened to see him and Brookshire riding along, which would he shoot first, the Ranger or the dude?

"You can come with me," Call said. "But it's up to you to keep up. I might not be able to stop and help you. You've got to try and keep up."

"Captain, I'll keep up—I'm a grown man," Brookshire said, a little insulted.

Call stood up and handed Brookshire the telegrams.

"We need one more man," he said. "I think I'll hire that lanky deputy."

"Oh, the tall fellow?" Brookshire asked, surprised.

"Yes," Call said. "You did say I could hire a man to make up for Pea Eye, didn't you?"

"Why, yes, provided he's not too expensive," Brookshire said. "How do you know he'll go? He has a job right here in town."

"The man looked restless," Call replied. "I expect he'll come."

11.

Doobie Plunkert cried so hard she ran completely out of breath. She stood in her own kitchen, gasping like a fish, her mouth open, trying to suck in air but mainly pouring out tears. Ted stood behind her, timidly patting her on the back, as if she were a baby who needed to burp.

The timid way Ted patted her was beginning to make Doobie angry. When Ted walked in and announced that he was going to El Paso, or possibly farther, to help some old lawman she had never heard of catch a bandit Ted had no business chasing, Doobie had been stricken to the heart. How could he, when she was already four months pregnant with their baby, a little boy, she hoped! She planned to name him Edward, after his father, but they would just call him Eddie, and he would be the light of their life.

Doobie had never, in her short married life of almost eight months, supposed that Ted Plunkert would leave her for any reason whatsoever; not leave her overnight, that is. So far, she and Ted had slept together every single night of their marriage. Of course, Doobie understood that accidents might happen; the milk cow might get loose, or one of the horses run away. In that event, Ted would have to go looking for them, and might not get back just when she wanted to go to bed. He might even be gone as late as midnight, as he was on the nights when he was required to watch the jail until all the saloons closed and all the drunks and bullies were rounded up.

Not having Ted beside her until around midnight was just one of those things you had to put up with if you married a lawman. Doobie was sixteen years old and married to a deputy sheriff; she expected to do her duty, even when she was lonely and could think of nothing but how happy it would make her if Ted would only get home, take his boots off, take his socks off, take his pants off and his shirt off, and get into bed and hug her tight.

The truth was, Doobie needed a lot of tight hugging. She had grown up poor; her mother had died when she was four, and the aunt and uncle who raised her were too poor and too busy to pay much attention to her. When Ted Plunkert began to pay attention to her, it was like a miracle sent from heaven—like the coming true of the best dream she had ever dreamed. He was just the sweetest man, willing to hold her tight all night long, except maybe for a few nights in July and August, when it was really too hot to hold anyone tight for very long.

Now Ted was leaving, after only eight months with her. It was the end of all her dreams, and she told Ted so, just before she burst into tears and cried so hard she lost her breath.

"Stop, honey. Stop, honey," Ted kept saying as he patted her timidly in various places. "We're just going after Joey Garza, that's all. Soon as the Captain catches up with him I'm coming right back here, to my darling."

But neither Ted's words nor his pats had any power to soothe Doobie. Ted was going away. He was going to leave her alone all night; maybe weeks and weeks of nights. It was the end of her happiness, the only true happiness she had ever known, and it was all happening because the old lawman had butted in where he wasn't wanted and persuaded Ted to go with him.

The thing that hurt the most, after the fact that Ted wouldn't be there to hug her tight for many, many nights, was that Ted hadn't even asked if he could go. One of the nicest things about Ted was that in all matters involving their domestic life, he let her be boss. Even before they married, he let her boss, and in fact, even offered formally to let her boss.

"I'm too busy, I've got my deputying," he said. "You look after the rest of it."

Ted had kept his word, too. If Doobie wanted to go to church on Sunday, they went; if she didn't, they didn't. If it was a fine day and she felt like wading in the river, Ted went with her, took off his boots, rolled up his pants legs, and waded in the river with her.

Doobie loved it, that she got to be the boss. During her hard life with her aunt and uncle, she had been more like a slave than a boss. In her marriage, though, Doobie tried very hard to make good decisions about what to cook, or when to clean, or how to doctor Ted when he got an ailment, usually the grippe.

She tried hard, and she had convinced herself that she was doing a good job and that Ted was happy; because she was convinced that she was doing a good job, it hit her all the harder when Ted walked in and announced that he was leaving in an hour. He said it matter-of-factly, as if he were telling her it might rain.

Doobie couldn't grasp it, at first. She thought she must have misheard, or misunderstood, or that she must still be asleep, having the worst dream of her life, instead of the best.

When Doobie had to admit that it was true, that it wasn't a dream or a misunderstanding, she started crying and cried until she ran out of breath. It was a worse shock than her mother's death. When her mother died, she had been young, and her mother had always been sick. There had been so little happiness that it wasn't very different when her mother went. The big difference was that her Aunt Gladys slapped her frequently. Her mother had never slapped her in her entire life.

But it was certain, Doobie knew immediately, that it was going to be a very different life, now that Ted wasn't going to be there to hold her tight, every night.

"Stop patting me on the back!" Doobie said, vehemently, when she started breathing again and could speak. At that point, she still had a little bit of hope that Ted would change his mind.

They had a happy marriage, all eight months of it, and Ted probably had no idea that his going away would upset her so. After all, he had no reason to go away and no place to go away to, not until the old lawman showed up.

Doobie had long realized that Ted's way of thinking was different from her own. What she needed to do was let him know how strongly she felt, and make it clear how much she needed him to stay with her. She had been told, by her one good friend, Susanna Slack, that men were a little dumb, in some ways. Susanna maintained that they didn't understand the first thing about how women felt; mainly, Susanna believed, men didn't even care to try to understand the first thing about how women felt. That had never sounded exactly right to Doobie. Maybe Ted didn't really understand how she felt, but he was willing to let her be the boss of their family life, and that amounted to pretty much the same thing.

Now, though, in her shock and misery, Doobie was forced to consider that Susanna had been right, after all. Ted Plunkert didn't know a thing about how she felt.

"I guess I better go round up some bedding," Ted said, as her tears were subsiding. "The Captain's in a hurry to get going."

"The Captain, who's he?" Doobie said, furious. "He's just some old man I never heard of. I don't see why you think you have to go with him."

"Why, it's Captain Call," Ted Plunkert said, shocked. He knew his wife hadn't had the advantage of much schooling—he himself hadn't had much, either—but he had not supposed her ignorance to be so profound that she would never have heard of Captain Call.

"I never heard of Captain Call, I tell you!" Doobie yelled. "I never heard of him! He don't live here, why would I have heard of him?"

"Why, it's Captain Call," Ted Plunkert repeated. "Everybody's heard of him. He's the most famous Texas Ranger of all time," Ted said, still shocked. He was a little embarrassed for Doobie. It was almost as bad as if she had told him she had never heard of air, or the moon, or something. He had lived along the border all his life, and along the border, the Captain was about as well known as air, or the moon.

"Well, *I* ain't heard of him, why do you have to go?" Doobie asked. She was ready to plead and beg, if she had to.

"Doobie, there's no why to it," Ted explained, patiently. "The Captain asked me to ride with him. That's it."

"If he asked you, you could have said no," Doobie pointed out, in what she thought was a reasonable, even a calm voice. "He ain't the president. He can't just order you to run off and leave your wife."

"Doobie, I swear, he's Captain Call," Ted said again. "You don't just go around saying no to him."

Doobie was silent. She didn't want to be angry, but she felt herself getting angry—very angry.

"Besides," Ted added, "it's a big honor to be asked to ride with him. I expect it's about the biggest honor I've ever had in my life, or ever will have."

"What if you ain't back when the baby is born?" Doobie asked. "What if you don't never come back? What if you never even see our little Eddie? If you go off and get killed, little Eddie might never even get to have a daddy."

"I guess I better round up that bedding," Ted said, trying to be patient. In fact, he was becoming a little exasperated. His private belief was that Doobie had temporarily lost her mind. Instead of feeling honored that Captain Woodrow Call, the most famous Texas Ranger of all time, had singled him out from all the men in Laredo and asked him to go up the river with him, all Doobie could do was cry and complain. After all, the great man could have asked Bob Jekyll to go with him. Bob was the sheriff, and had a better claim to such an honor. But Captain Call had walked around Bob Jekyll and had chosen him. It ought to have been the proudest moment of their marriage, and yet, all Doobie could do was bawl like a heifer.

Of course, he loved Doobie. No man could ask for a better little wife. Her biscuits were first-rate, and she could even repair boots, if the holes in the boots weren't too big. Ted sincerely hoped she would soon get over being out of her mind. She had no business suggesting that he might have turned down Captain Call's offer. Of course he couldn't refuse Woodrow Call, just because Doobie chose to bawl like a heifer for an hour. It was very inconsiderate of her, Ted thought. After all, he did have to gather up his bedding, and could have used some help. He didn't get any help, though. Almost an hour had passed, and he had to rush. One consequence of the rushing was that he forgot his slicker, an oversight that was to cause him much misery, on the trail.

Doobie Plunkert stood at the back door of their little house and watched hopelessly as Ted and the old Captain and the fat little Yankee rode away. She felt her heart breaking; she didn't think she would be able to endure the ache. If Ted had just once turned in the saddle and waved at her, it would have made the ache a little easier to bear. Even when he was just walking down the street to do his deputying, Ted would sometimes turn and wave at her. The fact was, she loved him so much that she could miss him acutely, even when he was just down the street. Often, she had an urge to run visit him at the jail, just to see if he still looked the same, or if his smile was as sweet. But Doobie could never indulge herself when she had this longing. Sheriff Jekyll had made it plain, the one time she stuck her nose in the door, that it was the last time he expected to see her at the jail. He lectured Ted so severely about his wife's behavior that Ted told her that evening never to go near the jail again.

"There's rules," he told her that night. He was gentle about it, but Doobie's feelings were still a little hurt. All she had wanted to do was peek at her husband, to be sure he looked the same.

Now, watching him ride north along the river with two strangers, one of whom, in her view, was no more than an old killer, Doobie cried again. She cried until she was cried out. She felt sure that little Eddie was crying too, inside her. There were rules, just as Ted had warned her, and the main one seemed to be that men could leave when they chose to. They could close doors to jails and other places, when they wanted to, and not wave when they left their wives to go off on manhunts.

They could do any and all of those things, and worse, for all she knew.

All the same, though she didn't like the rules, Doobie really wanted Ted to come back. That night, without him to hold her tight, she had many dreams, and tossed and turned, but the best dream she had was that the bandit they were after, Joey Garza, came riding into Laredo to surrender, so that Ted and the Ranger and the Yankee didn't have to go at all.

Doobie's dream was so vivid that she could even smell her husband, Ted Plunkert. He smelled of saddle soap. Only that morning he had taken it into his head to saddle-soap his old saddle. It gave off a good smell, saddle soap. Smelling it in her dream made Doobie remember what a good man Ted was, and how kind he had always been to her.

The best part of the dream, though, was that Ted not only smelled of saddle soap; Ted was there. He snuck into the bedroom, as he always did when he came in late; he took off his boots, took off his pants, took off his shirt, and climbed into bed to hold her tight, as she always hoped he would, not just for one night but throughout her whole life. Doobie tried to stay in her dream, to hide in it, but she grew more and more restless; she began to have moments of wakefulness, began to suspect that her dream was just a dream. She tried to fight off waking up, to burrow deeper into the dream, but it didn't work. Despite herself, she woke, opened her eyes, and knew the worst, immediately. Ted Plunkert wasn't there.

He wasn't there, just wasn't there. One day, when she had no reason to expect trouble, or even to be the tiniest bit worried, her life with Ted Plunkert had ended.

"No it ain't, honey. He's just gone on a job," her friend Susanna, told her a little later that morning. Doobie had been so upset that she had run down the street, barefoot and sobbing, and flung herself into Susanna's arms.

"He'll never come back. He'll never come back, I know it," Doobie kept saying, between fits of racking sobs.

"He'll come back," Susanna said. "He'll come back, Doobie."

In fact, she wasn't so sure. She couldn't really say it with much conviction, because only the year before, her husband, John Slack, by consent one of the best cowboys to be found anywhere near the Rio Grande, had ridden out one morning to brand a few calves—work he had done hundreds of times in the twelve years of their marriage—and had never come back, not alive, that is. A calf he had just roped turned directly under his horse while the horse was in a dead run. The horse's front legs buckled, and he fell in such a way that it drove John Slack's head straight into the ground, breaking his neck. He died instantly, and since then, Susanna had been a widow.

At least you've got his child, Susanna thought wistfully, as she held her sobbing friend. She and John had hoped for a child, hoped year after year; but no child came, and now she had nothing of John Slack except a few notes he had written her while they were courting, and of course, her memories, memories of being married to the best cowboy in the Rio Grande Valley. They had once hoped to have a ranch, as well as a child, but now John was dead, and Susanna had neither. She had been forced to move to town and take a job clerking in the general store, to support herself.

Doobie would not be comforted. Remembering her own loss made Susanna a poor comforter, anyway. Soon, she was crying, too.

"He won't come back, he'll never come back," Doobie said, again and again. She had never been so convinced of anything as she was that her husband, Ted Plunkert, was gone for good. Little Eddie would never know his father. She would never again have a husband, to hold her tight in the night.

"I was going to give him a new saddle," Doobie said, hopelessly, to Susanna. Indeed, she had been skimping and saving for just that purpose. She had paid down the immense sum of eight dollars to old Jesus, the local saddlemaker. She had discussed Ted's new saddle with Jesus in great detail. Doobie had even begun to take in sewing, to pay for the saddle. Old Jesus had promised it to her by the spring.

Doobie's dream was that someday Sheriff Jekyll would move away and Ted would be sheriff of Laredo. She thought Ted would be a wonderful sheriff; maybe little Eddie could be his deputy, when he grew up. She wanted Ted to have a saddle worthy of the sheriff of Laredo.

Now that little dream was lost, too. Jesus had already started on the saddle. Maybe the best thing she could do would be to let him finish it. It could be little Eddie's saddle, one day.

"I hate that old man Call," Doobie said. She felt weak from crying so much and so hard, but not too weak to hate what she hated. She had only seen the old man from a distance; the Yankee, too; but she hated them both. They had ridden in and taken her Ted. She hoped they were both killed, and that the buzzards ate their guts.

"Who does he think he is anyway, just to come here and take people, like that?" she asked Susanna.

Susanna was ten years older than Doobie. She had heard many stories about Captain Call, for the cowboys were always talking about him. But it had mainly just been men talking. She had not paid much attention. Doobie coming in so upset had upset her, too, and now it was almost time for her to go to work.

"I think he was an Indian fighter," Susanna said.

"I wish the Indians had killed him, then," Doobie said bitterly.

"Don't think about it," Susanna advised.

She soon had to leave for her job in the store. Doobie walked back home barefoot, not caring how she looked, not caring about anything. She wished an Indian would ride into town and kill her. It would be easier than suffering. But then, she remembered that she had to stay alive so that little Eddie could be born. It seemed hard, but she would have to do it. She would have to do it without Ted, too. Yesterday, he had been there; today he was gone, and he would not be back. Ted was not very tough. Doobie knew that. He would not be very hard to kill. Somebody would kill him—this Joey Garza, or someone else. She knew it in her bones.

Doobie walked on home and hid in her bed all day, wondering who would be the one to bring her the news, and how long it would be before it came.

12.

As a girl of ten, Maria had been given a crippled pony—not a true pony, but a small, spotted horse that had injured itself badly on some barbed wire strung by the men who owned the big ranch across the river. The men had been careless with their wire, and the little horse had become entangled in a coil and had cut one foot so badly that everyone thought it would lose its hoof. The villagers in Ojinaga were hoping that old Ramon, who owned the horse, would kill it and make horse-meat jerky.

That was what the people of Ojinaga wanted, but that was not what Ramon wanted. Ramon, though already an old man, wanted Maria, who was only ten. Ramon had a wife named Carmila, a quarrelsome woman liked by no one, but liked least by Ramon, who'd endured her angry eyes and acid tongue for thirty years. Now Carmila was sick; it was thought she had a tumor in her womb. As the tumor grew, Carmila became even more angry and spiteful, and refused to be with Ramon. She told him she thought he had put the tumor in her womb out of spite because she would bear him no more children. She had already borne him thirteen.

Denied relations with his wife, Ramon's thoughts turned more and more to Maria, whose breasts were already budding. One day, noticing that Maria came every day to pet the crippled horse, the horse he had been thinking of making into jerky, Ramon impulsively gave it to Maria. He was not just being generous; he was preparing the way for a serious courtship. As soon as Carmila died, he meant to go to Tomas, Maria's father, and ask for her hand.

That plan failed, because Tomas and his oldest son and son-in-law got caught in Texas with twenty stolen horses. A Ranger troop led by Captain Call and Captain McCrae caught the men, and they were hung within an hour of their capture. Ramon considered, and decided not to take back the horse, which could walk fairly well, and even trot, although it had only three good legs.

When the news came that her father and brother were dead, Maria took her horse, whom she called Three Legs, and walked far down the river, farther than she had ever gone before. She never rode Three Legs, but she loved him more than anything else in her life. Every day, she made a poultice for his wounded hoof, hoping it would heal. But a tendon had been severed when Three Legs got caught in the wire; with the tendon cut, the leg could not heal.

During her time on the river, mourning for her father, Maria ate mesquite beans, and nibbled carefully at prickly pear apples. Once or twice she was able to scoop a little fish out of the water. The fish she ate raw. Once she caught a small turtle, meaning to eat it, but instead, she kept it for a few days and let it go. During the day, she walked with Three Legs, as he foraged. During the worst of the heat, she found shade. Often she looked across the river, at the hated place called Texas, where men killed other men over a few horses. She wanted to kill all the men who had hung her father and brother. She did not suppose it would ever be in her power to kill them, but she vowed to do it if she could.

At night, she looked at the bright stars, sleeping little, listening to the river. She did not understand rivers. Where did so much water come from? She wondered if the river began in the sky, where the rain lived. On some days she didn't eat at all, though always, she drank the cold water of the river.

Ramon was furious with Maria, for going away with the horse he had given her. He wanted to find her and beat her, but in the end, he was too lazy to go look for her. It didn't bother Ramon that Tomas and his boy had been hung. They were sloppy thieves, and it was no surprise to him that the Rangers had caught them and hung them. They had known the danger before they crossed the border. Horse thieves had to hang. That was the law on either side of the river.

It angered Ramon that a girl of ten would take it upon herself to leave, without asking anyone, and with a horse he had given her. Carmila, his wife, was dying—she might go any day now. Her stomach was blue and swollen. She could not keep food down. All Ramon could think about, during Maria's absence, were her little budding breasts. He wanted to touch fresh young breasts, not the tired sacks that Carmila had.

Finally, Maria walked back to the village. The mesquite beans were gone, and she was hungry.

Two days after Maria's return, Ramon caught her in the cornfield. She was feeding Three Legs corn from her hand. Maria greeted Ramon with a friendly smile, but one look at his face told her that Ramon was not in a friendly mood. She knew little about men and women. She was shocked when Ramon simply shoved her down in the cornfield and began to pull at her clothes. She screamed, and Ramon hit her; she screamed again and he hit her again. Maria thought he had gone berserk when he tried to pry her legs apart. No one in the village came. Maria was weak from her fast, and Ramon was strong. Also, Maria was so shocked at the change in Ramon, who had been her neighbor all her life, that she did not know what to do. She thought his wife's illness must have driven him insane. He was acting like a crazy man. His face was twisted, he bared his teeth, and he was ready to hit her again if she tried to scream.

Maria gave up. Her life had become nothing but pain. She was surprised by Ramon's pleasure, which soon dripped out of her, along with her own blood. While he still held her down, Ramon told Maria that he wanted her to live with him now. Carmila would soon be dead. As soon as she died, he would marry Maria. Even as he crushed her into the dirt, Ramon was eager to let Maria know that his intentions were good.

Maria was almost more shocked by what Ramon told her than by what he had done to her. She did not want to marry Ramon, or anyone. What had happened in the cornfield frightened her and hurt her, but it also taught her something. It taught her what men really wanted of women. What they really wanted was what Ramon had just taken from her.

Carmila died the next day. Two days after her funeral, Maria's mother, Silvana, told Maria that Ramon had asked to marry her. Silvana thought Maria should do it. Ramon had money— not much, but more than they had. Maria had two younger brothers and a little sister. They were mouths that Silvana had to struggle hard to feed. She did not think much of Ramon, but he was no worse than most men. If Maria married him he might be kind to her family, to Silvana and the little ones.

Again, Maria was shocked. She knew that her mother was tired. Silvana had worked hard all her life, she had lost a husband and a grown son. She had given up. Maria knew what it was to give up, for she had given up in the cornfield, given up because she was afraid a crazy old man might kill her.

Still, Maria had no intention of marrying Ramon, or anyone.

"He is a bad man," Maria told her mother. "He did a bad thing to me." She had not meant to tell about the bad thing, but she could not hold back.

Silvana was saddened by this news. It confirmed a fear that she had had for two years: Ramon was not to be trusted around Maria. Silvana cried, but not for long. It was only one more sorrow, heaped on many others, so many that Silvana could not cry long for any of them.

"He is not as bad as some men," Silvana pointed out.

"He is a bad man, he bit me!" Maria said. She showed her mother a mark on her shoulder, a mark Ramon had put there with his teeth.

"He is not even as bad as your father," Silvana said. "Your father did worse things. Marry Ramon, Maria. It will help us eat."

But Maria wouldn't, not even if they all starved.

Silvana had to tell Ramon that Maria had refused. She was a stubborn girl, stubborn enough to deny her mother's wish.

Ramon did not take this news well. He cursed Silvana, and he told her he did not think she had asked Maria. He was only seventy-two, and he had given the girl a horse; crippled, it was true, but still a horse. How many men in Ojinaga were wealthy enough to give a ten-year-old girl a horse?

After that, Ramon watched Maria constantly. He became obsessed with her. Sometimes he even crawled up to her window at night, hoping to see her undress. He watched the cornfield, meaning to catch her again and repeat what he had done. Soon, he was convinced, Maria would accept him. She was not experienced. If she would consent, or if he could catch her, she would realize that he was a good man. Soon she would welcome his attentions, he was convinced of it.

But while Ramon was watching Maria, Maria also watched him. She would not be caught again, as she had been caught when she thought Ramon was her friend. Now she knew what he was, and he was not her friend. Perhaps no men would be her friends, not if they went crazy, as Ramon had, every time they wanted to go between her legs. Not if all they wanted was to make her serve their pleasure. She was determined that Ramon, for one, would never have that pleasure with her again. Her dead brother had left an old machete behind when he went to Texas on the raid that led to his death. The machete was dull, but Maria carefully sharpened it on the grindstone until its blade was as keen as a razor. She began to wear the machete in its scabbard over her shoulder. Whenever she led Three Legs into the cornfield in search of fodder, she carried the machete in one hand.

One day, when Silvana had gone to the river to wash clothes, Ramon snuck into her house, hoping to take Maria by surprise. Instead, he found her just inside the door, in the dim kitchen, her machete gripped in both hands.

Ramon cursed her bitterly, then. But he didn't challenge her knife. He was too slow, and his eyesight was not good. Maria

[141]

might cut him badly before he subdued her; he might bleed to death, or get an infection in the cut. Many men he knew had died from infections in the cuts they received in fighting. Ramon did not plan to lose his life because a ten-year-old girl cut him with a machete.

That afternoon, when Silvana was back, Ramon came over and offered to buy Maria. He could not get the girl off his mind. He felt that the rest of his life would be a sour thing if he could not have Maria. He wanted her so badly that he offered Silvana two hundred pesos for her. Two hundred pesos was an unheard-of price for a girl so young and inexperienced.

To Ramon's surprise and chagrin, Silvana countered by offering herself, in Maria's stead.

"She doesn't want you," Silvana said. "She won't marry you. Take me. I am your neighbor and I need a husband."

Ramon was outraged. He wanted the girl, not the mother.

"You are too old," he said. "Almost as old as Carmila. Sell me the girl."

"She won't go with you. She'll cut you when you're asleep," Silvana said. "Tomas's mother was part Apache. Maria is like her. They are not afraid to cut men."

"I didn't know Tomas's mother," Ramon said, a little daunted. He did not like Apaches. But he still wanted Maria, and he said so.

"No, she won't marry you," Silvana repeated. "Take me. I am not so old."

Silvana had not expected to offer herself to a man who wanted her daughter, but then, she had not expected many things that had happened in her life. This was just one more surprise, and it would help her feed her children.

Ramon spat, and turned away in disgust. He did not want any more old women.

The next morning, a gunshot woke Maria. Fear went through her heart. She ran outside with the machete, but she was too late. Ramon had shot Three Legs. He didn't make him into jerky, though. He just led him out beyond the cornfield and shot him.

Maria cried until she couldn't cry anymore. When her mother came to comfort her, she stopped crying and became like a stone. It was another lesson about men: they wanted only one thing, and they were vengeful if they didn't get it, or enough of it. Later, she was to learn that if someone else got what they wanted, they were even more vengeful.

A few weeks later, Ramon changed his mind and took Silvana. He had begun to be a little bit afraid of the girl; after all, she was part Apache. She might cut him in his sleep. Whenever he looked at her, he saw hatred in her eyes, black hatred. He began to avoid her, especially to avoid her hating eyes. Her hatred was too black. She might be a witch. He began to be fearful that Maria would sneak in and cut him in his own house. She was only a filthy Indian. He had been a fool to want her.

Silvana was not so old, after all. She did not smell bad, as Carmila had. She was a decent Mexican woman, and she had something of the beauty her daughter had. Ramon didn't want to marry her, but he took her into his house. Her brats had to stay in her house, though. He gave her a little money for their food, but he didn't want them underfoot.

Silvana's younger children, the two boys and the little girl, stayed with Maria in Silvana's house. Maria became their mother. They saw little of Silvana, once she became Ramon's woman, although his house was only a few steps away.

Maria forgave her mother. She knew that Silvana was only tired. She had accepted Ramon because her spirit was weary and dying. Only a woman whose spirit was dying would submit to a man like Ramon.

When Ramon killed Three Legs, Maria felt that her spirit might die, too. She had loved her horse more than anything. But her spirit didn't die. Her hatred kept it alive, hatred of Ramon, and for a time, hatred of all men. They were creatures of violence, brutes. Maria planned to live alone. She would raise her brothers and sister, but she did not plan to live with a man, as other women did. The only way a man would have her was if he was quicker and stronger and took her, as Ramon had.

[143]

Silvana gave Ramon two more children. Much of the time, they lived with Maria and the other little ones. Maria felt sorry for her mother, because her spirit was so damaged. She helped her mother as much as she could. But she never turned her back on Ramon. All she gave him was the hatred in her eyes.

In time, Ramon came to fear Maria as he feared his own death.

In the matter of men, though, Maria was wrong. She never expected to be with one willingly. But the years passed, and then Carlos Garza rode into town. He was then a vaquero who worked in the south. She saw him looking at her, and when he spoke to her in his soft voice, she felt a change inside her. A few days later, she went with Carlos willingly and even eagerly. Only later was Maria to learn that Carlos's soft voice belied his jealous nature. Soon after she went with him the first time, Carlos gave her a horse, a little white gelding who was too slow for cattle work. Maria named her little horse Chapo, because he was so short.

The day after Carlos gave Maria the horse, the two of them rode together, far down the river, past the place where Maria had gone to mourn her father. They entered a canyon whose great cliffs rose over the river. Carlos Garza looked especially beautiful to her that day. She was eager for him, more eager than she had ever been before.

In the time of their ride, Joey was conceived.

After Carlos gave her Chapo, Maria was never without a horse. Maria traded work for corn, in order to feed her boy and her horse.

Joey was six when Juan Castro sold him to the Apaches. He was gone two years. Maria had begun to give up before her son came back, and once he did return, she found she had to give up again, though in a different way. Juan Castro had traded away a good boy, a child she loved, but the boy who came back was not even a child she knew. No one knew Joey Garza. He was the most beautiful boy in the village; the girls looked at him, and hoped.

But they hoped in vain. It was to be that anyone who invested hope in Joey Garza hoped in vain. From the time he was ten, he often left the village, to be gone for a month or more. Maria wondered if he went back to the Apaches, if the Indian ways were stronger than her ways. Once she asked him if he went to the Apaches. Jocy merely looked at her, smiling.

"Why do you care?" he asked.

"You're my son," she said. "Can't I be curious? I wonder about you."

"I don't go to the Apaches," Joey said. "If I ever go to the Apaches again, it will be to kill the ones who beat me."

Later, by accident, Maria found out the truth. Joey went down the river, as far down as Laredo, and he went to steal. He was a thief, and a gifted one. Olin Roy told her about Joey's thieving. Olin said that Joey had found a cave, somewhere in the mountains north of Boquillas. Olin had glimpsed Joey once, at dusk, on the Mexican side of the river. Joey had been carrying a fine saddle, with silver trappings; the silver shone in the late light. Olin knew the saddle was stolen, because only two nights earlier he had stayed at the home of the hidalgo Joey stole it from. The old man thought an Indian had taken it, because there were no horse tracks leading to or from his ranch. There were no tracks at all.

It was a long way from the hidalgo's ranch to the mountains near Boquillas. And yet Joey was there, by the river, carrying the saddle. It was a thing an Apache could do. Apaches had little use for horses. They walked, and they left no tracks.

Olin Roy camped near the river that night, meaning to see if he could find Joey the next day. But Olin didn't find him. There were many caves in the high, limy cliffs, and the mountains rolled back for many miles into Texas, where the river made its great bend. Cougars lived in the caves, cougars and even a few grizzly bears.

Olin told Billy Williams what he had seen, and Billy told many others. Soon a legend was born, the legend of Joey Garza's cave. It was said that Joey was filling a cave with things he had stolen: rifles, fine spurs, fancy bridles, ivory combs and jewels, stolen from the bedrooms of rich ranchers on both sides of the river.

The river was no boundary to Joey. He crossed it as he would cross any stream.

Olin told Maria what he had seen. He loved Maria, and knew that she worried about her son. He also knew that things had not been good between mother and son since Joey returned from the Apaches.

"When he left here he was on a horse, a sorrel he got from Ramon's son," Maria said, in response to Olin's news. "When he came back, he was walking. He leaves on horseback—he returns on foot. Or he leaves on foot and returns with a horse. He's a boy I don't understand."

"Maybe Joey eats the horses. Apaches do, you know," Olin said, when he was discussing the matter with Billy Williams. "It's a long way from Ojinaga to Laredo, but Joey steals from Laredo like it was a candy store."

"If he steals horses, then it's better that he eats them," Billy said. He had always liked Joey. He thought he was a good boy, but strange. Being strange was not something he could hold against anyone; after all, he himself was strange.

"Life makes everybody strange, if you keep living long enough," Billy told Maria, once.

Maria disagreed. "I am not strange," she said. "I could be a happy woman, if I had a little help."

"Well, I'll help you," Billy said. "You name it, I'll do it."

"If you really wanted to help me, I wouldn't have to name it," Maria said. "You'd be doing it right now."

She smiled when she said it, though.

Billy Williams felt disquieted. They had just eaten a good meal, cabrito and frijoles. What could it be that Maria wanted help with? He considered asking, but in the end, he didn't. He got drunk instead

Maria had almost no money. She worked as a midwife for food, for herself and Rafael and Teresa. Her two brothers had run away to Texas, and her little sister had died one winter; she got a sickness in her chest and died within a week. Maria had to work hard to see that there was enough food for Rafael and Teresa. When Joey returned from his journeys, he always had money. He wore it in a belt that went across his shoulders, like the belt of the machete she had once carried to defend herself against Ramon.

It angered Maria that her son would not share his money, not even the few pesos it would have taken, every week, to keep his family in food. Besides her midwifing, Maria did washing and cleaning, so as to be able to give corn and frijoles to her children.

Joey liked for his mother to wash his clothes, because she did it well. When she did them, they were clean and soft. Joey took the soft, clean clothes as his due. He never offered to pay for the food he ate, and he took no notice of his brother and sister at all, unless he was in the mood to torment one of them.

One day when Maria was tired and angry—an old man she cooked for had tried to poke his bony hand between her legs, and when she shoved him away, he spat at her—she challenged Joey about the cave.

"I hear you have a cave full of treasures near Boquillas," she said. "Is that true?"

Joey looked at her insolently, as he always did when questioned. Who was this woman to ask questions of him? She was a woman who had whored with four men. Perhaps there had been even more.

"Where do you go, when you go?" Maria asked, when Joey said nothing. She felt like slapping him, maybe punching him with her fist. Rafael and Teresa, her damaged children, loved her. Even Rafael would come to her bed and try to speak to her, to express his little hopes. If he had a new chick, he would bring it to his mother and offer it to her as a present, cupping it tenderly in his large hands. Teresa would come to her bed to cuddle with her every morning. If Maria was sad, if tears leaked from her eyes, Teresa would whisper to her and wipe the tears away.

"Don't worry, Mama," Teresa said. "I am here. Rafael is here. We will take care of you."

It made Maria angry that her children who had no gifts—one who could not see, the other who could not reason—would help her with their love; while Joey, the brilliant one, the one whose mind was quick as a young deer, whose eyes were blue, whose teeth were so white that girls and even grown women melted at his smile—Joey gave nothing, not even little scraps of information. Maria did not really much want his money; what she wanted was his help.

"Someone saw you near Boquillas," Maria said. "Near the cave where you keep the treasures."

"I don't have a cave," Joey said. "I go to Piedras Negras, not Boquillas. There is nothing in Boquillas."

Maria thought of following Joey to his cave. She didn't believe him when he said he didn't have one. She didn't want his money for herself, she wanted it for her children. She had heard that in the City of Mexico, there were doctors who could cure many ills. It was said that there were doctors who could make blind people see. She wanted to take Teresa to such a doctor. It saddened her that her little girl had never seen the beauty of the world.

Also, she had heard that there were doctors who could help people whose minds were incomplete, or whose thoughts could not stay in order. She wanted to take Rafael to such a doctor, so that someday he could think like other people.

Maria wanted to take her children and go and seek the great doctors, in the City of Mexico, but she had no money. Joey had money. Maria wished he could be generous and give her what she needed, but she knew he never would. Joey was not generous, and not interested in her life or the lives of his brother and sister. He was only interested in himself.

"You help no one," she said to Joey one day, bitter.

"I help myself," Joey said.

"Are you the only one in the world?" Maria asked. "What is wrong with you?"

Joey didn't answer. He left, as he always did if she asked questions.

The day Maria rode off to Crow Town to warn Joey that Captain Call, the famous manhunter, had been sent to kill him, Billy Williams sobered up and made food for Maria's children.

[148]

As he cooked and set the plates, Billy felt sad. He should have gone with Maria, although he was nearly as blind as Teresa. He would have gone if Maria had asked him, should have gone, even though she hadn't asked. He was too old for places such as Crow Town. Going there might mean his death, but it also might mean Maria's death. He would worry now until the moment he saw her again. He wondered if Maria had refused him because he was a Texan. After all, her husbands had been Mexican. He didn't know if that had been her reason. Probably he had made some mistake and Maria had turned away from him instead of toward him. He ate his frijoles in sadness; he was old; it was too late. The large boy crooned, the little blind girl chattered. Billy thought it would be enough if Maria could just escape harm, if she could return from Crow Town to her children. His job was to stay sober and take care of her children.

Later, though, when Maria's children were asleep on their little pallets, the power of the lost, never captured love became too much for Billy. He couldn't bear it, not sober. And he began to get drunk again.

13.

"Now you wish you'd gone, don't you?" Lorena said.

Pea was standing just outside their back door, looking across the plains. It was past time to get the team hitched, to begin the day's work, but he was just standing there, looking across the plains. A norther had blown in around morning, and it was going to be a cold ride to school. But that wasn't what worried Lorena. For nearly a month after sending Call off without him, Pea Eye had worked with a will. But then, his will began to falter. Usually, he was out of bed and at work in the kitchen, getting a fire started or the boys up or making a beginning at breakfast, before she finished feeding Laurie and hauled herself from under the covers. Ten minutes more in bed, to gather her energies for the day, was something Lorena had come to count on, but she was able to count on it only because Pea was so good about getting up and getting started with the early chores.

He still got up and made a start on things, but with only half a will. He made mistakes, put one boy into another boy's clothes, burned the porridge; he seemed to be distracted, or in a daze, or something. Instead of saving her time, he cost her time, all of it spent correcting his mistakes.

The same distractedness stayed with him throughout the day. Clarie complained that he gave hay to the horses, but forgot the milk cow. He went off to work, as he always did, but instead of working from dawn until dark as he had to if the farm was to flourish, he would come home in the middle of the afternoon. Often, she would find him in the barn, when she returned from school. He would have taken a harness to the work bench, meaning to repair it, but then he didn't repair it. He would just hold it, and go into his daze.

Lorena let him be for three weeks. She had days when she didn't concentrate so well, either. Sometimes, she forgot things too, or did them badly, or just felt lazy. She didn't fret that much about human inconsistence, for she was human, and inconsistent herself.

But after a time, Pea's distractedness began to irritate her. They all had their work; she wanted him to do his, as she did hers. Hard work was the basis of their life. In the past, when Pea had gone off with Call, she and Clarie had worked harder than ever, so they would still have a life and a farm when Pea got back. They did well, too. They couldn't do all the field work, but otherwise, they kept things going so well that sometimes, it took a week or two to adjust to having Pea back. None of the stock died, the barn didn't burn down, and the essential things got done.

Picking up the slack when Pea Eye was gone was one thing; having to pick it up when he was there was vexing. Even more vexing was the cause of his distraction: he wished he had gone with Captain Call.

Lorena stepped outside, in the cutting wind, and repeated herself.

"Now you wish you'd gone, don't you?" she said again.

"I wish the Captain hadn't gone," Pea Eye said. "I wish he'd quit."

"Quit and do what?" Lorena asked. "He doesn't know how to do anything but kill."

"That ain't fair, Lorie," Pea Eye said. If there was one thing he hated to do, it was argue with Lorena, his wife, about Captain Call, his old commander. Yet that was exactly what he was doing, and in a cold wind, too.

[151]

"It *is* true," Lorena said. "Maybe in the days of the Indian troubles there was a need for a man like him."

"You know there was. Look what Blue Duck did, and he was just one man," Pea Eye said.

I don't need to remember what Blue Duck did," Lorena said. "I taught myself to forget it. Clara taught me about forgetting things like that."

"Why, he never bothered Clara," Pea Eye said. He, too, tried not to think about the terrible time when Blue Duck, one of the worst outlaws ever to terrorize the plains, had kidnapped Lorena. Gus McCrae had rescued her and she had survived; she had recovered, and become his wife. What had happened with Blue Duck was the kind of thing that happened to people all over the frontier, in those days. He himself had fought over twenty engagements with Indians, and the first one had frightened him the most. It was known to locals as the Battle of the Stone Houses. The Indians fired the grass and stole the Rangers' horses, putting them afoot in territory where it was easily possible to starve. They hadn't starved, but Pea Eye had been a little deaf in his left ear ever since, the result of a terrified Ranger firing his rifle into the smoke, when the smoke was so thick he was unaware that Pea Eye was kneeling only a yard away.

Those had been hard times. Without the Captain's and Gus's leadership, Pea Eye doubted that he would have been alive to try dirt farming on the plains.

Clara Allen, though, lived in Nebraska. So far as he knew, she had never been taken by anyone as bad as Blue Duck.

"Clara has things to forget, too," Lorena insisted. "There's other kinds of bad things besides what happened to me. All three of her boys died. We got three boys. How would we be if all three of them died?"

"Oh, Lord, don't even mention it," Pea Eye said. "Let's get back in the house."

He felt chastened. Of course, losing children was worse than being half deafened in a fight; the thought of his children dying was not something he even wanted to let his mind approach.

[152]

Lorie, as usual, was right. Life was hard for women, too, even though they didn't often have to go into battle.

"Clara has more to forget than I do," Lorena said, saddened by her own statement and by the memory of Clara's kindness— and Clara's sadness, which, now that Clara was older and had seen her girls marry, only seemed to sit on her the more heavily, judging from the letters she wrote Lorena. At least Clara loved horses, and had her herd to work with.

"If I was to lose three children, I'd give up," she told her husband. "If I even lost one child, I might give up. But Clara lost all her boys, and she didn't give up. And everything she did for me she did after her grief."

"I wasn't saying anything bad about Clara," Pea Eye said. "I guess if it hadn't been for her, we might not have come together, and I wouldn't have none of this. I'm obliged to Clara, and I always will be. I didn't have nothing but the clothes on my back, and she helped me. I ain't the kind of man who forgets the folks that helped him.

"It's just that Captain Call is one of the folks who helped me," he said. "Now he came asking for my help, and I didn't go. I can't not feel that's wrong, even though I know I'd feel wronger if I went."

"Not wronger—more wrong," Lorena corrected.

All of a sudden, without her wanting it or even expecting it, tears flooded her eyes, tears of anger and hurt. It would never be finished, the trouble over Call, not while the Captain was alive, it wouldn't.

"Go!" she said, vehemently. "Go! I want you to. I'll never really have you while he's alive, and neither will the children. Go! And if you get killed, good riddance!"

Pea Eye looked at her, stunned.

"I don't want to go," he said. "I told you why and I told the Captain why. Since we been married, I ain't really wanted to go."

"Haven't really wanted to go!" she corrected him, again. "Haven't!"

Pea Eye just looked at her, bewildered. He saw her tears and

[153]

her anger, but didn't really understand that she was trying to correct his grammar.

"I didn't go," he pointed out. "I didn't go. I didn't want to, neither. It's just that I feel bad for the Captain. I can't help it."

Lorena turned away. It was a subject she was sick of. She didn't speak another word to Pea, before leaving for school. But the sad look in his eyes, when she and the children left, made her feel sorry all day, and as soon as she got home she went down to the barn, where she found him trying to straighten a horseshoe. He was not that good with tools, Pea wasn't. Clarie could often fix things that left Pea Eye at a loss.

But seeing him holding the shoe in his hand—it seemed to Lorena that he was just making it more bent—touched her. He was not mechanical, or even very competent physically. It was a wonder he had survived, in a place where physical competence was so important. Yet his very lack of skill in areas where most frontiersmen excelled, moved her. It always had. Pea Eye was a man she could do things for, and he would let her do things for him. He accepted her instruction gratefully, whereas most men she had tried to instruct, in even small, unimportant matters, had usually bristled and become angry; in some cases, even violently angry. But Pea Eye had no violence in him, and he surrendered meekly and tried to pay attention when she or Clarie was trying to show him how to do some simple task.

"I didn't mean that about good riddance if you didn't come back," she said. "I'm sorry I said it. I was just mad."

When Lorena apologized to him, which she did almost every time she got mad at him, and she got mad at him fairly often, Pea Eye felt even more unhappy. Lorena oughtn't to be having to apologize. In his eyes, Lorie was never wrong. If they disagreed, he was the one who was wrong. In the matter of the Captain, he had to feel doubly wrong: in relation to Lorena and his family, if he went; in relation to the Captain, if he didn't.

But this time, it seemed, he felt even worse. The Captain had looked old, when they met by the train. In fact, the Captain was old. He oughtn't to be chasing bandits, at his age. Of course, ordinary bandits, of which there were a great many still running loose in the West, would give the Captain no trouble, even at his age.

It was just that the Garza boy didn't sound like an ordinary bandit. Pea Eye had run into Charles Goodnight while at the blacksmith's in Quitaque, and Goodnight had been startled to see him.

"Thought you went with Call to run down the Garza boy," he said, looking gruff.

"No, my family's got too big," Pea Eye said. Charles Goodnight was a stern fellow, even when he wasn't being gruff. Being even slightly in his disfavor was not comfortable.

"I've got a new little one, and my wife has to teach school," Pea said, though he felt explanation was hopeless. All the good reasons he could muster for not going with the Captain weren't likely to be good reasons to Mr. Goodnight. He would doubtless view them as the Captain had—excuses, made by a man who had no stomach for conflict, anymore.

"I don't care to know the details," Goodnight said, looking critically at the hoof of a horse that had just been shod.

"Well, the Captain went away, with the man from the railroad," Pea explained. "That's a young boy he's after. I doubt he'll give the Captain much trouble, the young ones never do."

"You're scarce on your facts," Goodnight said, lifting the hoof so high that the horse almost fell over. Goodnight was a big man. Though old, he could still lift most of a horse, if it was necessary.

"What facts?" Pea Eye asked. "We don't hear that much news, out at the farm."

"They estimate Joey Garza has killed over thirty men, and that's just the ones who've been found," Goodnight said. "There may be more who haven't been found and never will be found. He shoots a German rifle with a telescope sight. They say he can kill at five hundred yards, which is farther than most people can see. Half the line riders west of the Pecos may be dead, for all we know. Who's going to find a line rider, if he's shot fifty miles from the bunkhouse? Who would even miss one? Line riders don't come back half the time, anyway."

Pea had seen rifles with telescope sights. They had been available for many years. But they were too slow for most of the rangering action, and so he had never fired one. The notion that a man could be killed at five hundred yards, other than by a freak shot such as the famous one Billy Dixon had made during the Adobe Walls fight, was difficult to grasp. Most of the killing he had seen had taken place at distances under thirty yards, and in many cases, under twenty yards. Five hundred yards was about the distance from Lorie's schoolhouse to the Red River. He himself could see a bull, or a buffalo, at that distance, but that didn't mean he could hit it if he shot at it.

"Good Lord, I hadn't heard any of that," he told Goodnight.

"You ought to have gone with your Captain," Goodnight said bluntly. "This is a time when he might need an experienced man."

"Well, I swear," Pea Eye said. He felt bad in his stomach, suddenly. Mr. Goodnight was probably right. He should have gone.

"I guess the Captain will manage," he said, guiltily.

"In my opinion, Woodrow Call is a fool, to be pursuing young killers at his age," Goodnight said. "I'm his age, and I ain't pursuing young killers."

Pea Eye was silent. His sense of guilt was swelling within him. He had become sick at his stomach, just from the weight of the old man's displeasure.

"Is he that dangerous, this boy?" Pea asked.

"The whole Comanche nation would take a year to kill thirty men, and that would be in a good year, too," Goodnight replied, looking at Pea Eye solemnly.

Then, as if suddenly weary of his thoughts, or perhaps even of thinking, Goodnight set the gelding's foot down, and mounted him.

"There's always a time when you don't win," he said. "With me, it's lawyers. I've never won against any lawyer, not even the dumb ones. But lawyers just rob you legally. They don't shoot German rifles with telescope sights."

Pea Eye had met only two lawyers. One of them lived in

Quanah and had drawn up the deed when he and Lorena bought the farm.

"There's always a trip you don't come back from," Goodnight said. He turned his horse, as if to leave, and then turned back again, stood up in his stirrups, reached in his pocket and found several coins, which he handed to the blacksmith.

"Were you just going to let me ride off without paying you?" he asked the young blacksmith.

"Yes, sir," the blacksmith, Jim Peeples, replied. It would never have occurred to him to ask Charles Goodnight for money.

"Well, that would have been a damn nuisance," Goodnight said. "Then I'd have had to ride the whole way back to pay you. If you want to thrive in business, you better learn to speak up."

"Yes, sir," Jim Peeples said, terrified. He had never supposed Charles Goodnight would speak to him at all, much less lecture him. It was a little like being lectured by God, or at least, by the prophet Moses. Jim Peeples was a Baptist. He read the Bible every night, and much of Sunday, too. He didn't really think he had a clear picture of how God looked, but he did think he could imagine the prophet Moses fairly accurately. In Jim Peeples's opinion, Moses had looked a lot like Charles Goodnight.

Goodnight looked down at Pea Eye. The man had made a remarkable walk, nearly a hundred miles, naked, through the Cheyenne country to find Call and bring him to where his wounded partner, Augustus McCrae, lay dying. It was a great thing, in Goodnight's view, that walk. Not too many men, in his experience, had achieved a great thing, even one. Very few ever achieved more than one, he knew. He had led men himself, many men. Men as faithful as Pea Eye had been to Call had served with him until they fell, and the best of them had fallen. Goodnight was a married man himself, but had no children. He had always wondered what it meant, to have offspring. How would it affect his leadership, his ability to go and keep going, his attitude toward the dangers of the trail? It hadn't happened, but he didn't suppose it would have simplified matters if he had. In a time of danger, he had sometimes thought of his wife, but he always thought of his men. He did not worry too much about his wife. He had never supposed himself to be a very good husband; he had always been too busy. His wife was an able woman, and would probably be happier with someone more settled, if something happened to him. But he had never had to worry about children, and the man who stood before him did have to worry about children.

"I suppose your wife don't like it," he said.

"Don't like what?" Pea Eye asked. He was a little surprised to find himself in such a lengthy discussion with Charles Goodnight, a man known all over the West for his dislike of long conversations.

"You and Call," Goodnight said. "Divided loyalties don't appeal to women, not that I've noticed."

"I ain't divided, I'm loyal to them both," Pea Eye replied.

"That would be fine if Call was bunking with you," Goodnight said. "The fact is, he bunks with me, when he bunks, which ain't much. He sure don't bunk with you, though. Now, he's in Mexico, chasing a boy with a German rifle and a dern good eye, if he can shoot people at five hundred yards."

Pea Eye didn't know what to say. Captain Call had been in danger much of his life, but Pea Eye, in the years he had been with him, had never really considered that the Captain might be killed. That was Goodnight's point, though—the Captain might be killed.

"You think Joey Garza could kill the Captain?" he asked.

"Yes, I do," Goodnight said, and turned and rode away.

Pea walked back to the house with Lorena, after her apology. They had a good supper. The children were peaceful, for once. Lorena read the boys stories until they fell asleep. Little Laurie liked to listen to the stories, too; at least, she liked to listen to her mother's voice while her mother was reading. Her little eyes were so bright. She waved her hands but she was very quiet while Lorena read.

It was a fine evening, but in the middle of the night, Pea Eye woke with a start. He was shivering, as if with a chill. It seemed to him that death was in bed with them. When he had been trapped with Gus under the cutback in Montana, his death almost a certainty, he hadn't given it much thought. He had too much to do, keeping alive, to worry about dying. Then, on the last day of the long, cold, hungry walk out, he had begun to feel that perhaps he *was* dead; in the dark of the last morning, he had felt that Deets, his friend the black cowboy, was walking beside him, guiding him. Deets was dead; if he was with Deets, he must be dead too.

But he hadn't been. Within a few hours, Pea Eye found the herd, and Deets, if he was there, went back to the place of ghosts.

Now, though, with Lorena beside him and their five children in the house near him, Pea Eye faced death as a thought and as a fact, in a way he never had. Far south, below the border, Captain Call might be facing it, even at that moment. Little Laurie might be taken, the next time she had the croup. Lorie might be taken, the next time she bore a child. What would it mean, if any one of them died?

Lorena knew Pea Eye was awake. She had awakened while he slept, for he was restless in his sleep and had scraped one of her legs with a toenail. He was lazy about cutting his toenails and rarely cut them until she had complained two or three times.

But it wasn't the scrape from the toenail that bothered her. A bad dream had come, from the past, from the time when she had been with bad men. She always tried to pull herself out of such dreams as quickly as possible. Better to face those memories awake, with thoughts of her husband and children to support her, than to let the dream carry her far down, into the depths of pain and fear.

"Lorie, I'm scared," Pea Eye said. "I'm so scared, I've got a chill."

Lorena put her arms around him. Indeed, he was clammy, as if sweating out a fever. His skin was cold.

"Maybe you're getting what Georgie has," Lorena said. Georgie had been running a high fever for several days.

"I'll get you warm," she said, pulling her body close to his.

"I ain't cold outside—it's inside," Pea said, though he was

glad Lorie was lying close to him. It had seemed a miracle, the first time she had drawn him into her body. It still seemed a miracle that he, who had never been able to rise higher than the rank of corporal, could be wanted by a woman as fine as Lorie, and have the warmth and the pleasure of her body, in the bed at night, through his life. She was generous with him. He knew from the complaints of other men, that all women weren't so generous. He put his arms around her and held her, grateful and warmer, but still frightened.

Lorena liked it that she could comfort Pea Eye so easily, just by taking him into her arms. She hoped she wasn't with child. It was too soon, for she was still tired from Laurie. But if she was, she did not plan to stop wanting her husband because of the inconveniences of pregnancy.

Lorena knew that Clara Allen must be very wise to have advised her to marry Pea Eye. She had never expected to marry any man, or even to share a bed with one and want him. Too much of her life had been spent at the mercy of men she didn't want, even of men she despised; or in having to refuse the love of decent men—Dish Boggett was the main one, although there had been others in Ogallala—whose feelings she couldn't return.

Why she had been able to return Pea Eye's love, she really didn't know. In a way, she thought Gus might have wished it. He and Pea had been friends. But perhaps that was silly. Gus had been as jealous as anyone, in his way. Still, Gus had loved Clara, and herself as well, and Pea had been his corporal, and Clara her own best friend. Something had caused her to want Pea. Perhaps it was only his simple, honest need. And she still wanted him, which was more of a blessing than many people had in life. More than Clara had herself; she'd had no men since her husband's death, years before.

That made it all the harder to turn loose, though, to allow him to do his duty by old Captain Call. She might have to turn loose yet, probably would have to, but she still wanted to fight it, woman against man. That was what it was, too: woman against man. Her body, her spirit, her affection and passion, the children she and Pea shared, the *life* they shared on the farm that had cost them all her money and years of their energy. It was that against the old man with the gun, and the way of life that ought to have ended. Probably there was more to it—it involved the loyalty of fighting men to one another and to their leader, but Lorena gave that no respect, not where Pea Eye was concerned. He was a gentle man. He should never have been a Ranger, should never have had to deal out violence. There were many men who dealt out violence naturally. Old Call should never have had the use of one like Pea, a man who was comfortable with gentleness, who would spend hours taking prickly pear stickers out of the boys' hands, working at each one gently until he got it out.

Pea had never been meant for military life. He had turned out of it eagerly, happily, into a life with her. He loved best the days in the summer, when she didn't have school to teach, when they could work together at some of the lighter tasks around the farm. He had driven a wagon all the way to Amarillo to get lilac bushes for her to plant, and had helped her cover the little plants against the biting northers and the freezes of February and March.

She ought to win, Lorena knew. She held him in her arms, put her legs over his. She wanted him to know that there was more life with her; more children, if he wanted them; and more of her love.

But Pea Eye was staring past her, even as he held her tight.

"It's like I dread something," he said. "I dread something, Lorie." He whispered it. Pea was always nervous about waking the children. His voice, when he whispered, was exactly like Georgie's voice, when Georgie whispered his little secrets into his mother's ear.

Lorena felt some dread herself. She was only one woman, and she could only do so much. She knew she came first in Pea Eye's affections. It wasn't that he loved the Captain and not her. She had thought much about this subject—it had dominated their marriage, in a way—and the fact she couldn't change was that the Captain had been there longer, in Pea Eye's life. He was there first, and not by a week or two, either, but by almost three decades. That was the fact she couldn't eliminate. She could change her husband's habits, and she had, but she couldn't change his history, and it was in his history that the problem lay.

"I ought to go find him," Pea Eye whispered. "He's an old man. I ain't."

"You aren't," Lorena corrected. But then, what was the point of correcting his grammar if he was going to Call? Good grammar wouldn't save him, and saving him was what mattered most, now.

The dread that Pea Eye felt crossed into Lorena. They were both gripped by it, husband and wife. Lorena had watched him go away several times, always with irritation, but never with such trepidation. She hated to see him leave, but always before, she had assumed he would return. She didn't know why this trip should be so different, and neither did Pea Eye. Yet they lay together, equally troubled, equally frightened.

"At least I get paid in cash," Pea Eye said.

"I don't care if you get paid in cash," Lorena said. "Cash can't hug me. It can't make me a baby. It can't be a father to Augie and Georgie and Ben and the girls."

"Well, it won't have to," Pea said. "I'll come back."

"I don't believe you, this time," Lorena said. "If you go you won't come back. We'll never lie in the bed like this, again. I'll get old and I won't have you, and neither will the children."

Pea Eye said nothing. He had begun to have wild thoughts, one being that the Captain was already dead. That would mean that he didn't have to go. But of course, if the Captain had been killed, he would have heard about it, and he hadn't.

Lorena didn't say a thing, either; her thoughts were disordered, too. If Pea got killed, she would probably have to turn Dish Boggett down again. He kept a store in New Mexico and was still single, unless he had recently married. If Pea got killed, Dish would soon hear of it and ride over to court her. He wasn't a bad man; in fact, he was a good man. But she didn't want him, never had, and all the tea in China wouldn't change that.

I wish this would stop, she thought. I wish it would stop. It's going to drive me crazy, if it don't stop.

In the morning, they were both as drained as if they had done three days' work. Clarie had to deal with everything, including the chores and the younger children, too.

"What's wrong, Mama?" she asked, disturbed. "What's wrong, Pa?"

Neither parent would say. When Clarie went out to milk, Lorena made one last try.

"What makes you think you can find him?" she asked. "He's been gone nearly a month. He could be in the middle of Mexico by now. He could be as far away as the Pacific Ocean."

"I expect I can find the Captain," Pea Eye said. "People notice, when he's around. Roy Bean or somebody will know where he is."

"Go on, then, today," Lorena said. "Go now. I can't stand another night like last night. Go right now, before I leave for school."

Pea Eye got his slicker and his rifle and walked down to get his horse.

"You're going to ride?" Lorena asked, when he came back. "You could take the train. He took the train."

"No, I'll ride. I might not find a trustworthy horse down on the border," Pea said. Patches, his big bay with white spots, was a trustworthy horse.

Pea Eye kissed each of his children goodbye. All of them cried, Clarie the most. She was a big, strong girl. The boys cried themselves out, and Laurie cried because everybody else was crying.

Lorena went in and got ready for school. She dressed slowly, very slowly. Slowly, very slowly, she put her lesson books in order. Usually, she just threw them in her bag and sorted them out once she got to school. But this morning, she put them in order, carefully and slowly, as if her sanity or even her life depended upon keeping her schoolbooks in the correct order.

It was all she could do, once she got outside, even to raise her eyes to her husband. But she did, just briefly. His eyes, though troubled, were the same honest eyes that had won through her reluctance, long ago, in Wyoming. She kissed him briefly, gave him a long, tight hug, and then, moving stiffly, like a woman whose back has been injured, helped her children into the buggy and drove away to school. The children all looked back at their father, but Lorena didn't. She kept her eyes fixed on the plains ahead.

Pea Eye put a little salt and pepper in a sack, stuck a small skillet in his saddlebags, and stood at his back door a minute, wondering when he would see them all again, his loved ones, already almost out of sight to the north.

Then he mounted Patches, made sure his rifle and scabbard were tight, and turned himself south, toward Mexico, to go to the assistance of Captain Woodrow Call.

14.

On his way into Mexico, Call stopped to say goodbye to Bolivar. The old man had been with him a long time. Seeing him brought back memories, good and bad, of the Ranger troop and the Hat Creek outfit: memories of Gus and Deets, Pea Eye and Newt, Call's son. Only after the boy's death, in Montana, had Call been able to admit that Newt had been his son. Now, with the boy several years dead, it made Call sad to think of him. He had fathered a son, but had not been a father to him, although Newt had lived with the Hat Creek outfit most of his short life. He had lived with the outfit, but as an employee, not a son. Now it was too late to change any of that. The memory of it was a sore that throbbed every time his mind touched it. Bolivar, who had not many more years to live, was so woven into Call's memories of earlier days that Call had begun to hate leaving him behind, although Bolivar was an old, frail man who could not travel hard and perhaps ought not to travel at all.

But leaving him behind had become, to Call, like leaving his own life behind.

"*Capitán*, the bell! I can still ring the bell!" Bolivar said. He had a desperate look in his eye and a quaver in his voice. He saw that the *capitán* was about to leave without him. The two gringos with him were mounted, and there was a pack mule, well laden. It meant the *capitán* was going, perhaps never to come back.

The bell he referred to was the dinner bell, near the livery stable in Lonesome Dove, a business that Call and his partner, Gus McCrae, had once owned. Bolivar had summoned them all to his never very appetizing meals by whacking the dinner bell with a broken crowbar. As he grew older and less in control of his mind, he sometimes rang the bell whether he had made a meal or not. He often rang it when there was no one in hearing to come and eat the meal he had made. Beating the bell with the broken crowbar took his mind off the disappointments of life. The bell rang so loudly that it almost deafened him, but he continued to beat it fiercely, nonetheless. His life had contained many disappointments, and he needed something to make him forget them, even if he was deafened in the process.

Call, and Bolivar, too, regretted that the Hat Creek outfit was gone. What they had in common now was their regret. But the outfit *was* gone. Some of its members were dead, and those still living were scattered up the rivers and across the plains. Newt and Deets and Gus were no longer alive, and Call had the feeling that Bolivar might not be alive, either, when he returned to Laredo.

"That old man needs a haircut," Deputy Plunkert said, as they were leaving Nuevo Laredo. The old man's white hair hung almost to his shoulders.

"He tried to stab the barber with the scissors, the last time anyone tried to cut his hair," Call explained.

"I'd rather see him with hair down to his ankles than to trust him with anything he might hurt somebody with," Brookshire said. He remembered, with rue, that Bolivar had grabbed a shotgun out of his hand and killed the best mule with it. He was glad Bolivar was being left behind; he had been a little worried that Call might relent and let him come with them, something that would not have pleased Colonel Terry.

The fact that Captain Call immediately left Texas and crossed into Mexico startled Deputy Plunkert a bit. His personal preference would have been that they continue to travel on the Texas side of the river. He himself was not comfortable being south of the border, particularly if he was in the vicinity of Laredo itself. As a deputy, with his own badge, Ted Plunkert had participated in the hanging of several Mexicans. He had to shoot two Mexicans personally, and had to whack various Mexicans around a good bit. After all, it was his job, and the community expected it of him. He knew that, as a result of his very diligence, he had made himself not merely unpopular but hated, south of the border. Deputy Plunkert knew, too, that Mexican families were often vengeful, going to much trouble to avenge friends who had been wounded or killed. The deputy was prepared to make it clear to anyone who asked that he would be more comfortable on the Texas side of the river.

"There's a fair road up to Del Rio," he said, only to be immediately slapped down by the Captain.

"We're not going to Del Rio," Call said, bluntly. "I prefer to avoid settlements, when I can. There's too much gossip, in settlements. We don't want the Garza boy to know we're coming, if we can help it."

Deputy Plunkert didn't answer, but he found the Captain's position discouraging. Before going five miles from his home, he had begun to entertain some powerful second thoughts.

He had never supposed that the Captain would just jump right into Mexico. Of course, he knew they might have to cross into it sometime, but he had assumed that they would be several hundred miles up the river before that happened. His own bad reputation was mainly local. Five or six hundred miles upriver, they would be less likely to run into Mexicans who might be carrying a grudge. Now, though, they were right in the thick of the Mexicans who carried the hottest grudges. It was going to affect his peace of mind.

Also, he'd had a few hours in which to get a better look at his traveling companions. In Laredo, he had been so in awe of Captain Call that he had scarcely been able to look at him at all. In fact, except for a glance at the beginning, he hadn't looked at him. The man's aura was such that merely hearing his name blinded most people, as it had blinded him.

Now, though, riding across the empty, dusty country, the hero's aura had dimmed somewhat. The deputy saw that he was traveling with an old, stiff man, a man who had a hard time lifting his leg high enough to catch his stirrup. Captain Call had a gray, weary look about him, the look of a man who wasn't young, and wasn't healthy.

The Yankee traveling with them was just a raw dude, of course. He looked silly in his new boots and hat and pants, loaded down with guns. The fact that Captain Call would set out to catch a killer with such a man in tow made Deputy Plunkert wonder about the old man's judgment.

The deputy had a sudden, powerful urge to change his mind. He wanted to declare a mistake, go home, snuggle up to his wife, Doobie, and kiss her until she wiggled with desire. Now he had set out on a long journey, with an uncertain outcome. When would he get to enjoy Doobie's wiggling again? Why had he thought he wanted to leave? It had all been because the old Captain enjoyed such a blinding reputation. Doubting him was like doubting the sun.

Now that they were riding together, Call didn't seem infallible, or even very active. He just rode along, saying as little as possible. The deputy began to toy with various acceptable ways of saying that he had changed his mind. But none of the lines of talk he toyed with sounded as if they would be acceptable, either to Call or to the general community. And there was no denying, the general community posed a problem. Backing out of a chance to ride with Woodrow Call could ruin a man's reputation forever, with lawmen and citizens alike, along the border. But his reputation might survive. He just had to come up with some honorable reason for needing to go home. A lame horse would do it, but to his irritation, the horse he was riding showed no trace of lameness.

As Deputy Plunkert was happily contemplating returning to his eager wife, Captain Call suddenly turned in his saddle and looked hard at him.

"Do you want to quit, Deputy?" he asked. It seemed to him that the deputy had developed a faltering manner, and developed it quickly. If the man was going to quit, he wanted him to quit now. It wasn't admirable, but it wasn't a crime, either. Like Pea Eye, the deputy had a wife. They were going in pursuit of a youth who might kill them all. The man had not hesitated in making his decision. Now, he probably had second thoughts.

"Quit?" Deputy Plunkert said, stunned. The old man had suddenly read his thoughts.

"Yes, that's what I asked," Call said. "Do you want to go back to your wife?"

"Doobie? Why, she'll get along fine without me, I expect," the deputy replied.

"Then you don't want to quit? You're sure?" Call asked.

"Why, Captain, no. I signed on and I'm staying on," Ted Plunkert said. It amazed him that he couldn't seem to help lying. What he heard himself say to the Captain was exactly the opposite of what he had just been feeling, the opposite of what he had planned to say. But he couldn't help himself. Saying the truth wasn't possible, not when Captain Call was looking at you, hard.

"What do you think, Brookshire?" Call asked. Though skeptical of Brookshire at first, he had come to respect the man's judgment in some areas. He might be a fool about hats, but he wasn't such a fool about people.

One of Brookshire's boots was rubbing his heel so badly that he wasn't capable of giving much thought to anything else. He was wondering whether he'd have a heel left, when they got to camp that night. Also, he was suffering from a touch of his blowing-away feeling again. He had supposed that he had that feeling well under control, for it hadn't afflicted him since they reached the brushy country around San Antonio. But they were not in San Antonio now. They were not in the brushy country, either. To his eye, Mexico looked even emptier than Texas, emptier, and more forbidding. The night before, he had slipped over to Nuevo Laredo and purchased a few minutes with a Mexican girl, and the experience had been a disappointment. The girl had been inexpensive, but she had also been skinny and had a sad look in her eye during their brief commerce. The poverty in Nuevo Laredo had been a surprise to him too. He had read about Juarez, and Emperor Maximilian, and had expected at least a little splendor. Even in Canada, a country he disliked, there would occasionally be some splendor, at least in Montreal. But there seemed to be none, in Mexico. There were just sad women and children, and old men who gave him unfriendly looks.

"You're buying their daughters, or it might be their wives," Call had said, when Brookshire mentioned the unfriendly looks.

Now the Captain was soliciting his opinion about Deputy Plunkert, and the fact was, Brookshire really didn't have one. The man had been a hasty choice, in his view, but that didn't necessarily mean he had been a bad one.

"It's your expedition, or your Colonel's," Call reminded him. "Do you think we ought to keep this man, or send him back?"

"Captain, I can't go home!" Ted Plunkert said. He was nearing panic. It was as if his deepest thoughts were suddenly being held open to public discussion, a fact that appalled him. Once the Captain had fixed him with the hard look, Ted Plunkert remembered who he was: a deputy sheriff, well respected in Laredo, Texas. Now that he remembered himself, he had begun to feel irritated at Doobie, his wife. It seemed to him that it was mainly her fault, that he had wavered that morning. She had cried so, at the thought of his going, that it weakened him and made him less resolute than he normally was. If Doobie had any serious consideration for him, she should comport herself a little better when he had serious business to attend to. And there couldn't be business more serious than attending to whatever Captain Call might require of him.

Doobie had nearly caused him to make a mistake of the sort that could ruin him forever as a lawman, and he meant to speak to her sharply about it, when he got home. He himself might consider that Captain Call looked old and stiff, but that wasn't the general opinion, along the border. Most people, of course, never saw the real Captain Call, the very one he was riding with into Mexico. Most people only knew the man by reputation, as the Ranger who had protected the border south of Laredo for so long.

Captain Call had protected the border from bad Mexicans, bad Indians, and bad white men, too. Life was changing, along the border. It was becoming more or less settled. For many years, though, the thought of Captain Call had enabled many people to sleep better at night. They would not soon forget him, and most of them would never know that he was a man who had trouble lifting his leg high enough to catch his stirrup.

Now that he had strongly reiterated his desire to go, Ted Plunkert couldn't imagine how he could ever have contemplated quitting, although, in fact, he had contemplated exactly that very thing, not ten minutes earlier. He had never quit anything in his life, unless you counted cotton farming, and that was not a job he had chosen. He just happened to be born on a cotton farm.

"I came to ride the river with you, Captain," he said. "It's something I had always hoped to do. I sure ain't going home now."

Call turned back in his saddle, and let the matter go. Many men wavered, as they were riding into danger. They thought about their own deaths too much, or imagined injuries and pain that might never come. That was what excessive thinking could do, even to men who were moderately brave. Often, the same men, once in a conflict, settled down and fought well. Pea Eye himself had always been a reliable, if not a brilliant, fighting man. Yet he was the most nervous man in the company until hostilities commenced. He was almost too delicate for the rangering life. Call had concluded as much on more than one occasion, but had never quite gotten around to letting the man go. On the trail of Indians or bandits, Pea was prone to headaches, heartburn, upset stomachs, and runny bowels, all of it from nerves, Call was convinced.

Call felt a brief anger, because Pea hadn't come with him. But he knew that his anger was wrong, to a degree, and that he needed to let it go. Pea Eye had long since done his share, more than his share, of dangerous traveling with Call. If he now preferred his wife and children and dirt farming, that was his right.

That night, they camped on the monte, ten miles south of the river. Call had made a snap shot at a small javelina and hit it, so they had young pig to eat. After eating, he sat a little apart, thinking about the task ahead. He had not yet made up his mind where to take up the hunt—take it up seriously, that is. He thought he should probably cut up the Rio Grande, past the great bend, and start hunting there. The boy had bought his fancy rifle in Mexico City, and he had stopped a train in Coahuila, and another in Van Horn, Texas. That showed a remarkable propensity for travel, in a boy so young. It also showed that Joey Garza could cover country. The boy was said to be from a village north of Boquillas, a poor village, it was said. Not many Mexican boys from poor villages would travel to Mexico City to secure a German rifle. It took some thinking about.

"Do you ever get upset before a fight, Captain?" Deputy Plunkert asked. He addressed himself to the Captain, although the man sat apart, because he did not feel comfortable talking to a Yankee. So far, he had addressed only a few words to Brookshire, mainly yes and no, when the man asked him a question.

"No, I can't say that I fret much," Call said.

"Now, that's brave," Brookshire said. "When I was in the War, I was scared all the time. I was only in the hospital corps, too, I wasn't shooting at anybody. But I kept having them bad dreams."

"What'd you dream?" the deputy asked. He himself was often afflicted with bad dreams.

"Mainly of having one of them big shells come in low and knock my head off," Brookshire said. "That very thing happened to a man I know. He was from Hoboken and his name was Johnny Lowe."

"Bad luck, I suppose," Call said.

"Yes, I'd say it was bad luck," Brookshire said. "The man gave me his biscuit, the morning it happened. He said he was too nervous to eat. He was afraid his stomach would gripe him, if he ate the biscuit. Johnny drove the wagon we hauled the wounded in. Off he went, while I stayed by the mess and ate his biscuit. While I was sipping coffee, General Grant rode by. That was the one time I saw General Grant. Then, me and Jackie O'Connor went down the road in a buggy, squinching down as best we could. The shells were just whistling around us like ducks. Most of them hit in the trees. They broke off a world of limbs. We weren't five minutes down the road, when we saw a bunch of the boys standing around the wagon Johnny had been driving. We thought maybe they were looking at a dead Reb, but no, it was Johnny, and his head was gone. There was just a red bone, sticking out between his shoulders."

"Oh, Lord," Ted Plunkert said. "That's awful. It was just a bone?"

"Yes, a red bone," Brookshire said. "I suppose it was the end of his spine."

"Oh, Lord," Ted said, again. "His neck bone?" The detail he didn't like was that the bone was red. Of course, all the bones were inside you, where the blood was, but he still felt himself getting queasy at the thought of red bones.

Call listened with some amusement—not that the incident hadn't been terrible. Being decapitated was a grisly fate, whether you were a Yankee or not. But then, amusing things happened in battle, as they did in the rest of life. Some of the funniest things he had ever witnessed had occurred during battles. He had always found it more satisfying to laugh on a battlefield than anywhere else, for if you lived to laugh on a battlefield, you could feel you had earned the laugh. But if you just laughed in a saloon, or at a social, the laugh didn't reach deep.

In this case, what mainly amused Call was the contemplation of how amused his old partner, Augustus McCrae, would be if he could see the crew he was riding out with on his manhunt. Augustus had a well-developed sense of humor, too well developed, Call had often felt. Yet he missed Augustus's laughter as much as he missed anything else in his life. Gus enjoyed the predicaments of his fellowmen, and would have laughed long and hard at the spectacle of Call, Brookshire, and lanky Ted Plunkert.

"Joey Garza shoots a rifle, not a cannon," he observed. "If he takes your head off, he'll have to do it with a knife or a saw."

Deputy Plunkert ignored the part about the knife and the saw. Captain Call was only joking, probably. So far as he knew, the Garza boy had not cut any heads off, but there were plenty of other, less dramatic injuries to worry about.

"They say that rifle of his will hit you between the eyes even if you're a mile away," the deputy said. Several people he had talked with claimed that Joey Garza made kills at a distance of one mile.

"Half a mile, about," Call said. "I doubt the part about hitting between the eyes. If he's sensible, he'll shoot for the trunk. It's a bigger target."

"Well, half a mile, then. How do you expect to beat him?" Ted asked.

"I expect to outlast him," Call said. "He's young, and he's likely impatient. There's three of us, and he's alone. He might get impatient, and make a big mistake."

"The truth is, he's killed several passengers at a distance of about five feet, with his pistol," Brookshire reminded them. "Oh, I've no doubt he can shoot the German rifle. But he's done damage with some short shots, too."

"Why, he robs trains and makes people get off and hand over their watches and tiepins," Ted Plunkert said. "Some of the passengers are armed men. Why don't one of them try to shoot him? Then, the rest of them could jump him."

"I've wondered about that myself," Brookshire said. "You'd think somebody would try him, but they don't. They just stand there like sheep and let themselves be robbed."

"That's the effect of reputation," Call said. "Once you get one as big as this boy's, people think you're better than you are. They think you can't be beat, when the fact is, anybody can be beat, or make mistakes. I never met an outlaw who didn't make mistakes. I guess Blue Duck didn't make many, but he was exceptional."

"Joey Garza hasn't made any mistakes, not one," Brookshire said.

"Why, I'd say he has," Call said. "He broke the law—your Colonel's law, particularly. That was his mistake, and now he's got us hunting him."

"I guess I was talking tactics," Brookshire said. "He just seems to know when to show up, and when not to. If there's a company of soldiers on the train, he don't show up."

"That's just common sense," Call said. "I wouldn't show up, either, if I saw there was a company of soldiers on the train. That don't make the boy General Lee."

Deputy Plunkert was still thinking about the red bone, sticking out of the dead soldier's neck. Once he got such a troubling picture in his mind, he sometimes had a hard time making the picture go away. It was as if it got stuck, somewhere in his thinking machine. It might be a good picture that got stuck; several having to do with Doobie's young body got stuck just before they married.

But it was the bad pictures that seemed to get stuck the hardest, and stay stuck the longest. Being sucked down into quicksand was one bad picture Ted Plunkert had trouble with. There were patches of quicksand in the Rio Grande, and the deputy had a deadly fear of them. Not being able to breathe because quicksand was filling up your mouth and your nose was a bad picture, but not as bad as the picture of a red bone sticking out of a man's neck. He wished Brookshire had never told the story. It was just like a Yankee to talk about things civilized people would have the good sense to leave undiscussed.

"How did General Grant look?" Call asked. He had always had a curiosity about the great soldiers: Grant and Lee, Stonewall Jackson, Sherman.

"Well, he looked drunk and he was drunk," Brookshire said. "He won that War, and was drunk the whole time."

Call said nothing, but again, he remembered his old partner, Gus McCrae. Gus, too, could fight drunk. Sometimes he had fought better drunk than he had fought sober.

"I'd feel better if somebody could steal that rifle from that boy," Deputy Plunkert said. "A mile's a long way to be killed from."

"Half a mile," Call corrected, again.

Brookshire was wondering if Katie's legs would be any fatter when he got home.

"I'd still like to know who the second robber is," he said. "The one that struck that train out in New Mexico."

"I'd like to know that too," Call said.

15.

In Crow Town, Joey lived with three whores. He didn't use them for his pleasure—he never used women for his pleasure. The white whore was named Beulah. She had come south from Dodge City with a gambler named Red Foot. The nickname resulted from the fact that another gambler had become enraged and tried to stab Red Foot in the heart. But, being drunk as well as enraged, he took a wild swing, toppled out of his chair, and finally managed to stab Red Foot in his foot. Red Foot was very drunk too, and didn't notice at first that he had been stabbed completely through his foot. He only noticed the injury when someone pointed out to him that his right boot was full of blood. He looked down, saw that indeed the boot was full of blood, and fainted.

A few days later, he and Beulah left Dodge City and moved to Crow Town. The place was said to be booming; it was going to be the next Dodge. Red Foot and Beulah planned to open a whorehouse and get rich. But when they arrived, they saw at once that Crow Town was not booming. The rumors they had heard were lies. The population was low, and the few people who lived there were clearly too poor to support a whorehouse, or any other business, except a saloon.

Unable to face any more travel, Beulah and Red Foot stayed. Red Foot drank too much, and he had a tendency to pass out at inopportune moments. He had even passed out when playing cards, and cards were his profession.

Joey Garza was a different story. Beulah, twenty-eight years old and well traveled in more ways than one, had never seen a male as beautiful as Joey. His walk, his teeth, his hands, were beautiful. Red Foot was aging, and unreliable. Beulah hoped that Joey would take an interest in her, and he did. He asked her to come and live in his house, or a house he had taken as his. In Crow Town, houses often came to belong to the best shot. Joey didn't have to shoot anyone to acquire his house, though. A killer named Pecos Freddy passed through Crow Town the week before Joey arrived, and he ended up killing three Mexicans—the father, mother, and brother of the two young whores who ended up living with Joey and Beulah. The young whores, Marieta and Gabriela, were so saddened by the deaths that they didn't care, at first, whether they lived or died. They knew they would die soon, if they continued to live in Crow Town, but they had no money, no means of travel, and no hope.

When Joey appeared, they simply gave him the house, a two-room hut with low ceilings, and hoped that he would let them stay. He did, and he soon let Beulah stay, too, but he didn't share his bed, or even his room, with any of them. The three women slept on the floor in the larger room. Even that was better than sleeping with Red Foot, Beulah decided; another of Red Foot's unreliabilities was that he frequently wet the bed. He said it was because a horse had kicked him once, in a bad place. Beulah didn't know about that, but she did know that she was tired of waking up in a bed full of piss. The floor in Joey's house might host an occasional scorpion or centipede, but at least it was dry.

Joey let the women stay because he needed someone to cook and wash clothes. Beulah cooked, and Marieta and Gabriela kept his clothes clean. Joey Garza was by far the cleanest person in Crow Town. He insisted that his clothes be washed frequently, a difficult demand in a town where there was little water. Every three days, Marieta and Gabriela tied sacks of clothes and bedding onto a small donkey someone had lost. Then they trudged eleven miles through the sandhills, to the Pecos, where they washed the clothes, hung them on chaparral bushes to dry, and took them back to Joey. Often, they had to return to Crow Town by starlight.

Marieta and Gabriela were chubby girls, and they didn't expect much. Both had been whores since they were ten. Walking to the Pecos and washing Joey's clothes was an easier life than either had hoped for. It didn't bother them that Joey didn't want them. He was a *güero*, and *güeros* were often strange.

Beulah, though, was bothered by Joey's indifference. In her experience, if men didn't want you, they left you. Joey was the only person in Crow Town who had money. If he left, what would she do? Red Foot hated her now. He was a jealous man, and he would undoubtedly try to have his revenge the minute Joey Garza left. In his bitterness, he had already told her he would tie her to a tree and leave her tied until the crows pecked out her eyes. Beulah didn't really believe that crows pecked out people's eyes, but she didn't take Red Foot's threats lightly, either. He was perfectly capable of doing something horrible to her, and he probably would, if he got the chance.

It occurred to Beulah one day that Joey's tastes might be complex. She had known men whose tastes were complex; the most common complex taste, in her view, was for extra women in the bed. Maybe that was what Joey would like—all three of them in bed at once.

If there was even a chance that it might work, Beulah wanted to try. She talked it over with Marieta and Gabriela, both of whom were skeptical.

"Three women at the same time?" Marieta said. "He don't even want one woman."

"No, but he might like three," Beulah insisted.

Gabriela, the youngest, didn't like the idea at all. Whoring was bad enough. What Beulah suggested only sounded worse. Gabriela had become a whore when she was ten, but she didn't look at men. Once, her own uncle had forced her to look at him. He twisted her arm and beat her until she looked at him, but usually, she just looked away and pretended she wasn't there. Sometimes, while she was looking away, the men stole back the money they gave her. Gabriela never got to keep much of the money, anyway. Her father had taken it, while he was alive, and now Marieta took it.

"If he don't want us, he won't feed us," Beulah said. In her experience, that was how men were.

Later, the two girls talked it over. They didn't want to disappoint Beulah, who had been good to them, in their time of grief. The girls didn't like Crow Town. The wind blew very cold in winter. It was always dusty, and the men were rough. But in Mexico, they had nothing. Neither of them wanted to go back to Mexico.

"If he don't want us, he won't feed us," Marieta said, echoing Beulah. She was willing to defer to Beulah's judgment. Beulah was older, and knew more about men.

The next night, at Beulah's suggestion, they all got undressed except for nightgowns. The girls' gowns were only of thin cotton, but Beulah's was silk. She had bought it long ago, in Kansas City. When they went in to Joey, he was cleaning his fine rifle with a rag. The look in his eyes, when he saw them come in, was not friendly. He didn't speak.

"You could have us all three," Beulah said, timidly. From the look he gave them, she knew that her idea had not been a good one. She had mentioned it to Red Foot, to see what he thought, and Red Foot certainly liked it.

"I'd take three whores over one whore anytime," Red Foot said. "I'm a man that likes whores." That was true. The whores in Dodge City had profited greatly from Red Foot's interest.

Joey was different, though. He was a colder article, Beulah thought.

"I don't want three fat women," he said, to Beulah. "You cook. Marieta washes clothes. Gabriela don't have to do nothing."

"Well, why don't she?" Beulah asked, stung. She had already begun to be a little jealous of Gabriela, and now she felt even more jealous.

[180]

"Because she's pretty," Joey said, closing the conversation.

"He's in love with you," Marieta said to her sister, later. "He's rich, too. He has a cave full of money."

Joey did like to look at the young whore Gabriela. He liked it that she was so modest. That was the way women should be. But, other than admiring her looks and her modesty, he had no need for her.

During the day, Joey often sat for a while in the town's small, dirty saloon. At first, the gamblers who passed through always pestered him. They had heard of his robberies and knew, or thought they knew, of his wealth. They wanted him to go robbing with them, so they could have wealth, too. Joey was successful, far more successful than any of them. He was feared, and they, too, would have liked to be feared. They tried to be friendly with him, to suggest robberies in which he could share. Each of them knew of a bank that would be easy to rob, or a stage office, or something.

Joey ignored all their offers. He didn't trust any of the men. Also, he didn't need them. There was a boy in Crow Town who was slightly lame, but active. His name was Pablo, and he was twelve. Twice Joey took Pablo with him, so he would have someone to hold his horse during the robberies. He didn't like to tie his horse, and he didn't trust it to stand, either. If he had to leave in a hurry, having to untie a horse or look for one that had walked off would not be good. Pablo was his solution to the problem of the horse. Pablo liked Joey. Being chosen to go with him was the happiest thing that had happened to Pablo in his life. He did a good job, too, always leading Joey's horse to the handiest place for him to mount. Pablo thought Joey was the greatest man alive. He would have been proud to give his life for him.

Except for the services of Pablo and the three whores, Joey wanted nothing from the people of Crow Town. They were a rough lot, and also dumb. In his view, only smart people had a chance in life, and only smart people deserved a chance. Most of the men who stopped in Crow Town stayed drunk the whole time they were there. The cawing of the crows drove them to it.

Joey didn't mind the cawing, for he liked the crows. They were smarter than most people, in his view. Newcomers, maddened by the sound of cawing or the smell of crowshit or the wheeling of the thousands of birds, sometimes went berserk and tried to shoot the crows. They emptied pistols at them, or rifles. They missed, of course. Even when they tried shotguns, they missed. Not once did Joey see a crow fall. They were so smart that they didn't even lose a feather when the crazy men shot at them.

When Joey was in the saloon he sat alone, at a small table near the door. He wanted to be able to leave quickly if some of the stupid white men began to stab one another, or fire guns.

Joey drank coffee, when he sat in the saloon. Occasionally, he would put a spoonful of whiskey in the coffee, on days when the dust made him cough. He had taken a fine fur coat from off the gentleman who had the private car, and when the wind blew cold, or the dust was blowing, he pulled the fur collar of his coat high around him and was warm. Men envied him the coat. If he had not been watchful, one would have killed him for it. But he was watchful, and he liked it that he was envied.

Besides the coat, he also had a good blanket that had belonged to a cowboy he shot at a great distance. It was the longest shot he had made, since coming back from the City of Mexico with his gun. When Joey rode over to rob the corpse, he measured the distance; it was nearly six hundred yards. It gave him a good feeling, to be able to strike a gringo dead at such a distance. Finding that the cowboy had a fine blanket made him feel even better. The man was not young. He lay with his mouth open, when Joey reached him. Joey noticed that his teeth were false, so he took the false teeth, along with the blanket.

The cowboy had been about to ride into Presidio, when Joey killed him, and the shot was made at the last light of the day. No one in Presidio had noticed that the man was coming, and no one saw him fall. Joey waited until it was dark to measure the distance and rob the man. The bullet had taken off much of the cowboy's skull. The man wore a large pistol, which Joey used to smash the skull open a little more. Then he took a cup from the dead man's saddlebags and filled it with his brains.

[182]

When it was darker still, he walked into town, holding the cup full of brains. He went to the jail and carefully set the cup inside the door. The deputy who had only one ear was there, but he had his boots off and was sleeping soundly. Joey planned to cut the man's throat, if he woke up, but he didn't wake up, and on impulse, Joey stole his boots. He left the dead cowboy's false teeth in the cup of brains. Then he rode off happily. What he had done was not as bad as some things he had seen the Apaches do to dead white men. His only nagging worry was that he had seen a cat in the jail. The cat had opened its eyes and looked at him when he set the cup inside. It occurred to him that the cat might eat the brains and spoil the surprise he had planned for the hard sheriff and the one-eared deputy.

Later, in Crow Town, Joey learned that the cat had not eaten the brains. The one-eared deputy woke up, looked in the cup, and puked on the floor of the jail. Later, in the street, the deputy puked some more. The deputy thought at first that it might be the work of Apaches, but there were no Apaches anymore. The *Federales* had killed all the Apaches in Mexico, and those in the United States had been removed to Indian territory. Many people on the border had even forgotten Apaches, and what they did to people. When Joey left the dead cowboy's brains in the jail in Presidio, people began to talk about him as if he were the devil, not just a *güero*, a Mexican boy who was almost white. Only some of the older men and women remembered the Apaches, and how they cut.

One day, when Joey had been in Crow Town three weeks, Beulah came in with an antelope haunch she had bought from the old hunter Ben Lily. The old man walked the West endlessly, killing bears and cougars. He had started his lifelong hunt in Louisiana, and was now in west Texas, killing bears and cougars as he went. He ate what he could, and sold the remainder in order to buy cartridges with which to kill more lions and bears. His aim was to kill all the lions and bears between the Gulf Coast and Canada. By his reckoning, he was not yet half done. Thousands of lions and bears still lived, in the great West, and Ben Lily meant to kill them all. Antelope didn't interest him, but antelope made good eating, and could also be sold profitably in rough villages such as Crow Town.

Beulah looked scared, when she came in with the haunch. Her hands were shaking as she got ready to fry it.

"Why are you scared?" Joey asked.

"I saw old Ben," Beulah said.

"He only hunts, he won't bother you," Joey said. He was hungry, and he wanted Beulah to settle down and cook his meat.

"It ain't Ben," Beulah said. "Wesley Hardin's here. He showed up yesterday and killed that nigger that worked for the blacksmith. Wesley put a gun to my head, once. I was in Fort Worth then."

"Why?" Joey asked. "So he wouldn't have to pay you?"

"He didn't do nothing to pay me for," Beulah said. "He just likes to see people look scared. It don't matter to him if it's a man or a woman. He just likes to see people look scared."

Later, Joey went to the saloon, carrying his rifle. He never left his rifle. In Crow Town, all the people were thieves, and he did not intend to risk his fine gun.

A skinny man was sitting at the table next to his. It was the only other table in the saloon. The man wore a dirty black coat and had ugly skin, blotched and red, and it peeled in places from the sun and the wind. The man had thin, brown hair. Joey could see scabs on his scalp and on his hands as well. The man's foot twitched as he sat at the table, drinking whiskey. He didn't have a fine rifle, either, just a plain revolver, stuck in his belt.

Nonetheless, the killer John Wesley Hardin was the first gringo Joey had met in a long time whom he didn't take lightly. The man didn't even look at him, when he came in with his rifle. Wesley Hardin was not impressed, or even interested, which was unusual. Few people in Crow Town, or even travelers passing through, missed any chance to steal a look at Joey Garza.

But Wesley Hardin, the killer, didn't look. He was chewing tobacco and spitting the juice on the floor, although the saloon was provided with two brass spittoons.

Joey had barely sat down, when John Wesley Hardin looked up, but not at him. He looked up at the local blacksmith, whose name was Lordy Bailey. Lordy walked in the door, a large hammer in one hand, and went straight to Wesley Hardin's table. The blacksmith was a large man with a heavy black beard that was so long, he had to tuck it into his overalls while working his forge. He was not afraid of anyone, including Wesley Hardin. When he walked up to the table where the famous killer sat, Lordy was frowning, though John Wesley Hardin looked at him pleasantly.

"It's costing me fifty cents to get a grave dug for that nigger boy," Lordy said. "You shot him. I think you ought to pay the fifty cents."

"Why bury a nigger?" Wesley Hardin said. His voice had a tone in it that Joey hadn't heard before. It was a crazy tone. Wesley Hardin's eyes were cool, but he was scratching his scabby wrist with his other hand. Joey thought the blacksmith was very foolish, for speaking to the killer so brusquely. He would probably be murdered for his rudeness, and it would serve him right. His prices were high, and his work was not particularly skillful.

"We all need to be buried," Lordy said. "Do you think my nigger ought to just lay there and stink up the town?"

"Drag him off a ways," Wesley Hardin suggested. "That big pig might come along and eat him for you. It would save you the fifty cents."

"I paid fifty dollars for that nigger," Lordy said. He began to flip the big hammer up in the air, and caught it when it came down, without even looking at it. He made the big hammer seem light as a twig.

"I figure that's fifty dollars and fifty cents you owe me," he added. "Fifty dollars for the nigger, and fifty cents for burying him. Give it over."

"You're a fool if you paid cash for a nigger, in these days and times," Wesley Hardin said. "You don't have to buy niggers, anymore. It's not even legal. Abe Lincoln freed them. All you have to do now is *take* a nigger, if you see one you want."

[185]

"I paid for this one and you owe me," Lordy insisted. "Give over the money."

"You're an ignorant sonofabitch, and you don't know the law," Wesley Hardin said. He began to get worked up. His twitching foot twitched faster.

"Here you buy a nigger you didn't have to buy, and because I killed him, you come in here disturbing my morning," he went on. "I could kill you seven times before you could drop that goddamn hammer on your toe. Don't be playing with that hammer in here. The ceilings are too low. Go outside if you want to play with your hammer."

He took the plain revolver out of his belt and pointed it at the blacksmith, but the blacksmith was too angry to back down.

"You owe me, give over the money," he repeated, for the third time.

"You sonofabitch, I heard you," Wesley Hardin said. "If you want to live, get gone. If you'd rather die, flip that hammer again."

"I don't think you're the killer you claim to be, Hardin," Lordy said. He was wondering if he was quick enough to smash the man's head in with the hammer before he could pull the trigger.

"I don't claim nothing," Wesley Hardin said. "I don't claim one goddamn thing. Last time I was in jail, they kept me in nine years and whipped me a hundred and sixty different times. I stood it, and here I am. They whipped me because I wouldn't submit, and I *won't* submit. I hated the goddamn jailers, and I could kill you and nine like you and never even belch. I've left about forty widows so far, I guess, and I've killed a few bachelors, too. You're welcome to try me any time you want to try me."

Lordy decided that, after all, the risks were unwarranted.

"I'd like to smash in your goddamn skull, but I'll leave the pleasure of killing you to Captain Call," Lordy said. "I don't know if he'll choose to bother about a scabby old turd like you."

"Woodrow Call?" Wesley Hardin asked. "Why would he want to kill me? He arrested me once, but it was just because of a little feud I got into in Lampasas. Call ain't the sheriff of Crow Town. He don't even live here."

"No, but he's coming," Lordy said.

The news seemed to excite Wesley Hardin, the killer. His tone got crazier.

"Coming to Crow Town, Captain Call?" he said. "Why, that's bold, for an old shit his age."

"He's coming, but he ain't after you," Lordy said. "You ain't important enough, anymore. You're just an old killer waiting to die."

"Why's he coming, then? Does he expect to clean out the town?" Wesley Hardin asked.

"He's coming for the *güero*," Lordy said. "He's coming for Joey, here."

Joey didn't smile, or even indicate that he had heard the conversation. But he felt pleased. Billy Williams had told him many tales of Call's exploits. He had no fear of the man, though. No old gringo, however famous, was likely to interfere with his plans, not for long, anyway. But it interested and pleased him, that he had robbed enough and killed enough so that the Americans were sending their best bounty hunter after him. That was satisfying. It meant he had scared the Americans, and hurt them by taking their money.

John Wesley Hardin had noticed Joey come in. He was certainly a pretty boy, too pretty to last, Hardin thought. His clothes were too clean. In such a place, it was irritating to see a boy with clothes that clean. The rifle he kept with him was certainly exceptional, though. John Wesley had never killed with a rifle. He usually killed at close range, with his revolver, firing two or three shots right into the midsections of his enemies. He liked the way the heavy bullets kicked the life out of them. He liked their looks of shock, when they fell down and saw the blood spreading underneath them. He also liked to be looking at them when they died. That way, they would know that John Wesley Hardin had killed them personally. He had never killed a man from ambush, or from any great distance at all.

The notion that Woodrow Call would come all the way to Crow Town for this boy, this *güero*, was interesting, though. The boy must have vexed the rich men a good deal, for them to call out the old Ranger.

He looked at the boy and met a pair of cold, blue eyes.

Lordy Bailey, the blacksmith, was still standing there, with his hammer. Joey thought the man was a complete fool. He should go, while he was alive.

"You still owe me," Lordy said. "There's no reason I should give you a nigger to kill."

"I hate idiots like you," John Wesley Hardin said. He cocked his revolver and shot the blacksmith right in the gut. Then he shot him again, at about the point where his beard tucked into his overalls. He cocked the gun a third time, and shot the man in the gut again.

Lordy staggered backward, but didn't fall. He felt surprised. Hardin had seemed to be calming down. Lordy had not really expected him to shoot. Now he had been shot three times. He felt puzzled; he had meant to leave, but had waited a little too long. He didn't feel anything, just puzzled.

Joey Garza didn't move. It did not surprise him that the scabby old man had shot the blacksmith. He himself would have done it much sooner. But he knew better than to call attention to himself while the scabby killer had a gun in his hand.

"Wait—don't die," Wesley Hardin said, to Lordy Bailey. "You forgot to tell me how you knew Call was coming."

He was mildly annoyed with himself for having shot the man fatally before securing that piece of information. Most men, once shot a time or two, were so shocked to find themselves dying that they lost their power of speech.

"Famous Shoes told me," Lordy said. For a moment, the fact that he could still talk reassured him. Perhaps he hadn't been shot, after all. It was such a comforting thought that he believed it, for a second. He dropped his hammer, and reached down to pick it up. But his hand wouldn't grip. He could see the hammer, but he couldn't grasp it. At that point he sat down, being as careful as possible. All he wanted to do was pick up his hammer and leave.

"Don't sit there and die, you damn bastard," Wesley Hardin said. "Go outside and die. Nobody wants you dying in here."

"Oh," Lordy said, disturbed to have been caught in a breach of etiquette. He started to sit up, but instead, slowly toppled over and lay on his side, on the dusty floor.

"I thought I told you not to die in here, you ugly sonofabitch!" Wesley Hardin said. His temper was rising. The blacksmith had done nothing but vex and disobey him.

"If you weren't already nearly kilt, I'd take a bed slat to you—it might teach you some manners," he added.

Lordy Bailey realized he had made a serious error, bringing the black man to a town Wesley Hardin frequented. He was well known to dislike black men.

"Ought not to have . . ." he said, but then his tongue stopped working, and he felt a great loosening inside himself. He rolled on his back and stared upward until the light became dark.

Patrick O'Brien, the bartender, walked over and looked at Lordy.

"He's dead, and we're without a blacksmith," Patrick said.

"Good, I disliked the bastard," Wesley Hardin said. "He thought I ought to pay for his nigger, the damned idiot!

"Drag him out, boy," he said, addressing the order to Joey. "He'll soon stink up the place if we leave him long."

Joey met the scabby man's look, but didn't speak.

"Goddammit, is everybody stubborn in this town?" Wesley Hardin asked, his face splotchy with anger.

Patrick O'Brien felt a little worried. Many of his customers had killed a man or two, but not since he'd opened the bar had he had two men in it who were as dangerous as Wesley Hardin and Joey Garza. Between them, they had killed a fair number of men. It was early in the day, but already a man lay dead on the barroom floor.

It occurred to the saloonkeeper that Wesley Hardin, a selfish fellow who didn't take much interest in other people, might not realize how dangerous Joey Garza was.

[189]

"This is Joey Garza," he said. "He's the one they sent Call after."

Joey looked Hardin straight in the eye. He wanted to study the man, and would rather not have to kill him. But that was up to Hardin. He would kill him, if it became necessary, with his bowie knife. He had watched Hardin shoot the blacksmith. Hardin had managed it, but he was quite slow, Joey thought. An Apache would have killed the man with a knife, in half the time or less, and Joey modeled himself on the Apache when it came to killing. Joey knew he could slip behind Hardin and cut his throat with one move and one stroke.

But he didn't want to kill the man, and he also knew it would not be wise to underrate him, just because he was a scabby old gringo. Wesley Hardin had killed many, many men; the fact that he had been a little slow with the blacksmith didn't mean he would be slow if his own life was really at stake. The blacksmith had posed no threat. But Hardin was a killer, like himself. He should not be underestimated.

Wesley Hardin got up, picked up the blacksmith's legs, and slowly dragged him outside. The crows set up a cawing the minute the door opened. The blacksmith was a heavy man. Hardin had to stick his revolver back in his belt and use both hands, in order to drag him out.

"O'Brien, get your donkey and drag that heavy bastard off," he said, when he came back. He was winded from his effort, and his face had gone pale.

"Wes, you need to hold your temper," Patrick O'Brien said. "That was the only blacksmith within a hundred miles."

Wesley Hardin didn't take kindly to censure. He frowned at the Irishman.

"I might shoot every man, woman, and child in this stinkin', nigger-bird town, and then you wouldn't need a goddamn blacksmith. How's that?" he asked.

Wesley Hardin turned to Joey with an angry look.

"You could help me wipe this nigger-bird shithole off the face of the earth, if you're such a killer," he said to Joey. "You kill the men, and I'll take care of the women and the brats."

"Wes, there's only two children in town, and they're mine," Patrick O'Brien said. He had meanwhile taken the precaution of arming himself with a shotgun. When Wes Hardin was in one of his irritable moods, it was wisest to be armed.

"I wasn't speaking to you, you damn pig!" Wesley Hardin said, giving the man a violent stare. "I was speaking to the notorious young killer, here."

For all Hardin's jumpy manner, his eyes, when he looked at Joey, were clear. He might twitch, but he wasn't really agitated, not in the part of himself that sized up men and situations.

The boy, the *güero*, gave back an empty gaze. Joey let his eyes meet Hardin's, but in Joey's eyes there was nothing. Only distance, a distance deep as the sky.

"Why would they send Woodrow Call after a pup like you?" Hardin asked. But he let no insult into his voice.

"Because I steal money from Americans," Joey said.

"You're right—it's the money, not the killing," Wesley Hardin said. "They don't care who gets killed, out here in the baldies. It don't cost the damn pigs a cent for us to kill one another out here. Why would they care? Out here west of the Pecos, it's fine to kill, but you better not steal from no trains coming from the east, where the damn Yankees keep their money.

"How much did you get?" he inquired, in a calmer tone. "I heard it was a million, and I heard it was the army's money."

Joey looked at the man coolly, with his distant eyes. Did the old killer really expect him to tell how much money he had stolen?

In fact, he had buried the payrolls only a few miles from where he stole them. He didn't know how much he had taken, he just knew that the money was too bulky to carry very far. He was not such a fool as to bury it all in one place, either. He hid it in snake dens; the Apaches had taught him how to find them. They often ate snakes, when they could get nothing better.

He didn't have the time to carry so much money to his cave, nor did he want to. The money was not very interesting to him. His cave was for beautiful things. Everything he stole, he wrapped well. He had taken two hundred gunnysacks from a hardware store in Piedras Negras, to the puzzlement of the man who owned the store. The man could not understand why anyone would take gunnysacks, when there were guns and axes to steal.

Joey took the sacks because he needed them to wrap his treasures. That was also why he had taken the fancy sheets from the rich man who had the fur coat. He didn't want to sleep on the sheets; he wanted them for wrapping, so that his many silver objects would not grow dingy in the cave. At another hardware store in San Angelo, he found some excellent wooden barrels, and he hired an old man named Jose Ramos to help him take the barrels on donkeys into the mountains. He left them in one cave, an empty one, to fool old Ramos, and later came back and carried them, one by one, to his own cave, which was three days away.

Then he packed his well-wrapped treasures in the excellent barrels, where they would be safe from rats and varmints. He already had more than one hundred watches, and nearly as many rings. One of his regrets was that there were so few women on the trains, because women had nicer things than men. They had beautiful combs of ivory, and necklaces and bracelets, even jewels to hang in their ears. Joey kept all the women's things together. When he went to his cave, he would spend whole days unwrapping his treasures, one by one, holding them and letting the light play on them. They were far more interesting than the money.

Knowing that he had the treasures and that he could go there and enjoy them, was a deep satisfaction to Joey. Lately, he had begun to steal things with little value—ladies' hairbrushes, or letter openers—simply because he liked to touch the ivory or shell that they were made from.

The quality of his treasures was not something he intended to talk about to a killer such as Wesley Hardin, though. He decided he didn't like the nosy old gringo, who asked the kind of questions his mother asked. The killer was a man to be watched, that was all.

"I guess you're feeling closemouthed today, are you, boy?"

Wesley Hardin asked. Of course, he had not expected the *güero* to tell him how much money he had taken from the trains.

"You'd do better to talk to yourself, Wes," Patrick O'Brien said. "My ears get tired, just from listening to you cuss, when you're in a temper."

"Be glad you can hear me—it means I ain't shot you yet, Pat," Hardin said. "I can cuss old Lordy now, as much as I want to, but he won't hear a whisper."

Joey picked up his rifle and started to leave. He would rather look at the pretty young whore, Gabriela, than at the scabby old killer with the splotchy face.

"Hold on, I'll offer you a little free advice," Wesley Hardin said. "They say you have a tendency to steal, which is a more dangerous habit in these parts than the habit of killing. One thing you ought to be careful of, when you're out stealing, is to stay clear of Roy Bean. He can't abide a thief. If he catches you with money on you, he'll hang you promptly and keep the money. He's hung five men that I know about, for no better reason than that they had money in their pockets, and he wanted it."

"He won't hang me, but I might hang him," Joey replied. He said it merely to meet the challenge in the old killer's voice. But once he began to consider it, the idea grew on him. Roy Bean was known to be a hanging judge. Roy Bean cared little for justice, or so Joey had been told by Billy Williams. Joey cared little for justice, himself. He couldn't blame the judge for that, and he didn't care that the judge wasn't fair.

"I think I will hang him," he repeated. "It might be pleasant."

John Wesley Hardin was startled, and he wasn't a man who startled easily. This pup of a boy had just had an idea that he should have had himself: hang Roy Bean. That old fart had it coming to him, had for years.

"Why, that's original," Wesley Hardin said. "I expect that would make the newspapers. Old Call might get fired, for letting it happen."

"Do you know Famous Shoes?" Joey asked. The old man was a tracker, a Kickapoo. No one knew where he lived; somewhere in the Sierra Madre, it was thought. Billy Williams had known Famous Shoes for many years and thought him the best tracker who ever lived. He even knew how to track birds, as they flew. Even the Apaches respected Famous Shoes, and the Apaches yielded up little respect when it came to tracking. They considered themselves the best, but admitted that if anyone was better than they were, it was Famous Shoes. Some Apaches thought that the reason Famous Shoes was such a brilliant tracker was that he was part eagle. Someone had seen him bringing the eggs of an eagle down to his camp, where he ate them. It was because of the eagle's eggs, some thought, that Famous Shoes could see so well. No one in the West could see farther, or more clearly, than the old Kickapoo. In earlier days, he had been employed up and down the border by whites, Mexicans, and Indians alike, to help recover children who had been stolen, or sold into slavery. Famous Shoes never failed to find the children, even when he was put on the trail months late. He could not always recover the children, for his skill was only in tracking. But he always found the children. A man who could track the flight of birds and even follow eagles to their roosts, in order to take their eggs, would have no difficulty in tracking a raiding party that had come to take slaves.

"I have seen Famous Shoes a few times," Wesley Hardin said. "If I see him again, I'll kill him, and if I'd known he was around I'd have been out hunting for him yesterday."

"Why?" Joe asked. "He's an old man. You wouldn't need to fear him."

"He's an old man, but his eyesight ain't failed him," Hardin said. "Suppose I kill the wrong fellow, someone who ain't just scum, and the law comes after me again? If they hired old Famous Shoes, they'd find me, too, and if there's more of a damn posse than I could shoot, I'd be back in prison again. And next time, they'll beat me to death."

He suddenly turned his back to Joey and pulled off his coat and shirt. His back was crisscrossed with scars, every inch of it.

"The time I went for the warden and tried to knock the sonofabitch's head in, they gave me five hundred lashes. I wasn't awake for but about two hundred of them, though."

"They will not do that to me," Joey said.

Wesley Hardin stuffed his shirttail back in his pants. He turned to Joey and smiled. "If they get you in jail, then they can do anything they want," he said. "If they want to beat you with a damn whip, they will."

"They won't get me in jail," Joey said. The sight of the man's scarred back had impressed him.

"Then you better kill Famous Shoes, and kill him next," Wesley Hardin said. "That's my recommendation."

"Why him? I don't even know him," Joey replied.

"He's a hired hand. He tracks for anybody that'll pay him," Wesley Hardin said. "Woodrow Call might pay him to find you. If he's set to find you, he'll find you. Famous Shoes don't miss."

Joey Garza smiled. "I don't miss, either," he said. Then he took his fine rifle and left.

16.

When Famous Shoes decided to take a walk, it was usually a long one. He didn't like to walk where there were *Federales*, because the *Federales* killed Indians. The presence of *Federales* distracted him, and took away some of the pleasure of his long walk. To avoid them, he walked north through the Madre until he was out of Mexico, before turning east. He had decided to go to the Rio Rojo and live on it a few weeks, as his people had once done. He was an old man, and one day soon, he would have to give up his spirit. He thought it would be fitting to go to the Rio Rojo, where his people had once lived. It was his view that the Kickapoo people would be living along the Brazos and the Rio Rojo still, if the Comanche and the Kiowa had not been so hard to get along with.

But the Comanche and the Kiowa did not like the Kickapoo people, or any other people, and it was not easy to live with the Comanche or the Kiowa if they disliked you. They killed so many Kickapoo that the old men decided the tribe had better move, or soon there would be no tribe.

Now the Comanche were gone, and the Kiowa, too. Famous Shoes could go visit the land of his fathers without unpleasantness. He walked east, toward the pass of the north. In a few days, he would be on the great plain. He wanted to visit the several forks of the Brazos—the Salt, the Clear, the Double

[196]

Mountain fork and the Prairie Dog fork—to see if the river had moved far from where it had been when he was a boy. He had known the Brazos when he was young. He liked to watch it wander, and make itself new channels.

While Famous Shoes was walking east near Agua Prieta, he crossed a track that frightened him so much that he wanted to crouch down. It was a track he had not seen in many years: the track of Mox Mox, the manburner. The Apaches called him The Snake-You-Do-Not-See, for his habit of catching people unawares, and burning them. Particularly, he liked to burn young children, but he would burn anyone he could catch, when he wanted to burn.

Mox Mox, The Snake-You-Do-Not-See, had stopped to urinate along the trail Famous Shoes was walking. Famous Shoes thought he had better hurry on to the Rio Rojo before Mox Mox found him. He walked for two days, sleeping only a few minutes at a time.

When he came to the Rio Rojo, he walked east along its wide, sandy banks for two weeks. On the old river, he felt better. The Snake-You-Do-Not-See had not struck him. He wanted to make contact with the spirit of his grandfather, if possible. His grandfather had lived and died on the low, sandy banks of the Rio Rojo.

Though Famous Shoes walked for days along the river, he did not meet the spirit of his grandfather. The old man had not liked the Comanche, and Famous Shoes decided that his grandfather's spirit had become impatient for the Comanche to be taken, so impatient that his spirit left its home and went to live somewhere else. Probably, he would make contact with his grandfather as he walked south, amid the forks of the Brazos. But that might not work, either. His grandfather had been an unpredictable man, and all his wives had complained of his impatience and unpredictability. He left when he felt like leaving, and told no one where he was going or when he might return. He was apt to walk south and then change his mind and walk north. There was no confining the man. Famous Shoes, too, was in the habit of walking where he chose and when he chose. He might get up one morning and walk for three months.

Once, when he was younger, he had decided to walk north, to the place the ducks and the geese came from and returned to every year. He knew the birds could travel much faster than he could, and that he would have to get a big jump on them if he was to visit them in their home in the north. He started early in the spring, thinking he would be in the place the birds returned to, when they returned. He had been told that they nested at the edge of the world. An old Apache man who, like himself, took an interest in birds, told him that. The old Apache believed that the ducks and geese, and even the cranes, flew to the edge of the world each fall, to build their nests and hatch their young.

Famous Shoes wanted to see it. In his dreams, he saw a place where all the ducks and geese came to nest. It would be noisy, of course; so many birds would make a lot of racket. But it would still be worth it.

What defeated the plan was that Famous Shoes did not really enjoy cold weather. It was cold enough in the Madre, and even colder on the plains, north of the Rio Rojo. But those colds were as nothing to the cold Famous Shoes began to encounter as the fall came, in the far north. He had walked to the top of the plain, and into the wooded country. As the days shortened, he began to see strings of geese overhead, and thought that he must be getting close to the great nesting place at the edge of the world.

But then, it seemed to him, he reached the edge of the world without getting to the nesting place. He passed through the great forests, and came to a place where the trees were only as tall as he was, and Famous Shoes was not tall. Ahead, he could see horizons where there were no trees at all, and only a few plants of any kind. There seemed to be only snow ahead of him. He survived by knocking over fat birds and slow rabbits, but the snow was becoming painful to his feet, and the diminishing vegetation worried him. With no wood to make fires, he knew he might freeze. Also, it was only fall. The real cold was ahead.

Reluctantly, Famous Shoes stopped when he reached the place of the last tree. He looked north, as far as he could see, wondering if the edge of the world was only a day or two away. A day or two he might risk, but he knew it would be foolish to go to a place without wood, when the great cold was coming. Overhead, the sky was thick with ducks and geese, going to the place Famous Shoes wanted to go. He heard them all night, calling to one another as they neared their home. He was annoyed with the geese, for he felt that they should appreciate how far he had walked, out of an interest in them, and that some great goose should come down and help him go there. The old Apache man claimed that he had once seen a white goose big enough for a man to ride. Famous Shoes didn't know if the story was true, for the old Apache man had been a little crazy, and was also fond of mescal. He might have been drunk, and the liquor might have made the goose grow into a goose that a man could ride. But if there was such a goose somewhere, it too must be on its way home. Famous Shoes waited a whole day by the last tree, his feet aching from the snow, hoping the great goose would see him and recognize his appreciation of the greatness of birds and alight and fly him to the big nesting place. Also, while he was there, he meant to look off the edge of the world and see what he could see.

But no great goose came, and Famous Shoes was forced to turn back, before his feet were frozen. A few days later, by great good luck, he killed a small bear. He made moccasins from the bear skin and hurried south, hoping to get to a place where there was good firewood before the blizzards came. Three days later, when he had just made it into the forests, a great blizzard did come. Famous Shoes had carried much of the meat of the little bear with him, and he ate it while the blizzard blew.

Months later, when he was still far from his home in the Madre, Famous Shoes saw the geese and the ducks overhead, flying south again. It seemed to him that their calls mocked him, as they flew above him. For a time, he became bitter, and decided he didn't like birds, after all. They didn't care that he had walked a whole year, just to see their nesting place. He resolved to take no more interest in such ungrateful, unappreciative creatures.

But once back in the Sierra Madre, watching the great eagles that lived near his home, Famous Shoes gradually lost his bitterness. In the presence of the great eagles, he became ashamed of himself. Two or three of the eagles knew him, and would let him sit near them; not too near, but near enough that he could see their eyes, as they watched the valleys far below. Their dignity made him feel that he had been silly, to expect the ducks and geese, or any birds, to take an interest in his movements. He knew himself to be a great walker—he was not Famous Shoes for nothing—but what was that to any bird? The geese and the great cranes could fly in an hour distances it would take him a day to cover. The eagles and the hawks could see much farther than he could, and even the small birds, the sparrows and the cactus wrens, could do the one thing he couldn't do: they could fly. That was their greatness, not his, and his walking must seem a poor thing, to them.

Famous Shoes was grateful to the eagles for letting him sit near them and recover himself from his long journey. He needed to recover from the vanity of thinking that he was as special as the birds. He did not deserve to see the great nesting places, nor to look off the edge of the world. He was only a man, of the earth and not of the sky, and his skills were not the skills of birds.

It was on his return from the Rio Rojo, across the Quitaque, that he came upon the track of a horse carrying his old friend Pea Eye, in the mud of a little creek. Famous Shoes had known Pea Eye for a long time, since the days when the Rangers rode the border. He could tell Pea Eye's track anywhere, because Pea Eye favored his left stirrup and the horse track went deeper on the left side, particularly on the rear hoof. It puzzled him to discover Pea Eye traveling south, for he understood that Pea Eye had a woman and several children, and a farm. Yet, he was leaving. Famous Shoes knew that Pea Eye's woman was a teacher. He meant, someday, to have her teach him to read the strange tracks in books. Those were the only tracks he had never been able to master. For many years, he had carried a small Bible with him. It had been given to him by an old man who carried many such books in a wagon, and gave them to Indians. The old man's name was Marshall. He had come among the Apaches when Famous Shoes was there, trying to persuade an old medicine man named Turtle to give up a little white girl he had captured in a raid. Turtle wouldn't give up the girl. His own wife was shriveled and had no interest in him, and he needed a young girl. The money Famous Shoes offered, money provided by the little girl's family, was not as important to Turtle as the little girl herself. Turtle patiently explained this to Famous Shoes, who understood it well enough. His own wife had lost interest in him, forcing him to find girls at a time when he would rather have been concentrating on other things. But he had been younger then, and in those days, lack of a woman often caused his concentration to wander.

So he accepted Turtle's explanation, and did not try to take the girl, even though her family missed her and had paid him well to find her.

Mr. Marshall, the white man with the Bibles, did not accept Turtle's explanation as to why he needed the little girl, although it was a valid one, in Famous Shoes' opinion. Marshall tried to buy the girl from Turtle, despite the fact that Turtle had told him plainly that he would not sell her.

When Marshall saw that he would not be allowed to buy the white girl, he became angry. He began to say bad words, and make the Apaches feel bad. But a young Apache named Long Thorn lived up to his name by taking a bayonet he had picked up after a battle and sticking it all the way through Mr. Marshall, who soon died. It was agreed that Long Thorn had acted properly. The white man had become abusive, and deserved to be stuck with a bayonet. The Apaches could eat the horses that pulled the white man's wagon, but the load of books with meaningless tracks in them was a different matter. Marshall had told them that the books came from the god who made all the whites. There were many whites, and they were rich; the god must be powerful, if he had made them all. It might anger him if the book with his tracks in it was not treated properly, but the Apaches had no idea what they would have to do to treat the book properly. By accident, someone tore a few pages out of one of the books and threw them on a campfire. They burned so well that the Apaches decided to keep the books and use them to start fires. If the god who made the whites was offended, they would have to live with his wrath. But after a few days of starting fires with the pages from the Bibles, the Apaches decided that this god was too busy making whites to care what they did. After that, they relaxed and soon forgot the god altogether. They even forgot about Marshall, although they ate his horses and found them to be tasty.

Famous Shoes was given a Bible, in lieu of the little white girl. He would rather have had the girl, but he took the Bible and pored over it for years, in his spare time. He had never seen tracks as strange as the tracks in his Bible. After much study, he could see that the little tracks were individual, as were the tracks of all animals. Even worms and snails made tracks that were unlike those of other creatures.

But in the end, Famous Shoes could make nothing of the tracks that were supposed to lead the whites to the spirit world. Famous Shoes would have liked to see a picture of the white man's god, but there were no pictures of him in the book. What this god's ways might be, Famous Shoes could not imagine. If he was wrathful, like his minister Marshall, then Famous Shoes was not interested in knowing too much about his ways.

One time, Famous Shoes showed the Bible to the old judge, Roy Bean, a white man who enjoyed hanging people. Famous Shoes had always kept to the law and had no fear of Roy Bean. He didn't steal, and it was well known that Roy Bean was harshest on thieves and had a tendency to be tolerant of murder. Famous Shoes had rarely murdered, either, only a time or two when he was younger and had less control over his passions. Now that he was older, he had his passions under control to such an extent that it was not really accurate to call them passions anymore. If he had a passion left, it was for the flight of the eagles. Fortunately, near his home in the Madre, there were many eagles whose pure, beautiful, soaring flight he could study at his leisure.

"Why, this is the Bible. It tells you about Jehovah and his angels," Roy Bean said, when Famous Shoes handed him the book. Roy Bean was drunk; this was often the case, and he was not really eager to enter into conversation with a talkative Indian.

"What is an angel? I have never seen one," Famous Shoes replied.

"Nobody ain't. That is, they ain't if they're alive," Roy Bean informed him, testily.

"Where is heaven?" Famous Shoes asked.

"It's the place you go to when you die, if you've been good," Roy Bean said. "You ain't been very good, and I ain't, either, so I doubt either one of us will ever see an angel."

After a little more questioning, Roy Bean let slip the exciting fact that angels were men with wings. Famous Shoes had always suspected that there might be men with wings, somewhere. If he had been willing to risk freezing to death when he was near the edge of the world, he might have looked over the edge and seen these men with wings, flying around. Perhaps they would have helped him grow wings himself, so that he could fly off the edge of the world, as the great eagles flew off the cliffs of the Madre.

Then Roy Bean got so drunk, he couldn't talk. Before his tongue grew too thick to manage, Roy Bean became irritated with Famous Shoes for referring to the words in the Bible as tracks. It did seem to Famous Shoes that they resembled certain tracks, such as the track of the centipede, or of certain delicate birds who skimmed the water's edge for their prey.

"They're words, not tracks, you damn Indian!" Roy Bean insisted. "They're words, like I'm saying to you, now."

"But words are made from breath. How can they live in such a thing as this book?" Famous Shoes asked.

He might as well have asked his question of an eagle, or of the moon, for Roy Bean had not only lost interest, he had lost consciousness as well.

Famous Shoes kept the book for several more years, but he never learned to make much of the little tracks. Finally, he left the book on the ground, and a golden eagle came and tore out many of its pages to use to line its nest. That was a good use for such a book, Famous Shoes thought.

Later, though, he learned from the great Captain Marcy, for whom he had scouted when he was younger, that Roy Bean had been right: the little tracks in the book were words. Even when he learned this, Famous Shoes didn't regret giving the book to the golden eagle. The eagle had made better use of it than he had.

Seeing Pea Eye's track made him remember that Pea Eye's woman was a teacher, who well understood the words in books. This gave Famous Shoes an idea. He might go and stay with Pea Eye for a few weeks, and ask his woman if she would teach him how words got into books, and how to know one word from another, simply by its tracks. It should not be too different from knowing each animal or lizard by its tracks. It might be that Pea Eye's woman could explain words to him, and even help him understand the ways of the god of whites. Among his people, the Kickapoo, respect for the gods caused most people to behave well, at least to behave well most of the time. But the same did not appear to be true of whites, most of whom behaved as if they knew no god and had no guidance stronger than their own passions, when it came to deciding how to behave.

When he found Pea Eye's track, in the little creek on the Quitaque, Famous Shoes saw that Pea Eye was about a day ahead of him. He knew that, as a traveler, Pea Eye was rather lazy. He was timid about snakes, and did not really like to move around in the darkness, which was necessary if a man wanted to cover much country. Also, once Pea Eye went to sleep, he didn't wake up quickly. Thus, though Pea Eye was mounted and had a day's start, Famous Shoes reckoned to catch him somewhere near the Clear Fork of the Brazos. And he did.

He walked quietly into Pea Eye's camp early one morning, when the stars were still out and the moon was about to go to sleep. Famous Shoes did not like to disturb anyone, so he sat quietly until Pea Eye began to stir. As was common with whites, Pea Eye had made a much larger campfire than was necessary. Several coals were still glowing. Famous Shoes fed twigs and small branches to the coals, until the fire itself woke up and burned again.

When Pea Eye heard the fire crackling, he managed to open his eyes. Famous Shoes sat beside the campfire, looking at him. He was a tiny old man and was wearing the same dirty bandanna around his head that he had been wearing the last time Pea had seen him, several years before.

"Would your woman help me learn to read?" Famous Shoes asked, to get the conversation started.

"Well, more than likely," Pea Eye said. "She's been meaning to teach me, but I've got so much farming to do that I ain't learned yet. I know my letters, though."

"I will go home with you, then," Famous Shoes said. "We can learn to read together."

"You sure did slip in quiet, didn't you?" Pea Eye said. "I guess if this was the old days and you was a Comanche, I'd be scalped by now.

"There's coffee there, if you want to make some," Pea Eye added. Famous Shoes was not a Comanche, nor a bad Indian of any kind, and he himself was in no danger of being scalped. The thought made him feel so relaxed that he figured he might just doze for another minute or two, while Famous Shoes made coffee. He did doze, but when he finally woke up, the sun was in his face and he had the feeling he might have dozed for more than a minute or two. A jackrabbit was cooking on the fire, and he himself had certainly not provided any jackrabbit. Famous Shoes must have caught one, skinned it, and cooked it, a process that would have taken more than a minute or two, although the old man had always been efficient, when it came to camp chores.

"If you are chasing somebody, I don't think you are going to catch up with them, unless they are crippled," Famous Shoes said. "When you eat this rabbit, we should go."

"Okay, you can come with me," Pea Eye said, hastily shaking

his boots, in the hopes of emptying out whatever bugs or scorpions might have crawled into them during the night. It would have been safer to sleep with his boots on; but when he did that, he got cramps in his legs, often such bad cramps that he had to get up and stamp around in order to loosen the cramps.

"The thing is, we'll have to put off the reading lessons for a while. I ain't headed home," Pea Eye said. "I'm going to look for the Captain. I got a late start, and don't have no idea where he is. You'd be the perfect compañero because you could track him if we ever cross his tracks."

"He likes to keep his money," Famous Shoes said. Captain Call had never paid his scouts very liberally. "I'm not sure he would pay me, if I help you find him. He might think I'm too old to need money."

"It wouldn't be his money, though. He's working for the railroad now," Pea Eye said, uneasily. "There's a Yankee with him. I expect the Yankee would pay you."

Pea Eye did remember that the Captain, though respectful of Famous Shoes' great skill in tracking, thought the man put too high a price on his services. There had been more than one dispute over money, and in the end, Famous Shoes stopped tracking for the Rangers.

Memories of this old conflict made him feel uncomfortable, and just when he had been enjoying a feeling of comfort, the first he had experienced since leaving Lorie and his children. It would be nice to travel with Famous Shoes; he didn't mind doing the cooking, and he would be a great help in locating the Captain.

Still, there had been that friction, in the past. The Captain might not be altogether pleased to have him show up with Famous Shoes.

"Where do you think the Captain is?" Famous Shoes asked.

"On the border, somewhere," Pea Eye said. "He's supposed to catch a bandit named Joey Garza."

"Oh," Famous Shoes said. "Maria's son."

"Whose son?" Pea asked.

"She is a woman in Ojinaga," Famous Shoes said. "Joey is her son. I think he went bad."

"I guess he did," Pea Eye said. "Charlie Goodnight says he's killed over thirty people. If Charlie Goodnight says it, I expect it's true."

"I was in Ojinaga when the *Federales* killed Maria's first husband," Famous Shoes said. "She is a good woman, but she does not have good luck. I'm afraid the hard sheriff will kill her someday."

"What hard sheriff?" Pea Eye asked. "Does the woman live in Texas or Mexico?"

"In Mexico, but the hard sheriff doesn't care," Famous Shoes said. "He kills many people who live in Mexico. He wanted to hang me once for stealing a horse, although I don't ride horses."

"Why'd he think you stole it, then?" Pea Eye asked.

"I was eating part of it when he caught me," Famous Shoes replied. "A snake bit the horse on the nose, and its nose closed up and it died."

"I'd need to be half starved before I'd eat a snake-bit horse," Pea Eye said.

"I didn't eat its nose," Famous Shoes said. The whites, even nice ones like Pea Eye, had absurd prejudices. The only danger the dead horse had caused him came from Doniphan, the hard sheriff. Doniphan had marched him back to Presidio, meaning to hang him, but a fire broke out and burned up the saloon and part of the church. Doniphan had been afraid that the fire might burn his jail. It was a windy day, with smoke blowing everywhere. In the smoke and confusion, Famous Shoes escaped. It was Maria Garza who had given him a little jerky, so that he might hurry back to the Madre, where the hard sheriff would never come.

"Where'd you get this rabbit? I didn't see one all day yesterday, or I would have shot it," Pea Eye said. It was a tasty rabbit. He thought about the border. It was far away, and he had to pass through some bleak country, too. It would be real handy to have a traveling companion such as Famous Shoes, a man who was adept at catching game, and cooking it too.

There was another factor to be considered, too, and that had to do with his own deficiencies as a tracker and a plainsman. Charlie Goodnight told everybody he met that he had never been lost, day or night, rain or shine. But this was certainly not a claim Pea Eye could make. He himself had been lost all too often; in particular, he had a tendency to lose his bearings on cloudy days. In truly rainy weather, he was even worse. He had even been known to confuse north and south, on rainy days. He thought he could find his way to the border simply by counting the rivers. But once he got to the border, then what? He would have no way of knowing which direction the Captain was headed, or even whether he was in Mexico or in Texas. In normal times, he could locate the Captain simply by asking the locals. The Captain was a man people noticed. But along much of the border, there were no locals. If the Captain was in Mexico, Pea Eye had his doubts about his skill in finding him. That problem had made him anxious from the moment he left home. What if he had left the farm and upset Lorena and the children and still didn't manage to locate the Captain in time to help him? What if the Garza boy outsmarted the Captain and wounded him or something, while Pea Eye was still miles away, looking in the wrong place? The Captain might even be killed, and if that occurred, Pea knew, he would never forgive himself.

With Famous Shoes along, some of that anxiety would be removed. Famous Shoes could find anybody, anywhere in the West, and could find them more quickly than anyone else. Even the Captain, who thought Famous Shoes too expensive, was quick to admit that the old Indian was without equal, when it came to tracking.

"I think it's eyesight," the Captain said. "He can see better than us."

That remark had been made on a nervous occasion, when everyone in the Ranger troop thought they saw Indians kneeling in the prairie grass far ahead. Everyone, including the Captain and Gus McCrae, had peered hard across the prairie and concluded that there were Indians ahead, preparing an ambush. Famous Shoes took only one quick look and shook his head.

"Not Indians," he said. "Sagebrush." And so it had proved to be, when they reached the point where they thought the ambush had been planted.

"Come with me to the border," Pea Eye said. "If the Captain won't pay you enough, maybe I can trade you reading lessons or something, when we get back." He said it, hoping that Lorena wouldn't mind too much, when he actually showed up with the old man.

"Good," Famous Shoes said. "If your woman will teach me to read, I won't take wages from the Captain."

It was such a relief to know that the matter of the expense had been settled, or settled, at least, until Lorena had her say in the matter, that Pea Eye finished the tasty jackrabbit and was saddled and ready to go within ten minutes. It was a bright day, and the gray plain south of him for once didn't seem so bleak.

Famous Shoes, as usual, walked far ahead.

17.

"I didn't like the War," Brookshire said. "I never understood why it was happening. Nobody ever explained it to me. They just stuck me in uniform and sent me off. My mother cried, and my sister cried, and my father told them to dry up, I was just doing my duty."

They were camped far out on the monte, in Mexico. Call had decided to swing west, toward Chihuahua City. They had run into a small troop of *Federales*, who told them Joey Garza had been seen in Chihuahua City. Call didn't necessarily believe it, but he swung west anyway, to put some distance between his party and the river. Too many people traveled the river country, or lived in it. Even in the long, hundred-mile stretches where there were no villages, there were still people—Indians, travelers, prospectors. In his lifetime on the border, Call reckoned that he had run into at least fifty people, lost souls mostly, who were looking for Coronado's treasure. Call didn't know much about Coronado, just that he had been the first white man to travel through the region. He had made the trip a long time ago, and Call had never been certain that he knew exactly where Coronado had gone. Some reports put his route as far west as the Gila, but others thought he had just gone straight up the Rio Grande. A few even argued that he had started at Vera Cruz and come out at Galveston.

Whichever route the man had actually taken, Call doubted that he had come up with much in the way of treasure. He might have collected a little silver, if he got into the Navajo country, but Call himself, in nearly forty years on the border, had encountered mostly poor people who had no treasure.

Avoiding the river made sense to him. Also, he had never traveled very deeply into Mexico, and he wanted to see it. Brookshire worried, and the more he worried, the less Call hurried. He kept an eye out for tracks. Deputy Plunkert tried to help, but it soon became evident that he was no tracker. About all he had ever tracked, before the expedition, was lost milk cows. More and more, the deputy missed the comforts of home; in particular, he missed Doobie's biscuits, which she made every morning and had ready for him, hot and buttery, when he got up.

"How come you to miss the War, Captain?" Brookshire asked. The likelihood of combat, sometime in the near future, had stirred old memories. He remembered the screams of the men whose limbs had to be amputated, quickly, on the battlefield. He remembered the sound the saw made, as the surgeons cut through bone, and the dull groaning of the men in the hospital tents as they awoke every morning, to face another day without an arm or a leg, or both legs, or an eye, or whatever part was missing. Those memories had ceased to trouble him, during the quiet years in Brooklyn.

"Somebody had to stay around and keep the Comanches in check," Call said. "Otherwise, I guess they would have driven the settlers back to the sea. They drove them back nearly a hundred miles as it was, with us after them all the time. There was trouble from the south, too."

"Still is. We should just take Mexico and be done with it," Deputy Plunkert said. "If we owned it, we could make the people abide by the law."

Call ignored the remark. He thought it ignorant.

"I wish I could have fought in the War," Deputy Plunkert said. "I would have been happy to kill a few Yankees."

"That's not polite, there's a Yankee right here at this campfire," Call said. "Mr. Brookshire fought for his side. You can't blame him for that."

"Why, no, I meant other Yankees," the deputy said. It embarrassed him that the Captain had dressed him down in front of a fat little Yankee such as Brookshire. The man had lost a little bit of his girth, once the diet had dropped to frijoles and not much else. But he hadn't lost any of his Yankeeness, not in Plunkert's view.

"That damn Abe Lincoln oughtn't to have freed the slaves, neither," the deputy said. He was feeling aggrieved because no one was taking his side, not even the Captain, the man he had left home to assist.

"What was your opinion on that question?" Brookshire wondered, looking at Call.

"Oh, I grew up poor," Call said. "We would never have had the money for a slave."

There had been a time when Gus McCrae had wanted to abandon the Rangers and rush back east to fight Yankees, for he had gotten it in his head that Southern freedoms were being trampled, and that the two of them ought to go fight; this, despite the fact that they had more fighting than they could handle, right where they were.

Call himself had never caught the fervor of that War. The best man he had working with him at the time was black— Deets, later killed by a Shoshone boy, in Wyoming. He had known people who had owned slaves and mistreated them, and he would certainly have fought to keep Deets from being owned by any of the bad slaveholders; but he could not have fought with the North, against his region, and was content to stay where he was, doing what he was doing. No one in his right mind would have wanted fiercer fighting than the Comanche were capable of. Gus McCrae's problem was that he liked bugles and parades. He had even tried to persuade Call to hire a bugler for the Ranger troop.

"A bugler?" Call said. "Half these men don't have decent saddles, and we're lucky if we have forty rounds of ammunition apiece. Why waste money on a bugler?"

"It might impress the Comanche. They've got some sense of show," Gus retorted. "That's your problem, Woodrow, or one of them. You've got no sense of show. Ain't you ever heard of esprit de corps?"

"No, what is it, and how much does it cost?" Call asked.

"I give up! You don't buy esprit de corps, you instill it, and a good bugler would be a start," Augustus said.

The argument had taken place north of the Canadian River, when they were chasing a party of Comanche raiders who were, to put it plainly, smarter and faster than they were. The Rangers' horses were winded, and the men so hungry that they were wading around in the icy Canadian, in February, hoping to catch small fish, or frozen frogs, or anything that might have a shred or two of meat on it. Two days before, they had eaten an owl. The men had been cutting small strips of leather off their saddles and chewing on them, just to have something in their mouths. Gus was standing in zero weather, with a norther blowing so hard they could barely keep a campfire lit, talking about buglers.

They didn't catch the raiders, who were carrying two white children with them, and they never hired a bugler, although Gus McCrae was still talking about it, nearly ten years later, when the Civil War finally ended and the Indian wars were beginning to wind down.

As for the great and terrible Civil War, Call's main sense of it was derived from seeing people who came back from it. Several Rangers who had served under him left to go fight Yankees. But those who returned were blank and mostly useless. One boy named Reuben, who had lost an eye and an arm at Vicksburg, did more than anyone to make that conflict vivid to Call.

"Captain, you don't know," Reuben said, looking at Call sadly with his one eye. "When we get into it with the Comanches, maybe it's ten or fifteen of us, and fifteen or twenty of them, all of us shooting at one another. But in the big fight I was in, it's thousands and thousands on both sides, and cannons and smoke and horses running around half kilt. I seen one horse come by with just a leg in a stirrup, no rider—it's terrible. I got one eye left, and one arm, and I'm one of the lucky ones. All but three of the men I started soldiering with are dead."

Brookshire had been worrying a good deal about the train robbery in New Mexico. Who could the second robber be? He had no answer, and neither did Captain Call.

"The other robber could be anybody," Call told him. "This is a free country. Anybody can rob a train if they can make it stop. Trains travel through some lonesome country. If I was a mind to be a criminal, I can't think of an easier way to start than robbing trains."

"I've always tried to be honest," Deputy Plunkert said. "I stole some pecans once and cracked them with my teeth, but I was just a boy then."

There was something about being so far into Mexico that made the deputy feel hopeless. He had never been very good at finding his way in new country, which was one reason he had made his life in Laredo. The town was well supplied, and there was no need to go anywhere. Now that he was married to Doobie, there was no need even to cross the river for girls.

But he had been swept away by his desire to be a Ranger, something he had always dreamed of being, and now he was deep in the middle of a country he didn't like, with two men who weren't nearly as easy to get along with as Doobie. And one of them was a Yankee, to boot. Sometimes, riding through the empty country, where in a whole day they might not even see a bird or a rabbit and had nothing to eat but a little jerky and frijoles, and had even been instructed to parcel out the water in their canteens, the deputy wondered if he would ever get back to Doobie, or his friend Jack Deen, who liked to hunt wild pigs. Something had carried him away; something he hadn't expected. He hadn't even known Captain Call was in Laredo, or that he was hunting Joey Garza. It was like a wind had swept through Laredo one afternoon, carrying him away with it. Would there be another wind, to carry him back home? In his sad moments, Ted Plunkert didn't think there would be a homing wind. He felt that he had made one simple, wrong move, but one that could never be corrected. He resolved to be very careful, to give himself the best possible chance. But he didn't know, and he didn't feel hopeful.

They rode into Chihuahua City on a freezing, windy day, when the streets were nothing but swirling dust. The old women in the marketplace, where they stopped to secure provisions, were wrapped in long, black shawls, and the shawls were spotted with dust. One old woman had killed three lizards and was offering their meat for sale. It revolted Ted Plunkert, that a people would be so degraded as to eat lizards, and he said as much to the Captain.

"I've eaten lizard," Call said. "I've eaten bobcat and I've eaten skunk." The deputy had lived in settlements all his life, and had no notion of what sorts of things men would eat when they were hungry, really hungry.

Brookshire rode over to the telegraph office. Call found a barber, and he and the deputy both had a shave. Call enjoyed his, but Deputy Plunkert was nervous. Allowing a Mexican such a good opportunity to cut his throat was not easy for the deputy. But the Mexican shaved him clean and didn't offer him any trouble. Of course, Chihuahua City was a long way from Laredo. Around Laredo, any Mexican barber would have been glad to cut his throat.

That was another strange thing about travel. You went among people who had never heard of you. Ted Plunkert had lived in Laredo all his life, and everybody in Laredo knew him on sight, even the Mexicans. He had been living there when Doobie was born, and kept on living there until she grew up and got old enough that he could marry her. Being in a place where people didn't know him was unusual, but so far, no injuries had resulted.

When Brookshire came back from the telegraph office, he had six telegrams, and he looked sick.

"Your color ain't good," Call observed. "I guess if I was your doctor, the first thing I'd advise you would be to stay away from telegraph offices. Every time you go into a telegraph office, you come out looking sick."

"Yes, and there's a reason," Brookshire said. "There's a bunch of news, and not a word of it good."

"What's the worst?" Call asked.

"The worst is that my wife died," Brookshire said. "Katie died. . . . I never expected it." Before he could get a grip on his feelings, he found himself crying, even dripping tears on the telegrams. He hurriedly thrust them at the nearest man, who happened to be Deputy Plunkert. Katie was dead; pneumonia had carried her away. She was already buried, too. He would never see her, nor speak to her, again.

"I swear," Call said. "That is bad news. I'm sorry to hear it. I wish now I'd sent you back from Amarillo. You might have been a help."

"It's too late. . . . Katie's gone," Brookshire mumbled. It was the most shocking thing that had happened to him in his life. He and Katie had discussed his death several times, for he was fourteen years older, and it would only be natural that he die first. That was what they had expected, what they had discussed. He had supposed she would go right on being alive, doing her sewing, putting up with the cat, and making meals for him when he got home. On Sundays, they often ate out.

That was how Brookshire had supposed it would be. Someday, he would pass away. If Katie missed him for a while, that was natural, but in all likelihood, her distress wouldn't last long. She would soon take his death in stride and be able to continue with her life in fairly good order. Certainly, she would be a help with her sister's children, for they themselves had none. Often, her sister's children had stayed with them, and on three visits out of four, there would be emergencies or crises. Katie was never more useful than at such times. She knew how to judge the seriousness of fevers, and never gave a child the wrong medicine. Brookshire was not nearly so useful in crises involving children. Katie was never more irritated with him than when he gave a child the wrong medicine or misjudged the dosage. She felt strongly that he ought to learn to dose children correctly, even though they didn't have any children of their own.

Now all that had been turned upside down. Katie had died,

not he, and he had no choice but to receive the news in a gritty, cold, Mexican town, where he had been sent by Colonel Terry, to do a job he was in no way fit for.

"You're my overseer, Brookshire," the Colonel told him, the day he left. "See that the Captain doesn't waste time and doesn't waste money. I want the Garza boy stopped, but I don't want unnecessary expense. You're a competent accountant, and I'm depending on you. Keep your ledgers neat."

The Colonel, who had lost an arm in the War, did not shake hands with him when he left. The Colonel rarely shook hands with his employees. He had the notion that people caught diseases by shaking hands. He avoided it, unless he was with the President, or the governor, or the mayor of New York, or some such higher-up.

Now Brookshire had gone too far from home, and he had tried to do his exact duty, only to have Katie catch something and be the one to die. She would never again complain of his erratic dosing, when her sister's children were ill. It was a hard thing to accept, real hard. Brookshire struggled to regain control of himself, but he couldn't. He wept and wept.

Deputy Plunkert quickly handed the telegrams to Captain Call. He was surprised to see that a Yankee would cry so, over a wife. He had heard that all Yankees were cold with their women, but this one, Mr. Brookshire, had tears running all down his face. The old Mexican women in the market, wrapped in their shawls against the sand and the wind, were watching the man silently, as if they, too, were surprised by his tears.

"If you like, we'll stop for a day. It's hard to travel when you're grieved. I've done it," Call said.

"No, read the telegrams," Brookshire said. With Katie dead, the only thing he had to cling to was duty. He had to keep thinking of duty, or he would be lost.

Call took the telegrams from Deputy Plunkert and read them. In the last years, he had improved his reading considerably. Charlie Goodnight had books in his house, fifteen or twenty, maybe. Call had been inside the Goodnights' house just once, to visit them. He had not paid much attention to the books, but

[217]

Goodnight had one that had just come in the mail a few days before. It was called *A Texas Cowboy, or Fifteen Years on the Hurricane Deck of a Spanish Pony*—on its cover, it had a picture of a man sitting on a pony that was clearly not Spanish. The book was by Charlie Siringo, a kind of ne'er-do-well who had cowboyed a little and rangered a little, while gambling and drinking steadily, at least in the years when Call had been aware of him.

It was a surprise that such a man had written a book, but there it was.

"I want you to read it and tell me if you think there's anything true in it," Goodnight said. "I think it's all yarns, myself."

Call read the book and agreed with Goodnight. It was all yarns, but what else would anyone expect from a braggart like Siringo?

Reading Siringo's lies had improved his reading, though. He had even thought of stopping by Goodnight's house to borrow another book, in order to keep in practice. He had heard that General Crook, whom he had once met, had written a book. General Crook would be far less likely than Charlie Siringo to fill a book with lies.

Call took his time, and read the telegrams carefully. Then he reread them, in order to give Brookshire time to recover a bit from the terrible news he had just received. Four of the telegrams were from Colonel Terry. The first was merely an inquiry:

Where are you? Stop. Report at once.

The second was in a similar vein:

Important that you report at once.

The third telegram was the one Call studied the longest. A train had been stopped in Mesilla, near Silver City, New Mexico. It had been carrying only three passengers, but all three had been killed and their bodies burned. A witness, a Zuñi man, had been killed and scalped, but not burned. It was not the work of Joey Garza. A local tracker said seven men were involved.

The fourth telegram from the Colonel offered reinforcements. Call, if he accepted the job, could hire as many men as he needed, catch the Garza boy, and then go to New Mexico to deal with the new threat.

The fifth telegram was from Goodnight, a surprise to Call: first, that Goodnight would take the trouble; and second, that he could guess where Call was going accurately enough to have a telegram waiting for him. Of course, Charles Goodnight was no fool. He had not lasted as long as he had by being ignorant. His telegram was as terse as its author:

> Mox Mox is alive. Stop. He's your manburner. Stop. Your deputy is on his way. Stop. Famous Shoes tracking for him. Stop. Mox Mox burned four of my cowboys. Stop. You may not recall. Stop. Available if needed. Stop. Goodnight.

The final telegram was the one with the sad news about Brookshire's wife. Call folded them all and put them in his shirt pocket. The one about Mox Mox he meant to study later. Mox Mox was a renegade from the country north of Santa Fe. News that he was alive, and evidently had a gang, was startling. The man had supposedly been killed some ten years earlier in Utah, by a Ute Indian. Call remembered that rumor, and he also remembered the four Goodnight cowboys Mox Mox had killed and burned, in the days when Mox Mox had been a junior member of Blue Duck's gang of roving killers. Goodnight had pursued the man then, pursued him all through New Mexico and into Arizona and Utah, but had met with one of his rare defeats. Mox Mox had vanished into the canyons. It was not long afterward that news came of his death at the hands of the Ute. Not a word had been heard of him since. Now he was alive and in New Mexico, and he had a gang and was picking off trains. It did complicate the search.

Balancing the complication, though, was the news about Pea Eye, news that Call found very gratifying. The man was loyal, after all. And, if he had old Famous Shoes with him, Call would not have to go looking for his deputy. The two of them would just show up one day.

Brookshire, though still wobbly from his tragic news, was watching Call closely. Katie was dead, and he had only his job to think about now. He wanted to get on with it. He wanted to know what Call's opinion was about the other telegrams.

"Are we going after the new robber, Captain?" he asked.

"He's not a robber—he's a killer," Call said. "He kills men and then burns them. Sometimes he don't bother to kill them before he burns them."

"He burns people?" Deputy Plunkert said, shocked. "Burns them when they're alive?" He had heard of Indians torturing and burning people, in the old days, but this wasn't the old days, this was his own time.

"Yes, he burns them to death, in some cases," Call said. "I don't know much about the man. I had about quit rangering before he showed up. He killed some of Goodnight's men, but that was in Colorado. I've never been there.

"His name is Mox Mox," he added.

"What kind of a name is that?" Brookshire asked.

"Just a name," Call said. "Your Colonel wants us to lope up and catch him, after we subdue the Garza boy.

"There's some good news, too," he added. "Pea Eye is coming, so we'll have reinforcements. He's bringing a tracker with him—or rather, the tracker is bringing Pea. I know the old man, he's a Kickapoo. There's nobody better, but he's not cheap. I don't know if your Colonel will want to finance him or not."

"Why, how much does a tracker cost?" Brookshire asked. He was weak in the legs, had a headache, and felt as if he would just like to be alone in a nice hotel room for a while, in a hotel where they could bring him brandy and where he could sleep on sheets and not have the wind and sand blowing in his hair all night, nor hear the coyotes howl. He had a sudden urge, now that they were in a city of sorts, to be inside, away from the wind and sand and sky, away from Call and the hostile deputy who never spoke to him unless he had to.

Still, he was a salaried man. Even though Katie, who had

been a good wife, was dead, he was not his own master. Colonel Terry wanted action and he wanted reports. "Remember, Brookshire, I'm a man who likes to keep his finger on the pulse," the Colonel had said, as he was leaving. "Keep those telegrams coming."

"I don't know how much Famous Shoes thinks he's worth, nowadays," Call said. "If he could write, he'd have his bill ready the minute he arrives. He'll be the first to tell you he don't work for free."

"I'd just like a general figure," Brookshire said, wondering why the old women with the dirty shawls were watching him so intently. More and more, he wished for a hotel room, but from the look in the Captain's eyes, he knew it was not likely to be. The Captain had the look of a man who was in no mood to linger.

"Now there's two bandits and two killers," Brookshire said. "Which one do we start with?"

"Joey Garza," Call said. "That's who I was hired to catch. The manburner is another story. There's supposed to be law in New Mexico now. Let them stop him."

"What if they can't? Do we have to do it?" Deputy Plunkert asked. Here was another bad picture about to get stuck. The thought of burning men had got stuck in his mind; he wanted to dislodge it, but he could not. He had once helped remove the bodies of two old women who had burned to death when their house caught on fire. He could still remember how the burnt flesh smelled, and how the ashes stuck to their faces. That had been his most horrible duty since becoming a lawman. The thought that there was a killer named Mox Mox, who burned people routinely, was very disturbing. More and more, it seemed to Deputy Plunkert that he had been swept out of his life by an evil wind. The wind was blowing him farther and farther away from home. He looked at Captain Call, and he looked at Brookshire. He felt almost like a boy, in relation to the two men. He was young, and they were not. They were even older than Sheriff Jekyll, who had been his boss. Being in a city where there were only Mexicans was disquieting too, even though these were Mexicans who knew nothing about him. He was in the path of an evil wind, and he felt that he would never get home.

"I want to buy some binoculars, if we can find any," Call said. "Then we can provision ourselves and leave."

"Where will we go next?" Brookshire asked. "I'd like to send Colonel Terry a telegram."

"Presidio," Call said. "I think the Garza boy comes from around there. Famous Shoes might show up there, too. Then, we'd have Pea Eye."

"How would he know to show up there?" Brookshire asked. "We didn't even know we were going there ourselves, until just now."

Call smiled. "That's the tracker's skill," he said. "It ain't all just looking at the ground and studying tracks. Famous Shoes will think about it and watch the birds and talk to the antelope and figure it out. Pea's no tracker. I expect it would take him six months to locate us, on his own."

In a hardware store, he purchased some field glasses. They were not the highest quality, but they would have to do. He was about to leave the store, but turned back and bought two extra rifles. He rarely burdened himself with extra equipment; a blanket and a Winchester and one canteen had seen him through many engagements. This time, though, he felt it might be wise to carry a couple of extra guns. Goodnight's telegram had made him think twice about what lay ahead. Mox Mox was a complication. Call did not intend to go after him, but it might not be a matter of going after him. Mox Mox might come to Texas, for all anyone knew.

Also, Pea Eye had never owned a reliable gun, and Famous Shoes rarely went armed. He moved too fast to be carrying weapons. The extra Winchesters would come in handy.

As they left the store, Call handed the receipts to Brookshire, who carefully folded them and put them in his shirt pocket. The day had turned cold, and the sky was the color of steel. It was nearing evening; Brookshire still entertained the hope that they would spend at least one night in a hotel of some sort. But the Captain had not mentioned a hotel. He was securing the provisions, tying them onto the pack animals.

Ted Plunkert, for once, shared an opinion with the Yankee, who had mentioned to him, hesitantly, that it would be very nice to spend one night in a bed, inside a building.

"Yes, I don't much care what it's like, as long as it's inside," the deputy said.

But when Call was satisfied that the packs were secure, he mounted his horse and looked at the two men, both standing by their mounts.

"I guess we ain't staying the night. Is that right, Captain?" Brookshire asked.

"Why, no. Your boss wants results, ain't that correct?" Call said.

"That's correct," Brookshire replied.

"There's a full moon tonight, and we should take advantage of it," Call said. "The horses are rested. We should be able to make it to the Rio Concho."

"How far is that, Captain?" Brookshire asked.

"I suppose about fifty miles," Call said. "If we don't strike it tonight, we'll strike it tomorrow."

Neither Brookshire nor Deputy Plunkert looked happy. Of course, Brookshire had lost his wife; he could not be expected to recover from such a blow immediately. But there was a full moon, and Call didn't want to waste it.

"Mr. Brookshire, I think it's better that we go on," Call said. "I'm sorry about your wife, but lagging won't bring her back. We'd better go get your boss some results."

"Well, that's good," Brookshire said. "That's exactly what the Colonel wants."

"I'm confident the Garza boy's not west of us, and I don't think he's south, either," Call said. "I think he's east and north. This is where the hunt starts. We haven't been in any danger, so far, but that might change in a day or two. I want you both to keep alert. He's got that German rifle, don't forget it. We'll be going through country where there's not much cover. You both need to keep alert."

[223]

"Do you think Joey Garza knows we're coming, Captain?" Brookshire asked.

"I expect so," Call said. "If he doesn't know it now, he'll know it by the time we cross the river."

"Who'll tell him?" the deputy asked.

"Why, I don't know," Call said. "He's an intelligent young bandit. I expect he'll know we're coming."

"What do you think? Will he try to pick us off?" Deputy Plunkert asked. He noticed that the Captain was frowning at him. Brookshire, the Yankee, had already mounted; he looked miserable, but at least he was already on his horse.

Ted Plunkert hastily mounted too.

"I don't know what he'll try. Let's go to Texas," the Captain said, turning his horse.

By the time the full moon appeared, they were well out of Chihuahua City. The moon shone on a landscape that seemed to be emptier than any of the barren country Brookshire had ridden through since coming to Texas. There was nothing to be seen at all, just the moon and the land. The wind soared; sometimes spumes of dust rose so high that the moon shone bleakly through them. At other times the dust cleared, and the moon shone bright—so bright that Brookshire could read his watch by its light. At midnight, they struck the Rio Concho, but the Captain neither slowed down nor looked back. He kept on riding toward Texas.

The blowing-away feeling came back to Brookshire, but it came to him laced with fatigue and sadness over the loss of his wife, Katie, a nice person. He felt heartsick at the knowledge that he would never see Katie again. His heartsickness went so deep that the blowing-away feeling didn't frighten him. It would be fine now, if he blew away. He would not have to face the Colonel and explain the exorbitant expenses that might accrue.

In Brooklyn, in his work as a salaried man, Brookshire had never paid much attention to the moon. Once in a while, on picnics, he might admire it as it shone over the East River, or the Hudson, if they went that far to picnic. But it hadn't mattered to him whether the moon was full, or just a sliver, or not there at all.

Once they were on the black desert in Mexico, Brookshire saw that the Captain had been right. The full moon, in the deep Mexican sky, was so bright that traveling was as easy as it would have been in daylight. Brookshire was still a salaried man, but he was also a manhunter now, a manhunter hunting a very dangerous man. He was heading into Texas with Captain Woodrow Call, and he would probably do well to start paying more attention to the moon.

Part
II

The Manburner

1.

Lorena was reading a letter from Clara when Clarie came in to tell her that Mr. Goodnight was at the door.

In the letter, Clara was urging her to make a beginning in Latin, advice that caused Lorena to feel doubtful. She thought she could do quite well with English grammar now, but she didn't know if she was up to Latin, or if she ever would be. The baby had been sick most of the time since Pea Eye left, and she had been sleeping tired and waking tired, worrying about the baby and worrying about Pea.

"Mr. Goodnight?" Lorena said. Though he had given the money to build the school she taught in, Lorena had only met Mr. Goodnight once or twice, and he had never visited her home.

"Why would he come here? Are you sure it's him?" she asked. She felt unprepared, and not merely for the study of Latin, either. At that moment, she just felt low, and her feet and hands were cold. Usually, letters from Clara cheered Lorena, but this one made her feel more aware of her shortcomings. She knew herself to be a competent country schoolteacher, but somehow, the Latin language felt as if it should belong to a better order of person than herself, a farmer's wife with five children, no money, and no refinements. If Latin was anything, it was a refinement.

"Learning may be the best thing we have. It may be all that we can truly keep, Lorie," Clara wrote in the letter, along with news about her girls and her horses.

Lorena read that sentence several times. In fact, she read it again, even after Clarie delivered her information. She felt her daughter's impatience, but she was reluctant to lay aside her letter, to go and attend to Charles Goodnight, the great pioneer.

"Ma, he's waiting—he already took his hat off!" Clarie said, annoyed at her mother's behavior. Mr. Goodnight was on the back steps, hat in hand. Why was she sitting there like that, reading a letter she had already read five or six times? Laurie had just taken the breast, and her mother had scarcely bothered to cover herself, even though the baby was now asleep. What was wrong with her?

"Ma!" Clarie said, deeply embarrassed.

"Oh hush, don't scold me, I've been scolded enough in my life already," Lorena said. She buttoned her dress and put the letter under a book—*Aurora Leigh* it was; she had ordered it from Kansas City—and went to the kitchen door. The old, heavy man with the gray hair and the gray beard stood there, patiently. A big gray horse waited behind him.

"I was busy. I'm sorry you had to wait," Lorena apologized, opening the door for him. She had heard that Goodnight was severe with women, but she had seen no sign of it in his behavior toward her. Despite her past, he had approved of her as a schoolteacher. Not everyone wealthy enough to simply write a check and have a schoolhouse built would have been so tolerant.

"I hesitate to bother you, ma'am," Goodnight said.

"Come in, I can offer you buttermilk," Lorena said, holding the door open.

Goodnight immediately came in and took a chair in the kitchen.

"I know you've got your duties, I'll be brief, though I would like the buttermilk," he said. "If I had been born in different circumstances, I could have made a life of drinking buttermilk."

[230]

Lorena poured him a large glass. He drank half of it and set the glass down. Clarie peeked in at the door. She couldn't resist. Everyone talked about Mr. Goodnight, but she had only seen him once before, at a picnic, and he hadn't stayed around long cnough for her to get a really good look at him.

"That's a fine-looking young lady there—I understand she helps out with the teaching," Goodnight said.

"Yes, she's a great help," Lorena said. Clarie blushed, so unexpected was her mother's compliment; she had made it to the great man, too!

"I'm shaky at some of the arithmetic," Lorena admitted. "Clarie grasps fractions better than I do."

Goodnight drank the other half of the buttermilk and set the empty glass back on the table.

"I expect I could chase a fraction from dawn to sunset and never come near enough to grasp it," he said.

Then he looked firmly at Clarie. The three boys, hearing an unfamiliar voice in the kitchen, were huddled behind her, peeking along with their big sister.

"I'll have to ask you young'uns to excuse us older folks," he said. "I've got a private matter to talk over with your mother."

"Oh," Clarie said. She immediately retreated, taking the boys with her. Georgie she had to forcibly drag by the collar. He had developed the ill-mannered habit of staring at guests.

Lorena felt a sudden alarm. Had something happened to Pea?

"No, your husband's fine, as far as I know," Goodnight said, seeing the alarm in the woman's eyes. He felt sympathy for her, and much admiration. It was well known that she had not missed a day of school since taking her job. She arrived every day, in her buggy, in the coldest weather and in the muddiest weather, too. He himself had always been more vexed by mud than by cold, and so was Mary, his wife. Skirts and high-button shoes were a great nuisance when it was muddy, Mary claimed, and he didn't doubt it a bit.

This young woman had strength, and she didn't neglect her duties; that he admired. He felt uneasy, though, at the nature

[231]

of the inquiry he had come to make. The uneasiness had kept him at home for two weeks or more, since he had first been told that Mox Mox, the manburner, had appeared again. This woman had a difficult past; he knew that, but he didn't care. Life was an uneven business. He knew himself to be of a judgmental nature—too judgmental, his wife assured him. But with the schoolmarm, he had no urge to pass judgment. She was not the only woman in the Panhandle to have had an uneven life, and her performance with her pupils had been splendid, in his opinion. Her past was between her and her husband. Goodnight was not a preacher, and he had no mission to save the world, either.

"You're sure he's not dead?" Lorena asked. She couldn't help it. She'd had several bad dreams, since Pea Eye left, and in all of them he was either dead or about to be.

"If he is, I haven't heard it," Goodnight said.

"Then what is it, Mr. Goodnight?" Lorena asked. "What is it?"

"It's Mox Mox," Goodnight replied.

Lorena knew then why it had taken an old man, known all over the West for his abruptness, so long to come to the point. Her first urge was to run and lock her children in the bedroom, where they couldn't possibly even hear the name Goodnight had just spoken.

At the same time, she felt too weak to stand up. A rush of fear broke in her such as she had not felt for many years.

Goodnight saw it—the woman had come into the kitchen a little flustered, some color in her cheeks. But the color left her, as soon as he spoke Mox Mox's name. It was as if the blood had suddenly been milked from her, with one squeeze.

"But he's dead, ain't he?" Lorena asked. It was the first time she had slipped and said "ain't" in many months.

"I thought so myself, but now I ain't so sure," Goodnight said. "I've never seen the man myself, and I believe you have seen him. That's why I've bothered you and took the risk of upsetting you."

He paused, watching the young woman bring herself under

control. It was not a simple struggle, or a brief one. She stared at him, wordless. She was plainly scared, too scared to hide it. Finally, to be doing something, he got up and helped himself to another glass of buttermilk.

Seeing Mr. Goodnight pouring himself the buttermilk brought Lorena back to herself, and just in time. For a second, she had felt a scream starting in her head, or had heard, inside herself, the piercing echo of many screams from the past. She felt cold and clammy, so heavy with fear that, for a second, she didn't know if she could move. During the hours when she had been a captive of Mox Mox and his boss, Blue Duck, she hadn't been able to move, and the terror that she felt during those hours was a thing that would never leave her. The name alone had brought it all back. Mr. Goodnight must have known it might, or he would not have hesitated.

But the man was in her kitchen, he was her guest, and there was such a thing as manners. Even though her deepest urge was to gather her children and run—run to Nebraska, or farther— she knew that she had to control herself and try to help Charles Goodnight, for the very sake of her children.

"I'm sorry, I'm bad scared, it caused me to forget my manners," she said. She gripped the edge of the table and squeezed it with the fingers of both hands. She needed something that would steady her, something to grip. But the spasm of fear was stronger than her grip. Despite herself, she kept trembling.

"It don't take much muscle to pour buttermilk," Goodnight said. "I regret having to put you through this."

"Why are you? Mox Mox is dead," Lorena said. "Pea Eye heard it years ago. He was killed in Utah, or somewhere.

"He's dead. . . .ain't he?" she asked. "He's dead. Everybody said it."

"I chased him to Utah myself," Goodnight said. "He burnt four of my cowboys, in Colorado, on the Purgatory River. Three of them were boys of sixteen, and the fourth was my foreman. He'd been with me twenty years. I chased Mox Mox, but I lost him. It's a failure I've regretted ever since. Two or three years later, I heard he was dead, killed by a Ute Indian."

[233]

"Yes, it was a Ute that killed him," Lorena said. "That's what Pea Eye told me."

Goodnight watched her shaking. He wished he could comfort her, but he had never been much of a hand at comforting women. It wasn't one of his skills. He drank the second glass of buttermilk, looked at the pitcher, and decided not to have a third.

"I think Mox Mox is alive," he said. "Somebody's been burning people in New Mexico."

"Burning what kinds of people?" Lorena asked, still gripping the table. It was all she could do to keep from jumping up and gathering her children and running before Mox Mox could come and get them all.

"Whatever kind he catches," Goodnight said. "He stopped a train and took three people off and burned them. That was three weeks ago.

"There ain't that many manburners," Goodnight added, after a pause. "The Suggs brothers burned two farmers, but Captain Call caught the Suggs brothers and hung them. That was years ago."

He paused again. "Mox Mox is the only killer I've heard of who makes a habit of burning people," he said, finally.

Lorena was silent. But in her head, she heard the screams.

"If I've got the history right, when Blue Duck took you from the Hat Creek outfit, Mox Mox was still running with him," Goodnight said. He spoke with caution. He had known several women who had been captives, several women and a few children. Some of them babbled about it; others never spoke of it; but all were damaged.

Though used to plain speech, he knew that there were times when it wasn't the best way to talk. This woman, who worked so hard for the ignorant, raw children of the settlers, in a schoolhouse he had built, had been a captive, not of the Comanche, but of Blue Duck, one of the cruelest renegades ever to appear in the Panhandle country. And Mox Mox, at various times, had run with Blue Duck. He himself had never seen either man. This woman had seen one of them for sure; perhaps she had seen both. He wanted to know what she knew, or as much of it as she could bear to tell him.

Rarely, in his long life, had Goodnight felt so awkward about asking for the information he needed. Lorena was not one to babble. What she felt, she mainly kept inside. Her fingers were white from gripping the edge of the table, and her arms shook a little; but she was not behaving wildly, she was not screaming or crying, and she was also not talking.

"Mox Mox is a white man and he's short," Lorena said. "One of his eyes ain't right, it points to the side. But the other eye looks at you, and one's enough."

Goodnight waited, standing by the stove.

Lorena took a deep breath. She felt as if she might strangle, if she didn't get more air into her lungs. She remembered that was how she had been then, too, the day Blue Duck led her horse across the Red River and handed her over to Ermoke and Monkey John and all the rest.

But not Mox Mox. He hadn't been there then. He had arrived later; how many days later, Lorena wasn't sure. She wasn't counting days, then. She hadn't expected to live, and didn't want to, or didn't think she wanted to.

Then Mox Mox arrived. He had three Mexicans with him, and a stolen white boy. The little boy was about six. He whimpered all night.

When Gus McCrae rescued her, she hadn't been able to speak, and she had never since spoken of that time to anyone— not much, anyway.

Particularly, she had never spoken about the little boy.

"Mox Mox wanted to burn me," Lorena said. "I'll tell you, Mr. Goodnight. I'll tell it today. But don't ever ask me about it again. Is that a bargain?"

Goodnight nodded.

"He's small," Lorena said. "He wasn't big, like Blue Duck, and he's got that eye that looks off. He wanted to burn me. He piled brush all around me and he poured whiskey on me. He said that would make me burn longer. He said it would make it hurt worse. He rubbed grease in my eyes. He said that would be the worst, when my eyes fried. He poured whiskey on me and he rubbed that grease in my eyes."

"But he didn't burn you," Goodnight said. "I'm surprised. It's our good luck and yours."

"Blue Duck wouldn't let him burn me," Lorena said. "Blue Duck wanted me for bait. He let him pile up the brush, and he let him squirt and rub grease in my eyes, but he wouldn't let him burn me. He wanted to use me to catch Gus McCrae. He wanted to catch Gus real bad, but then Gus killed half his renegades, and Blue Duck left."

"What about Mox Mox?" Goodnight asked. "I guess he didn't stay for the fight with Captain McCrae, did he? He left, like his *jefe*."

"Yes . . . he left with his Mexicans," Lorena said.

She stopped.

"I've never told nobody this. . . . I don't know if I can, Mr. Goodnight," Lorena said.

"Don't try, " Goodnight said. "You don't need to. I'll tell this part, ma'am. He didn't burn you, but he burned the boy, didn't he?"

"How'd you know?" Lorena asked, looking at him in surprise.

"Because I found what was left of that boy, and buried him," Goodnight said. "Six months later, that devil burned my cowboys."

"I'm glad somebody else knows," Lorena said.

"Well, I know," Goodnight said. "I found the remains. The boy's parents showed up at my headquarters about a year later. They were still looking for their child."

Lorena began to tremble so hard that Charles Goodnight stepped over and put a hand on her shoulder. He had steadied horses that way; perhaps it would have the same effect with this woman.

"You didn't tell them, did you?" Lorena said. "You didn't tell them what happened, did you?"

"I told them their son drowned in the South Canadian River," Goodnight said. "I usually try to stick to the truth, but these poor folks had been hunting that boy for a year. I thought the full truth was more than they needed to hear. Anyway, the child was dead. They wanted to go to the grave, and I took them. I'm thankful they didn't try to dig up the child."

"You did right," Lorena said. "You shouldn't have told them no more than you did."

They were silent. Lorena was still trembling, but not so badly.

"I wasn't a mother then," Lorena said. "I'm a mother now. Mox Mox did the same things to that child that he said he would do to me. He whipped him and he poured whiskey on him, and he rubbed grease in his eyes. Then he piled brush on him and burned him."

She had said it, said it for the first time. She looked up at Goodnight, the old man of the plains.

"Were the Indians that bad, with people they caught?" she asked.

"They were," Goodnight said. "Those were bloody times, the Indian times. But you said Mox Mox was white."

"He was white—a mean, little white man," Lorena said. "He whipped that boy till there wasn't an inch of skin on his body. Then he burned him."

"It ain't often you find two bad ones of the caliber of him and Blue Duck, running together," Goodnight said. "But you said Mox Mox had his own gang?"

"Three Mexicans," Lorena said. "They left with Mox Mox, when Blue Duck wouldn't let him burn me."

Goodnight was about to speak when Lorena's voice quickened.

"I still hear that boy screaming, Mr. Goodnight," she said. "I'll always hear that child screaming. I'm a mother now. He was about the age of Georgie . . . about . . . the age of Georgie."

Then a convulsion of sobbing seized her, and she got up and stumbled out of the room, her arms clutched about her chest, as if her very organs might spill out if she didn't clutch herself tightly enough.

Goodnight looked at the buttermilk again, and again decided

against another glass. Though he was old, and should have been used to all suffering, to any misery that life could place in his path, he had never accustomed himself to the deep sobbing of women, to the grief that seized them when their children died, or their men. He had no children. His cowboys were his children, but he had not given birth to his cowboys; it must surely make a difference. He went out the back door, into the stiff wind, and stood by his horse, waiting until the young woman had recovered sufficiently to fend for herself and her children.

A little boy came out and walked up to him.

"My m-m-mama is crying," he said, looking at Goodnight. The boy didn't seem to be particularly upset. He was just reporting.

"Well, I expect she needs to. . . . Let her bawl," Goodnight said.

"My b-b-baby sister cries all the t-t-time, but I don't cry," the little boy, Georgie, stammered.

Two more boys came out, one older, one younger. They stood together. All were barefoot, though it was cold outside. Then the large girl came too, carrying the baby. She looked scared.

"Mama's screaming in there," the girl said. "Why is she screaming like that? She's never screamed before."

Indeed, when the wind lay for a few seconds, Goodnight could hear Lorena screaming. They were wild screams. He supposed captive women must scream like that, during the worst of it. But he had never been a captive, nor a woman, and he could only suppose.

"I brought some bad news; I'm afraid it's greatly upset her," Goodnight said. "She'll probably be better, presently."

Unless she isn't, he thought. People had lost their minds over less than the schoolmarm had endured.

"I hope she stops," one of the older boys said.

"It wasn't about Pa, was it?" Clarie asked.

"No. I have no reason to think your father has had any difficulty," Goodnight told the girl. He was not used to talking to young people, and found it a strain. But in the calm intervals, between the surges of wind, he could still hear Lorena, as could the children, and she was still screaming. Then the wind would return and whisk her screams away.

"Do you ever c-c-cry, mister?" the bold Georgie asked.

"Seldom, son, very seldom," Goodnight replied.

"Is it b-b-because you have a b-b-beard?" Georgie asked. He liked the old man, though he certainly didn't have much to say.

"Yes, I expect that's the reason," Goodnight said.

There was an interval. The wind lay, briefly. They heard no screams.

"She's stopped. Do you think I should go see about her, Mr. Goodnight?" Clarie asked.

"No, let's just wait," Goodnight said. "I expect she'll come and get us when she wants us."

They were all silent for a minute, as the wind blew.

"It's chilly weather to go barefoot in," Goodnight said. "Don't none of you have shoes?"

"We got a pair apiece," the older of the boys replied. "Ma don't like us to put 'em on until we get to school, though. She thinks it's wasting shoes."

"G-g-got any horses that's for k-k-kids to ride?" Georgie asked. "I b-b-been wantin' a horse."

"Georgie, it's Mr. Goodnight," Clarie said, mortified. Georgie had practically come right out and asked him for a horse, with their mother screaming in the house.

"That's fine, miss," Goodnight said. "A cowboy needs a horse."

"Well, d-d-do you have one, m-m-mister?" Georgie asked.

Clarie resolved to box him soundly, when she got the opportunity. She had an urge to go in the house and see about her mother, but she hesitated to leave Georgie alone with Mr. Goodnight. There was no telling what he might ask for next.

"Why, I'll have to inspect my herd," Goodnight said, amused. "I wouldn't want to give a cowboy like you just any horse."

"M-m-make it brown, if you've g-g-got a brown one," Georgie said. "B-b-brown's my f-f-favorite c-c-color!" His stutter became worse when he got excited.

[239]

"Would you come back in, please? All of you?" Lorena asked, from the doorway. "I'm so sorry I drove you out in the wind."

"It ain't the first breeze I've felt," Goodnight remarked. Evidence of her sobbing was in Lorena's face, but she had put a comb in her hair and seemed composed, more composed than she had been even when he arrived.

"You children go into the bedroom. You, too, Clarie," she said. "I have to talk to Mr. Goodnight a minute more. Then, we'll try to get back to normal."

"Ma, Georgie's been asking Mr. Goodnight for a horse," Clarie blurted out. She didn't want to go in the bedroom. She wanted to report on Georgie's misbehavior first.

"Where he's going, there are plenty of horses," Lorena said. "Don't question me now. Go in the bedroom."

The children went, obediently.

"I'm sending them off to Nebraska," Lorena said, the minute she knew the bedroom door was closed. "I have a friend there. She'll take them till this is over.

"I thought it *was* over, or I wouldn't have been living nowhere near here," she added. "He told me if I ever had children, he'd come and burn them, like he burned that little boy. It was the last thing he said to me, before he and his Mexicans left."

"I should have stopped that man a long time ago," Goodnight said.

"You didn't, though," Lorena said. "He burned your cowboys, despite you. I won't take a chance with my children."

"Don't blame you," Goodnight said. "You've got a fine brood. I like that talkative little boy, he takes up for himself."

"He's going to Nebraska, and so are the rest of them," Lorena said. "As soon as I can get them packed and on a train, they're going. Mox Mox is a bad man, Mr. Goodnight. He's not getting a chance to torment any of mine."

"I thought all the mean wolves was about killed out, in this country," Goodnight said. "I thought that man was dead, or I would have stayed after him. Of course, maybe he is dead. Maybe this manburner is somebody else."

"I can't take that chance, not with my children," Lorena said.

"Now my husband's gone too, and it's my fault. He ain't a killer, and he has no business hunting killers with Captain Call, not anymore."

Goodnight felt a little uncomfortable. After all, he had urged the man to go, though it was none of his business. Once again he wondered when he would ever learn not to meddle in other people's business. The woman was right. Pea Eye was not a killer, and had no business having to deal with a Joey Garza, or a Mox Mox.

"There's something else," Lorena said. "I think we ought to close the school, until this ends. If Mox Mox showed up, he might burn all the children. He's capable of it—he might pen us in and burn us all. I won't risk it for my children or for anybody's."

"What if I set a guard?" Goodnight asked.

"No," Lorena said. "If I had known he was alive, I'd never have started the school. When he's dead, and I know it, there'll be time for studying and teaching. But not until I know he's dead."

"I better go myself and stop him, then," Goodnight said. "That way, when it's done, I'll know it's done, and so will you."

"Let Captain Call do it," Lorena said. "I'm sure that sounds bold. I have no right to give you orders. I've no right even to make suggestions. But you came here and asked what I knew, and I told you. I have seen that man, and you haven't. If I were you, I'd let Captain Call do it."

"It was my men he burned," Goodnight said. "It's my responsibility, not Call's."

Lorena didn't respond. She felt she had overstepped as it was, by saying what she had said. She thought she was right, and had said what she felt.

Besides, part of her mind had already begun to occupy itself with the logistics of flight: getting the children's things together, finding neighbors who might take their animals, or hiring a helper to live in the house and look after things. There was no time even to write Clara. Lorena knew she would not draw an easy breath until the children were gone and safe. Clara would

[241]

be surprised, when five children got off the train expecting to live with her. But Lorena knew Clara would take them. Since her daughters' marriages, Clara had been too much alone, anyway. At least it seemed so, from her letters. Having children in the house again might not be the worst thing for her.

"I expect you think I'm too old to subdue the man," Goodnight said. He was annoyed, and surprised at his annoyance. But the definite way the young woman had come down for Call and not for him, stirred something in Goodnight; the competitor, perhaps, or just the male. In his long years as a pioneer, he had always *led*, no matter how long, how difficult or how ugly the task. He had always led. He had been the man to do the job, whatever that job was. He was vain enough to think he was still the man who could do the job, whatever it happened to be, although his own vanity annoyed him, too.

"No, you're not a killer," Lorena said. "I know you may have killed to survive, but you're not a killer. Mox Mox is a killer, and so is Captain Call. Send a killer after a killer. That's why I said it. I wasn't thinking about your age.

"Besides, people here need you," she added. "This whole part of the country needs you. You're the man who built the school, and I know you've built others, too. You brought the doctor here. You paid for the courthouse. You're needed. Nobody needs Captain Call."

"Well, the rich men need him," Goodnight said.

"Yes, because he's a killer," Lorena said. "That's why they need him. He's as hard as Blue Duck, and he's as hard as Mox Mox."

"He's got that other boy to catch first," Goodnight reminded her.

"Mr. Goodnight, I've got to start packing," Lorena said, standing up. "I've got to go to the school and dismiss my pupils. They'll want to know why, and I'm going to tell them. Then I've got to hunt up somebody to do the chores here, for a while. Then I've got to pack. I want to start for Amarillo tonight. I want my children out of here, now."

"You'll be in a regular lather, before you get all that done,"

[242]

Goodnight said. "I expect I could stop the train for you, at Quanah, and I'll send a wagon and a cowboy or two to help you get to the train."

"Much obliged," Lorena said. "And could you lend me a weapon? All my husband left me with was a shotgun. Of course, he didn't know about Mox Mox. I've never even said that name to him."

"I can lend you several guns, but I doubt you'll need them, once you're on the train for Nebraska," Goodnight said.

"My children are going to Nebraska, I'm not," Lorena replied.

"Not going?" Goodnight said. "Why not, ma'am? You're the one he nearly burned. I doubt that he's in six hundred miles of here, but six hundred miles can be crossed. If anyone has a right to be scared, it's you. Why not leave with your children?"

"Because I have to find my husband and bring him home," Lorena said. "I should have set my heels and kept him, but I didn't. It's my place to go bring him back."

"Now, that's rash," Goodnight said. "If you'd like me to lend you something, why not accept the loan of a man who knows the country and can go get your husband and bring him home?"

"None of your cowboys married him," Lorena said. "I married him. He's a good man, and I need him. Besides, he won't mind anybody but me, unless it's the Captain. I'm going to go find him, and he's going to mind me, particularly now."

Charles Goodnight, rarely quelled, felt quelled this time. He knew determination when he saw it. He ceased to argue, but he did promise to send two cowboys with a wagon, to get her to the train at Quanah. As he was preparing to leave, he told Lorena he wanted to provide each of her boys with a horse, when they returned.

"I do like the way that talkative little boy takes up for himself," he repeated.

"Don't forget to send me the gun," Lorena said. "I don't want to be going south without a gun."

2.

Riding to Crow Town across the empty land, Maria began to wish she would never have to arrive. The happiest moments of her life had often been spent alone, with her horse. From the time of Three Legs, she had always loved going away alone, with her horse.

To avoid Presidio and Doniphan, the hard sheriff, she rode up the river for two days before crossing into Texas. She saw mule deer and antelope, many antelope, but no people. It was cold, and the north wind sang in her face. At night, she persuaded her spotted horse—she called him Grasshopper, because he had a way of suddenly springing sideways—to lie down, so she could sleep close to him and share his warmth.

Twice she saw trains moving across the long plain. The trains did not seem to be moving very fast; no wonder Joey could rob them. The locomotives pulled only two or three cars. They were just little trains, moving slowly across the endless line of the horizon. Maria had ridden a train only once, to go to her mother when her mother was dying. It had rattled so badly that she had been unable to think.

Grasshopper did not like the new country, and he shied at many things. Once, a tumbleweed surprised him, and he bucked a few times. Maria was amused, that he was so skittish; she didn't think he could throw her. She enjoyed it, when Grasshopper was naughty. He was irritated with her for bringing him so far from the cornfield. But he obediently lay down at night, so Maria would be warm.

As she rode east, through the sage and the thin chaparral, Maria wondered about herself. Why was she traveling so far, for a boy who didn't care about anyone but himself? She should just let Joey go. There was a hopelessness in what she was doing, and Maria felt it strongly. She should stay at home and help Rafael and Teresa, for they were loving children. With them, even though they were damaged, she could be happy as a mother, and they could be happy too.

But Joey was different. He would not yield her even a moment of affection. She wondered if he blamed her for Juan Castro, and for the fact that he had been sold to the Apaches. It seemed to Maria, remembering before that time, that Joey had been a good boy. He played with other children, and she could tease him and hug him.

But when Joey came back, there was no touching him, and he never smiled, unless he was looking at himself in the mirror. Maria wondered if it was wrong to blame the change in Joey on the Apaches. Perhaps the coldness had been in him earlier. Perhaps it came from her grandfather, a cold old man who did not speak a word to his wife, Maria's grandmother, for seven years, because he blamed her for the death of their first son. What was in Joey could have come from that old man.

Maria rode on toward Crow Town, across the great, empty Texas plain. When she came to the Pecos, with its steep banks, she followed it north for two days, before she could find the courage to cross it. Since the time when the lawmen tied her to the mule and almost drowned her in the Rio Grande, she had had a fear of water that she could not control.

But she knew that Crow Town was east of the Pecos; she would have to cross it somewhere. As she rode along, fearing the river, Maria felt her motherhood to be a cold chain linking her to Joey, who wanted nothing from her and had no love for her or interest in her. If she drowned crossing the Pecos, Joey might not ever know, and might not care if he did know. Why did she think she had to risk the water, in order to warn him that the famous lawman was coming after him? Was it only because she had given birth to him? Did that mean she could never be quit of the pain of such a son? Would her obligation always be so hard and so unredeemed?

Grasshopper did not like the Pecos, either. Every time she found a cut in the brushy banks and tried to force him down it, he balked, sulked, whirled, tried to resist. Because Maria was so frightened herself, she let the spotted horse defeat her, several times. They went on up the plain, following the west bank of the river.

The cold was deepening, ever deepening. The clouds were gray, like the sage grass. Maria awoke so stiff with cold that she could hardly mount. In the mornings, the chaparral thorns were white with frost, and the water in the Pecos was black from cold.

One morning, Maria decided to cross. She felt that if she didn't cross that day, she would give up and stop trying to be a good mother to Joey and go home. It might be for the sake of her father's memory, and her brother's, that she was coming to warn Joey. He might not care himself; he might think he was a match for Captain Call. He might even feel complimented that such a famous man had been summoned to kill him.

Maria broke a limb off a dead mesquite tree to use as a whip. Rarely had she needed to strike her horse, but this morning, when he refused to take the water, she beat him with all her strength until, finally, unable to turn in a narrow cutbank, he made a convulsive plunge into the dark water. It was so cold that Maria feared she might pass out. Her fingers became too numb to hold the bridle. She hung on to Grasshopper's neck with both arms as he struggled out of the water and up the thin cut in the east bank.

On the whole journey, she had not allowed herself a fire. She did not feel it was wise to build a fire in the Texans' country. A fire might bring her someone she didn't want. It might bring her cowboys, or killers, or lawmen.

But this morning she built a fire, in order not to freeze. Sleet began to blow, and her clothes were wet. She was so numb in her hands and feet that she thought she might die if she didn't get warm. The air felt cold inside her when she breathed. She broke off small limbs of mesquite and made herself a little fire, while Grasshopper grazed on the cold tufts of grass.

Suddenly, Grasshopper threw up his head and neighed. Maria was too cold to stop him. She knew there were wild horses in Texas. Perhaps he had only neighed at one of them. She had the revolver Billy had given her in her saddlebags. She got it out, but her fingers were stiff from the cold water. She might not be able to shoot well, if she had to shoot.

Then, to her relief, the old Kickapoo Famous Shoes appeared out of the sleet. He moved, as always, at his own gait, a walk that was almost a trot.

Famous Shoes saw at once that Maria was almost frozen. He thought he had better make coffee. Fortunately, Maria had coffee and an old, bent pot with her. She was trembling from cold. She had made a fire so small that it warmed only part of her.

When Maria saw Famous Shoes making coffee, she felt relieved. The old man was peculiar; he appeared and disappeared at whim. But he was competent. He had offered to take her deep into the Madre once and hide her from the lawmen, when they were being rough with her. Maria had refused his offer. She would not be driven from her children by any lawmen. If she ever had to go to the Madre, she would take Rafael and Teresa with her.

Then Grasshopper neighed again, looking to the north, where the sleet came from.

Famous Shoes saw Maria's concern, and understood it. There were many bad men in Texas. He gave her a cup of boiling coffee. Just holding the hot cup would make her hands feel better, and the coffee would warm her insides.

"I am traveling with Pea Eye," Famous Shoes said. "His woman is going to teach me to read. His horse is a little slow. I was looking for a place to cross the river when I found you."

"Who is this man? I don't know him," Maria said.

"He is a friend of the Captain—you remember?" Famous Shoes said.

"The Captain who hung my father?" Maria asked.

"That one," Famous Shoes said. "Now he is looking for Joey. Did you know that?"

"Why would I be here, freezing, where the Texans could get me, if I didn't know that," Maria said. "I am on my way to warn Joey. Now you bring me one of the men who is going to kill him. Why didn't you let me freeze?"

"Pea Eye doesn't know you," Famous Shoes assured her. "Joey is in Crow Town, anyway. We didn't go there because if we had, one of the bad men might have killed us."

The coffee made Maria feel a lot warmer. The tin cup was so hot she had to hold it with a part of her skirt or her hands would have burned. When she realized what Famous Shoes was telling her, she grew angry.

"Why are you bringing men to kill my son?" she asked. "I thought you were my friend."

"I have been to the Rio Rojo," Famous Shoes said. "I was looking for my grandfather, but his spirit had wandered off. I don't know where it lives. I was coming to Ojinaga to see you. I thought you might have some corn. Then I met Pea Eye, who is my old friend. He doesn't know where he is going. I don't want him to get sick, so I am helping him."

"I don't care if he gets sick. I don't want him to kill my son," Maria said. "How far away is he?"

"He is a few miles north," Famous Shoes said. "He wanted to sit by the fire and drink more coffee. I came on to the river to find a crossing."

"Here's the crossing—you found it," Maria said. "Go on across it and go away, and take this killer with you. Don't be bringing killers to murder my son."

Famous Shoes felt irritated. He had built up Maria's fire, and made her coffee. Now she was demanding that he leave. While she was talking, telling him to leave, he remembered something that had almost gone out of his mind while he was traveling.

Seeing the track of Mox Mox, The-Snake-You-Do-Not-See, had made his mind too busy to work properly.

As he was nearing the Pass of the North, Famous Shoes had gone to see old Goat Woman. She was a woman who had the power to see ahead to the future. Maria knew her. When her mother had been dying in Agua Prieta, she had gone to see old Goat Woman, to find out how long her mother might live. Goat Woman went to the river and caught frogs and read their guts. Famous Shoes found it strange, that the guts of frogs could show the future, but he knew it was true. Old Goat Woman had been right too many times. She lived with her goats in a little dwelling of sticks, not far from the river. Famous Shoes always went to see her when he traveled through the Pass of the North. It was good to stay in contact with people who could see ahead. When she had a great need to see far ahead, not just a day or a week or a month but years, Goat Woman didn't rely on frogs. She killed one of her own goats, and read its guts.

What she had told him on this visit was that Maria's son would kill Maria unless someone killed him soon. Goat Woman had seen this in the guts of a frog and had become so worried that she killed one of her own goats, to check the information. But the guts of the frog and the guts of the goat agreed: Maria's son would kill her.

Goat Woman liked Maria. She had known and liked Maria's mother, too. She did not like the news the guts gave her. Famous Shoes didn't like it, either. He wasn't even sure he believed it, although he knew Goat Woman had strong powers.

"You might be wrong," he suggested. "We are all wrong, sometimes. Maybe the guts are trying to fool you."

"Maybe," Goat Woman said.

"Do they ever try to fool you?" Famous Shoes asked.

"No," Goat Woman replied. "But sometimes, I get confused and don't see what is plain."

"Can anything change the future?" Famous Shoes asked. He rarely got a chance to talk to Goat Woman, who knew about many things he would like to understand.

"Yes, the stars," Goat Woman said. "The stars can change the future. But I don't think they'll change it for Maria."

Now he was actually with Maria, who was wet and cold beside the Pecos. He knew what old Goat Woman knew, and Maria didn't, although it concerned Maria's own death. She didn't want him to take the killers to her son, but if he didn't do it and do it quickly, her son might kill her.

It was a dilemma that made his mind tired. Usually the sleet freshened him, but this morning he did not seem very fresh. He didn't know what to do.

Maria was warming up, and as she grew warmer, she also grew more and more angry. She had been grateful to the old man for saving her from freezing. But when she discovered that he was leading Captain Call's deputy, she stopped being grateful. She wanted the old man to take the deputy far away.

"I want you to go," Maria said. "This deputy might show up any time. If he sees me here alone, he will figure it out and tell the Captain."

"The Captain will figure it out anyway," Famous Shoes said. "I can't fool him. He's the Captain. All he does is kill men."

"Maybe, but you don't need to help him," Maria said. "Let him catch Joey himself, if he can."

"All right, I will leave," Famous Shoes said, very annoyed.

"Thank you for your help with the coffee. Now go away," Maria said. "I don't want this man to see me. I have to help my son."

"If you are in Juarez, you should see Goat Woman," Famous Shoes said. He was outraged. He had kept the woman from freezing, and now she was sending him away, all because of a boy who would kill her someday. She didn't seem to understand that he was old and had to make a living. Also, he wanted badly to learn about the tracks in books. Pea Eye's woman might teach him, if he stayed with Pea Eye and brought him home.

But he couldn't say much to Maria, without revealing what he had heard from old Goat Woman.

"Next time you cross this river, you need to build a bigger fire," he said.

Then he remembered the tracks, near Agua Prieta.

"The-Snake-You-Do-Not-See is alive," he said. "You need to be careful. Don't let him get you and burn you."

"The-Snake-You-Do-Not-See?" Maria asked. She remembered hearing that there was such a man, and that he was evil, but she didn't know much about him.

Famous Shoes turned back up the river to find Pea Eye. It was a nuisance. He had been happy to see Maria, when he found her soaking wet and freezing, but she had been disagreeable and had made him feel confused. If he took Captain Call to Joey Garza, it might save her life. But if he took the Captain to Joey, Maria would hate him, although Joey was a bad son and meant his mother no good. It was a confusion that he didn't know whether to mention to Pea Eye. He would have to think about it when he found him.

Maria stayed by the fire until she was dry. She thought at one point that she saw a rider to the north; perhaps it was the man Famous Shoes was with, Pea Eye. She didn't know what to do. She thought she might try to slip away quickly, on Grasshopper. But then she lost sight of the man—if it had been a man. She wasn't quite sure she had seen him. Perhaps it had only been an antelope. The air was still full of sleet, and it was hard to see clearly, very far.

No rider appeared, so Maria wrapped up in her poncho and made her way into the sandhills, toward Crow Town. The sleet rattled on the chaparral bushes, but soon, over the rattling, she heard the sound of crows, and began to see them, sitting on the cold bushes or in the little skinny black mesquite trees. The crows cawed at her as she rode. Grasshopper didn't like it. He would have liked to go away from the crows, but Maria wouldn't let him. Soon there were crows all around them, in the trees and in the air. As she got closer to the settlement, the wheeling, gliding crows seemed thicker than the sleet.

The settlement, when she came to it, was just a few bumps on the plain. There were several low houses, none of them much higher than the hills of sand. Smoke rose into the air, mixing with the sleet, rising high with the crows.

Joey's house was easy to find, because his black horse grazed behind it, hobbled to a long rope. There was not much to graze on, just a few little sage bushes and a tuft or two of grass. The horse lifted its head when it saw Grasshopper. The two horses had met the last time Joey was in Ojinaga. The black horse neighed, and when he did, a chubby young Mexican woman came out the door. When she saw Maria, she quickly retreated. A second later, a white woman came out. The woman was shivering; she wore only a thin housecoat. But she waited politely for Maria to speak.

"Is my son here?" Maria asked. She did not dismount.

"Joey Garza," she said, in case the woman was stupid and could not think who her son might be.

"Joey, yes," Beulah said. "He's here, but he ain't awake."

"Wake him and tell him his mother is here," Maria said. "I have some news he needs to know."

"You can come in. I ain't going to wake him," Beulah said. "He don't like it when people wake him up."

Maria got off Grasshopper and pushed into the little house. The white woman had a smell. It must not be easy to wash, in such a place, where there was much sand and little water, Maria thought. She did not look like a bad woman, the white woman; she was not young, and she was frightened.

Inside, two fat Mexican girls sat on a pallet, trying to huddle under one blanket.

There was another room. The low door to it was shut, but Maria pushed it open. Joey, her boy, was asleep, under many blankets. The room was dim. She could just see Joey's face, a young face, so young that for a moment she saw him merely as her son, the child she had borne, the child she loved. He was still only a young boy. Perhaps it was not too late to save him, to help him become decent.

"Joey, wake up, you need to leave," she said, touching his shoulder.

Joey did wake up, and the moment he looked at her, the hope that had been rising in Maria sank again and vanished. There was only bottomless cold in Joey's eyes.

"This is my room. I don't like women in here," Joey said. "Get out."

Maria felt anger surge up. She wanted to deliver the slap that would make him good, or at least make him realize he was in danger. She had ridden five days and crossed the freezing river for him, and all he had for her was a look that was as cold as the black waters of the Pecos. It was not a thing she could take patiently—not from her own child.

"Goddamn you, leave!" Maria yelled, slapping him. "Get up and leave. They've sent the great killer for you. Call. Go down into the Madre and go quick, or you'll be dead!"

"You leave," Joey said. "Don't come where you're not invited, and don't hit me again. You're a stupid woman. You've ridden all this way to tell me what I already knew. I know about Captain Call."

"You don't know about him," Maria said. "You just know the name. He took my father. He took my brother. Now he will take my son, and it's because my son is stupid, so stupid he thinks he can't die."

"No old gringo will kill me, and no old gringo will make me run to the Madre, either," Joey replied.

"Then you're dead, if you think that way," Maria told him. "I will go home and tell your brother and sister that you died. They love you, even though you don't care about them."

"You'll tell them a lie, then," Joey said. "I won't die. Call will die, if he comes here. He'll die before he even knows that his death is coming."

Maria turned away. She went back to the room where the three women waited, uneasily. She saw that they were all frightened, the two fat girls and the tired, smelly woman.

"Is there any man here he listens to?" she asked. "Is there anyone who can make him listen?"

"John Wesley Hardin, if it's anybody," Beulah said. "John Wesley's killed all those people. I think Joey likes him. But John Wesley's crazy."

"I don't care. Where is he?" Maria asked.

"He never sleeps, I guess he's in the saloon," Beulah said. She felt afraid of the Mexican woman. Her eyes were angry. When she came in from the storm, her dress and her hair had been covered with sleet, but she hadn't seemed to care. She had walked in and awakened Joey, which nobody did. Maybe the woman was his mother, maybe she wasn't, but in the eyes of the three women, she was scary. Gabriela was so scared, she wanted to hide under her blanket; Marieta was too cold to care. She shivered and sniffled. Not many women came to Crow Town. A woman who appeared out of an ice storm might be a witch woman.

Maria left the house. Her head was hurting. She felt she might be feverish, from almost freezing in the black water. In her fever, she could not control her thoughts. She didn't know where Captain Call was, but in her mind he was close, so close that he might come and kill Joey that very day if she didn't do something quickly. She saw smoke coming from the roof of another low, lumpy building. Maybe that was the cantina. A row of crows sat on the roof of the building. The row went all the way around the low roof. Now and again, a crow would fly up, wheel, come back to the building and take its place in the row. When the crows flapped their wings, a little rain of sleet fell from their feathers.

Maria heard a snort and looked around to see a large pig following her. The pig was the color of sand. She had the pistol that Billy Williams had insisted she take. She took the pistol and pointed it at the pig. The pig was not just large, it was giant. Maria's hands felt a little warmer. She was in a better state to shoot than she had been back when Famous Shoes showed up. The pig snorted again, but it didn't charge her. She had seen pigs charge people in Ojinaga, when the pigs were angry for some reason. She didn't know whether the great sandy pig was angry, or when it might charge her.

The pig stopped and looked at her, but again, it didn't charge. Maria turned and trudged on toward the cantina. It was hard to walk. The sand seemed to fill the street. There were no horses outside the cantina, though Maria saw a glow under the uneven wooden door. Perhaps the wild man was there, in the cantina, the man Joey might listen to.

When she was almost to the cantina, she heard the great pig snort again, and when she turned, it was trotting toward her. Without thinking, she pointed the pistol at the pig and shot. She wanted to scare it away, and she knew sometimes loud noises frightened pigs. When the church bell rang in Ojinaga, the pigs and goats became nervous for a bit. She did not expect to hit the pig, with the sleet blowing. She had not shot a pistol since Benito's time. He had enjoyed shooting and would let her shoot with him, although he was stingy about bullets and did not want to let a woman use too many of them.

To Maria's surprise, the big pig slid forward on its snout, almost at her feet. Then it rolled over, a great hill of hair, and some blood ran out its nose. She waited for the pig to get up. One of its legs was twitching; then it stopped. The giant pig was dead.

The door to the cantina opened, and two men stepped out. One was skinny and had scabs on his face. The other was an older man and he limped. Both looked taken aback. The great pig lay dead, and a woman with sleet in her hair stood over it with a pistol in her hand.

The scabby man was not pleased. The older man just looked surprised.

"You killed our pig—what kind of wild slut are you?" the scabby man asked.

"I'm Joey's mother," Maria said. "If you're his friend, I would ask you to tell him to leave and go to the Madre. Captain Call is coming. I don't know where he is, but I think he's close."

"How close?" Wesley Hardin asked.

"I don't know. His deputy is over by the river," Maria answered. "Famous Shoes is taking him to meet Call."

"That old Indian ought to be shot," Wesley Hardin said.

"She kilt the devil pig," Red Foot said. "I can't believe it. Hundreds of people have shot at that pig. Now this woman just walks into town and shoots the sonofabitch dead."

"I guess the killer instinct runs in the family," Wesley Hardin said. "It's too damn breezy to stand out here worrying about a dead pig."

He looked hard at Maria. She thought he looked crazy. He reminded her of old Ramon, when he was in one of his fits.

"Come on inside, but I'll take the gun," Wesley Hardin said, reaching for Maria's pistol.

She drew back. "Why do you want my gun?" she asked.

"I don't like to be inside small buildings with women who shoot pistols, that's why," Wesley Hardin said. "You just killed the local pig. You might do the same to me, if I get unruly."

"Not if you'll help my son," Maria said. The man was still reaching for her gun, and she still drew back.

"No, thanks, I live for myself," John Wesley replied.

"Captain Call will kill him," Maria said. "For all you know, he might kill you, too."

"No, they ain't paying him for me, they're just paying him for your boy," Wesley Hardin said. "Call's economical. He don't kill just anybody that needs killing. He just kills when he's paid."

Then he grew enraged; his splotchy face turned red and white.

"It's too damn cold to be standing in the wind. Give me the gun and come in, if you want to discuss your son."

"If I come in, it will be with my gun," Maria said.

The scabby man seemed to lose interest in taking her pistol from her. He looked again at the dead pig.

"I wish there was some way we could charge people that want to come and look at this pig you killed," he said, shivering. He kicked the pig a time or two; his boots had holes in them. Maria could see his toe through one of the holes.

"These Texans are superstitious," he said. "They think this pig was the devil. I could have killed it years ago, and I would have, too, if it had ever bothered me. I figured it was more interesting to let it live, so people would have something to be scared of."

Maria followed him into the low building. No more was said

about taking her pistol. There seemed to be a thin trail of blood leading into the cantina, yet the dead pig lay outside, in the sand.

The cantina smelled of tobacco, spit, and whiskey. The limping man had his boot off. The trail of blood had come from his foot. The man did not look well. He was shaking, and his sock was soaked with blood.

"What's wrong with his foot?" Maria asked.

"I stomped it. The sonofabitch is a card cheat," Wesley Hardin replied. "What's the news, other than that Woodrow Call is on his way to Crow Town?"

"The-Snake-You-Do-Not-See is alive," Maria said. "Famous Shoes saw his track."

"Oh, Mox Mox?" Hardin said. "He won't bother me. I'm meaner than he is. It's bad news for anyone else who crosses his path, though. He's meaner than most folks."

Maria saw him looking at her as a man looks, although she was dirty from her ride. She was glad she had kept her gun.

"There's a bed in that corner," Wesley Hardin said, pointing. "Come crawl in it with me."

Maria thought she should have known that was what he wanted when he invited her into the cantina. Killers she had known had not wanted women much. Their interest was in other things, as Joey's was.

She said nothing, but she was glad she had her gun.

"You're a fine one," Hardin said. "You come in here and kill our best pig, and you ask me to help your killer son, but you won't crawl in bed with me, even though I asked you polite. Have you got some old punch you bed down with, down in Mexico?"

Maria remembered that Billy Williams had warned her about Crow Town. It had been foolish for her to bother the killer at all. She didn't know why she had thought he might help.

"A dollar and a quarter, then?" Wesley Hardin asked. "Red can pay you. He owes me money. If he wants to throw in seventy-five cents for himself, he can have the second turn and you'll be two dollars richer before you even eat breakfast."

Maria turned and walked out the door. The killer gave her a hot look, but he didn't follow. He was shuffling cards.

She walked past the dead pig, and went to Joey's house. When she pushed inside, her feet and hands were cold, although it had only been a short walk. The woman who smelled was crying, and so were the two girls. The door to Joey's room was open. He was gone, and so was his rifle. Maria ran out of the house, hoping he was still in sight; maybe he would at least let her ride with him for a while, out of the bad town.

But Joey wasn't in sight, and neither was Grasshopper. Joey was gone, and he had stolen her horse. Maria felt that she must be the most foolish mother in the world, to ride so far in the winter, into the place of the Texans, for such a boy. Now she was afoot, and tired, in a town where the men were hard. Call was coming, and The-Snake-You-Do-Not-See was somewhere around.

Maria began to weep, at her own folly. She knew her son. She should never have given him a chance to steal her horse. Now she was really in trouble. She remembered the killer's hot look. She would have to cross the cold river again, to get back home, and this time she would have no horse to warm her at night.

"Did he say anything when he left?" she asked the white woman, once both of them had stopped crying.

"Maybe he just went to hunt antelope," she added.

"He didn't say nothing. He don't usually say nothing, in the morning," Beulah said. "I didn't want to make him mad, so I didn't ask. He gets real mad if you ask."

"Yes, he thinks somebody crowned him king," Maria said. "Do you have any food I could take?"

The white woman looked hopeless.

"We don't have no food," she said. Her face was streaked with tears. She, too, had made a mistake in coming to Crow Town, Maria thought. Probably this white woman had made many mistakes. Now she wasn't young, she smelled bad, and she was in a bad place with no food. It would not be easy for her, or for the fat girls, either.

"I'm going to Mexico. Do you want to go home with me?" Maria asked the two girls. If the three of them traveled together, it might be warmer. Then she remembered the pig she had killed—there was her food.

The girls were very young. They looked scared.

"We don't have nobody, in Mexico," Gabriela said. Her sister seemed numb. She wouldn't speak. "We don't have nobody here, either. We don't have nobody."

"Do you know anybody with a horse we could borrow?" Maria asked. "I killed the pig, but he is too big, I can't drag him. I can butcher him, but I can't drag him. I need a horse, for a little while."

At home, she had always done the butchering, whether of pigs or of goats. None of her husbands were good at it. Benito wouldn't even try to butcher. He hated blood, and butchering would have made him sick. Then, in the end, he was butchered himself, and hung like a carcass, his own blood draining.

"I'll get Red's horse," Beulah said. "He don't feed it much. I don't know if it can drag a pig."

Then Beulah realized what Maria had said. She had killed the pig! She had killed *the* pig, the devil pig.

"She killed the pig!" Beulah told the girls. "She killed the pig!"

The girls looked stunned. They had both feared the pig, particularly when they had to go into the bushes. The pig watched them; it liked their droppings. Marieta couldn't grasp it. She thought the woman must be a witch, to be able to kill the great pig.

Maria went with Beulah to get the horse. She hitched it to a rope tied to the pig's feet and, urging the skinny horse, dragged the pig slowly to Joey's house. The horse was afraid of the dead pig, and kept shying and flaring its nostrils. It would have liked to run, but hitched to the pig, there was no way for it to run.

There was no tree to hoist the pig, but Maria didn't care. She wanted the blood; it would be easier to get if she hoisted the pig, but she couldn't. She found a knife in the house. She sharpened it on a rock as best she could, and let the pig's blood drain into a rusty bucket. It was not easy to handle so much blood. Maria finally found three buckets and filled them all with the pig's blood. She took the liver and the sweetbreads and then began to cut the meat into strips. The blood was still warm, and soon she was covered with it. The white woman and the two girls got excited at the thought of so much meat. Some of the other women in the village heard that the pig was dead, and came to watch the butchering. Two of them were old Mexican women whose men had worked for the railroad until they died. They lived in Crow Town because they were too old and too weak to go anywhere. But they knew about making jerky, and they had better knives than the one Maria had found. She told them they could have meat, for there was far too much to carry on her journey.

The wind got colder, but the women were excited at the thought of the meat. Also, their great enemy, the pig, was dead, and they would eat him. They were all covered with blood. At one point, John Wesley Hardin came to the place where the butchering was taking place, and stood looking at the excited, bloody women for a few minutes. He said nothing; he just looked. The women's arms were black with blood, as they cut deeper and deeper into the carcass of the great pig. The women were so hungry that they sliced bits of liver and sweetbreads and ate them raw. Maria didn't care. She wanted only to get her jerky and start back for Ojinaga. She missed her children, Rafael and Teresa. She knew she would not be able to smoke the jerky very well. It would be half raw, but it would keep her from starving as she walked home.

By the end of the morning, every woman in Crow Town was behind Joey's house, helping Maria finish butchering the giant pig. All of them carried off meat, and then came back and helped Maria smoke hers over a little fire. They were beaten women, none of them young; only Gabriela and Marieta were young. Most of the women were old, within sight of their deaths. They had been thrown aside by their men, or their men had died, leaving them in this bad place, too spiritless to move on. All of them, even the oldest, had sold themselves, or tried, to the men who passed through Crow Town.

[260]

Now they were excited, and not just by the meat. The pig had frightened them all. He had made their dreams bad, made them scared when they had to squat in the bushes. They had seen the pig eating dead men, on Hog Hill. They knew that when they died, the pig would eat them, too. Nobody would care enough about them to bury them deep enough, and the pig could even root up corpses that were buried deep.

But now the tables had been turned, and it was all thanks to Maria. She had arrived out of the storm and had killed their enemy, the great pig. They had wet their arms with his blood, eaten raw bites of his liver, and waded in his guts, which spilled from his belly and spread over the ground when Maria opened it. An old Comanche woman whose husband had been shot by Blue Duck many years before knew how to strip the guts. She sliced the long, white pig gut into foot-long sections, stripping what was in them into a bucket.

"Don't eat that, there could be people in it, parts of people," Beulah said. She had never liked the old Comanche woman, whose name was Naiche.

Old Naiche was a tiny, wizened woman. She stood up to her shins in the pig guts, merrily pulling up stretches of gut, cutting off sections, and stripping the sections into her bucket.

Beulah knew the pig must have parts of people in its intestines. It sickened her that old Naiche would fill a bucket with the contents of the guts.

As the women worked, the men of the town came, in ones and twos, to watch the spectacle. None of them said anything. They stood in the wind, watching the bloody women cut meat.

Though she continued to work, Maria kept one eye on the men. They were all watching her, and their eyes were hostile. She knew she would have to leave Crow Town that night, as soon as she had enough jerky to see her home. She was a new woman; the men who watched her cut the pig were tired of the women they had, if they had any at all. Their women were worn out. Except for the two Mexican girls, they were all women whose hearts had died within them. They were broken and they didn't care what men did to them anymore. Men had used them until they had used them up. The women were excited that the pig was dead, but their excitement would be brief. In the next day, or two days, or a week, they would just be broken women again.

Maria knew the men would be after her soon. They would be angry because she had stirred up their women. Most men didn't like women to be stirred up, about a dead pig or about anything. Life was much easier when women were broken, when they didn't dare express a feeling, whether happy or sad. It was not something to question; it was just how men were.

By the middle of the gray, cold afternoon, the work was finished. There was nothing left of the great feral pig except its hide, its hooves and its bones. Old Naiche had even taken its eyes. She dropped them into a bucket with the strippings from the guts and hobbled off to her small hovel with them. Then she came back and got an armful of the sections of gut she had cut. The plentitude of guts made old Naiche happy. It reminded her of the buffalo times, long before, when she had often waded in piles of guts.

In the late afternoon, as the winter sun was setting, the sleet turned to snow. Maria felt a bitterness growing in her toward Joey, her son. He had sneered at the trouble she had gone to warning him, and then he had stolen her horse. She had not expected thanks when she journeyed to Crow Town. Joey did not thank people, for nothing they did made him grateful. But she had not supposed he would steal her horse, and leave her on foot in such a place in the winter, among Texans. It was a cruel thing. It made her wonder if her son wished her dead. It was a long way back to Ojinaga, and there were many perils. With Grasshopper, she stood a better chance. Without a horse, it would be very difficult. She might freeze, or she might be taken by men who would be rough with her.

There were horses in Crow Town; Maria had seen five or six. Some of the men who came to watch the butchering were mounted. But Maria had no money, and could not buy a horse. If she stole one and they caught her, she would be hung. That was for sure, they would hang her when they caught her. If there were no trees, they would stretch her between two horses until her neck broke or she strangled. She had seen the *Federales* hang men that way. They had stretched Benito's brother, Raul, between two horses. They had pulled so hard that they almost pulled Raul's head off. A Mexican hanging, the Texans called it, although they used it too, if they were too far from a tree.

Maria decided to walk. That way, she could at least hide in the sage. She searched Joey's room, to see if she could find anything useful. She thought he might have left some money, but there was no money. Gabriela and Marieta tried to stop her from searching, for they were scared of Joey.

"He don't like nobody to be in his room," Marieta said. "He'll beat you, when he comes back."

"I can beat, too," Maria said.

All she could find to take was one blanket and a good knife. She wrapped all the meat she could carry in a sack. While she was packing, the women of Crow Town began to crowd into the house. All were wearing what coats they had. All carried parcels of meat. Only old Naiche didn't come. Beulah had put on her coat too. Marieta and Gabriela had not dressed warmly. They looked scared.

Beulah spoke for the women.

"We want to go when you go," she said. "We don't want to stay here. We're all going to die, if we stay here."

"You might die harder, if you go with me," Maria warned. She did not want to lead the women across the bad land, between Crow Town and Mexico. The meat would not last. She had only three bullets left for her pistol. The women did not look strong. They would freeze or starve, or drown or give up. Her statement had been the truth: dying in Crow Town would not be good, but dying in the borderlands in winter might be worse. At least in Crow Town, there would be shelter.

Then she remembered the railroad. It was only two days' walk south, or a little more. The women might make it to the railroad. Then maybe a train would stop for them. She had seen two trains. She didn't know what made trains stop, but she thought that maybe a train would stop for the women, if they waved at the men who drove the train.

It was a hope, at least. Maria could understand that the women did not want to die in Crow Town. It was not a good place. The crows flew through the snow, or walked in it. Three sat on the bare ribs of the great pig. As the cold deepened, the cawing of the crows seemed to grow louder. Maria felt feverish. She would have liked to rest in Joey's bed for a day or a night, but she was afraid. If the men caught her, they would not care that she was feverish. They might tie her and keep her until she became like the other women in the town. Her heart might die within her, as their hearts had.

Maria couldn't risk that. Her children needed her. Even now, she worried that Billy Williams wouldn't take care of them well enough. Rafael might be growing thin, for sometimes he forgot to eat. Teresa was careless sometimes, and burned herself on the stove. What if she had burned herself badly? Who would hold her in the night and help her with the pain?

"I will take you to the railroad, if you will try to keep up," Maria said. "That's the best I can do. I have to leave you at the railroad and go home to my children."

When the time came to leave, Marieta and Gabriela wept. They had no warm clothes; they didn't want to go.

"My feet freeze, even when I'm in the house," Marieta said. "I don't want to walk in the snow."

"I want to wait for Joey," Gabriela said. "He don't have no one else to help him."

"Joey thinks she's pretty," Marieta said. She was bitter that her sister had been favored. She didn't like Joey anymore. But her feet got very cold, just sitting in the house. Someone had told her that if your feet froze, they had to be cut off. She was afraid that if she went with the woman, her feet would freeze. The person who told her what happened to frozen feet was Red Foot, who sometimes visited her. He would only pay her a dime, but it was a dime at least. Red Foot liked to be behind her; she could hear him panting in her ear, like a dog. He said frozen feet had to be sawed off with a saw.

"Me and Gabriela, we better stay," Marieta said.

"Don't be weak," Maria said. The two girls were just girls, not too much older than her own girl. She didn't want to leave them to the rough men. If she had to take the women, she would take the girls, too.

"These men will use you till you're sick," Maria said. "I will wrap your feet so they won't freeze."

While the girls sat, looking scared, she cut up sacks and wrapped their feet in many layers. She found an old pair of chaps that had worn thin and used the leather to make tight wrappings around the sacks. She didn't think the girls would freeze, for the worst cold didn't come with snow.

When Maria was ready, all the women looked scared. It was dark and the snow was still blowing. Some of the women wanted to wait until morning, but Maria wouldn't hear of it.

"Do you want a parade?" she asked, angrily. She had enough responsibilities, without these women balking.

"You know what we are to these men," she said. "Look between your legs—that's what we are. That's why they even let us be alive. Do you think they will let us all walk off, and not do something about it?"

Then she thought of old Naiche. She was Indian, Comanche. Probably, the women had not asked her to go. When Maria inquired, several of the women claimed not to know where old Naiche lived. Finally, Beulah told her.

Maria went through the snow to the little hovel of dirt and branches where Naiche lived. The shelter was made of thin mesquite branches, bent together at the top. There were many spaces between the mesquite limbs, but old Naiche had covered them with some of the rotten buffalo hides. It was a flimsy dwelling, so low that Maria had to go almost to her hands and knees to get through the opening. The wind sang through the small, smoky room, but Naiche didn't seem to mind. She sat with her bucketful of strippings and her armful of guts. Now and then, she would dip into the bucket and nibble from the squeezings of the dead pig.

"I don't see well, no more," Naiche said, when Maria stooped low and came in. "Too much smoke."

"We're leaving. You should come with us," Maria said. "I will take you to the railroad. It's not a long walk. This is not a good place for a woman."

Old Naiche shook her head.

"The train don't have no place to take me to," she said. "All my people are dead."

"They are not all dead," Maria replied. "Billy Williams says there are many of your people, in the Territory. The train could take you to them, if you will get up and come with me."

"No, there are only whites in the world now," old Naiche said. "I have all this food. You got it for me. I want to stay here and eat this food."

"Bring it, I'll help you carry it," Maria said. She knew it was no use, trying to save a woman as old as Naiche, but she wanted to try. The women of Crow Town were too sad. Even with her eyes half gone from smoke, the old Comanche woman had more life left in her than any of them. She didn't seem discouraged, to be living in a small hovel made of mesquite sticks, with rotten buffalo hides to cover it and protect her from the cold breath of the norther.

"Come, try," Maria said. "I don't know what will become of you if I leave you here with these men."

"I don't worry about these men," Naiche said. "Look. I'll show you what I have."

She bent, and began to dig with her hands by the little fire.

"This fire don't go out," she said, as she was digging. "I only let it go out in the summer, when it is hot. When the norther comes, I let the fire burn so my scorpions won't freeze."

Naiche uncovered a pit, so near the fire that the glow of the coals lit it. Maria looked in and saw that the pit was full of scorpions. She didn't like scorpions; she didn't count, but there were many scorpions in Naiche's little pit, and also a few of the long centipedes with the red legs. Old Naiche had made a roof over the pit, with little sticks and a badger skin to cover it and keep the scorpions in.

"When they sting me, it don't hurt," Naiche said. "If men are bad, I will go around and put scorpions in their clothes. I did it to old Tommy, because he stole my tobacco. When he was drunk, I put three scorpions in his pants, and they stung him where he is a man."

Old Naiche grinned. She had few teeth. Maria, too, was amused, at the old woman's vengeance and her cleverness in keeping a pit of scorpions near her fire. Billy had once told her that the Apaches sometimes kept scorpions because they needed their poison.

"Are you Apache?" Maria asked, thinking she had made a mistake about Naiche's tribe.

"No, but I was given to an Apache," Naiche said. "I lived in the Bosque Redondo, but I didn't like it. I ran away."

"Run away again," Maria said. "I will take you to my home. I have two children who are damaged. My girl is blind and my boy cannot think too well. Come to my home, and I will take care of you. We'll leave the others at the railroad, but you can come to Mexico with me."

But again, Naiche shook her head.

"My time is coming," she said. "It will come when I finish this food you gave me. I do not want to go away and miss it. When you miss your time, then you cannot rest.

"Besides, I like the crows," Naiche added. "I have one that comes to my house and tells me secrets. That is why I know I have to stay here and wait for my time. She is up there now, my crow."

Maria had no more time. She saw that she could not persuade the old woman, and she needed to be far from town with the other women when morning came. Maybe if it was still snowing, the men would be too lazy to follow the women. That was her hope, and her only hope. The women she was taking away were ugly, dirty, and weary, but they still had the places between their legs. The men wouldn't like losing those places. Maybe they would pursue them, and maybe they wouldn't. But Maria had to go, and go at once.

"I will give you this advice," she said to Naiche. "Do not put your scorpions on the killer with scabs in his hair. He don't care about women. He will sting you worse than you sting him."

Old Naiche didn't answer. She looked into the smoke, the smoke that had ruined her eyes. Again she dipped her hand into the bucket of strippings from the pig's guts.

Maria crept out. The snow had stopped, which made her fearful. She had to hurry, and she had to get the women moving. Several crows sat on top of old Naiche's hut. Maria wondered which one was the crow that had told the old woman secrets. She wondered, but she did not have time to find out. The snow had stopped. She had to get the women and the two scared girls, and go.

3.

When Mox Mox and his seven men rode into Crow Town, he made the men ride their horses back and forth over old Naiche's little brush shelter, trampling her to death.

At first, the horses shied, and didn't want to crash through the shelter. Mox Mox pointed to a sandhill, about one hundred yards away.

"Go to the top of it and blindfold them shittin' horses," he instructed. "Head them for this brush and keep on spurring."

Old Naiche heard. While the men were blindfolding the horses, she tried to crawl out, but Mox Mox was waiting for her with his leaded quirt. He quirted her in the face until she gave up. She crawled back into her hut and waited for the hooves to bring her darkness. Soon she heard the horses coming hard. The crows began to caw. Naiche tried to be ready, but she had begun to feel regret for not going with Maria. It was a sharp regret, so sharp it made it hard for her to be ready.

But the horses were coming hard, whether or not she was ready. Naiche clawed open her little pit and dug quickly with one hand into her scorpions and centipedes. She raked a handful of them up and shoved them under her blanket. Perhaps one of them would bite The-Snake-You-Do-Not-See. The horses were closer. Naiche still had scorpions in her hand when they crashed through the branches of mesquite.

The hooves did not immediately bring her death, though they broke both her hips and crushed one hand.

"She's still stirring—ride again," Mox Mox said. The seven men wheeled their horses and rode again, and again. Because they couldn't see, the horses were frightened. Soon the men stopped racing. They merely spurred their mounts, causing them to jump into the broken branches. The rotten buffalo robes were soon kicked away, the mesquite branches broken.

"I guess that will teach her," Hergardt said. He was German, the largest of the seven men. He was also, by common consent, the dumbest. Hergardt was so dumb he often put his boots on the wrong feet. He was strong and would pull his boots on without looking, as easily as most people pull on socks. Later, he would wonder why his feet hurt.

Hergardt rode a big bay horse. The other men dismounted and began to pile the broken mesquite limbs into a pyre, but Hergardt kept riding his horse back and forth over the body of old Naiche.

"What will it teach her?" Mox Mox asked him, looking at the body of the dead woman. A hoof had broken her neck. "I could cook you for a week and it wouldn't make you smart," Mox Mox said. "Being burnt just teaches you that you're burnt."

Mox Mox had found Hergardt in San Francisco, when he returned from his years on the sea. He had gone to sea to escape Goodnight, who had pursued him all the way to the Great Salt Lake. Mox Mox knew he could not go back to the Southwest for a while. Goodnight had been too persistent. Mox Mox put out the story of his death at the hands of the Ute, and went to sea for seven years.

Hergardt was making his living as a wrestler when Mox Mox docked in San Francisco. He wrestled all comers for a dollar a bout. Mox Mox began to promote him and soon had the price up to ten dollars a bout, although Hergardt was far from invincible. Many smaller, quicker men beat him.

"You deserve to be burnt, but it wouldn't teach you nothing," Mox Mox observed. "Stop riding over her. She's dead. It's time to light the fire, Jimmy."

[270]

Jimmy Cumsa lit the branches. He was a Cherokee boy from Missouri, very quick in his movements; almost too quick, in Mox Mox's view. Mox Mox liked to have a sense of how his men worked together, if there was a fight. Six of them he could keep up with, but Jimmy Cumsa—Quick Jimmy, they called him— was so swift that Mox Mox could seldom anticipate him. He would see Jimmy in front of him one minute, and the next minute, Jimmy would be behind him.

"Watching you burn people would teach me something, Mox," Jimmy said. "It would teach me not to stay around you too long."

"You been around me for a year. What keeps you, if you don't like my ways?" Mox Mox asked.

Jimmy Cumsa didn't answer. He was watching the hut burn. The old woman's thin garments began to burn too.

He knew it irritated Mox Mox, when he didn't answer a question, but Jimmy Cumsa didn't care. He did not belong to Mox Mox, and didn't have to answer questions. Jimmy was careful of Mox Mox, but he was not afraid of him. He had confidence in his own speed, as a rider, as a runner, and as a pistol shot. He was not an especially good pistol shot, but he was so fast it fooled people, scaring many of them into firing wildly, or doing something else dumb, that would cause them to lose the fight.

Mox Mox killed short people because they reminded him of himself—that was Jimmy Cumsa's theory. He killed tall people because he envied them. He could be a killer, but he could never be tall. He could never be blond, because he had red hair; and he could never look you straight in the eye, because one of his eyes was pointed wrong. It looked out of his head at an angle. Mox Mox hated being short, regretted that smallpox had scarred his face, and was sorry that he was not blond, but the thing he hated most about himself was his crooked-looking eye. His greatest, most elaborate cruelties were reserved for people with well-set, bright blue eyes. When Mox Mox caught such a person, male or female, he tended to do the worst things to the eyes. If the person with the perfect blue eyes was tall and blond, then so much the worse for him or her.

Jimmy Cumsa wondered if fire was so hot that even dead people could feel it burning them. He had seen corpses twitch, while Mox Mox was burning them. It seemed to Jimmy that might mean even the dead had some feelings, enough feelings that they could respond to the heat of a fire.

Mox Mox had probably killed the old Comanche woman because she was short. She was about the same height as Mox Mox himself. Burning flesh smelled sweet—that was a fact soon learned, if you rode with Mox Mox. It didn't matter why he had killed the old woman; she was definitely dead. The flimsy branches of her little hovel didn't make much of a funeral flame. She wasn't going to be burned very completely, Jimmy knew that.

Mox Mox didn't seem to be paying much attention to this fire, or to the old woman's burning. Most likely, that was because she was dead, and couldn't scream and plead. When people screamed and pleaded, Mox Mox got icy cool. He was like the sleet at such times. Never once had he spared a person he wanted to burn, not since Jimmy had ridden with him. It didn't matter how loudly they pleaded, or how much money they offered him.

Peon got off his horse and began to piss into the flames. Peon was another runt, a little taller than Mox Mox, but not much. He had grown up in a swamp in Mississippi, and he slunk along, looking furtive and dirty, like some old swamp dog.

The two Mexicans were anxious to get the burning over with, so they could go to the cantina and drink. Oteros kept looking at the horizon, as if he expected to see a posse coming for him, with their hang ropes out.

Oteros was not afraid of Mox Mox, either. He was with him because he admired his business sense. He had met Mox Mox in jail, in San Luis Obispo. Mox Mox was about to be hung, for killing a boy. Oteros had very long arms and managed to reach out of his cell with one of his long arms and catch the jailer as the man was walking past with a plate of beans for an old bank robber who was being kept in the jail. Oteros held firmly to the jailer's collar until he could get his pistol and beat his head in.

Mox Mox got the jailer's keys, and the two of them left. Oteros had been with Mox Mox ever since.

"I don't like these crows," Oteros said. "Why did we come here? There are too many laws in Texas."

"He means lawmen," Peon said. He understood Oteros and liked him, although Oteros was the most violent of the seven men and as likely to kill friend as foe when his temper was up, as it often was.

"He thinks there are too many lawmen in Texas," he repeated, in case Mox Mox missed his point.

"There may be too many lawmen in Texas, but there's still too many Apaches in New Mexico," Mox Mox said. "I'd rather fight any lawman in the world than some old Apache with one eye and a weak bow. I'd kill the lawman, but the one-eyed Apache would probably kill me."

"You, but not me," Oteros said. "I have killed many Indians and I will kill more if I see any."

"Go kill Goodnight, if you want to kill a tough old wolf," Mox Mox said. "The sonofabitch chased me a thousand miles, and he'd do it again if he knew I was alive."

"Well, he'll find out, if we come over here and start cooking people," Jimmy Cumsa said.

"We won't be cooking too many until Goodnight is dead," Mox Mox said. "I do want to kill that Mexican boy who robbed those trains with the payrolls on them. We've robbed three trains and ain't took a payroll yet. That boy's beating us to the money. If we could take a payroll, we could hire enough men to clean out a state."

"A state?" Jimmy asked. "You want to kill all the people in a whole state? I never knew you had that kind of ambition, Mox."

"Which one would you take, if you was to take a state?" Peon asked.

Mox Mox had given no detailed thought to the conquest of a state. He'd merely been reflecting on the army he could raise if he had a million dollars to spend. It was rumored in Juarez that the Garza boy had taken a million dollars in payroll money off the trains he had robbed.

"I might take Wyoming," Mox Mox said. "I could take it and be governor of it. Then, I'd hang all the dirty sonsabitches I didn't like."

"There wouldn't be a soul left in the state, if you hung all the people you didn't like," Jimmy Cumsa said. "I don't notice that you like too many people, Mox."

"I don't, for a fact, and you're getting to be a prime candidate for hanging yourself," Mox Mox said. Sometimes Quick Jimmy let a little too much contempt leak into his voice, when he spoke to his boss. Jimmy didn't like very many people himself, but he paired up with Pedro Jones when they hit a town and decided to seek women. Pedro Jones had a Yankee father and a mother who came from far down in the Indian country below the City of Mexico, by the ocean. Pedro carried a seashell with him, in his saddlebags. At night, by the fire, he would often sit holding the shell to his ear. He liked to listen to the sea, for he had grown up by it. Listening to its faint echo in the shell reminded him of a time when life had not been so harsh.

Pedro had become a criminal by accident, at a time when he lived in Vera Cruz. He was very tight with his money and had begun to strangle the whores he went to see, in order to save what they cost. It seemed to him a reasonable practice. There were many, many whores in Vera Cruz, and he had only strangled a few and beat in the heads of one or two more. He had only killed the last few because of drink, but the authorities had not accepted his excuses. A whore who was in love with him helped him break out of jail and he went west, across Mexico and then north into Arizona Territory, where Mox Mox found him. Pedro had killed an old woman who wanted to charge him too much for his supper. Old as she was, the authorities still took offense, so that Pedro was forced to flee along the Gila.

Manuel had been in jail with Pedro, and fled with him when he escaped. Manuel was a simple horse thief who was too lazy to run as far as it was necessary to run when he stole horses from the gringos. He stayed with Mox Mox and his gang because he didn't like traveling alone. He thought Mox Mox's habit of burning people was repugnant, and he always rode off a mile or two and tried to take a nap, while the people screamed out their pain. But he stayed with the gang because it eliminated the problem of being lazy and getting caught. He could make fires and he could cook; those were his main jobs with Mox Mox. He was rarely asked to take much part in the killing, and had been very reluctant to ride his horse over the hut of the old Comanche woman, although he had not known the woman personally. It seemed to him dangerous to race seven horses at the same time, and make them smash a hut, even a small one. Running horses often fell anyway. His own brother had his skull broken because a running horse had fallen in a rocky place with him on its back.

"They say Joey Garza can shoot you from a mile," Jimmy Cumsa said. "They say he don't miss."

"I don't miss, either," Mox Mox said. "You miss because you don't aim—you just shoot. If I hadn't adopted you, I imagine you'd have been plugged by now. Let's go find somebody who knows where this wild boy's at. I want to kill him before he takes any more payrolls away from us. Then, we'll go get Goodnight."

At the saloon, Oteros and Manuel stayed outside. Pedro Jones went in, but came right back out. He disliked low rooms. Peon went in, hoping Mox Mox would buy him whiskey, but Mox Mox didn't mention buying whiskey for anyone. Hergardt and Jimmy Cumsa also went inside. Hergardt's head came within an inch of the ceiling, when he straightened up.

A white man with a splotchy face, a cripple, and an Irishman were in the saloon. Mox Mox recognized John Wesley Hardin at once, from photographs he had seen in newspapers. Seeing him in person was a surprise. Mox Mox hadn't supposed he could walk into a saloon in the sandhills and come upon a famous man.

"Ain't you Hardin?" he asked, feeling that he was addressing a peer.

"Mind your own business, you cross-eyed runt," Hardin said. He had stepped outside and surveyed the gang briefly. Red Foot had limped in and informed him that they were trampling old Naiche to death.

"Well, there goes the last woman," he observed, to Patrick O'Brien. "This place has got the curse of doom upon it. If I was you and had a business in a place like this, I'd move it."

"Wes, I just got a load of whiskey in last week," Patrick pointed out. "It's the wrong time to move."

Mox Mox was so startled by John Wesley Hardin's insulting reply that he didn't do a thing. He took the other table, and told the Irishman to bring him whiskey. There were only two chairs at his dirty little table, and Jimmy Cumsa took the second chair. Jimmy was amused by the killer's reply to Mox Mox. Such talk was music to his ears. He had described Mox Mox exactly: a cross-eyed runt.

Hergardt was left standing. He didn't seem to mind or to notice, but John Wesley Hardin noticed.

"You're too big to be inside—go outside and wait," he said, to Hergardt. "Or else sit down. You're blocking the light. I can scarcely see my cards."

"There ain't no chair for me," Hergardt informed him.

"Then sit on the floor, you damn German," Wesley Hardin said. "If you don't get out of my light, you'll soon be enjoying a few holes in your liver."

He pulled his revolver out of his belt, and laid it on the table.

Despite the insult that had been offered him, Mox Mox found that he admired Hardin's temerity. Hardin was the most famous killer in the Southwest, after all. Finding a man who would say exactly what he pleased was a novelty, and of course, Hardin's reputation was far greater than his own. Hardin had the habit of killing, and he had gone to prison for it and survived, untamed. Mox Mox decided to overlook the insult. He wanted to get to know Wesley Hardin, but more than that, he wanted Hardin to accept him as a peer. Being called a cross-eyed runt was nothing new anyway. In his years at sea, when he was often the smallest man on the ship, he had been called worse things.

The epithet was inaccurate, of course. His eyes didn't cross. One was pointed at an angle to the other. People who called him cross-eyed were not very observant.

[276]

"Now, be friendly, Hardin," he said. "I've got seven men here, and we're after the Garza boy."

"As to that, seven is not enough," Hardin said.

"Well, counting me, it's eight," Mox Mox said.

"No, you have to subtract the Mexicans, because they undoubtedly can't shoot," Wesley Hardin informed him. "Then, you subtract this giant, who's blocking my light, and the reason you can subtract him is because I'm about to kill him if he don't sit down. I won't stand for dim light. I killed a blacksmith on that very spot a few days ago, and he wasn't near as tall as this lunkhead, and didn't block near as much light."

"Sit down, Gardt, don't you hear Mr. Hardin?" Mox Mox said.

"Going outside would be even better," Wesley Hardin said. "That way, I wouldn't have to look at three hundred pounds of stupidity while I'm trying to concentrate on my cards."

"I'll play you cards, if you're shorthanded for a game," Jimmy Cumsa said. The man John Wesley had a droll habit of speech. If he had been offering employment, Jimmy would have accepted it on the spot. There was little conversation to be had out of the present gang, although Pedro Jones became garrulous at certain times.

"I guess you would, you goddamn Cherokee," Hardin said. "Or are you Choctaw?"

Jimmy Cumsa just looked at him. The man had a surprisingly rough tongue. He didn't seem to realize that he was badly outnumbered, or else he just didn't care.

"Is the Garza boy here?" Mox Mox asked. With a man as unpredictable as John Wesley, it seemed best to come to the point. He might fly off the handle and kill Hergardt, and Gardt was useful when there were heavy things to lift.

"The boy ain't, and what's more, his mother ain't, either," Hardin said. "She came here and killed the big pig that was eating the corpses, and then walked out of here with all the cunt, except that old thing you just killed with your damn nags."

"Why, that old Comanche woman was too old to pester," Mox Mox said.

"Old or not, and Comanche or not, she was the last woman left in Crow Town, and your action was unwelcome," Wesley Hardin said. "We don't like strangers who trample our women."

"You're a sonofabitch," Mox Mox said—respectful as he was of Hardin, he was beginning to be riled by his tone.

"You must have run wild so long, you don't realize you can be killed," Hardin said. "I've done been hung twice, to the point where I passed out, only they cut me down too soon. I could be killed by a knife if it was stuck in my liver or my jugular. I could be shot by a bullet, and if it was thirty-caliber or heavier, it would probably do the job and I'd be dead. I could be bit by a snake that was filled with poison spit, or I could ride under a lightning bolt or fall down drunk and split my head on a rock."

He paused, but only to peer hard at a card that had come out of the deck he had just been shuffling.

"That ace don't belong in this deck, it's got six or seven already," he said, laying the card aside.

"What I doubt is that I'll be killed by a damned squint like you, or a Choctaw boy, or this damn ignorant anvil of a German you brought in," Hardin said.

"Maybe you ought to leave the anvil here," he added, considering Hergardt for a moment. "We need a blacksmith, and he's got the heft for it.

"I won't kill him till he thinks it over," he added, in a charitable tone.

"Then you'll never kill him, because he'll never think it over," Jimmy Cumsa said. "Gardt can't think, and he couldn't shoe a horse if he had a week."

"He can't even shoe himself," Mox Mox said.

"Well, if he's useless, move him out of the light, then," Hardin said.

"Move, Gardt," Mox Mox said. "Go outside and dig a hole or something."

"Ain't you the man Charlie Goodnight chased to Utah?" Wesley Hardin asked, looking at Mox Mox. "Old Charlie's still kicking. I expect when he hears you're in Texas, he'll come and chase you back to Utah again."

"No, we're going to get him," Mox Mox said. "I intend to kill the Garza boy first, because he's costing me money."

"Get Woodrow Call, while you're getting," Wesley Hardin said. "They sent him after Joey Garza."

"Who did?" Mox Mox asked, surprised.

"The railroad, of course," Hardin replied. "I expect him to show up, any day. Call won't bother me because there's no money in it, but he'll probably catch you and hang you properly."

"Who's he talking about?" Jimmy Cumsa asked.

"An old Ranger," Mox Mox said. "He don't worry me. He never caught Duck, and he'll never catch me."

Wesley Hardin suddenly sprang up from the table and hit Hergardt in the temple with his pistol as hard as he could. He hit him accurately. Hergardt fell right behind Jimmy Cumsa's chair. Hardin glared at Mox Mox. Jimmy Cumsa almost pulled his gun, but decided at the last second that it might not be a wise move.

"That was like whacking an ox, I hope my weapon's intact," Hardin said. He was calm again. He looked his pistol over, and then cocked it and put it back on the table, in front of him.

"Call never caught Duck, but he caught me a couple of times, back in my feuding days," Wesley Hardin said. "I was pretty disagreeable, in my feuding days. Then Call went off and hung the Suggs brothers, up in Kansas. The Suggs were as mean as you, if not meaner."

"You don't have no idea how mean I am, you scabby sonofabitch," Mox Mox said. He was tired of insults. Besides, Jimmy Cumsa was hearing it all. He had to speak up, or let Jimmy think he was afraid of Hardin.

"Oh, you cook some chicken you drag off a train now and then," Hardin said. "I expect most of them are just fat Yankees. You could fry a hundred of them and it wouldn't impress me."

He seemed amused by Mox Mox's anger.

"What would impress you?" Jimmy asked. He could tell Mox Mox wasn't going to stand for much more. He wanted to ask a few questions before the killing started, if it did.

"Well, you've got three problems," Hardin said. "Joey Garza, Charlie Goodnight, and Woodrow Call. Take 'em in any order you like. When you've killed any one of the three, come back, and I'll buy you and all your damn Mexicans a drink."

"You don't think we can manage it, do you?" Jimmy asked.

"No, I don't," Hardin said. "You're just a bunch of chicken fryers."

"We've been in the papers," Jimmy said. "The papers say we're the worst gang ever to hit the West."

He was becoming annoyed himself at John Wesley Hardin's evident lack of respect.

"I guess you want me to bow to you, because you got your name in some damn newspaper," Hardin said. "I wouldn't give a nickel's worth of dogshit for the whole bunch of you, and I don't care what it says in the papers. If you want to sit here and drink, do it quietly. Maybe I won't have to whack you like I whacked that lunkhead."

"No, if we ain't wanted, we'll depart," Mox Mox said, standing up. "When I come back, I'll bring you three heads, and then I'll expect an apology for your rude behavior, Mr. Hardin."

Hardin was studying his cards. He didn't look up.

Mox Mox waited, but Wesley Hardin seemed to have forgotten their existence.

"Why don't we go back in and kill him?" Jimmy Cumsa asked, when they were outside. The horses had all been dumping; several piles of horseshit steamed in the dirty snow. Pedro, Peon, Manuel, and Oteros all looked drunk. They had gone to the back of the saloon and helped themselves to some liquor in Patrick O'Brien's storeroom. Each of them had drunk a bottle.

"The way to think about Hardin is that he's crazy," Mox Mox said. "Having him alive is like having another weapon. He might kill anybody, at any time. If Call wandered in here, Hardin might kill him for us. Or, he might kill Goodnight."

"I thought you wanted to kill Goodnight yourself," Jimmy said.

"I'd like to, but if Wesley Hardin happens to kill him first, I wouldn't shit my pants."

"I thought you wanted to do it yourself," Jimmy repeated.

Mox Mox took his horse and walked off. He led his horse behind the saloon and helped himself to two bottles of Patrick O'Brien's whiskey. Patrick came out while he was doing it, and held out his hand.

"That's six bottles you owe me for," he said. "Your men took four. I sell a lot of whiskey out my back door."

"It's convenient, I guess," Mox Mox said. He handed over the money. He wanted to stay friendly with the Irishman. In his experience, it was bad policy to offend saloonkeepers.

The real reason Mox Mox led his horse behind the saloon was because he needed a place to mount that wouldn't require him to jump for his stirrup in front of the men. He found just the thing, too, a little lump of sand about two feet high. Usually he managed to mount from the uphill side, so he wouldn't have to jump for the stirrup. That was the awkward thing about being short; he could never forget it. If he was mounting out on the flats, where there was no uphill side, he had to jump for the stirrup, whether he liked it or not.

When he rode back around the saloon, all the men were mounted except Hergardt, who had just crawled out the door. He sat in the snow, crooning a German song he sometimes sang when he was unhappy. Some blood ran out of his ear, on the side where Hardin had hit him.

"Get up, Gardt. We're off to catch that Mexican boy," Mox Mox said.

Hergardt stumbled up, but fell flat down again before he could reach his horse. Manuel and Oteros managed to hoist him to his feet, but Pedro Jones and Jimmy Cumsa had to help, in order to get him flopped over his horse. Hergardt caught his reins, but dropped them. Pedro Jones had to lead Hergardt's horse.

The mesquite limbs from what had once been old Naiche's hut were still smoldering as Mox Mox and the seven men rode out of Crow Town. The crows were cawing, and the bitter wind still blew.

4.

Brookshire had attended Princeton College for a year. He hadn't the head for it, and knew he hadn't the head for it, but his mother had ambitions for her children: she was determined that he become a college man. She made him a suit, so that he would not look so much like a plain Hoboken boy, and she scraped and scrimped to save the money to send him.

They were not rich, but his father had a decent job on the railroad. He was foreman of the railroad yard in Queens; it had not been Colonel Terry's yard, not then.

Brookshire had only stayed a few months at Princeton College. Even his mother was forced to accept the sad fact that he didn't have the head for it. In later years, it was only in her bitterest moments, after she discovered that his father, like the Colonel, had a Miss Cora tucked away in Queens, that she railed about her son's failure at Princeton.

As he rode up the Rio Concho, with Captain Call and Deputy Plunkert, Brookshire had occasion to remember Princeton College, and to reflect on it. The wind grew colder, and what might have been only a soft snow in the East became a sharp sleet that bit at his face like bees.

In Princeton College, they had talked a good deal about civilization. Those who attended Princeton College were, of course, among the civilized. The New Jersey countryside had been civilized too, though Brookshire hadn't thought much about the civilized New Jersey landscape, or civilization in general, until he found himself freezing on the Rio Concho with Captain Call.

Up to that time, civilization had just been a fancy word that preachers and professors and politicians bruited about.

It wasn't just a word to Brookshire anymore. It was something he had left, and it involved comfortable beds and gas heaters and snug brick buildings, to keep out the wind. It involved meat that had been sliced by a well-trained butcher, and purchased at a butcher shop and cooked by Katie, his wife, now sadly gone, leaving him with no one to cook his chops for him.

Nothing that the professors at Princeton College would have been prepared to call civilization existed on the Rio Concho. Indeed, on the cold stretch where they were, nothing human existed, except themselves. At least the old women in Chihuahua City, staring out of their dusty shawls, had been human. Here, there was only the earth, the sky, and the wind. When night came, it took them an hour to gather enough scanty brushwood to make a decent fire.

The night the ice storm hit, it was so cold that even Captain Call didn't pretend to sleep. They all huddled by the fire, trying to keep it alive. At times, the wind surged so that it seemed the fire might blow away.

Brookshire had never expected to be this cold, and yet, he reflected, only a month before he had been sweltering in Laredo.

"A few weeks ago, I was the hottest I've ever been," he told the Captain. "Now, I'm the coldest. It ain't ever moderate down here, is it?"

Deputy Plunkert had given up talking. Every time he opened his mouth, the air came in, so cold that it made his teeth hurt down to the roots.

"No, it's not moderate, much," Call said. His knee pained him. The morning before, he had let a mule kick him. Usually he was quick enough to sidestep such kicks, but he hadn't sidestepped this one.

More worrisome to him was the fact that the joints of his fingers had begun to swell, when it got cold. For most of his life, he had paid no attention to weather; weather was just there. He never let it interfere with his work or his movements. In time, the weather would always change, but the work couldn't wait. Now, it seemed, weather was interfering plenty. When the cold struck, his wrist joints became swollen, and the joints of his fingers, even more so. It had happened to a lesser degree the winter before, and a doctor in Amarillo had told him he had arthritis. The only remedy the doctor suggested was that he wear a copper bracelet, advice Call ignored. Now he wished he had tried it. His finger joints were so swollen on the cold mornings that he had an awkward time buttoning his pants, or pulling his saddle straps tight. Knotting the packs onto the mules had ceased to be a simple task, with his joints so swollen. He tried letting Deputy Plunkert pack the mules, but Deputy Plunkert could not tie a knot that would hold.

Just the day before, they had spotted a mule deer—a big doe. They needed meat, too. Call yanked his rifle out of its scabbard and tried to get off a shot, only to find that the knuckle of his trigger finger had swollen so badly he had to force it through the trigger guard. When he finally got his finger on the trigger, the doe was two hundred yards away, and Call missed.

Sitting by the gusting fire with Brookshire and the deputy, Call rubbed the knuckle. It had not become any less swollen. They still needed meat, too. They were living on jerky, and a few tortillas that were stiff as leather. He looked at the knuckle and was shocked by its size. He thought he might possibly have a thorn in it; mesquite thorns could cause swelling in a joint. But he looked closely and could find no sign of a thorn.

It was worrisome. Neither Brookshire nor the deputy was a particularly good shot. He himself was not an exceptional shot, but had usually been able to bring down meat when it was vital. It occurred to him that he might have to take the trigger guard off his rifle. At least he might have to if the intense cold didn't break. He could not remember having been so uncomfortable in cold weather, though he had spent a winter in Montana on the Milk River, where temperatures of forty below zero were not uncommon.

"Well, none of us are as young as we used to be," Brookshire remarked.

Call had never thought much about age. Charlie Goodnight liked to talk about it, but Call found the talk tedious. He was as old as he was, like everyone else; as long as he could still go when he needed to go, age didn't matter much. He was still able, within reason, to do what he had a mind to do. But he'd had a mind to kill the large doe, and he hadn't. Of course, he wasn't an exceptional shot. He had missed mule deer before, but the fact that he had missed this one just when he had, was troubling. They were just coming into the home country of the young bandit, a boy with a keen eye and a German rifle with a telescope sight. Getting a knuckle stuck in a trigger guard would not be wise, in a contest with Joey Garza.

"How cold do you have to be to freeze?" Deputy Plunkert asked. Though he hated to open his mouth and let the cold attack the roots of his teeth, he had begun to worry constantly about freezing and wanted to ask. Coming with the Captain was the worst mistake of his life. If he were to freeze to death on the Rio Concho, it would serve him right. But he still didn't want it to happen.

"We won't freeze," Call said. "We can squeeze in with the mules if it gets much worse."

Deputy Plunkert had a private agony that he had not shared with his traveling companions. The day before, when they faced the freezing wind, he had put on all the clothes he had brought with him. He was wearing two pairs of pants, and several shirts. With so much clothing on, and his hands half-frozen anyway, it had proven difficult to get himself fully unbuttoned when a call of nature came in the night. He thought he was free, but when the piss started to flow it turned out that he wasn't—a good measure of piss went between one pair of pants and the other. The cold deepened and the piss froze, making a shield of ice along one thigh. The weak fire barely warmed his hands. It made no impression on the shield of ice.

Shortly after that calamity, the Yankee, Brookshire, came to his aid by loaning him an extra pair of gloves he had brought along. Brookshire noticed that the deputy kept dropping his reins, because his hands were so cold he couldn't hold them. He offered the gloves, and the deputy gratefully took them. He knew he would be more grateful too for his wife Doobie's warm body, the next time he got to lie beside it.

"Are you sorry you came with me, Mr. Brookshire?" Call asked. He knew the Deputy was sorry *he* had come; his every motion and statement made that clear. But Brookshire was a more complex fellow. He had adapted to hardship far more easily than Call had expected him to. Once out of the heat of Laredo, he had not uttered a word of complaint, and he tried to handle his share of the chores efficiently. Call had come to admire him. It could not be easy to go from the comfortable life of the city to what they were experiencing on the Rio Concho. Yet it was the deputy—the native—who was feeling worse.

"No, I ain't sorry," Brookshire said. "Katie's gone now. I'd just as soon be here." He could not think of his wife without tearing up, though he quickly wiped away the tears when they came.

"This way, I feel about as bad outside as I do inside," he said. "It's nice to be shut of the Colonel for a while, too. I imagine he's pretty jumpy by now, wondering what became of us. I hope he ain't fired the whole office."

The thought came to Brookshire that if he ever did make it back to Brooklyn, he might take the train down to Princeton College, just to walk among the buildings for an afternoon. He supposed other Princeton men had gone to the West, and come back, though he didn't know any. He couldn't claim to be a Princeton man anyway; he hadn't had the head for it, and had to quit and take a job in an office. Still, he had a sense that he would like to see the place once more, to look at the gray buildings and the great trees. If he did go, it would be because he had managed to survive a place where no one gave a thought to civilization. Survival was all they had time for, and numbers of them failed even at that. It would be good to see Princeton again, after the Rio Concho. If he was fortunate enough to find another wife, and marry and have a boy, he thought he might want to send him to Princeton College. If he could marry a smart wife, perhaps he would have a boy with the head for Princeton College. Brookshire began to ruminate about his boy, and what his name might be. He thought he might want to name him Woodrow, after the Captain; that, of course, was a matter that would have to be discussed with his new wife.

The next morning, they came to the Rio Grande. Near its banks was a little village. Call had a distant memory of the place. He and Gus McCrae had once hung some horse thieves not far from it, on the Texas side. The village was called Ojinaga, as he remembered. He and Gus had brought the bodies home. Other Ranger captains considered that foolish, for they thought it invited ambush or revenge. But he and Gus had sometimes done it anyway, on the occasions when the village was close. The men hung were, in most cases, the only ones capable of ambush, and having the bodies made it easier on the womenfolk.

Call had never expected to return to Ojinaga. He remembered the bitterness in the eyes of some of the village women. But that was a common thing, along the border. He saw the bitterness whether he was returning bodies or not.

Now life had brought him back to Ojinaga. As they rode to the well, in the center of the little plaza, he was surprised to see old Billy Williams standing outside a small adobe house. Billy seemed to be sniffing the air—it was a scout's habit—but what was more surprising was that he held the hands of two children. One was a large boy, and the other a girl of ten or twelve who seemed to be blind. Billy himself didn't appear to be very keen of sight, either. The large boy had a look that suggested he might not be fully right in the head.

Call turned his horse and rode over to the three people. He had never been a great admirer of Billy Williams, but after three hard nights along the cold river, it was comforting to come across an old acquaintance.

"Why, hello, Billy," Call said. "That is you, isn't it?"

"Woodrow, where have you been?" Billy asked. "We've been expecting you for a week."

That was unwelcome news.

"Why would you be expecting me?" Call asked.

"Why, everybody knows you're after Joey," Billy Williams said. "It's the talk of the whole West."

"I wish the whole West would shut up, then," Call said. "Do you know Joey Garza?"

"I know him," Billy said. He saw no point in not admitting it.

"This is his brother and sister," he added. "This is the house he grew up in. His mother, she's gone."

"Oh, are these your children?" Call asked, surprised by the news he had just been given. He had heard that Billy had a woman in Mexico.

"They ain't, no," Billy said. "I'm just watching them. Ain't that Deputy Plunkert, from down in Laredo?"

"Yes, that's him," Call said.

"What are you dragging him along for, he's worthless," Billy said. "I wouldn't hire him to shovel out shit, if I had a livery stable full of it."

"I needed a man," Call replied. "I was hoping he might turn out to be a fighter."

"No, he's just a jailer," Billy said. "I've been arrested in Laredo quite a few times, but always by Sheriff Jekyll. All Plunkert does is ladle out the beans they feed you, when they feed you."

"This town looks familiar to me," Call said. "I think I was here before, with Gus. We hung three horse thieves and brought them home."

"Yes, to this house," Billy said. "You hung Maria's father and her brother and a brother-in-law. It's just as well Maria's gone. She ain't forgot."

"In that case, I suppose she's gone to warn her son. Or have you warned him already?"

"Well, I told Maria you were coming," Billy said. "She thought Joey might be in Crow Town, so she left. The weather turned cold, but she made it to Crow Town, I know that much."

"Oh, did a crow tell you?" Call asked.

"No, Famous Shoes told me," Billy said. "He's waiting in Presidio, with your man."

[288]

"Well, that's good news," Call said. "Deputy Plunkert can go home now, if he wants to. I'd far rather travel with Pea."

While the men were talking, Teresa listened. Though she herself was not frightened, she could tell that the man frightened people. Billy's voice sounded different, when he was talking to this man. The man's voice wasn't loud, but it was rough. Teresa felt interested—she wished the man would stay with them a little while. She liked the way the man's voice sounded, even if it was rough. From time to time, she felt the man watching her; it was her belief that the air changed, when people watched her. She wanted to whisper to Rafael, about the man. She wanted to lead Rafael amid the sheep, to whisper about the strange man who had just come to Ojinaga. Teresa thought the man might be a king, from the way he made the air different when he looked at her. It was very interesting to her. She was glad her mother wasn't home, because her mother always made her go in the house when strangers came.

It pleased her that Billy knew the man. Perhaps he would visit them again, in the next days, so he could talk to Billy.

"If you care for his brother and sister, then I guess you must be a friend of Joey Garza's," Call said. He wanted what information he could get, but he had traveled the border a long while and knew better than to try and twist loyalties.

He felt the little girl was watching him, but of course, that was wrong thinking; she was blind, she couldn't watch him. But she was an unusually pretty, appealing child. There was something in her quick expression that was unusual. He knew blind children were often very smart, and he suspected that this little girl was one of the smart ones. To be blind must be a sadness for anyone, of course. There would be little hope for the girl, in such a poor village, even though she was clearly going to be a beauty. Some man might marry her for her looks alone, Call supposed.

"I know Joey," Billy admitted. "I knew him when he was a youngster. He was likable then. I have not seen him much since he took up killing and train robbing. I doubt it's improved his disposition."

"I expect not," Call said, waiting. Perhaps Billy would let slip something useful; or perhaps not.

"Joey's smart, and he's lived with the Indians," Billy said. "He outran the Apaches, and they couldn't track him, neither. You won't locate Joey easy, unless he decides to come at you and present a challenge."

"Famous Shoes can track him, if the railroad can afford his fee," Call said. "I imagine the old man is still expensive."

Call sat watching the sprightly girl. He wished he had a bauble to give her, a ribbon, or a locket, or some such trinket. Of course, she wouldn't be able to see it, but she could feel it.

The boy's face was puffy, and he drooled a little. He made a sound, now and then, like the sound a goat would make. It made Call wonder about the mother. What could she be, to produce a beautiful blind girl, an idiot, and a killer? He only dimly remembered the three men he and Gus had hung. The border had an abundance of horse thieves then; probably it still did. He had forgotten many of the ruffians he'd had to deal with. It seemed an odd turn of the wheel, that he should come back after so many years to the very house where he and Gus had brought the three bodies.

It was still very cold, and Brookshire was anxious to get across the river, to see if there were telegrams from his Colonel. Call could not linger too long, just in the hope that Billy Williams would tell him something useful. It might be that old Billy didn't really know anything useful about the young killer.

He thought he might try one more question.

"I've heard there's a cave," Call said. "It's said the Garza boy carries everything he steals, and hides it in a cave. Has anyone you know seen it?"

"Nope," Billy said. He knew he had to be careful in his statements. If Maria found out he had said something that gave Joey away to his pursuer, she would drive him out of Ojinaga, or else kill him.

"I don't think there's no cave," he said, lying.

"He's taken a passel of stuff," Call said. "It's got to be somewhere."

Billy didn't answer. For all he knew, Joey could have ten caves. Olin Roy had seen him carry a saddle into the mountains once, but that was as close as anyone had ever come to Joey's treasure.

"Well, I expect I'd better go locate Pea Eye," Call said. He looked again at the sprightly little girl, and turned his horse.

Later, Teresa took Rafael into the sheep herd and told him that an unusual man had come. Rafael had been there too, of course, but often he did not know of many things that happened in his presence, until Teresa told him. She stroked her baby chicken and helped Rafael suckle one of the sheep who had just lambed and had much milk.

"I think he must have been the king," Teresa told her brother. She wasn't sure what a king did, but her mother had read her two storybooks, and one of the books had stories about a king.

"I think he must have been the king," she said again, as Rafael sucked the ewe.

5.

Famous Shoes had not wanted to go into Presidio.

"The hard sheriff will arrest me," he told Pea Eye. "He thinks I stole a horse. It was a long time ago, but he will remember."

"We've got to have shells," Pea Eye reminded him. "If we don't get shells, we'll starve and never find the Captain."

They'd had a hard trip across the Pecos country. The cold was bitter, and the antelope stayed just out of range, tempting Pea Eye to shoot time after time at animals he couldn't hit. They'd had no food at all for the last thirty miles.

"You're working for the Captain now," Pea said. "You're like a deputy. Doniphan won't arrest no deputy of Captain Call's."

But Doniphan, the hard sheriff, came with the one-eared deputy, Tom Johnson, and pointed rifles at them in the hardware store. Doniphan wore a long mustache and carried two handguns, besides the rifle. The one-eared deputy had a red face, from drink. His life had not been easy since Billy Williams shot off his ear. People mocked him, and Doniphan, his boss, had no sympathy. As everyone on the border knew, Doniphan had been born without sympathy.

"We're here waiting for Captain Call," Pea Eye said, when he saw the rifles pointed at them. "We're both deputies. We've been hired to help the Captain bring in Joey Garza."

"This Indian is a horse thief," Doniphan said. "He's escaped me once, because of a fire. He won't escape me again."

"He's called Famous Shoes because he walks everywhere," Pea Eye told him. "He wouldn't steal a horse because he don't use horses. The only use he'd have for one would be to eat it."

"Stealing horses to eat is still stealing horses," Doniphan said. "Start walking toward the jail."

"I have never stolen a horse in my life," Pea Eye said. "Why are you arresting me?"

"Because you're with this horse thief," the sheriff answered. "You might be a horse thief, too."

Pea Eye went along to the jail. He felt bad about Famous Shoes. He should have come into the town alone and bought the cartridges. He had ignored the old man's advice, which was foolish of him. Almost every time he ignored someone's advice, whether it was Lorena's or Mr. Goodnight's or the Captain's or Famous Shoes', he had cause to regret it.

Doniphan put the two prisoners in separate cells.

"Once I hang this old red nigger, and I'll get to it quick, you can go," Doniphan said. "I suspect you're a criminal, but I can't prove it."

The next day, several people came to the jail and stared at Famous Shoes. Doniphan had let everyone know the man had been recaptured. He decided to keep the old man on display for a week, as a form of publicity. His boast was that no criminal escaped him. Now he had recaptured the one man who had escaped him. He decided to hang him publicly, as an example. Normally, he would just have taken him out and yanked him up and let him choke; normally, an old Indian with a taste for horseflesh would not have merited a public hanging. But Famous Shoes' escape was the only escape there had been from Sheriff Doniphan's jail, and he wanted it to be known up and down the border that he had avenged it.

Pea Eye's repeated claim that Famous Shoes worked for Captain Call merely annoyed Doniphan. He left the old man without food for two days, to show his annoyance. When Pea Eye tried to share his frijoles with him, Doniphan moved Famous

Shoes a cell away, so that Pea Eye couldn't pass him the food.

"Why are you starving him?" Pea Eye asked. "All he done was eat a dead horse, and that was years ago."

"He evaded the law—my law," Doniphan replied. "He deserves worse than starving, and he'll get worse than starving, too."

Famous Shoes said nothing. Talking to the hard sheriff was a waste of breath. He began to regret having left the Madre. He knew that his time was near, but was sorry that it might be the hard sheriff who put him to death. He had hoped to die near the Rio Rojo; even though he had not made contact with the spirit of his grandfather, the spirits of many of the Kickapoo people were there, along the river. It would have been a better place to give up his spirit than the jail of the hard sheriff.

Famous Shoes was old, though. He had lived past the time of his people. He knew that few men got to choose the place of their going, or of their coming, either. Only the wisest old men and women of the tribe were able to determine when or where to accept their deaths. Only the wise could do that, but even with those few wise ones, there had to be more than wisdom. For wisdom, in his view, had ever been a downward path: luck was better than wisdom, while one was alive. It was mainly the lucky who got to die in the right time, or the right place, or so Famous Shoes felt.

He himself had been lucky, for he had lived in the lands of the Mexicans and also the lands of the whites. Both peoples hated Indians, yet he had lived a long life. His main regret was that he had not kept his last wife. She had grown dissatisfied and left him, just as he was beginning to appreciate her attentions. He missed her sorely for many years, and still missed her, when he thought about her.

Also, he would have liked to know how to read. It seemed that his dream of having Pea Eye's wife teach him would be frustrated. The one-eared deputy, who didn't hate him as much as the hard sheriff, let him have an old piece of newspaper that had the book tracks on it. Famous Shoes tried his best, for what he thought might be the last time, to make sense of the tracks on the paper, but it was no use. He lacked instruction, and he had to give up.

Every time Pea Eye mentioned the Captain, Sheriff Doniphan got a cold look in his eye, and the look in his eye was not very warm to begin with.

"I doubt he'll show up, and if he does, I'm apt to lock him up, too," he told Pea Eye. "He's just an old bounty hunter—he ain't the law. He's too old to catch that Mexican boy, anyway."

"Well, Charlie Goodnight don't think so," Pea Eye said. He thought that name, at least, might impress Doniphan, but the truth seemed to be that nothing impressed Doniphan.

"He's another one that's too old," Doniphan said. "These old buffalo need to be put out to pasture. They won't be catching no more swift bandits, and if they come round me, I'll send 'em home."

In fact, now that Joey Garza had become such a sought-after outlaw, Sheriff Doniphan had developed a plan to catch the young robber himself. The boy's mother had been in his jail once already, although Doniphan had been gone at the time, delivering a man to the penitentiary. Now she had gone to Crow Town, to warn her son, but she would have to come back sometime, and when she came back, Doniphan meant to arrest her. What his deputies had done to her then would seem like child's play, compared to what he meant to do to her now. Next, he would find her son and kill him. There would be no capture and no trial. There would just be a bullet, or two, or three.

Doniphan didn't suppose it would hurt his reputation to dispatch Joey Garza; in fact, it would make it. After that, every border killer from Matamoros to Juarez would know that Joe Doniphan was a sheriff to be reckoned with. The people would stop talking about old-timers like Woodrow Call and Charlie Goodnight; when it came to modern lawmen, Joe Doniphan would be the first name that came to mind when trouble on the border was being discussed. The next time they needed a federal marshal to clean out Crow Town or any other nest of ruffians, his name would likely be at the top of the list.

Sheriff Doniphan was in the midst of just such a dream of glory when Captain Call walked in, with a Yankee at his heels. The one-eared deputy, Tom Johnson, saw him coming and quickly stepped in to alert the sheriff.

"I think it's old Call," he said. "I've never seen the man, but I think it's him."

Doniphan was startled. He had not expected the old man to appear. He got up and put on his hat. After all, the man had been a great Ranger once. Showing him a little respect wouldn't hurt.

Call had seen too many country sheriffs to be much interested in what he heard about Sheriff Doniphan. Presidio was a small town, in a remote spot on the border. Few criminals of the first class would have any incentive to pass through it. The man had probably harvested his reputation by arresting local thieves, or men who got drunk and shot their best friends. Local law work was mostly of that order. When told at the hardware store that Doniphan had arrested Pea Eye and Famous Shoes, Call had been irritated, but not overly so. At least Pea Eye was there, and the old tracker was still with him.

When he stepped into the jail, Doniphan held out his hand, but Call ignored it.

"Let those men out—you had no business arresting them," Call said bluntly. "They were sent to help me bring in Joey Garza, and you need not have interfered with them."

Sheriff Doniphan was surprised that such an old man would take such a sharp tone with him. He didn't appreciate it, either. It was not the kind of talk he was used to hearing, in his own jail. The Yankee looked mild, but old Call didn't.

"I know who to arrest, I reckon," Doniphan said. "This Indian's going to be hung, in a few days. He's a known horse thief. I'm sure you've hung a good many like him, yourself."

"Famous Shoes has never been known to ride a horse, much less steal one," Call informed him. "Anybody who knows anything about this part of the country knows that. Pea Eye has been my deputy for thirty years, and he's never been a lawbreaker."

"He came into town with a criminal, and that's breaking the law, for me," Doniphan said, irritated by the old man's tone. He felt his temper rising. Who was this old fellow, to walk into his jail and start giving orders?

"Here," Call said, handing Doniphan a telegram. "This is from the governor of Texas. I heard you were a stubborn man, so I asked Mr. Brookshire to have Colonel Terry wire the governor. I done it as soon as I heard these men were in your jail. I done it to save time. We're provisioned, and we need to go. There's been another train robbery, near San Angelo."

Doniphan took the telegram, but he felt himself growing angrier. He was too angry to read. Old Call had gone around him, without even speaking to him.

Doniphan wadded up the telegram unread and tossed it on the floor. Tom Johnson, though well aware that his boss was temperamental, was appalled. They had never received a telegram from the governor before. They had never even dreamed of receiving one—at least, he hadn't. Now Joe Doniphan had received one and wadded it up without even reading it.

He hastily picked it up and attempted to smooth it out. It was from the governor, and it ordered Sheriff Doniphan to release Call's men and give him every assistance.

Call watched the sheriff, who had grown quite red in the face. He had secured the telegram as a matter of correct procedure. He knew that local sheriffs were apt to be touchy about their authority. Call supposed, from what he had heard, that Doniphan was likely to be touchier than most. So he had asked Brookshire to wire his boss and had used the time it took exchanging telegrams, to provision well. Again he had offered to release Deputy Plunkert from his duties, and again the deputy, though half frozen and permanently melancholy, had refused to be released. Now that they were back in Texas, Ted Plunkert felt that conditions were sure to improve. He resolved to stay with Captain Call, whatever it meant.

Call had not supposed that Doniphan would be obdurate enough to defy an order from the governor of Texas, but it seemed the man was just that stubborn.

[297]

"Sheriff, it *is* from the governor," Tom Johnson said. "Don't you want to read it?"

"No, I don't, and when I wad something up, I want it left wadded up!" the sheriff said, highly irritated with his deputy.

"Goddamn the governor, and goddamn you," the sheriff said, addressing himself to Call. "You don't come in here and order me to let criminals out of my own jail."

"They aren't criminals, and you've overstepped," Call said. "Let them out."

"I'll let your man go the day I hang the Indian, and I'll hang the Indian in my own good time," Sheriff Doniphan said.

Call saw a ring of jail keys hanging on a hook near the sheriff's desk. He walked over and took the ring and went to the cell where Pea Eye sat. He saw the sheriff draw his gun, but paid it no mind; he didn't expect the man to shoot. After all, he had his back to him, and there were five witnesses in the room.

The third key he tried opened the cell. Then Call found the key that freed Famous Shoes.

"They're dead men if they step out of them cells," Doniphan said. "I don't tolerate escapes."

Brookshire, watching from just inside the door, felt that the Captain might have made a mistake. The sheriff didn't seem to be a relenting man. In that respect, he reminded him of Colonel Terry. The fact that the Captain was just ignoring the sheriff made Brookshire nervous. If the sheriff pulled the trigger, everything would change. Doniphan might shoot them all; he might even shoot his own deputy. He looked to be a man who acted only for himself, as Colonel Terry did. Brookshire wondered if the Captain had miscalculated. If so, Call exhibited little concern.

Then, to Brookshire's astonishment, Call flattened the sheriff with a rifle. He whacked him right in the neck with a hard swing. He hadn't been carrying a rifle, though there were several in a gun rack along the wall. Somehow the Captain, who usually moved slowly and stiffly, had walked right in front of the sheriff, ignored his cocked pistol, pulled loose a rifle, and hit the sheriff with it.

The minute he struck the blow, the Captain seemed to change. He didn't stop with one blow, although Doniphan was knocked flat, and his pistol went skittering across the floor of the jail. Call continued to hit the sheriff with the rifle. Once, when the sheriff turned to try and escape, the Captain knocked him in the ear with his boot, so hard that Brookshire would not have been surprised if Doniphan's head had flown off.

"Stop, Captain, he's subdued," Pea Eye said, though he knew the Captain wouldn't stop. He rarely went off into such a storm of violence, but when he did, it was almost impossible to stop him. Once, in Ogallala years before, the Captain had launched himself at a sergeant who was quirting Newt. Before that storm ended, the Captain had almost killed the man by pounding his head against an anvil. Gus McCrae had stopped it by roping the Captain and pulling him off the bloody sergeant with his horse.

There was no Gus, no rope, and no horse, but Pea Eye knew the Captain had to be stopped somehow, or else Sheriff Doniphan would be dead. Once the storm of rage took him, the Captain could no more stop hitting and kicking than a blizzard could stop blowing. Pea Eye saw the Captain lift the bloody rifle for what might be a fatal blow, and flung himself at Call—there was no waiting, and no choice.

"Help me, you've all got to help me!" Pea Eye yelled. He partially deflected the rifle with his arm as the blow fell that might have killed Sheriff Doniphan.

The one-eared deputy, Tom Johnson, tried to grab one of the Captain's arms, but was immediately knocked back. Pea Eye concentrated on the rifle, trying to keep the Captain from splitting Doniphan's skull with it. He managed to hang on to one arm, but he knew it wouldn't be for long.

"Somebody's got to rope him, it's the only way," Pea said, looking desperately at the Yankee.

"Here, ride your horse up, give me your rope!" Brookshire yelled out the door to Deputy Plunkert, who, though taken by surprise, immediately spurred his horse up the few steps to the porch of the jail. He handed Brookshire his rope.

[299]

"I'll get it on him, then you pull," Brookshire said. He was trembling from the shock, but he managed to make a loop in the end of the rope. He got close enough to the Captain to get the loop over one of his feet as Call was trying to step free of the fallen sheriff so he could kick him again.

"Pull!" Brookshire yelled. He had never seen such a killing frenzy take any man. Merely witnessing the destruction of the sheriff made Brookshire's breath come short, and his heart pound uncomfortably. But he knew he had to get the rope on some part of Call, or the sheriff of Presidio would be dead.

Deputy Plunkert dallied the rope around his saddle horn and backed his horse along the narrow porch until it grew tight. He soon discovered, to his amazement, that Captain Call was on the other end. He held a bloody rifle in one hand, and for a moment, looked as if he wanted to club Brookshire with it. But he didn't. He shook Pea Eye off and then shook the rope off his foot. He broke the bloody rifle over the hitch rail and threw the two parts of it into the street.

Call went back inside, dragged the bloody, unconscious sheriff into the cell where Famous Shoes had been, and locked it. He took the big ring of keys outside and threw them into the cistern at the end of the porch. When he passed Pea Eye, Brookshire, and the one-eared deputy, each drew back a little, as they might if a bear had just approached them.

"When he comes round, tell him the next time he points a damn pistol at me, he'd better shoot," Call told the one-eared deputy. "I won't tolerate rude threats of that sort."

"Yes, sir," Tom Johnson said.

Privately, he was not sure Sheriff Doniphan would come around. Men had died from much less punishment than the Captain had just dished out. The sheriff's mouth was leaking blood, and not slowly, either. One whole side of his face seemed to be caved in, and his long mustache was just a line of blood.

Call knew that his violent fighting temper had gotten the best of him again, but he did not pretend to regret his attack on the sheriff, who had pulled a gun and threatened to shoot two valuable men, and in defiance of the governor's orders, too. He would have liked to do worse than he had done, but he'd gotten enough of a grip on himself to refrain from dragging the man out of his cell and finishing him.

What he did do was pick up the telegram the frightened deputy had dropped. He put the telegram on the sheriff's desk.

"Remind him that I was following the 'governor's instructions," Call said. "Read him the telegram."

"Yes, sir," Tom Johnson said again. "I'll remind him. I expect he'll listen, this time."

"Yes, if his ears ain't burst," Pea Eye said. "The Captain caught one of his ears a pretty good lick."

"We're provisioned, let's go," Call said. He felt that he had returned to normal, but the men were looking at him oddly— all the men but Famous Shoes, who had found a half-eaten plate of beans and was eating them.

Pea Eye saw the Captain looking at Famous Shoes in a testy way, and thought he had better explain.

"He wasn't allowed no food for two days, that's why he's into them beans," he said.

Famous Shoes could not understand why the foolish white men had kept the Captain from killing the hard sheriff. It was very foolish, in his view. The sheriff had been about to shoot them all, and he might try it again, if he lived. Famous Shoes was not sure the sheriff would live, though. The Captain had dealt him some hard licks, mostly to the head. The way the Captain's anger came reminded Famous Shoes of old Kicking Bird, a Comanche chief given to terrible furies. When Kicking Bird went into a rage, he was apt to injure anyone near him, including members of his own tribe. He was a great fighting man, but he fought so hard that he lost track of who it was he was fighting and merely killed everyone near him. Once, he had grievously wounded his own brother, while in such a rage.

"We need you to help us track this Garza boy. Are you available?" Call asked. He noticed there was quite a bit of blood on the floor of the jail. The one-eared deputy would have to get out his mop, once they left.

"Yes," Famous Shoes said. "You don't have to pay me, either. Pea Eye's woman is going to teach me to read. That and something to eat will be wages enough, this time."

"Hired, I guess, if Pea Eye's wife agrees," Call said. "Let's go."

Deputy Plunkert, who had spurred his horse onto the porch of the jail with no difficulty in response to Brookshire's plea, had great difficulty getting the horse to go back down the steps. Pea Eye finally whacked the animal a time or two, and the horse jumped as far out into the street as it could, nearly knocking down one of the waiting pack mules when it landed.

Call was composed by this time. He wanted to get started, and not waste an afternoon. The men were all subdued, all except Famous Shoes, who was already half a mile ahead of them, proceeding at his customary rapid pace.

Brookshire felt so weak that he could barely mount. The shock of seeing Captain Call suddenly hit the sheriff with the rifle, and then continue to hit him, had been almost too much for his system. He felt very tired, and once more thought wistfully of how nice it would be to spend the night in a decent hotel. That was not to be, though, not for a while. They had already left Presidio behind them.

The thing that troubled Brookshire most was that his memory of the incident was incomplete. He had been watching the Captain carefully, hoping Call was not misjudging the sheriff's temper; yet, somehow, his eyes had failed him. He didn't see the Captain walk from the cells, past the sheriff, to the rack of rifles. Whatever happened had happened too fast, or else his brain had cut off for a moment, or something. One minute the Captain was releasing Famous Shoes; the next, there was the sound of the rifle barrel hitting the sheriff. Brookshire considered it spooky. He couldn't explain it.

He had no doubt about one thing, though: Colonel Terry, in his wisdom, and he did seem to have wisdom, had clearly chosen the right man for the job at hand. The Garza boy would need more than a German rifle with a telescope sight when the

Captain caught up with him. If the boy was smart, he would just surrender, and not let himself in for the kind of punishment that had just befallen the unfortunate Sheriff Doniphan.

It took the one-eared deputy, Tom Johnson, and such towns-people as gathered to help, over three hours to fish the jail keys out of the cistern. Fortunately, the hardware store had a big magnet that was used to sort nails, and with the aid of the magnet, tied to three lariat ropes, the keys were finally brought up.

Sheriff Joe Doniphan was still unconscious when they opened the cell. He was conscious only fitfully for the next several days. His right jawbone was broken in seven places, and his palate damaged. He lost all his teeth on that side of his mouth, and eventually had to have his other teeth pulled in order to bring his bite into balance.

Also, three ribs were broken, and one leg. The leg was set improperly. The local doctor was so worried about the jaw that he made a hurried job of the leg, the result being that Sheriff Doniphan limped for the rest of his life. He resigned as sheriff a month after the beating. No one, including his wife, could stand to see his mashed-in face. He retired to his house and sat in the bedroom most of the day, with the shades pulled, whittling sticks. He didn't whittle them into any shape, he just whittled them away. The memory of his own inaction, at the fatal moment, was what haunted the ex-sheriff most. He had been holding a pistol, cocked and pointed right at the old man. He could have shot him at any moment, and justified it on the grounds that Call was helping a known criminal escape. Of course, the telegram from the governor was awkward; Deputy Johnson had preserved it, for the townspeople to see. But Doniphan could have argued that he never saw it, and had reason to suspect its authenticity.

The point was, he hadn't shot. He had let an old man whip him nearly to the point of death, with one of his own guns, in his own jail, in front of five people. He hadn't shot; he had just stood there.

It was a failure the former sheriff, Joe Doniphan, couldn't live with. The next time he lifted a gun to shoot, a little less than a year after the beating, but long after the pursuit of Joey Garza had ended, it was to put a .45 caliber bullet into his own brain. His wife, Martha, was in the kitchen, rolling biscuit dough. When she heard the gun go off in the bedroom, Martha was glad.

6.

Doobie Plunkert had only gone by the jail to see if there was any news of Ted; after all, Sheriff Bob Jekyll was known to be lazy. He didn't care whether Doobie had any news of Ted, or whether Ted was alive or dead, for that matter. He wouldn't walk up the street to her house to bring her news, even if he had any.

Doobie knew there probably wasn't any news, though; there hadn't been a word, since the day Ted left. It seemed to Doobie that he had now been gone most of the time since they married. She had even begun to forget bits and pieces of her early married life, though her early married life had happened less than a year ago. It was just that the terrible loneliness she felt, now that Ted was gone, had cut her off from her own good memories.

Doobie knew that when Ted finally came home, they would be the happiest couple in the world. And she would know what to do the next time some old sheriff rode into town and tried to take her husband away. Next time, Doobie was determined to fight, and she meant to win, too. Next time, she wasn't going to let her husband go.

But chill day after chill day passed, with no word from Ted at all, or of Ted, and Doobie had become a little desperate. Every day, she went to the little post office in the back of the hardware store, hoping there would be a letter. She knew Ted wasn't much for writing, since it was all he could do to make a sentence. But still, he might pass through a town that had a post office, and he might be tempted to write her at least a note, so she would know he was alive.

She knew Bob Jekyll didn't really want her coming around the jail, whether Ted was on duty or not, but the jail was the place news would be most likely to show up. The hunger for at least some word of her husband gnawed at Doobie so deeply that she couldn't stop showing up at the jail, just to peek in and ask Sheriff Jekyll what he had heard. Captain Call was a famous man; surely there would be some news of the Captain and his party, sometime.

In the nights, Doobie began to be prey to even more terrible fears. What if Ted was lost? What if the whole party had starved, or been killed by Indians? She knew there were still wild Indians in Mexico—what if they had killed Ted in a place where no one would even find his body? What if she had the baby and it grew up and neither of them ever heard another word about Ted Plunkert in the whole of their lives?

Doobie tried to make herself stay away from the jail, but on days when she was particularly worried, or had had a particularly bad night, it was hard. Her feet just seemed to take her in the direction of the jail, the one place where there might be news.

Doobie never supposed, not for one moment, that Sheriff Jekyll might take this wrong. She felt he must know that the one and only reason she pestered him was because she loved her husband so much, and was desperate for news. Everyone in Laredo, Texas, knew how much Doobie Plunkert loved her husband. They were the happiest young couple in the community. That was common knowledge.

Doobie had seen Sheriff Jekyll looking at her that way once or twice, that way men looked at women. It was part of being a woman, she supposed. Men just would look at you, that way. Susanna Slack, her best friend, told her it was merely the way of the world. Men looked at Susanna that way too, although she was an older woman. Doobie hoped that Sheriff Jekyll and the men of Laredo in general might be a little more respectful in their manner of looking, once it became obvious that she was enceinte; they should not be casting disrespectful looks at a woman who was soon to have a baby.

When Doobie realized that Bob Jekyll was looking at her that way more intently than usual, and was even moving toward her, she tried to dart back out the door of the jail to safety, but she was a step too slow. Bob Jekyll caught her arm and started dragging her toward a cell with a cot in it. The jail was completely empty, too; there was not a single prisoner, not a soul for Doobie to cry out to.

"You keep coming here—now, shut up!" Bob Jekyll said, as he dragged Doobie toward the cell. When Doobie opened her mouth to scream, Bob Jekyll punched her so hard it stunned her. He had been standing right by the door, looking at her with that look, when she stepped inside the jailhouse, full of hope that there might be some news of Ted.

Doobie didn't want to be punched again. She was afraid Bob Jekyll might hit her in the stomach and injure her baby. She was inside the cell, pinned to the cot, before she started fighting again. She had never hoped to see any man on earth except her husband with his pants pulled down, but Sheriff Jekyll had his pants down, and he was pulling at her drawers. Doobie tried to claw him, but when she did, he punched her so hard again that she lost consciousness for a minute. When her head cleared a little, Sheriff Jekyll was there, doing what only her husband had the right to do.

Doobie gave up then. A sorrow came to her as deep as the bone, for everything was lost now; even her baby was lost. Sheriff Bob Jekyll had destroyed her virtue, and her future, too. It wouldn't even matter if Ted came back now, for he would never forgive her. Perhaps he would not even believe her when she said she only went to the jail hoping for news of him. Even if he did come back, their happiness was lost.

Doobie became so hopeless that the sheriff grew disgusted with her. As soon as he had pleased himself, he told her to get out of his jail and stay out. He went over to his desk and didn't look at Doobie again.

He hadn't torn her dress; only her drawers had been ripped. Doobie didn't know what his punches had done to her face, but at least she could walk the few blocks home dressed respectably. One or two people even spoke to her, as she hurried up the street. Doobie managed a good morning to them, though it wasn't a good morning. What it had turned out to be, in the course of a few minutes, was the last morning of her life.

Doobie loved Ted Plunkert with all her heart and would never have done anything to bring dishonor to him. The knowledge that she mustn't let dishonor stain their marriage helped her keep a firm resolve. She wanted to die as quickly as possible, before she weakened. She thought about writing Ted a note, but dismissed that notion at once. She would never be able to explain; it would be better to let Ted think she had just gone crazy from loneliness, from missing him. She wasn't going to burden her husband with the awful truth.

Doobie couldn't help but cry. Now she knew how swiftly all the good things of life could be lost. Her marriage was lost, and her baby; compared to those griefs, the loss of her own physical life seemed minor. She only wanted to hurry with dying. She didn't want someone to come and interrupt her before she could do what she had to do. She ran to her kitchen and quickly dug out the rat poison.

Laredo was overrun with giant brown pack rats that lived under houses and also under the giant piles of prickly pear. Sometimes the Mexicans stuffed the ratholes and set the piles of prickly pear afire. Once the fire burned down, they dug out the rats and ate them.

Doobie thought that was a horrible practice. She hated the rats, and considered that one of her own duties as a housewife was to keep their little house free of them. She spread the rat poison carefully around all the places a rat might get in. Once in a while, a rat would die under the house, and she and Ted would smell it, but mainly, the rats ran off to the river to die.

Doobie felt very calm about what she had to do, until she

started trying to eat the rat poison. She got a big spoon and tried to eat it straight down, like the oatmeal she sometimes made Ted in the mornings. But rat poison wouldn't go down like oatmeal, and it only made her gag. When it got moist, it stuck to her teeth and to the roof of her mouth, and became very hard to swallow. Doobie stopped being calm and became frantic. What if she failed to die and Ted had to come home to a wife who was no longer worthy, a wife who had carelessly let her virtue be lost to the lust of Sheriff Bob Jekyll? Ted Plunkert would never get over such a thing. Doobie knew she mustn't let him know. It would be a terrible failure if she let Ted find out the truth. She thought about hanging herself, but that was chancy, since she had never been very good at tying knots. If she tried to hang herself, somebody might find her while she was still alive.

Ted had explained to her that water helped the rat poison work. When the rats ate the poison, it made them thirsty and they ran off to the river to drink. Then the water made the poison work, and the rats died.

The minute she remembered what Ted had told her, Doobie took the big can of rat poison and a cup and went out her back door. The river was only two streets away. She walked toward it swiftly, hoping no one would see her or speak to her. She made it to the river unobserved, and began to stuff poison in her mouth and then drink water. Then, it occurred to her that she could mix the poison with water. She began to scoop water into the cup and mix it with poison. After that, the whole business went more quickly. It was working, too—Doobie began to feel a pain inside, down in her belly. It was as if something with sharp claws was pulling on her guts. She cried at the thought that her baby might be feeling the clawing too. But she kept scooping poison into the cup and filling it with water. She drank and scooped poison and drank. It was her way of doing right by Ted. The worse the clawing hurt, the more sure Doobie was that she would triumph. Ted would be sad when he found out that she was dead, but he wouldn't have to try to live down the terrible thing that had happened. He would get over her death, in time, but neither of them would ever be able to put right what had happened in the jail.

Doobie's hand got shaky. She began to spill the poison when she tried to scoop it into her cup. Some of it spilled into the river. It was yellow, and it flowed away with the brown water.

Doobie had not been paying attention to anything but drinking the poison, but as the clawing got sharper, and it felt as if her insides were being ripped by claws and squeezed together at the same time, she happened to see a dead rat lying at the edge of the water, only a few yards away. Its mouth was open, and she could see its ugly teeth. It lay with most of its body in the water, and its brown fur was wet. Maybe the rat had died from eating some of the very poison she was drinking down.

In just a few minutes, Doobie hoped, she would be as dead as the rat. She might roll into the river, just as it had. She might be wet too, when people found her. But she didn't want that, she didn't want to be found all wet and messy. She began to crawl farther from the water. The bright sun began to affect her. She wanted to hide her eyes from the sun. She began to curl up, in order to hide her eyes. But when she curled up, the pain in her gut became unbearable. She tried to straighten up again, but the pain in her belly was now just as bad, no matter how she lay or sat, no matter whether she was curled or straight. For a second, Doobie wanted to give up. She wanted to run to a doctor and have him give her something to stop the pain. But she couldn't run, or even stand. She began to roll around and had soon rolled back down to the river's edge. One of her feet knocked over the can of rat poison, but not much spilled because there wasn't much poison left in the can. Doobie had eaten or drunk most of what had been in it. She didn't feel good at all anymore; she didn't feel anything but a clawing, needling pain. She tried to cry out, but the poison gummed in her mouth so that she could only make a weak sound, a sound no one passing would even hear.

Doobie continued to make a weak sound, no louder than a rat's squeak, until her voice stopped and she made no sound at all.

7.

On the coldest night, the night of the great ice storm, Maria thought she and all the women might freeze. The fires she made sputtered and blew out. The two old Mexican women were almost dead anyway. Maria had to go back and find them. One of them had fallen three miles behind the group. Maria hunted wood and kept the fires going, but ice had covered everything, and her hands and feet got very cold.

"Don't make me go no farther. I'd rather give up and die," Cherie said. Her real name wasn't Cherie, but she was so cold, and had stopped using her real name so long ago, that it didn't matter what it had been. Patrick, the saloonkeeper, had brought her to Crow Town, only to abandon her for another woman. She had been there five years, and she'd had to struggle so hard that she lost her memory of other places.

The women were convinced that they would all die. They didn't believe they would live to reach the railroad, and several of them had ceased to care. Gabriela and Marieta were numb, their feet so cold they couldn't feel them. Beulah kept trying to stop. Maria had to push her and prod her to keep her going.

They had not even crossed the Pecos yet; Maria kept angling away from it, hoping for a warmer day before she had to try to bring the women across. She had fixed her mind on saving the women, though she didn't know any of them. Getting them

safely to the railroad had become important to her. She had
taken them out of the town, even though she hadn't wanted to
at first. But she had accepted their need to go, and now she felt
she must supply the will to keep them traveling, despite the
bitter cold. She herself had often had to search for will, in hard
times. When the men from Texas pretended to hang her, she
had tried to make her will stop, so she could die. She had wanted
to elude them, that way. Again, when they were degrading her,
she would have liked for her will to stop. She would have rather
not been alive anymore. And, as she had lost hope with her
husbands, each in turn—except for Benito, she had never lost
hope with Benito—she had sometimes wished in the night that
she could just stop breathing, and not be there in the morning
and have to get out of the bed in hopelessness to deal with the
man who was making her hopeless, week after week and year
after year.

It was in those times that Billy Williams had proven himself a
true friend. He would cajole her over to the cantina, make her
drink until she felt like dancing, or dance until she felt like
drinking. Somehow, Billy could make her laugh. That was a
rare thing too, for a man to be able to make her laugh. With
women, Maria laughed; with her children, she laughed; but
rarely did she laugh with a man. She only laughed with Billy
Williams.

The lack of laughter in her life was a thing Maria held against
men. She felt she had the temperament to be a happy woman,
if she was not interfered with, too much. She knew that it was
her fault that she let men interfere with her; yet if she didn't,
there was nothing, or at least there was not enough. She wanted
a man to lay with, except if she wanted a man once, she would
want him many times. She liked to take pleasure from men, and
liked to give it, but when she gave men that pleasure, they came
to need it and then to resent her because they needed her.
When that happened, the interfering began. Maria didn't know
why men resented the very women who gave them the most
pleasure, and gave it generously. It was foolish, very foolish, of
men to resent the good that came from women. Still, they did.

Thinking of Billy Williams, and all the times he had made her laugh, kept Maria's mind off the icy ground and the sheaths of ice on the mesquite limbs she broke off to keep the fire going. She made three fires, and kept them all going herself. The women were too tired and numb to move. She put the women in a little triangle, between the fires.

But it was bitter cold, and even three fires were not enough. It was too cold, and the women were too tired and broken. Maria knew she had to do something else, or the women would give up and begin to die.

She thought about the things she talked about with the women of her village, when they were washing clothes together or cooking for a little fiesta. Those were times when she and the women were apt to get bawdy and talk about the embarrassments or the rewards of love. None of the women huddled between the fires looked as if they had known love recently. Men might have used them, especially the young ones, but that was different. The women might not be able to remember a time when love had been an exciting thing, but Maria decided she wanted to make them try. It was a long time until dawn, and they had nothing but three small, sputtering fires to get them through the night. There had to be something more. Maybe she could get the women to tell stories about their lives. Maybe the memory of times when life had been exciting would make them want to live through the freezing night.

"Tell me about your first man," Maria said. She addressed the question to Beulah.

"What?" Beulah said. She thought she must have heard Maria wrong.

"I want to know about your first man," Maria said.

Then she looked at Cherie.

"I want to know about yours, too," she said. "My first man was a vaquero. He came riding into town, and when he got off his horse and walked to the cantina, his spurs jingled. From the time I heard his spurs, I knew I wanted to be his woman."

"Oh, Lord," Cherie said.

Maria waited. Marieta and Gabriela paid no attention; they had not even heard Maria's words. But the oldest woman in the group, a thin, old woman named Maggie, showed a spark of interest. Maggie had been one that Maria had to go back for several times. Once, Maria had found her kneeling by a little bush. She was crouched behind the bush as if she expected it to keep the cold wind from biting her.

Yet Maggie had recovered a little. She looked at Maria with curiosity.

"Did you get the vaquero?" Maggie asked.

"Yes, he was my first husband," Maria said. "We had good times—but then, he got mean. I still remember the sound of his spurs, the first time I saw him. When I think of him now, it's the spurs I remember."

"I was married to a circus man, first," Maggie said. "Mostly, he was a juggler. He could keep seven barbells up in the air at the same time, when he was sober."

"Where did you live?" Maria asked.

"Boston, for a little while," Maggie said. "Then he took me to New Orleans. He was going to marry me, but he never did. Them mosquitoes in New Orleans was bad. I'd get so I wanted to drown myself, rather than be bit by them mosquitoes."

"They're bad in Houston, too," Beulah said. "It's swampy down there in Houston."

"Jimmy drunk too much to be a juggler," Maggie said. "He'd drink all night and then the next day, he'd miss two or three of them barbells." Maggie chuckled, at the memory.

"Them barbells are heavy," she said. "I couldn't even juggle two. If one was to crack me in the head, I wouldn't be able to walk straight for a week."

"You can't go off with men and expect them to marry you," Beulah said. "That's the mistake I kept making. Now, here I am, an old maid."

Several of the women looked at her when she said it. Beulah realized that her last remark must have sounded a little odd. She smiled at herself.

"Well, I mean, I never married," she explained.

Maggie, now that she had begun to talk, wasn't interested in listening to anyone else.

"Jimmy cracked himself in the head so many times that he got where he couldn't walk the tightrope," she said. "He wasn't no tightrope walker anyway, but he wanted to be the star of the show. I told him to stay off the dern tightrope, but he didn't listen to me. I started up with a trick rider about that time. Jimmy found himself a high yellow woman, but she had a temper, and Jimmy didn't want nothing to do with women who had tempers."

"Didn't you have a temper?" Maria asked.

"No, I was just a girl then," Maggie said. "I was all in love, and I wanted to do whatever Jimmy wanted me to. I didn't put up no fight, but that high yellow woman did."

All the women, even Marieta and Gabriela, were listening to Maggie. Maria had not expected it to be Maggie who talked; she thought Maggie was too far gone. But that proved to be a misjudgment. Maggie had some spirit left. She knew everybody was listening to her, and she liked the attention.

"What was the trick rider like?" Maria asked.

"He was just a trick rider," Maggie said. "He could stand on his head on a horse, with the horse running full speed, but he wasn't no good with women. I got tired of the circus life and ran off with a smuggler. He was my first husband, and he took me to sea. We'd be rollin' around in one of them narrow bunks and sometimes we'd roll one way and the ship would roll another, and we'd go sailin' right out of that bunk."

She cackled at her own memory. "That was forty years ago, that I married Eddie," Maggie said. "I'm surprised I can still remember him. He got caught smuggling niggers, and they hung him."

"Was it a crime to smuggle niggers?" Cherie asked. "I thought back then you could buy them and sell them any time you wanted to."

"You could, but Eddie wasn't buying them," Maggie said. "He was smuggling stolen niggers. I can still remember them nigger women, howlin' down in the bottom of that ship. Eddie and the boys would lash 'em good, trying to get them to shut up when they was coming into port. But they would keep on howlin'. That was how Eddie got caught. I told him he ought to just smuggle buck niggers. The bucks didn't howl as much. But Eddie never listened to me, and he got his neck stretched, as a result."

"Men don't listen," Beulah agreed. "I could have made Red Foot rich, if he'd listened to me when we were in the saloon business, in Dodge. I told him it was time to go to Deadwood. They say nearly everyone who opened a saloon in Deadwood in those days got rich. There's just more loose money where there's miners.

"But we come to Crow Town instead," she added. "Red heard it was booming, but there sure wasn't no boom when we got there."

Maggie was so eager to talk by this time that she could hardly check herself and wait for Beulah to shut up.

"The circus was in St. Louis when Eddie got hung," Maggie said. "I went up to Vicksburg on one boat, and then I rode on another boat that had a train on it."

"A train?" Cherie asked. "Why would a train be on a boat?" She decided the old woman was telling lies and nothing but lies. She had thought as much back in Crow Town, too. Old Maggie did nothing but lie. Cherie didn't resent it, particularly. Maybe the old crone actually believed everything she said. Anyway, listening to her brag about all the men she'd had was something to do while they were sitting and freezing.

"It wasn't the whole train, it was just the locomotive," Maggie said. "They were taking it upriver somewhere. I couldn't sleep because I got to worrying that the locomotive would bust loose and sink the boat. We got to St. Louis, though, and the first person I saw when I got off the boat was Jimmy. He had almost cut his nose off. It was sewed on, but it didn't look right, and it never did look right after that."

"Was it a woman that cut his nose off?" Maria asked. She had heard that among the Apaches, such things occurred.

"No, it was the tightrope," Maggie said. "Jimmy kept trying to walk it, but he was wobbly from hitting himself in the head too many times with them barbells. He fell off the tightrope, and it hit him right under the nose and nearly cut his nose off."

"What's a circus?" Marieta asked. She didn't understand the talk of barbells and jugglers.

"Did you ever get up to Deadwood?" Beulah asked. "I still have a hankering to go."

"No, I worked on a riverboat," Maggie said. "I went up and down the river I don't know how many times, until I got tired of hearing the water slosh. Then, I married another fool who got hung, and then I married Ross. I was soon wishing they'd hang Ross. He beat me so bad, I couldn't turn over in my own bed. Ross had fists like bricks."

"How did you get rid of him?" Sally asked. Sally was about Beulah's age. She had two big moles just above her upper lip.

"Ross stepped on a nail and got blood poisoning and died," Maggie said. "It saved me. He would have broken every bone in my body if he hadn't stepped on that nail."

Maggie smiled, and cackled again. She looked like a wicked old woman, but she was still alive, and she liked to talk.

"I didn't go to Ross's funeral. I didn't figure I owed Ross nothing," she said. "But a few days later, I went to the funeral of one of my girlfriends. Three days later, the preacher that preached it came up and asked me to marry him. That's how pretty I was, when I still had my looks. I never knew preachers liked women that much, until the Reverend Jonah got ahold of me."

"They do—one got after me, too," Beulah said.

As Maggie and Beulah talked on, a tiredness began to come to Maria. She had kept the women going for three days, leading them, encouraging them, going back for them. She had gathered most of the frozen wood they burned, and she had made the fires. She heard Maggie talking about her preacher, and Beulah about hers, but Maria began to lose the names that went with the stories. The sound of the women's voices lulled her. It was better to hear women talk, even if she was too tired to listen, than to have only the silence and the cold. Maria would have liked to be fresh, to tell some of her own stories too, but it would have to be another time, when they all reached the railroad and were safe.

Maria's eyes grew so heavy she could not watch the fire. She slumped over, and her serape slipped off her shoulders.

Sally, who was closest, got up and wrapped the serape back around Maria, pulling it tight so it would not slip off again. She fed the fire a few sticks, from a pile Maria had gathered. Maria had come back for Sally when Sally was freezing, and Sally didn't want her to sleep cold.

"She's tuckered out," Maggie said. Then she went on to tell the women about some of the peculiarities of the Reverend Jonah, the preacher who had loved her in St. Louis, long ago when she still had her looks.

8.

When Lorena got off the train in Laredo, the first thing she saw was a funeral procession, and the first person she spoke to was Tinkersley. As she stepped out of the little railroad station and stopped to watch the funeral procession—it seemed as if everyone in town was following the wagon that had the coffin in it—a tired-looking older man in a slick, brown coat looked at her, and stopped and looked again.

"Why, Lorie," he said. "Could it really be you?"

Lorena supposed the mayor must have died. She had never seen such a lengthy funeral procession, in a town the size of Laredo. Even in Ogallala they would have had a hard time getting so many people to march behind a coffin. She looked again at the man who had called her by her name. He had few teeth, and bags hung halfway down his cheeks. He wore a sporty hat, but it was not new. A rat or something had chewed a piece out of the brim.

"Lorie, it's me, Tinkersley," the man said. "It's you, ain't it? Tell me it's you."

"I'm Lorena, I'm married now," Lorena said. Tinkersley ran whores and gambled. No doubt he was still running whores and gambling, though not so prosperously as he had been when she knew him. Tinkersley had brought her to south Texas, when she was a young whore. In a San Antonio hotel room, during a fight, he had bitten her on the upper lip, leaving a faint scar that she still had.

Now here he was in Laredo, watching a lengthy funeral procession. She saw a familiar light come into his eyes, from looking at her. She wanted to immediately put it out.

"I've come here to look for my husband. He's with Captain Call, or at least, I hope he is," she said. "Who died?"

"Her name was Doobie Plunkert. She was well liked in the town," Tinkersley said. "I liked her myself, although we only met once. That's why I lent my whores, for the singing.

"I run the whores in this town," he went on. "They wanted a big singing for Doobie, so I lent them six girls. I just kept back two, to take care of the customers until the funeral is over."

Lorena saw the whores, in a group, well behind the coffin hearse, with some more churchly-looking women marching just ahead of them, right behind the wagon.

"I'm surprised they'd let whores sing at a proper funeral," Lorena said. "Was the woman a whore?"

"No, she was the wife of a deputy sheriff. He's gone with old Call, too, like your husband," Tinkersley said. "Sheriff Jekyll raped Doobie, and she took poison and died. It's a pity. The man could have bought a whore, and spared poor Mrs. Plunkert."

The young woman must have felt hopeless, Lorena thought. She hadn't wanted her husband to find out what happened. Lorena set down her valise, leaving it on the railroad station platform, and began to walk along with the funeral.

Tinkersley, after a moment's hesitation, fell in with her.

Lorena didn't try to stop him. What Tinkersley did didn't matter. She supposed it was even rather nice of him, to let his whores sing at the funeral. He probably charged the church a fee, or tried to, but at least he let them sing.

"What kind of poison?" Lorena asked.

"Well, rat poison. She drank most of it in water," Tinkersley said. "They found her by the river. She wasn't quite dead at the time. It was the doctor who noticed that her drawers were torn, and that somebody had hit her a lick or two. They found a little ribbon from her dress in a cell in the jail, and that's what nailed the sheriff."

Lorena regretted that the train had come in when it did. She would rather not have known about the death of Mrs. Plunkert. They had never met, of course, but Lorena had been alone, in south Texas, in rooms that were no more than jails, with men who were no different from the sheriff, and who were certainly no better. She had no way out then, and only one way to survive; many times, it had seemed to her a close bargain. In even worse times, when she was taken by Blue Duck and given to the men of Ermoke's band, and then threatened with burning by Mox Mox, she had been reduced to one wish: that there was some way to be dead, and be dead quickly. Although the circumstances of Mrs. Plunkert's travail might seem lighter, Lorena knew they had not seemed at all light to the young woman who had so promptly taken her own life. Mrs. Plunkert must have felt that her happiness and her husband's happiness were forfeit anyway. She had become hopeless. Lorena knew enough about hopelessness. She did not want to be reminded of it, not even a hopelessness experienced by a young woman she had never met.

What the death of Mrs. Plunkert meant was that hopelessness was always there. There was never a way or a time one could be safe from it. If Pea Eye died, or one of her children, she knew she would have to feel it again.

"Lorie, you don't know her, you ain't expected to attend the funeral," Tinkersley said.

"I want to attend the funeral, but I'd rather you didn't accompany me," Lorena said.

"But you didn't know the woman," Tinkersley said. He felt a sudden deep need to stay with Lorena. Seeing her had reminded him of the regret he had nursed for years, when he'd left her and lost her. He had even journeyed to the little town of Lonesome Dove, where he heard she worked, hoping to get her back. But he came too late. She had left with the cow herd and the cowboys, for Montana.

Now, through a miracle, she had stepped off the train in

Laredo, right in front of him. He didn't want to leave her. When she told him she didn't want him to accompany her to the funeral, he fell back a few steps, but he didn't let Lorena out of his sight.

The cemetery was just a plain piece of ground, dusty, without a bush or a tree to lessen its plainness. Most of the grave markers were wooden, and many of them had tilted over, or fallen flat altogether. One of the whores, the smallest, a slip of a girl with curly brown hair, had a beautiful soprano voice.

When she sang "Amazing Grace," her voice rose over all the other singers, the other five whores and the few churchwomen. Her voice was clear as the air. They sang "Rock of Ages," and then "Will the Circle Be Unbroken." Three hymns at a funeral was unusual, Lorena thought. Yet, despite the cutting wind, the mourners seemed reluctant to leave. When the women finished the last song, they looked around, wondering if they should sing more. It was odd, Lorena thought, that no one was hurrying away.

The young whore with the beautiful voice finally spoke to one of the churchwomen, and the women began to sing "There's a Home Beyond the River."

The young soprano poured her heart into the song. No doubt she had an inkling of how Mrs. Plunkert had felt. That, at least, was Lorena's view. The girl's voice was so strong and pure that it silenced the other singers. One by one, the other whores and the churchwomen fell silent, and the beautiful voice of the whore with the curly hair soared on, in lonely lament for the lost life of a woman the young whore had not known, and perhaps had not even met.

When the song ended, the mourners turned away from the grave, and an old Mexican man with a shovel began to push in dirt around the coffin.

"At least she had a right pretty funeral," Tinkersley said. He fell in with Lorena as she was hurrying back to the station, anxious to secure her valise. Tinkersley was seeking to make small talk, or any talk, that would persuade her to allow him to stay with her for a while.

"Get away from me, Tinkersley," Lorena said. "You done nothing but hurt me, when we was together. I don't want you to be walking with me. I'm here to find my husband."

"But, I bought you pretty dresses," Tinkersley protested. "I took you to the fanciest shop in San Antonio."

"So you could sell me for a higher price," Lorena reminded him. "Get away from me. I don't like remembering none of that."

"Lorie, I was just hoping we could visit," Tinkersley said. "I know I done you badly. I came back to find you, but you were gone north with Gus McCrae."

Lorena didn't speak to Tinkersley again. She just ignored him. He walked with her, pleading, until they were nearly back to the station, but Lorena didn't say another word. She scarcely noticed him, in his slick coat, nor did she listen to his excuses or his pleas. She felt a great longing to be with her husband. Most men would make excuses all day and all night for their failings, but Pea never did. When Pea did something that hurt her feelings, he accepted his error and suffered for it until she had to take him in hand and try to coax him and tease him back into a good humor. She had to convince him, each time, that what he had done was only a small error, not the unforgivable act he believed it to be. Marriage was often vexing, that was all.

Now, with the funeral over, she wanted to gather such information about where Captain Call might be as she could. She wanted to catch up with Pea and bring him home, before one of the bad men in the world did something to hurt him.

It was not until that night, in her small, chill room in the drafty hotel, that Lorena's thoughts returned to the dead woman and the funeral. She remembered the young whore who could sing soprano, and a deep sadness came with the memory. In a building not far away, the young whore with the beautiful voice was back being a whore. The churchwomen who had spoken to her at the funeral wouldn't allow themselves to speak to her in their day-to-day lives. She was just one of Tinkersley's whores, as Lorena herself had been, once.

The only thing that was true in the four hymns the girl had

sung was the music itself, Lorena thought. Neither the whore nor the dead woman over whose grave she'd sung had received any grace at all, to draw upon; nor did they have any rock to stand on; nor any circle to shelter or protect them.

As to the home beyond the river, Lorena didn't know. She just wanted to find her husband and bring her children back from Nebraska. She wanted the six humans she was responsible for to be back again in their home, where she could watch over them.

At the telegraph office in the late afternoon, she had been given one good piece of information by the elderly fellow who worked the telegraph. Several telegrams had poured in for Captain Call, instructing him to hurry to San Angelo. Joe Garza had struck there, only the week before.

The next morning, at breakfast—she was the only woman in the small hotel dining room—Lorena happened to overhear a conversation that sent her heart leaping. Two Texas Rangers were at a table talking, and she heard the name Call mentioned.

The Rangers had looked at her hard when they walked in and saw her alone in the dining room, but Lorena had not sent her children away and traveled so far to be balked by hard looks from lawmen.

She got up and went over to their table.

"Excuse me, I heard you mention Captain Call," she said. "My husband is his deputy. I'd be grateful if you'd give me any news of the group."

The men looked surprised. The larger one rattled his spoon in his coffee cup; he was uncomfortable talking to women in public places.

"Don't know much, ma'am," he said, finally. "Call nearly killed a sheriff in Presidio. They don't know yet whether the man will live. Call was getting his deputy out of jail and just went wild. He got his deputy and an old Indian he uses to track down bandits."

"That's my husband. He oughtn't to have been in jail, he's never broken the law," Lorena said.

"Well, you don't have to break much law out in Joe Doniphan's part of the country," the large Ranger said. "He'd arrest you for spittin', if he didn't like your looks."

"I guess Captain Call didn't like his looks," the other Ranger said.

"Thank you, I appreciate the news," Lorena said, politely.

She went back to her table in a happier frame of mind. Pea was alive, and with the Captain. She didn't like the Captain, but he was able enough. He would protect Pea until she found him.

When the two Rangers left the room, they didn't look at Lorena so hard. They even stopped for a moment, and tipped their hats.

9.

The evening of the second day, as the party traveled east from Presidio, Call, Brookshire, the two deputies, and Famous Shoes climbed out of the Maravilla Canyon just at dusk and made a camp. The winter sun was filling the canyon behind them with red light.

"That old man who kills bears is coming with his dogs," Famous Shoes remarked. "I saw his track on the Salt Fork of the Brazos, but then, he was going north. I did not expect him to be coming this way."

"If it's Ben Lily, he don't ask nobody's opinion when he changes directions," Pea Eye said. Twice the old bear hunter had turned up at their farmhouse on the Red River, on his way to kill cougars in the Palo Duro Canyon. He had killed the last bears in the Palo Duro years before, but there were many cougars, and from time to time, Ben Lily rested from his lifelong bear hunt and killed cougars for a while instead.

"I'll feed him, but I won't feed his dogs," Call said. "It don't take that many dogs to run lions, and I doubt there's any bears left in Texas for him to run. He's killed them all."

A few minutes later, they heard the baying of six or seven dogs. In the still, silent night it was hard to tell how far away Ben Lily and his dog pack might be.

"He is like me, no horse," Famous Shoes said. "I doubt he

can finish off the lions, in the time he has left. He is an old man."

"Who's this?" Brookshire asked. He had never heard of the person they were talking about, though that fact was not particularly odd. Six months ago, he had scarcely even heard of Texas, and could not have named one living Texan. Now he knew several Texans in person, and several more by reputation.

"He's a hunter, he don't do nothing else," Pea Eye said. "I don't guess he ever has done nothing else."

"They say he hunted all the bears out of Louisiana and Arkansas before he come here," Deputy Plunkert said. Since leaving Presidio, the deputy had been in a lighter mood. They were on their way to San Angelo, which was not that long a distance from Laredo. If they were successful and captured the Garza boy promptly, he might be on his way home within two weeks. Just being north of the border made him feel a lot better about life. Once he got home, he meant to plan his life so that he never had to enter Mexico again. If necessary, he and Doobie would move north, to San Antonio, or even Austin, to avoid the possibility that anything would require him to cross the border again.

As the winter night deepened and the half-moon rose, they heard the baying of Ben Lily's dogs, coming closer.

"If the man travels so much, maybe he'll know something," Brookshire suggested. "He's coming from the east, and the last robbery was east, unless there's been one we don't know about."

"No, he won't know anything, he only pays attention to bears and lions," Call said. "Humans don't interest him. If he was on the track of a bear or cougar and a train was being robbed right in front of him, I doubt he'd even stop to look."

Many times, over the years, Call had encountered the hunter, but on no occasion had he gotten any cooperation from him. Ben Lily expected to get information, not give it. He had no use for civilizations, nor for society, nor individuals, and was even impatient with his dogs. All he liked to do was kill bears. He only hunted lions to pass the time, or to earn a little money now and

then, from ranchers who wanted lions or wolves cleaned off
their ranches.

.Toward midnight, the horses and mules began to snort and
whinny. They pulled at their picket ropes. Call got up and went
to quiet the animals, and when he had them calm, he walked
east about a mile, meaning to intercept the dogs. Ben Lily usually traveled with a pack of eight or ten, and eight or ten dogs
running into camp might spook the horses so badly that one or
two might injure themselves. Call had only a sidearm with him.
He did not expect trouble. Ben Lily's dogs were usually shy of
humans, since they rarely saw any, other than the old hunter
himself.

Call's hands were aching. He wished he had a little whiskey,
although he had never been a drinker, really. Augustus, his
old partner, had been the drinker. But in the last few winters,
particularly if he happened to be at home in his shack on the
Goodnight ranch, Call had taken to using a glass or two of
whiskey in order to help him sleep. A doctor in Amarillo had
assured him that a glass or two would be medicinal. Even with
the whiskey, he frequently awoke as early as two a.m., and had
little to do but pace around the cabin until dawn came.

The next whiskey to be had was at Judge Roy Bean's saloon,
three days away. Call had not yet decided whether to pay the
judge a visit. He wasn't quite as uncooperative as Ben Lily—
nobody was as uncooperative as Ben Lily—but he ran him a
close race. Roy Bean was cranky, and in his conversation, he
never strayed far from the subject of money. On the other hand,
little that occurred on the border escaped his attention. A visit
to Roy Bean would take them out of their way. The train had
been robbed near San Angelo. But of course, the Garza boy had
time to be back in Mexico, or perhaps back in Crow Town,
depending on which way he had felt inclined to go. The next
train stopped by the boy might be leaving Saltillo, or Tucum-
cari, or almost anywhere.

While Call was thinking of Roy Bean and his harsh tongue,
the dogs began to bay again. This time, they sounded farther
away than they had the last time they howled. Perhaps they

were running ahead of the old hunter, on the spoor of a lion, and maybe the lion had doubled back.

Just as Call was settling down to enjoy his solitude—he still liked to separate himself from the camp for an hour or two, at night—Famous Shoes came walking through the moonlight. Call felt a little irritated. He needed his solitary hours. They helped him clear his head, and think through the next few days of whatever campaign he was waging. Why wouldn't the old Indian stay put? Call slept little, but Famous Shoes, who was older, slept even less.

"Now those dogs are going east," Famous Shoes said. "I think they must be chasing a mule deer."

"No, they would have run it down by now if it was a mule deer," Call said. "That many dogs will run a mule deer to death pretty quick."

Famous Shoes ignored the correction, which he thought invalid. It could well be a large, well-fed mule deer who was not ready to die just because Ben Lily had come along with his dogs. The mule deer might have had a long start, too. But Famous Shoes saw no point in arguing with the Captain. Call did not accept argument, from his men or from anyone.

"They could be after those two wolves whose tracks I saw this morning," he replied. "The dogs might be running those wolves."

Famous Shoes had just stopped speaking when they heard the sound of gunshots, coming from the direction where they had last heard the dogs. There were many gunshots. In the Indian days, Call had been competent at counting gunshots, for it was a way of estimating the enemy's strength. But he was out of practice. He would have guessed that about forty shots were fired. In a lull, they heard the yelping of one of the dogs. It had been wounded in the gunfight, probably.

There were four or five more gunshots, scattered, and then silence.

"Somebody shot those dogs, that's what I think," Famous Shoes said. He was a little agitated. The flurry of shots had been an unwelcome surprise. It took several men to shoot that many dogs so rapidly. But what kind of men would shoot dogs in the middle of the night?

"Listen a minute," Call said. "They could have been shooting at whatever the dogs were chasing. If that's it, they weren't Ben Lily's dogs. Ben Lily travels alone and shoots a rifle. What we heard were mainly pistol shots."

They listened for fifteen minutes. There were no more gunshots, and no dogs howled.

"They probably shot the dogs. I'd like to know why," Call said. "Let's go to camp."

When Call got back to camp, all three men were sound asleep. Probably that was because the weather had warmed up. For the first time, they weren't so freezing cold.

Call expected no better of Brookshire or Deputy Plunkert, but he was irritated with Pea Eye. It was a small lapse, but a lapse nonetheless. As long as he and Pea Eye had been camping together, they had consulted about night duties—who would sleep first, who would sleep second. Never before, no matter how tired he might be, had Pea Eye just gone to sleep without discussing these arrangements. Of course, Call had lapsed himself, by leaving the camp without assigning a watch. But he had done that often, through the years, and when he did it, Pea Eye always stayed awake until he returned.

It wasn't like Pea Eye, going to sleep in dangerous country. It made Call wonder if urging Pea Eye to leave his family and join him had really been wise. He had done it from habit. Pea Eye was the last of his men, and one of the few people Call trusted. It had seemed natural to call on him, and it had disturbed him when Pea Eye refused to come.

Now he found that having him along disturbed him almost as much. Pea Eye wasn't behaving like himself. It might be because he was no longer the Ranger that Call had known and counted on for so long. He was a farmer and a husband, with the habits of a farmer and a husband, rather than the habits of a fighting man. Probably Pea Eye had been right, in deciding to stay with his family. Loyalty had made him change his mind, but foolishly, and too late. If he wasn't going to be able to be the competent Ranger he had been, then staying home was the better choice.

Pea Eye woke up the minute Captain Call reentered the camp, and immediately realized that he had been derelict.

"Oh, dern, I dropped off," he said. "I intended to stand watch."

"Well, Famous Shoes was up, and so was I," Call said. "Somebody just shot Ben Lily's dog pack, if them dogs we've been hearing really belonged to Ben Lily. If they weren't, I'd like to know who would be running in these parts, with eight or ten dogs."

Pea Eye felt such embarrassment at having gone to sleep that he scarcely attended to what the Captain was saying. He had no intention of going to sleep, when the Captain left the camp. The Captain always left the camp, for an hour or two in the evening. When he returned, the two of them would work out watch duties, for what remained of the night. Pea Eye usually stood the first watch.

But this evening, he had simply gone to sleep. The Captain didn't mention it. He had even been polite enough to change the subject, but Pea Eye knew he would remember it. The very fact that he hadn't been reprimanded made Pea Eye feel at a loss. In fact, he had been feeling at a loss from the moment the Captain led them out of Presidio. Pea Eye should have been feeling fine. With Famous Shoes' help, he had been able to connect with the Captain with only a minimum of travel. The Garza boy was probably east of them now. The whole job might be over soon, and he could go right home, back to Lorie and the children.

But Pea Eye didn't feel fine. He felt awkward; maybe he had irritated the Captain too much, by refusing to go with him initially. Maybe the Captain, as he got older, was becoming even harder to please. At no time had he been easy to please.

But whatever it was, there was a difference in the way he and the Captain were, and it made Pea Eye all the more homesick. He felt he had been foolish, after all, to leave home. The Captain had promptly recruited another deputy, and he had the

Yankee, Brookshire, as well. The Yankee seemed to be fairly competent. He had made the campfires, both nights, and had done it well. The other deputy was no good at packing horses or mules, but was handy enough at unpacking them. There was not much for Pea Eye to do. Standing watch was one area where his experience would have been useful, but he had gone right off to sleep and hadn't even heard the shots that killed Ben Lily's dogs, if they were Ben Lily's dogs.

All this made Pea Eye feel gloomy. He felt that he had stopped knowing how to be useful. He often felt that way at home, too. Lorie was as good at what she did as the Captain was at what he did. Pea Eye wasn't as good as either one of them, at anything. It made him wonder why the Captain had wanted him along in the first place.

Call was sufficiently alarmed by the sound of so much gunfire that he woke Brookshire and Deputy Plunkert. He also put out the fire. In the brilliant darkness, on the long plain, even a speck of fire as small as theirs could be spotted by an experienced eye from many miles away; as many miles, at least, as an experienced ear could hear a dog bark.

Call could sometimes distinguish calibers of weapons, if the firing was slow, but the men who shot the dogs hadn't been firing slow. The forty shots had been fired in a minute or two. Call thought he heard six or seven guns, but that was a guess. There could have been ten or more, or there could have been only three or four.

Famous Shoes had not returned to camp. The man seldom waited for instructions, and he was apt to rove all night, when he was on a scout.

"Where's our Indian?" Brookshire asked. He had taken a liking to the old man, although he wasn't exactly businesslike. When he noticed that Brookshire had a book or two in his baggage, Famous Shoes had started pestering him to teach him to read. The old man seemed to think it was something he could start doing immediately, if only he were given the right clues. Famous Shoes had even insisted that Brookshire dismount, so he could show the Yankee a number of animal tracks and iden-

[332]

tify them. He seemed to think that Brookshire ought to be able to instruct him in reading just as quickly. When Brookshire attempted to explain that the two things weren't the same, Famous Shoes became irritated. Then Brookshire made the mistake of mentioning sentences. Famous Shoes immediately started asking him to explain what sentences were. Brookshire felt sure that he knew what a sentence was, but he found it damnably difficult to explain the sentence to the old Indian.

He liked the old man, though. It astonished him that a man Famous Shoes' age could travel faster on foot than the rest of them traveled horseback. He stayed ahead of them all day, moving at his strange little trot.

The four of them watched the rest of the night, but there was no more shooting. About dawn, Call thought he heard something, a kind of cry or keening. But he couldn't figure out what might be making it.

"Could it be an eagle?" he asked Pea Eye. "They say eagles scream, but I've never heard one."

Pea Eye heard the sound only faintly. He had no idea what it was.

Before it was fully light, Call had them headed toward the east.

"What about Famous Shoes?" Brookshire asked. "Shouldn't we wait for him?"

"He's a tracker, we don't have to wait for him," Call said. "He'll find us."

Famous Shoes did find them, about an hour later. He was down in a little ravine, and he had Ben Lily with him. The old hunter was shaggy, filthy, and mad.

"It was the manburner," Famous Shoes said, as he trotted up out of the ravine. "He has seven men with him."

"He burnt my best dog," Ben Lily said. "Kilt all nine of them, and burnt one alive."

"That's what we heard, I guess," Call said. "That's the sound a dog makes when it's being burned alive."

"He wanted to burn me," Ben Lily said. "I hid in a snake den. His men shot my dogs. They roped old Flop and burnt him."

[333]

"Not to eat, though," Famous Shoes said. "You can see—the dog is a little ways ahead."

Ben Lily sat on a rock, unkempt and bewildered. Call offered to let him ride one of the pack horses, if he wanted to come with them, but the old man didn't even answer. He sat on the rock, shaking his head and mumbling.

"I think he's gone loco," Famous Shoes said quietly, to Call.

"He's always been loco," Call said. "Now he's old, and he's lost his dogs. If I were him I'd quit, but I ain't him."

Call went over to the old hunter, who seemed stunned by the calamity that had befallen him in the night. He held an old Winchester; apart from two cartridge belts, he seemed to have no equipment. Ben Lily was reputed to be an exceptional shot, exceptional enough to have killed more than two thousand bears and an unreckoned number of mountain lions. Call remembered him as having keen, mean eyes. This morning, his eyes seemed vague.

"He burnt old Flop," Ben Lily said. "Old Flop was my best dog."

"You're lucky he didn't burn you, Mr. Lily," Call said. "You'd better follow along with us for a day or two, until we know where he is and where he's going. Next time, you might not make it to the snake den."

The old man shook his head. He wore a ragged cap, which looked as if it had been made from a wolf skin. He kept putting it on, and then taking it back off.

"I'm going to Santa Fe," he said. "I got to get some new dogs."

"You won't need them, if Mox Mox catches you," Call said. "You better come with us until we stop him."

"I got to get some dogs," Ben Lily repeated. "I can't run no bears or tree no lions without some dogs."

"I can't take you against your will, Mr. Lily, but you'd be wiser to come with us," Call said. "This man's not your ordinary killer. He's the manburner."

Ben Lily paid no attention; he was looking to the southwest, toward the distant mountains. His eyes seemed blurred and tired, but Call supposed they might clear quickly enough if he had a lion, or better yet, a bear in his sights.

"Them mountains are full of lions, but there ain't no bear," he said. "I be going on to Wyoming, I guess. There's bear up there in Wyoming."

He stood up and looked around, as if surprised to see that he was among people and not dogs.

"That killer kilt my dogs," he repeated. "I best go to Santa Fe."

His eyes turned to the northwest; he stared at the distances.

"You could go with us to Roy Bean's," Call suggested. "He usually has a few dogs."

"No, I don't like Bean," Ben Lily said. "His dogs are just hounds. One mean lion could run them all off. I won't hunt with dogs that run from lions."

"Be careful, then," Call said, but the old man either didn't hear him, or didn't care to respond. He put his Winchester on his shoulder and climbed out of the ravine, heading north. Though he seemed stiff in his movements, he kept moving north and was soon out of sight.

Brookshire couldn't get used to the way people behaved in the West. The old man had no blanket, or kit of any kind. No doubt he had matches somewhere about his person, but otherwise he was setting out to walk hundreds of miles, in the wintertime, with nothing but a gun and two cartridge belts, and in country where there were at least two deadly killers on the loose.

"He just hunts?" Brookshire asked.

"Yes, all his life," Call said. "I never heard of him doing anything else."

"If he was born today, he'd have to do something else," Deputy Plunkert said. "There wouldn't be enough varmints to satisfy him. I've never even seen a wild bear. The circus come once and it had a little bear, but it was tame."

"You're right," Call said. "Mr. Lily's worked himself out of a job, where bears are concerned, unless he heads for Alaska."

Call felt some sadness as he watched Ben Lily disappear into the sage and the distance, his rifle on his shoulder. It was unlikely that he would ever see the old man again. Call had never liked him, really. The two of them had probably not exchanged a hundred words in all their various brief meetings over the years. Ben Lily would talk of nothing except what he was hunting at the time, and Call hunted only for practical purposes and had nothing to say about it.

But Ben Lily was one of the old ones of the West. Ben Lily and Goodnight and Roy Bean and a few others. None of them were particularly likable, although Charles Goodnight had become friendlier than Call had ever expected him to be. But all of them, and those like them who had fallen—Gus McCrae and old Kit Carson, the Bent brothers, Shanghai Pierce and Captain Marcy—had been part of the adventure. Gus McCrae had declared the adventure over before the Hat Creek outfit had ever crossed the Yellowstone. A few days after he said it, he had gone off adventuring and been killed. Gus had been both right and wrong. The exploring part of the adventure had ended, but not the settling part, and settling, in the time of the Comanche and the Cheyenne and the Apache, had plenty of adventure in it.

Now, the settling had happened. Ben Lily and Goodnight and Roy Bean and, he supposed, himself—for he, too, had become one of the old ones of the West—were just echoes of what had been. When Lily fell, and Goodnight, and Bean and himself, there wouldn't even be echoes, just memories.

Call mounted up, feeling that he had begun to miss Ben Lily, a man he had never liked. Yet, a time or two in his life, he had even missed enemies: Kicking Bird, the Comanche chief, was one. Missing Gus McCrae, a lifelong friend, was one thing; missing Ben Lily was something else again. It made Call feel that he had outlived his time, something he had never expected to do. Now he had begun to listen for echoes, an unhealthy form of distraction when there were still men in the country who burned people and dogs.

It was an unhappy thought, but soon it might be that the bad men, the Wes Hardins and the Mox Moxes, would be all that was left of the West as it had been. The bad men, in the end, were the ones who wouldn't settle.

A few miles farther on, Famous Shoes showed them the burned dog. It was large—part mastiff, Call reckoned. Its four feet had been tied together, and its mouth wired shut. The fire hadn't been hot enough to consume the animal, but it had been thoroughly seared. Even its teeth were black.

Brookshire looked at the dog, got off his horse, and threw up. Deputy Plunkert took one quick look and rode on by. He stopped fifty yards farther on, but kept his back to the group. Pea Eye looked, and felt more than ever at a loss. He had seen far worse sights than a burned dog, in his days with the Rangers, and he knew men did bad things to other men. That was an old lesson, learned and learned well in the Indian wars.

Pea Eye realized that he was just tired of it, tired of such sights and such memories. He had been feeling tired since he'd had to help pull Captain Call off Sheriff Doniphan. Pea Eye didn't want to see the Captain beat a person to within an inch of his life, even if the person deserved it, as the sheriff had. He didn't want to see burnt dogs or burnt people, or people with bad gunshot wounds in the belly, or any of that. What he wanted to see was Lorena, his wife, nursing their baby at the breakfast table. He wanted to see his three little boys, and his big girl, Clarie; his big girl, that all the boys were already wanting to court. He wanted to hold his wife in his arms, not bury corpses of people killed by outlaws. It was time for all that to be over. It should have already been over, at least where he was concerned. He had never had the appetite for it, and now he really didn't have the time for it, either. He had different work to do.

Famous Shoes studied the tracks for a while, and Call dismounted and took a look too. The tracks went east—eight men and two extra horses.

"They don't hurry," Famous Shoes remarked.

"No, I guess they wouldn't," Call said. "If they hurried, they might miss something Mox Mox wants to burn."

He felt uncertain as to how to proceed. The killers were within twenty-five miles of them, probably, and there were eight of them. If Mox Mox would take the time to stop and burn Ben Lily's dog, then killing was probably their main object, though no doubt they would rob, too, when the opportunity arose.

Call's instinct was to go after Mox Mox at once. It wasn't the job he had been hired to do, but Mox Mox was between him and the job he had been hired to do. Besides, the eight killers were a danger to anyone they encountered, wherever they were. If they had the leisure to burn a dog, they were not expecting either resistance or pursuit.

Call was traveling with a largely untried troop, though. Pea Eye would probably fight well enough, when the time came— he always had—but the others might just get in the way. Brookshire had indulged in a good deal of target practice on the trip. He was a fair shot at stationary targets, but of course he had never shot at a living target, much less one that could shoot back at him. Deputy Plunkert was also a question mark. By his own admission, he had scarcely left Laredo in his whole life. What he would do in a running fight was anybody's guess; get himself killed, probably.

"The manburner has a big man with him," Famous Shoes said. He had found a track that was as deep as any track he had ever seen. "His horse is tired, from carrying him."

"That's good. Big men make easy targets," Call said. "Once we shoot the big one, we'll only have seven to worry about. We won't be so badly outnumbered."

Brookshire felt that the clock of his life had run backward, to the time of the War. The sight of the burned dog did it. In the War, the sight of dead horses, some of them scorched, some with their stomachs burst open or their innards spilled, upset him more than seeing the bodies of men. He didn't know why they upset him more; they just did.

In the time he had traveled with the Captain, Brookshire had thought often about their quarry, Joey Garza. Joey had killed, and in fact, he killed often, but he killed with a bullet. It scared him to think of Joey crouched behind a rock somewhere, looking at him through a telescope sight, ready to end his life with a bullet. Still, it was a bullet; Katie dying of her sickness probably suffered more than he would suffer if Joey Garza did kill him.

But the man who had burned the dog, this Mox Mox, was different. Joey was a killer; Mox Mox must be a maniac. Brookshire had observed Captain Call over a fair stretch of time, and had much confidence in his abilities. The man was a little stiff in the morning, but he kept going. He had no tendency to recklessness, that Brookshire could detect. He consulted Brookshire fully when there were decisions to be made. Brookshire had confidence in the Captain's ability to locate and subdue Joey Garza. He thought Call could do it, and do it handily.

But Mox Mox was a maniac, and he had seven men with him. He wasn't interested in killing with bullets, either. What he was doing went beyond stopped trains, passengers who lost their valuables, and Colonel Terry's profits. The thought of Joey Garza left Brookshire scared, but the thought of Mox Mox left him terrified.

Call knew he had a ticklish decision to make. He could keep the men with him, try to catch up with Mox Mox, and hit him in force, such as the force was. Or, he could go alone, and hope to ambush Mox Mox and the men himself. The fact that he would be one against eight didn't disturb him much. Very few men could fight effectively, and of the eight there might be only one who was formidable. Blue Duck had been formidable, but from what Call could remember of the Goodnight trouble, Mox Mox had merely been mean. No one seemed to think much of his abilities as a killer. He had led Goodnight a merry chase, and had eluded him, but in that instance, he had a week's start. The main problem in attacking Mox Mox and his men alone was to determine which one had the ability. That was the man to kill first.

His only source of information, at the moment, was Famous Shoes. The old tracker had walked off to the east and was squatting on his heels, smoking. Call loped out to where he rested. It was time to decide.

"He's got a giant with him, you said," Call remarked. "Who else has he got?"

"Three Mexicans who spur their horses too much," Famous Shoes said. "Their horses jump when they spur them. The manburner himself is small. He makes little tracks when he is burning something."

"That's three Mexicans, the giant, and the manburner," Call said. "That's five. What about the other three?"

"There's a Cherokee," Famous Shoes said. "He has the best horse, and his horse is not tired."

"What makes you think he's Cherokee?" Call asked.

"Because I know him," Famous Shoes said. "I tracked him once before. He stole a woman that Quanah Parker wanted to marry. His name is Jimmy Cumsa. He is very quick. I tracked him two years ago, and he is still riding the same horse. He takes good care of his horse. I think he is a better killer than the manburner."

"If you tracked him, why didn't Quanah get him?" Call asked.

"I don't know," Famous Shoes said. "I tracked him to Taos Pueblo. But Quanah had to go somewhere on a train, for many days. I think he went to see the President. When he came back, he was too busy to go get Jimmy Cumsa."

"That leaves two," Call said.

"I don't know where the last two come from," Famous Shoes admitted. "One rides a pacing horse—he is not a good rider and his horse is not strong. The other man is small. He rides a little ways apart. Maybe the manburner doesn't like him too much."

The other men came and joined them. Brookshire looked sick. Deputy Plunkert looked scared. Pea Eye was calm enough, but it was clear to Call that the man's heart wasn't in what he was doing.

Call decided not to leave the men. When the time came to strike Mox Mox, he would leave them, but he wanted them to be in a more protected place before he left. If he sent them alone to Roy Bean's, with Famous Shoes to guide them, they might make it and they might not. Even if they traveled by night, they would be vulnerable. Ben Lily had been traveling by night, and he had still lost his dogs, and nearly his life.

"We'll go to Bean's," Call said. "We'll find out what he knows. Then I may separate from you for a few days and see what I can do about these killers."

They started at once, but all morning, Call felt torn. He felt he should break off and go, while he was so close to the killers, but he feared for the men. They were all grown men, and he should let them fend for themselves; he'd often had to leave men in dangerous situations. This time, though, he didn't feel he should leave them. He didn't want to come back and find them burnt, like Ben Lily's dog.

Brookshire was relieved, when the Captain said he would stay with them. Looking around him, he could see nothing but an endless distance. It seemed that the West just kept opening around him, into greater and ever greater distances. When he thought the horizons could get no farther away, he awoke to horizons that were yet farther. Brookshire had a compass, but he didn't use it. Captain Call was his compass. Without him, Brookshire doubted that he could find the will to keep himself going across the empty country, toward the dim horizon. He would simply stop, at some point. He would just stop and sit down and wait to be dead.

Also, he had seen the burnt dog. If the Captain left them, it wouldn't be simply a matter of keeping going, of pursuing the long horizons until they yielded up a town, a place where there might be a hotel and a train. It was no longer just the emptiness, and the blowing-away feeling, that Brookshire had to fear—not anymore.

The manburner was there. Probably he was within the vast rim of horizon that encircled them at that very moment. Brookshire felt deeply grateful to the Captain, for staying with them. He had come to feel that he might not mind dying so much, if dying just meant a bullet.

But Brookshire had seen Ben Lily's dog. He did not want to die as the dog had died. He did not want to be burnt.

10.

"That Indian owes me a nickel—if he's on your payroll, fork it over," Roy Bean said, before Call and his party had even dismounted. He was sitting in the weak winter sunlight, outside his saloon, wrapped in a buffalo robe. He had a cocked pistol in one hand, and a rifle across his lap; the rifle barrel stuck out from under the robe. A shotgun was propped against the wall of the saloon, within easy reach. "What sort of drink would only cost a nickel?" Call inquired.

"He don't owe me for a drink, he owes me for some lotion," the judge said. "He come up lame one time, and I let him rub some lotion on his foot and forgot to charge him for it. It was a fine lotion. It cures all ills except a weak pecker."

Call gave Roy Bean the nickel. Until he was paid his full bill, whatever it might be, there would be little chance that he would dispense much information.

"I stepped on a little cactus with thorns like the snake's tooth," Famous Shoes said. "He gave me some of his lotion, and I am still walking. I will pay the nickel, although I don't have it with me right now."

"Brookshire's boss will pay the nickel," Call said, not surprised that the first thing they received at the Jersey Lily Saloon was a bill of several years' standing.

"Put it in your ledger, Brookshire," Call said. "I'm sure your

Colonel will be glad to contribute a nickel to the man who kept our tracker healthy."

Brookshire had lost interest in the ledger, and had not kept it current, although they had made substantial purchases in Presidio. He had, on one or two occasions, even torn pages out of it and used them to help get the campfires started. Somewhere along the Rio Concho, he had stopped feeling that he lived in a world where ledgers mattered. Colonel Terry still belonged to that world, and would always belong to it. The Colonel, like the old judge, would be quick to demand his nickel, even his penny.

But Brookshire had passed beyond the world of ledgers, into a world of space and wind, of icy nights and brilliant stars, of men who killed with bullets and men who burned dogs. In order to keep his accounts at night, Brookshire would usually have had to thaw out the ink, and then thaw out his fingers sufficiently to be able to write. It was hard to see the lines on a ledger by the light of a small campfire, and it was hard to be correct in one's penmanship when one's fingers were frozen. The Colonel was a stickler for good penmanship, too. He didn't like to squint or puzzle over entries when he was examining a ledger, and he had said so many times.

Now, looking back into Mexico from the front of Judge Bean's saloon, the Colonel's strictures no longer seemed to matter. Brookshire had other disciplines to concern himself with, such as making campfires that would last the night without wasting wood. Captain Call was as strict about campfires as the Colonel was about penmanship.

"Are you expecting a war party?" Call asked the judge. "You seem to be thoroughly armed."

"I expect perdition, always have," the judge replied. "I keep this building at my back, and several guns handy, in case perdition arrives in a form that's susceptible to bullets. I expect it will come in the disease form, though. I'm susceptible to diseases, and you can't shoot a goddamn disease."

"If this is still a saloon, we'd like whiskey," Call said. "We've had a cool ride."

They had scarcely left the canyon before another norther had sung in behind them. The cold cut them badly, although they rode with their backs to the wind.

The judge reluctantly took them inside the saloon. Once settled warmly into his buffalo robe, he hated to be disturbed. Most conversations, even in the coldest weather, were conducted outside, with him speaking from inside his robe.

The saloon had only one table, and it was so tilted on its crooked legs that a drink placed on the uphill side would quickly slide to the downhill side and off onto the floor, unless the drinker kept a grip on his glass.

Call bought whiskey for everyone; only Pea Eye refrained. Lorena was very severe with him, in the matter of drink. In his lonely cowboy days in Montana, he had taken to drinking for an hour or two every evening. Once married, he continued the practice for a while, from nervousness, but Lorena soon put her foot down. Since the day she had put her foot down, Pea Eye had very few drinks, norther or no norther. He did take a beer, though. Fortunately, Judge Bean had a few. Famous Shoes requested tequila—the judge also had plenty of that substance— and drank almost a pint, as if he were drinking water. Deputy Plunkert fell asleep just as the judge was refilling his whiskey glass. It promptly slid toward the edge of the table, but the judge himself caught it at the last minute.

"I'll pour this back in the bottle until your man wakes up," Roy Bean said.

The judge had quick, crafty eyes. Rumor had always placed him on the wrong side of the law. Call had not been the only one surprised when Roy Bean assumed his judgeship. To be fair, though, no one seemed to quite know what laws the new judge had broken. Some thought he smuggled gold for powerful Mexicans; others thought he stole gold from the same Mexicans. Call thought the gold rumors were probably exaggerations. For one thing, Roy Bean lived a long way from anyplace where gold could be used or deposited, and gold was heavy. To Call, Roy Bean had more the manner of a skillful gambler. Becoming a judge, in a region where few people had much fondness for the law, was in itself a gamble.

"I hope you catch the Garza boy next week," Roy Bean said. "This week wouldn't be too soon, neither."

"I'll catch him, but I doubt it will be this week," Call said. "The last train he robbed was near San Angelo, and I imagine he kept traveling. We'll have to see if Famous Shoes can pick up his track."

"There are very few competent marksmen in this part of the country," Roy Bean said. "This boy is a competent marksman and he's affecting my profits.

"The truth is, my profits are way down," he added, glumly.

"Oh, how's that?" Call asked.

"The Garza boy shoots people who might come here and drink," the judge replied. "There's other problems, too. I used to be able to sit outside and concentrate on business matters, without having to worry that somebody a mile away on a hill might plug me while I'm concentrating."

"There's no hill within a mile of you, and half a mile would be a more likely distance for a rifle shot, anyway," Call said. "No rifle I've ever seen will shoot accurately much farther than half a mile."

"Yes, but you ain't a competent marksman yourself, and you don't know everything!" Roy Bean said sharply. "Charlie Goodnight has always thought he knew everything, and so did your damn partner, and so do you."

"Well, I've known a few fine shots," Call replied, mildly. "I've never known you to worry about killers, before. There are safer places to live than along this border if you're the sort to let killers disturb your naps."

"I have weathered a number of killers, but I resent Mexican boys with rifles that can shoot that far," Roy Bean said. "If you catch him for me, I'll hang him in a wink."

"That boy ain't the only reason you ought to start napping indoors, with your door locked," Call said. "Have you heard of Mox Mox?"

"Yes, Wes Hardin said he was around," Roy Bean said. "Who's he singed now?"

"Ben Lily's best dog," Call replied.

"Not Flop," Roy Bean said, visibly startled. "Why would the sonofabitch burn a dog?"

"Why would he burn a person?" Call asked. "Because he likes to, that's why."

"Did he get Ben?" the judge asked.

"No, but they killed every dog he had," Call said. "I'm thinking of going after him first, before he causes any more harm."

"Go get him," Roy Bean said. "Leave these men here. They look like they need to thaw out. I'll cut the whiskey to half price while they're visiting with me."

Guarding you, you mean, Call thought, but he didn't say it.

"Mox Mox has seven men with him," Call remarked.

"Hardin says the Cherokee boy is the only one with any fight," Roy Bean said. "Take a slow aim and eliminate him first. That would be my advice."

"Quick Jimmy," Famous Shoes said.

"Yes, Hardin said he had a rapid way about him," Roy Bean said.

"I didn't know you were friends with John Wesley Hardin," Call said.

"I ain't—nobody is," Roy Bean replied. "He come down here to see if I had a whore. Joey Garza's ma went to Crow Town and walked off with all the women. Hardin got restless for a whore and came to see me."

"When?" Call asked.

"Last week," Bean said. "He says Crow Town's emptied out, since the women left."

"Joey Garza's mother went to Crow Town and took the women?" Call said. "Took them and went where with them? She wasn't home when we came through Ojinaga. Billy Williams was looking after her other children. She has a pretty little girl, but the child is blind."

"I ain't met the woman, but I expect she's a beauty," Roy Bean said. "Billy's been in love with her most of his life, but she won't bend. Olin Roy's partial to her, too, but she won't have Olin, neither."

"I would have thought Huerta or somebody would have finished Olin by now," Call said. "Dabbling in Mexican finance is chancy work."

Call remembered the little blind girl with the quick expression, standing with Billy Williams. He rarely noticed children, but he not only remembered the blind girl, he could picture her vividly in his mind. He wondered about the mother. Few women would be bold enough to go to Crow Town. This woman had not only gone, she had led the women of the community away. She had produced the blind girl, the idiot boy, and Joey, and if Bean was to be believed, had captured and held the affections of Billy Williams and Olin Roy, two men who had not been noted for the constancy of their attachments. Olin was a smuggler who spoke good Spanish, and Billy Williams was more or less a roving drunk.

Still, some women seemed to be able to get holds on the most unlikely men. Pea Eye, for example, had never seemed to be the marrying kind. He had never sought out women, that Call could remember, when they were in towns. But here was Pea Eye, married, and happily so, it seemed.

"I don't understand the business about the women," Call said. "She just rode into town and rode out with them?"

"Nope," Bean said. "She rode in on a spotted pony, but Joey stole it and left her afoot. She and the women walked out."

"I met her on the road when she was almost there," Famous Shoes remarked. "She got very cold in the sleet storm, crossing the Pecos. I built her a fire, but she was angry with me and wouldn't let me stay."

"Did she know you were working for me?" Call asked.

"Yes, and she don't want you to kill Joey," Famous Shoes said. "She don't want me to track him for you."

"I didn't know you knew her," Call said.

"Her name is Maria," Famous Shoes said. "She saved my life the first time the hard sheriff wanted to hang me.

"She was too angry when I met her this time," he repeated. "I built the fire and left her."

"He's an ungrateful son, if he stole her horse and left her afoot in a place like Crow Town," Call said. "Not many women would ride into Crow Town."

"Or cross the dern Pecos, either," Pea Eye said. "Not when it's icy. I'd call that brave."

"Well, the boy is her son," Call said. "Even if he stole her horse, you can't expect her to want him dead."

"I don't know the woman—she can like it or lump it," Roy Bean said. "Her son's a thieving, murdering lawbreaker. You better go catch him, and plow Mox Mox under, too, if you have the time."

"This is your jurisdiction, Judge," Call reminded him. "I was just hired to catch Joey Garza. What I'd like to know is where his mother took the women."

"Wesley said she took 'em to the railroad," Roy Bean said. "He was upset. He said he would have shot her on sight if he'd known she was going to take away the whores."

"Where is Hardin, while we're talking about killers?" Call asked.

"No idea—he left," Roy Bean said. "I ain't his butler."

The judge had produced one bottle of brandy and asked an inordinate price for it, but Brookshire bought it anyway. He drank it until the edges of the little room became blurred, which didn't take long. Now the Captain was talking about yet another killer, a famous one this time. Even in Brooklyn there were people who had heard of John Wesley Hardin.

Brookshire kept drinking the brandy. He drank until he could hardly see the Captain, who was sitting not two feet from him. Deputy Plunkert was snoring; the warmth of the room had put him right to sleep. It seemed to Brookshire that they were traveling in circles. Every curve took them farther from civilization and produced another killer. The whole thing had started with a train robbery; now it involved three men who, among them, had killed the equivalent of a company of soldiers. Killers were multiplying, whereas Captain Call wasn't. There was still only one of him.

"They say the Garza boy has a cave full of valuables, down in

Mexico," Roy Bean said. "They say he takes everything he steals and hides it there."

"I expect that's a rumor," Call said.

"It's nice to think about, though," Bean said. "If I could find myself a cave full of treasure, I could retire from the bench and move to England, and if I was in England, I could watch Miss Lily Langtry perform on the stage every night of the week."

Call paid no more attention to Judge Bean. The only interesting information he possessed came from John Wesley Hardin, and it concerned Joey Garza's mother. If there was a way to find Joey, it probably involved the mother, not the cave. Sooner or later, Joey might come home. The fact that he had stolen his mother's horse might not mean much. Mothers had been known to overlook worse behavior than that. Joey might decide to bring the pony back someday. He knew he was being chased, and might want his mother to hide him.

Soon all the company was asleep, except for Pea Eye. Famous Shoes had drunk a second pint of tequila. He curled up under the table and slept soundly. Brookshire was out, his head fallen into his arms. Deputy Plunkert was snoring soundly, his head tipped so far to one side that his hat had fallen off. Pea, who'd had only one beer, seemed a little glum, but he was not drunk.

The smelly old judge had taken his buffalo robe and gone back outside.

Call motioned to Pea Eye, and the two of them went out into the cold air.

"I'm going to split off," Call said. "I hate to do it, but we've got two different threats to deal with, and I don't think they'll line themselves up like dominoes and wait for us to knock them over."

He'd had a feeling that the Captain might be about to leave. It always made Pea anxious when the Captain left to perform some task alone. When the Captain wasn't around, things were apt to go wrong. Several horses might turn up lame at the same time, or a man might develop pleurisy, or the hunters might be unable to bring in any game.

"I guess it will upset Brookshire," Pea Eye said. It was easy to see that Brookshire set great store by the Captain's judgment.

"Yes, I expect so," Call said. "But he's a grown man, and he knows how to make a fire.

"You'll have to watch that you don't fall asleep on guard duty," he added, mildly. "The others haven't had your experience. You don't want to let anybody slip up on you."

"Not with the manburner on the loose," Pea Eye said. "Where do you want us to go?"

"Go back to where we were, only circle down into Mexico," Call said. "You'll be safer, at least from Mox Mox. That village just across from Presidio is where Joey Garza's mother lives. I think that's where we'll catch him."

"What if he gets there before you do?" Pea Eye asked.

"Wait," Call said. "Circle south of the village and camp on the Rio Concho about half a day away. I'll find you."

"That don't sound too hard," Pea Eye said.

But the melancholy wouldn't leave him; it only got stronger. The Captain was going one way, and sending him another. It was a sign of trust, that the Captain would leave him in charge of the men. There was nothing exceptional about splitting up a company, either. That had happened many times, in the old days.

"This is not the end of the world," Lorena often told him, when she was trying to boost his spirits after some quarrel or mistake. "It's not the end of the world, Pea. Just pick up and keep going."

Pea Eye felt that Lorena didn't understand how much their fights or his mistakes saddened him. She would get busy with the children, or start studying her schoolwork, and the quarrel would go out of her mind. She would become cheerful again so quickly that it would make Pea Eye feel a little lonely. Hurts didn't go out of his mind that quickly, particularly if he was the cause of them. They seemed to settle in his throat, like gravel in a chicken's craw. Often, his feelings of absence or confusion would linger so long in his breast, while Lorena and the children went on with their lives, moving around him as if he wasn't there, that Pea Eye had a hard time feeling he was in their lives at all. He would begin to feel he was just some stranger who happened to be staying where his family lived. Often, too, it would not be until the next day, when some child jumped in his lap or came to him with a problem, that he would recover a sense of being connected to them.

As the Captain went about preparing to leave—they had bought a couple of extra rifles in Presidio, and the Captain took one of them and a good supply of ammunition—Pea Eye felt the same sadness tightening his throat that he felt at home when Lorena tried to assure him that his world wasn't coming to an end.

Lorena could say that to him all she liked, but her saying it didn't take away Pea Eye's feeling that the world might be coming to an end anyway. As he grew older, he felt more keenly how hard it was to know anyone. Lorena and the Captain, in turn, let him stay with them and share their lives. But Lorena and the Captain were complete, in a way that he wasn't, and being complete, they didn't realize how partial he felt. He was not as good as they were, not as smart and not as strong. They might know him, but he felt he would never be much good at knowing them. Often, in bed at night, listening to Lorena breathe and feeling her body warming his, tears would come to his eyes, from the sense that he didn't know his Lorena. He didn't, and he never would. He felt grateful, though, that she was letting him stay with her, and glad that they had the children and the farm.

But it didn't mean that the world wasn't coming to an end, or that it wouldn't.

Pea Eye didn't attempt to tell the Captain how he felt, though. The Captain was preparing to leave, and he didn't linger when he had someplace to go.

"I'll meet you on the other side of the river," Call said. "If I don't have too much aggravation with Mox Mox, I wouldn't think I'd be gone much more than a week."

"Don't neglect any killers," Roy Bean admonished. He was swaddled in his buffalo robe, the cocked pistol still in his hand.

"You oughtn't to leave that pistol cocked," Pea Eye said, as they watched the Captain lope away to the east. "You might have a bad dream and jerk and shoot your knee off."

"It might rain whores out of the sky, too, but I doubt it," Roy Bean said.

11.

Joey Garza watched Captain Call's departure through a telescope he had taken off the train from San Angelo. The telescope
had belonged to an old man with stringy gray hair, who protested so much when Joey took it that Joey shot him. He had
not intended to kill anybody when he stopped the train; he'd
only wanted to add to his treasures. If the old man had surrendered the telescope peacefully, Joey wouldn't have killed him.
The old man claimed to be a teacher. He said he taught about
the stars, and needed the telescope in order to study the stars.
He was bound for Fort Davis, where the stars were easier to see,
or so he said. He offered to give Joey all his money if Joey would
leave him the telescope.

"You see, I can't get another, not in these parts," the man
said. "I had to send to England for this one."

Joey thought he was just a disagreeable old man, so he shot
him and took the telescope and the money, too. Apart from two
or three good watches, the telescope was the only thing on that
particular train that Joey felt was worth stealing. He hoped that
by going east, closer to the cities of the Texans, he would find
better things on the trains he robbed. But if San Angelo was
any example, this theory was no good. The train mainly held
cowboys, who were being sent to some large ranch. None of the

cowboys had anything of value. Sometimes Joey took fine spurs, but the spurs these cowboys wore were of no interest. Even their saddles were poor. So he took the telescope, and the little stand that it rested on, killed the old man, and left.

That night, he used the telescope to look at the stars. He had to admit that the old man had been telling the truth. The telescope brought the stars much closer. When Joey pointed it at the moon, the results were even better. He could see what seemed to be mountains on the moon. The surface of the moon looked a little like the country where the Apaches had taken him. It was pretty bare.

The best use of the telescope, though, was to look at men. He concealed his mother's spotted pony in a gully, before pointing the telescope at Roy Bean's door. By adjusting it a little, he could see with great clarity. He saw the famous Captain Call come out with his tall friend, and get ready to leave. He saw the Captain take an extra rifle, and even saw that Judge Roy Bean kept his pistol cocked.

It annoyed Joey, that the Captain left his men behind. There were four of them; three were still inside. If they stayed, he would have to kill them before he could hang the judge, but he didn't want to kill them while the famous bounty hunter, Captain Call, was close enough to hear the shots.

It meant waiting, which Joey hated. He wanted to hang the judge, and then follow Captain Call and shoot him. Once Call was dead, he intended to go to Ojinaga and steal his brother and sister. It bothered him that his mother gave them so much attention. He meant to steal them and give them to the manburner, if he could find him. If the manburner wanted to burn them, that was fine with Joey. They were damaged anyway, too damaged to deserve all the attention his mother gave them. They were merely the products of her whoring. Stealing them would show her what he felt about her low behavior. If the manburner had no interest in burning them, Joey meant to take them deep into Mexico and give them away, to someone who wanted two slaves. He would take them so far away that his mother would never find them, and if he could find no one who wanted them for slaves, he might take them to his cave and throw them off the cliff behind it.

To his relief, the men Captain Call left at the saloon didn't stay long. The tall man went back inside and got them. There were two more white men, and old Famous Shoes. The two white men looked drunk. One of them was so drunk that he had difficulty mounting. But eventually, they got started. Famous Shoes led them across the river and took them north. Probably the Captain had sent them to catch him, when he came home. If that was the plan, it was silly. He might not go home, and even if he did, white men who were so drunk they couldn't mount their horses were not going to catch him. He could ride in and steal his brother and sister while they were in the cantina, getting drunk again. They would never see him, or even know he had been there.

Of course, Famous Shoes might find his tracks and track him. Joey decided he had better kill Famous Shoes, at some point; the old man was the last tracker in Mexico capable of tracking him to his cave. It would be best to kill him soon, before some gringo hired him to find the cave. Joey knew that the cave was becoming a legend among the gringos. Soon men would begin to hunt for it. But the cave was deep in the mountains, up a canyon where horses couldn't go. With Famous Shoes dead, the treasure in his cave would be safe for years.

When Captain Call and the men had been gone a few hours, Joey got out his rifle and looked through the telescope at Judge Roy Bean. The old man had gone inside and got himself a bottle of whiskey. He sat with his back to the building, holding his pistol in his lap. The whiskey bottle, he set on a little rock beside his chair. There was a shotgun propped against the wall and a rifle under the buffalo robe. The old man had brought some kind of newspaper out of the saloon and was reading it in the fading sunlight. It was a large newspaper; when the judge held it up to read, all Joey could see was his legs.

Joey leveled the rifle and shot Judge Roy Bean right through the newspaper, low down, a belly shot. Roy Bean leapt up and began to fire his rifle wildly, as much at the sky as at anything in particular. Joey shot him in the shoulder, so he would not be able to shoot the rifle well, and then he shot him in the leg, causing him to crumple. The old man tried to crawl over to the shotgun propped against the wall, but as he reached for it, Joey shot him in the arm. Joey was surprised that the old man struggled so, after being shot in the belly. He was plainly a tough old man, but that would only make matters worse for him. Joey got on his mother's spotted pony and rode up to the saloon. He could see the rifle and the shotgun, but he couldn't see the pistol. Joey thought the pistol was probably under the newspaper the judge had been reading when he shot him in the belly. The wind was blowing the newspaper away. Several pages were stuck on prickly pear piles, between the saloon and the river.

Roy Bean managed to prop up against the wall of the saloon. He had his pistol, but when he pointed it at Joey and tried to shoot, the pistol didn't fire. The old man was breathing heavily —he tried again to shoot the pistol, but again, the pistol didn't fire. The trigger wouldn't pull. Joey had his own pistol out and was ready to shoot, but he didn't want to kill Roy Bean with a gun if he could avoid it. He had other plans.

Roy Bean grew so irritated with his pistol that he started hitting it against the wall. The joke was on him, he knew. He had kept the pistol on cock for so long that it had rusted tight. It seemed to him that it had been on cock for ten years or more— foolish behavior. Now, the young Mexican had him. He was belly-shot, had a broken shoulder, a ruined leg, and a smashed arm. He couldn't move well enough to get inside his saloon, where he had a good stabbing knife. The young Mexican rode right up to him, and made a loop in a rawhide rope.

"You arrogant pup, do you plan to hang me? Go away," Roy Bean said. "I'm the one that hangs people around here. I'm the law west of the Pecos, or ain't you heard, you damn cub?"

The next moment, he was choking so badly he couldn't talk. Before he even realized the boy was moving, Joey Garza had slipped off his horse, flipped the rawhide noose around his neck, and jerked it so tight it almost crushed his Adam's apple. Roy

Bean felt a burning anger at Woodrow Call, who could have stayed put with his men for a day or two, and given Joey Garza time to pass on by. The boy had outsmarted Captain Call, and now look!

But the pain in his throat grew so severe that it cut off his anger along with his breath. Joey got back on his spotted pony, and Roy Bean found himself being pulled up toward the roof of his own saloon. The boy had flipped the rawhide rope over the chimney and was backing his horse away, pulling the judge slowly upward. When his feet left the ground, he twisted slightly, trying to get a hand under the rawhide rope. But the rawhide was unforgiving; he felt scalding bile flood his throat.

Roy Bean struggled and twisted. He felt that if he could just get one breath, he might yet struggle out of the noose and live. But Joey Garza slowly backed his horse, pulling Roy Bean higher, pulling the noose tighter. The rawhide was like steel. Roy Bean twisted again. He thought he might crawl up on the roof and get free, but he only had one hand. His lungs burned badly; the air seemed like black water. Call's man had been right about the pistol—he shouldn't have kept it on cock all those years. The Mexican boy backed the horse another step, pulling him so high that his head mashed against a roof beam that protruded from his wall. Black water flooded the world, where the air should have been.

When the old man's kicking and twisting began to slow, Joey got down and carefully gathered up the pages of his newspaper. The wind had scattered them badly, but Joey took his time and got them all. There was a bullet hole through the paper, and the prickly pear had torn it a little, but it was all there. Joey folded it carefully and put it in his saddlebags. There was a picture in it of a lady who wore many jewels. Maybe someday he would stop a train with a lady on it who had jewels he could take to his cave.

Then he went inside the saloon and looked around, hoping old Bean owned something worth stealing. The old man was still kicking and twisting—once or twice, Joey heard him thump against the wall. There was not much in the saloon, though.

The only thing he found that he considered worth taking was a silver picture frame.

The frame sat on a whiskey box by the old man's bed. The woman whose photograph was in the picture frame seemed to Joey to be the same woman whose photograph was in the newspaper, the one whose jewels he wanted to study. But the light in the little room was dim; he wasn't sure. He took the picture with him.

There was nothing in the saloon except cases of whiskey. A knife hung on a peg inside the door, but it was an old knife. Its blade had been sharpened so many times that it was as thin as the moon, when the moon was only a sliver.

Joey took the knife and used it to cut open Roy Bean's clothes. The old man was dead. He hung just beside his own doorway. Joey wanted to see where his first bullet had gone in. It had struck just below the navel. The old man had been tough as a javelina, Joey decided. Not many men would struggle that hard, after being shot below the navel.

Before leaving to take up the trail of Captain Call, Joey stood up in the saddle and crawled onto the low roof, in order to snub the rawhide rope more securely to the chimney. He wanted to make sure that Judge Roy Bean would be hanging by his own door when the next traveler showed up at the Jersey Lily Saloon, hoping for a drink.

12.

Charles Goodnight sat until past midnight, studying the fire in his kitchen fireplace. Winter was always severe on the plains, but this winter was unusually severe. It drizzled and then froze; drizzled and then froze; by Christmastime, there had been three big snows, which was rare. The cowboys rode long days, trying to keep the cattle from drifting too far from his range. Goodnight himself was in the saddle fifteen hours a day, most days.

His wife, Mary, was gone visiting a sister; otherwise, he would have been chided for working too hard. With Mary gone, the kitchen was about as much of the house as he needed to use. There was a cookstove as well as the fireplace, but he rarely cooked, himself. Now and then, he singed a beefsteak, and ate it with strong coffee. Muley, his ranch cook, had a kitchen in the big bunkhouse, where the cowhands ate. Muley, like many ranch cooks, was intolerant of suggestion or restriction. Every once in a while, when Goodnight took a meal with his cowboys, he was in the habit of speaking his mind. But if Goodnight made a habit of eating with his ranch hands too often and putting in his two cents about the food, a habit that visibly annoyed Muley, the result would be that Goodnight would rise up some-day and fire Muley for insubordination. It would be a severe aggravation if he had to fire him. Adequate ranch cooks were at a premium in the Panhandle. He would have to go to Amarillo, if not farther, to find a replacement.

The fire in the little kitchen fireplace gutted and blew, as the wind sang over the chimney. Northers had been almost constant for the past month. Day after day, the plains would be coated with a thin sheet of ice, as a result of the freezing drizzle.

Goodnight rarely slept more than three hours a night. The bulk of the night he spent in the kitchen, drinking strong coffee, figuring a little, and thinking. When Mary was home, she slept her eight hours, like a log. If she woke at all, it was usually to complain that he was burning too much kerosene in the lamp.

"I can't figure in the dark," he told her often, pointing to his account books.

"Nor in broad daylight, either," Mary said. "Figuring ain't your strong point, Charlie. If all you're going to do is think, then turn off that lamp and sit in the dark and think. You don't need light to think by, do you?"

Often, he obeyed rather than quarrel; it was dangerous to quarrel with Mary, when she was sleepy. If the quarrel got too vigorous, she might wake up, in which case she would press the quarrel all through the next day. She was capable of pressing one for a week or more, if she was aggravated enough. Such quarrels were a great waste of energy, and a good reason for spending as much of life as possible on horseback. Once a quarrel broke out, it was like a prairie fire—neither reason nor patience could extinguish it. Mainly, it had to be left to burn itself out. Many times he had thought such a quarrel burned out, only to have it flare up again as a result of some chance remark, and consume another hundred acres of his time.

But Mary wasn't there to complain about his extravagant waste of kerosene, this time. No one was there. In rummaging through his desk that afternoon, looking for a hardware bill that he had evidently mislaid, he came across an old brand book, dating from the days long before, when he and his partner, Oliver Loving, had first ranched in Colorado.

Perusing it now in the kitchen, with the fire guttering and the wind singing, was a chastening experience, testament to the uncertainties of the cattle business and of human existence as well. Not only was his old partner, Oliver Loving, dead, but so were a large majority of the cattlemen and trail bosses whose brands were recorded in his book. Those who weren't dead had mostly gone bust in the cattle business. They were farming now, or selling hardware in the small towns scattered about what had once been the great open range. Many of them had been good and able men; competent, resourceful, and good companions on the trail. But they hadn't lasted. Some got busted up by half-broken horses. Some drowned in foolish, impatient attempts to cross unfordable rivers. Others had taken sick and quickly and quietly expired. Perhaps they worked in the rain and sleet too long; the next day, they had a sniffle, the sniffle became pneumonia, and they died.

The book contained over four hundred brands. As he turned through its pages, Goodnight kept a little tally of those brands that were still active, used by the same cattlemen who had used them during the trail-driving days. He found only eight brands whose owners were still alive and in the cattle business. Those were the toughest of the tough, or the luckiest of the lucky.

Goodnight knew himself to be among the luckiest of the lucky; he had fought Indians for over twenty years and never received a scratch. Bullets had killed men fighting at his very elbow, but no bullet had ever struck him. He had taken herds across almost one hundred waterless miles, and not starved. He had raced to turn stampedes, in pitch darkness, over broken country on unreliable horses, and had not once fallen or been thrown. He had been in barrooms and other crowded situations with outlaws who would shoot you if they didn't like the way you removed your hat; yet, he had removed his hat pretty much as he pleased and had never been shot.

He knew he was fortunate, not merely because none of his own blood had ever been spilled in battle, but because he himself had spilled only a minimum, considering the circumstances under which he had to operate. He had killed three Comanches and one Kiowa, and hung three determined horse thieves, a modest tally by the standards that had prevailed on the frontier in his youth.

A man like Woodrow Call, a lawman most of his life, had far more on his conscience, when it came to taking life, than he himself had.

It was Call, mainly, that Goodnight had on his mind, as he sat in the kitchen by the little fireplace. That night, after consuming his lightly singed beefsteak, he had taken his rifle from behind the door and cleaned it. He did the same with a .44 Colt he had carried daily until a year or two before, when the spread of the settlements had made such a frontier artifact unnecessary, unless one was on a trip. Goodnight knew that it had mainly been the fact that he was there, on his ranch with his wife and cowhands, that had encouraged the first trickle of settlements into the Panhandle. Thereafter the trickle had increased; soon the trickle grew until there were towns and villages and sufficient law that sidearms gradually ceased to be a part of everyday dress.

All his cowboys still wore pistols, of course; they claimed they kept them to use on snakes, but in fact, few of them could shoot well enough with a pistol to hit a rattlesnake in under ten shots at point-blank range.

The cowboys wore the guns from wistfulness, Goodnight supposed. They wanted to feel that they were living in a West that was still wild. It was harmless nostalgia, for the most part; as long as they didn't injure themselves or the livestock, he put no strictures on their use of firearms.

But the Panhandle was no longer the wild West—not by a long shot. The cowboys could play and posture all they wanted to, adjusting their holsters and practicing fast draws. The fact was, they were herdsmen, not gunfighters, and it would be colossal bad luck if their herding ever brought them into contact with a real killer, of the sort that had once been common in the West. If any of his cowboys were that unlucky, they would certainly be killed. Roping and branding and riding pitching horses was no preparation for dealing with deadly men.

Goodnight had cleaned the rifle and oiled up the pistol restlessly, with a troubled mind. He could not get Lorena, the young schoolteacher, out of his thoughts. She had left to find her husband; and her husband, at Goodnight's own insistent urgings, had left first, to go to the assistance of Captain Call. Goodnight had a nagging feeling about the whole business—it nagged him so severely that he had scarcely slept, for three nights. If Mary had been home, she would have been having conniptions, at the thought of all the kerosene he was burning in the kitchen lamp.

The fact was, there still were deadly men in the West, and there was a vast space in which they could operate. The country between the Pecos and the Gila was still mostly no-man's-land. Its emptiness made it a magnet for killers, and at least two of some determination were operating there right now. Mox Mox was probably only a paltry bandit, with a few horse thieves for companions, but he was the man who had piled brush on four cowboys and burned them to death near Pueblo, Colorado. And he had been ready to do the same to Lorena.

The Garza boy didn't seem to be as morbid, or afflicted with the need to burn, but he, too, was a deadly killer who executed his victims at random, and without remorse.

Goodnight felt oppressed by his own thoughts. He had made a serious mistake, when he hectored Pea Eye at the blacksmith's in Quitaque. He had been too blunt, and had acted as if things had to be as they had been in the past. Lorena did not stay a whore; no more did her husband have to stay a Texas Ranger. Except for the meeting at the blacksmith's, these two people, both a credit to their little community, would be at home with their children, the husband farming, the wife teaching school. And, what was most important, they would both be safe.

Now, they were far from safe. They were in the great emptiness of the Pecos country, where Mox Mox and the Garza boy were, too.

Perhaps Woodrow Call would eliminate the outlaws. He had eliminated a good number, some of them formidable, in his day. But he couldn't be everywhere, and he couldn't work miracles. He was one man, trying to find two killers in a big country.

Goodnight had supposed that he was past having to take up the gun. He hadn't had a serious encounter with an outlaw in twenty years. He had thought that sort of conflict behind him; certainly, Mary thought it behind him. If she had been home, he would not have been able to clean the rifle without a debate, probably vigorous. Mary believed in professionals: cattlemen ought to raise cattle; bankers ought to handle money; lawmen ought to deal with outlaws; and wives ought to run their households without interference from the men.

But Mary wasn't home, and anyhow, although he had often let Mary slow him, she had never stopped him, not when he felt he had a task that he should do.

"No, and God and his lightning bolts don't stop you either, Charlie," Mary had observed once, when he was about to leave for Colorado, in uncertain weather.

The weather was uncertain again, but Goodnight had never let weather interfere with him. No one who worked on the plains could afford to bend to weather, if they hoped to accomplish anything.

At four a.m., Goodnight strapped on his pistol, put his rifle back in its saddle scabbard, and went to the lots to catch his horse. It was sleeting again. Dawn was nearly three hours away, but he was restless. He had decided to go, and was soon saddled and ready.

There was a light on in the bunkhouse kitchen. Muley, for all his flaws, at least wasn't lazy. He was in the kitchen, arms white with flour, making biscuits for the cowboys, all of whom were still asleep except his yawning foreman, Willie Bascom, who was sitting up in his bunk trying to pull on his stiff boots.

"Breakfast ain't ready, I just got up," Muley said, the minute Goodnight stepped in the door.

"Fry some bacon. I have to leave, and I hate to travel on an empty stomach," Goodnight said. "I hope that won't interrupt your schedule too much."

"I usually fry the bacon last, but I guess you're the boss," Muley said.

"I was the last time I wrote you a paycheck," Goodnight said.

Goodnight poured his own coffee, since Muley hadn't offered to. The bacon was soon crackling and spitting grease. Willie Bascom came over and accepted a cup of coffee. He had his boots on, but did not look happy to be up.

"I didn't think we was branding till tomorrow," he said. "I guess I lost shut of a day."

"No, you're branding tomorrow," Goodnight said. "I hate to desert, but it's just the branding. You can handle it yourself."

"Don't see why not," Willie Bascom said.

"What's taking you off in a sleet storm?" Muley asked. Another habit he shared with many ranch cooks was inquisitiveness. It was not so much that he didn't mind his own business; he just didn't recognize that there was any business that wasn't his.

"I'm going on a wolf hunt," Goodnight said. He finished his bacon and his coffee. Cowboys were just beginning to crawl out of their bunks.

"These biscuits will be ready in another few minutes," Muley said. "You might as well wait and eat a few—you can't see to shoot a wolf when it's this dark, anyway."

"No, I'll have to do without the biscuits," Goodnight said.

Despite the weather, he was impatient to leave. He had saddled his best horse, a big roan named Lacey. The horse's coat steamed as the snow melted on it.

"He had his pistol on," Muley remarked, once Goodnight left. "That's the last time I'll offer him biscuits, if he's always going to be in such a hurry."

"It's been five years since I've seen him wear his pistol," Willie Bascom said.

By the time the cowboys finished their breakfast, Goodnight was many miles to the south. The sleet had gotten heavier, but he didn't notice. He had too much on his mind.

13.

By the time Maria reached Ojinaga, her feet were badly cut from the icy, stony ground. Since leaving the railroad, Maria had walked without shoes. The train took the seven women east; the conductor was reluctant, but not so reluctant that he would leave seven women to die in the cold.

By then, Maria's shoes were gone. The wet snow and icy weather cracked them. She cut up the bag she had carried the jerky in and wrapped her feet in the sacking, but the sacking was thin and wore out within a few miles.

From then on, Maria was barefoot. She went slowly, avoiding cactus, trying not to cut herself on rocks or ice. Her food gave out when she was three days from the river. Since leaving the railroad, she had not seen a single human being.

The conductor had offered to take her to Fort Worth. What did one more woman matter? He told her she was a fool, to try to walk to Mexico in such weather. Mox Mox had taken two children from a ranch near Comstock. He could be anywhere. Any day, he might appear with his men and catch her. Speculation was that he had already burned the children, a boy of nine and a girl of six. If he caught Maria, she could expect a hard death.

The conductor grew irritated with the woman when he saw that she wasn't going to take his advice. Maria merely looked at him, without expression, when he offered to take her on the train. He didn't like sullen women. Who was she, that she could turn down free passage to Fort Worth?

"My children don't live in Fort Worth—I would just have to come back," Maria said. She wanted to be polite. After all, the man had accepted the seven women.

"You've got no shoes," the conductor pointed out. Despite rough travel, the Mexican woman was good-looking. Once she was on the warm train and had some food in her, she might become friendlier. Perhaps she could be persuaded to show her gratitude for what he was doing for her friends.

"You've got no shoes," the conductor said, again. He felt like dragging her onto the train. It would be a kindness, in the end. It might save her life.

"No, but I have feet," Maria said. She saw how he was looking at her—men were always men. She had intended to ask for a little food, but when she saw the conductor's look, she turned and walked away from the train. Men were always men—she would have to find food elsewhere.

But she found no food. Only the sight of the mountains gave her the strength to keep walking. Her children were west of the mountains. Crossing the Maravilla Canyon was very hard, though. She had to crawl up the far side.

The day before Maria got home, she saw three cowboys in the distance. She hid in the sagebrush until they were out of sight. They belonged to the big ranch. Perhaps they would remember her; if so, it might be hard. She was too tired and too weak to be worried with cowboys. If they were too hard on her, she might forget her children and die. She still wanted to take her children to the doctors, so that Rafael's mind and Teresa's eyes might be fixed.

It seemed a big thing to hope for, though. She was tired and hungry, alone, and with no money. Even if she got home, she would have no money. But it was only her hope for her children, however farfetched that hope might seem, that kept her will strong and gave her strength to keep putting her torn, swollen feet on the hard ground. Rafael and Teresa had no one but her to think ahead for them, to consider how their lives might be if she could take them to the great doctors who knew how to cure eyes and fix minds.

Finally, Maria saw the curve of the river. She crossed well below Presidio. She did not want the hard sheriff to find her, just as she was almost home.

Teresa heard her mother's footsteps and went running to her, though the chickens squawked loudly at such an interruption. Rafael stumbled after his sister, carrying a young goat he had taken as a pet.

While Maria was still holding her children in the road, Billy came out and told her that Captain Call had destroyed the hard sheriff, beating him with a rifle.

"That's right," Billy Williams said. "Joe Doniphan's done for. He's had to quit. You can walk right through the middle of Presidio and not a soul will bother you."

"Did you see Call?" Maria asked.

"I reckon I did," Billy said. "Call and a Yankee and a deputy from Laredo came riding up the Concho and stopped right at this house."

Maria saw that her children were healthy. Teresa's hair had not been brushed well, and Rafael's shirt was not as clean as she would make it when she washed his clothes. But they were healthy. Billy had done a good job. Maria smiled at him, to show that she was not without gratitude. Since leaving the railroad, she had been thinking bad thoughts about men. She had left her children with this man, and he had cared for them well, although she had never been with him in the bed. Whatever his disappointments, he had been decent, and he had cared for her children. It was a thing she would not forget. She meant to try and help Billy a little, once she was rested. He was an old man, he drank too much, he didn't keep himself clean, and he was not very well.

Now, though, she felt frightened for Joey. Captain Call had found her village, and even her house.

"Did Famous Shoes bring him here?" she asked. The old tracker was not to be trusted. He liked money too much.

"Nope, never got this far," Billy said. "Famous Shoes and another deputy were in Joe Doniphan's jail when Call showed up. Joe wouldn't let 'em out. He pulled a gun on Call, and that's when Call started whipping him with the rifle barrel."

"Did you tell Call anything about Joey?" Maria asked, suspiciously. When it came to Joey, she trusted no one.

"No, why would I?" Billy asked. "Do you take me for a lawman?"

"I'm sorry," Maria said. "Let's go in the house. I need to heat some water, and I need to eat."

Billy and Teresa made her soup. She took a little, but she felt feverish and did not take much. The next day, Billy killed a baby goat—not Rafael's pet—and fed her some of the tender meat. Maria's fever got worse, though. For more than a week, she tossed with it, too weak to get out of her bed. Billy and Teresa cared for her, giving her a little soup, and bathing her face with cool rags.

Maria's mind flew around, while the fever burned or chilled her. She saw Joey hanging from the rock where Benito had died. In a dream, Benito came to her as a baby and tried to suck her breast. She dreamed about Captain Call beating the hard sheriff with a rifle—only the hard sheriff changed into Joey. It was Joey who the Captain beat.

When the fever broke and Maria could look clearly at the world again, Billy Williams was asleep on the dirt floor by her bed. He had a bottle of whiskey beside him, but had drunk only a little. The bottle had fallen over, and whiskey was seeping out. Billy slept with his mouth open. To Maria, he seemed older than he had seemed when she took the fever. He looked gray, as if he had no blood.

It was a chilly morning. When Maria got up, she covered Billy Williams with the serape she had been using for herself.

"Mother, a man came and looked at me," Teresa said. She was glad that her mother was out of bed.

"What kind of man?" Maria asked.

"A gringo—he is the one who is hunting Joey," Teresa said. "I could feel him looking at me."

Again, Maria felt frightened. Call had destroyed the hard sheriff. He was hunting her son. What business did he have, coming to her house and looking at her daughter?

"Go in the house, if he comes back," Maria said. "Don't let him look at you. He is a bad man. He wants to kill Joey. Don't ever let him look at you."

"He said I was pretty," Teresa said. "He didn't do anything bad."

"He was right—you are pretty," Maria said. She hugged her daughter. They sat in a chair by the table. Rafael came in with his pet goat and sang the goat a little song. Maria held her daughter in her arms for a long time. Someday, Teresa would be a woman, but Maria didn't want that time to be soon. She held her daughter tightly. Rafael sat down by Maria's chair, holding his goat in his lap. Maria stroked his hair. Then she held Teresa tightly. Teresa liked it, when her mother held her close, in her warm arms.

Maria wished that this could be their life forever, just herself and her children sitting in her warm kitchen together. If such a time could be the whole of life, then life could be happiness. If Teresa could remain a child in her arms, then Teresa would never know the deep sorrows of womanhood, sorrows as deep as the cold water in the village well. She sniffed her daughter's neck. Teresa still smelled like a child. She did not smell like a woman, yet. Rafael had stopped changing. Unless she could find a doctor to fix his mind, Rafael would always be a boy. He would not know many of the sorrows of men.

But Teresa was growing; only her eyes were arrested. Teresa had heard Captain Call's compliment, and remembered it. She would not always fit in Maria's arms, and she would not always smell like a little girl. Maria meant to hold her as long as she could. Joey might be evil; he might be lost. Rafael might always be young in his mind. But Teresa was whole; she lacked only sight. Someday, she would escape from her mother's arms and walk out in her beauty into the world of sorrows.

Maria didn't want it to be soon.

14.

Call had a sense that someone was behind him, but if so, it was someone smart. After two days, the sense was so strong that Call doubled back twice. If it was the Garza boy, Call might surprise him. Even if he didn't surprise him, he could probably strike his track and determine whether the boy was alone.

In the course of four days' travel, he doubled back three more times, but he didn't surprise Joey Garza, and he struck no track.

Yet, the sense that someone was behind him wouldn't leave him. It became a conviction, though none of his maneuvers produced the slightest evidence of a pursuer. Anyone following him would have had to be on horseback, and horses left tracks. But there were no tracks. If it was the Garza boy, then he was a formidable plainsman. In the cold night, Call rode a circle, hoping to glimpse a campfire, but there was no campfire, either.

It was vexing, because it made him distrust his own instincts. Maybe he had slipped a notch, as a tracker; or maybe he had just begun to imagine things. Never before had he followed his instincts and come up totally empty.

All he could do was travel cautiously. At night, he made no fires; he slept little, and kept his horse saddled and the bridle reins in his hand when he lay down. During the day, he kept as much space around him as possible. He tried to stay a mile or more from any cover that might shelter a killer with a fine rifle and a telescope sight. He whirled his horse often, hoping to catch a flash of reflection on a spur or a bridle bit, but he saw no reflections.

He was alone; yet, he knew he wasn't.

Then it occurred to him that perhaps the boy wasn't on horseback. Perhaps he was a runner, like Famous Shoes, or some of the celebrated Apaches. If so, he was bold indeed. Few men of experience would voluntarily put themselves afoot in such country, in the wintertime. Few would be able to do without fire to rest by, in the freezing night.

Call's own hands ached terribly, in the mornings. Three days passed without his even unsaddling his horse. He was afraid he might not be able to pull the saddle straps tight again, with his sore hands. When the horse grazed, he walked with him. One night, he napped on his feet, leaning against the horse for warmth. He took the trigger guards off both rifles; his knuckles were too swollen to fit through them.

On the fifth day, he crossed the trail of Mox Mox and his men. They were traveling toward Fort Stockton. The trail was fresh—the gang had just passed. In fact, to the northwest, Call did see a flash, as the sun struck some piece of equipment.

Call checked the loads in both rifles and took his extra Colt out of the saddlebags. It was midafternoon. He turned northwest, on the easily followed track of the killers. He put his horse into a lope, debating with himself about the timing of his ambush.

He could try to overtake them that day; his mount was fresh enough. If he could kill Mox Mox and the Cherokee, the others might run. But he needed good light to shoot by, and he also needed to be close. He was not shooting a German rifle with a telescope sight. He was confident of his marksmanship, but only if the range and the light were favorable. If he attacked at night, as Gus had once attacked Blue Duck's camp, it would all be guesswork, and anyhow, he had never been as reckless on the attack as Gus McCrae.

Within an hour, it became apparent that catching up with the gang would be no trouble. They were idling along. Call soon had to drop back and veer west of them to lessen the danger of being observed. He decided then to try to close the gap and hit them as they made camp. They didn't know he was following them, and might not immediately set a guard.

The outlaws were even lazier than Call judged them to be, at first. It was only a little past midafternoon when they made camp. Call walked his horse for the last three miles, as he approached. He was one against eight, and he wanted to be as meticulous as possible in what he had to do.

He could not expect to thunder in and kill eight men, or even cripple them sufficiently to remove them as a threat. Above all, he had to try to kill the fighter, Jimmy Cumsa, first.

As Call cautiously moved, foot by foot, to within two hundred yards of the camp, he heard a child scream. It was a rude surprise—Mox Mox must have taken a child from some farm or ranch, in his marauding. The outlaws had not even made a campfire yet; surely they couldn't be burning the child.

But the child continued to scream, as Call crept closer. The child's screams rang in Call's ears, echoing other screams, heard years before. On one of his first forays against hostile Indians, when he was a young Ranger, the troop had surprised a little cluster of Comanche, on the Washita. They recovered two young white captives, both girls. Just before the Rangers raced down on the camp, one of the little girls screamed. An old Comanche woman was beating her with a stick. Call shot the old woman, the only female he ever killed in his years of battle. The little girls had lost their minds, from the cold and the beatings. The one the old woman was beating recovered and married; the other one was never right.

When Call got close enough to look over a low ridge, down into the camp where the child was screaming, he saw that Mox Mox had two children, a boy and a girl. They were bound together by a short length of chain. Mox Mox was quirting the boy savagely, whipping him in the face. The little girl seemed too terrified to even whimper, but the boy screamed every time the quirt struck him. Call looked first for Jimmy Cumsa, but saw at once that he had no clean shot at him—the Cherokee was among the horses, preparing to hobble them for the night. The three Mexicans, the giant, and a small man were standing idle, easy targets. But the giant was standing between Call and Mox Mox, watching him quirt the child. The eighth man Call couldn't immediately see, which worried him.

Call had never seen a man beat a child so savagely. What the old Comanche woman on the Washita had done to the young girl was merely rough, compared to the whipping he was witnessing. Call felt he had to act quickly; otherwise, Mox Mox might whip the boy's eyes out, or even kill him with the quirt. There was no time to plan; he had to shoot, if he wanted to save the child's eyesight and possibly his life. He could not shoot the Cherokee first, or the manburner, either. He had to act, if he hoped to save the little boy's vision.

Call shot the giant man first, hoping he would fall clear and give him a clean shot at Mox Mox. But the giant staggered, leaving Mox Mox mostly hidden. Call went ahead, risked one shot and hit him, but Mox Mox did not fall. Even before he could lever a third shot, he heard horses racing away and knew that Jimmy Cumsa was escaping. The Cherokee had taken two horses and was hanging between them; Call couldn't see him at all.

He shot again at Mox Mox and hit him in the shoulder; then Mox Mox, too, was among the horses. The three Mexicans and the small man were running for their rifles, which had been propped against their saddles. They were slow, perhaps drunk. Call shot all four of them and put them down, not for good, probably, but down.

Mox Mox couldn't ride as well as Jimmy Cumsa. Even without a broken shoulder, he could not have handled animals well enough to hang between two horses, but he managed to do the next best thing, which was to spook all the horses and raise a dust. Call snapped a shot at one of the horses Jimmy Cumsa was escaping with; the horse went down, but the Cherokee didn't go down with it. He switched to the other horse and struggled into the saddle. Call shot again, but by then the range was long and the bullet kicked up dust.

[374]

One of the fallen Mexicans was trying to run to his horse, but his horse was carrying Mox Mox away. Call shot the Mexican again and then threw one more shot at Mox Mox. He could scarcely see him, for the dust, but he thought he hit him in the leg. The big man was stirring, so Call shot him again. What nagged him was the eighth man—where could he be? Almost as the question registered in his mind, he saw a man trying to pull up his pants, a good distance beyond the camp. He had been shitting and was trying to get his pants up so he could run away, when Call saw him. He was a long way from camp, but Call took a slow aim and brought him down.

Mox Mox and Jimmy Cumsa were far out of range, but still going. Maybe they would keep running, but there was also a chance they would return and make a fight of it. It would depend on how badly Mox Mox was wounded, and whether he was disposed to fight. Jimmy Cumsa had run from Quanah Parker; probably he would run again, but that was not a certainty.

Call reloaded, took both rifles, stuck one in his belt, and with a pistol in one hand and a rifle in the other, leading his horse— he had to hold the bridle reins in his teeth—came down into the camp. Of the six men down, only the last one, the one who had been shitting, was dead; when, a little later, Call walked out and turned him over, he found a boy in his late teens, with black teeth. The other men he had to dispatch with his pistol, which he did quickly. He was not in a position to take prisoners, much less to nurse wounded outlaws who would only recover to be hung, if they recovered at all.

Call had no difficulty freeing the children. The short chain that held them was only fastened with wire. The little boy was still moaning; his face ran blood. Call washed the blood away with water from one of the dead men's canteens. One of the boy's eyes had swollen shut, probably from being hit with the tip of the quirt. The eye itself did not appear to be hurt, and the other eye was not damaged. The cuts on the boy's face were deep, but he was young, and he would recover.

The little girl grabbed Call's leg and clung to it so tightly he had to pull her arms loose in order to lift her up.

"Want Ma. . . ." she said. "Want Ma. . . ."

The little boy had stopped moaning. He seemed numb. He looked at Call with his one open eye gratefully, though.

"He said he'd whip my eyes out," the boy said. "He said he'd burn Marcie."

"He's gone—he won't put your eyes out and he won't burn your sister. Can you stand up?"

The boy stood up. He was shaky, from the shock of the violence, and probably from lack of proper food. But he could walk.

The horse Call shot was on its feet again; it stood pawing the ground, about a hundred yards away. It was saddled. If it was not too badly injured, it might do for the children. Call was keenly conscious that he needed to move, and move at once. The ridge that had provided his cover before the fight would provide the same cover for the Garza boy, who, if he was following, would undoubtedly have heard the shooting. All Joey Garza would have to do would be to crawl up behind the ridge and shoot; he wouldn't need his telescope sight. Call and the children were within easy range.

"Stay a minute, I need to catch this horse so we can go," Call told the children. He left them standing together. The little girl tried to run after him, but the boy grabbed her arm and pulled her back.

Call caught the wounded horse easily and was relieved to see that its wound wasn't crippling. The wound was in the neck. It was bleeding profusely, but he could stop the bleeding, and the horse could carry the two children. Fort Stockton was not more than forty miles away.

"Mister, have you got a biscuit?" the boy asked, when Call returned, leading the horse. "Me and Marcie ain't had no food. That squint-eye wouldn't give us none."

Call rummaged quickly in the dead men's kit and found some jerky and a few stiff tortillas. He gave them to the children.

"This is all I can do for now," Call said. "We have to leave here. Can you ride a horse?"

"I guess I can," the boy said, with some pride. "Pa got me Brownie when I was three, and I'm nine now."

His wounds were still running blood. The whole front of his shirt was stained with it. But that could be attended to later, when they were safe.

"We have to move," Call said. "We ain't safe here. The man who quirted you might come back."

"Why didn't you kill him, mister?" the boy asked.

"I tried—I hit him," Call said.

"I wish you'd kilt him," the boy said. "He said he'd burn Marcie."

Call gathered up serapes from the dead men. He wrapped the children well, against the cold, and put them on the wounded horse. Probably neither of the children had been warm in days. The little girl shivered so badly that Call thought he might have to tie her to the horse, but he didn't. It wouldn't do to have her tied to a horse if there was another fight.

He took several blankets and what food he could find. At the last minute, he discovered a piece of antelope haunch, wrapped in some sacking. That was lucky. He cut off two pieces and gave them to the children, to gnaw as they rode.

He decided to lead the wounded horse. With Mox Mox and Jimmy Cumsa somewhere ahead of him, perhaps waiting in ambush, and with Joey Garza behind him, if it was Joey Garza behind him, he needed as much control over the animals as he could get.

"What's your name?" Call asked the boy, before he mounted.

"Bob," the boy said. "Bobby Fant."

"Why, son . . . is Jasper your pa?" Call asked. "Jasper Fant?"

"That's our pa. How'd you know his name, mister?" the boy asked. His wounds had stopped bleeding and had crusted over. Call had packed some sand in the wound in the horse's neck, and it was no longer bleeding so badly.

"Your pa worked for me once," Call said. "We went to Montana together. I didn't even know he had married. Last I heard of him, he was in Nebraska."

"Nope, we live out by Comstock now," the boy said.

"Say, are you Captain Call?" he asked, his eyes widening. He even got the swollen eye open, in his amazement.

"Yes, I'm Captain Call," Call replied.

"Pa always talks about you," the boy said. "He said if anyone ever took us, he'd get you to find us, even if it was Indians that got us."

"Well, it's your good luck that I did find you," Call said. "You hold on to your sister and don't let her fall off.

"We may have to ride all night, Bob," he said. "There's a town we can get to tomorrow if we don't stop. Once we get there, you'll both be safe and I can send you home to your ma and pa."

"Want Ma. . . ." the little girl said again. "Want Ma. . . ."

"You'll have her," Call said. Despite being wrapped in two serapes, the little girl was still shivering, chilled through by the long cold, Call supposed.

"Don't let her fall," he said again, to the boy.

'Oh, I don't guess Marcie will fall off. She's got her own pony, back home," the boy said.

Call took the lead rope and headed immediately into the widest space he could find, well away from the ridges. He was glad that Fort Stockton was no farther than it was. It was bitter weather, and the children had gone through a brutal experience. They might sicken yet, and probably would. He wanted to get them to a place where there were warm houses and a proper doctor. They seemed to him to be remarkably plucky children. That was even more remarkable in view of the fact that their father was Jasper Fant, a man who complained constantly about his ills, real or imagined. He had been a Hat Creek cowboy and had made the drive to Montana. His main terror was of drowning, but it took only a sniffle to bring out Jasper's complaints.

Night fell, and Captain Call kept riding. He stopped now and then to check on the wound in the horse's neck. The little girl had gone to sleep, propped against her brother's chest. Bobby, the boy, was wide awake.

"We're gonna keep going," Call told him. "Gnaw on that meat and give your sister some if she wakes up."

"My hands are freezing off," the boy said. "I wish it wasn't so cold."

"Keep your hands under the blanket," Call said. "I can't stop and make a fire. Mox Mox might find us."

"That squint—I wish you'd kilt him," Bobby said.

"Well, I didn't, but I might yet," Call said.

Call rode on, trying to knot an old bandanna around his neck to protect it from the cutting wind. The little gun battle had been badly handled, he knew. Bobby Fant was right to reproach him for not killing Mox Mox. The boy's screams had caused him to rush what he ought not to have rushed. It would have been wiser to let the boy endure the whipping for another few seconds. The large man might have moved out of the way and given him a clear shot at Mox Mox. He might even have had a clear shot at Jimmy Cumsa, if he had waited a minute more to start firing.

As it was, he had rushed, and the result of his rushing was that he had killed the six incompetents and let the two really dangerous men escape. It was foolish behavior. He had rescued the children, but he hadn't removed the threat. He should have kept his mind on the prime object, which was to kill Mox Mox. Jimmy Cumsa might be deadly, but he hadn't been leading the pack, and he didn't quirt children for his amusement.

Another truth, just as discouraging, was that he had not shot well. Only the boy who had been caught with his pants down had been killed cleanly, with one shot, and that was probably luck. All the others had required two or more bullets. It was poor shooting, and yet he'd had all the advantages: not a shot had been fired at him, he had been shooting from less than fifty yards' distance, and he had taken the men completely by surprise.

Call blamed his swollen knuckles. Also, he wasn't as sure of his eyesight as he had been. If the men had been better fighters, he would have been in trouble. If Mox Mox and Jimmy Cumsa had taken cover instead of running, the outcome of the struggle might have been different.

Call often picked over battles, in his mind. There were few fixed rules. Once men started shooting at one another with deadly intent, strategies and plans were usually forgotten. Men acted and reacted according to their instincts. Experience didn't always tell; veterans of many battles made wild, inexplicable mistakes. Even men who remained perfectly calm in battle did things that they could not make sense of later, if they survived to rehash the battle.

But, right or wrong, it was done. At least he had Jasper Fant's children, and they would survive, if he could get them to a warm place soon enough.

As Call rode on, the cold grew more intense. His mind returned again and again to the shooting. It troubled him that he had shot so poorly. Augustus McCrae, given similar advantages, would probably have killed all the men with a pistol.

Before the night ended, the children got so cold that Call had to stop and risk a fire. He could barely gather sticks with his stiff fingers. The children's feet were so cold that Call knew he was risking frostbite if he didn't do something. Fortunately, there was enough scrubby brush that he soon had adequate wood. He made two fires and put the freezing children between them. The crusted blood on the boy's face was icy. He had been plucky when first rescued, but had gone into a kind of shock and couldn't speak. The little girl was so cold she was past whimpering.

Call built up the fires and kept them flaming as the children slept. He himself hunkered near the flames only a few minutes at a time. It was so cold that he doubted any killer would be vigorous enough to take advantage of them. But he couldn't be sure, and he didn't want to get too warm himself. When he hunkered by the fire, fatigue began to suck at him, a deep fatigue. He was accustomed to sleeping in snatches; squatting, leaning against a horse; he had even slept riding, if the country was flat and the horse reliable. In the Indian-fighting days, he had tried to acquire the abilities and the endurance of his foes.

He wanted to be able to do anything a Comanche could do, or an Apache. Gus had scoffed at the notion. He said no white man could live as an Indian could, or travel as fast, or subsist on as little.

Probably Gus had been right about that. And if he hadn't been as able as the best of the Indians when he was young, there was little hope that he could compete with one now. Joey Garza was Mexican, not Indian, but many Mexicans were part Indian, and there was a rumor that the Garza boy had lived with the mountain Apaches for several years. The cold might not affect him; once, it would not have affected Call, either.

With things so uncertain, it wouldn't do to give way to fatigue, or to nap too long by the campfire. He might wake up to discover that his throat had just been cut.

In the morning, the frost was so heavy that Call had to scrape ice off the saddles. The children were so cold they couldn't eat. He decided that he had better tie them to the horse. Though there was a band of red on the eastern horizon, the sun was soon blanketed by heavy clouds, and the cold remained intense.

The wounded horse was stiff—it could barely move, and not rapidly. Fortunately, when they had been riding an hour, Call saw a few plumes of smoke to the northwest, clear in the freezing air. The smoke was coming from the chimneys of Fort Stockton.

A little later, he saw more smoke, on the eastern horizon. This smoke moved westward, and it came from a train. Call couldn't see the train, but he knew the railroad was there, for nothing else would be moving under a plume of smoke.

The wounded horse slowed to a walk, and then to a slower walk. A little before midday, the horse stopped. It could go no farther. By then, the town was no more than five miles away. Call left the horse; perhaps it would walk on in, under its own power, once it had rested for a day. He put the children on his horse, only to have his horse come up lame a mile or two farther on. A needlelike sliver of ice had cut its hoof.

But the town was not far. The little girl had recovered a little, and now and then asked for her mother. Bobby Fant, his face a horror of frozen cuts, had not spoken all day. Call took his time, walking the lame horse slowly. He didn't want to have to carry the children, or abandon his guns and equipment.

When they were only two miles from the town, they came upon two sheepmen, butchering sheep to sell in Fort Stockton.

"Dern, where'd you folks spring from?" the older sheepman said, when he saw Call leading the lame horse with two children on it.

"From far enough away that we'd appreciate a ride to somewhere these young ones can warm themselves," Call said.

"We'd more than appreciate it," he added. "We'd pay a good fare if you'd take us in your wagon the rest of the way to town."

"Mister, you don't have to pay us nothing—we was about to haul these carcasses in anyway," the younger sheepman said. They were shaggy men, in great buffalo coats, and they had three huge dogs with them. It had been the barking of the dogs that led Call to the wagon. There were no grazing sheep visible, though, just six bloody carcasses piled up in the wagon.

Call chose to walk behind the wagon, leading his lame horse. The young sheepman said there was a rooming house on the main street in town.

"It ain't fancy, but it's got beds," he said. "Who done that to that boy's face?"

Bobby Fant's face had gotten worse during the night. It was swollen, and some of the cuts still leaked blood, most of which froze on his cheeks.

"A man named Mox Mox done it," Call said. "I shot him, but I don't think I killed him."

"Somebody ought to kill the sonofabitch, then," the older man said. "I've seen rough stuff out here on the baldies, but I've never seen nothing like that—not done to a child."

Call carried Bobby Fant into the little frame rooming house. The young sheepman got off the wagon for a minute and carried the girl, who was whimpering for her mother.

A woman stood just inside the door, looking out at them through the pane of glass. Call could just see her; she was blond. The young sheepherder brought the little girl in first. By the time Call eased through the door with Bobby Fant, the woman had already taken the little girl in her arms and was whispering to her.

Call couldn't hear what the woman was whispering. The fact that the blond woman had appeared so suddenly behind the pane of glass startled him a little. The woman looked familiar. He thought for a moment she might be the children's mother, Jasper Fant's wife, though he hadn't even known Jasper Fant had a wife until yesterday, and how the woman could have anticipated them and got to Fort Stockton was a mystery.

When the woman saw Bobby Fant's face, she drew in her breath.

"Mox Mox done that, didn't he, Captain?" she asked, touching the boy's cuts gently with her fingers. "Did you kill him, Captain?"

"Well, I hit him," Call said. "I doubt it was mortal, but it might slow him enough that I can catch him."

"Bring the boy to my room," the woman said. "I just got off the train and was about to have a bath. I've got hot water waiting. I'll put them both in the bathtub. It'll warm them quicker. Then I can wash those cuts."

The woman started up the stairs with the little girl. Call thanked the young sheepman and began to climb the stairs, carrying Bobby Fant. The moment he stepped into the warm rooming house, he had begun to feel tired, so tired that it was a strain even to carry the child up one flight of stairs. He was wondering, in his fatigue, how the woman had known who he was—and how she knew about Mox Mox.

It was not until the blond woman paused at the top of the stairs and looked down at him, the little girl in her arms, that Call realized who she was: she was not the children's mother, she was Pea Eye's wife.

"My Lord, you'll have to excuse me," he said, embarrassed. "I didn't recognize you."

Call could not quite remember when he had last seen Lorena; in Nebraska, it seemed to him. She had been a young woman then. Of course, many years had passed, and she would have to be older. But the fact that she was so much older that he hadn't recognized her, left him feeling at a loss.

"You don't need to be embarrassed," Lorena said. "You kept Mox Mox from burning these children, and you brought them out. That's enough."

He carried the boy into her room where, indeed, a bath was steaming.

"Put him on the bed," Lorena said. "Just put him on the bed. I'll take care of these youngsters. You better go get a little rest yourself."

"Yes, I'm weary," Call said. In fact, he felt so weary that he could hardly carry the child across the small room.

"I'm mighty surprised to see you," he added. He felt that he ought to say more, but he didn't know quite what.

"I came looking for my husband," Lorena said. "I was hoping you'd have him with you."

"I don't, but I know where he is," Captain Call said. "He ain't far."

The woman's face brightened, when he said it. He went downstairs and got a room key, though later, he was unable to remember getting a key or even going to the room.

When he woke up, fully clothed on a bed, many hours later, it was worry about his horse that caused him to wake. He had forgotten the horse completely, once he entered the rooming house, and had just left it standing in the street. He looked out the window, but could see nothing. It was pitch-dark. He wondered if anyone had done anything about his horse.

15.

Lorena didn't leave the children all day, except to walk down the street and find a doctor who could treat Bobby's face. Fortunately, there was no damage to either eye. The boy could see fine, but some of the cuts on his cheeks were so deep that the doctor told her he would probably always bear the scars.

Lorena was not sleeping much, and did not expect to sleep much until she knew that Mox Mox was dead. The sight of Bobby Fant's face was enough to keep her awake. It reminded her too vividly of the little boy who had not been lucky enough to be rescued, the boy Mox Mox had burned in her place. That boy's death cries still echoed in her mind, and she remembered the deep, grinding fear she had felt as she waited for it to happen to her. The fear had been so nearly unbearable that it made the other things the men did to her seem a small business. She had trained herself over the years not to remember that fear. If she dwelt on it, even for an hour, it paralyzed her and made it difficult for her to do her schoolwork, or be a wife, or even do her motherly chores.

When she looked out the door of the rooming house and saw Captain Call coming, she had been shocked at how decrepit he looked. Pea Eye had mentioned, casually, that the Captain wasn't quite as spry as he had been, but the comment hadn't prepared her for how the man actually looked.

Lorena had not seen Call since the morning, long before, when he had left Clara Allen's house with Gus McCrae's body. The man had not been young when he rode off that morning, but neither had he been the old man who walked stiffly into the rooming house in Fort Stockton. Of course, her daughter Clarie was fifteen years old, and Call's departure from Clara's on his trip back to Texas with Gus's body had occurred two years before she married Pea. She had not seen Captain Call in nearly twenty years. She should have been prepared for him to be old.

She just hadn't supposed he would look so stiff and worn out. Of course, he had traveled a long distance with two children, in the bitter cold. He had probably been traveling since the day Pea Eye had refused to go with him. Younger men than Captain Call would have been tired.

The day after he arrived with the children, Call was too tired even to go downstairs. He knocked timidly on Lorena's door and asked if she could request the lady who owned the rooming house to bring him some food. He also asked if Lorena would inquire about his horse. Had it been stabled and fed?

Lorena got him food, and was able to assure him that the local sheriff had taken charge of his mount. The lameness wasn't serious, and the horse would be ready to travel in a few days. Call seemed reassured. He considered it a serious lapse, that he had forgotten to stable his own horse.

"It was so warm, I guess I fainted," he said. "I don't recall going to bed. I don't usually forget to stable my horse."

"You saved two children," Lorena pointed out, again. "There's people here who aren't busy that can take care of your horse."

"Well, it's my horse," Call said. "I have always looked after my own mounts."

"My seven-year-old can unsaddle a horse and feed it as well as you can, Captain," Lorena said. "But my seven-year-old couldn't save two children from Mox Mox."

Call took the point—he didn't mention the horse again, for fear of irritating Lorena.

But he didn't forget the lapse, either. It took him a day and a half to feel refreshed enough to walk down to the livery stable and inspect the horse himself. He felt he ought to get moving, for none of the work he had set out to do had been accomplished. Mox Mox wasn't dead, or if he was, no one had found him. And he was no closer to catching Joey Garza than he had been when he left Amarillo. Brookshire would be having fits about the delay, and his boss, Colonel Terry, was probably having worse fits.

On the third day, Jasper Fant arrived with his wife, to take his stolen children home. To Call's surprise, Jasper had grown bald; he had also grown a belly. His wife was a small woman, of the wiry type. Her name was May.

Both parents gasped when they saw their son's face. The wiry little mother held her children and sobbed. Jasper turned a violent red.

"Why, the damned killer, why did he do it, Captain?" Jasper asked.

Lorena stood with Call, watching. The little girl clung to her mother's neck so tightly that the woman couldn't speak. Jasper and May had been on a train for two days. They had left as soon as the telegram came, telling them that their children were alive.

A few hours later, the little family got on the train to go home. May tried to thank Call, but broke into such sobs of gratitude that she couldn't get the words out. Jasper grasped his hand and held it until Call was afraid they'd miss their train, although they were standing two steps from it.

"I hope you kill that squint, mister," Bobby Fant said, as his father was helping him onto the train.

"Many thanks, Captain," Jasper said. "We won't none of us ever forget what you've done. Me and May, we won't forget it. If you're ever down in Comstock I hope you'll stop and make a meal with us."

"I will," Call said, glad that the train was leaving. He couldn't get over how bald Jasper was. Earlier, in the trail-driving days, the man had been somewhat vain about his hair.

"They're lucky," Lorena said, as she and the Captain were walking back to the hotel. "When Blue Duck had me, Mox Mox wanted to burn me. Blue Duck wouldn't let him—he wanted me for bait. But Mox Mox caught a boy somewhere, and he burned him in my place."

"Why, I never knew that," Call said. "Gus never told me— I'm surprised he kept it from me."

"I didn't tell Gus," Lorena said. "I didn't tell my husband, either. I told Mr. Goodnight, just before I left to come on this trip. He was the first person to hear about it, and you're the second."

"You told Charlie Goodnight?" Call said, amazed. "Did he come around and ask?"

"That's right," Lorena said. "He came around and asked. When can we go to my husband?"

"He's in Presidio, or he's near there," Call said. "There's no train, and not much of a road. We'll have to go horseback."

Call fell silent. He knew that Lorena had every right to go to her husband. Traveling the distance she had traveled already, and riding a train when two notorious train robbers were on the loose and every train liable to being stopped, showed unusual courage. Call was happy to relent and let Lorena take Pea home. The man's heart wasn't in law work anymore, if it was law work they were doing. It was better that he quit lawing for good, and take care of his wife and children, and his farm.

"Captain, I hope you don't doubt that I can ride," Lorena said, seeing the man hesitate. "I rode all the way to Nebraska, with that cow herd you and Gus drove. And I lived with Clara Allen for three years, on her horse ranch. I can ride and I'll keep up. The cold don't discourage me. I want to go to my husband. If you're going to Presidio, I want to go with you."

"Oh, it ain't the riding or the cold," Call said. "I'm told you drive a buggy every day to teach school—Charlie Goodnight told me that. He admires you. Riding to Presidio won't be much colder than driving your buggy to school, in the Panhandle."

"What is it, then?" Lorena asked. "I can leave now. I'm packed. What is it?"

As she asked the question, the sheriff of Fort Stockton, the fellow who had stabled Call's horse, saw them and practically ran toward them.

"Captain, did you get the news?" he asked.

"Why, no, I guess not," Call said. "What news?"

"Joey Garza killed Judge Roy Bean," the skinny sheriff said. "He gut-shot him and then strung him up to his own chimney. Hung him. That's the news."

"When?" Call asked.

"Maybe a week ago, about," the sheriff said. "Nobody knows exactly, because nobody was there when it happened."

"I was there about then, but I left," Call said. "Pea Eye and Brookshire and Deputy Plunkert were there, too, but they left right after I did."

"A sheepherder found him," the sheriff said. "Came by to get a bottle of whiskey and there the man hung, right by the door of his own saloon."

"That boy must have been watching," Call said. "He must be clever at hiding. I looked, and I didn't see him."

"The sheepherders are all scared now," the sheriff said. "They're bringing their sheep closer to the towns."

"I don't know what good that will do them," Call said. "They could run their sheep right here in the main street, and he'd still kill them, if he's that good at hiding."

"Are you sure my husband left?" Lorena asked. The fear that had been with her for weeks rose up in her throat again.

"Well, he was saddled and ready when I rode off," Call said. "Brookshire was drunk and Deputy Plunkert and Famous Shoes were napping. But I imagine they left—your sheepherder didn't find but one body, did he?"

"Nope, just one," the sheriff said. "Just old Bean. He was a tough old rooster, but I guess he's cawed his last caw."

"I want to go, Captain," Lorena said. "I don't want my husband shot, somewhere out in the wastes. There might not even be a sheepherder to find him."

"I sent them into Mexico, so they'd be safe," Call explained. "I think the Garza boy came this way. I think he followed me, but I could never catch him at it. He's a damn clever boy, to ambush Bean like that."

"That's the end of Judge Roy Bean, I guess," the sheriff said. He felt slightly at a loss. He was hoping the great Ranger would want to talk it over, or perhaps ask his opinion about the best way to catch Joey Garza. He and his deputy, Jerry Brown, had figured out just how to do it.

But the old Ranger and the blond woman scarcely blinked at his news.

"I'm much obliged to you for looking after my horse," Call said. Then the two of them turned and walked back down the street. To the skinny sheriff, old Call seemed stiff, and far too slow to catch a swift young bandit such as Joey Garza. That was a job, in the sheriff's view, for much younger men, men about the age of himself and his deputy, Jerry Brown.

Call didn't speak as they were walking back to the rooming house. The fear was in Lorena's throat, not merely for Pea Eye's life, but fear that the Captain wasn't going to take her with him.

"Captain, I can ride," Lorena repeated. "I can ride day and night, if I have to. I did it when we trailed those cattle, and I can do it now."

"Ma'am, that was not my objection," Call said. "I'd like you to come."

Call meant it, too. Lorena had come a long way, at some risk. She deserved to get to see her husband, and as soon as possible. The bond of a husband and a wife was one he had never had, and didn't understand, but he could tell, both from Lorena's behavior and from Pea Eye's, that it was a strong bond. He had come to admire Lorena, for the quick way she took charge of Jasper's children. She had given them excellent care.

Also, he wouldn't mind the company, in this instance. Traveling alone had always suited him. It was only this winter that it had come to suit him less. He was rather sorry that he had left Mr. Brookshire behind. He had come to like Mr. Brookshire.

"What is your objection then, if you have one?" Lorena asked.

"I don't know that I can protect you—that's it," Call said. "I let the Garza boy slip right by me and kill Roy Bean. Then, I let

Mox Mox get away. That's two poor performances in a row. I just don't know that I can protect you."

To his surprise, Lorena took his arm as they walked down the street.

"Did you hear me?" Call asked, fearing that he had not stressed the risk quite enough.

"I heard you, Captain," Lorena said. "I need to go find my husband. He's the one you ought to be protecting. Help me pick out a good horse, and let's go."

Lorena's look was determined, and her step determined too. What she said startled Call, but by the time she walked him past the saloon and the hardware store, he had come to see that she was right. Lorena had been taken by Blue Duck and held two weeks; but she had survived and recovered. More than that, she had educated herself, and was rearing a family.

But Pea Eye had depended on him and Gus until the time when he came to depend on Lorena herself. Pea was able enough when he was given clear orders, but only when he was given clear orders. No doubt Lorena was well aware of that characteristic, too. Pea Eye was not accustomed to acting alone. It was doubtful that he could have found his way to Presidio so promptly if he had been without the help of Famous Shoes.

Call picked out a strong mare for Lorena, and bought her an adequate saddle. An hour later, the two of them rode out of Fort Stockton, the strong wind at their backs.

The skinny sheriff and his deputy, Jerry Brown, stood in the empty, windy street, and watched them leave. The skinny sheriff was a little disappointed. The old Ranger had not been friendly at all.

"Now where are they going?" Deputy Brown asked.

"Why, I don't know, Jerry—they're headed south," the sheriff said. "I didn't ask them their route, and they didn't mention much."

"We don't get women that pretty in this town, not often," Jerry Brown said. "I ain't seen one that pretty since I come out here, and I been out here six years. I wish she'd stayed a little longer."

"Why?" the sheriff asked, surprised that his deputy was being so forward. "You don't even know the woman."

"No, but I might have met her in a store or somewhere," Jerry Brown said. "I might have got to say hello to her, at least.

"I'm a bachelor," he added, though the sheriff knew that.

But soon, the Ranger and the pretty woman were swallowed up by the great blue distance to the south, and Deputy Jerry Brown, who was a bachelor, went back into the jail and spent the windy morning playing solitaire.

Part
III

Maria's Children

1.

"Don't go off and leave me here, you goddamn Cherokee rascal!" Mox Mox said.

He wanted to kill Jimmy Cumsa and wanted to kill him badly; but he had no weapon and was sorely wounded, to boot. In the scramble to get away from Call, his pistol had fallen out of its holster. He had been flopped over his horse, and somehow, the gun got jerked loose.

Mox Mox bled and bled, and coughed and coughed as they ran. He was shot in the lung, which he knew was bad. Every cough caused a pain like needles sticking in him. Then Jimmy Cumsa rode up beside him and took his rifle. The scabbard had Mox Mox's blood all over it, but Jimmy took the rifle and scabbard anyway. Mox Mox had no pistol and was too weak to stop Jimmy.

Mox Mox rode on, as far as he could. He only had the one horse, but when the herd spooked, Jimmy had managed to keep three horses ahead of him. He had four mounts; he could run a long way.

"Let me switch, Jim—I need a fresher horse," Mox Mox said, as his horse began to tire, but Jimmy Cumsa didn't answer, or offer him a fresh horse, either.

Finally, his mount faltered, trying to climb out of a gully. They had ridden some twenty miles. The horse stumbled back to the bottom of the gully and stood there, shaking. It was dusk; Mox Mox could barely see Jimmy Cumsa, who was in the process of shifting his saddle to one of the extra horses, the big sorrel that had belonged to Oteros.

Mox Mox slid carefully to the ground. He coughed, and the needles stuck him. He was trying to get matches out of his saddlebags, when Jimmy Cumsa came over and started to help him. Mox Mox took a step or two back, then staggered and sat down.

"Build a fire, Jimmy—it's chill," he said, but again, Jimmy didn't answer, and he wasn't helping, either. He simply transferred Mox Mox's saddlebags with the matches in them and a little food and ammunition to another horse.

"Build a fire," Mox Mox said, again. "We'll freeze if you don't build a fire."

"Nope, no more fires for you, Mox," Jimmy Cumsa said.

"Why not? What's wrong with you?" Mox Mox asked.

"Not near as much as is wrong with you," Jimmy Cumsa said. "I ain't shot in the lung, and I ain't dying. You're both, Mox. Building you a fire would be a waste of matches, and I ain't got the time to waste on a man that's dying anyway."

"I ain't dying, I'm just shot," Mox Mox said. "I'll live if I can get warm."

"Hellfire will warm you, Mox," Jimmy Cumsa said, mounting Oteros's big horse. "You'll cook plenty warm down in hell, like all those people that you put the brush on and burned."

Mox Mox realized then that Jimmy Cumsa meant it. He was not going to help him. He was going to leave him there to die, with a bleeding lung and no matches, in weather that was bitter.

"I should have killed you long ago, you Cherokee dog," Mox Mox said. "I should have shot you in your goddamn sleep."

"You wouldn't have got me, even in my sleep," Jimmy Cumsa said. "I could be sound asleep, or drunk, and still be quicker than you. That's why I'm called Quick Jimmy."

"You damn snake, get off and make me a fire," Mox Mox said.

"I ain't the snake," Jimmy Cumsa said. "You're the one they call The-Snake-You-Do-Not-See. Only old Call seen you. He didn't get much of a shot, but he still killed you."

"I ain't dead, I'm just shot, goddamn you!" Mox Mox said, again. "Make me a damn fire or leave me the matches, if you're in such a goddamn hurry. I'll make my own fire."

"I am in a hurry," Jimmy said. "I want to be a long way from here when the sun comes up, Mox. That old man might still be coming. He killed seven of the eight of us, unless Black Tooth got away, which I doubt."

"He ain't coming, he's got those children," Mox Mox said.

"Well, I don't believe I'll take the chance," Jimmy Cumsa said. "If he does come, he'll find you frozen, or else bled out. I never thought a man that old could beat you, Mox, but I guess I was wrong."

Mox Mox knew that his only chance was to rush Jimmy Cumsa, grab his gun or grab the reins of one of the other horses —grab anything that might help him survive. There must be brush in the gully that he could find and make enough of a fire to keep himself alive, even if he had to crawl. He staggered up and tried to make a run at the horses. If he could just get one fresh horse, he might make it. But the needles in his lungs were sharper than ever, and he couldn't control his legs. He ran a few steps, but fell before he got near a horse. When he finally did get to a horse, it was the one Jimmy Cumsa had just run for twenty miles. It was as useless as his own.

Mox Mox had a small knife in his belt, the one he used to cut meat. It was his only weapon. He managed to get it out; with luck, he might stick Jimmy and cut him badly enough that he would fall off his mount. But when he lunged with his knife at where he thought the Cherokee was, Jimmy Cumsa wasn't there. He had taken the reins of the extra horses and ridden out of the gully. Mox Mox wanted to slash him to death for his treachery, but there was no one to slash. He could hear the clatter of the horses as Jimmy Cumsa loped away. But in a moment the sound grew faint, and in a few more minutes there was no sound at all, except his own breathing. In the sudden

[397]

stillness, the sound of his own breathing shocked him. His breath bubbled, as a cow or a sheep or a buffalo bubbled with its last breath.

Mox Mox felt a bitter rage. An old man had come out of nowhere and shot him and all his men, except Jimmy Cumsa, and now Jimmy had deserted him, left him to bleed to death or freeze in a gully. How dare the old fool! If he'd only had a moment to turn and fight, he could have rallied the men and caught Woodrow Call and burned him. He could have shot him or stabbed him or quirted him to death. Old Call had just been lucky to get in such a shot. It was Jimmy Cumsa's fault for messing with the horses when he should have been standing guard. None of the men, in fact, had been alert. It served them right that they were all dead—all except Jimmy, the one who had ridden off and left him to die.

Mox Mox crawled to where his horse stood, caught the stirrup in his hand, and pulled himself to his feet. His only chance was to mount and make the horse keep going. Maybe there was a house somewhere that he could get to, someplace where there were matches, so he could build a fire. A fire would save him. He had built wonderful fires over the years, fires hot enough to warm him on the coldest nights, hot enough to burn anyone he had on hand to burn. If he could just get to a place where he could make a fire, a wonderful warm fire, the bubbling in his breath might stop and he would get better and live.

He pulled himself up slowly and managed with great difficulty to get himself into the saddle. But when he tried to spur his horse out of the gully, the horse refused to move. He jerked when he was spurred, but only took a step or two, and then stood there quivering again.

Mox Mox wouldn't stand for it; even his horse wouldn't obey him. He still had the small knife in his hand. In his rage, he began to stab the horse as hard as he could. He stabbed him in the neck and slashed at his shoulders. Then he stabbed him in the flank—he would *make* the animal go where he wanted it to go! He slashed at the horse's flank until the animal finally bolted and tried to flounder up the sides of the gully. But the sides of the gully were too steep. In the dark the horse lost its footing and fell, rolling over Mox Mox as it slid back to the bottom of the gully. Mox Mox slid after it, and as he did, the horse kicked at him, catching him hard in the leg. When Mox Mox tried to stand, he heard his leg crack. He tried to stand up, but the leg wouldn't support him.

In his bitterness and rage at Call's good luck and his own defeat, Mox Mox hadn't fully felt the cold. But with his leg cracked and his breath bubbling, he could scarcely move. Soon, the savage wind began to bite. Mox Mox began to think of cutting himself in order to feel the warmth of his own blood. But when he put the knife down for a moment and tried to ease himself into a more comfortable sitting position, the knife slid down the slope, out of his reach. He eased down a little ways himself, but he couldn't find the knife.

The blood seeping out of his chest began to freeze on his shirt. When he put his hand on his side, his blood was cold. He wanted a fire, but there was no fire and no way to make one. The coyotes began to yip in the cold distance. Mox Mox listened. He thought he heard horses coming from far away. He listened as hard as he could. Maybe Quick Jimmy had been teasing him; he was known to be a teaser. Maybe Jimmy would come back and build him a good crackling fire. Even if the horseman was old Call come to get him, the man might at least build him a fire and keep him alive through the night.

Mox Mox listened hard. Once or twice, he thought he heard the horses in the cold distance. But mainly it was just the coyotes yipping. The wind died; it was cloudless and very cold. Mox Mox reached again for the knife. Better to cut himself than to freeze to death. But he still couldn't find the knife, and when he reached for it, he began to slide and then to roll over. He rolled to the bottom of the gully. There was not even a bush to crawl behind. The two exhausted horses had walked away. It might have been his own horse whose hoofbeats he had heard. There was no warmth anywhere—only the yipping of the coyotes and the yellow of the shining stars.

[399]

2.

Mexico was colder on the second trip than it had been on the first, Brookshire thought, and it had been sufficiently cold the first time.

Every night he felt nervous about shutting his eyes, for fear that he'd freeze in his sleep. They made roaring fires—he soon used the last of his ledger books, even burning the covers getting the fires started—but the fires didn't warm the ground, and the ground was where he had to lay himself down to sleep.

The Captain's departure had shocked Brookshire badly, that and the fact that they had been ordered back into Mexico on the vague hope that Joey Garza would show up at his mother's house. They had already been to his mother's house, and the young bandit hadn't been home. If the plan was to lie in wait for him, then they might as well have waited for him when they were there the first time.

Now Captain Call, the one man in the whole of the West that Brookshire had confidence in, wasn't even with them. Often in his life when he had failed to restrain his taste for brandy, things had slipped off course. Now it had happened again. Things were twisting farther and ever farther off course, it seemed to him. The old Indian seemed irritated at having to make a long detour into Mexico to get back to the village. He trotted so far ahead of them during the cold days that Brookshire more than once concluded that they had been abandoned. Colonel Terry was going to think it a very odd way of proceeding. The Colonel had only wanted one bandit apprehended, and quickly. He was going to be mighty aggravated that so much time had passed without results.

Normally Brookshire would have been in a sweat at the thought of the Colonel's aggravation. But it was impossible to sweat when it was as cold as it was, and anyway, Colonel Terry, who usually entered Brookshire's thoughts at least once every five minutes, now entered them less and less often. When he did enter them, he did so less vividly. Colonel Terry had become mainly a memory from a different life. Brookshire didn't know whether he would ever return to that life, or ever see the Colonel again.

He rode along obediently, though. He tried to keep himself in order and not let the blowing-away feeling seize him too strongly. There was not much else he could do. They were in Mexico, and keeping up with Famous Shoes was task enough for the moment. Vegetation was sparse, and by midafternoon, Brookshire would begin to be nervous about finding enough firewood to keep a good fire going through the night. He tried to keep the location of substantial bushes and trees firmly in mind, so he could return to them and make a fire out of them if he needed to.

Deputy Plunkert had been deeply upset when Pea Eye told him they were going back into Mexico. It was the one thing he had never intended to let happen; and yet, when the moment came to resign and go home, he rode numbly back across the Rio Grande, behind Pea Eye and Brookshire and old Famous Shoes.

Deputy Plunkert looked down the river when he was in the middle of it. Laredo was down there, and Doobie was down there. If he just turned left and followed the winding stream, he could not miss getting home. The river would lead him right to it, if some Mexican didn't kill him first.

That was the catch, though. To get home by way of the river meant going straight through the vicinities where he was most unpopular. Even on the Texas side of the river, there were places where he was rather unpopular.

Tired as he was, Ted Plunkert didn't feel up to coping with his own unpopularity. It was better to remain a part of the Captain's expedition. Once the bad outlaws were finished, caught, and hung, the Captain had promised to send him home on a train. The thought of the comfort to come was enough to keep him going.

Pea Eye had no interest in Mexico, but he didn't fear it. The Captain had given him clear orders, and all he had to do was follow them. In order to follow them, all he had to do was keep up with Famous Shoes. The old man was unusually irritable, but he hadn't deserted them yet. Even if he deserted them, Pea Eye felt confident that he had enough ability to tell east from west. He could find his way back to the river, and eventually get where he had been told to go.

The third night, as they were making their campfire behind a little spur of rock, Famous Shoes came walking in from one of his swings through the country ahead.

"Olin is coming," he said. "He was about to make camp when I found him. I told him we already had a camp, so he is coming here."

Pea Eye only vaguely remembered Olin Roy. Once in a while, long before, accident had thrown him into the same vicinity as the Ranger troop. He camped with them now and then. Pea Eye could not recall Olin's occupation, if he had one. Not every traveler did have an occupation, and a good many of those who had one wouldn't reveal it. All he remembered about the man was that he was very large.

"Has he lost any weight?" he asked Famous Shoes. "The way he was back then, a horse could hardly carry him all day."

"He weighs too much for his horses," Famous Shoes said. "He is easy to track, though."

When Olin Roy rode into camp he didn't look very impressive to Deputy Plunkert or to Brookshire, either.

"I thank you," he said, formally, when Brookshire offered him a cup of coffee.

After that, he merely sat by the fire in his old greasy clothes, saying little.

"The weather's cold, ain't it?" Pea Eye said, rather at a loss as to how to address the big man.

"It could be colder—I've seen it colder," Olin said. He regretted letting Famous Shoes tempt him into making camp with the travelers. They were pleasant enough and generous with their coffee, but on the whole, he felt he did better camping alone. The necessity of making conversation didn't arise, since no conversation was required when he camped by himself. Making conversation with perfect strangers was to Olin an irksome task. Pea Eye wasn't a perfect stranger, of course, but neither was he someone Olin felt he could easily talk to. The only two people in the world he could talk to easily were Maria and Billy Williams, and even when alone with Maria, he rarely said that much. He usually just sat and listened as Maria talked, or he watched her brush her little girl's hair.

At such times he wished that life was different, and that he could marry Maria and be a settled man. It was not possible, of course—Maria had no interest—but if matters had been different, Olin felt he would have been a happier man. There was no one who touched him as deeply as Maria, though he had never been her husband or a member of her family and had not had the pleasure of watching her with her children as a steady thing.

"Been anyplace special?" Pea Eye asked. The Captain had appointed him the leader of the group, which made him more or less the host; and as host, he felt he ought to try to prompt at least a little conversation.

"Well, Piedras Negras," Olin said.

"I've heard that was a rough town," Deputy Plunkert said.

"No, it ain't," Olin replied. "Of course, Wesley Hardin's there now. Any town he unsaddles his horse in is rough. But he just came for whores. I imagine he'll move on soon."

"Why, we heard he was in Crow Town," Brookshire said.

"He was, but Maria took the whores and left," Olin said. "That's when Hardin left. He likes places where there's whores."

After that, conversation lagged.

[403]

Brookshire couldn't think of a thing to say. He was wondering if the fire would last the night.

Olin thought the group was rather odd. In his years of travel, mostly in Mexico, he had grown used to having odd groups turn up—Englishmen or Germans, prospectors, gunrunners, schemers of various kinds.

But this group was Woodrow Call's posse, it seemed; they were the men who were after Joey Garza. They seemed like harmless fellows, and it was difficult to believe that any of them were gifted manhunters. The Yankee mostly shivered. Pea Eye was an old Ranger who should have retired from the business long ago. The other man Olin didn't know; he had introduced himself briefly, but had mumbled his name so low that Olin didn't catch it. Even with old Famous Shoes to track for them, there was little likelihood they would ever get within fifty miles of Joey Garza, and if they did, it would only be worse for them.

Joey had a cold nature. There was no accounting for it, either. His mother was generous and warm. But wherever he got it, Joey had a cold nature. If the men did happen to stumble on him, Joey would make quick work of them.

"What's the news from down the river, then?" Deputy Plunkert asked. It seemed to him that he had been gone from his home for years. He suddenly had a hunger to hear the news from Laredo. The large man had been down the river as far as Piedras Negras, and perhaps he had heard something from Laredo. A bank robbery or a lynching might have occurred since he left, or a store might have burned down, or one or two of the older, more famous ranchers might have died.

"I didn't stay in Negras long enough to gossip," Olin said. "Having Hardin in town makes me uneasy. He don't look like much, but he's a wild one."

"Any news from Laredo?" Deputy Plunkert said. "That's where I hail from."

"Yes, they put that damn Sheriff Jekyll in his own jail," Olin said. "I hope they hang the rascal. There's no excuse for forcing a woman."

"Bob Jekyll's in our jail?" Ted Plunkert said, very startled. "I'd say that's news."

The first part of Olin's comment had startled him so much that he hadn't quite taken in the second part. The thought of Bob Jekyll locked in their jail was so astonishing that he hadn't yet started thinking about the nature of his crime.

"I guess some little gal came in asking about her husband, and the damned scoundrel forced her," Olin said. He had seen an Apache girl forced once, during the Indian times, and the sight had sickened him. Over the years whenever he thought of it, it sickened him. He knew that Maria had suffered something like that about the time that Joey started killing. From time to time, he considered going to Texas and taking vengeance on her attackers. The men who used the Apache girl had shot her when they were through. Maria hadn't been shot, at least. But the thought of her suffering troubled him whenever he remembered it. Maria was the only woman he had tender feelings for. She should be exempt from such abuse, and if he did encounter the cowboys who attacked her, he planned to take their lives.

Suddenly Deputy Plunkert got a bad feeling.

"A woman asking about her husband . . ." he repeated. Who but Doobie, of all the young women in Laredo, would go to Bob Jekyll to ask about her husband?

"Do you recall her name?" he asked; of course, there were other young women in Laredo. Other husbands might have strayed. In fact, husbands strayed fairly often. Most of them just got drunk and fell in a ditch to sleep it off. Maybe it was another woman with a stray husband, who Bob Jekyll had forced.

"Why, no," Olin said. "I don't recall hearing her name. The poor thing took rat poison and died. They're trying the sheriff for murder, but I doubt he'll hang, myself."

"Oh, Lord!" Ted Plunkert said. Something gripped him more powerful than the cold: the fear that it had been Doobie. He had been Bob Jekyll's deputy until he'd quit and gone off with Captain Call. Who but the deputy's wife would be going to the jail to inquire?

"She died?" he asked, in a weaker tone.

To everyone's amazement, Deputy Plunkert suddenly sprang up and went stumbling over to the horses. He looked like a crazy man.

"It was my wife. . . . I fear it was her . . ." he said, and then he mounted and went racing off in the darkness, to the south.

"Now, that's bad luck," Brookshire said. "I believe I saw his wife as we were leaving Laredo. She was a pert young thing."

"Ted oughtn't to run his horse at night, not in this rough country," Pea Eye said. "There's bluffs down the river that a horse could go right off."

"I always despised that sheriff," Olin said. They heard the clatter of the deputy's horse, receding to the south. Olin felt embarrassed. Inadvertently, he had informed a man that his wife was dead. He more and more regretted letting Famous Shoes talk him into joining the camp. Now he had been the bearer of tragic news. If he had just gone on and made his own camp, the poor deputy would still be in ignorance of the fact that he no longer had a wife. Boy, he wished he had made his own camp, and built his own fire! He did not like to cause trouble, and yet he just did.

"Why, that's the devil," Brookshire said. They could scarcely hear the deputy's horse. What did the man think he was going to do, run the horse all the way to Laredo? It was hundreds of miles to Laredo. And what could he do when he got there? The poor young woman was no doubt long since buried.

Then Brookshire remembered that Katie, his own wife, was dead. Of course, her death had been normal; she had taken sick and died. There had been no abuse, and no rat poison. But still, his own wife was gone, and like Deputy Plunkert he would be returning to nothing, if he returned. The cold wind was blowing. It was always blowing.

Brookshire began to get a worse feeling even than the blowing-away feeling. It struck him that the expedition was cursed. He had lost his wife while on the trip, and now the same thing had happened to the young deputy, who should never have been hired in the first place. All Deputy Plunkert had done was ride pointlessly around Texas and Mexico, while his young wife was despairing and dying.

The search for Joey Garza was being pressed at a high price, and they hadn't come anywhere near the bandit yet. Now they were in Mexico, and Captain Call was in Texas. All that was being accomplished was that the wives were dying. He knew Pea Eye had a wife, too—when would the messenger appear to tell him that *his* wife was dead? Pea Eye's wife was a schoolteacher, he recalled. What if the manburner eluded Captain Call, as Joey Garza had, and burned up Pea Eye's wife along with some of the schoolchildren?

Brookshire remembered all his happy years with Katie, and began to sob. Ordinarily, he didn't cry in front of people, but this time, as when he first received the news about Katie, he couldn't help it. Sobs shook his shoulders. It embarrassed Pea Eye and Olin, but Brookshire didn't care. He couldn't stop. He was freezing, his wife was dead, and now the deputy's wife was dead. He was in a cold place, in a strange, forbidding country, hunting a bandit. How could it all have happened? He was an accountant in Brooklyn. Somehow a chain of events had got started, and now the events were less and less sensible, less and less like events that should be occurring in his life. For a week or two, he had enjoyed the adventure; he had even flourished. He mastered new skills, such as building fires. But the pleasure had all ended once he got the telegram informing him of Katie's death. Now it was all cold, fatigue, and pain. Where would it lead?

Brookshire remembered his first impression of Captain Call. He had felt that the man was too old for the mission he was charged with. He had looked too old that first morning in Amarillo. Brookshire had quickly gained confidence in the Captain, but now it was beginning to seem that his confidence had been misplaced, and that his first impression had been accurate. The Captain had pursued no clear plan. He had let himself be distracted by another killer. They had ridden through Mexico and then through Texas, without coming even within a hundred miles of Joey Garza, as far as he knew. It didn't add up, and

Colonel Terry would be quick to point out how erratically things had been managed.

But there was more at work than just cold and inconvenience and tactical mistakes. At home, behind them, the wives were dying.

"How far is it back?" he asked. He felt that he was in the grip of a sickness of some kind. He was in a place where nothing was rational and civilized, as it had been in Princeton College, or as it was in Brooklyn. He was in a place where people killed regularly, where killing was a day-to-day part of life. Of course, there were killings in Brooklyn, but very few. In Texas and Mexico, killing seemed to be almost constant. Brookshire had the feeling that he might go crazy if he didn't get back to a place and a form of life that were more familiar.

"Back where?" Pea Eye asked. He saw that the man was upset. Deputy Plunkert's departure had startled them all. It was terribly bad luck that Deputy Plunkert had to receive such news when he was hundreds of miles from home. The fact that it was rat poison that had killed his wife, not to mention what had happened with the sheriff, were facts that Pea knew must be hard to bear. If anything like that happened to Lorena, he himself would start racing off in the night, ready to shoot the first man he saw.

But he was not in a position to take Mr. Brookshire back to anywhere. They had to go on to Presidio, where the Captain expected them to be. That was a clear order.

"I expect we'll get to Presidio in about three days, if we don't have trouble," he said.

Brookshire didn't answer. He scooted closer to the fire and sat with his hands held over the flames. He was shivering and crying.

Famous Shoes didn't enter into the white men's talk. He was beginning to tire of white men, something that had happened often in his life. They pursued their business in strange ways, and got upset about things he didn't grasp. He had begun to doubt that he would stay with Pea Eye long enough to find his wife. He would like to learn about the tracks in books, but he was old, and the white men's habits were boring. Now one of the men had run off into the night, like a crazy thing. There were only two white men left; if he tracked Joey Garza for these two men, Joey would immediately kill them both. Famous Shoes thought he might tell his friend Pea Eye that his wife could teach him about the little tracks in the spring, when he went traveling on the Rio Rojo.

Famous Shoes didn't think Joey was in Mexico, and he was getting bored. He thought he might leave in a day or two and go back to the Madre. Eagles were more interesting than white men. It would be more interesting to go home and watch the eagles for a while.

3.

Goodnight was coming across the sand through the sandhills when he saw a solitary rider coming from the south. Crow Town was fifteen miles to the west; he could see a speckling of crows in the sky when he looked toward the winter sunset.

Coming across this particular stretch of country awakened quite a few memories. Until he noticed the rider Goodnight had been lost in revery, for he was crossing his own trail, the trail he and his old partner, Oliver Loving, had laid out many years before. In fact, he was on the exact spot where they had rested the cattle on the second afternoon of their ninety-mile waterless drive. A horse had died inexplicably, while they were resting. He had cut into the horse in an effort to determine what had killed it, but his work was to no avail. The horse had just died.

Goodnight had not expected to be crossing the trail so many years after Oliver Loving's death, and at dusk on a cold winter night to boot. But so it was.

If the rider he glimpsed was headed for Crow Town, he was likely to be the sort of man it would behoove a person to avoid. On the other hand, once you started avoiding people, you were apt to lose a lot of time. Even in the remote stretches along the Pecos River, a surprising number of people were apt to turn up. Decisions as to whether or not to go around a particular traveler needed to be made almost constantly.

Going around people had never been Goodnight's practice, and he decided he was too old to change. It was nearly dark, and the weather bleak; he was almost upon the man before he could make out much about him. When the rider was only thirty yards away, Goodnight saw that it was John Wesley Hardin. A second later, Hardin hailed him.

"Why, Charlie, dammit, you're out late," Hardin said.

"Out late, and far from home," Goodnight admitted. He himself had never had any difficulty with Wesley Hardin, but Hardin was a nervous man who was known to kill from whim. It wouldn't do to get too jocular with him. If you didn't manage the jocularity to suit John Wesley, he might flare up and yank out a gun.

"Are you still in the cattle business?" Hardin asked.

"Yep," Goodnight said. "Still in it. Why?"

"Thought you might want to switch to the crow business," Hardin said, in a whinny of a laugh. "There's a lot of fine crows around here, and they're going cheap. The best crow in Crow Town wouldn't sell for more than a penny."

"In fact, I'm looking for Woodrow Call," Goodnight said. "Any news of him?"

"Yes, and I'm the only man that's got it," Hardin said. "I ought to charge you for it, Charlie, since I've got a monopoly, but being as it's you, it's free. Woodrow Call done for Mox Mox."

"Now that's news, all right," Goodnight said. "Are you sure?"

"Sure as daylight," Hardin said. "I went down to Piedras Negras to whore, because the Garza boy's mother took the women out of Crow Town. I'm coming from Mexico, and I'm heading for Denver. I believe I can do better in Colorado than I'm doing in Texas."

"Where is Mox Mox?" Goodnight asked. "I want to see his body."

"I'm surprised you'd doubt my word, Charlie," Hardin said, with a touch of irritation.

"I don't doubt it, John," Goodnight said. "But I am determined to see the man's body. He burnt four of my cowboys, on the Purgatory River, and I want to be sure it's him, so I can stop chasing him in my head."

"Well, the sonofabitch froze to death in a gully about a hundred miles south of here," Hardin said. "Call killed all but one of his men about twenty miles farther on. All of them were laying there dead, except that quick Cherokee boy. Him and Mox Mox made a run for it, but Mox Mox was shot in the lights. He played out and froze. I expect the Cherokee is still running."

"Let him run," Goodnight said. "Call done a good day's work."

"No, he done a sloppy day's work," John Wesley said. "He's lucky he got the six men down, shooting as bad as he was. He knocked them over, but they were still kicking, and if any one of them'd had any fight they'd have got him. He had to finish them off with his pistol, which is a disgrace if you're in good range and have a decent rifle to shoot."

"The fact that he gave Mox Mox a mortal wound makes it a good day's work, in my opinion," Goodnight said.

"Mox Mox was just a mean bandit, Charlie," Hardin said. "I wouldn't call him a man of talent. The sonofabitch should have been a cook, since he liked fires so much. I could have killed him in a blink, and all his men, too.

"I wonder where that Cherokee boy has run to?" he added. "That Cherokee boy is quick, and he ain't wasteful. He didn't leave Mox Mox even so much as a match."

"I'd appreciate it if you'd direct me to that gully," Goodnight said. "I'd like to see the body before some varmint drags it off."

"Backtrack me for two days, and you'll run right into it, Charlie," Hardin replied. "It ain't more than twenty-five miles south of the railroad."

Goodnight was anxious to get going. He had been thinking about his old partner, Oliver Loving, a man he had cared for greatly, and with whom he had camped on the very spot where he was conversing with John Wesley Hardin. Oliver Loving, a fine cattleman, had been dead for many years; John Wesley Hardin, a pure killer and a man who respected no one, was still alive and still brash. It was not justice, it was just life.

[412]

"Well, I'll be going," Goodnight said. "Much obliged for the news. Once I've seen what's left of the manburner, I guess I'll go home. Captain Call done the job I ought to have done ten years ago."

"He done it, but he was lucky," Hardin said. "If you see him, tell him that for me."

"It might have been luck, and it might have been preparation," Goodnight said. "Call was always known for his careful preparation."

Hardin laughed his whinny of a laugh, again.

"He can prepare till doomsday. What he needs to do is shoot a little better," Hardin said. "He was just fighting louts. If he thinks he can saunter up to the Garza boy and be that lucky, then he ought to retire. The Garza boy will pick him off before Call even knows he's there."

"Have you met this boy?" Goodnight asked. He didn't necessarily believe what Hardin was saying; on the other hand, what he was saying couldn't be lightly disregarded. Wesley Hardin had been in several penitentiaries, and undoubtedly knew something about killers.

"Why, yes, he showed up in Crow Town," Hardin said. "That was before the whores left. I found him rather standoffish. I started to kill him, but then I decided it was the wrong day for hostilities."

"Why?" Goodnight asked.

"Well, it just was," Hardin replied. "I've got to the age where I don't tempt fate. At least, I don't if I'm drunk, and I was drunk."

He cackled, lit a cheap cigar, and left. Goodnight looked around; Hardin was the kind of fellow who prompted you to watch your back. But all he saw was a quick arc of red. Hardin had thrown the cheap cigar away.

Two days later, Goodnight found the gully and inspected the remains, which were a little scattered by that time. The buzzards had helped him locate the correct gully, in a country where there were many. Hardin had been right. The manburner was dead.

[413]

There was also a dead horse a few hundred yards from where Mox Mox lay; run to death, Goodnight felt sure. Mox Mox wore a noticeable belt—the belt buckle had a red stone of some kind set in it. Goodnight took the belt and put it in his saddlebags. When he next ran into Call, he planned to give him the belt. If Mox Mox had run far enough to ride a horse to death, Call might not even know that he had killed him. The belt ought to convince him.

Then, since he had ridden that far to see one body, he rode another twenty miles to the camp where the battle had taken place. He didn't have to search, either. He could see buzzards the whole way.

Goodnight had surveyed many battle sites. He could usually figure out what had gone on and what mistakes had been made, from looking at the scattered cartridges, the lost hats, and the dead bodies. In this case, he dismounted and inspected the area carefully. He was forced to conclude that John Wesley Hardin had been correct in his assessment: Woodrow Call had been lucky. Probably only his willingness to keep pumping in bullets while his opponents were confused, had saved him. There was cover within a few steps of the campsite. If one or two of the men had had any presence of mind, they could have quickly dug in and made a fight of it. They had horses, too; a couple of them could have flanked Call and cut him off.

They hadn't, though, and that was that. Looking around, Goodnight found something surprising—a small rag doll, such as a little girl might have. Mox Mox must have had captives and was probably going to indulge in his favorite pastime. But Call had killed him in time, and had probably taken the children to safety.

Goodnight debated going to look for Captain Call. What John Wesley Hardin had to say about the abilities of the Garza boy weighed on his mind. But after a time, he decided to let it be. Mox Mox, not Joey Garza, had burned his cowhands. He himself was not a manhunter, and he had a ranch to run. Woodrow Call was the manhunter. He had accepted the job; let him do it. If he couldn't, some posse would, eventually.

Besides, Goodnight had been brooding during the whole ride about the insolence of Muley, his ranch cook. He had decided to go home and fire the man, even if it did mean a trip to Amarillo and an irksome search.

Goodnight didn't like leaving men unburied. That had never been his practice, unless the fight was so hot that he couldn't afford to stop and attend to the civilities. He buried the scraps of Mox Mox. The meanness was gone now, and just bones and flesh remained. Goodnight unstrapped his little shovel and did the same for the six dead men.

Then he turned back north, toward the Quitaque. It was time to hang up the rifle. The manburner was dead.

4.

In the fight with Mox Mox, Call had somehow wrenched his neck. It began to pain him badly as he rode south with Lorena. At times it was as if his nerves were on fire, and he had to grit his teeth against the pain as they rode. He could hardly turn his head to the right at all, and he had to be cautious about turning it to the left, or a streak of fire shot up from his shoulder blade almost to his ear.

"It's just a nuisance," Call said, when Lorena asked whether he was well. She could see the strain in his face.

"We should have bought some liniment, when we had the chance," Lorena said. "Pea Eye's always getting sore in his back. He can't lift hay like he once could."

Call could not rid himself of the conviction that they were being followed. He had no evidence, but he could not relax. Every time he turned his head to scan the horizon behind them, the pain shot up his neck.

On the evening of the third day, they met a small horse herd being driven north by two cowboys. One of the cowboys, a tall fellow named Roy Malone, had a drooping mustache that reminded Call of Dish Boggett, the excellent Hat Creek cowboy who was now selling hardware in Lincoln, New Mexico. By coincidence, the horse herd was bound for the Chisum Ranch, not far from Lincoln.

"You're welcome to stop the night with us," Call told Roy Malone, but the cowboy shook his head.

"You don't stop for the whole night, if you work for Mr. Chisum," Roy said. "He likes things to happen prompt, if not a little sooner."

Call would have been relieved to have some help. As it was, he stood watch himself most of the night.

Lorena proved a competent traveling companion. They had bacon and coffee, acquired in Fort Stockton, and she had coffee made and bacon fried not long after they made camp. In the morning, she cooked them a bite of breakfast before first light.

"That cowboy reminded me an awful lot of Dish," Call said, as they ate. "I'd like to see Dish sometime. I never expected him to go in the hardware business."

"I wonder if he married?" Lorena said. Dish had been in love with her once; he had stayed in love for several years. It was a love she couldn't return, though—she just couldn't. Some traveler told her that Dish had taken a sledgehammer and used it to smash a heavy barrel of horseshoe nails, in his surprise and disappointment, when the news reached him that she had married Pea Eye. The traveler said that people in Lincoln were worried that Dish would lose his mind from disappointment, even though by that time, she hadn't so much as seen him in over three years.

Lorena didn't know what had kept her so stiff with Dish. She had just got stiff. For a time in Nebraska, he had brought her flowers and given her little presents, but it hadn't changed anything.

Then she fell in love with Pea Eye, who would never have ventured to choose a present for her, or pick her a flower, either.

"I guess I should have left Pea Eye at home," Call said, after they ate. "Then you wouldn't have had to make this long trip."

"It won't matter, once I get him back," Lorena said.

The way she said it made Call wish they could hurry along a little faster, or that Pea Eye would get wind that his wife was coming and ride to meet them. He felt he had run a miserable expedition so far; it was the most ineffective of his life. Three families had been inconvenienced, with as yet no progress at all in the matter of Joey Garza. Rumor in Fort Stockton had it that Joey had gone back to Coahuila, but no one really had the details, and Call didn't know how much credit to give the rumor. Now he regretted that he had taken Brookshire with him, or Deputy Plunkert, either. Colonel Terry would rightly be incensed at the long wait and the absence of results. Brookshire had lost his wife while on the trip, and Pea Eye had lost time from his farming. Lorena had to take leave from her schoolteaching. When they got to Presidio, he meant to send everyone home. From that point on, he would hunt Joey Garza alone.

Call wished his neck would ease up. He had rarely felt a pain more intense than the fire that shot up his neck if he moved his head a little too quickly. He also wished the cold would abate. In the morning, his hands were so swollen that he had increasing trouble doing the packing. Lorena saddled her mount and was ready to go before he could complete his chores.

When they got ready to start, Call noticed two horses standing a fair distance to the northwest of their camp.

"I wonder if those cowboys lost some horses," he said. "If they did, there'll be trouble when they get to John Chisum's. He's the kind of man who counts his horses, and he expects a full count."

He finished his coffee. Lorena was about done with her packing. Their breaths made clouds of steam; it was hard to see the knots they had to tie to secure their duffle.

"I think I'll just ride out and check the brands on those horses," Call said. "I don't know why those men would let those horses stray. They seemed like competent men."

He put his horse into a short lope. Before going a quarter of a mile, he surprised two mule deer, a doe with a fawn. They had been bedded down, but jumped up and scampered off. In the clear air he had misjudged the distance to the horses a bit; they were farther from camp than he thought. While Call was watching the mule deer, his horse shied at a badger that waddled out from behind a sage bush, practically at the horse's feet. The horse crow-hopped a time or two, just enough to cause Call to lose a stirrup.

He had the horse almost calmed down and was searching for the stirrup with his foot when the first bullet struck him, low in the chest. Careless, he thought; too careless, and now I'm shot. He whirled his mount and yanked his rifle from the saddle scabbard, but his hands were so stiff with cold that he dropped the weapon. Just as he did, a second bullet smashed his knee and evidently went through and wounded his horse, for the horse squealed and began to buck. A third shot hit his arm. Call was trying to hang on; he couldn't afford to be thrown, not with the bullets coming so fast and so accurately. They seemed to him to be coming from under one of the stray horses. Careless, he thought again. He's shooting from under the horse, and I rode right out to him. Then he lost his seat and was thrown hard, in the direction of the rifle he had dropped. Fortunately, he was able to reach the rifle. He had to work the lever with one hand, but as soon as he could sit up he began to fire in the direction of the horses. One of them raced away, but the other stood exactly where it had been, hobbled, probably, so the rifleman could shoot from underneath it, hidden by the sage.

There was a final shot—it brought down Call's horse.

All he could do then was wait, in the hope that the killer would be foolhardy enough to come and try and finish him off. After the shot that killed his horse, there was not a sound from the northwest. Call knew he would have to try and staunch his bleeding soon. He had been hit three times, and the bullets were heavy caliber. His left arm and right leg were smashed for good; the arm was practically shot off. When he looked at his knee, he saw bone fragments through the hole in his pants. The first wound, the one in the chest, was bleeding more than it should. If he didn't staunch it soon he might faint, and if he fainted, he was lost, and probably Lorena, too.

Call raked up a little sand and covered the chest wound with it, pulling aside his shirt. The sandy poultice quickly grew muddy with blood, but it was the only way he had of staunching the blood flow; he kept raking sand and patting it onto his chest.

He raised up only high enough to see that the hobbled horse was still there. Any higher he couldn't risk.

He felt a deep shame when he thought of Lorena, back at the camp alone. She would have heard the shots, and he hoped that she would run. There were ranches to the south. Perhaps she could survive long enough to reach one of them, if the killer didn't strike her, too. He had brought her with him, and then failed to protect her—the very thing he had mentioned, and the very thing he had feared. Now he himself might be dying. The chest wound probably involved a lung. He could feel the bullet like a nut inside him when he coughed. Call knew he should not have let the killer know that he'd got his rifle—that was another mistake. Now there was little hope that the killer, Joey Garza probably, would expose himself at all, and even if he was reckless and let himself be seen, Call knew it would only be luck if he could hit him, shooting one-handed.

He had botched the matter completely; everything was his fault. He had known in his gut that someone was following them, someone so clever that unending vigilance was essential. But the fact that the cowboys had apparently lost two horses, a normal thing, had distracted him to such an extent that he had just ridden out casually, as he would have under normal circumstances, to have a look.

Now a clever boy, shooting from under a hobbled horse, had done what all the fighters he had engaged with over four decades —Kicking Bird, the Comanche; the Kiowa Pedro Flores; and outlaws of all description, both Mexican and American—had failed to do. He was hit, and hit soundly. Probably only the fact that his horse was restive caused the first bullet to miss his heart. It hadn't missed it by much, at that, if it had missed it. Perhaps it was his heart's blood he was pumping out.

Once before, he had been hit by a bullet. That bullet was fired by an Apache, as Call was about to cross the Pecos River with Gus McCrae's body, on the long trek back from Miles City, Montana, where Gus had died. But that bullet had merely lodged in his side and had touched no vital organs. It was a nuisance, mainly; it pained him at times, but Call didn't regard it as a serious wound and had never bothered to have it cut out. The Apache had shot from a considerable distance, too; the bullet had been almost spent when it hit him. It didn't stop him from crossing the river, or from burying Gus McCrae where he had wanted to be buried.

Now Call knew he was so badly hit that he would be lucky to live. He didn't expect that he would live and didn't care, really, if he could only kill Joey Garza before he died. He felt that he had to kill him; it was the only way to provide any measure of safety for Lorena. And not just Lorena, either. There was Pea Eye and Brookshire and Deputy Plunkert to think of. The ease with which Joey Garza, if it was the young bandit, had drawn him in range, and the consistency of the shooting, was a shock. Shooting from under a horse was an old, old trick. The Indians had done it routinely. Call reproached himself bitterly for carelessness, for assuming the horses were strays. But he knew that he could reproach himself for a year and not alter the truth, which was that someone, Joey Garza most likely, had outsmarted him easily and shot him, probably mortally. What made the failure worse was that the burden of his error would be visited upon people who had depended on him. It would be visited on Lorena, and probably on Pea Eye and Brookshire and Deputy Plunkert, too.

Call remembered Mox Mox, and the Cherokee killer, Jimmy Cumsa. He considered the possibility that they had lured him out of camp. Perhaps it was Jimmy Cumsa who had shot from under the tethered horse. But Call didn't think so. Mox Mox was like most outlaws, careless and lazy. He had made camp in a place that laid him open to easy ambush. He had posted no guard. Nothing he had done had been smart or well planned.

Crouched behind a sage bush, one arm and one leg useless, Call felt a desperate need to slay his murderer before he died. He felt the wound in his chest; it seemed to him the bleeding was slowing. He might have an hour—he might have more—but he doubted he had much more.

He didn't think his opponent was Mox Mox, or the Cherokee,

either. They ran, and he imagined they would keep running. But someone had followed him, and waited while he was in Fort Stockton, and then had picked up the trail when he and Lorena left town. It was the sense that he was being followed that caused the terrible ache in his neck, Call was sure of that. Never before in his life had he been unable to backtrack and surprise a pursuer. Rarely had he encountered an outlaw with the patience to wait outside a town for three days, in bitter cold, until his prey took to the trail. Most outlaws acted on impulse. They rarely planned, and when they did plan, the slightest hitch was likely to cause them to abandon their plans. Many an innocent citizen had fallen because some bank robber saw a deputy sheriff approaching as the robbery was in progress. Usually, the robber started shooting; rarely was the deputy the one killed. Old ladies chatting with a teller got killed, or merchants who picked a bad time to make a deposit got killed.

Call knew that successful bandits had their reputations inflated by rumor. The press helped bandits get names for themselves. People in small towns, who were bored most of their lives, thought bandits were colorful. The newspapers printed the gossip, and pretty soon everyone on the frontier would get the notion that a certain bandit was invincible, when in fact, few of them were particularly able, or more than moderately smart.

But the person who had put three bullets in him in less than five seconds was exceptional. Call knew his first mistake had been a reluctance to believe that the Garza boy actually might *be* exceptional. He had assumed that his was just another case of inflated reputation. He had only begun to suspect differently when he hadn't been able to catch Joey Garza following him. Call had known it, when the boy had ridden up almost before he was out of sight, and killed Roy Bean.

Yet he hadn't acted on his knowledge. He had eaten Lorena's bacon, drunk her coffee, and loped out to check the brands on two horses, as if Joey Garza was any other killer.

He had failed in vigilance, and now he was paying for his failure. That had always been the way of the frontier. If you failed in vigilance, you usually died. Rarely would the frontier permit a lapse as serious as the one he had just made.

Call considered that he had always been able to draw on more will than most men possessed. He could keep riding longer and keep fighting harder than any man he had worked with. He had never considered himself brilliant, and as a rider or a shot he was only average. But he could keep going in situations where others had to stop. He had never quit a fight, and the fight he was in now demanded just that persistence of him. He might be dying, but he couldn't quit until he had killed his killer. If he failed, all his effort would have been futile, and the lives of people who trusted him deeply would, in all likelihood, be forfeit.

Call risked sitting up for a second to see if he could catch a glimpse of the rifleman. The hobbled horse was exactly where it had been. But Call saw no one—not a movement, not a hat, not a glint of sun on a rifle barrel.

He flattened himself on his belly and began to push the rifle ahead of him. He wished he could simply cut off the useless arm and the useless leg. The leg was the worst—he didn't look at his knee, but he knew it must be nothing but bone fragments. The pain was beginning, and when he moved, sharp points of bone tore at what flesh was left. The arm he didn't feel. He pulled himself along on his one good elbow. For a while he pushed the rifle ahead of him, but he soon abandoned the rifle and took out his pistol instead. If he got a shot at Joey Garza, it would likely be at close range. If it wasn't at close range, he would probably miss anyway, particularly if he tried to shoot a rifle with one hand.

Every few minutes, Call raised up. His vision annoyed him. He couldn't see sharply. He could see the horse but not the shooter. It angered him. His eyesight was no longer adequate to the work he had tried to do. No doubt Gus McCrae or Charles Goodnight, men renowned for the sharpness of their vision, would have seen the boy under the horse while still safely out of rifle range. Either one of them could have seen that the horse was hobbled, and have avoided the bullets. He had tried spectacles but found them irritating, and he had not provided himself with any for the trip. That little neglect was another reason he was shot and dying.

Call kept on crawling. The hobbled horse had been some two hundred yards away when the shots came. Call wiggled for nearly half the distance, the pain in his leg growing more terrible with every movement. He left a trail of blood on the sand and on the sage bushes as he crawled. But he began to grow weak, and he began to feel light-headed. He saw that he wasn't going to make it to the hobbled horse. He wouldn't last that long.

Besides, the boy might not even be there. He might have been so confident of the wounds he had given that he had simply slipped away. Call felt his strength failing. He had crawled a long way, but he was still just half the distance to the horse, and had still not caught one glimpse of human movement.

He decided to tempt the boy, if the boy was there. He would show himself; maybe the boy would want to laugh at him, taunt him, shoot him again. If so, Call might be lucky enough to get off two or three pistol shots. If he was very lucky, he might put the boy down.

It was a gamble, of course. He had never shot especially well with the pistol, and the Garza boy would not likely be such a fool as to come close. So far, the Garza boy had been no sort of fool at all.

But it was a chance—his only chance. In another few minutes, he might pass out. Already he had lost so much blood that his hand was unsteady. Call wished he had kept pushing the rifle. It would make a fair crutch, something to support him when he stood up. But he had foolishly left it. He would just have to teeter as best he could and hope the Garza boy would be amused enough to expose himself.

Very carefully, Call got into a sitting position. He had his pistol on cock. He got his good leg under him and rested a minute. When he tried to take a deep breath to steady himself, he coughed. Again, he felt the first bullet, like a nut in his chest.

But he gathered himself, wiped the sweat out of his eyes with his good arm, wiped the blood off the gun with his shirttail, and

[424]

slowly eased up. The hobbled horse was still hobbled. Call could see nothing beneath it.

Then he heard a movement to his left and shot three times at the sound. It had sounded like a human footstep—Joey Garza had probably been sneaking up to finish him. But to his immediate, bitter disappointment, Call saw that it was only the mule deer he had scared earlier. He had shot the big doe. She bucked a few times and ran off, the fawn bounding after her through the sage.

Call knew it was no good. It was a failure; a botch. Joey Garza had left. He might have already found Lorena and killed her. Perhaps Joey wouldn't bother with her. After all, he had killed the bounty hunter, and there would be no one to interfere with his robbing for a while. Perhaps the clever boy would just ride away.

But it was clear that all the options belonged to Joey Garza. Call couldn't see him, couldn't find him, couldn't affect his actions. He eased back down. He had begun to feel the dangling arm, as well as the shattered leg. He lay flat, concealing the pistol under his bloody shirttail. If the boy did happen to ride by to inspect the body, Call might yet get off a shot. But he didn't expect this to happen. His head was swimming. He was so light in the head that he felt he was off the ground. He seemed to be somewhere between the sagebrush and the moving clouds. He tried to keep his eyes open. He felt dreamy and tried to fight the feeling. He kept telling himself that any moment he might look up and see the Garza boy standing over him, or looking down at him from horseback. He had to try to stay alert. But his eyelids wouldn't obey. They kept closing, at first for only a fraction of a second. But then it seemed to Call that despite himself, he was floating away into the world behind his eyelids. They wouldn't stay open. They wouldn't.

In the world behind his eyelids, everything was white.

5.

When Lorena heard the shooting, she quickly took her pistol out of her bag. In Presidio, Captain Call had given her one of his rifles; she took that, too.

"If we get separated, you'd have a gun you might kill an antelope or a deer with," he had said.

"I've never killed a big animal," Lorena had replied. "I'd rather we didn't get separated."

Now they *were* separated. Lorena had trouble getting the heavy rifle out of its scabbard. She finally had to take the scabbard off the saddle to do it. She took the pistol and the rifle and crawled quickly into a thick clump of chaparral near the camp. The thorns were sharp and she got scratched in several places, but she didn't care. She clutched the guns and pushed on into the very center of the chaparral. If the shooter was Mox Mox and he had killed Captain Call, she meant to kill herself, or else fight so hard that Mox Mox would have to kill her to get her out of the brush. She didn't intend to be Mox Mox's prisoner again, not even if it meant losing the life she wanted to devote to her children. Clara and Pea Eye would have to raise the children. She would not live to let Mox Mox smear grease in her eyes again.

Lorena crouched in the brush listening, the pistol in her hand. After the first several rifle shots, there was a long silence.

She could only endure it. She didn't dare come out of her hiding place, although she knew it would be no hiding place at all to the killers if they came for her.

Then she heard three smaller reports—pistol shots, she supposed. Crouching, she remembered the night Gus had rescued her from Blue Duck and Ermoke. She remembered the shooting, and how she had hoped she would die somehow if Gus was killed. She felt that terrible feeling again. If Captain Call had fallen and left her to Mox Mox, she wanted to die. She wanted to have it over; her hope was that she would have the strength to shoot herself. She would have to not think too much of her children. She would have to let them pass in her mind to Clara and Pea.

But the cold hours passed, and Lorena heard nothing and saw nothing. There was not a movement anywhere. She twisted around and around in the thorny chaparral, hoping to catch a glimpse of the men who might be coming, so she could prepare.

But no men came. Lorena waited hours; four or more, judging by the weak sun. Finally she began to be a little less frightened. The terror that had tightened her chest and made it hard even to breathe began to loosen. It might be that no one was coming. It might be that Captain Call had killed Mox Mox, or the Garza boy, or whoever had been there. If he hadn't, someone would have come.

She kept looking in the direction Captain Call had taken. She knew he must be injured or dead, otherwise he would have returned. She began to feel that she should go look for him, but it was midafternoon, and the sun was dropping in its arc before she could conquer her fear sufficiently to crawl out of the chaparral. The thorns had made her feel at least a little bit safe. She was reluctant to leave them, but she knew she had to. If Captain Call was dead, it was time to know it. Then she would have to try and go on alone. She knew where the Rio Grande was. That morning, Captain Call had said they would be there in two more days. She thought she could survive two days and find her way, if no one caught her.

When she stood up she could see one of the stray horses. It

had not moved from where it had been that morning, though the other horse was gone. She mounted and rode toward the horse, her pistol in her hand. It took her only a few minutes to cover the distance to the stray horse.

The first thing she saw as she came near the stray was a dead horse: it was Captain Call's. Lying not far from it was a dead mule deer. As Lorena approached, a fawn bounded away.

Then she saw the Captain's rifle. There was blood on the sand near it, and a bloody trail leading toward the stray horse. Lorena dismounted and followed the trail of blood, pistol in hand.

When she found the Captain lying flat on his back behind a sage bush, a pistol lying near, she thought he was dead. Blood had pooled beneath him, some of it seeping out of a wound in his chest; the rest was from a smashed arm and smashed leg. She thought he was dead. She had better leave him and try to get to the river and find Pea Eye. But when she knelt by the Captain, she saw his eyelids flutter. He opened his eyes and his hand came up, as if he were about to fire a gun at her. Only he had no gun in his hand. The pistol lay not a foot away, beside his mangled leg.

Call saw that it was the woman, Pea Eye's wife. Her face had collected itself out of the whiteness he lay in. She had a horse behind her. He had almost shot at her, thinking she was Joey Garza—it was lucky he had lost hold of his gun.

"He got me, you go on," he whispered.

"Who got you—was it Mox Mox?"

"No," Call said. "Mox Mox would have come to burn me. It was the boy. I never saw a trace of him."

Then he fainted. His voice had been a feeble whisper. Yet he wasn't dead. How he had lived with such wounds and such a loss of blood was a mystery, though Lorena knew that people did survive the most terrible wounds, all the time. Gus McCrae could have survived, if only he would have allowed his legs to be taken off. Lorena had felt angry for years that Gus would not allow that; as if she would have stopped loving him because he had no legs!

Now the same violence or worse had been done to the Captain. If he lived at all, he would probably have to lose the leg and the arm. Lorena didn't know how she could move him without killing him. Yet she had to move him, or else build a fire where he was. When night came, he would freeze in his own blood if he had no fire.

Also, his horse was dead, and they had brought no pack animals. He would have to ride her horse, if he lived. Then she remembered the stray horse, still standing a hundred yards or so away. Maybe the stray was tame enough that she could ride him. Then the Captain could have her horse, if she could get him on it. She took the bridle off Call's dead horse and walked out to the stray. The horse, a buckskin, whinnied when she approached; she saw that he was hobbled. No wonder he had stood there all day. She slipped the bridle on, and the horse let her lead him back to where the Captain lay.

Then Lorena went back to their camp and moved it. She had been mostly packed anyway. There was just the coffeepot and the skillet and a few other things. She had waited in the chaparral too long, and now it was too late to move the Captain. The best thing she could do for him was to build a big fire and try to get a little coffee in him. If she kept him warm, he might live through the night.

Lorena spent the last hour of sunlight gathering wood. She wanted to keep the fire hot until morning. The Captain whispered now and then, but so low that Lorena couldn't hear what he was saying. He was still bleeding; she didn't expect him to live. His hands twitched, but otherwise he scarcely moved. At times, the Captain lay so still that Lorena thought he was gone. She would have to put her hand on his breast to determine that he was still breathing.

The only water she had was in the four canteens, and there was no creek or river near where they had camped. Lorena knew she ought to wash the Captain's wounds, but she was fearful of using up the water. If she couldn't move him for several days, they would need it. If she left him to go look for water, she might be unable to find her way back—she might only make their situation worse.

She decided finally to sacrifice one canteen. She boiled water in the coffeepot, and very carefully opened the Captain's shirt and cleaned the wound in his chest. The arm and the leg were more difficult, for she had to cut his shirtsleeve and pants leg away. Every time she moved the wounded limbs even a little, the Captain moaned. Once, when she was a little too rough with the leg, he cried out.

It was no wonder, either. His knee was nothing but splinters of bone, and the arm was not much better. Still, Lorena knew that it was the wound in his chest that threatened his life. The wound leaked only a little blood now, but a large bullet was somewhere in the Captain, near his heart, and that was bad.

Once in the night, Call woke. He had supposed Lorena was gone, but then he saw her putting sticks on the fire.

"You ought to go on," he said, again. "You can make the river. Pea Eye ain't far from the river. Just follow the Rio Concho into Mexico for half a day. You'll find him."

"Captain, I can't ride off and leave you to die," Lorena said. "If you die, I'll go—but not until then."

"Foolish," Call whispered. "I might linger for a week. I can't get well. I'd be obliged if you'd go."

"Am I such poor company?" Lorena said, trying to josh a little. His breathing was labored, and she didn't expect he would live.

"You've got a family, I don't," Call whispered.

"You need to quit talking and rest," Lorena said.

That was easy advice to take. Call found that just lifting his tongue to make words was heavy work. It was as hard as lifting the side of a wagon to fix a busted wheel. A few words, just whispers, and he had to rest.

In the night the sky cleared, and the cold grew more bitter. Just before first light, Lorena used the last of her wood. She could hear the Captain breathing; there was a rasp in his breath. She had to walk a long way to find an armful of frozen sticks. For a moment she thought she was lost; but luckily, it was still dark enough that she caught a flash of her own fire. She made it back to camp and fed the fire, holding her cold hands over it.

[430]

Despite the good fire, the Captain was shivering. Lorena managed to pull and tug until she got the saddle free of his dead mount. She wanted the saddle blanket. They had only three blankets, and she put all of them on the Captain, placing the heavy saddle blanket over them. She had to keep arranging the blankets, because the Captain became restive. When he shifted, he cried out from the pain in his arm and leg.

Lorena knew she had to choose from between lesser evils. She could try to get the Captain on a horse and take him with her, or she had to leave and hope she could find a town and get back with help before he died. Probably he would die in either event, from moving or from staying.

He was not a large man; in the years since she had last seen him, he had become older and smaller. She was sure he hadn't been so small when she had known him before her marriage. She felt sure she could lift him onto a horse, but whether the movement would kill him, she didn't know. When it warmed a little, she would have to make her choice.

She tried to feed Call a little coffee with a spoon, but he was shivering so that most of the coffee spilled onto his shirt.

"You need to take a little, it'll warm you," she said. But Call was unconscious; he didn't respond.

Lorena decided then to take him with her. If she could get him on a horse while he was unconscious, the pain might not be so sharp. A few buzzards were circling in the cold sky, attracted by the dead horse and the dead deer. Lorena's horse was an old black plug named Blackie. The Captain had chosen a solid mount for her, one that would not act up and throw her some cold morning.

She saddled Blackie and walked him over to the dead horse. The frost was so intense that the dead horse didn't smell, not yet. The corpse would make a good stepladder, she decided; it was the only one available to her. She didn't want to give herself time to think about the task too much. She didn't want to waver.

When she lifted the Captain, she was shocked by how little he weighed. Clarie, her fifteen-year-old, far outweighed him. She had been tussling with Clarie not long before they left

home, and had tried to lift her off the ground. It was all she
could do to lift her daughter and carry her a few steps.

Captain Call wasn't as heavy as Clarie, not nearly. It seemed
absurd to her that this man, old and small, was still the man
they sent after the meanest killers. They should have found a
younger manhunter long since, and Captain Call should have
been living a safer life.

That was wisdom come too late, though. As she was carrying
him to the horse, the Captain woke. He looked at the ground,
as if surprised that a woman was carrying him. But his eyes were
not focusing, for he was in great pain.

"Captain, do you think you can ride?" Lorena asked. "I
caught that other horse—I'll put you on Blackie."

Call blinked; the world was hazy. He saw the black horse
standing by the dead horse. Lorena was carrying him as if he
weighed nothing. The fact was, his weight had dropped in the
last few years. But not being on his own feet startled him. It
made him wonder if he was still himself. He had always had his
own feet on the ground. To be carried, even the few steps to the
horse, was like floating. He felt he was floating into another life,
a life so different from his old one that he wondered if he would
even have the same name.

"I ain't been carried since my ma carried me, I guess," he
whispered.

Lorena got his good foot in the stirrup. Call pulled up with
her help, but when he swung his bad leg over the saddle, he
yelled out; then he vomited and fainted.

At least he was on the horse, Lorena thought. He was unconscious. She cut his lariat into sections with the big bowie knife
he kept in his saddlebags, and then she tied him on.

The buckskin stray was jumpy when she first mounted, but
she walked him until he settled down. Captain Call was alive,
but only just. She didn't want any jumpy horses causing his
death. She led Blackie, and led him slowly. She hoped Call
would come to from time to time, to direct her if she strayed off
course.

Call did awaken several times during the day, but he was too weak to speak. The pain in his leg was so intense that he could not hang on to consciousness for more than a few minutes. Lorena checked on him frequently. She was hoping for directions, but Call's whispers were incoherent. He muttered a name, but she didn't catch it.

Lorena stopped well before dark. She wanted plenty of time to gather firewood. They stopped by a little creek with a trickle of water in it. She wanted to heat water and try again to wash the Captain's wounds. He had wet himself during the long day horseback. She knew she could never manage to change his pants with the shattered knee, but she could at least put him by the fire and dry him. The wound in his chest was still leaking blood. She cleaned that and then cleaned off the saddle; it was a bloody, smelly mess.

Lorena gathered an abundance of firewood and drank several cups of strong coffee. She gave the Captain some and he came awake enough to drink it gratefully. All they had was bacon. Lorena fried some, but the Captain only ate two bites.

"Dillard," he whispered. It was the name he had been muttering all day. But it meant nothing to Lorena.

"Dillard Brawley," Call said. "He was the barber in Lonesome Dove."

"Well, I never used a barber in Lonesome Dove," Lorena said. "I guess I never met him."

"A centipede got in his pants and ruined his leg," Call whispered. "Gus and me tied him to a table and cut his leg off. We had to—he would have died of blood poisoning, if we hadn't. You have to do the same, you have to cut my leg off."

"No," Lorena said. "That town can't be more than two more days. There'll be a doctor there to tend to your leg."

In his haze during the ride, Call remembered Gus McCrae's wounded legs and how they looked before he died. Both Gus's legs had turned black, and Gus's wound had been nowhere near as bad as his. During the day, a great clot of blood had formed on Call's splintered knee. The bullet had hit just below the knee, but had gone upward and wrecked the kneecap. Lorena had tried to wash the clot, but it looked so bad that she had concentrated on doing the other wounds first. The bone fragments were like needles.

Then she remembered the one-legged man in Lonesome Dove; he had come in the bar sometimes. He had a hoarse voice.

"Was Dillard the man with the hoarse voice?" she asked.

Call nodded. "He ruined his voice, screaming, when we took the leg off," Call whispered. "We thought he'd faint, but he never fainted. He just screamed his voice away."

Lorena concentrated on washing the wounded arm; she hoped the Captain would forget about the leg, though she knew the pain must be too great to allow for forgetfulness. She was not squeamish. Clara had sometimes been in demand as a midwife, and Lorena had gone with her to help. She had also helped castrate horses when the ranch was shorthanded, and she had helped birth foals, as well as babies. She had felt the pains of childbirth five times herself, and she didn't faint at the sight of blood, even a lot of blood. She had seen injuries, some of them horrible. She had once bandaged the arm of a farmer who had been mangled in a haying machine, and she had several times cut fishhooks out of her own children.

But she didn't want to have to be the one to remove Captain Call's leg. Better to travel night and day until they reached a settlement where there was a qualified doctor. The knee looked so bad that she was even indecisive about cleaning it. Still, there was Gus and his death to remember. The clot on the Captain's knee was black.

Lorena thought about it until her mind went numb. She tipped over by the hot fire and slept a little.

In the morning when she awoke, the Captain was looking at her out of feverish eyes. Lorena looked at the leg and then looked away.

"You might bleed to death," she said.

"I didn't yet," Call whispered. "I ain't handsome, like Gus. I've got no women to lose. If I have to be one-legged, I will. I want to live to kill that boy."

Lorena felt a flush of disgust. The man was all but dead and might be dead before a day passed, or even an hour. He could barely whisper and his arm was ruined; he had a bullet in his chest that made his breath sound like a snore. Yet he still wanted to kill. The sympathy Lorena had felt for him in his pain, went away. Not all of it, but much of it.

"You ought to think of a better reason to live than killing a boy," Lorena said. "If killing is the only reason you can think of to live, then you might as well die."

Call was surprised by the anger in Lorena's voice.

Lorena was surprised by it herself. It came from memories and from times long past, from things she had felt about Gus, and things she had felt about Jake Spoon. The very man before her, Captain Call, the man with the ruined arm and leg and the deep chest wound, had himself hung Jake Spoon, his friend. If Gus McCrae hadn't killed to save her, she would have died alone at the hands of cruel men, long years before. She would have had no husband, no children, no pupils. Killing was part of the life they had all lived on the frontier. Gus's killings had saved her, but Lorena still felt a bitterness and an anger; not so much at the old, hurt man laying by the campfire as at the brutal way of life in the place they lived. She and Clara sometimes daydreamed of making a trip to England together to see civilization. They meant to visit Shakespeare's birthplace, and to see a play. They had amused themselves in the Nebraska evenings by imagining what they would say if they happened to meet Mr. Browning on the street, or Mr. Carlyle.

Yet here she was, not with Clara in a theater or a nice hotel in London, but on a bleak prairie, with not even one house within a hundred miles, caring for an old killer who wanted her to cut his ruined leg off so he could get well and kill again. She had studied and educated herself, but she had not escaped. When she looked around and saw where she was and remembered why she was there—because this man had taken her kind husband to help him kill a train robber—she felt a deeper anger still.

"I'm tired of it," Lorena said. "I'm tired of it, Captain! You oughtn't to have taken my husband. He's not a killer. You and

Gus were the killers. I loved Gus McCrae, but not like I love my husband. Our children love him and need him. You oughtn't to have taken him from us."

Call was sorry he had said anything; better to have stayed quiet until he died. Lorena was risking her life to help him, and Pea Eye was risking his life too; and yet he had angered her. There was justice in what she said, too. He shouldn't have taken her husband. He had taken him and wasted weeks of his time and put his life in jeopardy, and for nothing.

"The Garza boy is a killer," he whispered.

"I don't care," Lorena said. "There's killers and killers and killers out here. My husband's got nothing to do with that. You should have let him be."

Call remembered the fury Clara Allen had directed at him in Nebraska, as he was leaving her ranch with Augustus's body to bring it back to Texas. Now another woman, and one who was putting herself to great trouble to save him, was just as angry, if not angrier. He didn't know what the flaw was in his speech or in himself that brought up such anger in women.

But the fury was up in Lorena. He saw it in her eyes, in the way her nostrils flared, in the stiff way she held herself.

"You remember what I was, Captain," Lorena said. "I was a whore. Two dollars was all I cost—a dollar on Sunday. I don't know how many men bought me. I expect if you brought them all here, they'd about fill this desert. I expect they'd nearly make an army."

Call remembered well enough. Gus and Jake and Dish and many men in Lonesome Dove had visited Lorena. In those days, cowboys rode fifty miles out of their way to visit Lorena.

"But I'm not a whore now," Lorena said. "I'm a married woman. I'm a mother. I teach school. I didn't stay what I was— can you understand that? I didn't stay what I was! Clara cared for me, and she showed me a better way."

Call didn't know what was wrong. Lorena had clenched her fist, and if he had been well she might have hit him. But the Garza boy was a killer, and a deadly one: he killed frequently and without pity, so far as Call knew. He had been hired to stop the boy's killing. That was his job. Getting well in order to do what he had been hired to do seemed a reason to live; though when he took stock of his actual condition, he knew it was unlikely that he would ever go on the hunt for a killer again. He probably wouldn't live anyway—why was the woman so angry?

"I'll cut your leg off!" Lorena said. "I'll cut it off now! If you die, then you'll have been killed by a killer like yourself. But if you live, you oughtn't to stay a killer. I didn't stay a whore!"

In her anger she thought she could just take the big knife and cut the ruined leg off. But when she actually prepared for the task, she cooled quickly. Call was feverish and barely conscious. When he saw Lorena take the knife he wondered, in a dim, faraway state of mind, if he should have made the request. He and Gus together had a time getting Dillard Brawley's leg off, and they'd had a saw. A knife wouldn't cut bone. If the joint was shattered, as it seemed to be, she might cut there. But she would have to nick the knife blade first to make a kind of saw.

"Hit the knife on a rock, hit hard," Call said, weakly. "You need to nick it a little, so it'll saw.

"Once you've nicked it, sharpen it," he added, in a whisper. "There's a whetstone in my saddlebags."

Lorena found the whetstone. She hit the knife blade hard against a rock, again and again. Finally she made a few small nicks along the blade. Then she sharpened the big knife for several minutes. Captain Call had his eyes closed. Lorena hoped he was unconscious. She filled the coffeepot with water and heated it; then she poured the water over his knee until most of the black clot was gone. She knew she had to cut at the joint, and she wanted to see as clearly as she could.

"Captain, I oughtn't to do this," Lorena said. "I don't know how to take a leg off."

"If I die, it'll be the bullet that killed me, not the knife," Call whispered. "It won't be none of your fault."

"That's how you feel, maybe," Lorena replied. "I'm the one that will be doing the cutting. If this don't work, I'll be questioning my judgment for a long time."

Time and again in her marriage, Lorena had watched Pea

[437]

Eye put off decisions. He would hem and haw, and lean one way and then another, and try to weigh the pros of a given matter against the cons. Usually he would keep on weighing the pros and cons for several weeks, or even months, until one day Lorena would have had enough of his procrastination. She would whirl and make the decision herself, annoyed that she hadn't gone on and made it weeks before.

She was at such a point with the Captain. He was only just barely alive. His leg was ruined. Either she had to carry him on and hope she found a doctor before he died, or she had to cut.

Without speaking to Call again, she made her decision—she cut. She grasped his thigh with her left hand to hold it steady, and she cut. Call moaned; he was too weak to manage a scream. He was in a hazy, hot state. He moaned twice, and then boiling red water seemed to settle over him.

Lorena was glad he was unconscious. She didn't want him looking at her with his feverish eyes while she labored to remove his leg. It *was* labor, too; the hardest, apart from childbirth, that she had ever done. In no time it seemed she had blood to her elbows. The knife became slippery, so slippery that Lorena had to wipe off the handle several times. The flesh cut, but the bone was unyielding. She sawed and sawed, but it seemed that she was only scraping the bone. The Captain was bleeding heavily again, and it seemed to Lorena that he must be almost drained. He might be bleeding to death even, as she cut.

Lorena became desperate. She began to saw with both hands, bearing down on the knife as hard as she could. Blood ran so thick that she couldn't see the groove where she had the knife. Her arms were weary up to the shoulders from pressing and sawing. Once when she paused just a moment, the Captain rolled over. She had to turn him back and then wash the blood out and find the cut in the bone. She began to hate the blood: it was everywhere—on her, on her dress, on the Captain's shirt. It made the knife so slippery she couldn't hold it in the groove. She wanted to take a rock and smash the leg off somehow. Her shoulders ached, and a pain shot down her back from the effort of bearing down on the knife. She remembered Clara, and how

[438]

she had worked when they were pulling a foal out of a young mare. Clara's arms would be red to the shoulder from reaching into the mare to turn the foal. She would go home bloody from her shoulders down, but she never quit and she rarely lost a foal. Lorena knew she couldn't quit, either. She had started and she had to finish. She sawed on and on, though she had little hope that she would succeed or that the Captain would live.

Then Lorena realized she was sawing dirt. It was dirt as soaked with blood as she and the Captain were, but it was dirt. The leg was off. Lorena was so exhausted that she couldn't move. She knew she would have to tear up a dress to make a bandage, for it was all she had. But she was too weak to move. She didn't know what to do with the severed leg. She had cut it off, but she didn't want to touch it or even look at it. She didn't want to bury it or be near it. What she had done had been too hard. It had brought her so close to death that the thought of death was comforting. She had known that feeling before—life could be so harsh that the thought of death seemed to offer the only comfort. It wasn't good to be so close to death, because death might suck you in. She got to her feet finally, and walked away a few steps to be farther from the Captain. She felt she wanted to be away from him and away from what she had done.

She walked some distance from the fire and sat down on a large rock. She was covered with the Captain's blood. She didn't know if he was even alive, and she would soon have to go find out. But for a moment she needed to stay apart, for if she didn't she might lose her mind. She had come so close to death that she had forgotten everything else, forgotten that she was a married woman with children to raise. She had to stay apart to remember who she was and what her life was. She had to remember her children and her husband. She had to pull back from the place of blood and killing.

Lorena sat for nearly an hour, feeling empty. She knew the Captain might be dying—bleeding to death as she sat—but she could not do a thing about it. She had done what the man had asked. Most of her life she had struggled to do what some man asked, but she was through with that. She could do no more.

Only Pea Eye, her husband, didn't ask her for things she had to strain to do. Pea Eye never asked for anything. Sometimes it irritated her that he asked for so little.

But when she calmed down some, what she felt was a great longing to see Pea, her husband. She needed to see him. Once she found him, then she could rest.

When Lorena stood up again, she found that she had hardly any strength in her legs. It was hard even to walk back to the campfire, but she did. Captain Call was still alive and still unconscious. She didn't want to touch the severed leg. She pushed it away with a stick, tore up her spare dress, and bandaged Call's wound as best she could. Then she saddled the horses and packed the few things there were to pack. She went to the little creek and filled all the canteens, moving very slowly. She seemed to have no strength. Getting the Captain on the horse was going to be hard. She began to wish he would just die, so she wouldn't have to bother. Lifting him was very hard, but the Captain roused a little once he was in the saddle. He steadied himself, though he didn't speak and didn't seem to know where he was. Lorena was not sure he even realized she had cut off his leg.

The leg lay by the smoldering campfire where Lorena had pushed it. Captain Call's boot was still on it. Lorena started to mention the boot, but what good was a boot if you didn't have the leg? She felt wrong; probably she should bury the leg. But she was too tired, too tired to bury it, or even to mention it. She barely had the strength to tie the duffle to her saddle. Pulling herself into the saddle was hard. When she reached over to take Blackie's reins, she felt a great urge just to put her head down on the horse's neck and go to sleep.

"We go south," Call barely whispered. He saw that Lorena was exhausted. He felt a throbbing pain, but it was less sharp than it had been.

"Captain, I left your leg," Lorena said, as they were starting.

Captain Call didn't hear, and didn't answer.

6.

The morning after Deputy Plunkert ran away in his grief Famous Shoes, who had been squatting by the fire napping a little, heard the approach of a stumbling horse. Olin Roy had risen early and departed. Olin had never been one to stay in camp very long.

Brookshire was already awake. Even though he was very tired, the cold was so intense that he generally huddled by the fire in the hours before dawn. Sitting up was more restful than laying on the cold ground.

"Pea Eye is a good sleeper," Famous Shoes observed. "I don't think he would hear a bear if one came along."

"Why, there ain't bears here, are there?" Brookshire asked. "The Captain didn't mention bears when we came through here before."

"In the Madre, where I live, there are many bears," Famous Shoes said. "There are not too many bears left along the river, but there are still enough that a bear could come along."

"If one came along, it would eat Pea Eye before he woke up," he added.

Brookshire was glad he had several guns with him. If a bear came into camp, he supposed he could hit it. The range would not be a problem.

[441]

"I think that horse I hear has something wrong with it," Famous Shoes said. "It's just stumbling along."

He got up and disappeared into the darkness. Brookshire had heard one or two faint sounds, but he couldn't identify them. If the old Indian thought they were made by a stumbling horse, he was probably right.

Famous Shoes was back almost immediately, leading Deputy Plunkert's horse, which was indeed crippled and without its saddle and bridle. Its right shoulder seemed to be broken, and a rear leg was injured as well. When Famous Shoes tried to inspect its rear leg, the horse squealed in pain.

The squeal woke up Pea Eye, who had been dreaming that it was Saturday afternoon at home. Lorena had been giving the boys their haircuts. All the boys hated having their hair cut; they considered it unfair that they should have to have their hair cut so often, since Clarie, their big sister, could let her hair grow as long as she liked. Nonetheless, Lorena insisted on cutting the boys' hair every other Saturday afternoon. She had ordered special hair clippers from a catalogue and had a special pair of scissors that she used to give haircuts with. The boys all complained that the clippers pinched them cruelly, but Lorena ignored their complaints.

After she finished with the boys, Lorena would cut his hair. Although the clippers did occasionally pinch a little, Pea Eye didn't mind Lorena's haircuts at all. He liked the touch of his wife's cool hands as she smoothed his hair and brushed it. He had a tendency to cowlicks. Lorena could never correct them, but she would often take several minutes at the end of each haircut, smoothing the remains of the cowlicks with her cool hands, trying to make him look presentable or at least acceptable, in case they felt like making the fifteen-mile trip to church on Sunday morning. Pea Eye would go into a happy reverie while Lorena cut his hair. He knew he was very lucky to have such a considerate and affectionate wife, one who would take time from her many chores to cut his hair and try to make it look good. He knew he didn't really look very good—he never had—it was all that much more a miracle that Lorena chose to give him such loving attention. He didn't know why she did, and he never allowed himself to expect it to continue; yet through the years, as the children grew, it seemed that it did continue.

It was so nice to see Lorena and the boys, even in a dream, that Pea Eye was reluctant to wake up and face the day. It was very pleasant to be with his family in his dream of Saturday afternoon. He could even see the clippings of brown hair—the boys had brown hair—all over the kitchen floor. Lorena would sweep up the hair cuttings as soon as she finished the haircuts. If she saw a particularly fetching lock from one of her sons, though, she might keep it and put it in her album of family memories.

"Why, it ain't too different from taking scalps," Pea Eye had observed once, when he noticed Lorie saving a lock of Georgie's hair.

"It is *too* different!" Lorena said. Then to his horror, she burst into tears.

"I just want a few curls of hair from my menfolks," she said, in a shaking voice. "I'd have it to remember you all by, in case something happened to any of you."

She cried hard, and Pea Eye felt miserable. Then she stopped crying. At least that was over, he thought. He regretted his careless remark about the scalps.

"Things happen to people, don't you understand that?" Lorena said, and began crying again, harder than ever.

Still, despite that painful memory, one of the many that had been caused by his slips of the tongue, it was hard to leave the peaceful dream of home and haircutting to come back to the cold world of Mexico. Deputy Plunkert's horse was back in camp, badly crippled. But where was Deputy Plunkert?

"I think his horse fell," Famous Shoes said. "It has blood on its head. I think it fell and hit a rock."

Sure enough, the horse had a cut place on its head.

"Could you backtrack this horse?" Pea Eye asked. "Ted Plunkert might be hurt."

"I think you should kill this horse—it can't walk any further," Famous Shoes said. "We can eat him."

Then he left. He was gone several hours. His absence made Brookshire nervous. Morning became noon, and then mid-afternoon. They were just sitting and waiting, and Brookshire hated waiting. At least when they were moving, he could convince himself that they were following a plan. It was the Captain's plan. On a day-to-day and hour-to hour basis it might seem pointless, but there was always at least the hope that the Captain might know what he was doing. He might yet catch Joey Garza, or kill him, thus ending the threat. After all, Brookshire had seen with his own eyes how quickly Captain Call had ended the threat of Sheriff Joe Doniphan. It had only taken him a few seconds once he got to it.

The few seconds that it would take him to end the career of Joey Garza might arrive just as unexpectedly. The hands of the clock would keep turning, and one day the Captain and Joey Garza would finally be in the same place. Then when that moment arrived, Joey Garza would be dead or captured, and Colonel Terry could get a good night's sleep, or at least start worrying about something else. Brookshire had never witnessed anything as violent as what Captain Call had done to the sheriff. He had seen the results of such violence during the War, but he had not actually seen the violence happen.

"I wish Famous Shoes would get back," Pea Eye said. He had already shot the crippled horse, but he didn't butcher it. They still had bacon, and a little venison from a small buck he had shot. He didn't feel he had to be reduced to eating horsemeat, not yet.

There were only two hours of sunlight left when Famous Shoes returned. Though he rarely seemed to show the effects of travel, this time he did. When he returned he wasn't trotting; he was walking. He had a belt in his hand, which he handed to Pea Eye. It was Deputy Plunkert's belt.

"That horse ran off a bluff," he said. "If the moon had been shining, he might have seen where he was going, but it was dark."

"How about Ted?" Pea Eye asked.

"He is dead," Famous Shoes said. "I buried him. I only had my knife to dig with, or I would have been back sooner."

"Good Lord, he fell that far?" Pea Eye said. "It must have been a high bluff."

"No, the fall only broke his hip," Famous Shoes said. "Some vaqueros came along and shot him and took his clothes. I found this belt, though. I think they dropped it."

Though the fire was blazing, Brookshire felt cold. A man who had been with them for weeks, who had been sitting around this very campfire on the night before, was now dead. He had run off in grief over the cruel death of his wife and now was dead himself, of a circumstance almost as cruel.

"He had a broken hip, and yet they shot him?" Brookshire said. "Who would shoot a man with a broken hip?"

"I think they were just vaqueros," Famous Shoes said, again. "They were probably poor. Their horses weren't shod. There were four of them, I didn't recognize their tracks. I think they were just vaqueros from the south. They probably wanted his guns and his saddle. I don't know if he was willing to give them up. He shot one time with his rifle—here is the empty cartridge. They killed him and took his clothes. Then they went south."

"All his clothes?" Brookshire asked.

Both Famous Shoes and Pea Eye looked at him as if he had asked a very foolish question.

"We ought to get a ways along tonight," Pea Eye said. "Those vaqueros might decide they want some more horses and guns. They might come back."

Famous Shoes was annoyed by his friend's ignorance. Hadn't he just said that the vaqueros had gone south? He had tracked them for two miles to make sure.

"We can camp anywhere," he said. "Those vaqueros are gone."

Brookshire didn't mention the deputy's clothes again, but he had his own view—and his view was that he preferred to imagine the deputy's dead body fully clothed. The man had come on a trip for nothing, lost his wife in cruel circumstances, and

[445]

then had been murdered himself in circumstances just as cruel. Deputy Plunkert had been a skinny fellow, and it was cold. Of course a dead man would not feel the cold, but Brookshire still didn't like to think of that skinny white body laying naked in the cold night. In his mind, he dressed Deputy Plunkert in the clothes he had been wearing when he rode sobbing out of the camp. Pea Eye and Famous Shoes were men of the West, and no doubt they were used to such harsh sights.

But Brookshire, an accountant from Brooklyn, was not.

7.

Joey was surprised and a little disappointed at how easily Captain Call had let himself be shot. He was still testing the range of the German rifle, and he had thought the Captain might be a man he should try to kill from the limits of the rifle's range.

He had followed Call from the day he left old Bean's. Within an hour of hanging the judge, Joey was on Call's trail and never lost it. He didn't come too close to the man, though. He held about ten miles back; even so, it was soon apparent that Call knew he was being followed. From tracks, Joey saw that he doubled back several times, both day and night, hoping to surprise him or at least pick up his tracks. If Call had doubled back a few miles farther, he would have picked up Joey's tracks, of course—no one could travel and leave no tracks at all.

The Captain only doubled back some five or six miles. He was after Mox Mox and his seven men, and evidently felt that he had no more time to spare for the one man who was following him, if it was one man.

Joey thought it impressive that the old man sensed he was being followed. Call had tried four times to pick up signs of his pursuer. It showed that he wasn't a fool. Joey was hanging far back on the day Call attacked Mox Mox. Joey heard the shooting, but from very far away and faint; it could have been hunters shooting.

But he followed, and then inspected the little battle site. It was evident that Captain Call was not an especially good shot. On the other hand, he had attacked eight men and killed six of them. Also, he had wounded at least one of the men who had escaped. He was not a particularly good shot, but he was willing to fight and he fought successfully.

When he left the scene of the fight, Joey decided to follow Mox Mox rather than Call. It was evident that Call was going to Fort Stockton. His trail could be picked up a little later.

But Joey only had to track Mox Mox about three hours before he came upon his corpse, laying in a gully not far from a dead horse. Probably old Call didn't even know he had killed the manburner, but he *had* killed him. Mox Mox would not be burning Rafael and Teresa. Joey would have to find another way to dispose of his brother and sister. If he couldn't find a rich man who would buy them for slaves—a rich man might consider them too damaged to make good slaves—he could take them to the mountains near his cave and leave them for the bears or the big gray lobo wolves. Or he could simply push them off a cliff. He meant to kill them, one way or another. Then his mother would know what he thought of her whoring. She would have to give him all her attention. She would wash his clothes and make them soft, and cook him tasty meals when he was in Ojinaga.

First, though, Captain Call had to be killed. He was old, but he could fight. He was to be respected, as John Wesley Hardin was to be respected. The Captain and the gunman were both men who didn't hesitate to kill. Before Joey hung old Bean, he had run into a vaquero from Chihuahua who told him that Call had beaten the hard sheriff, Doniphan, almost to death with a rifle. All the vaqueros on both sides of the river had lived in fear of the hard sheriff. He had been severe with everyone he ever caught.

Yet Call had easily beaten Doniphan. Call was a man to be approached with attention and skill.

Joey lingered outside Fort Stockton for three days, waiting for the Captain to leave. He was afraid Call might take the train and escape. He didn't know whether he should risk robbing a train with Captain Call on it. He would not be able to keep the man in sight, but to lose sight of him would mean taking a large risk. With most lawmen, Joey thought, he could rob the train anyway and depend upon his own quickness. But with Captain Call, quickness might not be the most important thing.

Then Captain Call had left town with the woman. It surprised Joey greatly that old Call would need a woman. When people talked about Captain Call, women were never mentioned. Joey had supposed Call was a man like himself, one who didn't need women and who didn't like whores.

That the woman was a whore like his mother, Joey had no doubt. He would have liked it better if Captain Call had continued to travel alone. Then he would have felt that he was stalking an equal. But no man who went with whores could be his equal.

Then the cowboys with the herd of horses appeared, and Joey changed his plans. He had been thinking of shooting the Captain from a very long range, but he thought the horses might help him get a little closer. He stole two horses from the cowboys in the night, and hobbled one of them near the Captain's camp. The Apache had often fired from beneath horses. He had heard that there were Comanche so skillful in approach, they could even fire from beneath the bellies of antelope or deer. He didn't believe that anyone, even a Comanche, could get close enough to an antelope to fire from beneath its belly. Even if an Apache wore the skin of an antelope and imitated its movements, the antelope would smell the man beneath the skin and run off. Some deer, though, were stupid. With deer it might be possible.

Joey had expected much more caution from Captain Call than the old man had exercised. He had been willing to risk a long shot. He was afraid if he waited too long, one of the cowboys might come back looking for the missing horses and muddle his plan.

But the Captain merely rode out carelessly, not noticing that one of the horses didn't move. A man who had hunted men all his life should know the difference between a hobbled horse and one that was loose. But the Captain had loped out within easy range. Perhaps his eyesight was failing him. It had been annoying that the lawman's horse was high-stepping and trying to pitch. Joey thought that his first shot was a little off because of the jumpy horse. It was not off much, though; probably it would be mortal. Then he shot Call in the leg and in the arm, and killed his horse. The big bullets would ruin the arm and the leg. Even if the chest shot didn't kill the old man outright, he would bleed to death or starve.

Joey had no interest in the woman. He watched with the spyglass as she crawled into the chaparral carrying the pistol and the rifle. Probably she thought he would come and try to whore with her. Or she may have thought that the Captain had been shot by a gang of men, in which case she had good reason to be cautious.

Joey didn't think much about the woman. She could stay in the chaparral until she starved for all he cared. His only concern was Call. He moved around with his spyglass until he could see the body, and he saw at once that the Ranger wasn't quite dead. His foot moved from time to time. Once he raised his good arm. Joey saw he had a pistol in his good hand, and that made Joey feel good. The old man was still wanting to kill him. He hoped Joey would come to rob his body, so he could shoot at close range. But Joey had no intention of coming any closer than he was. The Captain looked poor, and there was little likelihood that he owned anything worth taking to the cave.

Joey could easily have come in closer and shot at him again. He would not have needed to come into pistol range or even close to pistol range to end the Captain's life. But he didn't want to shoot again. He wanted the man to die from the first bullet. Almost all his kills had been made with one shot.

Still, if the old man somehow managed to live, it might be better. It might only enhance Joey's reputation. After all, the Captain had hunted him for more than a month and had never even seen him. If Call survived, he would be a cripple. His leg would probably have to be cut off, and his arm too. Everyone who saw him would know what it meant: Joey Garza had beaten the most famous manhunter in the West, beaten him and left him a cripple. It would be obvious to all who saw the old man that it was Joey's choice that Call lived. A man so injured would be easily killed. Better to let him live as a warning to other men who might be tempted to hunt him for bounty. He had destroyed Call as easily as Call had destroyed Sheriff Doniphan. Four shots, one for the horse—and the old king of the border had been cut down and made a cripple. Captain Call would no longer be a threat to even the most ignorant, careless outlaw. He would never again be thought capable of challenging anyone as able as Joey Garza.

Joey decided to wait through the night to see if Call lived until morning. He saw the woman come out of the chaparral and go to the place where Call lay. He watched her move camp; he watched her gather firewood. She was blond. Her hair came loose as she was bending to gather firewood, and she let it stay loose. Joey watched her closely through the spyglass. At one point she squatted, to relieve herself. Joey felt a disgust and stopped looking. She was just like his mother—she was only a beast, a whore.

The next morning, he watched the woman lift the Captain onto the black horse. She was a strong woman. When she came to catch the hobbled horse, Joey was only a hundred yards away. But the woman didn't sense him. He followed them all day, expecting Call to die at any moment. But when afternoon came and the woman made camp, the old man was still alive.

In the morning, Joey watched the woman cut off Call's leg. He was surprised that a woman would attempt such a bloody task with only a big bowie knife. Of course, his mother had always butchered the sheep and the goats they ate, and she even butchered pigs when they had pigs. She didn't mind being bloody, and neither did the blond woman who was cutting off Call's leg. Joey watched it all through his spyglass. Old Call was tough. He lost blood and then more blood, and yet he didn't die. When Joey had hacked off Benito's arms and legs, he had been unprepared for the spurting blood. He had turned his face away and struck with the heavy machete. Later he had thrown away all his clothes and snuck naked into his house. He didn't want to wear clothes that had blood on them. He couldn't let his mother wash the clothes. She might understand, then, that the blood had come from her husband.

Joey didn't think the blond woman was going to be able to take Call's leg off. She was tiring, and he could see her chest heaving. She stopped at times to rest, but she always returned to the task. Finally, when Joey had concluded that she wasn't going to succeed, she got through the bone and the leg came off. Then the woman walked away from the camp and sat on a rock to rest. For a second, Joey was tempted to shoot her—it would be a test for Captain Call, to see if he could survive with only one leg and no one to help him.

But Joey didn't shoot her. He watched her mount the buckskin horse and saw her ride away, leading the horse that Captain Call was slumped on.

It was a strange thing to see, a whore strong enough to cut a man's leg off. Joey watched them go and then put his spyglass back in its leather case. He imagined Captain Call would die somewhere on the trail to the south.

Now he had to go to Mexico and kill Call's men. They had come after him in his own country and he meant to see that such effrontery cost them their lives. After he killed them he thought he might go to Ojinaga, though he didn't intend to let anyone in the village see him when he got there.

Once he got home, it would be Rafael's and Teresa's turns to die. He thought he might steal a horse and then tie them on the horse. He could take them to his cave for a while to tease them. The idea of throwing his brother and sister off a cliff had begun to appeal to him. He would take them to his cave and see how he felt about it then.

8.

The day after Lorena amputated his leg, Captain Call developed a fever so high that Lorena felt sure he would die. She had nursed five children through many fevers, but in the very young, fevers came and went like clouds in the skies. As the children grew older, high fevers were more serious—Captain Call was an old man, and he was burning up. Even Lorena couldn't remember Georgie having fevers that felt as hot to the touch as Call's, and Georgie was prone to blazing fevers.

Call soon became incoherent. He mumbled, slumped over Blackie's neck. The leg bled, but not much. Lorena had used the last of her extra clothing for bandages, and she had no more cloth to make bandages with. She had no medicines with which to treat the fever. If Call died, he died. All she could do was keep pressing on, hoping to come to the river.

Lorena knew she was going in the right direction. She could tell that from the sun. But she was in a big country where she had never been before, and she didn't know how to aim for the town. It could not be a very large town. The country rolled so that she knew she might not be able to see Presidio, unless she spotted it from the top of a ridge. Captain Call had said it was on the Rio Grande. That was all she knew.

She stopped twice and tried to get the Captain to wake up and look around. If he could only glance around, he would probably figure out where they were and correct her if she was off course. He had mentioned that he had been over the country many times.

But Captain Call was lost in fever, more lost even than Lorena was in the vast country. She would have to keep going as she was going and hope to know which direction to turn when she came to the river.

They endured another cold night. Lorena was too tired to gather enough wood to see them through the night; the fire died well before dawn. She piled the heavy saddle blanket and all but one of the smaller blankets on the Captain, but it was not enough to keep him from shivering and shivering. Looking at him, so old and frail and sick, caused Lorena to feel pity but also puzzlement. What kept the man alive? Why didn't he just die? The big bullet was still in him, close to his heart. His leg was gone, and the wound had not been treated. If it got infected, he would surely die. His arm was also terrible. She wasn't going to try to cut it off; she wasn't up to another amputation. Any of the three wounds might prove mortal.

Yet the man still breathed. He burned with fever, he couldn't talk, and couldn't see, yet he breathed. Even if she wrestled him onto his horse and got him to Presidio and they found a doctor, what could the doctor do? And what would there be left for him if he did live? He couldn't hunt men anymore. He wasn't a rancher. He didn't farm. He had lived all his life by the gun, and now no one would ever want him for his fighting abilities again. Better that he died—he wouldn't have this suffering, and he wouldn't have to live as an old cripple.

Call had done what Gus McCrae wouldn't do. He had given up his leg in order to keep his life. For years, Lorena had wished Gus had chosen to live, to live anyhow, and she had been angry with him because he hadn't. But now, seeing Call, she wasn't so sure.

Riding over the barren ridges, leading the horse with the sick, feverish, diminished man on it toward a destination she didn't know if she could even locate, made Lorena feel doubtful. Gus might have taken the sensible option, after all. He was the

[454]

smartest man she had ever known, Gus McCrae. He had a fine, soaring imagination. Gus had not been able to put his imaginings in writing, as Mr. Dickens and Mr. Browning could, but he could speak them and he had spoken them to Lorena in the months they had been together. Gus had been himself—a full man. He'd had his flaws, and Lorena knew them. He was selfish at times past believing, as selfish as Pea Eye was unselfish. Gus knew himself. He knew how he wanted to be, and he had chosen in the critical hour not to accept being less.

Perhaps after all, Augustus McCrae had been right. But that was something Lorena could never know, not for herself and not for Gus. If Gus had lived, he would probably have married Clara; and if he had married Clara, Lorena would have had to take her heartbreak and go away with it. She could not have lived around their happiness. She might never have taken up her studies and never have been friends with Clara's girls. She would have left with her sorrow. She would never have married Pea Eye and would not have had her children. She would have drifted off, been an unhappy woman, and gone back to whoring, probably. By now she would be dead of discouragement. She would not have killed herself, but she would have found her way out of an existence that, without Gus, Clara, Clara's girls, or Pea Eye, would have become too heavy to carry.

The next morning, she saw the ribbon of river shining far ahead. But she saw no town. She had found the Rio Grande, but where was she, north or south of the town and the Rio Concho? She didn't know. When she tried to nudge Call out of his delirium, she failed again. He couldn't see, for his eyes were hot with fever.

Lorena crossed the river. She remembered that Call had said Pea Eye was half a day to the south. He had mentioned an old scout named Billy Williams who was staying in a little village in Mexico. The old scout might tell her the way or even lead her. Call had told her about Billy Williams before she cut his leg off. He must have known that he would be useless to her, even if he lived.

Lorena crossed the river and looked both ways. There was

nothing to see in either direction but the gray land. She had hoped for a spiral of smoke or an adobe hut, but there was nothing.

The choice was a coin toss: Lorena had to choose between two emptinesses. She chose to go north, for no better reason than that she was right-handed. For six hours she led the Captain's horse north, feeling more and more despairing, more and more convinced that she had made the wrong choice. She became seriously frightened. She had eaten the last of the bacon that morning, and had only enough coffee for two more camps. If she didn't find a settlement or a dwelling soon, she would wear out and give up. Her nerves had not recovered from the amputation, and she was exhausted but unable to sleep. She could not get warm, no matter how close to the fire she slept, and she had troubling dreams about her children when she did sleep. They were vague dreams, and she could not remember them clearly, but in all of them her children were under threat. Laurie was sick, or a horse was running away with Clarie, or Georgie had fallen down a well.

Lorena stuck close to the riverbank. If she wandered off and lost the river, it would probably be the end. Toward evening, as the weak sun began to sink, she thought she saw a movement near the river. There was a little rapid, and just above it she thought she saw a brown rock move. She had been nodding in her fatigue, perhaps even dreaming. Brown rocks didn't move.

When Lorena rode a little closer, she saw that an old Mexican woman sat by the river, just above the little rapid. She was wrapped in a brown serape and looked from a distance like a rock, but she was a woman. Call was slumped over his horse's neck, unconscious.

"I have seen that man before," the old woman said. "He was in our village. Who cut off his leg?"

"I did," Lorena said. "I had to."

"He is the famous Texas Ranger. He killed Maria's father," the old woman said. "He killed her brother, too. That was a long time ago, when my children lived with me."

"He was a lawman," Lorena said. "I need food and I need a doctor. He has a bullet in him. I need to find a doctor who will take it out."

"There is no doctor in our village," the old woman told her. "The butcher might take the bullet out—his name is Gordo. But he is lazy, I don't know if he would want to help a gringo. Maria can do many things. She might take the bullet out. But this lawman killed her father and killed her brother. Maria may not be willing to help him."

"I'll have to take the chance," Lorena said. "I'm out of food. Where is your village?"

"Go on the way you are going, it isn't far," the old woman replied.

Lorena wondered why the old woman had chosen to sit by the river. The dark was coming, but she was making no move to go home. Lorena thought she might be sick, and she felt she should offer to help her.

"If you're tired, you can ride my horse," Lorena said to her. "I can walk, if the village isn't too far."

"No, I want to stay here tonight," the old woman said. "My children live here. If you listen, you will hear their voices."

Lorena did listen, but all she heard was the splashing of the water in the little rapid. She decided the old woman must be crazy.

She rode on another mile, and soon saw the village. The setting sun shone on it. There were only some eight or ten small buildings, but after days of seeing nothing but the gray land, the sight of even one building would have been welcome.

It was welcome to the horses, too; they were hungry. Both of them tried to speed up, but Lorena held them back. She was afraid that a faster pace might jar the Captain and cause worse bleeding.

As she rode into the village, a few goats walked out to meet her, bleating. She saw a large boy and a small, slight girl standing with the goats. Both children were barefooted, despite the cold. The little girl was very pretty, but she moved oddly, holding her head to the side like a bird. Lorena was only a few feet away from them, when she realized that the little girl was listening, not looking. She was blind.

Behind the children, in the doorway of a small house, Lorena saw a woman with a butcher knife in one hand—probably she had been cutting meat for supper. A tall, older man with a slight limp came out and stood beside the woman. He looked American. Perhaps he was the scout Call had mentioned, the one who might take her to find her husband. She stopped, and the woman and the tall man came out to greet her.

"I have a wounded man," Lorena said to them. "I need help. If there's a doctor here, I'd appreciate it if someone would find him. This man has a bullet in him that needs to come out."

Billy Williams took the reins of Call's horse. He was shocked at how the man looked. He had seen many wounded men, but could not recall seeing anyone still breathing who was in worse shape than Call was in.

"It's Woodrow Call," Billy said, to Maria. "Somebody's about finished him."

Maria had the knife in her hand. She walked up to the horse and looked at Call. For years, when she was younger and the sting of her father's and her brother's deaths had been sharper, Maria had promised herself that she would kill Captain Call if she ever got the opportunity.

Now the opportunity was an arm's length away. They were planning to kill a goat, and Billy Williams had just sharpened the butcher knife. Maria hadn't spoken—Billy always grew nervous when Maria didn't speak. Her angers matured in silence. Then they came boiling up.

But Maria didn't raise the knife and she didn't strike. She looked at the blond woman on the other horse. It was easy to see that the woman had come a long way, for she looked cold and she looked tired. She looked as exhausted as Maria had felt when she got back from Crow Town.

"Get down," she said, to the woman. "Come into my house and eat."

Maria looked only briefly at the man tied to the black horse. He was an old man, and so wounded that he was only just barely alive. Though he bore the name of the man who had killed her father and her brother, Maria knew he was no longer that man, the one she had wanted to kill. She had wanted to kill him in his power because he had used his power wrongly. She wanted him to know that he could not simply kill people, good people, and be excused.

But the man who had wielded the power and done the killing was not the old, sick man on the black horse. To stab him now would be pointless—for she would not be stabbing the Captain Call she had hated for so long, but only the clothes and the fleshy wrappings of that man. She began to untie the knots that held him to the horse. The knots were slick with his blood.

"Take him in," she said to Billy. "Put a blanket down by the fire and put him on it. I want to look at his wounds."

Billy cut the bloody knots and lifted Call off the horse. Call moaned when his wounded arm bumped against the saddle horn. Teresa came over and stood beside Billy as he lifted Call.

"Is that the man who was here before?" Teresa asked. "I hear him breathe—is he sick?"

"Yes, he's sick," Maria said. She was unsaddling Call's horse. "Tell Rafael to drive the goats to the pen. We don't want the wolves getting them."

Lorena was stiff. She hadn't yet dismounted. She was trying to adjust to the fact that she had actually found the village. She had stopped believing that she would find any settlement, anyplace with people in it.

"Get down," Maria told her. "Billy will take care of your horse. You need to wash and you need to eat."

Lorena eased off the horse.

"I've come a long distance," she said. "I'm tired."

"Who cut his leg off?" Maria asked. Not until Billy lifted Call down did she notice the missing leg.

"I did," Lorena responded. "It was that or let him die."

"No wonder you are tired," Maria said. "Come into my house and rest."

[459]

It was a small house. There was a table with a lamp on it, two plain chairs, and some blankets spread on the dirt floor. But it was a house, so warm inside that before Lorena had been there five minutes, she began to nod.

The large boy brought in a bowl full of cold water for her from the well. Lorena splashed it on her face, trying to wake up. She saw Maria bending over Call. The old scout was there, too. They cut his shirt off and examined the wound in his chest. Then they looked at his arm.

"You should have cut the arm off, too," Maria told her, when Lorena squatted beside her.

"I was just too tired," Lorena answered. "It was just too much cutting.

"You have a pretty daughter," she added. The little blind girl was ladling food out of a pot. The girl moved around the house lightly, like a moth.

"Thank you," Maria said.

"Well, I ain't going in after that bullet," Billy Williams said. "That bullet is lodged in a bad place. Whoever takes it out needs to know what he's doing, and I don't."

"There's no doctor here?" Lorena asked.

"Just the butcher, and he's a butcher," Maria said. "Who shot this man?"

"Joey Garza, I guess," Lorena said. "Neither of us ever saw who it was. The man shot from under a horse. Captain Call said he thought it was Joey Garza, though."

Maria was silent. Her son would be very famous now; he had brought down the great manhunter. All the girls on the border would want him, though that would make little difference to Joey. He didn't like girls.

But Joey had avenged her father and her brother. He had crippled their killer, and there was no need for her to do more. She could even help the old man a little, though she knew she was not skillful enough to remove the bullet from his chest. She could probably cut off his arm if the butcher couldn't be persuaded to do it. Or they could send across the river for the doctor in Presidio. He didn't like coming to Mexico—the people were too poor to pay him—but he might come to treat Captain Call. He was a famous Ranger, not a poor Mexican.

"Do you know Joey Garza?" Lorena asked. She had seen the woman stiffen a little, when she said the name.

"He is my son," Maria said.

Lorena thought she must have misheard. Surely she hadn't carried Captain Call for three days across the wastes, only to bring him to the house of the boy who had tried to kill him.

"I am Joey's mother, but I am not like him," Maria said. She saw that Lorena was frightened.

"You need to rest," she added. "There is a bed in the other room. You can sleep without worrying. We will take care of your friend. We are not going to kill him. If I had meant to kill him, I would not have brought him into my house."

Lorena was so tired that she wasn't thinking or even hearing very well. She had to sleep soon, no matter what happened to Captain Call.

"Teresa, take her," Maria said.

Lorena followed the little blind girl into the other room.

"I cleaned your bed," the little girl said. "When you wake up, I will tell you a story."

"Why, thank you," Lorena said. "I like stories."

Then she stretched out on the low bed.

"Do you have any children?" Teresa asked, as Lorena stretched her stiff limbs.

"Five . . . I have five," Lorena said. Then, in a blink, she went to sleep.

Teresa sat on the bed beside her for a few minutes. She had ladled up some posole, but she knew the woman hadn't eaten any.

"You didn't eat your posole . . . wake up," she said, touching the woman. But the woman didn't wake up.

Teresa sat on the bed listening to the woman breathe. She was thinking about the story she would tell her when she woke up. It would be a story about the big spider that lived by their well. Sometimes she would put her hand on the ground and let the spider crawl over it. The spider never bit her, though a scorpion had bitten her once. She could hardly wait for the woman to wake up so she could tell her the story about the spider.

9.

When he robbed the train outside San Angelo, Joey made a discovery. What he discovered was that it was more interesting to him to frighten people than to kill them. He had made the passengers stand outside for an hour after he robbed them. He told them he would be watching through his spyglass, and he assured them he would kill the first one who moved before the hour was up. The people stood in terror for a long time. He had taken their watches, and he told them to look at the sun and mark the hour by its movements. But the people stood in the cold for almost three hours before any of them dared to move. They were afraid of being shot. In the end, Joey didn't shoot any of them. Through the spyglass he could see that the people were shivering—from fear, not from cold. Two of the men wet themselves. They were too afraid of his bullets even to move behind a bush.

Watching the passengers tremble was more satisfying than killing them. None of them were people of importance, and there was no distinction to be gained from killing people of no importance. Making people dead was easy, but it was no longer interesting to him.

Wounding Captain Call so badly and so easily was a triumph Joey knew he would never be likely to equal. But he would never need to equal it, so potent was the reputation of the man he had wounded. Even if he never shot another person or robbed another train, his reputation would grow and grow along the border and all through the West. He had ended the career of the most famous manhunter of all. People would still be talking about Joey Garza when he was an old man, even if he never killed or robbed again.

He planned to kill again, though, and quickly. He wanted to shoot Captain Call's three deputies. They were probably too inept to be a nuisance, but Joey wanted it known that he had wiped out Captain Call's whole party. That would build his reputation even higher.

Joey followed the blond woman all the way to Ojinaga. From time to time, he took out his spyglass and trained it on the horse carrying Captain Call. He expected to see that the old man had died. But every time he looked, he saw movement. Somehow the old man still lived.

When he saw the woman lead the horse upriver toward the village, he let her go and rode off a few miles into Mexico, where he made camp. He meant to travel up the Rio Concho and locate the deputies.

The next morning, a little before midday, he found their camp. They were almost a day's ride inside Mexico, and they seemed simply to be waiting. They were probably waiting for Captain Call. They didn't know what had befallen him.

Joey was surprised to see that there were now only two deputies and old Famous Shoes. He saw no reason to kill the old man. Probably the third deputy had met with an accident of some sort.

Joey studied the camp for a while with his spyglass, trying to decide on a method of attack that would provoke the utmost fear. After giving it some thought, he decided to shoot the horses and the two pack animals first. Maybe he could scare the men out into the desert. If he frightened them badly enough, he might not even have to shoot them. He could simply chase them into the desert, shooting now and then to scare them farther away from the river. When he had them exposed and lost, he could simply go away and leave them to freeze or starve to death.

Joey decided to wait until the next morning. Captain Call would not be coming to their rescue. Unless Famous Shoes happened to be wandering around tracking some animal, no one would know he was there. His shots would come as a complete surprise.

The next morning, Joey's first shot killed a pack mule just as Brookshire was trying to extract some coffee from one of the saddlebags. The mule fell in Brookshire's direction, knocking him back several feet and causing him to spill the coffee. Before he could scramble to his feet, a second shot killed the other pack mule.

Pea Eye had been frying bacon. A third shot kicked the frying pan into the air, causing sizzling grease to burn his hands and wrists. He got to his feet and began to run to his horse, only to have a fourth shot kill the horse before he could even grasp the bridle reins. Brookshire's big horse was the only mount left, but before Pea Eye could step over his own horse, which was down but still kicking, Brookshire's mount was knocked to its knees. It scrambled up and was shot again. Pea Eye was in agony from the pain of the sizzling bacon grease, but he knew he had to run for cover or he would be dead and past worrying about a little thing like burned hands.

"Run!" he yelled to Brookshire, who sat amid the spilled coffee, looking dazed. "Get a gun and run to cover!"

As he said it, Pea Eye realized he didn't have a gun himself. He had taken his pistol off because the scabbard was rubbing his hip raw, and his rifle was propped against his saddle. The pistol was closer, so he turned and grabbed it. Brookshire had picked up the big shotgun and was stuffing shells into his pocket.

"No, get a rifle, we need rifles," Pea Eye yelled.

Brookshire just looked addled. Pea Eye decided to try for his own rifle, so he ran back and grabbed it. Then he turned and headed down into the riverbed. Soon he heard Brookshire stumbling after him. Pea Eye ran for a hundred yards or more, then stopped and waited for Brookshire to catch up. He listened, but he could hear nothing other than Brookshire, as he stumbled on the rocky ground.

"Reckon it's him?" Pea Eye asked, when Brookshire caught up. "Reckon it's the Garza boy?"

"I don't know who it is," Brookshire said. The dying mule had slammed into him, knocking the breath out of him. He had somehow grabbed the shotgun and made it into the riverbed without having quite regained his breath. He stopped by Pea Eye and gasped for air. He realized he had not made a good choice in taking the shotgun. Carrying it was like carrying a small cannon. But he couldn't immediately spot his rifle or his pistols, and he didn't want to just stand there with a killer shooting mules and horses to death on either side of him.

A little creek cut into the Rio Concho not far from where they stood. It, too, was dry, but its steep walls were pocked, offering better cover than they had in the riverbed. As Pea Eye led Brookshire into the narrow creek, a memory flashed back to him of the time long ago in Montana, when he and the wounded Gus McCrae had hidden in a creek while they attempted to fight off the Blood Indians. Of course, this creek was dry and that creek had water in it, and he'd had to eventually swim out at night past the Indians and walk a long way naked to find the herd and bring the Captain back to where Gus was. Without the deep-walled creek, the Indians would have had them. A creek had saved him once, and perhaps the dry little Mexican creek would save him this time.

Pea Eye took off his hat and crawled up the creek bank to a spot that allowed him to look over the plain. He saw nothing. The only movement on the whole vast plain was a hawk, dipping to strike a quail.

Then Pea Eye remembered Famous Shoes. The old man hadn't been around when the shooting started. There was nothing unusual about that, though. Famous Shoes was rarely there in the mornings. He went off in the darkness to take a walk or track bobcats or badgers or anything else whose track he struck. He would just show up again later on in the morning. If they were traveling, Famous Shoes would just step out from behind a bush or appear out of a gully and fall in with them. Sometimes he would mention interesting tracks he had seen; other times he wouldn't say a word all day.

Now, though, they needed him. Pea Eye himself had never been in that part of Mexico before, and though Brookshire had come down the Rio Concho with Captain Call, he had no eye for landmarks and would be lost without expert help.

"All I know is that if we follow this river to the Rio Grande, we'll come to the village where Joey Garza's mother lives," Brookshire said. He had caught his breath, and his big shotgun was loaded. He had only managed to collect four shells. He had no idea what he and Pea Eye were going to do.

"I wish the Captain would show up," Pea Eye said. Often in the past, when he and some of the men found themselves in a predicament, the Captain had showed up and had taken matters in hand.

Now, though, it was just himself and Brookshire, and an Indian who might appear again or might not. Their horses were dead and likewise their pack animals. If they survived, they would have to walk out. On foot, the Rio Grande was at least three days away, probably more. They could go back to camp when it grew too dark for the killer to shoot, and provision themselves from the packs. They possessed adequate food and lots of ammunition. Also, they were right in the Rio Concho. Unless the killer forced them out of the river, there was not much danger that they would get lost and starve.

Still, Pea Eye felt nervous; but more than that, he felt scared. When the shooting had started, he'd done what he always did when shooting started: he had taken cover. Being shot at was always a shock, and it was not something he had ever gotten used to. It took a while for the shock to subside sufficiently to allow him to think. Sometimes it took a week or more for the shock to subside, but in this instance he wasn't with a troop of Rangers, and he didn't have a week in which to calm his nerves and take stock of the situation.

"Why did he shoot the horses and mules?" he asked Brookshire. That was a question that had nagged him even as he was running up the riverbed.

"Why didn't he just shoot us?" he asked. "We was standing in plain sight. Except for that big nag of yours, he killed all the animals with one bullet apiece. He could have shot us just as easy as he could shoot a mule. It don't make sense."

"Nothing makes any sense," Brookshire said. "This whole trip hasn't made any sense. The Captain ought to have caught this boy by now. He's taking much too much time. If it's the Garza boy shooting at us, then the Captain ought to be here.

"Maybe it ain't the Garza boy, though," he added. "Maybe it's the vaqueros who killed Ted Plunkert. Maybe they came back to get more plunder."

"No," Pea Eye said. "It was just one gun and one shooter, and I never caught a glimpse of him. If it was vaqueros, there would have been three or four of them, and they would just have rode in, blazing away. They wouldn't have shot the horses, either. They would have tried to shoot us. Then they'd have been two horses and two mules richer."

"Maybe he was trying to shoot us," Brookshire suggested. "Maybe he just missed and hit the horses."

"Nope, he hit what he aimed at," Pea Eye said. "He wanted to put us afoot, and he done it. What I don't know is why."

Brookshire felt dull. He had felt dreadfully frightened when the bullets started hitting the horses, and while he was running he had felt scared. He had expected a bullet to strike him at every step.

But no bullet had struck him down, and now he just felt dull. Over the course of the trip, he had gradually stopped being interested in his own fate. He knew he had made a great error in coming to Texas. He understood little enough of life as it was lived in Brooklyn, but he could make nothing at all of life as it was lived in Texas; or at least as it was lived by Captain Call and those associated with him. They had gone from somewhere to nowhere, accomplishing nothing along the way except the loss of Deputy Plunkert. All he had expected of the morning was a piece of bacon and a big cup of coffee. Why some maniac would suddenly shoot the very mule that carried the coffee, and the other mule and the two horses as well, was beyond him. It made no sense at all, but it was in keeping with everything else that had happened since his arrival in Texas. Captain Call, who seemed the most rational and most methodical of men and who was the most experienced manhunter in the West, had done nothing that made clear sense from the time they had left Amarillo together. The Garza boy was still free to do whatever he chose to do, including shooting mules and horses, if indeed he was the shooter. The only exceptional thing Call had done on the whole trip was beat a sheriff nearly to death. Admittedly, catching one quick boy in a vast country was a difficult task—but then, that was the Captain's work; his life's work, really. If he couldn't accomplish it in this instance, then he should have resigned.

Brookshire no longer believed, as Pea Eye seemed to, that the Captain was still in control of events. He didn't believe that he would simply show up in the right place at the right time and end the career of Joey Garza. While the Captain had been looking for him in Mexico, Joey had robbed a train in Texas. Now that the Captain was in Texas somewhere, Joey was in Mexico, shooting the mule that carried the coffee. It was a botch. When Colonel Terry heard about it he would be angry, and in this instance justifiably so.

Brookshire had almost stopped caring whether he lived or died. The cold had frozen the will to live right out of him. Katie, his excellent wife, was dead. In the past weeks, he'd had time to remember all the ways in which Katie had been an excellent wife. He was losing his ability to imagine Brooklyn and the office, and the good chops Katie had cooked him, and the cat, and the cozy house. What he had feared that first morning on the windy station platform in Amarillo had actually happened. He had blown away, into a dry creek in Mexico—cold every night, cold every day, wind all the time, sand in the food, sand in the coffee, no houses and no coziness of any kind. He had blown away; now he was so tired that the long struggle upwind, back to where he had once been, back to who he had once been, no longer seemed worth it. Let the young killer walk up and finish him. Maybe he would get off a shot with his eight-gauge, but he didn't expect to eliminate Joey Garza as easily as old Bolivar had eliminated their unfortunate mule.

"What do we do next?" he asked Pea Eye, though he didn't really expect Pea Eye to know. But they had to do something next. Or were they just going to stand in a drafty creek bed all day?

"We'll wait for dark and go back and get our supplies," Pea Eye said.

So they did—they stood in the dry, drafty creek bed all day. When they weren't standing, they squatted. Pea Eye wanted to wait until full dark to go back to camp and secure food and ammunition. It was the longest, dullest, coldest wait of Brookshire's entire life. It was cloudy, and he did not even have the distraction of watching the sun move across the sky. There was no distraction at all, and Famous Shoes hadn't come back from wherever he had gone.

"That's a little worrisome," Pea Eye said. "I'd hate to be out here in Mexico without our tracker, even if we have the river to show us the way."

"Well, ain't the river enough?" Brookshire asked.

"It's enough unless he flushes us out of it," Pea Eye said. "I just got the feeling that he wants us to run. I don't know why, though."

When full dark came they went to the camp, where they found nothing—only the four dead animals. Everything had been removed: the extra guns, the frying pan and coffeepot, the saddles, the packs, the blankets, everything. There were no matches, no knives, nothing. Brookshire stepped on a spoon that had been dropped in the ashes of the fire. The horse killer apparently hadn't noticed it, but it was the only thing he hadn't noticed. Brookshire gave it to Pea Eye, who stuck it in his shirt pocket, though they had no food that could be eaten with a spoon; no food that could be eaten, period, with or without utensils.

When Pea Eye saw that the camp had been cleaned out, his

fear came back more strongly. Any bandit would loot a camp and take what appealed to him. Some would take guns and some would take provisions, and some might take a saddle or a nice blanket. But in his experience, bandits rarely took everything. Bandits had to keep on the move. They didn't want to be burdened with things they didn't need or want.

This bandit had taken everything, though, and not because he wanted it. Their gear was unexceptional. He had taken it because he didn't want them to have it. He wanted to be sure that they were cold and hungry.

"Don't you even have a match?" Pea Eye asked. Brookshire occasionally smoked a pipe. Brookshire thought he might have a match or two in his shirt pocket, but in fact, he didn't.

"I guess I used the last one this morning," he said. "I had already smoked a pipe before the man shot the mule."

"It's going to be cold," Pea Eye said. "All we can do is get out of the wind and hunker down."

"We could walk," Brookshire suggested. "We're going to have to walk anyway. Why not start tonight? At least, it'll keep us warm."

"Well, we could," Pea Eye said. "I never liked traveling at night, but I guess it would warm us up."

They had scarcely left the edge of the camp before a shot rang out. It hit a rock not far from Brookshire's foot and whined away into the darkness. Another shot followed; Pea Eye heard it clip a bush near his elbow. He stopped, as did Brookshire. They were too startled and frightened to say a word. Their assailant was watching them, or listening, or both. The slaps of the shots had been fairly close. The horse killer was probably within fifty yards of them.

"We'd best go back to the riverbed," Pea Eye said.

"No, let him come and kill us," Brookshire said. "He's going to anyway. He knows right where we are. I guess he's listening. He's got our ammunition and food. He's just playing with us now. We don't have a chance, and he knows it. I've spent nothing but cold nights since I got to Texas. I'll be damned if I want to spend another cold night, squatting on my heels, just to get shot in the morning. He can shoot me now and spare me the shivering."

"No, Brookshire, don't give up," Pea Eye said. "Come back to the riverbed with me. We're armed still. While we're alive there's a chance. There's two of us, and just one of him. We might beat him yet, or the Captain might show up in the morning and scare him off."

"What if he's already killed the Captain?" Brookshire asked. "I expect he has, myself. The Captain's five days late, and you said he was never late."

"He ain't, usually," Pea Eye admitted. The thought that the Captain might be dead had occurred to him too, but he did his best to push that thought away. People had thought the Captain was most likely dead many times during the Indian wars. He himself had feared it on a number of occasions. And yet the Captain had always appeared. If they didn't give up, the Captain might yet appear again.

"Let's go to the creek," Pea Eye said. "Try it one more night, Brookshire. If we go to him, he'll shoot us, but if we go back, he might let us go."

"Go back where?" Brookshire asked. "There's nothing back that way except Chihuahua City, and we'd starve long before we got to Chihuahua City. I'd rather be shot than starve, and I'd even rather be shot than shiver all night. I'm tired of this shivering, and I'll tell Joey Garza so, if I see him. I'll tell Colonel Terry something, too, if I make it back to the office. Joey Garza can rob all the trains he wants to. Ned Brookshire is resigning. I may never hold another job with the railroad, but I'll be damned if I'll wander around Mexico any longer, freezing to death."

Brookshire meant it, too. He had blown away, but he wasn't a hat. He could try to walk back. If he didn't make it, so be it. The whole adventure had been a terrible mistake. Katie had died while he was on it. Captain Call, the manhunter everyone said was infallible, had been plenty fallible in this instance. Brookshire saw no reason to suffer passively anymore. He felt sure he could walk three days, even without food. He could make it to the village by the river. Then he was going to rent a buggy and drive somewhere and catch a train, one that would take him to New Orleans or Chicago and then home. He had seen the great West, and he didn't like it. There were plenty of accountants in New York—Colonel Terry would have no trouble finding a man to replace him. Perhaps next time, the Colonel would know to keep accountants where they belonged, in the office with the ledgers.

Pea Eye knew he ought to knock Brookshire out with a gun barrel and make an effort to save him. The Captain might show up at any time. Joey Garza might lose interest in the game and ride off.

"Brookshire, just wait one more night," Pea Eye said. "There's two of us, we might beat him. The Captain might come. One of us might get off a lucky shot. We'd do better sticking together. Just wait one more night."

"I appreciate the thought," Brookshire said. "But I've waited and waited, and now I'm going, killer or no killer. I can follow this river as well as the next man, I guess. Maybe I'll get through. If I don't get through, all I ask is that you send my love to my sister."

On impulse, he grasped Pea Eye's hand and shook it hard.

"Well, I don't know your sister," Pea Eye said. "I wouldn't know how to get word to her."

"Her name's Matilda Morris, and she lives in Avon, Connecticut," Brookshire said. "I regret that I had no time to write her before I left. Colonel Terry wanted me on the next train, and that was that."

He cocked both barrels of the big shotgun and walked past Pea Eye out of the camp. Pea Eye didn't hit him—knocking men out was a tricky business. He might misjudge the lick and hit too hard, in which case he would just cause unnecessary suffering. He couldn't bring himself to do it.

Brookshire went boldly out of camp. He walked along at a good pace, trying to maintain a staunch attitude. Sometimes in Brooklyn, if he was on the streets late and had to walk past bullies or louts, he found that the best method was just to walk along boldly and not give the bullies or louts the time of day.

Perhaps the same method would work with this Garza boy, if it was the Garza boy who had killed their animals. He did wish he were walking along the orderly streets of Brooklyn, with solid brick houses on either side of him. Just thinking of the solid brick houses of Brooklyn caused him to be seized by a moment of almost overwhelming longing to be back in his own place once more. If he could be in his own place, he felt that life would swing into firm shape in no time, even without his dear Katie.

Brookshire had to choke down his longing, though; he was in Mexico, not Brooklyn. He kept walking at a fast clip. If attacked, he planned to give a good account of himself and try to at least injure his assailant.

But when Brookshire, walking smartly along, heard the click of a hammer, it was just behind his head, close enough that whoever held the pistol could have stuck it in his hip pocket.

One more mistake on my part, Brookshire thought. He whirled and saw the boy standing an arm's length away, his pistol pointed at Brookshire's face. Brookshire knew he had no chance to swing up the big shotgun, and he was so numbed by his own folly that he didn't even try.

"At least I've seen your face," he said.

Joey Garza didn't answer. He pulled the trigger instead. One shot did it; he liked to be economical.

When Pea Eye heard the pistol shot, he knew the battle was over for Mr. Brookshire. He turned and hurried back to the little creek with the steep walls. The little creek was the only place that offered him any protection. There had been no blast from the big shotgun. The Garza boy was unscratched. Pea Eye knew he would have to fight him alone.

He stayed in the creek for an hour, then snuck back to camp, and with his pocketknife began to cut strips of horsemeat off the haunch of Brookshire's horse. He knew he might be in for a long siege. In Montana he had walked nearly one hundred miles with only a few berries to eat. He didn't intend to get that hungry again. There was no need to, either, with four dead animals right there. He sliced and sliced with his little knife. Before he went back to the creek, he had almost a week's supply of horsemeat stuffed into his shirt. If he had to walk out and make a long detour, at least he would have food.

Pea Eye wanted to last, and he meant to last. He had Lorena and his five young children to think of. He could not just hand himself up for slaughter as Brookshire had. His chances might be slim, but for the sake of his family he had to fight the deadly boy as hard as he could.

As the cold hours passed, Pea Eye had a terrible longing to be with Lorena and his children one more time. He wished they could all be together in their kitchen, talking. He imagined Lorena with her coffee cup and himself with his. Clarie would have brought in the milk; the boys would be in their chairs, a little sleepy probably; and Laurie would be in her cradle, which he could rock with his foot.

Pea Eye wanted badly to tell them all how sorry he was that he had left them. He wanted them to know how much he regretted putting Captain Call first, and not them. It had been a terrible wrong. He wanted them to know that never again would he put any duty before his duty to them, to Lorena and his children. He felt a great sadness at not being able to let his family know what he was feeling. If he was killed, they would never know how much he loved them and missed them. They would never know what he was feeling at this moment.

In his sadness at not being able to say to his family what he so badly needed to say to them, Pea Eye began to cry. He didn't know how he could have persuaded himself to leave them; and yet he had. If only it was himself having to pay for his mistake, he could have lived with it and died with it. But the bitterest knowledge was that his wife and children would be the ones having to pay for his error. No doubt they were paying already, and had been paying since the day he left the farm. The thought he found hardest to bear was that they might never know how much he loved them, or how keenly, how terribly he missed them.

He had left them, though, and he could not undo that fact. All he could do was clutch his rifle and hope that somehow he could prevail when the killer came. He had never risen higher than a corporal in his years with the Rangers. He knew he wasn't smart or an exceptional fighter, like the Captain or like Gus McCrae. But in this last fight, he had to be better than he had been. He had to fight well. He had to for his family's sake.

The long night passed slowly. Pea Eye was shivering in a cold dawn when he saw Famous Shoes coming along the creek.

"Is Brookshire dead?" he asked, when Famous Shoes arrived.

"Yes, Joey shot him," Famous Shoes said.

"When's he coming to kill me, then?" Pea Eye asked.

"He says if you will give him your boots, he will let you go," Famous Shoes said. "He doesn't think you will follow him without your boots."

Pea Eye considered that a poor dodge. He didn't entirely trust Famous Shoes anyway. The old man's services had always been for sale to the highest bidder. Pea Eye did not intend to give up his footgear.

"Why didn't he kill you?" Pea Eye asked Famous Shoes.

"He doesn't want to kill me. I am too old," Famous Shoes said. "Captain Call is in Ojinaga, but Joey shot his leg off. He thinks the Captain might die. It was your woman who brought him to Ojinaga."

"Lorena?" Pea Eye said, severely startled. "Are you sure?"

"It is your woman, she has blond hair," Famous Shoes said. "She cut the Captain's leg off. Joey saw it. Then she brought the Captain to Ojinaga."

"Well, I swear," Pea Eye said. "I wonder who's got the children?"

He was so surprised by the news that he almost forgot the danger of the moment.

"Joey wants me to bring him your boots," Famous Shoes reminded him.

"If the rascal wants my boots, let him come and get them," Pea Eye said. The knowledge that his wife was less than a day's ride away filled him with hope. If he could outfight the killer, he could look on Lorena's face again. It was a chance. He meant to use every ounce of fight he had in him to beat the killer and get back to his wife.

Long ago, Gus McCrae had teased the Rangers by calculating how much fight each man had in him, as if fight could be measured like oats or some substance that could be placed on a scale.

"Call, now, he's about ninety-eight percent fight," Gus had said. "Take away the fight and he'd be so weak, he couldn't mount his horse. But that's unusual. I'm only about forty percent fight myself. Pea, I expect you're about twelve percent or so, and old Deets about fifteen."

Twelve percent didn't sound like much to Pea, but he resolved to use every oat of it to struggle past the killer and get to the river where Lorena was. If she was there, it was because she had come to get him and take him home. She must have traveled all that way just to bring him home. It was amazing to Pea Eye that Lorena would go to all that trouble just for him. But since she had, he meant to see that she hadn't wasted her traveling.

"Where is Joey Garza?" he asked Famous Shoes.

"He is by the Concho," Famous Shoes said. "If you go toward the village, I think he will kill you. If you go the other way, he might let you go."

"I reckon I'll go where my wife is," Pea Eye said. "If she was home safe, I might run, but if she's here in Mexico, I guess I'll fight the rascal."

"Can I borrow your knife?" Famous Shoes asked. "I want to cut myself some of that horsemeat. I'm going to walk to the Madre, and I want to take some food."

Pea Eye lent him the knife. In a few minutes, Famous Shoes returned and gave him back the knife. He had a few strips of horsemeat tucked under his belt.

Pea Eye felt the blade of his knife and saw that it was a little dull. He took a thin whetstone out of his pocket and began to sharpen the pocketknife. As he was sharpening it, a thought struck him. Brookshire had walked off with the big eight-gauge shotgun. It was an ugly weapon, and no one but an inexperienced Yankee would have considered bringing it on a long expedition. Joey Garza was known to prefer pretty guns, and the eight-gauge was anything but pretty. Maybe he had neglected to take the shotgun from Brookshire. Maybe he had just let it lay.

"Did you see that big shotgun?" Pea Eye asked Famous Shoes. "Did Joey gather it up, or is it still there?"

"Joey didn't take it, it's there," Famous Shoes said. "He only took the man's watch."

Pea Eye wanted the shotgun. He didn't trust his rifle that much, and he knew he was inept with a pistol. But with an eight-gauge shotgun, if Joey Garza was fool enough to come in range, he ought to be able to pepper him, at least.

"Whose side are you on?" he asked Famous Shoes. "Mine or his?"

"I am going to the Madre," Famous Shoes said. "Joey might change his mind and kill me if I stay here. I don't know what he will do."

All Pea Eye could think of was the big shotgun. In his mind it had become the thing that might save him. He needed to figure out a way to get it without getting shot. He couldn't forget his wife. She was not far away, and he had to get to her. Joey Garza was the one thing in his way.

Pea Eye sat down and took his boots off.

"Take my boots," he said, handing them over to Famous Shoes. "Tell him I'm going away."

Famous Shoes didn't believe Pea Eye. He took the boots, but he felt nervous. "You don't want to go away," he said. "You like your woman too much to go away."

"That's right," Pea Eye said. "I oughtn't to have left her, and now I've got to try and get back to her."

"If Joey kills you, can I have your knife?" Famous Shoes asked.

Pea Eye gave it to him. "It's yours, one way or the other," he said.

Then he dug in his pocket and came out with a gold piece.

[478]

He knew Famous Shoes was greedy. It was a five-dollar gold piece; it might tempt him.

"This is yours," he said. "When you're walking back to Joey, stop a moment where Brookshire's body is. I need to know where to run to, to pick up that big shotgun. Just stop a moment, look down, like you're looking at a track."

Famous Shoes felt a little disquieted. Pea Eye didn't know Joey and didn't realize how coolly and easily he killed. Famous Shoes thought that Pea Eye liked his woman too much, so much that he might get killed trying to return to her. No one killed as easily as Joey Garza. Probably Pea Eye was being foolish. But Famous Shoes could not wait around all morning discussing the matter. He had to get to the Madre.

"I will take him these boots," he said. "If I come to the Rio Rojo in the spring, I will come and see you. If your woman is alive, maybe she will teach me about the tracks in books."

"I expect she'll be glad to," Pea Eye said. "That's what she does, she teaches school."

He let the old man get a fifty-yard lead, and then began to follow him up the riverbed. The rocks were sharp, but Pea Eye kept following. Famous Shoes passed where the camp had been. Buzzards had begun to circle, and a few were watching from the dry trees.

Famous Shoes went on. He thought Pea Eye was foolish to challenge Joey Garza. The man's liking for his wife was so strong that it had destroyed his reason. Famous Shoes expected that Joey Garza would kill Pea Eye long before Pea Eye got to the big shotgun. But he had taken the gold piece. When he came to Brookshire's body he stopped and bent over it for a moment, as if looking at a track, though there were no fresh tracks near the body. He paused and then went on, carrying the boots. Joey was not far, and Joey was watching.

Before he had gone two more steps, he heard Pea Eye running behind him. Even though he was running in his stocking feet, Pea Eye made a lot of noise. He was running toward the dead man. A moment later, Famous Shoes saw Joey stand up. When Joey stood up, Pea Eye began to shoot at him with his rifle. Joey Garza looked startled. He had not expected to be charged by the old deputy. He didn't have his rifle; it was on the horse. But he had his pistol, and he leveled it at Pea Eye and began to shoot. Famous Shoes saw that at least two of Joey's bullets hit Pea Eye—but Pea Eye was still running, and he was almost to Brookshire's corpse. Joey shot at Pea Eye again, but this time, he missed. He became nervous—why hadn't the old man fallen? He knew he had hit him solidly twice, but still he ran. Joey shot twice more, but both times he missed.

Pea Eye ran as he had never run before. He fired as he ran. He wished he could fly so as to get to the big gun faster. He felt that he was running to Lorena and his children. He saw Joey shooting, but he didn't feel the bullets when they struck him. He ran as fast as he could. He fired the rifle, but only in hopes of distracting the young killer. Mainly he ran, his eyes fixed on the spot where Famous Shoes had paused.

Only at the last moment, with Pea Eye still coming, did Joey remember the big shotgun. He had left it with the body, and the old Ranger was almost there. The fact that he had made such a simple, stupid error unnerved Joey. He shot once more, but only hit the running man in the foot. The running man was very close, and he should not have missed him. Yet he *had* missed him. Joey could not understand his own error: he had left a loaded gun by a corpse. It was a big, ugly gun, not worth keeping, but he should not have left it. His pistol was empty; all he could do was flee. As he turned to run for his horse, he saw the old deputy drop his rifle and scoop up the big gun. Then the heavy shot cut his back and he stumbled and fell. He sprang up and kept running, but he saw over his shoulder that the old man was still running toward him, holding the big shotgun. Joey was leaping for his horse when Pea Eye shot again. This time, the heavy bullets ripped his legs. In his pain he almost went over his horse, but just managed to hang in the saddle. He looked back and saw that the deputy had turned and picked up his rifle. There was no time to free the Mauser; the deputy might kill his horse if he didn't flee. He ducked onto the far side of his horse and put the horse into a run. Pea Eye's shot hit the cantle of the saddle. Before Pea Eye could aim again, Joey was racing away through the sage; soon he was out of range. He clung to the safe side of his horse, expecting that the deputy would shoot again and that his horse would fall. But the deputy didn't shoot again. Joey was bleeding from his shoulders to his heels, but he clawed himself back into the saddle and hung on.

Pea Eye went back and dug in Brookshire's pockets. He found the other two eight-gauge shells. He trusted the big gun a lot more than he trusted his rifle or his pistol. He knew he had hit the Garza boy with both barrels. It might not have been at a killing range, but it had probably damaged the young killer severely. Pellet wounds worked slow, but they worked, and all the boy's wounds were on his backside. Joey would not be able to dig the pellets out himself.

Pea Eye sat down to rest a moment. He was not far from Brookshire's corpse. As he rested, Famous Shoes approached and handed him back his boots.

"Take these boots," he said. "You hit Joey pretty good. I don't think he'll need them."

Pea Eye was experiencing a kind of disbelief in the course of events that he had just passed through. He was alive; moreover, he had hit the Garza boy twice with blasts of eight-gauge pellets, and the boy had run. He had driven off a prominent killer. The boy had shot at him six times with a revolver and hadn't killed him. He might yet see his wife's face and hold his children on his lap.

"Why, he was supposed to be a dead shot," Pea Eye said. "He missed me three times, and one shot hit my dern toes."

"I don't need this knife," Famous Shoes said, handing Pea Eye back his pocketknife. "Joey left his knife by his blanket, and his is better."

Pea Eye stuck his finger into the wound at his hip. It was the deepest of his wounds. It might be that his hip was broken, but the wound wasn't going to be fatal. The wound in his shoulder wasn't serious. Pea Eye looked at his foot and noticed that he had lost two toes.

Pea Eye looked at the body of Ned Brookshire. He remembered that the sister he was supposed to send his love to was named Matilda Morris; she lived in a town called Avon, but he had forgotten the name of the state. It was one of the Yankee states, he felt sure. Lorena would help him look it up. She would have to write the letter too, of course; he didn't imagine she'd object.

Mr. Brookshire had been the wrong man for the job he had been sent to do, but he had been a very decent man, Yankee or not. It seemed sad to Pea Eye that Mr. Brookshire would not get to know that Joey Garza was wounded and on the run. The long job might soon be finished. His Colonel would get to know, but not Brookshire himself. He should have stayed in camp. But if he had stayed, Pea Eye would not have been the one using the big shotgun.

"I reckon I owe my life to Brookshire, mainly," Pea Eye said, holding his finger in the deep wound in his hip. "After all, he bought the shotgun."

"I may take Joey's blanket too," Famous Shoes said.

10.

The doctor from Presidio did not want to cross the river and operate on someone in a Mexican woman's house. If word got out that he was treating Mexicans, he was sure to lose business. But when Billy Williams told him that Woodrow Call was the patient, he finally agreed to make the trip.

Call was in a fever of delirium when Billy and the doctor arrived. He had been in and out of the delirium for two days. In his dream the little blind girl, Teresa, was leading his horse down into the Palo Duro Canyon. The drop was almost sheer, but the little blind girl picked her way down the cliff, and the horse didn't stumble.

"Well, the Captain smashed Joe Doniphan, but now he's smashed himself," the doctor said, when he looked at Call. "I'll take the arm first. Then if he lives, we'll go after the bullet under his heart."

The doctor looked at Maria sternly. "It's too dark in this kitchen," he said. "Go borrow some lanterns."

Maria said nothing. She knew the doctor scorned her. When she went to borrow a lamp from Gordo the butcher, the butcher looked at her with similar scorn.

"Why don't you just kill the old gringo?" the butcher asked. "Remember what he was."

"I remember what he was," Maria said. "Joey ended that. I can't kill a sick man in my home."

"You should never have brought him into your house," the butcher said. He was a large man, and he had always coveted Maria. He had fathered twelve children, but his wife had died recently. The butcher kept looking at Maria, but he gave her the lamp. Maria decided that she would ask Billy Williams to return it. The butcher and two of his friends had tried to catch her by the river when she was younger. She had seen them coming and escaped on her horse. She did not intend to let him catch her now.

While the arm was coming off, Lorena began to feel faint. She was helping hold Call down, and she was afraid for a few minutes that she would have to leave the room. But she was needed. Maria and Billy together were not strong enough for the task.

In the bedroom, Teresa heard the old man moan. He moaned like the cows moaned, when they were being slaughtered. Teresa hoped the old man wouldn't die. He had told her that her name was pretty, and that she was pretty, too. His moans woke Rafael, who began to moan, too, from fear. Strange sounds frightened Rafael, but not Teresa. She knew that Lorena was helping her mother and Billy hold the old man. She had told Lorena her story about the spider, and Lorena, in turn, had told her a story about a rabbit. Teresa wanted Lorena to stay with them so they could exchange more stories. She heard her mother's hard breathing and Lorena's and Billy's. Once she heard the old man cry out, "Let me up!" But the hard breathing continued. They did not let him up.

When the doctor finished, Call was unconscious and scarcely breathing. The doctor decided not to try for the bullet near the heart. He knew that if he cut any more, the old man would probably die.

"He's lived this long, I reckon he'll keep on living," the doctor said. "If he does die, at least he killed the manburner first."

"What's that?" Lorena said. "Captain Call killed Mox Mox?"

"Yep, old Charlie Goodnight seen the corpse himself," the doctor said. "Didn't you know?"

"No," Lorena said. "I don't think the Captain knows, either. He told me he hit him, but I don't think he knows that the man died."

"Oh, he died as dead as anybody. Old Charlie seen the corpse," the doctor said.

"You keep the bandages fresh, and see that they're clean," he told Maria sternly, before he left.

The doctor's unexpected news made Lorena feel such relief that she had to go to a chair and sit. Her legs felt weak. In her most terrible nightmares, Mox Mox had one of her boys and was piling brush on him. That danger had passed, for her and for all the parents in the West. Her husband might be in danger still, but he wouldn't be burned. She was glad she had worked so hard to save the Captain. He had not caught Maria's son, but he had stopped the manburner.

"We don't hear enough news over here," Billy Williams said. "We'll have to tell the Captain when he comes to."

"I'll tell him," Lorena said. "He'll want to know—it might help him get better."

"I wonder why a man would want to burn up people like that?" Billy Williams said.

Lorena remembered Mox Mox. She had seen the excitement in his eyes when he quirted someone, or prepared for a burning. She knew why he liked to burn people. But she didn't tell that to Billy Williams.

Lorena was sitting in the kitchen with Maria, watching Teresa play with a white chick, when an old Indian man she had met a time or two before came to Maria's door.

"That man will be hungry," Maria said, when she saw Famous Shoes at her door. "Whenever he comes to my house, he is hungry. I have to make him some food this time. He built me a fire when I was freezing on the Pecos."

"Do you have any menudo?" Famous Shoes asked, as soon as he came to where the women sat.

"There is none today. The doctor has just been here," Maria

said. "I will catch a chicken and cook it for you, if you want to wait."

Maria saw that Famous Shoes carried a blanket Joey had used on his horse the last time he was in Ojinaga.

"That looks like Joey's blanket," Maria said. "Have you seen him?"

"Yes, Pea Eye shot him," Famous Shoes said. "He shot him with the big shotgun. Joey ran off. I don't know if he will live. He was shot pretty good."

"Pea Eye shot him? Where's my husband?" Lorena asked, jumping up. It was a day of two miracles: Captain Call had killed Mox Mox, and Pea Eye had wounded Joey Garza.

Then it struck her that maybe there was only one miracle. Maybe Joey had killed Pea Eye before escaping.

"Your husband is wounded," Famous Shoes told Lorena. "On a horse it will take you a day to go to him. I don't think he is wounded too bad, but he was shot in the hip. He can't walk good. He has the big shotgun, though. I don't think Joey will go back and bother him."

"I'm going now. I'll take him a horse," Lorena said. "I'll take the buckskin, and I'll lead Blackie. Pea Eye can ride Blackie back here."

"Wait for daylight. I'll send Billy with you," Maria told Lorena. "He'll find your husband."

Lorena felt awkward—it was her own husband who had wounded and maybe even killed Maria's son. But before Lorena could even thank her for offering help, Maria had gone out the door to catch the chicken she had promised Famous Shoes.

Maria stood in the darkness for a while, feeling a mixture of fear, sorrow, and shame. She wondered where her son was and what condition he might be in. She had come to like Lorena, in large part because of the kind interest she had shown Teresa and Rafael. She had asked Lorena to wait and had offered Billy as a guide, because she knew Joey was out there somewhere. Shotgun wounds rarely killed, and if Joey was not mortally wounded, he would just be angry. He would make short work of Lorena. Even with Billy along, it would not be a very safe trip.

Only three mornings earlier, Maria had discovered from Teresa that Joey had been to their village. He had caught Teresa near the field and told her that he would return soon and take her and Rafael away. He told her he would take them to a high cliff in the mountains and throw them off.

Teresa had no fear of the world, nor of her brother. She thought Joey was telling her a scary story, merely to tease her. Maria knew that what Joey had told Teresa was not just a story. She had gone in and told Billy Williams not to let the children wander to the field again. She told him not to drink whiskey, and to keep his weapons handy. She also told him why she was so concerned, for she knew her son meant what he had said. Joey had always been jealous of his brother and sister; once he had put spiders in Teresa's bed, and had also put a small rattlesnake in Rafael's blankets. But the spiders had not bitten Teresa, and the little snake had crawled away without biting anyone.

If Joey said he would throw Rafael and Teresa off a cliff, then he would try to do it. Joey was clever, as evil people sometimes were. Maria knew she would have to be very watchful to forestall her son. She didn't want to kill him; she could not bear the sorrow that would fill her if she had to kill her own child. But she meant to frighten him. Joey had seen her call up her rage, and he knew her rage was no small thing. But she would have to be very watchful, always. Joey was sly. Only Teresa had known, when he was near the village. He had come and gone, undetected, and had only revealed his presence to his blind sister. But the message he had given to Teresa was for his mother, not his sister. He wanted Maria to know that he meant to harm his brother and sister.

When Maria heard that Joey had been wounded, she wondered why she could not wish him dead. Some lawman would kill him, sooner or later. Why not let it end? Why was the bond so strong that it was a kind of torture? Joey hated her, though she did not know why. She had done nothing to deserve her own child's hatred. Maria had given up trying to understand the hatreds Joey felt. His hate was just there, as fire is there, as blood is there, or desire, or sorrow, or sadness, or death. For her, the fact that Joey hated her was one more painful sorrow, like Teresa's blindness, or like Rafael's poor sheep's mind.

But what if Joey *was* mortally wounded? If he brought his wounds to her, she would try to heal them, even though the lawman who had been hired to kill him, and the woman whose husband had wounded him, were both in her house. Joey was still her child.

In the morning, watching Lorena ride off with Billy Williams ahead of her, Maria wondered what the two travelers would find. Famous Shoes said Joey had shot the deputy three times. Lorena might ride up the harsh river, only to find that the husband she had come so far to save was already dead. At times, Maria wondered if life would be so full of sadness had she been born in some other place. Too much of the sadness of the world seemed to pass through Ojinaga, which, after all, was only a very small village. In cities there must be more sadness, because there were so many more people. She wondered how the people in cities could bear the weight of all the pain around them.

"I want to give him some frijoles. He needs to eat," Teresa said.

"Who?" Maria asked. "Your goat?"

"No!" Teresa replied, annoyed. "I don't feed my goat frijoles. I mean the old man. I want to feed him."

"He's very sick, I don't think he will eat," Maria said. Call had awakened only once since the operation. He was very weak and had shown no interest in food.

But Maria was surprised, a little later, to see her blind daughter sitting by Captain Call's bed, feeding him tiny bites of frijoles with a spoon.

11.

"I wish your husband had kilt Joey on the spot," Billy Williams said, as he guided Lorena up the Rio Concho. He had led a safe life for the past few years, and he had forgotten the feel of danger. But he felt it that morning, as they rode through the gray country leading two extra horses: one for Pea Eye, and one for Mr. Brookshire's corpse.

Call had awakened as they were getting ready to leave. Lorena told him that he had killed Mox Mox, but the Captain didn't seem to be able to take in the information.

"Who was it?" he asked; most of the names in his head were vague. He knew he ought to be clearer, but he could not make his head sort out the names. His brain was a jumble of memories, and he could not sort them out, although once in a while one name would come clear.

Brookshire was one name that came clear. When Lorena told him that Brookshire was dead, Call felt such sadness that tears rolled out of his eyes. In his years as a Ranger, he had rarely cried at death, though he saw much of it. But he could not stop himself from weeping about Mr. Brookshire, and he whispered a request about the body. He wanted it brought back so Brookshire could be buried decently. Brookshire had died for the railroad, and the railroad ought to pay to bring him home to Brooklyn, the place he ought not to have left.

"It was my mistakes that led to it," Call whispered, weakly. "I let him come, but I didn't protect him, and Pea Eye couldn't, I guess."

That Pea Eye and not himself had been the one to wound Joey Garza was another thing that churned in his brain and would not settle itself clearly. Pea Eye had always been a corporal; now he was a hero, though he might not be alive to know it. He himself had failed, but Pea Eye had succeeded, or nearly; he had paid a price, but he had succeeded. It was strange knowledge. At moments he was proud of Pea, for he had gone a long way toward finishing the job that Call had started. Pea hadn't wanted to undertake it, and had been sent into danger with inadequate instructions and very little support; yet he had prevailed. Call tried to imagine the fight, but his brain wasn't working well enough. Three or four times as Lorena and Billy Williams were getting ready to leave, Call forgot about Pea Eye entirely and asked them where they were going. Then he remembered Brookshire, and he cried again. Lorena knelt by the bed where Call lay and tried patiently to explain about Mox Mox, but the Captain couldn't grasp it. She mentioned Charles Goodnight, and Call remembered him, but he could not get his mind around Mox Mox.

"The Indian said Joey was badly wounded. Maybe he died," Lorena said to Billy Williams.

"No, Joey ain't dead, or I wouldn't be this jumpy," Billy Williams said. "I don't get jumpy for nothing. Joey's here somewhere, and he's got his rifle. We better use what cover we can find."

Lorena wasn't frightened. She wanted only to find her husband. No killer was going to stop her now. Pea Eye wasn't far away. By the next day, she would have him back in Ojinaga, safe. Famous Shoes had assured her several times that Pea Eye's wounds weren't mortal. Still, she wanted to hurry. She didn't want to arrive and find that the wounds had been more serious than the old Indian thought. She wanted to hurry, and she grew impatient with Billy Williams, who zigzagged from ridge to ridge and bush to bush. Billy spent too much time looking around, when what they needed to do was hurry.

Billy knew Lorena was impatient, and he couldn't blame her. But Maria had put her in his care, and when Maria entrusted him with something or someone, he tried to do his best to carry the task through responsibly. Maria was not a woman who trusted lightly; Billy knew she had not had reason to trust, in view of the course her life had taken. Whenever she *did* repose trust in him, whether it involved watching her children or looking out for livestock on days when she was washing, he tried to do his best. He meant to bring Lorena back alive, and her husband, too. That meant watching as best he could for Joey Garza.

Worse than his apprehensions for Lorena and himself was the fear that Joey would slip around them and strike at Maria in their absence. He would probably strike at her by taking one of her children, as he had threatened to do; one of the children, or both of them. He might even attack his mother. Joey had always been devilish, but he had not always been what he had now become.

"I don't know why Joey went so bad," Billy said to Lorena, as they rode. "I guess he just went bad, and then got worse."

When Billy Williams talked to her about Joey Garza, Lorena's only thoughts were of Maria, the mother, and how terrible the knowledge must be that her child had turned out a killer. Lorena could muster no interest in the young outlaw. He had almost killed the Captain and had wounded her husband. The world was full of mean people; trying to explain why they were mean was a waste of time. Better to accept it and guard against it. In her years as a whore, it had been brought home to her over and over again, in varied and painful ways, just how mean some men were. Some were only mean enough to hit, but plenty were mean enough to do worse things. It was not a long road from a beating to a killing, in her view. She had known several men who had taken that road. The sooner all of them were dead, the better place the world would be.

But it wasn't her husband's job to bring them to justice, not anymore.

Pea Eye was crouched in the creek when he heard the horses coming. He was nervous; it might be the vaqueros who had killed Ted Plunkert, in which case he would be easy pickings. His hip was paining him terribly, and he couldn't walk. Running him to ground would be an easy thing. He cocked the big shotgun, got out his pistol, and put his rifle near at hand. Of course, the horses had been rather far away; perhaps they would pass him by. But he had to be ready, in case they didn't. Famous Shoes had promised to go tell Lorena where he was, but Famous Shoes was not entirely to be counted on.

When he drove off Joey Garza, Pea Eye had felt elated. The odds looked good that he would live to see his wife and children again. But, in the long nights and long days, his confidence had slowly ebbed. He could scarcely move, and he had lost considerable blood. He had nothing to bandage himself with, and no way to go toward Lorena. He could only wait and hope; and as he waited, feeling weaker by the hour, his hope began to fail. He tried to hold up—after all, he was alive and he had driven off the young bandit—but despite himself, deep fears assailed him. It might be that in leaving home to come with the Captain, he had made a mistake that was too serious to correct. He had left his family, and the penalty for that might be a bitter end. He might have to die without speaking to them again. His deepest wish was to be able to make his feelings into words, words that could travel across the distances into the minds of his wife and his children. He wanted them to know his regret. If there was some way they could know how he felt, then dying would not be as bad. But he couldn't do that. The regret was with him, and the distances were real and they were great.

Pea Eye pulled a piece of horsemeat out of his shirt and began to gnaw on it. Several times in the days since Famous Shoes left, he had begun to give up and then had pulled himself back from giving up. He *must* not give up; Lorena would expect better of him than that. It was hard to choke the dry horsemeat down, but he had to try. He had to take what nourishment he could, to give himself the best chance if there was another fight.

Pea put the strip of horsemeat down for a moment in order to ease himself a little farther back against the creek bank. His hip pained him so that he dreaded any movement. The horses had come quite near. He only heard two. Their slow hoofbeats gave him the feeling that he was being hunted. He had the shotgun tilted upward. When he tried to sit up straighter, his hip hurt so badly that he passed out for a few seconds. He had done that once before on his long walk in Montana. He had passed out from hunger and fatigue, even as he kept walking. As he walked, he had the sense that Deets, the black cowboy, had come back from the dead to guide him. This time, though, he was not walking—he was only hoping to sit up straighter so as to get off a good shot at whoever approached, in case they were enemies. He took one hand off the gun for a second to pick up the piece of horsemeat and put it back in his shirt. It was no time to be eating, but he didn't want to waste the food, either.

Listening hard, Pea determined that there were four horses coming, not two. That was a bad sign, and it frightened him. He got the strong sense that the horsemen were hunters and that he was the hunted.

Then, before he could even stick the meat back inside his shirt, he saw Lorena, his wife, standing not ten feet from him. It was a miracle—it was as if the sky had opened up and dropped her into the little creek. It was Lorena, not a ghost. It was his wife.

"Why, honey, you found me," he said. He rarely called Lorena by such sweet names; only on her birthday sometimes, or maybe Christmas.

Lorena walked over and took the heavy gun from Pea Eye's hand.

"Would you take this?" she said, handing the gun to Billy Williams, who was only a step behind her.

"You came all this way and found me . . . and it's winter, too," Pea said to her, astonished as he always was that Lorena cared to bother with him.

Lorena had paused in the creek a moment, watching Pea Eye, before he saw her. The big gun was cocked, and she was afraid that if she startled him he might accidentally shoot her. Pea looked bad. One side of his face was caked with blood, though probably he had just scratched himself with a bloody hand. He looked very thin, and his face was twisted in pain. The bad hip wound hurt him with every movement, she could see.

But here was her husband, and he was alive.

"Why wouldn't I—we're married!" Lorena replied. Then she took the awful piece of meat out of his hand, knelt close to him, being careful not to bump his bad hip, and took him into her arms. It was the luckiest thing in her life, that she found him in time. The children would not be without him, and neither would she.

"We're taking you home, Pea," Lorena said. "There won't be no more of this fighting, not for you."

"No, I'm done with it, somebody else will have to do it," Pea Eye replied.

12.

Joey rode back almost to Ojinaga before he stopped to hide. His wounds had begun to hurt, and he knew they would only hurt worse, unless he could find someone to dig out the shot. He could not do it himself, for all his wounds were on his back and legs. He had pellets in his neck and pellets all the way to his calves. He had carefully cleaned out the deputies' camp; there might be medicine in the saddlebags. But he had had to abandon it all when the old deputy came running at him with the big shotgun.

Joey hated the old deputy. It was absurd that a man so old would attack him. He should have shot him and the other deputy long before with his rifle, when they had been traveling on the plain. He could have done it easily, and he should have. Killing their animals, scaring them, and trying to drive them into the desert to starve had all been foolish actions. He should have just killed them. But he had never supposed that one of them would be crazy enough to charge him; even the great Captain Call himself had not charged him. Neither had he supposed that he himself would be so stupid as to overlook a loaded gun. During all his months as a robber, he had been careful and had made no mistakes. The fact that he made no mistakes added to his reputation—it terrified people. They thought of Joey Garza as the bandit who made no mistakes.

But then he had made one, and a bad one. The old deputy had looked a fool, and he had looked incompetent. But he had *not* been a fool or incompetent. The shotgun had been the deputy's only chance, and he had remembered it and used it. The pellets making poison in his blood were his payment for being foolish. He had underestimated the old man. The Apaches rarely underestimated anyone. They knew that any living man might be dangerous if desperate enough.

Joey felt rage at the deputy, but he also felt rage at himself. Three or four more steps and the lawman would have killed him outright; he might still die if his wounds were not treated and cleaned.

But he was alive, and if he lived, he meant to return and kill the old deputy and Famous Shoes, too. Thinking over the battle, he remembered that Famous Shoes had stopped right by the body where the gun lay. He had shown the old man right where to run. Otherwise, Joey would have had ample time to get his rifle and kill the old fool. Probably the deputy had paid him well, for everyone knew that Famous Shoes liked money.

Before he went back to finish the old lawman, Joey had to get his wounds cleaned. He wanted his mother to do it. When she had done it and he was safe from infection, he would show her what she was worth by taking his brother and sister. He would not have time to take them to the cave and throw them off the cliff. They would receive a quicker death. He might drown them or kill them with rocks. Then he would go back and finish off the old deputy and Famous Shoes as well.

Joey was watching his mother's house when Billy Williams and the blond woman rode away. It surprised him that the blond woman had come to his mother's house and that she was still there. She must have brought the old Ranger to his mother.

Joey saw Billy lead the blond woman and two extra horses up the river he had just ridden down. They were going to get the old deputy, no doubt of that. Famous Shoes had already told him that the blond woman belonged to the deputy. He didn't know why they were taking an extra horse, though. The old deputy might be dead—Joey knew he had hit him at least twice —but if he was alive, he could only ride one horse.

He watched through his spyglass. Joey could have followed Billy Williams and the woman and killed them, but he didn't. His wounds hurt too much. His back and legs felt as if they had been skinned. He knew his mother would have to cut his clothes off, for they were stuck to him from all the bleeding.

Joey saw his mother come out of the house to watch Billy and the blond woman leave. He watched it all through his spyglass from a mile away. He saw that Famous Shoes was there as well, for he came out of the house carrying a blanket that Joey had left in his camp. When Joey saw the blanket, he grew angrier and angrier. He had never liked it when people took his things, and he had certainly not made Famous Shoes a gift of his blanket. The old Indian had simply taken it. Perhaps he believed that Joey would soon die from the shotgun wounds. Joey had known the old man all his life and had neither liked him nor disliked him. The old Indian was crazy; he came and went, walking all over the place for no reason. Often he disappeared into the Madre. When Joey had been a prisoner of the Apaches, Famous Shoes had sometimes come to their camp. The Apaches thought he was crazy too; otherwise, they would have killed him. They didn't like Kickapoo.

Famous Shoes had finally decided to hurry home to the Madre. He had told Billy Williams just where to find the wounded man. He had no more business in Ojinaga, or any town, for that matter. He wanted to go to the high mountains where he could track the great eagles with his eyes. Once when he was young he had trapped an eagle, killed it, and eaten its eyes, hoping the vision of the eagles would be his. In tracking, he needed to see things so small that his human eyes couldn't find them. He thought the eagle's eyes might help, but the effort was a disappointment. His eyes did not improve, and worse, the meal made him sick. But he forgave the eagles. It was not their fault that he had been foolish enough to hope that he could see with their eyes. He liked to sit on rocks and watch the eagles swoop far down, out of sight into the shadows of the deep valleys, to catch what they wanted to eat.

Famous Shoes left Ojinaga at a good trot, for he wanted to hurry home to the Madre. But he had not gone far before he saw a familiar track in front of him. It was the track of Joey Garza's horse. Famous Shoes immediately turned north. He wanted to go as far around Joey Garza as possible. Joey might have changed his mind, and he might be in the mood to kill him now.

He had gone only a few miles north when, to his dismay, the track of Joey's horse appeared in front of him again. Joey, too, was going north. Famous Shoes thought he had made a mistake in leaving Ojinaga so soon. He immediately turned and started back for the village. Joey was evidently not as badly wounded as he had supposed. It would be better to stay in the village for a few days, until Joey left or died.

But he had gone only a mile back toward the village when he saw the track of Joey's horse in front of him once more. Famous Shoes didn't think the horse was wandering loose and just appearing in front of him every time he turned. Once, Joey had let him look briefly through the great eye he carried with him, the spyglass. The great eye was even stronger than the eyes of eagles. With it, Famous Shoes could see all the signs he had been hoping to see when he trapped the eagle. But Joey had only let him look for a moment, and then he tied the great eye back on his saddle. If Pea Eye had managed to kill Joey, Famous Shoes meant to ask him if he could have the great eye. It would help him in his work.

That hadn't happened, though. Now Joey was angry, and the young killer was stalking him. Famous Shoes saw no point in walking any farther. If he was going to be killed, he might as well rest. He had done a great deal of walking since he had left for the Rio Rojo. There was no point in turning again, since Joey would just turn too, and appear ahead of him. It had been a mistake to take his blanket, for Joey might resent it. But Famous Shoes had seen the blast from the big shotgun knock Joey off his feet, and he had seen the second blast hit him when he

[498]

jumped for his horse. Famous Shoes didn't think a man could live long with so much lead in him. Lead was bad for the blood. Joey was young and strong and he might yet die, but so far, he was lasting.

Famous Shoes was sitting on Joey's blanket, singing the Kickapoo death song, when Joey appeared on his horse. From the front Joey looked well, but when he dismounted, Famous Shoes saw that the boy's whole back was raw. Much of his shirt had been driven into his body from the impact of the pellets. Pea Eye had shot him pretty good, just as Famous Shoes had thought. The lead would soon poison Joey's blood unless he got it out. It might already be too late.

But Joey had his pistol in his hand, and Famous Shoes kept singing. It was his bad luck that the pellets were not killing Joey more quickly. It meant that he himself would have to die. He saw no point in holding a conversation with the young Mexican; it was better just to sing. He thought an eagle might come and take his song to the Madre for him. Famous Shoes sang loudly, for he wanted the eagles to hear him if there were any around.

Joey walked close to him and held his pistol to the old Indian's head.

"Get off my blanket," he said. "And give me back my knife."

Famous Shoes moved off the blanket, but he kept singing. He took Joey's knife from his belt and handed it to him. He looked to the sky to see if any eagles were coming, but he saw no eagles. He thought of asking Joey if he could look through the great eye one more time. He thought if he looked through it, he might see where his spirit would be going when Joey shot him. But Joey did not like to lend his things, and he was not in any mood to allow Famous Shoes a few minutes with the great eye.

Famous Shoes sang his death song loudly. He wanted to send his spirit far away on the sound. He had been in the Valley of Echoes once, in the country of the Utes, and he knew that sound could travel far and live on in echoes, even after the person or the animal who made the sound was dead. He had once seen Ben Lily shoot a bear. The bear had not been shot well, and its cries traveled far away as it was dying. Famous

Shoes wanted his spirit to float high on his song; perhaps an eagle would pass and hear it and take it to the Madre.

As Famous Shoes was waiting for the bullet, singing proudly, Joey Garza turned away and got back on his horse. He had come to Famous Shoes with a cold face, the face of a boy who could kill and not think about it. But once he got his blanket and his knife, Joey's face changed. He tied the blanket back on his saddle and got on his horse. He turned his horse toward Ojinaga and didn't speak again.

Famous Shoes was so startled that he went on singing. He sang until Joey was out of sight. He found it hard to stop singing his death song, for he had already turned loose of his spirit and sent it away. It was hard to have to recall it and go on living. His spirit was far above him and it was reluctant to come back. Joey had been about to pull the trigger, but he had changed his mind. It was quite puzzling. Joey killed as easily as he himself walked. Yet in this case, he had changed his mind and had simply ridden off. Famous Shoes stopped singing, finally, but he did not get up for a while. He had to wait for his spirit to come back; it came slowly, like a bird fluttering down.

When his spirit was back with him, Famous Shoes stood up —but he did not turn toward the Madre. He followed Joey's track, which went toward Ojinaga. He knew it was not safe; after all, Joey might change his mind again. His cold mood might return when he remembered that Famous Shoes had signaled Pea Eye where the big shotgun was, the shotgun that had driven lead and cloth into Joey's body, sickening his blood.

But Famous Shoes was curious. He wanted to know what Joey was doing, and he wanted another look through the great eye. If he followed and waited, he might get to see through the great eye again.

13.

Joey headed toward Ojinaga and his mother, for he wanted to make her take the pellets out of his body. He felt sick, so sick that he had lost interest in killing the old Indian. The wounds were like fire. They were making him feel so bad that he had lost his pride in killing. Joey had never expected to be injured himself, certainly not by an old man who could scarcely shoot a rifle. He felt such weakness in his body that he had difficulty mounting his horse; he could not waste his strength killing crazy old men. Once his mother had cleaned his wounds and he was well again, he would dispose of Rafael and Teresa. Then he would have his pride back. No more would he overlook loaded guns; he would no longer make mistakes. He thought he might go back near the City of Mexico and rob more trains. It would be nice to take some silver and some jewels back to his cave.

Soon after Lorena and Billy Williams left the village, the shoe-maker came for Maria. His name was Jorge, and he had a very young wife—too young, Maria thought. Her name was Negra. Her parents were rough people; they had married Negra to Jorge when she was only twelve. Now, barely thirteen, she was with child, and her time had come.

Jorge urged Maria to come to his wife quickly. Negra had already been in labor for more than a day. Maria had been to their home six times to check on her already. It was her practice to check often when a child was coming. She did not like surprises, although she often got them. There was no way of knowing how a birth would go until it happened—birth and death were alike in that way.

It was not a day when Maria wanted to leave her children. With luck, Billy Williams would be back that night or the next morning with the wounded man. Maria wanted to stay near Rafael and Teresa in case Joey came. The shoemaker's house was not far, but it was not her house, and Joey was quick in his evil. There was no one in the village that Maria could trust, now that Billy was gone. Captain Call was feverish, and he mumbled words that made no sense. Sometimes he was conscious, but he was too weak to even lift his head. When he had to relieve himself, Maria and Lorena had taken turns assisting him. He tried to fight them off with his one hand, but they helped him anyway, directing his water into a jug. Maria would have to do it herself now that Lorena was gone. And Call would accept all other attentions only from Teresa.

But Call could not help her guard against Joey, for he was too weak and in too much pain. If Joey came while she was helping Negra in her labor, Joey would probably finish off the Captain —with a knife, with a rifle butt, with anything handy.

"Maria, she is screaming—I'm scared," Jorge said.

Maria got ready to go. Negra was only one year older than Teresa, and she was small in the hips. It would not be an easy birth, and if Maria was not skillful, both Negra and her child might die. Maria felt a deep uneasiness: she could not refuse to help a child have a child, just because she was worried about Joey. Negra's baby was there, and Joey was not. She had to go, but she was very worried. She took her sharp knife with her when she went, and she made Rafael and Teresa go with her. Rafael drove his goats the short distance to the shoemaker's little house.

Teresa was very reluctant to leave Call.

"I want to stay with the old man," she said to her mother. She had taken a great liking to Captain Call, and he to her. Teresa was the only one who could get him to eat in his few moments of lucidity. Teresa would sit by him for hours, whispering stories in his ear and bathing his face with a wet rag to cool his fever.

"You can't stay with him, not now," Maria said. "You have to stay near me. We will be back this afternoon, I hope. Then you can be with the old man."

"But he might die if I leave," Teresa said. "I am his nurse."

"But I'm Negra's nurse, and we have to go now," Maria said. "Bring your chickens. Don't worry about the old man. He will be here when we get back."

Before she left, Maria took a cowbell. Their cow had died, and she had not been able to afford to replace her. When they all got to the shoemaker's house, Maria put the bell around Rafael's neck. It was a little awkward; the bell was for a cow, not for a boy. But Maria didn't know what else to do.

"Stay where I can hear the bell," she told them both. "If your brother Joey comes, ring the bell and run to me. Do not let him catch you, whatever you do."

Rafael took a few steps amid the goats, and the bell tinkled. He began to moan. Rafael was easily frightened, for anything out of the ordinary upset him. A bell around his neck was out of the ordinary, and it made him feel anxious.

"I don't want you to be too long," Teresa told her mother. "I want to go back to see Señor Call. He is my friend."

"He was not your grandfather's friend," Maria told her, but right away she regretted saying it. Teresa knew nothing of those troubles, and besides, bringing Call into the house had been Maria's decision. She had not expected Teresa or anyone to make friends with him, but Teresa often did things Maria would not have expected her to do. Teresa found a little storybook of Joey's and pretended to read it, although she could not see. She made up her own story while holding the book.

"I like Señor Call—do not talk bad about him," Teresa warned.

"I'm not talking about him, I'm talking about Joey," Maria said. She caught her daughter's face in her hands and brought it close to hers. Often that was the only way to get Teresa's attention when she was being willful. Only when she felt her mother's breath on her face would Teresa heed her.

"I have to help Negra have her baby," Maria said. "I want you to be careful and if Joey comes, you run. Your brother doesn't make jokes. I'm afraid he will hurt you if he comes."

"I will run away from him if he comes," Teresa told her mother casually, as if she could not imagine such a thing happening to her.

"Run, but make Rafael ring the bell," Maria told her daughter. "Make it ring loud, and I will come. Don't forget."

But she was afraid that Teresa would forget. Teresa wasn't afraid of her big brother. Rafael was afraid, but Rafael might not be able to remember to ring the bell if he became frightened. Some days, Rafael could not remember anything at all.

While Maria was talking to Teresa, Negra screamed. The scream poured out of the little hut into the empty streets of the quiet town. Gordo the butcher heard it; he had just butchered a pig and was hauling it up so he could gut it. The pig had screamed too, when he hit it in the head to kill it. The butcher had been drunk the night before, for with his wife dead he was lonely. He drank often, and in the mornings his work was not always precise. Gordo had not struck well, and the pig screamed when he hit it and when he cut its throat. He had not noticed before that the wild scream of a dying pig was so much like that of a woman in labor.

"Maria, can't you come?" Jorge begged. "Negra is dying." He came out of the little house shaking. His face was tortured with worry. Maria had seen many husbands in such pain. They did not know that their wives were not really dying; though sometimes the husbands were right—the wives did die, and their babies too.

Maria knew she could not delay any longer. She had to do her work, but she could not make her worry go away.

It was six hours before the baby came. Negra had been in labor a long time, and Maria's fear was that the young girl would become too weak to help. The girl's small, unprepared body would have to force the baby out without help from the mother's will. Already, Negra's will was almost exhausted. Maria had to sit with her patiently, soothing her and coaxing her to rest between pains. Negra was terrified of the pain; she thought she must be dying. Maria soothed her and explained to her that it was the necessary pain of childbirth.

"Soon you will have a fine baby," Maria told her. The water finally broke, and Maria became hopeful. The baby was turned properly and did not seem to be too large. She had sent Jorge away. She did the work with two women, old sisters who had made their lives together. They were crafty old women, and greedy. Each wanted to outlive the other so as to get the other's possessions. They had seen many children born and were indifferent to Negra's pain. From time to time they smoked tobacco, in little cigarettes they rolled themselves. Soon the floor of the little room was littered with cigarette papers the old women had dropped. But they knew the business of birth and helped efficiently when the pains came. Their names were Juana and Josia. Some people thought they were twins, for they looked very much alike. But each denied being the other's twin, and each claimed to be the younger sister.

"She was two when I was born," Juana claimed.

"She is a liar, she will go to hell," Josia said. "She was already three when I was born."

Maria didn't particularly like the old sisters. They were rude to one another, often having loud, harsh arguments just when the young mothers needed quiet. But they were the only ones she could find who knew what to do during difficult births, and so she called them in. They looked at life with skeptical eyes, which sometimes irritated Maria. She felt she knew as well as any woman that life was a thing of sadness; but it was not all sadness, and there were times for hope. And one time for hope was when a baby was being born.

Maria herself always began to have hopes for the babies she birthed, as soon as she saw them. Perhaps as they grew they would be lucky, have health, find good women or men to marry, rise above poverty, and be spared disease and loss. Few *were* spared. But each time when the baby was in her arms and the

[505]

moment of peace came, Maria let her hopes rise. She smiled at the little child and bathed it in warm water. She wanted to welcome it to life; perhaps it would be one of the lucky ones.

So it was when Negra's baby finally came—it was a boy. Maria was tired, but she liked the look of the little male child. He cried with spirit, the spirit of life. Maria smiled at him and whispered to him. He was to be named Jorge, too, after his father. He was a fine boy, and Maria could not help smiling at him. The mother was asleep, too tired to need her smiles. The little boy wiggled and cried, and Maria took him outside to show him to his father. The tortured look left Jorge's face and he looked at his son with surprise, the surprise men so often showed when they saw that a living human had been created from the actions of love—actions they had taken long before and perhaps had forgotten.

"This is a good boy, I like the way he wiggles. He will give you lots of trouble when he grows up and can walk," Maria told him.

Then, as she was about to take the baby back inside so the old women could cleanse him of the birthing blood, Maria looked around for her children. Several times during lulls in the labor, she had gone out to speak to them briefly. They sat with the goats between the shoemaker's house and the butcher's shed. While the butcher was butchering the pig, Maria's children were just sitting.

"It's cold. I want to go back to Señor Call," Teresa said, each time. She was sullen, as she often was if her mother denied her her way.

"You can come in where I am, only sit in the kitchen," Maria told her.

"No, I don't want to sit in that kitchen. I would rather be cold," Teresa replied.

Then the crisis arrived, and Maria forgot about the children. Once when Negra was screaming, she heard the cowbell and was reassured. She had to concentrate on what she was doing, and she could not listen every moment for a cowbell when the little room rang with the full screams that came with a birth.

Now, though, with little Jorge safely born, she turned to look for Teresa and Rafael and didn't see them. The goats were still there, but not her children. She ran to where the goats were, scattering them in her fear. Then she saw the cowbell lying in the dirt. Joey had taken it off Rafael—why hadn't she known he would?

Fear chilled Maria so, that she almost dropped the baby. She ran with him to Jorge and thrust the baby into his hands.

"Take him to the sisters," she said. "Did you see Joey?"

"No—how do I hold him?" Jorge asked.

Maria had no time to instruct the new father; he would have to figure out for himself how to hold his son. She ran to the butcher, who had taken the pig's hooves and ears and was putting them in a sack. Most of the pig had been cut up. Parts were heaped on a bloody table, and other parts were piled on strips of sacking.

"Did you see Joey?" Maria asked.

"You are bloodier than I am, and I've butchered a pig," Gordo told her. He was a little disgusted with the woman, for she had blood all over her arms. Still, she was shapely, and she was his neighbor. When she cleaned herself up he thought he might go visit her, perhaps taking her a little sausage. He might ask her to make him menudo or some other tasty dish.

"No, Joey wasn't here," he told her.

Maria knew better—Joey had been there. She had to have help, and there was only Gordo, the butcher.

"He was here. He's taken my children," Maria said to him. "Come and bring a gun, don't wait!"

In the desperate hope that Teresa had disobeyed her and taken Rafael home, Maria ran to her house. She had her knife in her hand. Call was laying outside the back door when she got there. He had hobbled out, using a chair for a crutch, and he had a pistol near him. But the chair was too short to be a good crutch, and he had fallen again. He was lying on his back. His leg was bleeding, and his eyes were open.

"Did he come?" Maria asked.

"He came—I can't do anything," Call said.

"I can't do anything," he said, again. He was so weak that she

[507]

could barely hear him whisper, and it was surprising that he could even have hobbled the few steps he had.

Maria felt fear shaking her, more powerful than any fear she had felt in her life. She did not have time to move Captain Call back to bed. She grabbed his pistol.

"What did he say, señor?" Maria asked. "Did he say anything?"

"No," Call said. "He came in and looked at me and left. He's wounded."

"Not wounded enough. I have to take your gun," Maria told him.

Call lay in helplessness. He had wanted to kill the boy, but he had no strength and no way. The boy had simply looked at him insolently for a moment and left. He was not a large boy, but he had a cold look. Call had rolled off the bed, pulled himself up with the chair, and found his pistol. But it was no good. He was too weak, and he soon fell. The world was swimming, and he couldn't see well. He could not make himself rise, and even if he had risen it would have done no good. Joey Garza was gone. Call was helpless and he had failed, again.

Maria felt helpless too, because she didn't know where to look for her children. Joey could not have gone too far, since it had only been a short time that she last looked out and had seen Rafael sitting amid his goats. But where had he gone? If he had put the children on a horse, she would have no chance of catching them. She could not track a horse, and no one in the village could, either. Joey might take her children far away, where she could never follow or find them. She ran to the cantina. Two vaqueros were there drinking. Perhaps one of them had seen something.

But the two vaqueros were very drunk. They looked at Maria with disgust, as Gordo the butcher had.

"Go wash yourself, you stink!" one vaquero said.

Maria raised the gun at him. It was the wrong moment for a man to tell her she was not clean enough. When they wanted her she was always clean enough, even if it was the time of the month when she was bleeding.

She didn't shoot the vaquero, though; she didn't have time. She just pointed the gun at him and saw his eyes widen at the thought that he might be shot by a filthy, dirty woman. Then she ran outside. As she ran she heard a high, moaning bleat from the direction of the river. It was a sound like a sheep makes when it is dying. She had heard it many times when the butcher was killing sheep. But it was not a sheep she heard this time—it was Rafael, who had lived with the sheep and made the cries they made. The boys in the village often taunted him for it. They called him sheep boy, and they told him his father had been a ram. When too much fear seized Rafael, his moan became the screaming bleat that Maria now heard.

Maria ran toward the sound. She remembered that long ago, Joey had sometimes tricked Rafael into playing a drowning game. He would persuade Rafael to put his head underwater to watch the fish; then Joey would jump on his head and try to drown him. Only the fact that Rafael was strong had kept Joey from succeeding. Maybe that was what he was trying to do, drown his brother and sister. Maybe he was too weak from his wounds to take them all the way to the cliff where he had said he would kill them.

Maria fired the pistol in the air, for she wanted to make Joey think men were coming. She wanted to do anything to get him to stop, so that she could get there before he killed Rafael. She heard the bleating again and kept running toward the sound, feeling a terrible fear. Teresa was the weaker child and might already be dead, killed by her brother Joey. Joey might realize that Rafael was too strong to drown, and he might stab him or shoot him before she could find them.

Maria had two fears: one, that she might not arrive in time to save her children; and two, that the warp of her life might have forced her to the moment when she would have to kill her evil son. Her sweetest, most beguiling dreams were dreams in which Joey was good again, as he had been when he was just a little boy. But then she would awaken to heartache and discouragement so profound that it made her limbs heavy, for Joey was no longer a little boy and he was no longer good. Even in her

[509]

discouragement she had the wish that it would be someone else, not her, who met Joey in battle and defeated him.

Now the two fears came together in her, and she carried them both as she ran. She had the gun and the knife. If only someone else would come—the butcher, Jorge, the drunken vaqueros, anyone. But Maria looked behind her as she ran, and there was no one coming.

Guided by Rafael's high, bleating call, Maria ran through the thin mesquite until she came to the river, near the spot where old Estela sat to listen to her dead children. Joey had pulled Rafael and Teresa into the deepest part of the river. Rafael was soaked, but he was alive. When Maria got to the river, Joey was holding Teresa's head under in the deep water.

But Teresa was not dead. Joey had tied her thin legs with a rawhide rope, but Teresa's legs were still thrashing. Rafael's head was bleeding. Joey had beaten him, trying to knock him out so he could drown him; but Rafael had been too strong.

Maria shot the gun again, twice. She did not shoot at Joey, she just wanted him to stop. His back was to her when she came up, and she saw that his wounds were bad. When he turned to confront her, he looked pale. But he did not release his sister— he held her as if she were a large slick fish. Maria saw Teresa get her head up and gulp at the air and felt a moment of pride at how hard her girl was struggling for her life. Then Joey shoved her under again, but Teresa only wiggled harder. Her body looked like that of a struggling fish under the water. Maria saw old Estela, sitting on the other bank, watching. She was listening for her own children and did not seem to care that two of Maria's children were being drowned before her eyes.

Maria went into the water and shot again. The bullet hit a rock and whined away.

"Let her go!" Maria yelled at her son. "Who are you to be killing your own sister?"

Joey turned his head toward Maria briefly and gave her that cold look he had, the look that made her feel she was not there. Maria had always hated that look. She was his mother and she was there, but not to Joey's eyes—he kept trying to get a better grip on his wiggling sister. Drowning Teresa was what interested him, not the fact that his mother was threatening him with a gun.

Joey was glad his mother had come. He wanted her to see what he was doing. Catching Rafael and Teresa had been easy. He had tied them up and thrown them on his horse while the shoemaker's wife was screaming. It was irritating that Rafael's skull was so thick that even three blows with a rock had not weakened him enough that Joey could drown him. Joey had hobbled Rafael's feet; he could finish him later. He was annoyed with his sister, too. He had not supposed that she was so strong or could struggle so hard. Despite all he could do, she kept getting her head up, gulping air. He could not get a good enough grip on her neck to keep her under. Because of his wounds, he was not strong enough for the task he was trying to do.

Joey was not at all surprised that his mother had come. She had been working with the woman in childbirth, and she was as bloody as a wounded animal. The fact that she had old Call's pistol didn't worry him. His mother wouldn't shoot him, and even if she tried she would miss. When the drowning was over he would make her take the pellets out. Once that was done he would get his strength and his pride back, and would go near the City of Mexico and rob some trains with rich people on them. His mother had doctored old Call, for he had seen the old Ranger in bed in her house. Joey had started to kill him, but had felt the same indifference he felt when he let Famous Shoes live. It would be wasting a death to kill such a worthless old person. Who could take pride in killing such old, half-dead people? It was better to do what he was doing: avenge himself on the bloody woman who stood there pointing a pistol at him.

Maria shot one more time. It hit the water near Joey, but he didn't even look up. She had stopped expecting to scare her son. She shot in hopes that someone would hear and come to see what the shooting was about. Even if the drunken vaqueros came, it might be enough; then Joey might stop.

But Joey didn't stop. He had managed to get Teresa's body

between his legs, and he tightened his legs and used both hands to shove his sister's head under the water. Maria waded into the water and struck Joey high on the shoulder with her knife. Joey screamed—the wounds on his back were sore. He turned to his mother with a look of hatred. Maria struck again, high on his other shoulder. She only wanted to cut Joey enough so he would let Teresa go. When Joey turned again, Teresa wiggled free and sucked in air. She kept wiggling until she was out of reach. Joey grabbed for her, but Teresa was quicker. Even with her feet tied, she was as quick as a fish. Joey took a few steps toward her, but Teresa was already yards away. In the water she was quicker than he was.

In fury, Joey turned on Maria and drew his own knife. He would kill Rafael with the knife and then chase down Teresa.

Maria saw where her son's eyes were pointed. She put herself between Joey and Rafael. She still held her knife, but she didn't want to stab her son again. The wounds she had given him were light and were meant to distract him, not hurt him. She could help him recover and live. She would do it—take out the pellets of heavy shot, wash his wounds, nurse him, if only he would relent. He must relent, though. She would not give him her other children, his brother and sister.

"Stop this!" Maria cried. "You're hurt, you're weak! Stop this killing! Come home with me and let me wash you. I'll feed you and I'll hide you until you are well."

"Wash yourself, whore!" Joey said, in his cold tone. His eyes were like sleet. Maria held her knife high. Joey would not stop. He would not become her good son again. All she could do now was protect Rafael. Joey's cold look made Maria want to give up. Her son should not look at her with his look of sleet—it was a poor return for the care she had given and the love she had borne.

But it was Joey's look, and she could not change him. She had to give up. That way she could protect Rafael and Teresa, and she *would* protect them, no matter what she had to do.

When Joey came close, Maria raised the knife and tried to cut his arm; anyplace to slow him but not kill him. She saw Joey's knife but didn't feel it strike—not the first time, not the second, not the third.

"Leave your brother alone!" she screamed. "Leave him alone. Don't hurt your brother!"

Joey was trying to push his mother out of the way so he could grab his brother's hair, when the bullet struck him. He turned his head at the shot. Maria turned, too. They saw Gordo, the butcher, standing on the riverbank with his old carbine.

"Don't kill her, you rascal!" Gordo yelled. "Don't kill her—I might want to marry her!"

Across the river, Teresa crawled into the shallows, and old Estela hobbled over and helped her out of the water. Teresa was very frightened. Her mother had been right; Joey was bad. She was worried, for she heard shots and she could not see.

"Where is my mother?" she asked the old woman.

Old Estela's eyes were dim, and she couldn't see the far bank of the river.

"She is over there," old Estela said. "I think I hear her talking to my children."

Joey fell backward into the water. Maria cut Rafael free, and the two of them began to drag Joey to the bank where the butcher stood with his gun. Before Maria could get out of the river, she fell, too. She fell across her son's legs, and the river began to swirl her blood away.

14.

Gordo carried Maria home. She was awake, but he saw where she had been stabbed and knew she would not live. It angered him, for he had already begun to think of her as his wife and was looking forward to laying with her. She had eluded him when she was a girl, and now she was going to elude him again by dying. It was an aggravation, such an aggravation that he refused to bring her devil of a son's body to her.

"He's dead, Gordo," Maria said. "Bring him home."

The butcher ignored her. He also refused to lift Captain Call and bring him back inside the house. He put Maria on the bed, and as he went out, he spat on Call. Later, the two drunken vaqueros came to Maria's house and they, too, spat on him. One wanted to put a rope around the old man's neck and drag him to death, but the other vaquero argued that it would be better just to let the old man die. He was too famous. If they put a rope on him, the Texans might find out about it and hunt them down.

Teresa picked her way back across the cold river in fear. She was afraid her brother might catch her again and put her head in the cold, swirling river and let it suck her breath away. Twice when he held her, Teresa had feared that the river was going to suck all her breath away. But her brother didn't take her. She waded through the cold water, stepping on slick rocks. Teresa knew the path through the mesquites and was soon home. Rafael was inside, moaning. When Teresa felt his head, she found that it was wet and sticky. Her mother lay on the bed where Señor Call had been.

"Where is he, did he leave?" Teresa asked, concerned. Her mother had promised that Señor Call would be there when she returned home.

"He is outside," her mother told her, in a voice that was very weak. "Joey hurt me, and Gordo would not help me. Go find Jorge and ask him to come. He can move Señor Call back inside. Ask the old sisters if they would come to me."

The old sisters and Jorge came. Jorge put Call inside on a blanket. Teresa fixed some frijoles, but only Rafael ate a little. Her mother didn't want any, and Señor Call was not speaking. His mind had gone to sleep, as it often did.

Teresa began to be afraid for her mother. She heard her mother's breath, and it was as weak as Señor Call's. She was worried that they might both die. She was also afraid that Joey might come back and get her and Rafael. She knew now that Joey was bad, and she was very afraid. Having the water suck her breath had left her with a deep fear.

Maria felt her daughter's fear in the trembling of her small hands.

"Don't be afraid," she said. "Joey's dead. You are safe. Billy will come soon and take care of us. The old sisters will stay until he comes to help."

When the vaqueros realized that Joey Garza was dead and that Gordo, a stupid butcher, had killed him, they became bitter. They had had the chance to kill him too, but the bloody woman had pointed a gun at them and prevented them from having the glory of killing the young bandit. In their bitterness, they drank a lot of tequila and convinced themselves that they *had* shot Joey Garza. The butcher had only assisted. They found Joey's body in the river and shot it a few more times, then put a rope on it and dragged it through the village streets. In other places, one would believe that a greasy butcher had killed the famous young killer with a rusty carbine. But in Mexico and

Texas, the people would think it was two fearless vaqueros who had risked their lives to rid the country of a scourge. Their fame would grow; there would be songs about them. Only in Ojinaga would anyone even suppose that a village butcher had anything to do with it.

The vaqueros left Joey's body outside the cantina and went to Presidio to spread the news. They wanted to find someone to take their picture with the corpse.

Jorge and his brother brought Joey's body to his mother. His body was filthy and dirty and coated with dust from being dragged by the two vaqueros. Maria begged the old sisters to heat water and help her clean her son. She wanted his body to be clean, and she wanted him dressed in clean clothes, clothes that she had washed herself.

"He's my good boy again . . . please make him nice," she asked the old sisters. But the old sisters smoked and sulked and ignored her. They knew the dead boy was of the devil—to touch him might be to catch corruption.

Maria was weak, but she was determined that her son's body would be clean.

"Get out!" she cried at the old sisters. "Go roll your cigarettes someplace else."

She made Teresa heat water. When it was hot, she bathed the wounds on Rafael's scalp, working very slowly. Then she had Teresa and Rafael help her move to where Joey lay. Teresa brought her a knife, and with it Maria cut off Joey's clothes. She was very weak, and she had to stop often to rest.

Jorge came in for a minute and helped Maria clean Joey's body. He was very grateful to Maria, for his wife was alive and he had a fine son. He didn't know why Maria was still alive. She had three deep wounds in her chest, and the blood seeped through her dress.

"Mama, you're bleeding," Teresa said. "I feel it on my hands."

"Maria, you're hurt," Jorge said, thinking she might not realize how badly she was wounded.

"I want to put clean clothes on my son," Maria said. "I want to do it now." She ignored their fears, the fears of her child and

[516]

of the shoemaker. She felt very weak, but she wanted her son's body to be clean.

She was not strong enough to dress him, though, and Jorge did not like to touch dead bodies. Jorge began to shake and tremble at the thought of what he was doing. He wanted to be home looking at his fine son. He didn't like moving Joey's stiffening limbs in order to get him into clothes. They got the shirt on him, but that was the best they could do.

"Maria, just cover him," Jorge told her, before he left.

Maria had to stop with the shirt, for she was too weak to do more. She asked Teresa to get a blanket, and they covered Joey. Maria wept and wept for her son's lost life. Teresa felt her mother's tears with her fingers and tried to comfort her, but for Maria there was no comfort. She had tried to be a good mother, but she had not been able to make her son a good person. Joey had been killed while trying to murder his own brother and sister. That he had killed her didn't matter so much; his life had killed her already, his life and her life. Her mistakes had been too many and too profound, though she didn't know exactly when the mistakes had been made or what they were. She had gotten up every morning and made food and washed clothes and seen that her children were clean. She had tried to teach them good behavior, but still it had led to Teresa's blindness, and Rafael's poor mind, and the moment in the river when she had had to turn the knife on her own child. It was too hard— Maria wanted peace. She wanted to have all the pains and worries bleed quickly away, and to go into a sleep beyond dreams, beyond the need to be awake and wash and cook while knowing every day that so much was wrong.

When Joey was covered, Maria crawled back to her blanket, stopping several times to rest. She saw old Call watching her. That was another strange trick of life—that she should be dying in her own house, in a room with the man who had killed her father and her brother.

The children had run outside for a moment. They couldn't stand to hear the weakness in her voice, and they wanted to be away from the fear that their mother might die. They hid among the goats while Rafael tried to find the nanny goat he sometimes suckled. But he was too confused; he could not find her.

Call saw Maria crawling on the floor, dragging herself back to her blanket. He didn't know what had occurred, but he saw that the woman was badly injured. He remembered that the cold boy had come into the room and had looked at him insolently.

Maria did not like having the old man in her house. Taking him in had been another mistake. If she met her father and her brother on the other side, they would be stern and unforgiving. But Call was kind to Teresa, and perhaps if he lived he would be a friend to her.

Several townspeople came to see Joey's body. Maria lay on her blanket and did not speak. She could not afford to waste what strength she had left. Teresa and Rafael came back and sat with her, one child on either side. They were silent and afraid. Maria hoped that Billy would return soon this time. She needed him to hurry back with Lorena. It was for Lorena that she waited, in pain and in life. Maria was a mother; she had two children alive, two damaged children. She hoped Lorena would be kind enough to take them. There was no one in the village to take them, for the village was too poor. No one would want to feed them or keep them clean or wash their clothes. Teresa was pretty; men would soon find her and degrade her. Rafael would be teased and tormented. He would go hungry, for his blind sister would not be strong enough to protect him. For them, Maria held herself in life. Teresa brought her posole, but she could not eat. She saw Teresa feeding old Call and heard her whispering to him.

Long hours passed. Maria grew more and more tired, until she was so weak she despaired. She was about to ask old Call if he would make the request to Lorena for her. Would he ask Lorena if she would take her children? She knew it was a serious request, to ask another woman to raise her children. Lorena had five of her own, and it might be that her husband was dead. But Maria had no one else to ask. She was about to tell Rafael to pull her over nearer to Call, when she heard the horses coming to the house.

Then Billy Williams stood in the doorway; Lorena stood behind him. He came and knelt by Maria. Maria felt grateful to fortune, that she had Billy Williams to assist her. He had come back when he promised. He had many failings, but he also had fidelity—now he had brought her the person she most needed, the woman who might help her children after her death, when she could not mother them anymore. It was important that he had come back when he said he would—it was the best thing a man had ever done for her.

"Why, Mary, you ain't dyin', are you?" Billy asked. He was stricken in the heart. He touched Maria's face; it was cold. He had only left for a little more than a day, and now this!

"Go get drunk now, Billy," Maria whispered to him. "But don't forget my children. Please talk about me when you see them. Give them your memories. Tell them how I danced and laughed, when I was young and pretty . . ."

"Mary, you're still young and pretty," Billy Williams told her. It took his breath away to think that after all these years, Maria was going. He would be lost; he wouldn't know what to do.

Maria raised up and gave him a little kiss and tugged at his hair for a moment. He still had the long hair of the mountain man.

"Go on, Billy. Go get drunk," Maria whispered, again.

"Oh, Mary . . ." Billy sighed. He wanted to talk more—he wanted to say things he had never said to her. But Maria's eyes were tired and sad.

"You go on . . . obey me," Maria told him, quietly, but in a tone that he knew better than to argue with.

"Well . . . didn't I always?" he asked.

Lorena wanted the old man to go. She saw the dying woman looking at her, and she knew what Maria wanted to ask. She wanted the old man to go; yet, maybe he had been to Maria what Pea Eye was to her. It was not her place to rush him in his last moments with his love.

Billy Williams rose, looked at Maria once more, and stumbled outside.

Lorena knelt and felt Maria's pulse; it was barely there. That

[519]

the woman was alive at all was a wonder. But then, it was a wonder that Call still lived. Pea Eye was outside, tied to his horse and in great pain. She wanted to lift him down and bring him in, but she had to hear Maria's request first.

"Would you take them?" Maria asked, with a movement of her head, first toward Rafael and then toward Teresa.

"Yes, I'll take them," Lorena said firmly. She wanted to relieve the woman's deep doubt. Maria had made the request she herself would have had to make to Clara, if things had gone differently. And she might not have even gotten to speak it— she might have had to trust that Clara would receive it in her heart, and respond.

"I've got my husband back now, and I'll take them. I expect we can take care of all the children that come along," Lorena told her. She meant it too; she was firm. She had Pea Eye back, and together they could take care of all the children that came along.

Maria smiled. She looked at Rafael and put her trembling hand on Teresa's face.

"I've got to get my husband in. He's hurt. I'll be right back," Lorena said, softly.

She found Billy Williams outside, crying.

"I just went off for two days," he choked, "and now this."

"It was the wrong two days, but you couldn't know that," Lorena said. "Help me get Pea off, will you? He's hurting."

They lifted Pea Eye down, carried him into the small house, and put him down beside Call.

"There's not too many more places left to lay sick people or dead people in this house," Billy Williams mumbled. There were Joey and Maria, Call, and now Pea Eye.

Lorena went to Maria and saw that she was gone.

"The count's even now," she said quietly to Billy. "It's two that's sick, and two that's dead."

"Oh, Mary," Billy said, when he looked at her. He sat down on the floor and put his head in his arms.

Lorena made Pea Eye as comfortable as she could. He was unconscious, but he would live. On the ride back, despite his pain, Pea talked and talked, asking questions about their children. The fact that his children were in Nebraska kept slipping from his tired mind. Finally, to satisfy him, Lorena made up little stories about the children and what they were doing.

Then, when she had made her husband as comfortable as she could make him, Lorena went back across the small room, covered Maria, and sat with her two new children, the little girl who had no sight, and the large boy with the empty mind.

15.

In the morning, the vaqueros came back with a photographer they had found in Presidio. They wanted to have their pictures taken with the famous bandit they had killed. They had drunk tequila all night, telling stories about the great battle they'd had with the young killer. They had forgotten the butcher and the mother entirely; in their minds, there had been a great gun battle by the Rio Grande, and the famous bandit had finally fallen to their guns.

Billy Williams had obeyed Maria's last order: he drank all night, sitting outside the room where Maria lay. But the whiskey hadn't touched him, and when the vaqueros came straggling up from the river with the photographer and his heavy camera, loaded on a donkey—he planned to take many pictures and sell them to the Yankee magazines and make his fortune—Billy Williams went into a deadly rage.

"You goddamn goat ropers had better leave!" he yelled, grabbing his rifle. The vaqueros were startled into immediate sobriety by the wild look in the old mountain man's eyes. Billy Williams began to fire his rifle, and the vaqueros felt the bullets whiz past them like angry bees, causing them to flee. The photographer, a small man from Missouri named Mullins, fled too —but he could not persuade the donkey to flee. George Mullins stopped fifty yards away and watched Billy Williams cut the cameras off the donkey and hack them to kindling with an axe. George Mullins had invested every cent he had in the world in those cameras. He had even borrowed money to buy the latest equipment—but in a moment, he was bankrupt. There would be no sales to Yankee magazines, and there would be no fortune. George Mullins had ridden across the river, feeling like a coming man; he walked back to Texas owning nothing but a donkey.

All day people filed out of the countryside like ants, from Mexico and from Texas, hoping for a look at Joey Garza's body. But Billy Williams drove them all off. He fired his gun over their heads, or skipped bullets off the dust at their feet.

"Go away, you goddamn buzzards!" he growled, at the few who dared to come within hearing distance.

The people feared to challenge him, but they were frustrated. The body of the famous young killer lay almost in sight, and they wanted to see it. They wanted to tell their children that they had seen the corpse of Joey Garza. They hated the old mountain man; he was crazy. What right did he have to turn them away when they had come long distances to look at a famous corpse. He didn't own the body!

"They ought to lock up the old bastard!" one disgruntled spectator complained. He expressed the general view.

But no one came to lock up Billy. Olin Roy arrived out of deep Mexico in time to help Billy dig the two graves. Olin was silent and sad, for he, too, had loved Maria. The old sisters came and dressed Maria's body, but they would not touch Joey. Lorena finished the cleaning that Maria, in her weakness, had begun. Pea Eye watched with Famous Shoes, who had arrived in the night while Billy Williams sat drinking. The wounds in Joey's back were terrible, and Olin and Billy both believed they would have killed Joey, in time.

"Why, he was just a young boy," Pea Eye remarked. It always surprised him how ordinary famous outlaws turned out to be, once you saw them dead. People talked about them so much that you came to expect them to be giants, but they weren't. They were just men of ordinary size, if not smaller.

"Why, Clarie's bigger than he was," Pea Eye said. All that chasing and all that pain and death, and the boy who caused it hadn't been as big as his own fifteen-year-old.

"He had pretty hands, didn't he?" Lorena said. She felt sad and low. All Billy Williams's yelling and shooting made her nervous. She could not forget Maria's anguished eyes. What a terrible grief, to have a child go bad and never be able to correct it or even know why it happened. She wondered how she would live if one of her sons came to hate her as Joey had seemed to hate Maria.

It was not a direction Lorena wanted to allow her mind to go. She didn't want such darkness in her thoughts, for she had the living to tend to. She busied herself caring for Pea Eye, Captain Call, and the two children. She thought of Maria and her bad son as little as possible. There was no knowing why such things happened. Lorena had good sons, and she knew now how very lucky she was. To have an evil child come from her own womb would be too hard to bear; Lorena didn't want to think about it.

When Pea Eye's mind cleared and he had a good look at the Captain, he was shocked. Call was almost helpless. He let the little blind girl feed him, but otherwise, he simply lay on his pallet, barely moving. Of course, he *could* barely move without assistance. He only had one leg and one arm, and could not button or unbutton himself.

"You have to help him make water," Lorena told Pea Eye. "He hates for me to do it, but if somebody don't help him, he'll wet his pallet. Watch him and help him. We don't have any bedding to spare."

"Why, Captain, if there was many more people as bunged up as you and me, they'd have to build a crutch factory in the Panhandle, I guess," Pea Eye said. He was trying to make conversation with the silent man. He thought of the part about the crutch factory as a little joke, but Lorena glared at him when he said it, and Captain Call did not reply. He just stared upward.

Later, Pea Eye felt bad about having made the remark. He didn't know why he had even made it, it just popped out.

Though his hip pained him a good deal, Pea Eye could not help but feel good. His wife had found him, and they were together again. He wouldn't have to lose her, and he would see his children soon. Lorena was going to wire Clara to send them home when the time came for them all to go north.

The sullen doctor from Presidio had been persuaded to come and set Pea Eye's hip, but only because Lorena had gone to Presidio herself and refused to take no for an answer. She had waited sternly in the doctor's office until he saddled a horse and came back with her. He said Pea would be walking without a crutch in two months, just in time for planting. His shoulder was already almost healed, and the two toes Joey shot off he could do without. Mox Mox and Joey Garza were dead, but he himself had survived. He had also learned his lesson, and learned it well. He would never leave his family again.

"Why'd you have to say that about the crutch factory?" Lorena whispered to him that night. The remark had startled her. Pea Eye had never made a joke in his life—why that one at that time?

"He'll never forgive you for saying it, and I don't blame him," she went on. "You're just hurt, Pea. In two months you'll be as good as new. But the Captain is crippled for life. He's crippled, for life!"

"You better just shut up about crutch factories!" she whispered later, with unusual vehemence.

Pea Eye came to feel that his chance remark was the worst thing he had ever said in his life. His main hope was that the Captain would just forget it. But the Captain said so little to anyone that it was hard to know what he was remembering or forgetting. The Captain just lay there. He only fought when Pea Eye tried to help him relieve himself, struggling with his one weak hand. His struggles unnerved Pea Eye so much that he did a poor job the first time, and he made a mess. This incompetence annoyed Lorena to the point that she ignored the Captain's objections and helped him herself after that.

"You'll have to learn to do things for him, Pea," Lorena said. "He's helpless. He'll have to live with us for a while, I guess. I told Maria I'd take her children, and we've got them to think about, too. We're both going to have all we can do. You better make up your mind to start helping Captain Call. You have to help him now whether he likes it or not. You know the man. You worked for him most of your life. He don't like it when I help him. I don't know whether he just don't like me, or whether it's because I'm a woman, or because I was what I was, once . . . I don't know. But we're going to have all we can do, both of us, and the Captain ought to be your responsibility."

"Why, that little blind girl takes care of him pretty well herself," Pea said. Indeed, Teresa's attentiveness and the Captain's acceptance of it surprised him. He had never known the Captain to cotton to a child. He had never even come to visit *their* children, and he and Lorena had five.

Teresa brought the Captain his food and sat by him and fed him. She brought a rag and washed his face when he finished. If he wanted to turn on his side, he let Teresa help him. Often, she whispered to him and the Captain responded, though in a voice so low that Pea Eye could not pick up the words. The little girl was quick as a lizard. She could be across the room and out the door in a flash, and Pea Eye never saw her bump into anything.

Maria and Joey were buried in the two graves Billy and Olin had dug. Many people came; not for Maria, but so they could say they had seen Joey Garza buried. Billy and Lorena went across the river and got the coffins, plain pine boxes. They tried to find Mullins, the photographer, and return his donkey, but Mullins was drunk somewhere and could not be located. The collapse of his prospects proved too much for him. Billy Williams was a little abashed; it had all been the vaqueros' fault, not the photographer's. But they could not spend all day looking for a drunken photographer, so they took the donkey back to Mexico.

The old sisters and a few local women came to the burial, but very few men showed up. Gordo, the butcher, walked by sullenly and went home. He was still angry with Maria for being dead and thus unavailable for marriage.

"There ought to be singing," Lorena said. She knew Pea Eye couldn't sing, and Billy and Olin were unknown quantities when it came to hymn singing. She remembered the songs in Laredo, during the burial of the deputy's young wife. She had learned from Pea that the deputy was dead now, too; it made her want to go live in a country where not so much blood was spilled. She remembered how the whore with the curly hair had poured her heart into the song for the young woman, as if she had known how the deputy's wife must have felt, to want to take her own life. Though not confident of her own voice, Lorena resolved to sing alone if necessary. She began "There's a Home Beyond the River"—after all, the river was right there in sight—and to her surprise, Olin Roy joined her. He had a fine baritone voice. He sang so well that a few of the gawkers from Presidio were moved to join in.

That night, dark feelings burdened Lorena. She could not get Maria's horrible end to leave her mind. She tried to sleep, but could not. She lay beside Pea Eye on the pallet and began to shake. The feeling came over her that had made her want to die when Blue Duck took her and when Mox Mox prepared to burn her. Evil men or evil circumstances would come and prove stronger than all the good in her life. She had her husband back and would soon have her children with her, but in her fear, she could not help feeling that the reprieve was only temporary. Clara Allen herself had watched all three of her sons die. Two of Maria's children had afflictions, and the one who had been whole and beautiful was evil. He had murdered many men and, in the end, had even murdered the woman who had carried him in her womb. Lorena couldn't control her fear, for it came from places too deep and too real, from what she had known and what she had seen. She and her family were safe, but only for a time. Her children were still young, and disease could take them. Her boys were still small; one of them could be a Joey. She didn't expect it, but Maria probably hadn't expected it either, when Joey had been the age of Georgie or Ben.

The fear made Lorena restless. She got up, then lay down again. The room was too small to walk in. She could hear Pea

Eye's breathing, and the Captain's and Rafael's; the large boy snored in his sleep.

Billy Williams and Olin Roy were outside, drinking and smoking. In her restlessness, Lorena went out. She had never drunk much whiskey, but she wanted something that would dull her feeling—the feeling that there was no safety and that nothing could prevent things happening to her or her loved ones, things that were even worse than what had already happened. She knew she was lucky, for she was healthy, she wasn't dead, none of her children were sick, and her husband's wounds would heal.

But it was only temporary, her luck. The next Mox Mox might find her, or the next plague, or a storm or a fire or a war. Maria had been a kind woman, but her fate had been far from kind—her fate had been hard and her end terrible. It was a warning; but a warning for a condition which had no cure, or of a threat that there was no guarding against.

Lorena put on Pea Eye's coat and stepped out into the cold night. The two men sat a little distance from the house. They had made a small campfire and were staring into it, passing a bottle back and forth. Lorena walked out to the fire.

Both men saw Lorena coming and felt uneasy. She had been courteous to both of them and had made Billy Williams an ally forever because of her kindness to Maria. Maria would have died even harder had she not known that Lorena would take care of her children.

Billy and Olin had roamed the border country for most of their lives, and both of them remembered Lorena from other days when she had been a beautiful young whore in Lonesome Dove. Both had visited her. Olin Roy remembered the Frenchman, Xavier Wanz, who had loved Lorena so feverishly that he burned his own saloon and himself with it, in his grief when Lorena went north with the Hat Creek outfit. Neither had supposed they would encounter the woman so much later in life, married to the gangly Pea Eye. She was heavier and her fresh beauty had been worn away by life, but she was the same woman: she was respectable and competent by any standard.

She had amputated Woodrow Call's leg and brought him to safety across more than a hundred miles of desert. Few men would have been equal to that task. Now she was walking toward their campfire, in her husband's big coat. In the heat of action and the sadness of the last days, neither man had thought much about their earlier brief connection with Lorena. But now they wondered, separately, if she would remember that they had been among her many customers, long ago.

"Could you spare me a little of your liquor, gentlemen?" Lorena asked. "I'm feeling chill."

"Here, ma'am—we've got a fresh bottle," Billy said, handing it to her. "This one ain't been slobbered on."

Lorena took the full bottle and drank. The whiskey burned her throat, but she sat down by the campfire, tucked the coat around her, and drank anyway. Pea Eye's coat was a heavy gray capote, with a hood for rough weather. Lorena pulled the hood over her head and drank. The men had fallen silent, which annoyed her a little. It irritated her that men were so uneasy in her company most of the time. She had been courteous to these men—why had they immediately stopped talking when she arrived? Even Pea Eye was sometimes ill at ease in her company, for no reason she could understand. She was doing exactly the same thing as the men: sitting by a campfire drinking whiskey. Why wouldn't they talk?

"I don't mean to impose," Lorena said to them. "You don't have to choke off your conversation just because I'm here."

"We wasn't saying much anyway," Billy Williams told her. "We was just chatting about Mary."

"Tell me about her," Lorena said. "I didn't have time to get to know her very well."

"She was married four times," Billy Williams said. "Three of her husbands got killed, and the other one run off. I never cared much for any of them myself, but it was Mary who took them as husbands, not me.

"Then Joey went bad," he added.

"Was she ever happy?" Lorena asked.

"Mary? Yes, we used to dance a lot," Billy Williams remembered.

"I guess you both cared for her," Lorena said. "Seems like you did, or you wouldn't be here. Didn't either of you want to marry her?"

"Oh, I did," Billy Williams said. "She wouldn't have me, but we got along anyway."

Olin Roy remained silent. His disappointments in regard to Maria were too deep to voice.

"Were any of her husbands good to her?" Lorena wondered.

The two men were silent. They had known little of what went on in Maria's marriages. When she was with Roberto Sanchez, her face had often been bruised; apparently he was rough, though Maria had never mentioned it to either of them. Carlos Garza had been a vaquero, off in the cow camps with other vaqueros. Juan Castro had been cheap; besides her midwifing, Maria had done cleaning for white people across the river when she was married to him. Benito had merely been lazy; he seemed to have no malice in him.

But was Maria ever happy? Both could remember her smile, and the sound of her laughter, and the look on her face when she was pleased as well as when she was displeased. But was Maria ever happy? It was a hard question.

"She had her children," Billy replied. "She was good to her children."

Lorena asked no more questions. She felt she had been foolish to inquire. The two men were probably decent, as men went. Both had clearly been devoted to Maria, else why would they be here, reluctant to leave her grave? But how the woman had felt when she closed the doors of her house at night and was alone with one of her husbands and her children, was not something that men could be expected to know. What Maria had felt in the years of her womanhood was lost. Who would know what feelings she had struggled with as she lost four husbands and raised her children? How could men, decent or not, know what made a woman happy or unhappy? She herself had known little happiness until she had persuaded Pea Eye to accept her. Why

[530]

she felt she might be happy with Pea instead of with any of the other men who had sought her hand in the years after Gus McCrae's death was elusive, too. Lorena had thought she'd known what drew her to Pea Eye once, but now, sitting by the campfire in Mexico, she found she couldn't recover her own reckonings in the matter. She had been right, though, for she had known great happiness with Pea Eye and their children. Probably there was no explaining any of it; probably it had been mostly luck.

The night grew colder, and the stars shone even more sharply in the deep, inky sky. Lorena drank most of the bottle of whiskey. She knew that she would feel like her head was cracking in the morning, but she didn't care. The restlessness she felt had to be conquered; the deep fear inside her had to be dulled. She needed the fire of the whiskey and the numbness that finally came.

Even with the whiskey in her, Lorena could not stop thinking of Maria. She wished she'd had more time with her, time not so filled with violence and pain. There had been no time for the talk of women when there had been so many injured to attend to. Then Maria had become one of the injured herself. She'd had to save her strength for her final request.

Maria's eyes, at the end, haunted Lorena. She wanted to forget Maria's eyes, but she also wanted to know what Maria knew and what she had felt. She wished the two of them could have had even one talk about their lives. She wished it very much, but that wish could not be granted.

The white line of dawn began to show in the east, across the river. Soon, Lorena knew, she would have to go in, drunk or not, rested or not, and start tending to the injured and the children. It was too late for the knowledge she craved; she would never know much about Maria. That chance—an important one—had been lost forever.

The line of white to the east widened, and the lower stars began to fade. In that direction, only a few steps beyond where the goats were sleeping, Maria Sanchez lay buried, not far from the Rio Grande, in a narrow grave.

[531]

Epilogue

1.

Call's greatest embarrassment was that he could not stand up and walk outside to relieve himself. For a time he had no crutch and would have been too weak to use one, even if one had been available. He had to make water in a jug, and often was too weak even to do that properly. He had only his left hand, and his finger joints were still swollen so badly with arthritis that he couldn't work his own buttons. Mostly, Pea Eye helped him. But if Pea Eye was sleeping or had hobbled outside with Maria's children, Lorena came and assisted him matter-of-factly, ignoring his embarrassment and shame. She did it quickly, as she might have dipped water out of a bucket.

"We don't have the bedding to spare, Captain," she said once; it was her only comment on the matter.

At such times, Call wanted to take out his pocketknife and cut his own throat. But someone had taken his pocketknife, and even if he had had it, he doubted he could have made a clean job of it with only his left hand to use.

2.

Call spoke only to the little blind girl, Teresa. She insisted on caring for him and he accepted her help, although sometimes her girlish chatter tired him. She was very helpful to him; also, she was a young child, and blind. She could not see his stumps, or the black bruise that covered most of his chest, where the bullet was that the doctor had not been bold enough to remove. Call wished the man had made an attempt; perhaps then he would have died.

At least Teresa couldn't see him, and she hadn't known him as he had been. She sat by him and fed him, and while she fed him, told him little stories about spiders and rabbits. Her speech was like a birdsong, quick and light. Hearing her voice was Call's only pleasure. He never reproached Teresa or sent her away, even when he was weary or hot with pain. In the mornings he waited patiently for her; as soon as she awoke, Teresa would come over and put her cool hand on Call's forehead to see how bad his fever was.

3.

From the moment Joey Garza's three bullets struck, Call's only escape from pain had been unconsciousness. He clung to sleep, but his dozings became shorter and shorter. On the day he was wounded he had wanted to live; he wanted to finish the job he had been hired to do. He had never left a job unfinished in his life. Remaining himself, remaining who he was, meant finishing the job he had undertaken.

But as Captain Call floated in and out of fever and hallucination, the first thought that filtered into his consciousness each time he awoke was a sense of irrevocable failure—a failure that could never be redeemed. He could not finish the job; would never finish or even undertake such a job again. He had failed and was beyond making the failure good. He deeply regretted not doing exactly what Gus McCrae had done: letting the wounds finish him. His wounds had finished him as the man he had been. He clung to a form of life; but a worthless form. He had never enjoyed letting people wait on him; he had always saddled his own horse, and unsaddled it too.

But now people waited on him all day. Teresa brought him food and spooned it into his mouth. Lorena changed his bandages. Pea Eye, crippled himself, nonetheless had two hands and helped him into a clean shirt and fresh pants when the time came to change.

Call could not clear his mind sufficiently to bring what had happened into a clear sequence, or even to remember it all. He inquired about Brookshire and was told that his body had been taken to the undertaker's in Presidio, the day Lorena and Billy had gone to procure the coffins for Maria Sanchez and her son. It was still there, awaiting instructions. No one had had time to inform Colonel Terry of all that had occurred.

Some days, Call understood that he had killed Mox Mox; at other times, he thought Charles Goodnight had killed him—at least, Goodnight had been mentioned in connection with the death. He could not get the facts of Deputy Plunkert's demise straight in his mind, nor was it quite clear to him how Brookshire had died. The confusion only made his sense of failure worse: two men who should never have been with him in the first place, who had been cajoled into coming by Call's own misjudgments, were now dead. It was a sorry thing.

Call's one consolation was that Pea Eye had wounded Joey Garza, and had finished the job he had been hired to do. He didn't understand about Maria or the butcher, though—what did the butcher have to do with anything? But he did grasp that Joe had killed his mother, and that the feebleminded boy and the little blind girl would be going with them to the Panhandle, when he was able to travel. When that would be, no one seemed to know. Call continued to be very weak. It was a long trip to the railroad, and the trip would have to be made in a wagon. The doctor didn't think Call was up to it yet. Lorena didn't, either.

"I carried him this far and kept him alive," Lorena said. "I want him to survive the trip back. We'll just have to wait until he's stronger."

4.

One day, Lorena went to Presidio and came back with three crutches. One was for Pea Eye; the other two were for Call.

Call could only look at the crutches. He was just at the point where he could sit up without growing faint. Sitting up made it easier for Teresa to feed him. He couldn't use a crutch; not yet. Pea Eye used his immediately. He pulled himself up and crutched his way around the room.

Pea Eye seemed to be feeling fine. It was known throughout the border country that Pea Eye had fired the shots that stopped Joey Garza. The doctor had let it be known that the shotgun wounds would have killed Joey, in time. The butcher had happened to finish him, but Pea Eye had made possible what the butcher had done. Pea Eye was a hero on both sides of the river.

Lorena saw Captain Call looking sadly at the crutches. The old man scarcely spoke all day, except to the little blind girl. Lorena had ceased to be certain that she had done the old man any favor by working so hard to save him. She had only saved him for grief, it seemed. He was an old man with no prospects; it was clear that he would prefer to be dead. He just didn't know how to be.

"You'll get stronger, Captain," Lorena said. "You'll be using these crutches as good as Pea Eye, one of these days."

"I doubt it," Call said. He didn't want the crutches. How could a man on crutches mount a horse?

Later, though, Call realized that he had no need to mount a horse, and nowhere to go on one, if he did mount it. Teresa was telling him one of her spider stories, when the realization struck him.

Sometimes, for a minute or two, Teresa would draw Call into one of her stories. He would begin to be interested in the spider or the lizard or the rabbit Teresa was talking about. It was only a brief relief from thinking about his failure, but even a brief relief was welcome. He lived, or at least he breathed; yet he had no idea what his life would be. Listening to Teresa's stories was better than thinking about the disgrace of his failed attempt to catch Joey Garza, or about the two pointless deaths, or about the indignity of the future. Pea Eye had said he could come and live on the farm, with himself and Lorena and their children.

Call didn't want it. Yet, he had to live somewhere.

"I doubt I could be much help," he said, when Pea Eye made the offer.

Pea Eye doubted it too, but he didn't voice his doubts.

"You don't have to be, Captain—not for a while," Pea Eye told him.

5.

Famous Shoes stayed in Ojinaga for a week. He wanted the great eye, which was still tied to Joey Garza's saddle. The saddle was in a small shed behind Maria's house. Billy Williams kept an eye on the shed, for he was afraid that people would try to steal anything they could find that had belonged to Joey. Joey was a famous bandit; people would be looking for souvenirs.

Famous Shoes wanted the great eye badly. He knew that such an instrument, which allowed one to study the plains on the moon, must be very valuable. Yet he had done considerable tracking for the white men, and had only been paid the five dollars that Pea Eye gave him. That came under a different account, in Famous Shoes' reckoning. Pea Eye had given him the five dollars to show him where the big shotgun lay. The wages they owed him for tracking had not been paid. Captain Call was sick; his mind was not on the debt. No one's mind was on the debt except his own. Billy Williams was grieving for Maria, and he drank too much whiskey. Olin Roy had left. Billy Williams's eyesight was failing. Probably he would want to keep the great eye for himself, if it was called to his attention.

The old Indian waited several days, trying to decide who he should approach about the great eye. He was tempted to steal it, but white men sometimes became crazy when things they weren't using were stolen from them. They might follow him and shoot him. The saddle had belonged to Joey, Maria's son, and both of them were dead. The great eye belonged to no one, as far as Famous Shoes could see. Taking it would not be stealing; still, he did not want to do anything that would make the white men crazy.

Captain Call did not want to talk to anyone except the little blind girl. He had never liked Famous Shoes anyway, and would find reasons to deny him the great eye if he was asked. He would say it was worth too much, or that Famous Shoes didn't have that much wages coming.

One day, Famous Shoes decided to approach Pea Eye, who was outside mending a stirrup.

"I want to go to the Madre and visit the eagles," Famous Shoes told him. "If you don't want to pay me my wages in money, I will take the great eye instead."

"The great what?" Pea Eye asked.

"The great eye that Joey used," Famous Shoes replied. "It is tied to his saddle."

"Oh, that old spyglass," Pea Eye said. "Nobody's using it—I sure don't want to drag that thing around. I guess you can just have it, if that's what you want."

Famous Shoes could scarcely believe his good fortune. Billy Williams was at the cantina. Lorena had gone to the river with Rafael and Teresa to wash clothes. He went at once to the little shed and took the great eye.

Captain Call had his eyes shut, and he breathed hard, like a sick calf. White men had the habit of staying alive too long, in Famous Shoes' opinion. Captain Call ought to send his spirit on, now. It was time for him to visit the other place. He might find his leg and his arm, if he went there.

Without delay Famous Shoes left for the Madre, carrying the great eye. Now he would be able to see as well as the eagles; now he could track them through the sky.

6.

Pea Eye was through with his crutch before the Captain attempted to use his for the first time. Call was so sad that it was hard to be around him. Lorena finally cleaned out the little room that had been Maria's, and made him a bed in there. Too much had to be done, in the other room. She had to cook and clean, tend to the two children, feed Billy and Pea and the Captain—when the Captain would eat. Having to walk around the silent, suffering old man every time she needed to do something was beginning to get on Lorena's nerves. When they got him home to the farm, Pea would have to build him a room of some kind, away from the house. With two more children in their home, there would have to be some expansion anyway. Lorena accepted that they would have to care for Call—he had no one else—but she didn't want him sitting in her kitchen, hour after hour every day, looking as if he hated life. It would be bad for her children, and her own nerves couldn't take it. She ran a happy household, usually; she was not going to dampen her children's liveliness because of Captain Call's grief.

Once she installed him in Maria's bedroom, things were better. Teresa became his sole attendant: she didn't like for anyone but herself to go into Call's room, and Call didn't welcome others, either. Pea Eye would come in once in a while and attempt to talk to him, but Call scarcely responded. The events of the past weeks were twisted in his mind, like a rope that had not been coiled properly. He wanted to remember things clearly, to backtrack through the pursuit of Joey Garza until he located the moment of failure. But the effort was discouraging; he had followed up the available clues and deployed his resources in what seemed like an intelligent way. Perhaps he should not have let himself be distracted by Mox Mox. If he hadn't, though, Jasper Fant's two children would have died, and others as well, very likely. By most reckonings, Mox Mox was worse than Joey Garza had been.

What it came down to, Call concluded, was this: on the morning when he was injured, his eyesight had failed him. He hadn't once suspected that the buckskin horse was hobbled. He ought to have been alert to that possibility, but all he had seen were two horses grazing. His eyes had simply failed him. Horses moved differently, when they were hobbled. Earlier in his life, his eyes would have detected the difference. As it was, they hadn't. He should have had spectacles, but it had never occurred to him that his vision had fallen off so. He had always trusted his senses and had not expected any of them to fail him. To reflect that a cheap pair of spectacles might have prevented the loss of his arm and his leg was bitter knowledge, and he could not stop himself from brooding about it. His eyes had cost him himself: that was how he came to view it. Because of his untrustworthy eyes, he had been reduced to what he was now, a man with two crutches, a man who could not mount a horse.

Some days, all the Captain did was wait for Teresa. When she was with him, he sometimes stopped thinking about his mistakes. Teresa would be outside with the goats and the chickens, and would come back to him with news of their activities. The old hen with the broken beak had caught a large lizard. One of the little goats had stepped in a hole and a snake had bitten it. Now, they were waiting to see if the kid would live or die. Rafael was upset, and they listened to his moaning through Call's little window.

"Do you think it will die?" Teresa asked him. She had brought him his coffee.

"Probably it will, if it was small," Call said.

"If it dies, I hope it will see my mother," Teresa said. "She is with the dead. My mother will take care of Rafael's goat."

"I expect she will," Call replied.

7.

It was almost another month before Captain Call became strong enough to travel the rough wagon road to Fort Stockton. Pea Eye was in a fever of impatience to get home to his children. In all his years with the Captain, he had never known him to be sick. Of course, he realized that being shot three times with a high-powered rifle would set a person back considerably; he had been shot himself and knew what it was to feel poorly. But he was so accustomed to seeing the Captain well and hardy that it was difficult for him to accept the fact that Call simply would not become hardy again.

Pea Eye asked Lorena so often when she thought the Captain would be ready to travel that she finally lost her temper.

"Stop asking me that!" she snapped. "You ask me that five or six times a day and I've been telling you five or six times a day that I don't know. I don't have any idea when he can travel. All you have to do is look at him to know he's not able, yet. When that will change I *don't know!*"

"I won't ask no more if I can help it, honey," Pea Eye replied, meekly.

"You'd better help it!" Lorena told him.

The thought of taking the old, ruined man into her household worried her more and more. Teresa cared for him almost entirely. Call made it clear that he didn't welcome anyone else's help. Her boys were no respecters of others' wishes, though—they had always been curious about Captain Call, and they were not likely to be easily shut out. They would have to build Call a room of his own—but where the money would come from, Lorena didn't know.

Rafael had been more affected by Maria's death than the little girl seemed to be. Lorena had taken a liking to Rafael, and he to her. Every morning he would milk his goats and bring the milk in a little pot for Lorena. Often she noticed Rafael peeking into Maria's old room, looking for his mother; she would see him searching for her outside, amid the goats and chickens and the few sheep; sometimes he would search by the river, where Maria had gone to wash their clothes.

It made Lorena sad, to see the boy looking so forlornly for his mother. He was a large boy, but sweet; his main problem was that he could not attend to himself very well. He was always spilling things on his clothes, or sitting down in puddles, or forgetting to button his buttons in the mornings.

"My mother isn't by the river," Teresa told Lorena. "She is among the dead. Rafael doesn't understand where the dead live."

"I don't understand that too well, myself," Lorena said. "I know they're somewhere you can't see them."

Later, she felt bad about the remark. She had made it to a little girl who had never seen her mother.

"I dream of my mother," Teresa said. "I dream she is with me and my rooster."

8.

Billy Williams drove them to Fort Stockton, when Call was finally strong enough to make the trip. Billy knew a bartender in Presidio who owned a wagon he didn't need. He persuaded the bartender to lend it for the journey, promising to bring it back loaded with cases of whiskey.

"You ought to come with us to the Panhandle," Pea Eye told him. He and Billy had become fast friends, during the period of Call's convalescence.

"Come to the Panhandle. I'll make a farmer out of you," Pea Eye said.

"Nope, I imagine I'd miss Old Mex," Billy replied.

Gordo, the butcher, was annoyed when the wagon pulled away. Lorena had allowed Rafael to bring two goats. Teresa had her rooster, and three hens. Gordo didn't care how many goats and chickens the gringos took away; he was annoyed because they took the little blind girl. She was almost as pretty as her mother had been, and soon she would be old enough to marry. Of course, she was blind; she might be a poor housekeeper, and she might not cook well. But he could cook for himself, and cooking and housekeeping were not the only things to consider. The butcher thought he might have liked to marry the girl, if the gringos hadn't taken her away.

9.

Call hardly spoke during the wagon ride to Fort Stockton. He held on to the side of the wagon with his one hand. The bullet in his chest still pained him, and it pained him even more when he was jostled, as he was when they crossed the many gullies along the way.

Now and then they met travelers, cowboys mostly. Call dreaded such meetings; he dreaded being seen at all. Fortunately, though, the travelers weren't much interested in him. They were far more interested in Pea Eye. His victory over Joey Garza was the biggest thing to happen on the border since the Mexican War, and none of the cowboys were old enough to remember the Mexican War.

Pea Eye felt embarrassed by all the attention he was getting. What made his embarrassment even worse was that he was getting that attention right in front of the Captain. Pea Eye had always been just a corporal—it was the Captain who had killed Mox Mox and six of his men. He didn't feel right being a hero, not with the Captain sitting right there in the same wagon. The Captain didn't seem to mind, though. He didn't even appear to be listening most of the time. But Pea Eye was still embarrassed.

"Mox Mox was worse than Joey," Pea Eye told Lorena.

"Yes, he was worse," Lorena agreed. She started to tell her husband that she had been Mox Mox's captive, but she caught herself. That had happened before Pea Eye was her husband. He didn't need to know about it.

10.

They rolled into Fort Stockton beside the railroad. When they came to the dusty, one-room station, they saw a private car sitting by itself on the track.

"I wonder what swell came in *that?*" Lorena said.

They soon found out. The stationmaster emerged from the little building with a short, white-haired man with a curling mustache and a quick, restless walk. The two came right out to meet the wagon, though by the time they got there, the white-haired man was twenty yards in front of the station-master.

"I'm Colonel Terry, I've come to look for Brookshire—why ain't he with you?" the white-haired man said to Pea Eye.

"He started with you, I know that much, because I ordered him to," Colonel Terry said, before Pea Eye could think of a nice way to inform him that Mr. Brookshire was dead.

"It was a foolish order," Call said. The Colonel's manner irritated him. Lately, Call had used his voice so seldom that what he said came out raspy.

"What's that? Who are you, sir?" the Colonel asked.

"I'm Woodrow Call," the Captain replied. "Your man's dead. Mrs. Parker brought the body out, at considerable risk to herself. Mr. Brookshire's at an undertaker's, in Presidio."

"Well, his sister's been raising hell, trying to get us to find him

—so much hell that I came here myself," the Colonel said. "Did the man do his duty?"

"I reckon he did," Pea Eye said. "I wouldn't be here driving this wagon, if he hadn't bought that big shotgun."

"If he did his duty, then his sister will get the pension," the Colonel told them.

"It was a foolish order," Call repeated. "Brookshire was no fighting man, and he should not have been sent to chase bandits."

He looked at the Colonel and noticed a detail that had escaped him at first: the Colonel's empty right sleeve was pinned neatly to his coat.

"Now hold on, Call—I sent Brookshire to keep the accounts," Colonel Terry said. "*You* were the man sent to catch the bandit, and from the looks of you, you made a botch of it."

Pea Eye nearly dropped the reins. Never in his life had he heard anyone speak so bluntly to the Captain.

To his amazement, Captain Call smiled.

"That's accurate," Call said. "I made a botch of it. But Mr. Parker is an able man, and he finished the job for you."

"Grateful," Colonel Terry said, glancing up at Pea Eye briefly. His custom did not run to extended compliments.

"If Brookshire did his job, where's the ledgers?" he asked.

Call didn't answer, and Pea Eye wasn't too sure what the Colonel was referring to.

"Oh, them big account books?" he said, finally. "We used them to start fires, back when it was so cold. We was in a country where there wasn't no kindling, and very little brush."

Call looked over the side of the wagon at Colonel Terry. He recalled that after Brookshire's first little panic at the Amarillo station, the man had been an uncomplaining companion. He did not intend to let the Colonel abuse him.

"Where'd you lose your arm?" Call asked him.

"First Manassas," Colonel Terry said. He looked into the wagon and saw that Call had lost not only an arm, but a leg as well. He had been about to rethink the matter of the pension.

An accountant who burned the account books because of a little weather was not doing his job, in the Colonel's view. At least, he wasn't doing it well enough that his family could simply expect to get his pension. But Captain Call was a frosty sort. It was known that he had killed the manburner, Mox Mox, another sizable threat to the security of paying customers. Colonel Terry seldom paused for anyone; but Captain Call had a distinguished record, and it seemed he felt strongly about Brookshire. It was not the moment to harp on pensions, paid or unpaid, the Colonel decided.

"Brookshire's sister lives in Avon, Connecticut," the Colonel told them. He remembered that the Garza menace had been ended, and the primary goal had been accomplished. Perhaps Brookshire had been some help. The pension was a modest one anyway, enough to keep a widow or an old maid sister, if the widow or the old maid was frugal.

"Well, without those ledgers, it will be damn hard to get the books to balance," he said, annoyed as he always was by irregularities in regard to the accounting.

He surveyed the group in the wagon. There was Call, minus an arm and a leg; there was Mr. Parker and a handsome blond woman—very handsome, he decided upon taking a second look. Then there was a greasy old fellow in buckskins, and a Mexican boy with shaggy hair and eyes somewhat like a sheep's. There was a pretty little girl who appeared to be blind, plus a bit of a menagerie: two goats, three hens, and a rooster.

Colonel Sheridan Terry—"Sherry Terry," as he was known in the military, because of his thirst for sherries and ports—had an abrupt shift of mood. It seemed to him that the people in the wagon had had too much hard travel, and all of them looked dirty and all of them looked tired. He gave the blond woman the smile that had won Miss Cora's heart, and the hearts of not a few others, too. The blond woman was a beauty. If she had a wash, she might look better than Cora. The truth was, he had begun to grow a little tired of Cora.

"You people look like you need a wash," he said. "I expect

[553]

you've come a fair ways, in that old wagon. I'll make my bath available. Of course, you're welcome to go first, ma'am—you and the young lady."

Lorena had not been paying much attention to the palaver. She was too tired. She ached from her heels to her ears, for the jolting had been continuous for almost two hundred miles. The Colonel's speech was brusque, but then, most men's speech was brusque. She had been half asleep when she heard the Colonel offer his bath. Every time the wagon stopped jolting for even five minutes, Lorena was apt to go into a doze. She had never been in a private railroad car before, much less had a bath in one. From the outside the car looked pretty fancy—she wished Tessie could see it. Pea Eye had taken to calling Teresa Tessie, and soon they all were doing it—the Captain, too. At least Teresa could feel the warm water and enjoy the bath, though.

"My name is Lorena Parker, and the young lady's name is Teresa," Lorena said. "I can't think of anything we'd be more grateful for than a bath."

"Come along, then—it's just a step," Colonel Terry said. He reached up a hand, the left one, the one that had been spared. Lorena took it and stepped down. Then she helped Teresa out of the wagon, and the two of them followed the Colonel. His manner had changed, but not his gait. He was soon twenty yards ahead of Lorena and Teresa. The stationmaster walked with the womenfolk, at a more moderate pace.

"You reckon all Yankees walk that fast?" he asked.

11.

Billy Williams loaded the wagon with whiskey and started back for Ojinaga the next day.

"I ain't been gone but a week, and I already miss Old Mex," he said.

"I still wish you'd come home with us and try farming," Pea Eye said.

"Why?" Lorena asked. "You don't even like farming yourself. If you don't like it, why would you think other people ought to do it?"

Pea Eye didn't know what had prompted his invitation. He thought it might have had something to do with the fact that Billy Williams was a bachelor.

"He's by himself," he told his wife. "We'd be company for him."

"You'd be a bachelor yourself, if I wasn't bold," Lorena reminded him.

12.

Colonel Terry's generous mood lasted several days. He insisted that they all ride back to San Antonio as his guests. He arranged a separate passenger car, just for them and the goats and the chickens. The more he saw of Lorena, the more he realized how tired he was of Cora.

Just as they were leaving for San Antonio, the Colonel changed his mind and took them to Laredo instead. He needed to see the governor of Coahuila, and the errand couldn't wait.

"I think Mexico's the coming place," he told Call. "They've got minerals. All they need is railroads."

"Did it take you long to learn to get by without your arm?" Call asked. He didn't have much patience with Terry, but he did have some curiosity about the lost arm. The Colonel seemed to function briskly without it. Of course, he owned a railroad and kept a servant with him, to help him dress. Still, Call suspected the Colonel was the sort who would function briskly, servant or no servant.

"It took me five years," Colonel Terry said. "Fortunately, the War was on, and the War took my mind off it. My orderly did most of the work, but I did all the thinking. You can't worry too much about one arm when there's a war going on."

Call said nothing. He didn't feel brisk, and didn't expect to. The detour to Laredo didn't bother him, though it did bother

Pea Eye and Lorena. They wanted to get home to their children, but he himself had a little business to attend to, in Laredo. He wanted to find Bolivar, and see if he was well enough to come with them to the Panhandle. He could not simply leave the old man with the Mexican family—they were too poor, and he had promised them he would come back and get Bolivar when he could.

In Laredo he asked Pea Eye to hire a buggy. Pea lifted him into it, and they crossed the river into Mexico. Call had some difficulty remembering just where he had left Bolivar, but by making inquiries they finally found the little house.

The woman he had left Bolivar with could not conceal her shock, when she saw how the Captain looked. He was gray, and he seemed so old.

"Oh, Señor Call," she said. "Bolivar died. He died the day you brought him—the day you left to go up the river."

"Well, I'll swear," Call said.

He had brought some money. He paid the woman well, but he didn't say a word as Pea Eye drove him back across the Rio Grande. He seemed to sink into himself, so deeply that Pea Eye didn't even try to make conversation. He concentrated on driving the buggy.

"That's about the last of them," Call said in a whisper, as they were driving through Laredo.

"The last, Captain?" Pea Eye asked.

"The last of the Hat Creek boys," Call said.

"Well, Captain, there's me . . ." Pea Eye mumbled.

13.

As soon as Colonel Terry left for Saltillo to pay his business call on the governor of Coahuila, Lorena went directly to the telegraph office and sent two wires—one to Clara Allen in Nebraska, and the other to Charles Goodnight. She asked Clara to send her children home when it was convenient, and she asked Charles Goodnight if he would loan her enough money for rail passage for three adults and two children, from Laredo to Quanah. She wanted to ask Mr. Goodnight if he could possibly send a wagon and a cowhand to get them home from Quanah; but in the end, she didn't make that request. If they could just get to Quanah, they could scare up a wagon for themselves. Someone would get them home. It was the money for the tickets she needed most. She hadn't a cent, and neither did Pea Eye. The Captain had given most of his money to a Mexican woman, the one who had kept Bolivar. In any case, Lorena didn't want to borrow from Call. She was willing to take care of him, but she didn't want to be dependent on him for money.

She didn't intend to be in Laredo when Colonel Terry returned from Mexico, either. When the Colonel had offered to let Lorena and Teresa use his big brass bathtub, he had been courteous and had visited a saloon while they took their baths. But on the long trip to Laredo, the Colonel had begun to find reasons to invite Lorena into his private car. He had discovered that she was a teacher, and no doubt liked to read. He had quite a few books, in his private car. He had a man in New York who kept him supplied, for occasions when he traveled with lady guests. Now and then, he even liked to leaf through a book himself. He had the latest novels and such, and he felt sure he had some that Lorena might enjoy.

Lorena would have liked a book, but she didn't want to go back to the Colonel's private car. The Colonel visited them in their car, several times a day, and he never missed an opportunity to compliment her, to pat her, to lean too close, to breathe on her neck, or to look her hard in the eye. Lorena surrounded herself with children. She sat between Teresa and Rafael, but the Colonel still patted her, leaned over her, looked at her. Lorena put her arm around Teresa, when the Colonel was in the car. The one advantage to being blind is that she'll never see men's looks, Lorena thought.

Pea Eye found it surprising that the Colonel would be so friendly. From hearing Brookshire talk about him, he would not have supposed that the Colonel would be friendly at all. He even had his servant bring them food, from time to time. Giving them a whole car to themselves was plenty generous, Pea Eye thought. He mentioned it to Lorena, but Lorena didn't say a word.

Just before they got to Laredo, Lorena was walking back to the dining car. She was on her way to beg a little stale bread for Teresa's chickens, when Colonel Terry suddenly popped out of a sleeping compartment. He didn't say a word—he just grabbed Lorena's arm and tried to pull her into the compartment. Lorena dropped the bread plate, and it broke. The Colonel was strong: if he had had two hands, Lorena would have had a hard struggle. The Colonel wasn't expecting a struggle of any sort, though he supposed Lorena might fuss a little, as Cora sometimes did. But what did that amount to? Women would fuss a little; it was part of the game.

"Now, missy," he said, but the next moment his hand was pouring blood. Lorena had picked up a piece of the broken plate and had slashed him with it, across the top of his hand. The

[559]

Colonel let go his hold. Blood was streaming from the wound. She had cut him deep, and from the way she was holding the shard of plate, she would be capable of cutting him again.

"Why, you hellion . . ." he barked. "You cut my hand!"

"You see that one-legged man in the next car?" Lorena asked him. "You see Captain Call? I cut his leg off myself, with a bowie knife. I'll be glad to do the same for your one hand if you ever try to be familiar with me again, Colonel."

The Colonel looked scared. Men usually did, if you hurt them a little.

"I've got to see the governor of Coahuila tomorrow," the Colonel said, in a shocked voice. "What am I going to do about this hand? Can't you bandage me, ma'am? I'm pouring blood all over the floor."

"You're lucky it wasn't your throat," Lorena said. "One of these days, if I'm not left alone, I'm going to cut a man's throat, I expect."

Colonel Terry felt a little faint. Cora might fuss, but she never cut him. When Lorena went past him he drew back, which was wise. If he had touched her again, Lorena felt she might have cut him worse—far worse than she had done already.

14.

Charles Goodnight wired the money, and Clara Allen telegraphed that she was bringing the children home herself as soon as she could get a train. Lorena felt relieved. She hoped Clara would stay for a while. Clara was the one person she could let herself rest with.

When Lorena came back with the tickets, Pea Eye was startled. The Colonel had assured him that everything would be arranged; he himself would be taking them home to the Panhandle.

Captain Call hadn't spoken, since coming back from Nuevo Laredo. He seemed to have taken the news of Bolivar's death very hard. Pea Eye was surprised at just how hard the Captain took the news. When Bolivar had worked for them the Captain had usually been mad at him, the way Pea Eye remembered it. Bolivar was given to clanging the dinner bell with his broken crowbar, whether it was mealtime or not. The Captain hadn't liked it, either. But now he was so sunken that even Tessie couldn't get him to speak.

"The Colonel's due back tomorrow," Pea Eye reminded Lorena. "He's going to be right surprised when he finds out we left ahead of him."

"We're going today—don't lose the tickets," Lorena said, handing them to him.

15.

Colonel Terry turned red with anger when he returned from Coahuila and discovered that Lorena and her party had left ahead of him. What was a little cut on the hand? It was only a start—women's anger sometimes led to better things.

"Who let them go? Was it you, goddamn you?" the Colonel said, glaring at the elderly stationmaster.

"Why, Colonel . . . they had tickets," the stationmaster told him. "People with tickets can get on the train . . . it's just a matter of having tickets."

"Damn the tickets, and goddamn you, you're fired, get off my railroad!" Colonel Terry ordered.

16.

In San Antonio, Lorena stopped for a day to take Teresa to an eye doctor. The stationmaster in Laredo had noticed that the little girl was blind, and told Lorena the name of a doctor in San Antonio who could help people with poor vision. His wife's sister was shortsighted, and had gone to him and got some fine spectacles. Before that, she had been prone to mixing up the sugar and the salt. Her husband, his brother-in-law, had been about to leave her for it.

The eye doctor was a very old man. His name was Lee.

"No kin to the General," he told Lorena. He boiled his instruments for a long time, before examining Teresa.

"People think I'm kin to the General, but I'm no kin to the General," he said again, while waiting for the instruments to cool.

Teresa held her rooster—the old doctor had allowed it.

"Why, sure, what's the harm in a rooster, unless he pecks," he said.

When he was through, Dr. Lee took Lorena aside and told her that Teresa was incurably blind. Lorena went back to the train with a heavy heart. But Teresa had her rooster, and she seemed happy.

17.

North of Fort Worth, there was a delay. An old man had been crossing the tracks with a wagonful of pigs. The old man was deaf, and he didn't hear the train coming. The wreck killed the old man, and scattered pigs everywhere. One of the wagon wheels jammed under the locomotive, along with a dead sow; it took a long time to clear it. In the railroad station in San Antonio, Lorena had used a little of Mr. Goodnight's money to buy a book by Mr. Hardy. She read it while the train was stopped.

"It's about a girl called Tess," she told Pea Eye, when he inquired.

"I hope she wasn't blind, like our Tessie," Pea Eye replied.

18.

Call looked out the window at the grasslands, as the plains opened around them. Teresa whispered to him, trying to get him to talk; but he could not bring himself to speak, at least not often. There must have been a lot of rain that winter, for the cover was abundant. It would be a good year for the cattle herds.

The Captain could not imagine what he was going to do, in the years ahead. He would have to live, but without himself. He felt he had left himself far away, back down the weeks, in the spot west of Fort Stockton where he had been wounded. He had saddled up, as he would have on any morning. He had ridden off to check two horses, as he would have on any morning, as he had ridden on thousands of mornings throughout his life. He had been himself; a little stiff maybe, his finger joints swollen; but himself. He scarcely heard the gunshots, or felt the first bullet. That bullet and the others hadn't killed him, but they had removed him. Now there was a crack, a kind of canyon, between the Woodrow Call sitting with Teresa on the train and the Woodrow Call who had made the campfire that morning and saddled his horse. The crack was permanent, the canyon deep. He could not get across it, back to himself. His last moments as himself had been spent casually—making a campfire, drinking coffee, saddling a horse.

Then the wounds split him off from that self, that Call—he

could remember the person he had been, but he could not become that person again. He could never be that Call again. Even if he had kept his arm and his leg, he knew it would be much the same. Of course, having the arm and the leg would have been a great convenience, for he could earn a living if he had them. He could be far less of a burden. But even if he had kept the arm and leg, he could not have returned to being the Call who had made the campfire and saddled the horse. The first bullet had removed him from that person. That person—that Call—was back down the weeks, on the other side of the canyon of time. There was no rejoining him, and there never would be.

19.

The train reached the little station at Quanah after midnight. Teresa slept. Rafael had been moaning; he was having bad dreams. Call could manage his crutches a little, but he was very stiff from the long ride on the hard bench. Pea Eye had to help him up.

Charles Goodnight stood on the platform. Clara Allen stood there, too. When Lorena looked out the window and saw Clara, her heart leapt.

"Clara's here," she said, to Pea Eye. "We'll get to see our children."

"Oh my Lord!" Pea Eye exclaimed.

Lorena picked up Teresa and kept Rafael close to her side. She didn't want to scare him. He had the smaller of the goats in his arms.

"Hello—we've got two more children now," Lorena said, as she eased Rafael down the steps.

"What a pretty child," Clara said, coming closer to look at Teresa in the light from the station window.

"You must have traveled hard—you got here quicker than us, and we was in Texas to begin with," Lorena said. She freed an arm and hugged Clara. To her eye Clara looked older, and too thin.

Even with Pea Eye's help, Captain Call had difficulty getting down the steps with his crutches. He was embarrassed that he had to be met, and particularly by Clara Allen, who had never liked him. But she had traveled from Nebraska to bring Pea Eye and Lorena their children. That was doing them a considerable favor, he recognized.

"Pea, you've got to go back and get the other goat and Teresa's chickens," Lorena said. "I don't know what Tessie would do if we left that rooster on the train."

"I'll fetch the goat," Goodnight said. He was glad to have something to help with. The sight of Woodrow Call was a shock to him, though he was no stranger to wounded men. It was not so much the missing limbs as the look on the man's face that bothered him. But it was shadowy, on the platform; perhaps in the daylight he wouldn't look so ruined.

"I'm not much of a hand with fowl," he said. "Hello, Woodrow."

"Yes, hello, Captain," Clara said. "I'll get the chickens, Charlie."

"Why didn't he just die?" she asked Goodnight, when they were on the train. Goodnight had already picked up the goat, but looked as if he didn't know quite what to do about the chickens.

"I was never much of a hand with fowl," he remarked, again.

"I told you I'd get the chickens," Clara said, annoyed that he had simply ignored her question about Call. Goodnight had happened to be in the station in Amarillo, when she and the children arrived from Omaha. Clara remembered Goodnight from her childhood, for he had known her father well. He had been in Nebraska once and had bought ten horses from her. She went over and said hello. Since they were going to be on the same train, she thought he might be some help with the little ones, but that proved a false hope. Not only was Goodnight hard to make conversation with, he was as scared of the children as if they had been wildcats.

Clara picked the chickens up by their legs and carried them off the train. The hens and the rooster were outraged—Teresa had never carried them upside down. The hens began to squawk and the rooster to protest.

"What's wrong with my chickens? Don't carry them that way, give them to me," Teresa said. She had realized from the sound that the chickens were upside down.

It was only when Teresa reached for her chickens that Clara realized the little girl was blind.

20.

The five children were asleep in a heap on the floor, in a corner of the station. Clarie had her arms around them all. At the sight of his daughter holding her brothers and her sister, Pea Eye broke down. In his time of danger he had almost given up hope of seeing his children again. Yet there they were, all alive, all sleeping, on the floor of a railroad station. His big daughter was looking after them. It was more than he deserved, more even than he had hoped for, and he began to cry. Teresa's hens were still squawking, even though she had set them down. They were running around the station; one brown hen jumped up on the stationmaster's desk and scattered his papers.

"Here, scat—who are you?" he said. He was not used to such commotion at that hour. Usually no more than a cowboy or two got off the Fort Worth train.

"Oh, Pa," Clarie said, when she awoke and saw her father. Ben got awake and hugged his father, but waking up proved too much for Georgie and August. Both yawned heavily and went back to sleep. Laurie, the baby, opened her eyes and started to cry. She didn't know who the strange man was, hugging Clarie. Then her mother reached down and took her. There was an old man standing near who had only sticks for legs. Laurie looked at him curiously, as her mother hugged her.

21.

Goodnight had arranged for a cowboy to bring a wagon. The cowboy arrived at sunup, driving the wagon and leading two horses. The boys were awake by then. They chased the hens and played with the goats. They took to Rafael right away but were a little shy with Teresa, who held her rooster in her arms.

"There must be a doctor somewhere who could help that girl see," Clara told Lorena. Although she had just arrived in Texas, she was already beginning to dread the trip home, by herself. She had grown used to Lorena's children, and to having laughter and fusses in her house. There had been life in her house again; since her daughters left, it seemed to her, there had been no life in her house. It was hard for her, one aging woman, to bring life to a home. Yet how she missed it!

Goodnight mounted one of the horses; the cowboy mounted the other. Pea Eye took the reins of the team. It was still all he could do to keep from bawling, at the sight of his children and the familiar country.

"Many thanks for the loan of the wagon," he said, to Mr. Goodnight.

"You're welcome," Goodnight replied. He had not quite mastered his shock at the change in Woodrow Call.

"I'll soon repay that loan," Lorena told him. She had not told Pea Eye she had borrowed money. She intended to discuss it with Mr. Goodnight privately, but there had not been a moment when she could speak to him alone. She was a little worried about Pea Eye's reaction, but Pea Eye let Georgie sit on his lap and pretend to drive the team—he didn't hear the remark about the loan.

"We're branding today," Goodnight said. "In fact, we're branding all this week. When we're done, I'll trot over and check on the bunch of you."

He tipped his hat to the two ladies and turned his horse; he rode a few steps and then turned back to Lorena.

"Mrs. Parker, I hope you'll be opening the school again," he said.

"I'll be opening the school again, Mr. Goodnight," Lorena said to him. "I'll be opening it again soon."

"Well, I've got to git," Goodnight said. He had not gotten around to firing Muley, the cook; it was a matter that preyed on his mind, as he and the cowboy loped away.

22.

At first, they put Captain Call in a little granary in the barn. There was no other place for him. The granary was fairly clean; there had never been any grain in it, because they had never been able to afford any, and had so far failed to raise enough to store. The house itself was so crowded that Clara had to sleep in a hallway during her visit.

"This hall is fine," Clara said. "I won't have these boys evicted from their bedroom for an old lady."

"I bet they didn't sleep in a hall at your house," Lorena said.

"My house is bigger," Clara admitted.

Everyone was surprised at how quickly Teresa learned her way around the farm. She went to the barn every morning to take Call coffee and bacon, and she learned all the farm animals by sound. She rarely stumbled. Ben fought with her—he wasn't prepared for another girl to be living with them. It hadn't been in his plans. Teresa more than held her own in the fights, though. She was quicker in the head than Ben, and she confounded him with her retorts.

"The doctor in San Antonio said she'd never see," Lorena told Clara.

"He's just one doctor," Clara said.

23.

Call didn't mind bunking in the granary. Excepting Teresa, who came to him often to bring him food or tell him her stories, he didn't want to see people or be around them. He had a kerosene lamp, but rarely lit it. There was hay in the barn; he didn't want to take a chance at falling asleep, knocking the lamp over, and burning the barn down.

Three old cowboys, one of them a former Ranger, stopped by to see him in the first week. They wanted to congratulate him on having rid the country of Mox Mox; mainly, though, they just wanted to see him, to talk about old times.

Call was uncomfortable with the men, and he let them do the talking. He felt like an impostor. He was no longer the man who had lived the old times; he was no longer even the man who had killed Mox Mox. That man was not the cripple who lived in a granary, in a barn on the Quitaque. That man lived back somewhere in memory, across a canyon, across the Pecos; that man had been blown away, as Brookshire feared he would be, on the plains of time.

The cowboys felt awkward. The Captain clearly did not want to see them. They regretted coming, and they left, disquieted by what had happened to a man they had once regarded as invincible.

24.

His branding done, Goodnight came. He took a look at Call and the granary, and left. Three days later, two wagons full of lumber arrived, accompanied by six cowboys. Between sunup and sundown of the next day, they built Call a shack. They had brought with them the few possessions he had left in the little line cabin on the Palo Duro. It was just a shack, but it was better than an oat bin. Pea Eye helped with the work, although he was a poor carpenter. He soon hit himself with the hammer, raising a blood blister that was so large and painful, Lorena had to eventually cut off the nail.

She was grateful to Goodnight for the shack, for she had felt bad about putting the Captain in the barn. But she worried about the debt.

"I'll pay you back, Mr. Goodnight," she told him. "I expect it'll be a while, though. But we're good for it, eventually. I just don't know when."

"I'd take up a collection for Call, but I suppose it would embarrass him," Goodnight said. "He's ruined now, but there are plenty of people in this part of the country who would have been shot or scalped or robbed, if not for him. Or their folks would have been, if not them."

Lorena's mind was on the debt. In the back of her mind was

the knowledge, which she had not yet shared with Pea, that she was pregnant.

"We intend to pay you back, Mr. Goodnight," she said again, firmly.

"If Mrs. Allen needs a ride to the depot, and if you'll get word to me, I'll send a cowboy with a buggy," Goodnight said.

25.

Sometimes, if Teresa urged him, Call would hobble to the house for his meals. He and Clara rarely spoke. When the meal was finished, it was Teresa who got Call his crutches and helped him from his chair.

If Teresa was out of the room for five minutes, Call grew visibly anxious. He would look around for her.

"Where's Tessie?" he would ask, if Teresa was absent too long. "Ain't Tessie here?"

Teresa always walked with him, holding him lightly by the arm as he went back to his shack.

"He's formed an attachment," Clara said, watching. "It's an attachment to a female, too."

"Yes," Lorena said. "He wouldn't last long without Tessie."

Clara sighed. She knew she ought to be going home soon. It was time to geld the foals, and put the mares with stud. Yet she hated to leave Lorena's loud, lively household. Sleeping in a hall was better than sleeping in an empty house. Laurie would toddle out in the morning, and cuddle with her. Sometimes little August would come, asking for a story. If August came, Georgie soon followed. She would lay in a heap of children, sometimes for an hour. In Nebraska, August and Georgie had slept in her bed; the little girl usually slept with Clarie.

In the hallway, holding the bright little boy and the babbling girl, Clara daydreamed about changing her life. She realized she had lost touch, just from *not* touching. Her daughters had produced no grandchildren for her to hold or carry to bed. It didn't seem to her that her own life had ever been entirely normal, but at least during her years of child raising, she had had people with her, in her house and in her bed—people to touch.

Now that was lost. Lorena's children were the first humans she had held in her arms in years. It was not good, for from being lonely too long she had become resigned.

"No beaux?" Lorena asked one morning, when they were sitting in the kitchen, talking. The children had all run outside with Rafael to look for his goats. One of them had strayed, during the night. Lorena's children had become protective of Rafael, all of them. She didn't harbor much hope for that particular goat, though. The coyotes were too numerous and too hungry.

"No beaux," Clara admitted. "I expect it's just as well. I'm too set in my ways now. I doubt there's a man alive who could put up with me. . . .

"Even if there is such a man alive, he probably doesn't live in Nebraska," Clara added, a little later.

Lorena thought her old friend looked sad.

"You probably run all the boys off," she said. "You have to be gentle with menfolk, you know. They aren't tough, like us."

"Well, I did scatter a few, I guess," Clara said. "But that was years ago."

Rafael stumbled back in, crying; the remains of the goat had been found. The boys all wore long faces. Lorena hugged Rafael, and shushed him. They were planning to acquire a few goats soon, and Rafael could look after them.

26.

The day she was to leave for Nebraska, Clara walked down to say farewell to Call. He was sitting with Teresa outside his shack, whittling a stick. Teresa liked to feel the smoothness of the wood of the sticks, once Call had whittled all the knots away. He had smoothed her a number of little sticks to play with. Teresa touched them with her fingers, and sometimes she held one to her cheek.

"Well, I'm off to the depot, I guess," Clara said. "I wanted to say goodbye, Woodrow."

Call had been hoping Clara would come by, before she left. There was something he wanted to ask her. But he didn't want Teresa to hear his question.

"Tessie, would you go to the house and ask Mrs. Parker if I could have some coffee?" he asked Teresa. "I woke up with a headache—coffee usually helps."

Teresa handed him back the little smoothed stick and started up the path to the house. She was barefooted; the day was warm. She stepped on a grass burr and had to pause for a moment, standing on one leg in order to remove it from her foot.

"I've heard there were schools for the blind," Call said to Clara. "Do you know anything about them?"

"Why, no," Clara replied. "Tessie's the first blind person I've ever had in my life. But I can inquire for you, Woodrow."

"I'd appreciate it," Call said. "I've got a little money saved. If there's a way Teresa can get her education, I'd like to help. I believe she's bright."

"You're right about that—she's bright," Clara told him.

"If she goes away, I'm sure we'll all miss her," Call said.

"You most of all, Woodrow," Clara said.

Call didn't answer, but the look on his face said more than Clara wanted to hear or see or know about one human missing another. She shook his hand and turned toward the house.

A moment later, she grew irritated—unreasonably irritated. She turned back on the path.

"Call Lorena Lorena," she said, loudly. "You don't have to call her Mrs. Parker now."

"The man's trying, but he just rubs me the wrong way," Clara said, when she marched into the kitchen. Lorena was washing a cut on Georgie's hand. She wasn't paying much attention.

Later, though, she remembered the remark. She wondered what Clara had meant by it, and why she looked so angry when she came in.

27.

The bounty on Joey Garza was never collected. Colonel Terry sent a detective to look into the circumstances of his death, and the detective's research revealed that the fatal shot, the one that finished Joey Garza, had been fired by a Mexican butcher in Ojinaga, Mexico. Besides that, the butcher then claimed that Joey Garza's own mother had stabbed the young bandit, and that Joey had turned the knife on her and killed her, depriving the village of its best midwife.

Citing the careless loss of the ledger books, which made it impossible to compute the costs of the expedition accurately, the railroad halved Brookshire's pension. What was left was sent to his widowed sister in Avon, Connecticut.

The same sister received a long letter from a Mrs. P. E. Parker, of Quitaque, Texas. Mrs. Parker assured the grieving sister that the last words Mr. Parker had heard Brookshire say were to remember his sister and send her his love.

28.

Call discovered that he had a gift for sharpening tools. Even with one hand, it was a skill he more than mastered. One day, watching Pea Eye futilely trying to cut a piece of rawhide with a dull knife, Call reached out and took it from Pea. He had a whetstone, and he soon had a good edge on the blade.

From then on, Pea Eye and Lorena brought whatever needed sharpening to the Captain. He sharpened scissors and shovel blades. He sharpened axes and rasps, and scythes and awls, and planing blades. He even improved the slicing edge on the plows.

In time, the neighbors heard of Call's skill and began to ride over with bushel baskets full of knives and hatchets, for him to work on.

Lorena insisted that he order a wooden leg. They wrote off for catalogues. Finally, Call ordered one—to sharpen some of the larger tools properly, he needed to be able to stand.

When the leg came, Call found that he had to whittle it a bit to secure a smooth fit. He was shy about it, at first. No one but Teresa could be with him, when he put on his leg or took it off. She learned to tuck his pants leg expertly. She laughed at him if he stumbled, but Call did not mind. The truth was, the leg made a big difference. Now he could stand up and work all day.

Clara Allen promptly sent him some literature on schools for the blind. The best one seemed to be in Cincinnati. Call hadn't mentioned school to Teresa yet; the thought of sending her away was too sharp a pain. But he did discuss the matter with Lorena. Privately, Lorena was torn. She had had another boy, Tommy, and was pregnant yet again. The house was overfull. She and Pea Eye had paid Mr. Goodnight back for the train fare. She was still running the school by herself, except for Clarie's help with the math. Clarie was engaged to Roy Benson, and would be leaving soon. The farm was doing a little better, but they still had almost no cash money.

Lorena's concern when the school came up wasn't for Teresa, who had not only Maria's look but Maria's strength. Lorena wanted Tessie to have an education, and she wanted her to have a chance to support herself.

But Captain Call had no one but the girl. He scarcely knew Lorena's children; he scarcely knew *her*, or Pea Eye, even. He worked all day at his sharpening, but except for Teresa, he had no one. Even looking at the Captain, unless he was with Teresa, was painful. Often when he was looking at Teresa, Call had tears in his eyes. But otherwise, there was nothing in his eyes— he was an absence.

Lorena feared he would die, if Teresa left.

"Let's wait one more year, Captain," Lorena told him. "Let's wait one more year."

"I expect that's best," Call said.

29.

Charles Goodnight and a young cowboy named J. D. Brown were out looking for a stray bull one day. They finally found the bull on the Quitaque, dead; it had managed to strangle itself with a coil of barbed wire.

Now and again, if he was in the vicinity, Goodnight stopped by to pay his respects to Call and the Parkers.

They found Call standing in his workroom in the barn, sharpening a sickle that a farmer from Silverton had nicked badly while cutting hay. The blind girl was rounding up her chickens. There must have been fifty chickens, at least, and there were also more goats than Goodnight was accustomed to seeing anywhere. They visited a minute, or tried to. Call scarcely looked up from his work. He had several hatchets and an axe in a bucket beside him that he needed to sharpen, once he finished with the sickle.

Pea Eye was out plowing, but Goodnight and J. D. Brown took a glass of buttermilk with Lorena before they left. Lorena was heavy with child; she paid Goodnight twenty dollars against her debt on the shack he had built for Call.

On the ride back across the gray plains, the young cowboy —he was just twenty—looked rather despondent. Goodnight ignored his despondence for a while, then got tired of it. What did a healthy sprout of twenty have to be despondent about?

"What's made you look so peaked, J.D.?" Goodnight inquired.

"Why, it's Captain Call, I guess," the young cowboy said. He was glad to talk about it, to get his dark feelings out.

"What about Captain Call?" Goodnight asked.

"Why, wasn't he a great Ranger?" the boy asked. "I've always heard he was the greatest Ranger of all."

"Yes, he had exceptional determination," Goodnight told him.

"Well, but now look . . . what's he doing? Sharpening sickles in a dern barn!" J.D. exclaimed.

Goodnight was silent for a bit. He wished his young cowboys would keep their minds on the stock, and not be worrying so about things they couldn't change.

"Woodrow Call had his time," he said, finally. "It was a long time, too. Life's but a knife edge, anyway. Sooner or later people slip and get cut."

"Well, you ain't slipped," J. D. Brown said.

"How would you know, son?" Goodnight said.

30.

In the fall of the following year, Clara Allen was pawed to death by a piebald stallion named Marbles. Everyone was scared of the stallion except Clara; Marbles, a beautiful animal, was her special pride.

On the morning of the attack three cowboys, including Chollo, her old vaquero, the most experienced man on the ranch, had urged her not to go into the pen with the stud.

"He's mad today . . . wait," Chollo told her.

"He's my horse—he won't hurt me," Clara said, shutting the gate behind her. The stallion attacked her at once. Four men leapt into the corral but could not drive him off. They didn't want to shoot the stallion, for Clara would never forgive them for it, if she lived. Finally, they shot the horse anyway, but Clara Allen was dead before they could carry her out of the pen.

31.

"It's risky, raising studs," Call said. "She must have been good with horses, or she wouldn't have lasted this long."

Lorena shut herself in her room, when she heard the news. She didn't come out all day. But then the day passed, and dusk fell. Lorena still wouldn't come out. Pea Eye knocked on the door, just a little knock.

"Leave me alone," Lorena said, in a raw voice.

Sadly, Pea Eye turned back down the hall.

"Pea," Lorena said, through the door.

"What, honey?" Pea Eye asked, feeling a little hopeful.

"Feed the children," Lorena said.

Later, when it was bedtime, Pea Eye knocked his little knock on the bedroom door, again.

"Leave me alone, Pea," Lorena said. "Just leave me alone."

"But where'll I sleep?" Pea Eye asked.

"I don't know . . . wherever you drop, I guess," Lorena told him.

At a loss and worried, Pea Eye put the children to bed and walked down to the Captain's little shack. Tessie was sitting in the Captain's rocking chair, asleep. The Captain sat on his bed, his leg off, sharpening his pocketknife on a small whetstone.

"Lorie's taking it hard, about Clara," Pea said.

"Well, that's to be expected—Clara took her in," Call said.

There was only one rocking chair. After a minute, Pea Eye sat on the floor. He thought he might go sleep in the oat bin, since the Captain was no longer using it. He thought he might go, after a while. But he was used to his wife and his bed. He wasn't ready for the oat bin, not quite.

"Do you ever think of Brookshire, Captain?" Pea Eye asked.

"I rarely do," Call said.

"It's funny. I got to liking him, just before he was killed," Pea said. "He wasn't a bad fellow, you know."

Teresa woke up, gave the Captain a goodnight kiss on the cheek, and went to the house to go to bed. When she left, the Captain made it clear that it was time for him to retire, so Pea Eye picked himself up and went off to the barn. There were several mice in the oat bin, and a small snake, but Pea Eye soon chased them out. He had nothing to sleep on, so he went to the saddle shed and pulled out a couple of old saddle blankets, which he wrapped up in as best he could.

Sometime deep in the night he heard the door to the oat bin creak. Lorena came in and bent over him. She held a lantern.

"I'm better—come on back, honey," she said.

Pea Eye felt itchy. The saddle blankets had been covered with horsehair, as was only natural. Now he was covered with horsehair, too, which *wasn't* so natural; at least, Lorena wouldn't be likely to think it natural, particularly on a day when she was in a bad mood anyway. He had horsehair absolutely all over him, a fact which made him more than a little nervous. Lorena was picky about their bed. Once she had lifted both her feet and kicked him straight off onto the floor, because he had been cutting his toenails and had neglected to clean the clippings off the sheets to her satisfaction. Horsehair might offend her even worse than toenail clippings had.

But Lorena was going—he saw the lantern swinging, as she left the barn. Pea Eye got up, rather stiffly, and tried to brush as much of the horsehair off himself as he could. In the dark, he knew he was probably making a poor job of it. But Lorena was going; he wanted to catch up.

EPILOGUE

Pea Eye shut the door of the oat bin, to keep out mice and snakes, and, at moments nervous, at moments relieved—at least she had called him *honey*—he followed his wife back to their house.